Critical acclaim for Peter Robinson and the Inspector Banks series

STRANGE AFFAIR

'The gripping story . . . shows Robinson getting more adept at juggling complex plot lines while retaining his excellent skills at characterization. The result is deeply absorbing, and the nuances of Banks's character are increasingly compelling'
Publishers Weekly (starred review)

'An enjoyable mystery'
Sunday Telegraph

'Mr Robinson stocks [*Strange Affair*] with chapter-ending cliff-hangers . . . an addictive crime-novel series'
New York Times

'Peter Robinson is a mystery writer's mystery writer . . . I can't imagine a more flawless police procedural than *Strange Affair*'
Globe and Mail – Canada

PLAYING WITH FIRE

'A shotgun blast of northern realism . . .
Robinson brings a welcome injection of reality
to police investigation in his fictional Yorkshire,
if not the genre. God's Own County tastes all the
better with a dash of Canadian bitters'
Independent

'An engaging pleasure . . . Virtually every character
is etched with care, precision and emotional insight.
With each book, the quietly competent Alan Banks
gets more and more human; like red wine, he gets
better and more interesting with age'
Publishers Weekly

'A good, solid, satisfactory police story with
a host of well-depicted minor characters and an
intriguing protagonist'
Evening Standard

Peter Robinson grew up in Yorkshire, but now lives in Toronto.

His Inspector Banks series has won numerous awards in Britain, Europe, the United States and Canada.

PETER ROBINSON

STRANGE AFFAIR

&

PLAYING WITH FIRE

INSPECTOR BANKS MYSTERIES

PAN BOOKS

Strange Affair first published 2005 by Macmillan.
First published in paperback 2005 by Pan Books.
Playing With Fire first published 2004 by Macmillan.
First published in paperback 2004 by Pan Books.

This omnibus first published 2006 by Pan Books
an imprint of Pan Macmillan Ltd
Pan Macmillan, 20 New Wharf Road, London N1 9RR
Basingstoke and Oxford
Associated companies throughout the world
www.panmacmillan.com

ISBN 978-0-330-44678-5

Strange Affair copyright © Eastvale Enterprises Inc. 2005
Playing With Fire copyright © Peter Robinson 2005

3 5 7 9 8 6 4 2

A CIP catalogue record for this book is available from
the British Library.

Typeset by IntypeLibra Ltd
Printed and bound in Great Britain by
Mackays of Chatham plc, Chatham, Kent

Visit **www.panmacmillan.com** to read more about all our books and to buy
them. You will also find features, author interviews and news of any author
events, and you can sign up for e-newsletters so that you're always first to hear
about our new releases.

STRANGE AFFAIR

For Sheila

'Though our brother is upon the rack, as long as we ourselves are at our ease, our senses will never inform us of what he suffers. They never did, and never can, carry us beyond our own person, and it is by the imagination only that we can form any conception of what are his sensations.'

Adam Smith, *Theory of Moral Sentiments*

'A friend loveth at all times,
and a brother is born for adversity.'

Proverbs, 17:17

1

Was she being followed? It was hard to tell at that time of night on the motorway. There was plenty of traffic, lorries for the most part, and people driving home from the pub just a little too carefully, red BMWs coasting up the fast lane, doing a hundred or more, businessmen in a hurry to get home from late meetings. She was beyond Newport Pagnell now, and the muggy night air blurred the red tail lights of the cars ahead and the oncoming headlights across the road. She began to feel nervous as she checked her rear-view mirror and saw that the car was still behind her.

She pulled over to the nearside lane and slowed down. The car, a dark Mondeo, overtook her. It was too dark to glimpse faces, but she thought there was just one person in the front and another in the back. It didn't have a taxi light on top, so she guessed it was probably a private hire car and stopped worrying. Some rich git being ferried to a nightclub in Leeds, most likely. She overtook the Mondeo a little further up the motorway and didn't give it a second glance. The late-night radio was playing Ol' Blue Eyes singing 'Summer Wind'. Her kind of music, no matter how old fashioned people told her it was. Talent and good music never went out of style as far as she was concerned.

When she got to Watford Gap services, she realized she felt tired and hungry, and she still had a long way to go, so she decided to stop for a short break. She didn't even notice the Mondeo pull in two cars behind her. A few seedy-looking people hung around the entrance; a couple of kids who didn't look old enough to drive stood smoking and playing the machines, giving her the eye as she walked past, staring at her breasts.

She went first to the ladies', then to the cafe, where she bought a ham and tomato sandwich and sat alone to eat, washing it down with a Diet Coke. At the table opposite, a man with a long face and dandruff on the collar of his dark suit jacket ogled her over the top of his glasses, pretending to read his newspaper and eat a sausage roll.

Was he just a common-or-garden variety perv, or was there something more sinister in his interest, she wondered. In the end, she decided he was just a perv. Sometimes it seemed as if the world was full of them, that she could hardly walk down the street or go for a drink on her own without some sad pillock who thought he was God's gift eyeing her up, like the kids hanging around the entrance, or coming over and laying a line of chat on her. Still, she told herself, what else could you expect at this time of night in a motorway service station? A couple of other men came in and went to the counter for coffee to go, but they didn't give her a second glance.

She finished half the sandwich, dumped the rest and got her travel mug filled with coffee. When she walked back to her car she made sure that there were people around – a family with two young kids up way past their bedtime, noisy and hyperactive – and that no one was following her.

The tank was only a quarter full, so she filled it up at the petrol station, using her credit card right there, at the pump. The perv from the cafe pulled up at the pump opposite and stared at her as he put the nozzle in the tank. She ignored him. She could see the night manager in his office, watching through the window, and that made her feel more secure.

Tank full, she turned down the slip road and eased in between two articulated lorries. It was hot in the car, so she opened both windows and enjoyed the play of breeze they created. It helped keep her awake, along with the hot black coffee. The clock on the dashboard read 12.35 a.m. Only about two or three hours to go, then she would be safe.

•

Penny Cartwright was singing Richard Thompson's 'Strange Affair' when Banks walked into the Dog and Gun, her low, husky voice milking the song's stark melancholy for all it was worth. Banks stood by the door, transfixed. *Penny Cartwright*. He hadn't seen her in over ten years, though he had thought of her often, even seen her name in *Mojo* and *Uncut* from time to time. The years had been kind. Her figure still looked good in blue jeans and a tight white T-shirt tucked in at the waist. The long raven's-wing hair he remembered looked just as glossy as ever in the stage lights, and the few threads of grey here and there made her look even more attractive. She seemed a little more gaunt than before, a little more sad around the eyes, perhaps, but it suited her, and Banks liked the contrast between her pale skin and dark hair.

When the song ended, Banks took advantage of the applause to walk over to the bar, order a pint and light a cigarette. He wasn't happy with himself for having started smoking again after six months or more on the wagon, but there it was. He tried to avoid smoking in the flat, and he would stop again as soon as he'd got himself back together. For the moment, it was a crutch, an old friend come back to visit during a time of need.

There wasn't a seat left in the entire lounge. Banks could feel the sweat prickling on his temples and at the back of his neck. He leaned against the bar and let Penny's voice transport him as she launched into 'Blackwater Side'. She had two accompanists, one on guitar and the other on stand-up bass, and they wove a dense tapestry of sound against which her lyric lines soared.

The next round of applause marked the end of the set, and Penny walked through the crowd, which parted like the Red Sea for her, smiling and nodding hello as she went, and stood next to Banks at the bar. She lit a cigarette, inhaled, made a circle of her mouth and blew out a smoke ring towards the optics.

'That was an excellent set,' Banks said.

'Thanks.' She didn't turn to face him. 'Gin and tonic, please, Kath,' she said to the barmaid. 'Make it a large one.'

Banks could tell by her clipped tone that she thought he was just another fan, maybe even a weirdo or a stalker, and she'd move away as soon as she got her drink. 'You don't remember me, do you?' he asked.

She sighed and turned to look at him, ready to deliver the final put-down. Then he saw recognition slowly dawn on her. She seemed flustered, embarrassed and unsure what to say. 'Oh . . . Yes. It's Detective Chief Inspector Burke, isn't it?' she managed finally. 'Or have you been promoted?'

'Afraid not,' he said. 'And it's Banks, but Alan will do. It's been a long time.'

'Yes.' Penny got her gin and tonic and raised it to Banks, who clinked it gently with his pint glass.

'Slainte.'

'Slainte,' said Banks. 'I didn't know you were back in Helmthorpe.'

'Well, nobody put on a major advertising campaign.'

Banks looked around the dim lounge. 'I don't know. You seem to have a devoted following.'

'Word of mouth, mostly. Anyway, yes, I'm back in the old cottage. What brought you here?'

'I heard the music as I was passing,' Banks said. 'Recognized your voice. What have you been up to lately?'

A hint of mischief came into her eyes. 'Now that would be a very long story indeed, and I'm not sure it would be any of your business.'

'Maybe you could tell me over dinner some evening?'

Penny faced him and frowned, her brows knit together, searching him with those sharp blue eyes, and before she spoke, she gave a little shake of her head. 'I can't possibly do that,' she whispered.

'Why not? It's only a dinner invitation.'

She was backing away from him as she spoke. 'I just can't, that's all. How can you even ask me?'

'Look, if you're worried about being seen with a married man, that ended a couple of years back. I'm divorced now.'

Penny looked at him as if he'd missed the point by a hundred miles, shook her head and melted back into the crowd. Banks felt perplexed. He couldn't interpret the signals, decode the look of absolute horror he'd seen on her face at the idea of dinner with him. He wasn't that repulsive. A simple dinner invitation. What the hell was wrong with her?

Banks gulped down the rest of his pint and headed for the door as Penny took the stage again, and he caught her eyes briefly across the crowded room. Her expression was puzzled and confused. She had clearly been unsettled by his request. Well, he thought, as he turned his back and left, face burning, at least she didn't still look so horrified.

The night was dark, the sky moonless but filled with stars, and Helmthorpe High Street was deserted, street lights smudgy in the haze. Banks heard Penny start up again back inside the Dog and Gun. Another Richard Thompson song: 'Never Again'. The haunting melody and desolate lyrics drifted after him across the street, fading slowly as he walked up the cobbled snicket past the old bookshop, through the graveyard and on to the footpath that would take him home, or to what passed for home these days.

The air smelled of manure and warm hay. To his right was a drystone wall beside the graveyard, and to his left a slope, terraced with lynchets, led down step by step to Gratly Beck, which he could hear roaring below him. The narrow path was unlit, but Banks knew every inch by heart. The worst that could happen was that he might step into a pile of sheep shit. Close by he could hear the high-pitched whining of winged insects.

As he walked, he continued to think about Penny Cartwright's strange reaction to his dinner invitation. She always had been an odd one, he remembered, always a bit sharp with her tongue and too ready with the sarcasm. But this had been different, not sarcasm, not sharp, but shock, repulsion. Was it because of their age difference? He was in his early fifties, after all, and Penny was at least ten years younger. But even that didn't explain the intensity of her reaction. She could have just smiled and said she was washing her hair. Banks liked to think he would have got the message.

The path ended at a double-barrelled stile about halfway up Gratly Hill. Banks slipped through sideways and walked past the new houses to the cluster of old cottages over the bridge. Since his own house was still at the mercy of the builders, he had been renting a flat in one of the holiday properties on the lane to the left.

The locals had been good to him, as it turned out, and he'd got a fairly spacious one-bedroom flat, upper floor, with private entrance, for a very decent rent. The irony was, he realized, that it used to be the Steadman house, long ago converted into holiday flats, and it was during the Steadman case that he had first met Penny Cartwright.

Banks's living-room window had a magnificent view over the dale, north past Helmthorpe, folded in the valley bottom, up to the rich green fields, dotted with sheep, and the sere, pale grass of the higher pastures, then the bare limestone outcrop of Crow Scar and the wild moors beyond. But his bedroom window looked out to the west over a small disused Sandemanian graveyard and its tiny chapel. Some of the tombstones, so old that you could scarcely read the names any more, leaned against the wall of the house.

The Sandemanian sect, Banks had read somewhere, had been founded in the eighteenth century, separating itself from the Scottish Presbyterian Church. Its members took holy communion, embraced communal property ownership, practised vegetarianism and engaged in 'love feasts', which Banks thought made them sound rather like eighteenth-century hippies.

Banks was a little pissed, he realized as he fiddled with his key in the downstairs lock. The Dog and Gun hadn't been his first port of call that evening. He'd eaten dinner alone in the Hare and Hounds, then had a couple of pints in the Bridge. Still, what the hell, he was on holiday for another week, and he wasn't driving. Maybe he'd even have a glass of wine or two. He was still off the whisky, especially Laphroaig. Its distinctive taste was the only thing he could remember about the night his life nearly ended, and even at a distance the smell made him feel sick.

Could the drinking have been what put Penny off, he wondered? Had she thought he was drunk when he asked her to dinner? But he doubted it. He didn't slur his words or wobble when he walked. There was nothing in his manner that suggested he'd had too much. No, it had to be something else.

He finally opened the door, walked up the stairs and unlocked the inside door, then switched on the hall light. The place felt hot and stuffy, so he went into the living room and opened the window. It didn't help much. After he had poured himself a healthy glass of Australian Shiraz, he walked over to the telephone. A red light was flashing, indicating messages on the answerphone.

As it turned out, there was only one message, and a surprising one at that: his brother Roy. Banks wasn't even aware that Roy knew his telephone number, and he was also certain that the card and flowers he had received from Roy in hospital had come, in fact, from his mother.

'Alan . . . shit . . . you're not there and I don't have

your mobile number. If you've got one, that is. You never were much of a one for technology, I remember. Anyway, look, this is important. Believe it or not, you're the only one who can help me now. There's something . . . I can't really talk about this to your answerphone. It could be a matter of life and death.' He laughed harshly. 'Maybe even mine. Anyway, I'll try again later, but can you ring me back as soon as possible? I really need to talk to you. Urgently. Please.' Banks heard a buzzing noise in the background. 'Somone's at the door. I'll have to go now. Please call. I'll give you my mobile number, too.' Roy left his phone numbers, and that was that.

Puzzled, Banks listened to the message again. He was going to listen a third time, but he realized there was no point. He hated it when people in movies kept playing the same message over and over again and always seemed to get the tape in exactly the right spot every time. Instead, he replaced the receiver and took a sip of wine. He'd heard all he needed. Roy sounded worried, and more than a little scared. The call was timed by his answerphone at 9.29 p.m., about an hour and a half ago, when Banks had been drinking in the Bridge.

Roy's phone rang several times before an answering machine picked up: Roy's voice in a curt, no-nonsense invitation to leave a message. Banks did so, said he'd try again later, and hung up. He tried the mobile number but got no response there, either. There was nothing else he could do right now. Maybe Roy would ring back later, as he had said he would.

Often, Banks would spend an hour or so perched on the window seat in his bedroom looking down on the graveyard, especially on moonlit nights. He didn't know what he was looking for – a ghost, perhaps – but the utter stillness of the tombstones and the wind soughing through the long grass seemed to give him some sort of feeling of tranquillity. Not tonight: no moon, no breeze.

The baby downstairs started crying, the way she did every night around this time. Banks turned on the TV. There wasn't much to choose from: films, a chat show or news. He picked *The Spy Who Came in from the Cold*, which had started half an hour ago. That didn't matter; he'd seen it many times before, and he knew the plot by heart. But he couldn't concentrate. As he watched Richard Burton's edgy, intense performance and tried to pick up the threads, he found his mind wandering back to Roy's phone call, felt himself waiting for the phone to ring, *willing* it.

There was nothing he could do about it right now, but the urgency and fear in Roy's voice disturbed him. He would try again in the morning, in case Roy had simply gone out for the night, but if he couldn't get in touch then, he would head for London himself and find out just what the hell was going on.

•

Why did people have to be so bloody inconsiderate as to find bodies so early on a Saturday morning? wondered Detective Inspector Annie Cabbot. Especially when Banks was on holiday and she was on call. It wasn't only that she was losing her weekend – and detective inspectors don't get paid overtime – but that those first crucial hours of an investigation were made all the more difficult by people being, for the large part, unavailable, making information harder to ferret out. And this was a particularly beautiful Saturday morning; offices would be empty, services reduced as everyone loaded a picnic basket in the car along with the kids and headed for the nearest stretch of grass or sand.

She pulled to a halt behind the blue Peugeot 106 on a quiet stretch of country road halfway between Eastvale and the A1. It had been just after half-past seven when the station desk sergeant rang and woke her from an uneasy dream she forgot, and after a quick shower and a cup of instant coffee, she was on the road.

The morning was still and hazy, with the drone of insects in the air. It was going to be just the kind of day for a picnic by the river, dragonflies and the scent of wild garlic, perhaps a bottle of Chablis cooling in the water, maybe her sketchpad and a few sticks of charcoal. After a few nibbles of Wensleydale cheese – the type with cranberries was her favourite – and a couple of glasses of wine, it would be time for a nap on the riverbank, maybe a pleasant dream. Enough of that, she thought, walking over to the car; life had other plans for her today.

Annie could see that the car's left wing had made contact with the drystone wall, so much so that the wing had buckled and scratched and the impact had brought down a section of the wall. There were no traces of skid marks, no tyre tracks at all on the dry tarmac surface.

There was already activity around the Peugeot. The road had been closed to all non-police traffic, and the immediate area around the car had been taped off. That would cause a few problems when the tourists started to dribble in, Annie thought, but it couldn't be helped; the integrity of the scene had to be preserved. Peter Darby had finished photographing the body and the car and had busied himself videotaping the area. Detective Sergeant Jim Hatchley and DC Winsome Jackman, who both lived closer to the scene, were already there when

Annie arrived, Hatchley standing by the roadside and Winsome sitting half in and half out of the unmarked police car.

'What have we got?' Annie asked Hatchley, who, as usual, looked as if he'd been dragged through a hedge backwards. The little piece of tissue paper he had stuck to a shaving cut on his chin didn't help much.

'A young woman dead behind the wheel of her car,' said Hatchley.

'I can see that for myself,' snapped Annie, glancing towards the open driver's side window.

'Bit prickly this morning, aren't we, ma'am,' said Hatchley. 'What's up? Get out of the wrong side of bed?'

Annie ignored him. She was used to Hatchley's taunts, which had only grown more frequent since she had been made inspector and he remained a sergeant. 'Cause of death?' she asked.

'Don't know yet. Nothing apparent. No obvious marks, no bruising. And officially she's not even dead yet. Not until the doc says she is.'

Annie refrained from pointing out that she knew that perfectly well. 'But you've examined her?' she pressed on.

'I had a quick look, that's all. Didn't touch anything. Winsome checked for a pulse and found none. We're still waiting for Doc Burns.'

'So she could have died of a heart attack, for all we know?'

'I suppose so,' said Hatchley. 'But like I said, she's very young. It smells a bit fishy to me.'

'Any idea who she is?'

'There's no handbag, no driving licence, nowt. At least not as you can see looking through the windows.'

'I checked the number plate on the computer, Guv,' said Winsome, walking over from her car. 'The car's registered to a Jennifer Clewes. Lives in London. Kennington. Twenty-seven years old.'

'We don't know for certain it's her yet,' Annie said, 'so find out all you can.'

'Right, Guv.' Winsome paused.

'Yes?'

'Wasn't there another one?'

'Another what?' asked Annie.

'Another murder. Like this one. Young woman found dead near a motorway. The M1 not the A1, but even so . . .'

'Yes,' said Annie. 'I remember reading about it in the papers. I can't remember the details. Look into it, will you?'

'Yes, Guv.' Winsome walked back to her car.

Annie looked at Hatchley again. 'Has Detective Superintendent Gristhorpe been informed?'

'Yes, ma'am. Says to keep him up to date.'

That made sense, Annie thought. No point having the super come running down here if the woman had pulled over into the lay-by and died of a heart attack, brain aneurysm, or any of the other random failures of the flesh that cause sudden death in otherwise healthy young people. 'Who was first officer on the scene?'

'PC Farrier over there.'

Hatchley pointed to a uniformed police constable leaning against a patrol car. Pete Farrier. Annie knew him; he worked out of Western Area Headquarters, the same as she did. Had done for years, according to all accounts, and was a reliable, sensible bobby. Annie walked over to him. 'What happened, Pete?' she asked. 'Who called it in?'

'Couple over there, ma'am.' Farrier pointed to a man and a woman some yards away from the scene. They were sitting on the grass by the side of the road, and the man had his arm around the woman, whose head was buried in his chest.

Annie thanked Farrier and walked back to her car, took her latex gloves from the murder kit in the boot and slipped them on. Then she walked over to the Peugeot. She needed to have a closer look at the scene, gather some first impressions before Dr Burns arrived and started his examination. Already a number of flies had settled on the woman's pale face. Annie shooed them away. They buzzed around her head, waiting for the chance to get back.

The woman sat in the driver's seat, slumped slightly forward and listing to the left; her right hand grasped the steering wheel, and her left held the gearstick. Her seat belt was fastened firmly in place, holding her up, and both front windows were open. The key was still in the ignition, Annie noticed, and a travel mug sat in its holder.

The victim wasn't a big woman, but her breasts were quite large, and the seat belt ran between them, separating them and causing them to appear even more prominent. She looked to be mid- to late twenties, which matched Jennifer Clewes's age, and she was very attractive. Her skin was pale, and probably had been even before her death, her long hair was dark red – dyed, Annie guessed – and she was wearing a pale blue cotton blouse and black denim jeans. There were no apparent marks on her body, as Hatchley had noted, and no sign of blood. Her eyes were open, a dull vacant green. Annie had seen that look before, felt that stillness.

Hatchley was right, though; there was something very fishy about the whole set-up, fishy enough at least to warrant a thorough preliminary investigation before deciding upon the scale of the inquiry. As Annie examined the scene, she made mental notes of what she observed and thought for later use.

When Annie had finished, she walked over to the couple who had found the body. They were very young, she noticed as she got closer. The man was ashen and the woman he was holding still had her face buried in his shoulder, though she didn't appear to be heaving with sobs. The man looked up and Annie squatted beside them.

'I'm Detective Inspector Cabbot from Western Area Headquarters,' she said. 'I understand you found the car?'

The woman turned her face away from the protection of the man's shoulder and looked at Annie. She had been crying, that was clear enough, but now she just seemed shocked and hurt.

'Can you tell me what happened?' Annie asked the man.

'We already told the policeman in the uniform. He was the first to get here.'

'I know,' said Annie, 'and I'm sorry to make you go through it again, but it'll help if you tell me.'

'There's nothing to tell, really, is there, love?' he said to the woman, who shook her head.

'First off, why don't you tell me your names?'

'This is Sam, Samantha,' he said, 'and I'm Adrian, Adrian Sinclair.'

'OK, Adrian. Where do you live?'

'Sunderland.' Annie thought she'd noticed a hint of Geordie burr in his voice, though it was faint. 'We're on holiday.' Adrian paused and stroked Samantha's hair. 'On our honeymoon, in fact.'

Well, they'd certainly remember it for as long as they lived, Annie thought, and not for the right reasons. 'Where are you staying?'

Adrian pointed up the hillside. 'We're renting a cottage. Greystone. Just up there.'

Annie knew it. She made a note. 'And what were you doing down here by the road?'

'Just walking,' Adrian said. 'It was such a beautiful morning, and the birds woke us so early.'

They were dressed for walking, Annie noticed. Not professional ramblers with the plastic-covered Ordnance Survey maps around their necks, ashplants, boots and expensive Gore-Tex gear, but simple, sturdy shoes, light clothing and a rucksack.

'What time did you arrive here?'

'It must have been a bit before seven,' Adrian said.

'What did you find?'

'The car stopped in the lay-by, just like it is now.'

'Did you touch it?'

'No, I don't think so.'

Annie looked at Samantha. 'Neither of you?'

'No,' Samantha said. 'But you might have touched the roof, Adrian, when you bent to look inside.'

'It's possible,' Adrian said. 'I don't remember. At first I thought maybe she was looking at a road map, or asleep, even. I went over to see if she needed any help. Then I saw her, with her eyes open like that and . . . We might never have gone over unless . . .'

'Unless what?'

'Well, it was me, really,' Sam said. 'I mean, like he said, Adrian just thought it was someone pulled over to rest or look at a road-map.'

'But you didn't. Why not?'

'I don't know, really,' Sam said. 'It's just that it was so early in the morning, and she was a woman, alone. I thought we should make sure she was all right, that's all. She might have been attacked or upset or something. Maybe it was none of our business, but you can't just leave, can you, walk on by?' A little colour came to her cheeks as she spoke. 'Anyway, when we got closer we could see she wasn't moving, just staring down like that, and it looked like she'd hit the wall. I said we should go over and see what was wrong with her.'

'Did you know she was dead when you looked through the window?'

'Well,' said Adrian, 'I've never seen a dead person before, but you can sort of tell, can't you?'

Yes, Annie thought, having seen far too many, you can tell. *Nobody home.*

Samantha gave a little shudder and seemed to melt deeper into Adrian's embrace. 'And the flies,' she said.

'What flies?' Annie asked.

'On her face and her arms. Flies. She wasn't moving. She wasn't even trying to swat them away. I thought how much they must be tickling her.'

Annie swallowed. 'Were the windows open?'

'Yes,' said Samantha. 'Just like they are now. We really didn't disturb anything. I mean, we've seen Morse and Frost on television.'

'I'm sure you have. I just have to make certain. I don't

17

suppose you saw anyone, heard any other cars or anything?'

'No.'

'What did you do when you found her?'

'Rang the police.' Adrian pulled a mobile from his pocket. He wouldn't have had much luck with it around these parts a few months ago, Annie reflected, but coverage had been improved a lot recently.

'And there's nothing else you can tell me?'

'No. Look, we're just so . . . devastated. Can we go home now? I think Sam needs a lie down, and I could do with a strong cup of tea.'

'How long are you staying at Greystone?' Annie asked.

'We've got another week.'

'Stick around,' said Annie. 'We might want to talk to you again.'

Annie went back to rejoin Hatchley and saw Dr Burns's grey Audi arrive. She greeted him and they walked over to the Peugeot. This would be a difficult examination for Dr Burns, Annie knew, because the body was sitting upright in an enclosed space, and he could hardly move it before Dr Glendenning, the Home Office pathologist, arrived. She also knew that Dr Burns was aware the Scenes-of-Crime Officers would be eager to give the car a thorough going-over, so he was being extra careful not to touch any surfaces and damage any possible prints, even though he was wearing disposable gloves. It was the police surgeon's job only to determine and pronounce that the girl was dead – the rest was up to the pathologist – but Annie knew that Dr Burns would like to give her some idea of time and cause, if at all possible.

After feeling for a pulse and examining the woman's

eyes, then listening for a heartbeat through his stetho-
scope, Dr Burns confirmed that she was, indeed, dead.

'The corneas haven't clouded yet,' he said, 'which
means she's probably been dead less than eight hours.
I'm sure the flies have laid their eggs already, which
you'd expect to happen quite soon in summer with the
windows open, but there's no sign of advanced insect
activity, another indication we're dealing with a relatively recent death.'

Dr Burns slipped off a glove and slid his hand inside
the woman's blouse, under her arm. 'Best I can do as far
as temperature is concerned,' he said, noticing Annie's
curious glance. 'It does help give an approximation.
She's still warm, which confirms that death occurred
only a few hours ago.'

'It was a warm night,' said Annie. 'How long?'

'Can't say exactly, but I'd guess about five or six hours
at the most.' He felt the woman's jaw and neck. 'Rigor's
present where you'd expect it to be, and as the heat probably speeded that up, we're still working within much
the same parameters.'

Annie looked at her watch. 'Between two and four in
the morning, then?'

'I wouldn't swear to it, of course,' said Dr Burns, with
a smile, 'but that sounds about right. And don't tell Dr
Glendenning I've been making wild guesses. You know
what he's like about that sort of thing.'

'Any thoughts on cause of death?'

'That's a bit more difficult,' said Dr Burns, turning
to the body again. 'There are no visible signs of strangulation, either ligature or manual, and no petechial
haemorrhaging, which you'd expect with strangulation.
Also no signs of a stab wound, no blood that I can see,

at any rate. It'll have to wait until Dr Glendenning gets her on the table.'

'Could it have been a heart attack, or something like that?'

'It could have been. Heart attacks aren't so common in healthy young women, but if she had some sort of genetic disorder or pre-existing condition . . . Let's say it's within the realm of the possible, but unlikely.'

Dr Burns turned back to the body and probed gently here and there. He tried to loosen the woman's hand from the steering wheel but couldn't. 'That's interesting,' he said. 'Rigor hasn't progressed as far as the hands yet, so it looks as if we're dealing with cadaveric spasm.'

'What does it mean in this case?'

Dr Burns stood up and faced Annie. 'It means she was holding the wheel when she died. And the gearstick.'

Annie thought about the implications of that. Either the woman had just managed to pull into the lay-by when she died, or she was trying to drive away from something – or someone.

Annie stuck her head through the car window, uncomfortably aware of the closeness of the corpse, and looked down. One foot on the clutch, the other on the accelerator, gearstick in reverse and ignition turned on. She reached out and touched the travel mug. It felt cool.

As she moved back, Annie smelled just a hint of something vaguely sweet and metallic. She told Dr Burns. He frowned and leaned forward, apologizing that he didn't have a sense of smell. Gently, he touched the woman's hair and pulled it back to expose her ear. Then he gasped.

'Good Lord,' he said. 'Look at this.'

Annie bent over and looked. Just above the woman's

right ear was a tiny star-shaped hole, around which the skin was burned and blackened with a soot-like residue. There wasn't much blood, and what there was had been hidden by her long red hair. Annie was no expert, but it didn't take an expert to realize that this was a gunshot wound fired from fairly close quarters. And if there was no gun in sight, and the woman had one hand on the steering wheel and the other on the gearstick, then it could hardly have been a self-inflicted gunshot wound.

Dr Burns leaned through the window in front of the woman, feeling the other side of her skull for signs of blood and an exit wound. 'Nothing,' he said. 'No wonder we couldn't see anything. The bullet must be still inside her skull.' He stepped away from the car, as if washing his hands of the whole affair. 'OK,' he said, 'that's all I can do for now. The rest is up to Dr Glendenning.'

Annie looked at him and sighed, then she called Hatchley over. 'Inform Superintendent Gristhorpe that we've got what looks very much like a murder on our hands. And we'd better get Dr Glendenning and the SOCOs down here as soon as possible.'

Hatchley's face dropped. Annie knew why, and she sympathized. It was the weekend, but all leave would be cancelled. Sergeant Hatchley probably had plans to go and watch the local cricket team and have a booze up with the lads afterwards. But not now. She wouldn't even be surprised if Banks was called back, depending on the scale of the investigation.

She looked down the road and her heart sank as she saw the first media vans arriving. How quickly bad news travels, she thought.

2

Unaware of the excitement just a few miles down the road, Banks was up and around before eight o'clock that morning, filter coffee and newspaper on the table in front of him, mild hangover held at bay by paracetamol. He hadn't slept at all well, mostly because he had been waiting for the phone to ring. And he hadn't been able to get that song Penny Cartwright had been singing out of his mind: 'Strange Affair'. The melody haunted him and the lyrics, with their images of death and fear, troubled him.

His window framed a view of blue sky above the rising northern daleside, and the grey flagstone roofs of Helmthorpe about half a mile away at the valley bottom, dominated by its church tower with the odd turret on one corner. It was similar to his view from the wall by his old cottage, just a slightly different angle. But it failed to move him. He could see that it was beautiful, but he couldn't *feel* it. There seemed to be something missing, some connection, or perhaps there was a sort of invisible shield or thick fog between him and the rest of the world, and it dimmed the power of all he had held dear to move him in any way. Music, landscape, words on a page all seemed inert and impotent, distant and unimportant.

Since the fire had consumed his home and possessions four months ago, Banks had become withdrawn and taciturn; he knew it, but there was nothing he could do about it. He was suffering from depression, but knowing that was one thing, changing it quite another.

It had started the day he left hospital and went to look at the ruins of his cottage. He hadn't been prepared for the scale of the damage: roof gone, windows burned out, inside a shambles of charred debris, nothing salvageable, hardly anything even recognizable. And it didn't help that the man who had done this had got away.

After a few days convalescing at Gristhorpe's Lyndgarth farmhouse, he had found the flat and moved in. Some mornings he didn't want to get out of bed. Most nights he spent watching television, any old rubbish, and drinking. He wasn't drinking too much, but he was drinking steadily, mostly wine, and smoking again.

His withdrawal had driven the wedge even deeper between him and Annie Cabbot, who desperately seemed to need something from him. He thought he knew what it was, but he couldn't give it to her. Not yet. It had also cooled his relationship with Michelle Hart, a detective inspector who had recently transferred to Sex Crimes and Child Protection in Bristol, much too far away to maintain a reasonable long-distance relationship. Michelle had her own problems, too, Banks realized. Whatever it was that haunted her was always there, always in the way, even when they were laughing or making love. They'd been good for one another for a while, no doubt about it, but now they were down to the 'just good friends' stage that usually comes before the end.

It seemed as if the fire and subsequent spell in hospital had put his life on pause, and he couldn't find the play button. Even work, when he'd got back to it, had been boring, consisting mostly of paperwork and interminable meetings that never settled anything. Only an occasional pint with Gristhorpe or Jim Hatchley, a chat about football or the previous evening's television, had relieved the tedium. His daughter Tracy had visited as often as she could, but she had been studying hard for her finals. Brian had dropped by a few times, too, and now he was in a recording studio in Dublin with his band working on a new CD. Their first as the Blue Lamps had done OK, but the second was slated for much bigger and better things.

More than once Banks had thought of counselling, only to reject the idea. He had even considered that Dr Jenny Fuller, a consultant psychologist he had worked with on a number of cases, might be able to help, but she was on one of her extended teaching gigs – Australia this time – and when he thought more about it, the idea of Jenny delving into the murky depths of his subconscious didn't hold a lot of appeal. Maybe whatever was there was best left there.

When it came down to it, he didn't need any interfering shrink poking around in his mind and telling him what was wrong. He knew what was wrong, knew he spent too much time sitting around the flat and brooding. He also knew that the healing process – the mental and emotional process, not merely the physical – would take time, and that it was something he had to do alone, make his way step by weary step back to the land of the living. No doubt about it, the fire had burned much deeper than his skin.

It wasn't so much the pain he'd endured – that hadn't lasted long, and he couldn't even remember most of it – but the loss of all his worldly goods that hit him the hardest. He felt like a man adrift, unanchored, a helium balloon let float off into the sky by a careless child. What was worse was that he thought he ought to be feeling a great sense of release, of freedom from materialism, the sort of thing gurus and sages spoke about, but he just felt jittery and insecure. He hadn't learned the virtue of simplicity from his loss, had learned only that he missed his material possessions more than he ever dreamed he would, though he hadn't yet been able to muster up the energy and interest to start replacing those items that *could* be replaced: his CD collection, his books and DVDs. He felt too weary to start again. He had bought clothes, of course – comfortable, functional clothes – but that was all.

Still, he reflected, munching on a slice of toast and marmalade as he scanned the reviews section of the newspaper, things were definitely improving a little each day. It was becoming easier to get out of bed, and he had got into the habit of occasionally taking a walk up the daleside opposite his flat on fine mornings, finding the freshness and exercise invigorating. He had also enjoyed what he heard of Penny Cartwright's singing the previous night and was beginning to miss his CD collection. A month or so ago, he wouldn't even have bothered reading the reviews in the paper.

And now brother Roy, who hadn't even rung or visited him in hospital, had left a mysterious urgent message and had not called back. For the third time since he got up that morning, Banks tried Roy's numbers. He got the answering machine again, the recorded voice telling him to leave a message, and the mobile was switched off.

Unable to concentrate on the newspaper any longer, Banks checked his watch and decided to ring his parents. They should be up by now. There was just a chance that

Roy was there, or that they knew what was going on. He certainly seemed to keep in touch with them more than with Banks.

His mother answered and sounded nervous to be getting a call so early in the day. In her world, Banks knew, early morning phone calls never meant good news. 'Alan? What is it? Is there something wrong?'

'No, Mum,' Banks said, trying to put her at ease. 'Everything's fine.'

'You're all right, are you? Still recovering?'

'Still recovering,' said Banks. 'Look, Mum, I was wondering if our Roy was there.'

'Roy? Why would he be here? The last time we saw Roy was our anniversary last October. You must remember. You were here, too.'

'I remember,' said Banks. 'It's just that I've been trying to ring him . . .'

His mother's voice brightened. 'So you two are making it up at last. That's good to hear.'

'Yes,' said Banks, not wishing to disabuse his mother of that little scrap of comfort. 'It's just that I keep getting his answering machine.'

'Well, he's probably at work. You know how hardworking our Roy is. Always got something or other on the go.'

'Yes,' Banks agreed. Usually something about two shades away from being criminal. White-collar, though, which didn't seem to count as crime to some people. When Banks thought about it, he realized he really hadn't a clue what Roy actually did to make his money. Only that he made a lot of it. 'So you haven't heard from him recently?'

'I didn't say that. As a matter of fact he rang about

two weeks ago, just to see how your dad and I are doing, like.'

The implied rebuke wasn't lost on Banks; he hadn't rung his parents for a month. 'Did he have anything else to say?'

'Not much. Except he's keeping busy. He might be away, you know. Have you thought about that? He did say something about an important business trip coming up. New York again, I think. He's always going there. I can't remember when he said he was going, though.'

'OK, Mum,' said Banks. 'That's probably where he is. Thanks very much. I'll wait a few days and call him when he gets back home.'

'You make sure you do, Alan. He's a good lad, is Roy. I don't know why you two haven't been getting on better all these years.'

'We get along fine, Mum. We just move in different circles, that's all. How's Dad?'

'Same as ever.' Banks heard the rustle of a newspaper – the *Daily Mail* his father read just so he could complain about the Conservatives – and a muffled voice in the background. 'He says to say hello.'

'Right,' said Banks. 'Say hello back . . . Well, take care of yourselves. I'll call again soon.'

'Mind you do,' said Banks's mother.

Banks rang off then tried both of Roy's numbers again, but still no Roy. There was no way he was going to wait a few days, or even hours. From what he knew of Roy, under normal circumstances if he had buggered off somewhere and not bothered to ring back, Banks would have assumed Roy was sunning himself in California or the Caribbean with a shapely young woman by his side. That would be typical of him and his me-first attitude. As far as Roy was concerned, there was nothing in life you couldn't get through with a smile and a wad of cash. But this was different. This time Banks had heard the fear in his brother's voice.

He deleted the messages from his answerphone, threw a few clothes along with his toothbrush and razor into an overnight bag, checked that the lights were out, unplugged all the electrical items and locked the flat behind him. He knew he wouldn't get any rest until he got to the bottom of Roy's odd silence, so he might as well drive down to London and find out what was happening himself.

●

Detective Superintendent Gristhorpe called the meeting in the boardroom of Western Area Headquarters after lunch, and DI Annie Cabbot, DS Hatchley and crime-scene coordinator DS Stefan Nowak, along with DCs Winsome Jackman, Kev Templeton and Gavin Rickerd, sat in the high, stiff-backed chairs under the gaze of ancient wool barons with roast-beef complexions and tight collars. Their notes and files were set in neat piles on the dark polished table beside styrofoam cups of tea or coffee. Pinned to cork boards on the wall by the door were Peter Darby's Polaroids of the scene. It was already hot and stuffy in the room and the small fan Gristhorpe had turned on didn't do much good.

Soon, when the investigation got seriously underway, more manpower would be allocated, but these seven would remain the core team: Gristhorpe as senior investigative officer and Annie, who would do most of the field work, as his deputy and administrative officer. Rickerd would be office manager, responsible for setting up and staffing the murder room; Hatchley would act as receiver, there to weigh the value of every piece of information and pass it on for computer entry. Winsome and Hatchley would be the foot soldiers, tracking down information and conducting interviews. Others would be appointed later – statement-readers, action allocators, researchers, and the rest – but for now it was of prime importance to get the system into place and into action. It was no longer merely a suspicious death. Jennifer Clewes – if that was really the name of the victim – had been murdered.

Gristhorpe cleared his throat, shuffled his papers and began by asking Annie for a summary of the facts, which she gave as succinctly as possible. Then he turned to DS Stefan Nowak.

'Any forensics yet?'

'It's still early days,' said Stefan, 'so I'm afraid all I can give you at the moment is what we *don't* have.'

'Go on.'

'Well, the road surface was dry and there are no discernible tyre tracks from any other vehicle. Also, we haven't turned up any physical evidence – discarded cigarette ends, spent matches, that sort of thing. There are plenty of prints on the outside of the car, so that will take Vic Manson a while to sort out, but they could be anyone's.'

'What about *inside* the car?' Gristhorpe asked.

'It's in the police garage right now, sir. We should know something later today. There is one thing.'

'Yes?'

'It looks as if she was definitely forced off the road. The left wing hit the drystone wall.'

'But there was no damage to the right wing, at least not that I could see,' Annie said.

'That's right,' Stefan agreed. 'The car that forced her over didn't make physical contact. Pity. We might have got some nice paint samples.'

'Keep looking,' said Gristhorpe.

'Anyway,' Stefan went on, 'whoever it was must have got in front of her and veered to the left rather than come at her directly from the side.'

'Well,' said Gristhorpe, 'what do you do if you're a woman alone and a car comes up fast behind you on a deserted country road at night?'

'I'd say either you take off like a bat out of hell or you slow down and let him get by and put as much distance as possible between the two of you,' said Annie.

'Exactly. Only in this case he forced her over to the side of the road.'

'The gearstick,' Annie said.

'What?' Gristhorpe asked.

'The gearstick. She was trying to get away. She was trying to reverse.'

'That's the way it looks,' said Stefan.

'But she wasn't fast enough,' said Annie.

'No. And she stalled.'

'Do you think,' Annie went on, 'that there might have been two of them?'

'Why?' asked Gristhorpe.

Stefan looked at Annie and answered. It was uncanny, she thought, how often their thoughts followed the same pathways. 'I think DI Cabbot means,' he said, 'that if the driver had to put on the brake, unfasten his seat belt and pull out his gun before getting out, those few seconds might have made all the difference.'

'Yes,' said Annie. 'Though why we should assume a murderer would be so law-abiding as to wear a seat belt is stretching it a bit. And he may have already had his gun out and not bothered to turn off the ignition. But if someone was there to leap out, say someone in the back, with his gun ready and no seat belt to unfasten, then she wouldn't have had time to recover from the shock and get away in time. Remember, she'd probably be panicking.'

'Hmm,' said Gristhorpe. 'Interesting. And possible. Let's keep an open mind for the time being. Anything else?'

'Not really,' said Stefan. 'The victim's been taken to the mortuary and Dr Glendenning said he should be able to get around to the post-mortem sometime this afternoon. In the meantime, it still looks very much as if death was due to a single gunshot wound above the right ear.'

'Any ideas about the sort of weapon used?'

'We've found no trace of a cartridge, so either our killer was smart and picked up after himself, or he used a revolver. At a rough estimate, I'd say it's probably a .22 calibre. Anything bigger would most likely have left an exit wound.' Stefan paused. 'We might not have had a lot of practice with gunshot wounds around these parts,' he said, 'but our ballistics specialist Kim Grainger knows her stuff. That's about it, sir. Sorry we can't be a bit more helpful right now.'

'Early days, yet,' said Gristhorpe. 'Keep at it, Stefan.' He turned to the rest of the group. 'Has anyone verified the woman's identity yet?' he asked.

'Not yet,' said Annie. 'I got in touch with Lambeth North. It turns out their DI at Kennington nick is an old friend of mine, Dave Brooke, and he sent a couple of DCs to her address. Nobody home. They're keeping a watching brief.'

'And there are no reports of her car being stolen?'

'No, sir.'

'So it's still more than within the realm of possibility that the registered keeper of the vehicle is the person found dead in it?'

'Yes. Unless she lent her car to a friend or hasn't noticed it's gone missing yet.'

'Do we even know for certain that she was alone in the car?' Gristhorpe asked.

'No.' Annie looked at Stefan. 'I'm assuming that's something they'll be able to help us determine down at the garage.'

Stefan nodded. 'Perhaps.'

'Anyone run her name through our system?'

'I did, sir,' said Winsome. 'Name, prints, description. Nothing. If she ever committed a criminal act, we didn't catch her.'

'It wouldn't be the first time,' Gristhorpe said. 'All right, first priority, find out who she is and what she was doing on that road. In the meantime, I assume we're already making door-to-door enquiries in the general area of the incident?'

'Yes, sir,' said Annie. 'Problem is, there's not much *in* the general area. As you know, it happened on a deserted stretch of road between the A1 and Eastvale in the early hours of the morning. We've got people going from house to house, but there's nothing except a few holiday cottages and the occasional farmhouse within a mile each way of the car. Nothing's turned up so far.'

'Nobody heard the shot?'

'Not so far.'

'An ideal place for a murder, then,' Gristhorpe commented. He scratched his chin. Annie could see by the stubble that he hadn't shaved that morning. Hadn't combed his unruly hair by the looks of it, either. Still, personal grooming sometimes took backstage when it came to the urgency of a murder investigation. At least as far as the men were concerned. Kev Templeton was far too vain, of course, to look anything but his gelled, athletic and trendy best, not to mention cool as Antarctica, but Jim Hatchley had definitely taken a leaf out of Gristhorpe's book. Gavin looked like a train-spotter, right down to the National Health specs held together over his nose by a plaster. Winsome was immaculate in pinstripe navy trousers and matching waistcoat over a white scallop-neck blouse, and Annie felt rather conservative in her plain pastel frock and linen jacket. She also felt unpleasantly sweaty and hoped it didn't show.

Finding herself doodling a cartoon of Kev Templeton in full seventies gear, complete with the Afro and tight gold lamé shirt, Annie dragged herself away from her sartorial musings, admonishing herself once again for having difficulty concentrating these days, and got back to the matter in hand: Jennifer Clewes. Gristhorpe was asking her a question, and Annie realized she had missed it.

'Sorry, sir?'

Gristhorpe frowned at her. 'I said do we have any idea where the victim was driving from?'

'No, sir,' said Annie.

'Then perhaps we should set about canvassing all-night garages, shops open late, that sort of thing?'

'If the victim really is Jennifer Clewes,' Annie said, hoping to make up for her lapse in concentration, 'then the odds are that she came from London. As the road she was found on leads to and from the A1, which connects with the M1, that makes it even more likely.'

'Motorway service stations, then?' Kevin Templeton suggested.

'Good idea, DC Templeton,' said Gristhorpe. 'I'll leave that to you, shall I?'

'Wouldn't it be better to get the local forces on it, sir?'

'That'll take too much time and coordination. We need results fast. Better if you do it yourself. Tonight.'

'Just what I always fancied,' Templeton grumbled. 'Driving up and down the M1 sampling the local cuisine.'

Gristhorpe smiled. 'Well, it *was* your idea. And I hear they do a very decent bacon panini at Woodall. Anything else?'

'DC Jackman mentioned that there had been a similar crime some months ago,' Annie said.

Gristhorpe looked at Winsome Jackman, eyebrows raised. 'Oh?'

'Yes, sir,' said Winsome. 'I checked the details. It's not quite as similar as it appears on first glance.'

'Even so,' said Gristhorpe. 'I think we'd like to hear about it.'

'It was near the end of April, the 23rd. The young woman's name was Claire Potter, aged twenty-three, lived in North London. She set off at about eight o'clock on a Friday evening to go and spend the weekend with friends in Castleton. She never got there. Her car was found in a ditch by the side of a quiet road north of Chesterfield by a passing motorist the following morning and her body was found nearby – raped and stabbed.

The way it looks is that her car was forced into a ditch by her assailant. The pathologist also found traces of chloroform and characteristic burning around her mouth.'

'Where was she last seen?'

'Trowell services.'

'Nothing on the service station's closed-circuit TV?' asked Gristhorpe.

'Apparently not, sir. I had a brief chat with DI Gifford at Derbyshire CID, and the impression I got was that they've reached a dead end. No witnesses from the cafeteria or garage. Nothing.'

'The MO is different, too,' Annie pointed out.

'Yes,' said Gristhorpe. 'Jennifer Clewes was shot, not stabbed, and she wasn't sexually interfered with, at least not as far as we know. But you think there could be some connection, DC Jackman?'

'Well, sir,' mused Winsome, 'there are some similarities: stopping at the services, being forced off the road, a young woman. There could be any number of reasons why he didn't assault her this time, and he could certainly have acquired a gun since his last murder. Maybe he didn't enjoy stabbing. Maybe it was just a bit too up close and personal for him.'

'OK,' said Gristhorpe. 'Good work. We'll keep an open mind. Last thing we want is to let a serial killer slip through our hands because we don't see the connection. I take it you'll be activating HOLMES?'

'Yes, sir,' said Winsome. The Home Office Large Major Enquiry System was an essential tool in any major investigation. Every scrap of information was entered into the computer and connections were made in ways even a trained officer might easily miss.

'Good.' Gristhorpe stood up. 'OK. Any—'

There was a knock at the door and Gristhorpe called out, 'Come in.'

Dr Wendy Gauge, Dr Glendenning's new and enigmatic assistant, stood there, looking as composed as ever, that mysterious, self-contained smile lingering around her lips the way it always did, even when she was bent over a corpse on the table. Rumour had it that Dr Gauge was being groomed as Glendenning's successor when the old man retired, and Annie had to admit that she was good.

'Yes?' said Gristhorpe.

Wendy Gauge moved forward. 'I've just come from the mortuary,' she said. 'We were removing the victim's clothing and I found this in her back pocket.' She handed over a slip of lined paper, clearly torn from a notebook of some sort, which she had thoughtfully placed in a transparent plastic folder. 'Her killer must have taken everything else from the car,' Dr Gauge went on, 'but . . . well . . . her jeans were very tight and she was . . . you know . . . sitting on it.'

Annie could have sworn Dr Gauge blushed.

Gristhorpe examined the slip of paper first, then frowned and slid it down the table for the others to see.

Annie could hardly believe her eyes, but there, scrawled in blue ink and followed by directions from the A1(M) and a crude map of Helmthorpe, was a name and address:

Alan Banks
Newhope Cottage
Beckside Lane
Gratly, near Helmthorpe
North Yorkshire.

•

By the time his colleagues back in Eastvale were speculating as to what his name and address were doing in a
murder victim's back pocket, Banks was in London,
making his way through the early Saturday afternoon
traffic past the posh restaurants and Maserati showrooms
towards his brother Roy's South Kensington house, just
east of the Gloucester Road. It was years since he had
driven in London, and the roads seemed more crowded
than ever.

He had never seen where Roy lived before, he realized, as he drove under the narrow brick arch and parked
in the broad cobbled mews. He got out and looked at the
whitewashed brick exterior of the house with its inte-
gral garage next to the front door and a mullioned bay
window above. It didn't look big, but that didn't matter
these days. A house like this, in this location, would
probably fetch eight hundred k or more in today's
market, Banks reckoned, maybe even a million, and a
hundred k of that you'd be paying for the privilege of
having the word 'mews' in your address.

All the houses stood cheek by jowl, but each was
different in some detail – height, facade, style of
windows, garage doors, wrought-iron balconies – and the
overall effect was of quiet, almost rural charm, a nook
hidden away from the hurly-burly that was literally just
around the corner. There were houses on all three sides
of the cul-de-sac, and the red-brick archway, only wide
enough for one car, led to the main road, helping to
isolate the mews from the world outside. Beyond the
houses at the far end a tower block and a row of distant

cranes, angled like alien birds of prey, marred the view of a clear sky.

There were hardly any other cars parked in the mews, as most of the houses had private garages. The few cars that were on display were BMWs, Jaguars and Mercedes, and Banks's shabby little Renault looked like a poor relation. Not for the first time the thought crossed his mind that he needed a new car. It was a hot morning for June, hotter here than up north, and he took off his jacket and slung it over his shoulder.

First he checked the number against his address book. It was the right house. Next he pressed the doorbell and waited. Nobody came. Perhaps, Banks thought, the bell didn't work, or couldn't be heard upstairs, but he remembered hearing it buzz on Roy's phone message. He knocked on the door. Still no answer. He knocked again.

Occasionally, a car would pass by the archway, on the Old Brompton Road, but otherwise the area was quiet. After knocking one last time, Banks tried the door. To his surprise, it opened. Banks could hardly believe it. From what he remembered, Roy had always been security conscious, fiercely protective of his possessions, had probably been born that way. One of the first things he had done, as soon as he was old enough, was save up his pocket money to buy a padlock for his toy box, and woe betide anyone caught touching his bike or his scooter.

Banks examined the lock and saw that it was the deadbolt kind, which you had to use a key both to open *and* to close. Behind the door was a copy of that morning's *Times* and a few letters, bills or junk. He noticed the keypad of a burglar-alarm system just inside the hall, but it hadn't been activated.

To the left was a small sitting room, rather like a

doctor's waiting room, with a beige three-piece suite and a low glass-topped coffee-table, on which lay a neat pile of magazines. Banks flipped through them. Mostly business and hi-tech. Between the sitting room and the kitchen, at the back of the house, ran a narrow passage, with a door on the right, near the front, leading to the garage. Banks peeked in and saw that Roy's Porsche 911 was parked there. The car was locked, the bonnet cold.

Back in the house, Banks opened the door that led to a narrow flight of stairs and called Roy's name. No reply. The house was silent except for the myriad daily sounds we usually tune out: distant traffic, the hum of a refrigerator, the ticking of a clock, a tap dripping somewhere, old wood creaking. Banks shuddered. Someone had just walked over his grave, as his mother would say. He couldn't put his finger on what it was, but he felt a distinct tingling up his spine. Fear. There was no one in the house; he was reasonably sure of that. But perhaps someone was watching the place? Banks had learned to trust his instincts over the years, even if he hadn't always acted on them, and he sensed that he would have to move carefully.

He walked into the kitchen, which looked as if it had never been used for anything but making tea and toast. The whole downstairs – sitting room, passage and kitchen – was painted in shades of blue and grey. The paint smelled fresh. A couple of framed photographs in high-contrast black and white hung in the passage. One was a female nude curled on a bed, the other a hill of terraced brick houses leading down to a factory, its chimneys smoking, cobbles and slate roofs gleaming after rain. Banks was surprised. He hadn't known that Roy was interested in photography, or in art of any kind.

But then there was so much he didn't know about his estranged brother.

In the kitchen stood a small rustic wooden table with two matching chairs, surrounded by the usual array of counter-tops, toaster, storage cupboards, fridge, oven and microwave. The table was clear apart from an opened bottle of Amarone with the cork stuck back in, and, half hidden behind the bottle, a mobile phone. Banks picked up the phone. It was off, so he turned it on. It was an expensive model, the kind that sends and receives digital images, and there was plenty of battery power left. He tried the voicemail and text functions, but the only messages were the ones he had left. Was Roy the kind of person who would forget to take his mobile with him when he went out under normal circumstances, especially as he had given Banks the number? Banks doubted it, the same way he doubted that Roy would deliberately leave his front door unlocked or forget to turn on his burglar alarm unless he was really rattled by something.

A wine-rack stood on one of the counters, and even Banks could tell that the wines there were very high-end clarets, Chiantis and burgundies. Above the rack hung a ring of keys on a hook. One of them looked like a car key. Banks put them in his pocket. He checked the fridge. It was empty except for some margarine, a carton of milk and a piece of mouldy Cheddar. That confirmed it. Roy was no gourmet cook. He could afford to eat out, and there were plenty of good restaurants on Old Brompton Road. The back door was locked, and the window looked out on a small backyard and an alley beyond.

Before going upstairs, Banks went back to the garage to see if the car key on the ring fit the Porsche. As he had suspected, it did. Banks opened the driver's door and got in.

He had never sat in such a car before, and the luxurious leather upholstery embraced him like a lover. He felt like putting the key in the ignition and driving off somewhere, anywhere. But that wasn't why he was here. The car's interior smelled clean and fresh, with that expensive hint of leather. From what Banks could see, there were no empty crisp packets or pop cans on the back seat or cellophane wrappers on the floor. Nor was there one of those fancy GPS gadgets that would tell Banks what Roy's last destination was. In the side pocket was a small AA road atlas open to the page with Reading in the bottom right and Stratford-upon-Avon at top left. There was nothing else except the car's manual and a few CDs, mostly classical. Banks got out and checked the boot. Empty.

Next, Banks ventured upstairs, a much larger living space than downstairs because it extended over the garage. At the top of the stairs, he found himself on a small landing with five doors leading off. The first led to the toilet, the second to a modern bathroom, complete with power shower and whirlpool bath. There were the usual shaving and dental-care implements, paracetamol and Rennies, and rather more varieties of shampoo, conditioner and body lotion than Banks imagined Roy would need. He also wouldn't need the pink plastic disposable razor that sat next to the gel for sensitive skin, not unless he shaved his legs.

At the back was a bedroom, simple and bright, with flower-patterned wallpaper: double bed, duvet, dressing-table, drawers and a small wardrobe full of clothes and shoes, everything immaculate. Roy's clothing ran the gamut from expensive casual to expensive business, Banks noticed – looking at the labels: Armani, Hugo Boss, Paul Smith – and there were also a few items of women's clothing, including a summer dress, a black evening gown, Levi's, an assortment of short-sleeved tops and several pairs of shoes and sandals.

The drawers revealed a few items of jewellery, condoms, tampons and a mix of men's and women's underwear. Banks didn't know whether Roy was into cross-dressing, but he assumed the female items belonged to his girlfriend of the moment. And as there was nowhere near enough women's paraphernalia to indicate that a woman actually *lived* there, she probably just kept a few clothes, along with the items in the bathroom, for when she stayed over.

Banks remembered the young girl who had been with Roy the last time they met. She had looked about twenty, shy, with short, shaggy black hair streaked with blonde, a pale, pretty face, with beautiful eyes the colour and gleam of chestnuts in October. She also had a silver stud just below her lower lip. She had been wearing jeans and a short woolly jumper, exposing a couple of inches of bare, flat midriff and a navel with a ring in it. They were engaged, Banks remembered. He tried to remember her name. It was Colleen or Connie, something like that. She might know where Roy had gone. Banks could probably trace her from Roy's mobile's phone book. Of course, there was no guarantee that she was still Roy's fiancée, or that the clothes and toiletry items were hers.

Next to the bedroom, and quite a bit larger, was what appeared to be Roy's office, furnished with filing cabinets, a computer monitor, fax machine, printer and photocopier. Again, everything was shipshape, no untidy

piles of paper or yellow post-it notes stuck on every surface, like Banks's office. The desk surface was clear apart
from an unused writing tablet and an empty glass of red
wine, the dregs hardening to crystal. In a bookcase just
above the desk were the standard reference books –
atlas, dictionary, Dunn and Bradstreet, *Who's Who*.

Roy certainly kept his life in order, and Banks remembered that he had been a tidy child, too. After playing, he
had always put his toys carefully away in their box and
locked it. His room, even when he was a teenager, was a
model of cleanliness and tidiness. He could have been in
the army. Banks's room, on the other hand, had been the
same sort of mess he'd seen in most teens' bedrooms on
missing-persons cases. He'd known where everything
was – his books were in alphabetical order, for example
– but he had never fussed much about making his bed or
tidying the pile of discarded clothes left on the floor.
Another reason his mother had always favoured Roy.

Banks wondered if Roy's computer would tell him
anything. The flat-panel monitor sat on the desk, but
Banks was damned if he could find the computer itself.
It wasn't on or under the desk, or on the shelf behind.
There was a keyboard and a mouse, but keyboard,
mouse and monitor were no use without the computer.
Even a novice like Banks knew that.

Given Roy's interest in electronic gadgets, Banks
would have expected a laptop, too, but he could find no
signs of one. Nor a handheld. He remembered Roy showing off a flashy new Palm – one of those gadgets that do
everything but fry your eggs in the morning – at the party
last year.

Needless to say, there was nothing remotely so useful
as a Filofax. Roy would keep all that information on his

computer and his Palm, and it seemed that they were both gone. Still, Banks had the mobile, and that ought to prove a fruitful source of contact numbers.

There was a Nikon Coolpix 4300 digital camera in one of the pigeonholes behind the computer desk. Banks knew a little about digital cameras, though his cheap Canon was well below Roy's range. He at least managed to switch it on and figure out how to look at the images on the LCD screen, but there was no memory card in it, no images to see. He searched around the adjoining pigeonholes for some sort of image-storage device but found nothing. That was another puzzle, he realized. All the things you expect to find around a computer – Zip drive, tape backups or CDs – were conspicuous in their absence. There was nothing left but the monitor, mouse and keyboard, and an empty digital camera.

One other gadget remained: a 40GB iPod, another little electronic toy Banks had thought of buying. He dipped in at random, hearing snatches of arias here and a bit of an overture there. Banks had always thought his brother a bit of a philistine, didn't know he was an opera buff, that they might have something in common. From what he could remember, when he had been into Dylan, The Who and the Stones, Roy had been a Herman's Hermits fan.

One of the songs Banks stumbled across was 'Dido's Lament' from Purcell's *Dido and Aeneas*, and he found himself listening for just a little longer than he needed, feeling a lump in his throat and that burning sensation at the back of his eyes he always felt when he heard 'When I am laid in earth'. The upsurge of emotion surprised him. Another good sign. He had felt little or nothing since the fire and thought that was because he had nothing left to feel with. It was encouraging to have at least a hint that there was life in the old boy yet. He browsed through the iPod's contents and found a lot of good stuff: Bach, Beethoven, Verdi, Puccini, Rossini. There was a complete *Ring Cycle*, but nobody's perfect, he thought. Least of all Roy. Still, the extent of his good taste was a surprise.

The telephone was like a mini-computer system in itself. Banks managed to dial 1471 and find out that the last incoming call was the one he had made himself that morning before setting off for London. Unfortunately, Roy hadn't subscribed to the extra service that gave the numbers of the last five callers. Banks realized it didn't matter, as he had called at least five times himself. The phone was hooked up to a digital answering machine, and after a bit of dodgy business with the buttons Banks discovered three messages, all from him. The other times he'd called he hadn't bothered leaving one.

Banks thought he heard a sound from somewhere inside the house. He sat completely still and waited. What if Roy came back and found Banks going through his personal things and business records? How would he talk his way out of that one? On the other hand, Banks would be relieved to see Roy, and surely Roy would understand how his phone call had set off alarms in the mind of his policeman brother? Nevertheless, it would be embarrassing all around. A minute or two passed and he heard nothing more, so he put it down to one of the many sounds an old house makes.

Banks opened the desk drawers. The two bottom ones held folders full of bills and tax records, none of which seemed in any way unusual at a casual glance, and the top ones were filled with the usual stuff of offices:

Sellotape, rubber bands, paperclips, scissors, scratch-pads, staplers and printer cartridges.

The shallow central drawer contained pens and pencils of all shapes and sizes. Banks stirred them around with his hand, and one struck his eye. It was thicker and shorter than most of the other pens, squat and rectangular, rather than round. Thinking it might be some kind of marker, he picked it up and unclipped the top. It wasn't a pen. Where the nib should have been, instead he found a small rectangle of metal that looked as if it plugged into something. But what? Banks put the top back on and clipped the pen in the top pocket of his shirt.

The last door led to a large living room above the garage. It was the front room with the bay window Banks had noticed from the street. The colour scheme here was different, reds and earth colours, a desert theme. There were more framed black-and-white photographs on the walls, too, and Banks found himself wondering if Roy had taken them himself. He didn't know whether you could take black-and-white photos of that quality with a digital camera, but maybe you could. He could still dredge up no memory of his brother's interest in photography; as far as Banks knew, Roy hadn't even belonged to the camera club at school, and most kids did that at some time in the vain hope that whoever ran it would sneak in a nude model one day.

This room, like the rest of the house, was clean and tidy. Not a speck of dust or an abandoned mug anywhere. Banks doubted Roy did it himself; more likely he employed a cleaning lady. Even the entertainment magazines on the table were stacked parallel to the edge, Hercule Poirot style. A luxurious sofa-bed sat under the window facing the other wall, where a 42-inch

widescreen plasma TV hung, wired up to a satellite dish
and a DVD player. On looking more closely, Banks
noticed that the player also recorded DVDs. Under the
screen stood a sub-woofer and a front centre speaker,
and four smaller speakers were strategically placed
around the room. It was an expensive set-up, one which
Banks himself had often wished he could afford.

Banks walked to the fitted wall cabinets and cast his
eye over the selection of DVDs and CDs. What he saw
there puzzled him. Not for Roy the latest James Bond or
Terminator movie, not schoolgirl porn or Jenna Jameson,
but Fellini's *8½*, Kurasawa's *Ran* and *Throne of Blood*,
Herzog's *Fitzcarraldo*, Bergman's *The Seventh Seal* and
Truffaut's *The 400 Blows*. There were some films that
Banks could see himself watching – *The Godfather, The
Third Man* and *A Clockwork Orange* – but most of them
were foreign-language art films, classics of the cinema.
There were a few rows of books, too, mostly non-fiction,
on subjects ranging from music and cinema to philo-
sophy, religion and politics. Another surprise. In a small
recess stood one framed family photograph.

Banks studied Roy's large collection of operas on both
DVD and CD: *The Magic Flute, Tosca, Otello, Lucia de
Lammermoor* and others. A complete Bayreuth *Ring*
cycle, the same as the one on the iPod. There was a little
fifties jazz and a few Hollywood musicals – *Oklahoma,
South Pacific, Seven Brides for Seven Brothers* – but no
pop at all except for the Blue Lamps' debut. Banks was
pleased to see that Roy had bought Brian's CD, even
though he probably hadn't listened to it. He slid it out
and opened the case, wondering what it would sound
like on Roy's expensive stereo system. Instead of the
familiar blue image on the CD, he saw the words 'CD –

ReWritable' and that the disk held 650MB, or 74 minutes of playing time.

Banks stuck the CD in his jacket pocket and went over to sit on the sofa. Several remote-control devices rested on the arm, and when he had worked out which was which, he switched on the TV and amp just to see what the set-up looked and sounded like. It was a European football game, and the picture quality was stunning, the sound of the commentary loud enough to wake the dead. He turned it off.

He went back into the office and took the writing tablet from the desk and a pen from the drawer and carried them down to the kitchen with him. At the kitchen table, he sat down and wrote a note explaining that he'd been to the house and would be back, in case Roy returned while he was out, and asked him to get in touch as soon as possible.

He wished now that he had thought to bring his mobile so he could leave a number, but it was too late; he had left it on his living-room table next to his unused portable CD player, having got out of the habit of using it over the past few months. Then he realized he could take Roy's. He wanted to check through the entries in the phone book, anyway, so he might as well have the use of it in case Roy needed to get in touch with him. He added this as a PS to the note, then he put the mobile in his pocket. On his way out, he tried the most likely looking key and found it fitted the front door.

3

'**What do you** make of it, Annie?' Gristhorpe asked.

They were sitting in the superintendent's large carpeted office, just the two of them, and the sheet of paper lay between them on Gristhorpe's desk. It wasn't Banks's writing, Annie was certain. But beyond that, the whole thing was a puzzle. She had certainly never seen the dead woman before, nor had she ever heard Banks mention anyone called Jennifer Clewes. That in itself meant nothing, of course, she realized. In the first place, it might not be her real name, and in the second, Banks might well have been keeping many aspects of his life from her, including a new girlfriend. But if she was his girlfriend, why did she need directions and his address? Perhaps she had never visited him in Gratly before.

Was she new on the scene? Annie doubted it. The way Banks had been behaving lately, withdrawn, moody and uncommunicative, was hardly conducive to pulling a new girlfriend. Who would take him on, the shape he was in? And this woman was young enough to be his daughter. Not that age had ever stopped a man, but . . . Perhaps even more important was that she had ended up with a bullet in her head. Knowing Banks had its dangers, as Annie well knew, but it was not usually fatal.

'I don't know, sir. I'd say the most likely explanation is that it's her own writing. Maybe she copied it down over the phone. We'll be able to find out for sure when we get a sample of Jennifer Clewes's writing.'

'Have you been able to get in touch with DCI Banks?'

'He's not at home and his mobile's turned off. I've left messages.'

'Well, let's just hope he gets one of them and rings back. I'd really like to know why a young woman who was driving up from London to see him in the middle of the night ended up with a bullet in her head.'

'He could be anywhere,' Annie said. 'He is on holiday, after all.'

'He didn't tell you where he was going?'

'He doesn't tell me much these days, sir.'

Gristhorpe frowned and scratched his chin, then he leaned back in his big, padded chair and linked his hands behind his head. 'How's he doing?' he asked.

'I'm the last person to ask, sir. We haven't really talked much since the fire.'

'I thought you two were friends.'

'I like to think we are. But you know Alan. He's hardly the type to open up when he doesn't want to. I think perhaps he still blames me for what happened, the fire and all. After all, Phil Keane was my boyfriend. Whatever the reason, he's been very quiet lately. To be honest, I think it's partly depression as well.'

'I can't say I'm surprised. It happens sometimes after illness or an accident. About all you can do is wait till the fog disperses. What about you?'

'Me? I'm fine, sir. Coping.' Annie was aware how tight and unconvincing her voice sounded, but she could do nothing about it. Anyway, she *was* coping, after a fashion. She certainly wasn't depressed, just hurt and angry, and perhaps a little distracted.

Gristhorpe held her gaze for just long enough to make her feel uncomfortable, then he went on, 'We need to find out why the victim had Alan's address in her back pocket,' he said. 'And we can't ask her.'

'There's a flatmate, sir,' said Annie. 'The lads from Lambeth North got bored with hanging around outside and went in for a look. Jennifer Clewes was sharing with a woman called Kate Nesbit. At least there were letters there addressed to a Kate Nesbit *and* a Jennifer Clewes.'

'Have they talked to this flatmate?'

'She's not at home.'

'Work?'

'On a Saturday? Maybe. Or she might have gone away for the weekend.'

Gristhorpe looked at his watch. 'Better get down there, Annie,' he said. 'Let your old pal at Kennington know you're on your way. Find the flatmate and talk to her.'

'Yes, sir.' Annie stood up. 'There is one other thing.'

'Yes?'

Annie gestured towards the scrap of paper. 'This address. I mean, it *is* Alan's address, but it's not where he's living now.'

'I noticed that,' said Gristhorpe. 'You think it might be significant?'

'Well, sir,' Annie said, hand on the doorknob, 'he's been living at that flat in the old Steadman house for four months now. You'd think everyone who knew him – knew him at all well, at any rate – would know that. I mean, if it was a new girlfriend or something, why give her his old address?'

'You've got a point.' Gristhorpe scratched the side of his nose. 'What action do you think we should take?'

'About DCI Banks?'

'Yes.'

Gristhorpe paused. 'You say he's not answering his phones?'

'That's right, neither his home phone nor his mobile.'

'We need to find him, as soon as we can, but I don't want to make it official yet. I'll get Winsome to ring around his family and friends, see if anyone knows where he is.'

'I was thinking of dropping by his place – both of them – just to have a look around . . . you know . . . make sure nothing's been disturbed.'

'Good idea,' said Gristhorpe. 'Are you sure you're all right on this?'

Annie looked over her shoulder. 'Of course I am, sir,' she said. 'Why shouldn't I be?'

•

Out in the street, Banks tried knocking on a couple of neighbours' doors, but only one answered, an elderly man who lived in the house opposite.

'I saw you going into Roy's,' the man said. 'I was wondering if I should ring the police.'

Banks took out his warrant card. 'I'm Roy's brother,' he said, 'and I am the police.'

The man seemed satisfied and stuck out his hand. 'Malcolm Farrow,' he said as they shook hands. 'Pleased to meet you. Come inside.'

'I don't want to intrude on your time, but—'

'Think nothing of it. Now I'm retired every day's the same to me. Come in, we'll have a snifter.'

Banks followed him into a living room heavy with dark wood and antiques. Farrow offered brandy but

Banks took only soda. Much too early in the afternoon for spirits.

'What can I do for you, Mr Banks?' Farrow asked.

'Alan, please. It's about Roy.'

'What about him? Lovely fellow, that brother of yours, by the way. Couldn't wish for a better neighbour, you know. Cheerful, considerate. Capital fellow.'

'That's good to know,' said Banks, judging by the slight slur in his voice and the network of purplish veins around his bulbous nose that Malcolm Farrow had already had a snifter or two. 'I was just wondering if you had any idea where he's gone?'

'You mean he's not back yet?'

'Apparently not. Did you see him leave?'

'Yes. It was about half-past nine last night. I was putting the cat out when I saw him going out.'

Just after the phone call, Banks realized. 'Was he alone?'

'No. There was another man with him. I said hello and Roy returned my greeting. Like I said, you couldn't wish for a more friendly neighbour.'

'This other man,' said Banks. 'Did you get a good look at him?'

'Afraid not. It was getting dark by then, you see, and the street lighting's not very bright. Besides, to be perfectly honest, I can't say my eyesight's quite what it used to be.'

Probably pissed to the gills, too, Banks thought, if today was anything to go by. 'Anything at all you can remember,' he said.

'Well, he was a burly sort of fellow, with curly hair. Fair or grey. I'm sorry, I didn't notice any more than that.

I only noticed because he was facing me at first for a moment, while Roy had his back turned.'

'Why did Roy have his back turned?'

'He was locking the door. Very security-conscious, Roy is. You have to be these days, don't you?'

'I suppose so,' said Banks, wondering how the door had come to be unlocked and the burglar alarm unarmed when he got there. 'Where did they go?'

'Got in a car and drove off. It was parked outside Roy's house.'

'What kind of car?'

'I'm not very good with cars. Haven't driven in years, so I haven't taken much of an interest. It was light in colour, I can tell you that much. And quite big. Looked expensive.'

'And they just drove off?'

'Yes.'

'Had you see the man before?'

'I might have, if it was the same one.'

'Was he a frequent visitor?'

'I wouldn't say frequent, but I'd seen him a couple of times. Usually after dark, so I'm afraid I can't do any better with the description.'

'Was either of them carrying anything?'

'Like what?'

'Anything. Suitcase. Cardboard box.'

'Not that I could see.'

That meant that Roy's computer equipment must have been taken later, by someone with a key. 'You didn't see or hear anyone else call after that, did you?'

'Sorry. My bedroom's at the back of the house and I still manage to sleep quite soundly, despite my age.'

'I'm glad to hear it,' said Banks.

'Look, is there something going on? You say Roy's not come home.'

'It's probably nothing,' Banks said, not wanting to worry Farrow. He put his tumbler of soda down and stood up. 'You know, I'll bet they went off to some pub or other, had a bit too much. They're more than likely back at the other bloke's place right now, still sleeping it off. It is Saturday, after all.' He started moving towards the door.

'I suppose you're right,' said Farrow, following, 'but it's not like him. Especially as he'd only just got in.'

'Pardon?' said Banks, pausing in the doorway.

'Well, he'd just come back in, oh, not more than ten or fifteen minutes earlier, about quarter past nine. I saw his car, watched him park it in the garage. I must say, he seemed in a bit of a hurry.'

The phone call to Banks had been timed at 9.29 p.m., which meant that Roy had rung him shortly after he had arrived home. Where had he been? What was it he couldn't talk about over the telephone? While he was on the phone, someone had come to his door, and a few minutes later he had gone out again, most likely with the man who had rung his doorbell. Where had they gone?

'Thank you for your time, Mr Farrow,' said Banks. 'I won't trouble you any longer.'

'No trouble. You will let me know, won't you, if you hear anything?'

'Of course,' said Banks.

•

And why shouldn't I be all right with it? Annie thought as she parked at the top of the hill and walked towards the old Steadman house. Any romantic involvement she'd had with Banks was ancient history, so what did it matter whether he was seeing this Jennifer Clewes? Except that she was dead and Banks had disappeared.

Annie paused a moment on the bridge. It was one of those early summer days when the world seemed dipped in sunshine and life should be simple. Yet, for Annie, it was not without a tinge of melancholy, like the first sight of brown on the edges of the leaves, and she found her thoughts turning to the unresolved problems that haunted her.

There was a time, she remembered, when Banks had just come out of hospital, that there was so much she wanted to say to him, to explain, to apologize for being such a fool, but he wouldn't let her get close, so she gave up. In the end, they simply carried on working together as if nothing of any consequence had happened between them.

But something *had* happened. Phil Keane, Annie's boyfriend, had tried to kill Banks, had drugged him and set fire to his cottage. Annie and Winsome had dragged him out in time to save his life, and Phil had disappeared.

Officially, it wasn't Annie's fault. No blame. How could she have known? But she *should* have known, she kept telling herself. She should have recognized the signs. Banks had even hinted, but she had put it down to jealousy. She had never been so wrong about anything or anyone before. She'd screwed up relationships, but that sort of thing happened to everyone. Nothing like this. Complete and utter humiliation. And it made her angry. She was a detective, for Christ's sake; she was supposed to have an instinct for people like Phil Keane; she should have sussed him out herself.

In some ways what had happened to her was worse than the rape she had endured over three years ago. This was total emotional rape, and it stained her soul. Because she had loved Phil Keane, though she loathed to admit it to herself, now the very thought of him running his hands over her body, pleasuring her, penetrating her, made her feel sick. How could she have seen no deeper than the charm, the good looks, the keen intelligence, that all-embracing energy and enthusiasm for life that made her – and everyone else in his presence – feel special, singled out for grace?

Well, she knew now that beneath the charm was an immeasurable and impenetrable darkness – the lack of conscience of a psychopath fused with the motivating greed of a common thief. And a love of the game, an enjoyment of deceit and humiliation for their own sakes. But was his charm merely on the surface? The more Annie thought about it, the more she came to believe that Phil's charm was not simply a matter of surface veneer, that it was deeply rooted in the rest of his being, a tumour inseparable from the evil at his core. You couldn't just scratch the surface and see the terrible truth beneath; the surface was as true as anything else about him.

Such speculation shouldn't be allowed on a fine day like this, Annie told herself, battening down the anger that rose like bile in her throat whenever she thought about Phil and what had happened last winter. But ever since then, she had been searching for a hint as to where he might have gone. She read all the boring police circulars and memos she used to ignore, pored over newspapers and watched TV news, looking for a clue – an unexplained fire somewhere, a businessman conned out of his fortune, a woman used and abandoned – anything that fitted the profile she had compiled in her mind. But after over four months all she had was one false lead, a fire in Devizes that turned out to have been caused by careless smoking. She knew he was around somewhere, though, and when he made his move, as he surely would, then she would have him.

A young boy in short trousers, shirt hanging out, sat on the bank of Gratly Beck fishing. He'd be lucky to catch anything in such fast-flowing water, Annie thought. He waved when he saw her watching him. Annie waved back and hurried on to the Steadman house.

After checking out Banks's house, she would have to hurry to Darlington to catch a train to London. The three twenty-five would get her into King's Cross just after six, all being well. It would be quicker than driving, and she didn't fancy negotiating her way through the central London traffic all the way south of the river to Kennington. She would leave her car at Darlington station.

Annie passed the tiny Sandemanian chapel and overgrown graveyard and walked down the path to the holiday flats. Two houses had been knocked into one, the insides re-finished, to make four spacious, self-contained flats, two up, two down. She knew Banks had the one that looked out on the graveyard, because he had mentioned how apt that seemed, but she hadn't been inside. He hadn't invited her.

Though she knew it was futile, Annie rang Banks's doorbell. A tired-looking young woman holding a baby to her breast opened the door to the downstairs flat, having no doubt noticed Annie walking up the garden path.

'It's no use,' she said. 'He's out.'

'When did he leave?' Annie asked.

'Who wants to know?'

Annie pulled her warrant card from her handbag. 'I'm a colleague of his,' she explained. 'There's something important I need to talk to him about.'

The woman looked at her card, but she obviously wasn't impressed. 'Well, he's out,' she said again.

'When did he leave?' Annie repeated.

'About eight o'clock this morning. Just drove off.'

'Did he say where he was going?'

'Not to me. And I wouldn't expect him to.'

'Do you own these flats?'

'Me and my husband. We live in this one and rent out the others. Why?'

'I was wondering if I might have a look around. I assume you have a spare key?'

'You can't do that. It's private.' The baby stirred, made a few tentative burps. She rubbed its back and it fell silent again.

'Look,' said Annie, 'this really is important. I don't want to keep you here. I can see you have the baby to deal with, but I'd really appreciate it if you'd let me have a quick look in DCI Banks's flat. It would be so much less trouble than if I had to go and get a search warrant.'

'Search warrant? Can you do that?'

'Yes, I can.'

'Oh, all right, I suppose,' she said. 'It's no skin off my nose, is it? Just a minute.'

She went inside and returned with two keys, which she handed to Annie. 'I'll be wanting them back, mind,' she said.

'Of course,' said Annie. 'I won't be long.'

She felt the woman's eyes boring into her back as she opened Banks's door and walked up the staircase to the upper flat. At the top, she opened the second door and found herself in a small hallway with pegs for jackets and raincoats and a small cupboard for shoes and heavier clothing. A few bills and circulars sat on the table under the gilt-edged mirror.

The first door she opened led to the bedroom. Annie felt strange poking around Banks's flat with him not there, especially his bedroom, but she told herself it couldn't be helped. Somehow or other, he had become instrumental in a murder investigation, and he was nowhere to be found. There was nothing in the bedroom anyway, except a double bed, hastily made, a few clothes in the dresser drawers and wardrobe, and a cushioned window seat that looked out over the graveyard. Must be quite a pick-up line, Annie thought, if you fancied sharing your bed with someone. 'Come sleep with me beside the graveyard.' It had a sort of ring to it. Then she took her mind off images of shared beds and went into the living room.

On the low table in front of the sofa sat a mobile phone and a portable CD player with headphones. So wherever Banks had gone, he had left these behind, Annie thought, and wondered why. Banks loved his music, and he liked to keep in touch. At least, he *used* to. Looking around the room, she noticed there were no books and no CDs except the copy of *Don Giovanni*, a gift from the lads, which she had brought him in hospital. The cellophane wrapper was still on it. There wasn't even a stereo, only a small TV set, which probably came with the flat. Annie began to feel inexplicably depressed. She tried Banks's answerphone, but there were no messages.

The kitchen was tiny and narrow, the fridge full of the usual items: milk, eggs, beer, cheese, a selection of vegetables, bacon, tomatoes, a bottle of Sauvignon Blanc and some sliced ham – all of it looking fairly fresh. Well, at least he was still eating. A couple of cardboard boxes under the small dining table were filled with empty wine bottles ready for the bottle bank.

Annie glanced briefly in the toilet and bathroom, a quick look through the cabinets revealing only what she would have expected: razor, shaving cream, toothpaste and toothbrush were missing, so he must have taken them with him. Amidst the usual over-the-counter medication, there was one small bottle of strong prescription painkillers dated three months ago. Wherever Banks had gone, he clearly hadn't thought he needed them any more.

She stood in the centre of the hall, wondering if she could possibly have missed something, then realized there was nothing to miss. This was the flat of a faceless man, a man with no interests, no passions, no friends, no life. There weren't even any family photos. It wasn't Banks's flat, couldn't be. Not the Banks she knew.

Annie remembered Newhope Cottage and its living room with the blue walls and ceiling the colour of melting Brie, remembered the warm shaded orange light and the evenings she had spent there with Banks. In winter, a peat fire had usually burned in the hearth, its tang harmonizing with the Islay malt she sometimes sipped with him. In summer they would often go outside after dark to sit on the parapet above Gratly Beck, looking at the stars and listening to the water. And there would always be music: Bill Evans, Lucinda Williams, Van Morrison, and string quartets she didn't recognize.

Annie felt tears in her eyes and she brushed them away roughly and headed downstairs. She knocked on the door and handed back the keys without a word and hurried down the path.

•

Banks sat in a pub on the Old Brompton Road playing with Roy's mobile, learning what the functions were and how to use them. He found a call list, which gave him the last thirty incoming, outgoing and missed calls. Some were just first names, some numbers, and quite a few of the incoming calls were 'unknown'. The last call had been made at 3.57 p.m. on Friday afternoon to 'James'. Banks pressed the call button and listened to a phone ring. Finally someone picked it up and uttered a frazzled 'Yeah?' Banks could hear Bowie in the background singing 'Moonage Daydream'.

'Can I speak to James?' he said.

'Speaking.'

'My brother Roy Banks rang you yesterday. I was wondering what it was about.'

'That's right,' said James. 'He was ringing to make an appointment for next Wednesday, I believe. Yeah, here it is, Wednesday at half-past two.'

'Appointment for what?'

'A haircut. I'm Roy's hairdresser. Why? Is everything OK?'

Banks rang off without answering. At least Roy had been certain enough at 3.57 p.m. Friday of being around next Wednesday to make an appointment with his hairdresser. Banks had never done such a thing in his life. He went to the barber's and waited his turn like everyone else, reading old magazines.

Banks washed down the last of his curry of the day with a pint of Pride, lit a cigarette and looked around. It was odd being in London again. He had visited many times since he'd left, mostly in connection with cases he was working on, but with each visit he came to feel increasingly like a stranger, a tourist, though he had once lived there for over fifteen years.

Still, that was quite a while ago, and things changed. Down-at-heel neighbourhoods became desirable residences and once-chic areas went downhill. Villains' pubs became locals for the trendy young crowd and upmarket pubs started to go to seed. He had no idea what was 'in' these days. London was a vast sprawling metropolis, and Banks had never, even when he was living there, been familiar with it beyond Notting Hill and Kennington, where he had lived, and the West End, where he had worked. South Kensington might have been another city as far as he was concerned.

He turned his mind to Roy's disappearance, oblivious to the ebb and flow of conversation around him. He would run through the rest of the call list later, back at the house. He also wanted to check out the data CD. There were plenty of Internet cafes around, and some of them would even allow him to read a CD and print out material, but they were far too public, and anything he did would leave traces. He had violated his brother's privacy, but he felt he had good reason, whereas there was no reason at all to risk making any of Roy's secrets known to strangers.

He realized he didn't know anyone in London who owned a computer. Most of the people he had known there, criminals and coppers, had either moved, retired or died. Except Sandra, his ex-wife, who had moved from

Eastvale to Camden Town when she left him. Sandra would probably have a computer. But his last meeting with her had been disastrous, and she had hardly been a constant visitor in his days of need. In fact, she hadn't visited at all, merely sent her condolences through Tracy. Then there was the husband, Sean, and the new baby, Sinéad. No, he didn't think he would be paying any visits to Sandra in the foreseeable future.

He also couldn't go official with what he'd got for the same reason he couldn't use an Internet cafe: in case the disc held something incriminating against Roy. If Roy had been up to something dodgy, Banks wasn't going to shop him, not his own brother. He might give him a damned good bollocking and read him the riot act when he found him, but he wasn't going to help put him in jail.

There was one possible avenue he could explore first, someone who would probably be as interested in protecting Roy's reputation as he was. Banks stubbed out his cigarette and reached into his pocket for the mobile. He scrolled through the list of names and numbers in the phone book until he found Corinne. That was Roy's fiancée's name, he remembered, copying the number down into his notebook. Then he put the mobile back in his pocket, finished his drink and walked out to the street.

London was hot and sticky. Of all the places to be during a heat wave, this was not one he would have chosen. People were wilting on the pavements, and the air was redolent with the smell of exhaust fumes and worse, like rotting meat or cabbage.

Banks didn't want to tie up the mobile again in case Roy got his message back at the house and phoned, so he sought out a public phone box and dug out an old phone card from his wallet. He felt as if he were walking into the tin hut where the Japanese locked Alec Guinness in *The Bridge on the River Kwai*. Sweat trickled down his sides, tickling as it ran, sticking his shirt to his skin. Someone had crushed a bluebottle against the glass, making a long smear of dark blood. He could even smell the warm paper of the telephone directory.

Banks took out his notebook and dialled the number he had copied from Roy's mobile. Just as he was about to hang up, a breathless voice came on the line.

'Hello?'

'Corinne?' Banks asked.

'Yes. Who is it?'

'My name's Alan Banks. Roy's brother. You might remember me. We met at my parents' wedding anniversary party in Peterborough last October.'

'Of course. I remember.'

'Look, I'm down in London and I was wondering if we could get together somewhere and have a chat. Maybe over a drink or something?'

There was a pause, then she said, 'Are you asking me out?'

'No. Sorry. I'm getting this all wrong. Please excuse me. Blame the heat. I mean, that's why I thought a drink might be a good idea. Somewhere cool, if there is such a place.'

'Yes, it *is* hot, isn't it. What do you mean, then? I'm afraid I don't follow.'

'I just need to pick your brains, that's all.'

'I remember. You're a policeman, aren't you?'

'Yes, but that's not why . . . I mean, it's not official.'

'Well, you've certainly got my attention. You could

come over to the flat.' She paused. 'I've got an electric fan in the office.'

'Have you got a computer?'

'Yes. Why?'

'Great,' said Banks. 'When would be convenient?'

'Well, I've got a couple of meetings with clients this afternoon – I'm afraid free weekends are never a given if you're an accountant out on your own – but I should be done by early evening. Say five o'clock?'

Banks looked at his watch. It was half-past three. 'All right,' he said.

'Good. Have you got a pen and paper handy? I'll give you my address.'

Banks wrote down the address and listened to Corinne's directions. Just off Earl's Court Road. Not far from Roy's at all, then, though another world entirely. He thanked her again, escaped from the sweat box and headed back to the pub.

•

By the time Annie had walked over the bridge and along the lane to Banks's cottage, she had just about succeeded in regaining her equilibrium. The builders had got as far as restoring the roof. From the outside, the place looked perfectly normal, and one might even think someone lived there if it weren't for the lack of curtains and the overflowing skip. Because it was Saturday there were no workmen around, though given how slow they had been, Annie thought, the least they could do was put in a few extra hours to help get Banks back where he belonged. After all, they'd been on the job close to four months now.

It was the first time Annie had been back there since

the night of the fire, and just seeing the place evoked painful memories: the feel of the wet blanket she wrapped around herself; the fire bursting out as she broke the door open; the smoke in her eyes and throat; Banks's dead weight as she dragged him towards the door; Winsome's strength as she helped them over the last few feet, a distance Annie thought she couldn't make alone; lying there on the muddy ground spluttering, looking at Banks's still figure and fearing him dead. And, almost worst of all, remembering Phil Keane's silver BMW disappearing up the hill as Winsome had first turned into Banks's drive.

She took a moment to bring herself back to the present. Jennifer Clewes had Banks's address in her back pocket, but it was *this* address, Annie reminded herself. Why was that? She noticed tyre tracks in the dust, but they could have been anyone's. The builders', for example. And despite the sign that said Beckside Lane was a cul-de-sac *and* a private drive, cars often turned into it by mistake. Even so, she made certain not to disturb the tracks.

Annie walked up to the front door of the cottage. Though the building wasn't finished inside, she guessed that the builders would keep it locked to discourage squatters and because they might sometimes leave their expensive tools there overnight. Which was why the splintering around the lock immediately caught her attention. She leaned closer and saw that it looked fresh. The door was new and not yet painted, and the splintered wood was clean and sharp.

Annie's protective gloves were back in the boot of her car, so she used her foot to nudge the door open gently and kept her hands in her pockets. Inside, the place was a mess, but a builders' mess, not a burglar's, by the looks of it. The rooms were divided and the ceiling beams in place, and most of the plasterboarding had been finished except the wall between the living room and the kitchen. It felt odd to be standing there smelling sawdust and sheared metal rather than peat smoke, Annie thought. The stairs looked finished, solid enough, and after a tentative step she ventured up. The once-familiar bedroom was a mere skeleton, with builders' calculations and blueprints scrawled on the walls in pencil. The second bedroom was similarly bare.

She went back downstairs and out to the lane. As she walked away, she turned once more and looked back. *Someone* had broken into the cottage, and recently. She assumed the builders had locked up when they left on Friday, though she would have to check with them to be certain. It could have been thieves, of course, but that seemed too much of a coincidence. Annie realized that she would have to bring in Stefan Nowak and the SOCOs to see if they could establish any links between Jennifer Clewes's car and Banks's cottage.

If it was the same person who had killed Jennifer Clewes, Annie reasoned, then he must have got hold of Banks's address by some other means, because Jennifer Clewes had it in the back pocket of her jeans. Perhaps he already knew where Banks lived and, when he had guessed where she was going, and when he had got to a desolate, isolated stretch of road, he had shot Jennifer and then carried on to Banks's cottage. To do what? Kill him, too? It would certainly make more sense to handle them one at a time.

But Banks hadn't been there; he'd been about a quarter of a mile away, in his temporary flat. Had Banks any idea of what was going on? Was that why he had taken off so early in the morning? That was the big question, Annie realized, heading back up the hill to her car. How much did Banks know and how safe was he now? And she knew that she probably wouldn't find out the answer to either question until she found the man himself.

•

Corinne lived in the first-floor flat of a four-storey building, overlooking the narrow street, not more than fifty yards away from Earl's Court Road. She looked different from the young girl Banks met at his parents', he thought, as she greeted him at the door and asked him in. Her hair was longer, for a start, almost down to her shoulders, and it was blonde with dark roots. The little stud was gone from below her lip, leaving a small flaw in her clear skin, and she looked closer to thirty than to twenty. She also seemed more self-possessed, more mature than Banks remembered her.

'Come into the back,' she said. 'That's where the office is.' An electric fan stood on the table by the open window, slowly turning through about ninety degrees every few seconds, sending out waves of lukewarm air. It was better than nothing.

'Everyone seems to work at home these days,' Banks said, sitting in a winged armchair. Corinne sat at an angle to him, cross-legged, the way some women seem to prefer, and he guessed that this was the space she used to discuss business when clients called at the flat. A jug of water thick with ice cubes sat on the table between them, along with two tumblers. Corinne managed to stretch her upper body forward and pour them both a glass while remaining cross-legged. Quite a feat,

Banks thought, considering he couldn't even sit in that position comfortably in the first place. But Corinne seemed to move with a dancer's grace and economy that spoke of Pilates and yoga.

'They say tea's refreshing in hot weather,' she said, 'but the thought of drinking anything hot doesn't have much appeal at the moment.'

'This is fine,' said Banks. 'Thank you.'

Corinne was wearing a plain orange T-shirt tucked into her jeans, and she wore a Celtic cross on a silver chain around her neck. She was barefoot, Banks noticed, and her toenails were unpainted. Occasionally, as she talked or listened, her heart-shaped face would tilt to one side, she would bite her lower lip and her fingers would stray to the cross. Sunlight gilded the leaves outside the window and their shadows danced pavanes over the pale blue walls, stirred by the lightest of breezes.

'Well,' she said, 'I must say you had me all intrigued on the telephone. I'm sorry if I . . .'

'My fault entirely. I wasn't being clear. I hope you don't take me for the kind of man who goes chasing his brother's fiancée?'

She gave a brief, tight little smile that indicated to Banks that perhaps all was not as it should be in the fiancé department, but he let it go for the time being. She would get to it in her own time, if she wanted.

'Anyway,' he went on, 'it's Roy I want to talk to you about.'

'What about him?'

'Do you have any idea where he is?'

'What do you mean?'

Banks explained about the phone call and Roy's

absence. 'I got your number from his mobile,' he said. 'He left it on the kitchen table.'

'That's not like him,' she said, frowning. 'None of it is. I can see why you'd be worried. Anyway, to answer your question, no, I don't know where he is. Do you think you should go to the police? I mean, I know you *are* the police, but . . .'

'I know what you mean,' said Banks. 'No, I don't think so. Not yet, at any rate. I don't think they'd be very interested. There could be a simple explanation. Do you know any of his friends?'

'Not really. There was another couple we used to go out with occasionally, Rupert and Natalie, but I don't think Roy has a lot of close friends.'

Banks didn't miss the 'used to', but he let it go for the moment. There was a Rupert in Roy's mobile phone book. Banks would ring him eventually, along with the rest of the names. 'Do you know a burly man with curly grey or fair hair?' he asked. 'He drives a big light-coloured car, an expensive model?'

Corinne thought for a moment, then she said, 'No. Sorry. Rupert drives a slate-grey Beemer and Natalie's got a little Beetle runaround.' She turned up her nose. 'A yellow one.'

'When did you last see Roy?'

'A week last Thursday.' She fingered the cross. 'Look, I might as well tell you, things haven't being going all that well for us lately.'

'I'm sorry to hear that. Any particular reason?'

'I think he's been seeing someone else.' She gave a little shrug. 'It doesn't matter, really. I mean, it's not as if it was serious. We've only been going out about a year. We're not living together or anything.'

'But I thought you were supposed to be engaged?'

'I think that was part of the problem, really. I mean, I'd brought it up, and Roy's impulsive. Neither of us is ready for marriage yet. We called it off, went back to the way we were. That was when the trouble started, really. I don't suppose you can take a big step back like that and expect a relationship to continue the way it was, can you?'

So the engagement had been postponed, or demoted to going steady, and the relationship had cooled, like Banks' and Michelle's. Little brother up to his usual tricks. At least Corinne was to be spared the indignity of being wife number four. 'Even so,' Banks said, 'it must still hurt. I'm sorry. Have you any idea *who* he's seeing?'

'No. I don't even know if I'm right for sure. It's just a feeling. You know, little things.'

Well, Banks thought, there were a few possible names and numbers in Roy's mobile phone book and call list. 'How recently?' he asked.

'Just this past few weeks.'

'And before that?'

'Things were fine. At least, I thought they were.'

'Was there anything bothering him when you saw him last?'

'Nothing that I could see. He seemed much the same as ever. Except . . .'

'Yes?'

'Well, as I said, little things, things a woman notices. Forgetfulness, distance, distraction. That wasn't like him.'

'But he wasn't depressed or worried about anything?'

'Not that you'd know. I just thought he had someone else on his mind and he'd rather be with her.'

'What about drugs?'

'What about them?'

'Come off it. Don't tell me you and Roy never snorted a line, smoked a spliff.'

'So what if we did?'

'Apart from it being illegal, which we'll ignore for the moment, when you get into the drug world you get to meet some nasty people. Did Roy owe his dealer money, for example?'

'Look, it wasn't much. Just recreational. A gram on the weekends, that sort of thing. Nothing more than he can easily afford.'

'All right,' said Banks. 'How much do you know about his business dealings?'

'Not a lot.'

'But you are his accountant, right?'

'Roy takes care of his own books.'

'Oh. I thought that was how you met?'

'Well, yes,' said Corinne. 'He got audited and a friend recommended me to him.' She twirled her Celtic cross. 'Most of my clients are in the entertainment business – writers, musicians, artists – nobody really big league, but a few decent, steady earners. Roy was a bit different, to say the least, but I needed the money. And before you ask, everything was above board.' She narrowed her eyes. 'Roy once told me he was sure you thought he was a crook.'

'I don't think he's a crook,' Banks said, not being entirely truthful. 'I think maybe he stretches the law a bit, finds the odd loophole, that's all. Plenty of businessmen do. What I'm wondering, though, is whether he had any reason to run off. Was his business in difficulties?

Had he lost a lot of money, made some errors of judgement?'

'No. Roy's books were good enough for me and the taxman.'

'Look, I've seen his house,' said Banks. 'The Porsche, the plasma TV, the gadgets. Roy obviously makes quite a lot of money somehow. You said he makes it legitimately. Have you any idea how?'

'He's a gambler. He still plays the stock market to some extent, but mostly he finances business ventures.'

'What kinds?'

'All kinds. Lately he's been specializing in technology and private healthcare.'

'Here?'

'All over the place. Sometimes he gets involved in French or German operations. He has connections in Brussels, the EU. He also spends a lot of time and energy in America. He loves New York. Roy's no fool. He knows better than to put all his eggs in one basket. That's one reason he's been so successful.' She paused. 'You don't know your brother at all, do you?' Before Banks could answer, she went on, 'He's a remarkable man in many ways, a financier who can quote Kierkegaard or Schopenhauer at dinner. But he never forgets where he came from. The crushing poverty. He dragged himself out of it, made something of himself, and it's what drives him. He never wants to end up like that again.'

What kind of a line had Roy been spinning Corinne? Banks wondered. Their childhood hadn't been that bad. Admittedly, she had only seen the relatively decent council house his parents lived in now, and not the back-to-back terrace behind the brickworks where they had lived until Banks was eleven and Roy six. But even then 'crushing poverty' was pushing it a bit. They had always been fed and clothed and never lacked for love. Banks's father had always been in work until the eighties. What did it matter that the toilet had been outside, down the street, and the whole family had had to share a tin bath tub which they filled with kettles of water boiled on the gas cooker? They were no different from thousands of other working-class families growing up in the fifties and sixties.

'It's true we were never very close,' Banks admitted, slapping a fly from the knee of his trousers. 'What can I say? It just happens that way sometimes. We haven't got that much in common.'

'Oh, I know all about that,' said Corinne. 'I can't stand my younger sister. She's a snob and a misery-guts.'

'I don't hate Roy. I just don't know him, and I'm worried he's in some sort of trouble. Something that's made him run away in a hurry.' Banks remembered the CD he had found in Roy's Blue Lamps jewel-case and slipped it out of his pocket. 'I wonder if you could help me with something?'

'Of course.'

It didn't take Corinne long to put the CD in her computer and bring up the list of contents. The icons were JPEGs: 1,232 of them in all. Some were merely numbered, others had names like Natasha, Kiki and Kayla. Corinne opened her image viewer and set a slideshow going.

Banks was looking over her shoulder, hand resting on the back of the chair, when the images started coming up on the screen. The first showed a naked woman with a man's erect penis in her mouth, semen dribbling down her chin, a stoned look in her eyes; the next showed the same man entering the woman from behind, an obviously feigned look of ecstasy on her face. After that came several photos of an extremely attractive blonde teenager in various stages of undress and revealing positions.

That was enough.

Corinne abruptly ended the slideshow and ejected the disc. 'I suppose that just shows you that Roy isn't much different from most men, when you get right down to it,' she said, moving away from the computer. Banks could see that her face was red. She handed the disc back to Banks. 'Maybe you'd like to keep this?'

'Is that all that's on it?' he asked.

'Short of looking at all 1,232 files to make sure, I'd say that's a pretty good guess. Of course, you're welcome to check them all out, but not here, if you don't mind. I find that sort of thing a bit demeaning. Not to mention insulting.'

Well, Banks thought, it had been worth a try. Though he had nothing at all against images of naked women, either alone or with partners, he had seen enough of the sordid side of the porn business to know how bad it could get, especially if children were involved. From what he had seen, though, Roy's collection looked ordinary, the girls of age, if a little on the young side. In a way, it made him feel a bit closer to Roy to find out that he was only human after all, the dirty devil. If only their mother knew. But then his policeman's mind kicked in. If Roy had taken these images himself, on a digital camera, say, rather than simply downloaded them from the Internet, then he could be involved in a sleazy business.

'Did Roy have anything to do with Internet porn?' he

asked Corinne, forgetting that she might not be the best person to ask.

'Always ready to think the worst of him, aren't you?' she said.

'I can't see why you're always so quick to leap to his defence after what he's done to you.'

Corinne flushed with anger.

'Believe it or not, I'm trying to help,' said Banks.

'Well, you've got a funny way of showing it.' She looked towards the CD and made a face. 'Anyway, there's your evidence, for what it's worth.'

Banks took the CD. At some point he would examine it more closely, study each of the 1,232 images, just to make sure. Hotel rooms and outdoor locations had been identified from background features in Internet porn. One victim of child pornography in America had been identified from a blurred-out school logo on her T-shirt. If Roy *had* taken any of these pictures, there was a chance of finding out where he had taken them, and who the models were, should it come to that. But not here, not now.

He had just about run out of questions to ask Corinne, and he could see that she had become edgy, anxious for him to leave. Whether it was the effect of the images on the CD or something else, he definitely felt that he had outstayed his welcome. But as he put his jacket on, he remembered the pen-like object he had found in Roy's office drawer. Maybe Corinne knew what it was. He took it out of his pocket and held it out to her. 'Any idea what this is?'

Corinne took the object from Banks, eyed it closely and removed the cap. 'It's a portable mini-USB drive. 'For storing information.'

'Like that CD?'

'Same idea, but not quite as much space. This one's got 256 megs, not 700. Handy, though. You can clip it in your inside pocket, just like a pen.'

'Can we see what's on it?'

Corinne clearly wasn't comfortable delving into Roy's private affairs, especially after what she had just seen on the CD. Banks had been at his job for so long that he had got used to digging deep into a person's private life. As far as the police were concerned, there are no secrets, especially in a major investigation. He often didn't like what he found, but he'd developed a tolerance for people's little quirks over the years.

Most people, when you get past their facade of normality, have some sort of guilty secret, something they've tried to keep from the rest of the world, and Banks had come across most of them in his time, from the harmless hoarders of newspapers and magazines, whose homes were like labyrinths of tottering columns of print, to the secret cross-dressers and lonely fetishists. Of course, they were all grief- and horror-stricken, humiliated that someone had found out their little secrets, but to Banks it was nothing special.

Corinne's reaction made him realize for the first time in a while that what he did was unnatural and invasive. In the short time he had been with her, he had as good as implied that her ex-fiancé, *his* brother, was involved in drugs, illicit sex and fraud. All in a day's work for him, perhaps, but not for a basically nice person like Corinne. Had the job made him insensitive? Banks thought of Penny Cartwright again, and her violent reaction to his suggestion of dinner last night. Was it something to do with what he did for a living, the way he looked at the world, at people? She was a free spirit, after all, so did that make him the enemy?

Corinne plugged the USB drive into her computer. 'Here we go,' she said, and Banks looked over her shoulder at the monitor.

4

Shortly after half-past six that Saturday evening, Annie walked out of the Oval tube station, where she'd been crammed in an overheated carriage with about five million people on their way home from shopping or visiting friends and relatives, and headed down Camberwell New Road, past the park on the corner. Young lads with shaved heads and bare upper bodies lounged on the grass drinking cans of lager and flexing their tattoos, leering at every attractive woman who passed by. A group of younger kids had set up makeshift goals with their discarded T-shirts and were playing football. Just watching them made Annie sweat.

Then she saw Phil.

He was on the other side of the street, walking a dog, some sort of little terrier on a lead. But it was him, she was sure of it. The same lazy grace in his step, the casual but expensive clothes, chin up, slightly receding hairline. Hardly looking, she dashed into the road, aware of horns blaring around her, and she had almost made it across when his attention was attracted by the noise.

He paused and looked towards her, puzzled. Annie got to the pavement and stopped, oblivious to the cursing of the last driver who had barely missed her. It wasn't Phil. There was a superficial similarity, but that was all. The man bent to pat his dog, then with a curious backward glance, he carried on walking towards the traffic lights. Annie leaned against a lamppost until her heartbeat returned to normal, and cursed. This wasn't the first time she thought she'd seen him; she would have to be more careful in future, less jumpy. If she was going to be realistic about it, she had to realize that bumping into him in a street in London was the last thing that was likely to happen.

She was still wired from the train journey. She would have to calm down. She had just made the three twenty-five and had even managed to find a seat in the quiet car, but no matter how many windows had been open, it had still been too hot. And she had been thinking about Phil, which was probably why her mind had fooled her into thinking she had actually seen him across the street. Throughout most of the journey, she had read the tabloids, scouring the pages for any whiff of Phil, but had found nothing, as usual. She had to get a grip on herself.

Despite the rule of quiet, more than one mobile rang during the journey, and Annie could also hear the over-spill from someone's personal headphones. It had made her think of Banks, and again she started wondering where the hell he was and what he had to do with Jennifer Clewes's murder. According to the woman with the baby, Banks had left under his own steam that morning, but none of this explained what the hell was going on.

Annie found the house just off Lothian Road. The two DCs assigned to watch the flat were still sitting in the kitchen, the man with his feet on the table, shirtsleeves rolled up, chewing on a matchstick and reading through a pile of letters, and the woman sipping tea as she flipped through a stack of *Hello!* magazines. Two tipped cigarette butts lay crushed in a Royal Doulton saucer. Somehow, both detectives managed to look like naughty school kids caught in the act, though neither showed any trace of guilt. Annie introduced herself.

'And how are things in the frozen north?' asked the man, whose name was DC Sharpe, keeping his feet firmly on the kitchen table and the matchstick in the corner of his mouth. He looked as if he hadn't shaved in about four days.

'Hot,' said Annie. 'What are you doing?'

Sharpe gestured to the letters. 'Just nosing about a bit. Afraid there's nothing very interesting, just bills, junk mail and bank statements, all pretty much as you'd expect. No really juicy stuff. People don't write letters the way they used to, do they? It's all e-mail and texting these days, innit?'

Considering that Sharpe looked about twenty-one, it was odd to hear him being so critical of 'these days', as they were probably the only days he knew. But the irony in his tone wasn't lost on Annie, and the callous disregard which both of them seemed to display towards the victim's home angered her. 'OK, thanks for keeping an eye out,' she said. 'You can leave now.'

Sharpe looked at his partner, DC Handy, and raised an eyebrow. The match in the corner of his mouth twitched. 'You're not our guv,' he said.

Annie sighed. 'Fine,' she said. 'If that's the way you want to play it. My patience is already running a bit thin.' She took out her mobile, went into the hallway and phoned DI Brooke at Kennington station. After a few pleasantries and the promise of a drink together that evening, Annie explained the situation briefly, then went back into the kitchen, smiled at Sharpe and handed him the phone.

The moment he put it to his ear, his feet shot off the table and he sat bolt upright in his chair, almost swallowing his matchstick. His partner, who hadn't said a word so far, frowned at him. When the call was over, Sharpe scowled at Annie, his face red, turned to the woman and said, 'Come on, Jackie, we've got to go.' Then he made a show of swaggering as slowly as possible out of the house, and with one mean, backward glance mouthed, 'Bitch,' and stuck his middle finger in the air.

Annie felt inordinately satisfied when that little scene was over, and she sat down and poured herself a cup of tea. It was lukewarm, but she couldn't be bothered to make a fresh pot. One of the DCs had opened a window, but it was no use; there was no breeze to bring relief. An empty strand of flypaper twisted in what little air current there was over the sink.

While she was waiting, Annie took out her mobile and rang Gristhorpe in Eastvale. Dr Glendenning had finished the post-mortem on Jennifer Clewes and had found nothing other than the gunshot wound. Her stomach contents consisted of a partially digested ham and tomato sandwich eaten at least two hours before death, which bore out Templeton's theory that she had driven up from London and probably stopped at a motorway service station on the way. Glendenning wouldn't commit himself to time of death, except to narrow it down to between one and four in the morning. The SOCOs were still working the scene and would get around to examining Banks's cottage as soon as they could.

As it turned out, Annie didn't have long to wait for Jennifer's flatmate. At about a quarter to seven, the front door opened and she heard a woman's voice call out. 'Jenn? Hello, Jenn? Are you back yet?'

When the owner of the voice walked into the kitchen and saw Annie she stopped dead in her tracks, put her hand to her chest and backed away. 'What is it?' she asked. 'Who are you? What are you doing here?'

Annie took out her warrant card and walked over to her. The young woman studied it.

'Yorkshire?' she said. 'I don't understand. You broke into our house. How did you do that? I didn't see any damage to the lock.'

'We've got keys for all occasions,' said Annie.

'What do you want with me?'

'Are you Kate Nesbit, Jennifer Clewes's flatmate?'

'Yes,' she answered.

'Maybe you'd better sit down,' said Annie, pulling out a chair at the table.

Kate was still dazed as she lowered herself into the chair. Her eyes lighted on the saucer and her nostrils twitched. 'Who's been smoking? We don't allow smoking in the flat.'

Annie cursed herself for not getting rid of the butts, though their smell still lingered in the warm air.

'It wasn't me,' she said, putting the saucer on the draining board. She didn't know where the waste bin was.

'You mean someone else has been here?'

Annie lingered by the sink. 'Just two detectives from your local station. I had words with them. I'm sorry they were so rude. It was necessary to get in, believe me.'

'*Necessary*?' Kate shook her head. She was a pretty

girl, in a very wholesome, no-nonsense sort of way, with her blonde hair cut short, black-rimmed oval glasses and a healthy pink glow on her cheeks. She looked athletic, Annie thought, and it was easy to visualize her tall, rangy frame on horseback. Even the clothes she wore, white shorts and a green rugby-style shirt, looked sporty. 'What's going on?' she asked. 'It's not good news, is it?'

'I'm afraid not.' Annie sat down opposite her. 'Drink?'

'Not for me. Tell me what it is. It's not Daddy, is it? It can't be. I was just there.'

'You were visiting your parents?'

'In Richmond, yes. I go every Saturday when I'm not working.'

'No,' said Annie. 'It's not your father. Look, this might be a bit of a shock, but I need you to look at it.' She opened her briefcase and slipped out the photograph of Jennifer Clewes that Peter Darby had taken at the morgue. It wasn't a bad one – she looked peaceful enough and there were no signs of violence, no blood – but there was no doubt that it was a photograph of a dead person. 'Is this Jennifer Clewes, your flatmate?'

Kate put her hand to her mouth. 'Oh, my God,' she said, tears in her eyes. 'What happened to her? Did she have an accident?'

'In a way. Look, do you have any idea why she was driving up to Yorkshire late last night?'

'I didn't know that she was.'

'Did you know she'd gone out?'

'Yes. We were home last night. I mean, we don't live in one another's pockets, we have our own rooms, but . . . My God, I don't believe this.' She put her hands to her face. Annie could see that her whole body was shaking.

'What happened, Kate?' Annie said. 'Please, try and focus for me.'

Kate took a deep breath. It seemed to help a little. 'There was nothing we wanted to watch on telly, so we were just watching a DVD. *Bend It Like Beckham.* Jenn's mobile went off and she swore. We were enjoying the film. Anyway, she went into her bedroom to answer it and when she came back she said there was an emergency and she had to go out, to just carry on watching the film without her. She said she wasn't sure when she would be back. Now you're telling me she'll never come back.'

'What time was this?'

'I don't know. I suppose it'd be about half-past ten, a quarter to eleven.'

That was consistent with the timing, Annie thought. It would take about four hours to drive from Kennington to Eastvale, depending on traffic, and Jennifer Clewes had been killed between one and four o'clock in the morning, about three miles short of her destination. 'Did she give you any idea about *where* she might be going?'

'None at all. Just that she had to go. Right then. But that's just like her.'

'Oh?'

'What I mean is she wasn't very forthcoming about what she was doing, where she was going. Even if I needed to know when she'd be back, for meals and such. She could be very inconsiderate.' Kate put her hand to her mouth. 'Oh, listen to me. How terrible.' She started crying.

'It's all right,' said Annie, trying to comfort her. 'Try to stay calm. Did Jennifer seem worried, frightened?'

'No, not exactly frightened. But she was pale, as if she'd had a shock or something.'

'Have you any idea who made the call?'

'No. I'm sorry.'

'What did you do after she left?'

'Watched the rest of the film and went to bed. Look, what's happened? Did she have a car crash? Was that it? It can't have been her fault. She was always a careful driver and she never drank over the limit.'

'It's nothing like that,' said Annie.

'Then what? Please tell me.'

She'd have to find out sooner or later, Annie thought. She got up, took a couple of tumblers from the glass-fronted cupboard and filled them with tap water. She passed one to Kate and sat down again. She could hardly bear Kate's imploring expression, the wide, fearful eyes and furrowed brow, the tumbler shaking in her hands. When Kate heard what Annie had to tell her, her life would never be the same again; it would be forever tainted, forever marked by murder.

'Jennifer was shot,' Annie said in a soft, flat voice. 'I'm really sorry.'

'Shot?' Kate echoed. 'No . . . she . . . But I don't understand . . .'

'Neither do we, Kate. That's what we're trying to find out. Do you know of anyone who would want to harm her?'

'Harm Jenn? Of course not.' The words came out in gulps, as if Kate were desperate for air.

Kate put the glass down, but she missed the edge of the table. It fell to the floor and shattered. She stood up and put her hand to her mouth, then, without warning, her eyes turned up, and before Annie could reach her she crumpled in a heap on the kitchen floor.

•

'Look,' said Corinne, 'are you sure we should be doing this? These are Roy's private files, after all.'

'It's a bit late to get squeamish now,' said Banks. 'Besides,' he said, gesturing to the CD, 'maybe it's just more of the same.'

Corinne gave him a dirty look and turned back to the screen. 'Well,' she said, 'at least the drive isn't password-protected.'

'And given Roy's concern with privacy,' said Banks, 'that probably means there's nothing really confidential on it.' Or nothing *incriminating*, he thought.

'So what's the point?'

'Perhaps it's something he wanted me to find and read? He'd know I'd be no good at cracking passwords and such. Besides, I need anything I can get. Business contacts, activities, habits, anything.'

'There's quite a mix of stuff,' said Corinne, scrolling down. 'Some Word documents, Money files, Excel spreadsheets, Power-Point presentations, market-research reports, memos, letters.'

'Can you print it out?'

'Some of it.' Corinne started selecting files and the printer hummed into action. It was fast, Banks noticed.

'Can you also copy the contents to another thingama-jig?'

'You mean a removable USB hard drive?'

'Whatever. Can you do it?'

'Of course I can. Or at least I could if I had a spare one. Will a CD do?'

'Fine,' Banks said. 'Just as long as we have a copy. The CD as well.'

'What are you going to do with it?'

'I'm going to post them to myself,' said Banks. 'That way I'll have back-ups.'

'But it might mean nothing at all. Maybe Roy's just run off with his new girlfriend. Have you thought of that?'

Banks had. 'Look,' he said, 'it's true that I don't know Roy very well, and I'll take your word that he's an imaginative and bold businessman rather than a crooked one, but you didn't hear the phone call. He sounded *scared*, Corinne. Is that like him?'

Corinne frowned. 'No. I mean, I'm not saying he's a hero or anything, but he doesn't usually back down from difficult situations. Maybe he's been kidnapped or something?'

'Has he ever mentioned that possibility?'

'No. But you hear about it sometimes, don't you?'

'Not that often. But trust me,' Banks said, 'something's wrong. There are just too many loose ends. The missing computer, for a start. If someone went to the trouble to take Roy's entire computer and all the storage devices they could find, then doesn't that seem suspicious to you? They only missed the USB drive and the CD because both were hidden.' Hidden in plain view, Banks might have added, like Poe's purloined letter. 'According to the neighbour, when Roy got in the car with another man, neither was carrying anything. Someone must have gone back and taken the computer stuff between about half-past nine last night and the time I arrived early this afternoon.'

'Has it occurred to you that he might have come back and taken it himself?' Corinne asked.

'Why should he? Where would he have taken it? Besides, his car's still in the garage. He doesn't own another, does he?'

'No. Just his darling Porsche. You're right, if he went anywhere, he'd have taken the Porsche. He loves that car.'

'I don't suppose he has another house, does he? Somewhere he'd go if he had to make a run for it? A villa on the Algarve, perhaps?'

'Roy's not particularly fond of Portugal. And he doesn't own a place in Tuscany or Provence, or anywhere else, as far as I know. At least, he never took me to one. He loves travel and holidays but he says it's too much hassle owning property abroad. It ties you down to just one place.'

'He's probably right.'

Corinne bit on her lower lip. 'Now you've got me really worried.'

Banks put his hand on her shoulder, then took it away quickly, not wanting her to get the wrong idea. She didn't react. 'I'll find Roy,' he said. 'But let's have a look at some of these files first. They might help us find out where to start looking. You know more about his business affairs than I do.'

'That's not saying much. Anyway, there's nothing here that looks even the remotest bit dodgy.'

'How can you tell?'

Corinne faltered a little. 'Well, I don't suppose I can, really. As I said, the drive isn't protected or encrypted, and Roy's hardly likely to write down references to importing heroin, is he?'

'So there's no way of telling?'

As Corinne spoke, she opened and scanned various files. The printer was still running. 'Not from these files. Everything *looks* above board. I think if he were trying to hide that sort of thing, there'd be *something* to set off alarm bells. It's not that easy. Besides, as I've been trying to tell you, Roy's not like that.'

'What about the Money files?'

'Simple income and expenditure. Company profit and loss sheets. Investment returns. Bank statements. Some offshore banking. His finances are in pretty good shape.'

'Roy did a lot of offshore banking?'

'Anyone working at his level of income has to. It's a matter of keeping tax liabilities as low as possible. It's not illegal. Mostly we're looking at memos and correspondence here. You are, of course, welcome to examine them all at your leisure, especially as you took them in the first place, but I'd say you'd be wasting your time. Roy's on the board of a few hi-tech companies, mostly interested in miniature information-storage devices, like that USB hard drive, flash memory cards, that sort of thing. Given the way the world's going, with mobiles, digital cameras, PDAs, MP3 players, and various combinations, it seems a wise enough area to be in. Smaller is better. As a board member, he's paid dividends.'

'What else is there?'

'Recently Roy's become interested in private health-care. I remember him talking about it. Look.' She activated a PowerPoint presentation that extolled the virtues, and profits, of investing in a string of cosmetic-surgery clinics. 'He's on the board of a chain of health centres, a pharmaceutical company, a fitness club.'

'It all sounds very dull,' said Banks.

'I told you so. But guess who's the one with the Porsche.'

'No need to rub it in. Is there more?'

'A few market-research reports on health and hi-tech, the kind of reports you buy, the expensive kind.'

'I was hoping for a few names.'

'They're here,' said Corinne. 'Memos and letters between Roy and various directors and companies he was involved with. Julian Harwood, for example.'

'I've heard that name.'

'You might well have done. He's quite big in the private healthcare field these days. Directs the chain of clinics Roy's involved with. Anything from cancer to breast enlargement. Actually, Roy and Julian have been mates for years.'

'He's not a doctor, though?'

'No, a businessman.'

'Have you met him?'

'Uh-huh.'

'You don't sound impressed.'

'That's maybe because that's exactly what he sets out to do. Impress people. Frankly, I always found him a bit boorish, but it takes all sorts. It still doesn't make him a crook, though.'

'So you don't think there's anything in there to suggest that Roy was involved in any sort of illegal or dangerous business ventures?'

'You can see for yourself it all looks quite kosher. I don't know about dangerous, though.'

'What do you mean?'

'Well, just because it *looks* clean, that doesn't mean the hi-tech companies he worked with weren't selling illegal weapons-guidance systems to terrorists, or that the clinics weren't involved in genetic manipulation. Maybe the cosmetic surgery clinics gave gangsters new faces.'

Banks laughed. 'Like *Seconds*, you mean?'

Corinne frowned. 'I don't know what you mean.'

'It's a film. Rock Hudson. A man gets a new face, new identity.'

'Oh, I see. Well, I suppose my point is that they're not exactly going to announce things like that in letters six feet high, are they? It's a wide-open world. You should know that. Even the most innocuous-looking enterprise on the surface can turn out to be a whole different matter if you dig a little deeper.'

Banks did know that, and it didn't make him feel a great deal easier about Roy.

Corinne collected the pile of printed paper, put it in a folder and handed it to him. 'Here. Be my guest.'

Banks picked up the folder, put it in his briefcase and stood up. 'Thanks a lot,' he said. 'You've been very generous with your time.'

'Don't worry about it,' said Corinne. 'Just find Roy.'

'I will.'

'When you do, will you let me know?'

'Of course. In the meantime, you take good care of yourself. If you think of anything else, or there's anything you need, well . . . you can ring me on Roy's mobile. He left it on the kitchen table. That's how I got your number.'

Corinne frowned. 'That's not like him,' she said. 'Not like him at all.'

'No,' said Banks, and left.

•

Annie hadn't seen anyone faint since she was about nine, when one of the women at the artists' commune where she had been raised keeled over in the middle of dinner. Even then she overheard some of the adults talking later, and the general agreement seemed to be that drugs were the cause. In the case of Kate Nesbit, it was most likely shock, and perhaps the heat.

Remembering her first aid, Annie acted quickly and placed Kate's feet on a chair to elevate her legs above heart level to restore the flow of blood to the brain, then turned her head to one side so she didn't swallow her tongue. She leaned close and listened. Kate was breathing without difficulty. Lacking smelling salts – never, in fact, having seen or smelled any – Annie just made sure that Kate hadn't cracked her skull when she fell and then went over to the sink to pour another glass of water. She found a tea towel, dampened it with cold water and brought it over with the glass, then she got another glass of water for herself. Kate was stirring now, her eyes open. Annie mopped her brow then lifted her into a sitting position so she could sip the water. As soon as Kate said she felt well enough, Annie helped her back into her chair, then cleared up the broken glass before continuing the interview.

'I'm so sorry,' Kate said. 'I don't know what came over me.'

'That's all right. I'm just sorry I couldn't find an easier way to break it to you.'

'But *shot*? Jenn? I can hardly believe it. Surely that sort of thing doesn't happen to people like us?'

Annie wished she could say it didn't.

'What was it?' Kate went on. 'Robbery? Not . . . like that other poor girl?'

'Claire Potter?'

'Yes. It was on the news for weeks. They still haven't found the man. You don't think . . . ?'

'We don't know yet. Jennifer wasn't sexually assaulted, though.'

'Thank God for that, at least.'

'Her things are missing,' Annie said. 'Handbag, purse. So it could be robbery. Do you know if she carried much money with her?'

'No, never. She always said she could buy everything she wanted with her credit card or debit card.'

That was true enough these days, Annie knew. The only time people seemed to have a lot of cash on hand was when they had just withdrawn some from a cash-point. 'Look,' Annie went on, 'you shared the flat with Jennifer. You must have been close. I know you're upset, but I'm relying on you to help me. What was going on in Jennifer's life? Men. Work. Family. Friends. Anything. Think. Tell me about it. There has to be an explanation if this wasn't just some senseless random attack.'

'Maybe it was,' said Kate. 'I mean those things do happen, don't they? People killing people for no real reason.'

'Yes, but not as often as you think,' said Annie. 'Most victims know their killers. That's why I want you to think deep and tell me anything you know.'

Kate sipped some water. 'I don't know,' she said. 'I mean, we weren't that close.'

'Did she have any close friends?'

'There was this girl she used to go to school with, up in Shrewsbury, where she grew up. She came around once or twice.'

'Can you remember her name?'

'Melanie. Melanie Scott.'

Annie definitely got the feeling that Melanie Scott

wasn't on Kate's list of favourite people. 'How close were they?'

'They went on holiday together last year. It was before Jenn moved in, but she told me all about it. Sicily. She said it was awesome.'

'Do you have an address for Melanie?'

'I think so. She lives in Hounslow, I remember. Out Heathrow way. I'll be able to dig it out before you go.'

'Fine. What was Jennifer like?'

'Quiet, hard-working. And she really cared about people, you know. Maybe she should have been a social worker.'

In Annie's experience, the world of social work was hardly staffed by caring people. Well-meaning, perhaps, but that was a different thing in her mind. 'What about all those mysterious comings and goings?'

'That's just me being silly, really. I like to know where people are and when they'll be back. Jenn didn't always bother to let me know. But she wasn't a party girl, if that's what you mean, or a clubber. I think she was actually rather shy. But she was bright and ambitious. Like I said, she cared about people. And she was funny. I liked her sense of humour. We used to watch *The Office* on DVD together and we'd both crack up laughing. I mean, we'd both worked somewhere like that. We knew what it was like. I'll miss all that,' Kate added. 'I'll miss Jenn.' She started to cry again and reached for the tissues. 'I'm sorry. I just can't . . .'

'It's all right,' said Annie. 'Is that what you always called her? Jenn, not Jenny?'

Kate sniffled and blew her nose. 'Yes. It's what she liked to be called. She hated Jenny. Mostly people called her Jennifer, though. I don't know. She just wasn't a Jenny. Like I'm not a Katy or a Kathy, I suppose.'

And like I'm not Anne, thought Annie. Funny the way names, contractions especially, tended to stick. She had been Annie all the time growing up in the artists' colony, and only at university had people called her Anne. 'The two of you must have talked,' Annie said. 'What sort of things did she talk about?'

'The usual things.'

Christ, thought Annie, this was like trying to get water out of a stone. 'Did you notice any change in her mood or behaviour recently?' she asked.

'Yes. She seemed very nervous and jumpy lately. It wasn't like her.'

'Nervous? Since when?'

'Just this past week or so.'

'Did she tell you what it was about?'

'No. She was even more quiet than usual.'

'Do you think there's any connection between that and her reaction to last night's phone call, the late drive?'

'I don't know,' said Kate. 'There might have been.'

The problem was, Annie realized, that Jennifer's mobile had been taken along with everything else. Still, the phone-company records might help.

'Do you know which network she used?'

'Orange.'

Annie made a note to follow up, then asked, 'Do you have anything with her handwriting on it?'

'What?'

'A note or something? Letter? Postcard?'

Kate turned to a corkboard on the wall by the door. A number of Far Side cartoons were pinned there, along with a few postcards. Kate went over and unpinned one

of them, a view of the Eiffel Tower, and carried it over to
Annie. 'Jenn went to Paris for a weekend break in
March,' Kate said. 'She sent me this. We had a good
laugh because she got back here before it did.'

'Did she go by herself?' Annie asked, taking a photocopy of the note found in Jennifer Clewes's back pocket
from her briefcase to compare the handwriting.

'Yes. She said she'd always wanted to go on the
Eurostar and they had a special deal. She went around
all the art galleries. She loved going to galleries and
museums.'

To Annie's untrained eye, the handwriting looked the
same, but she would have to get an expert to examine it.
'Can I keep this?' she asked.

'I suppose so.'

Annie put the photocopy and the postcard in her briefcase. 'You said she went alone,' Annie went on, 'but isn't
Paris supposed to be the city of romance?'

'Jenn wasn't going out with anyone back then.'

'But she has been more recently?'

'I think so.'

'Just think so?'

'Well, Jenn could be very private. I mean, she didn't
kiss and tell, that sort of thing. But she'd been getting a
lot of calls on her mobile lately, and making a lot. And
she'd stayed out all night on a couple of occasions. She
didn't usually do that.'

'Since when?'

'A few weeks.'

'But this started before the odd behaviour?'

'Yes.'

'Did she tell you his name? I assume it was a he?'

'Good Lord, yes, of course. But she didn't mention any

names. She didn't even tell me that she *was* seeing someone. It was just a feeling I got from her behaviour. Intuition. I put two and two together.'

'But you said she seemed nervous and jumpy. That's hardly the way a new relationship is supposed to make you feel, is it? And why was she so secretive? Didn't you ever talk about personal matters, say if one of you split up with a boyfriend or something?'

'We've only been sharing six months,' said Kate. 'And nothing like that's happened to either of us in that time. There's that one bloke keeps pestering her, but that's all.'

'Who?'

'Her ex-boyfriend. His name's Victor, but that's all I know about him. He keeps ringing and hanging around. You don't think . . . ?'

'I don't think anything yet,' said Annie. 'Are you sure you don't know his second name, where he lives?'

'Sorry,' said Kate. 'It was over before we started sharing. Or Jenn *thought* it was.'

'What did she think about it? Was she frightened of him?'

'No. Just annoyed, that's all.'

'How did you two come to be flatmates?'

Kate looked away. 'I'd rather not say. It's private.'

Annie leaned forward. 'Look, Kate,' she said, 'this is a murder investigation. Nothing's private. What was it? An advertisement in the papers? The Internet? What?'

Kate remained silent and Annie became aware of the tap dripping in the sink. She heard water from a hose spraying in a garden beyond the open window and a child squeal with delight.

'Kate?'

'Oh, all right, all right. I thought I was pregnant. I did one of those home tests, you know, but I didn't trust it.'

'How does Jennifer come into this?'

'It was where she worked. She was an administrator at a private women's health centre. They specialize in family planning.'

'Like the British Pregnancy Advisory Service? Marie Stopes?' Annie remembered both of these from her own unexpected brush with pregnancy nearly three years ago, though in the end she had gone NHS.

'It's a new chain. There are only a few of them open yet, as far as I know.'

'What's it called?'

'The Berger-Lennox Centre.'

'And they perform abortions?'

'Not at the centre itself, no, but they have satellite clinics, and they arrange for abortions to be performed. That's not all they do, though. They cover the whole range, really, do reliable pregnancy tests, give advice and counselling, physical exams, arrange for abortions or put you in touch with adoption agencies, social services, whatever. They take care of everything. And they're very discreet. One of my friends at work told me about them. Why, do you think it's important?'

'I don't know,' said Annie. But the one thing she did know was that abortion was a red flag for a number of fringe groups, and that people who worked at such clinics had been killed before. 'Do you have the address?'

'In my room. I'll get it for you when I get Melanie's.'

'Fine,' said Annie. 'So how did the two of you meet? You said Jennifer worked in administration.'

'Yes, she ran the business side of things. We got talking in the office while I was filling out the paperwork, that's all. She was explaining it to me, how the system worked, that sort of thing. We just sort of hit it off. We're about the same age and I think she felt a bit sorry for me. Anyway, it turned out I wasn't pregnant, and she asked me if I fancied a drink to celebrate. When we got talking we found out that neither of us was happy living where we were, so we decided to pool our resources and share. We didn't know each other well, but we got along all right.'

'Where did she live before?'

'I'm not sure exactly, but it was near King's Cross. She said it was a really tiny flat and the area wasn't very nice. She didn't like walking there by herself at night. There are a lot of prostitutes and drug addicts on the street. Can I have another glass of water, please?'

Annie wondered why she was asking, why she just didn't go and get it herself. It was *her* flat, after all. Shock, probably. The poor girl looked as if she was likely to faint again at any moment. Annie went over to the sink and filled the two glasses. A fat bluebottle had got itself stuck on the flypaper and was pushing frantically with its legs, trying to get away, only succeeding in miring itself deeper in the sticky stuff with each new effort it made. Annie thought she knew what that felt like.

'Where did you live then?' she asked, handing over the water.

'Thank you. In Richmond. With my parents.'

'Why did you leave? Was it because you thought you were pregnant?'

'Oh, no. It wasn't anything to do with that. I never even told them. And the boy . . . well, he's long gone now. Richmond is just too far out. I was spending all my time commuting. I work in Clapham. I'm a librarian. It's only a couple of tube stops, and on a nice day I can walk if I've got enough time.'

'I see,' said Annie. 'Why do you think Jennifer was so secretive about this new boyfriend?'

'If you ask me,' Kate said, lowering her voice, 'I think he's married.'

That made sense, Annie thought. Jennifer probably wouldn't have bragged about a relationship with a married man. The fear of discovery was likely to make her nervous, on edge, and maybe the mobile was the safest way to communicate. No chance of getting his wife on the other end. 'But you have no idea what his name is or where he lives?'

'No. I'm sorry.'

'How did they meet?'

'I don't even know if I'm right about any of it,' said Kate. 'My mother always said I have too much imagination for my own good.'

'Guess. Where *might* Jennifer have met someone? What kind of places did she like to go? Nightclubs?'

'No, I've already told you she wasn't like that. Besides, she was usually too tired when she got back from work. She often worked late at the centre. I mean she'd go for a drink or a meal with friends from work now and then, and maybe the two of us would go to the pictures once in a while. Then there was her friend Melanie.'

'Could it have been someone she met at work?'

'It might have been. That's the most likely place, isn't it?'

Annie nodded. She knew that. Work was where she had met Banks and, in a way, Phil Keane. 'Why wasn't she out with him on Friday? It's the weekend, after all. People usually get together.'

'I don't know,' said Kate. 'She just said she was stopping in. She did say she was expecting a phone call at some time, but she didn't know exactly when.' Her face started twitching again as if she was about to cry. 'Should I have known? Should I have stopped her?'

Annie went over and put a hand on her shoulder. 'Calm down, Kate,' she said. 'There's nothing you could have done, no way you could have known.'

'But I feel so useless. Some friend I've turned out to be.'

'It's not your fault. The best thing you can do is try to answer my questions as clearly and calmly as possible. OK?'

Kate nodded but continued to sniffle and dab at her eyes and nose.

'This phone call came between half-past ten and a quarter to eleven?'

'Yes. I think so.'

'What about Jennifer's family?' Annie asked. 'Where do they live? How did she get along with them?'

'Fine, as far as I know,' said Kate. 'I mean, she didn't visit them that often, but they live in Shrewsbury. You don't when they're so far away, do you?'

'No,' said Annie, whose father lived even further away, in St Ives. 'Can you find their address for me, too? Now that we know it is Jennifer's body we found, someone will have to let them know what's happened.'

'Of course,' said Kate. 'I've got that one in my PDA. You know, in case of emergencies or anything. I never thought I'd need them for something like this.' She dabbed at her eyes again, fetched her shoulder bag and gave Annie the address.

Annie stood up. 'And now,' she said, 'can I have a look at Jennifer's room, while you dig out those other addresses?'

5

Banks left his car parked in Corinne's street, only a short walk from Roy's, took the District line from Earl's Court to Embankment and walked up to the main post office behind Trafalgar Square. There he bought a padded envelope and posted both CD copies – Roy's business files from the USB drive and the sex images – to himself at Western Area Headquarters. It was always a good idea, he thought, to have a back-up, preferably stored in a different location. He kept the original CD of JPEGs and the USB drive in his briefcase along with the papers Corinne had printed out for him.

After he had finished at the post office, he dropped in at the first newsagent's he saw and bought another packet of Silk Cut. While he was paying he noticed one of the headlines in the evening paper and looked closer. A young woman, as yet unidentified, had been found shot dead in a car outside Eastvale, North Yorkshire. No doubt if he'd been on duty he would have caught the case, but as things were, it would be Annie's. He didn't envy her having to deal with the media feeding-frenzy that guns always caused, but perhaps Gristhorpe would take care of the press, the way he usually did.

Banks lit a cigarette and started to walk. He had often done so when he worked on the Met, and sometimes it helped him sort out his feelings or solve a problem. Whether it did or not, he always enjoyed walking around the West End at night, no matter how much it had changed in character since his early days on the beat.

Outside the pubs, knots of people stood clutching pint glasses, laughing and joking. In Leicester Square, jugglers and fire-eaters entertained the crowds of American tourists in shorts and T-shirts who milled around drinking water from plastic bottles.

It was a sultry evening and the square was bustling, long queues for the Odeon, metal barriers up, some premiere or other and everyone hoping to catch a glimpse of a star. Banks remembered doing crowd duty there once as a young PC in the early seventies. One of the Bond films, *The Man With the Golden Gun*, he thought. But that had been a cold night, not far off Christmas, as he recalled, he and his fellow PCs linking arms to keep back the onlookers as flashbulbs popped (and they were flashbulbs back then) and the stars stepped out of their limos. He thought he saw Roger Moore and Britt Ekland, but he could have been wrong; he never was much of a celebrity-spotter.

Banks had loved going to the cinema back then. He and Sandra must have gone twice a week before the kids, if he was on the right shift, and sometimes if he was on evenings or nights they'd go to a matinee. Even after Brian was born they had got a neighbour to baby-sit now and then, until undercover work made it too difficult for him.

These days, he hardly ever went at all. The last few times he'd been to see a film, there'd always seemed to be someone talking, and the place was sickly with the smell of hot buttered popcorn, the floors sticky with spilled Coke. It wasn't so much like going to the cinema any more as it was like hanging out in a cafe where they showed moving pictures on the wall. There was a new multiplex in Eastvale, an extension of the Swainsdale Centre, but he hadn't been yet and probably never would.

Banks made his way into Soho. It was going on for nine now, still daylight, but the sun was low, the light fading, and he was hungry. He hadn't eaten since that wretched curry round the corner from Roy's place. Here the streets were just as crowded, outdoor tables at the restaurants and cafes on Old Compton Street, Greek Street, Dean Street, Frith Street overflowing. A whiff of marijuana drifted on the air, mingling with espresso, roasting garlic, olive oil and Middle Eastern spices. Neons and candlelight took on an unnatural glow in the purple twilight, smudged a little by the faint, lingering heat haze. Boys held hands as they walked down the street, or stood on street corners, leaning in towards one another. Beautiful young women in cool, flimsy clothing walked together laughing or hung on the arms of their dates.

Banks made it to Tottenham Court Road before the electronics shops closed and after little deliberation bought a laptop with a DVD-RW/CD-RW drive. It was light enough to carry easily in a compartment of his briefcase, and it would do everything he needed it to and more. It also didn't break his bank account, still bolstered by the insurance money from the fire. He took out the manual and various extra bits and pieces, put them in his briefcase, too, and left the packaging in the shop. After that, feeling hungry, he headed back to Soho.

On Dean Street, Banks found a restaurant he had eaten at once before, with Annie, and had enjoyed. Like all the others, the outside tables were crowded and the frontage was fully open to the street. Nevertheless, Banks persevered inside and was rewarded with a tiny table in a corner, away from the street and the noise. It was no doubt the least desirable table in the house as far as most people were concerned, but it suited him perfectly. It was just as hot inside as out, so location made no difference as far as that was concerned, and a waitress came over almost immediately with the menu. She even smiled at him.

Banks mopped his brow with the serviette and studied the options. The print was small and he reached for his cheap non-prescription reading glasses. He had found himself relying on them for reading the papers and doing crosswords more often lately.

It didn't take him long to settle on steak, done medium, chips and a half-bottle of Château Musar. He sipped at his first glass of wine while he was waiting for his meal and the rich, complex flavour was every bit as powerful as he remembered it. Annie had liked it, too.

Annie. What was he going to do about her? Why had he been behaving like such a bastard after what she had done for him? She was seriously pissed off at him, he knew, but surely if he really tried . . . maybe he could break through the barrier of her anger. Truth be told, things had been shaky between them ever since they'd broken up. He had been jealous of Annie's relationships, and he knew that she was jealous of his. That was partly what had made his curt dismissal of her in the hospital so unforgivable. But the circumstances had been exceptional, he told himself. He had not been in his right mind.

His steak and chips arrived and Banks turned his thoughts back to Roy. With any luck, he would turn up *something* from the computer stuff – why would Roy hide it otherwise? – a name, a company, something that would send him in the right direction. The problem was that he would more likely than not turn up *too* much, and Banks didn't have a slew of DCs to send out on the streets to filter out the red herrings. Perhaps he could go back and enlist more of Corinne's help. She had said she would be willing.

For a moment, a shadow of concern for Corinne passed over him with a chill, and he shivered. Had he brought her danger along with Roy's business secrets? But he was sure he hadn't been followed to her house, nor was there anyone on his tail now. She would be all right, he assured himself. He would ring her first thing in the morning, just to make sure.

He had only once had dinner with Roy, he realized as he bit into the juicy fillet. They saw one another in passing at family gatherings, of course, though there had been few enough of those over the years, and Banks had been at Roy's first wedding, but as far as the two of them sitting down to dinner together, there was only the one occasion, and the invitation had come out of the blue, for no particular reason that Banks could gather.

It was in the mid-eighties, when the financial world was reeling with the shock of insider-trading scandals. Whatever he was now, Roy was a stockbroker then, and in his Armani suit, with his hundred-quid haircut, he looked every inch the successful businessman, apple of his mother's eye. Banks had been a mess, much as he was now, he thought, aware of the irony. Approaching burnout in London, career and marriage held together by threads, he was waiting to hear if his application for a transfer to North Yorkshire had been approved when Roy rang him one day at the office – he wasn't even sure his brother knew where he lived at that time – and asked him if he was free for dinner at the Ivy.

The restaurant was packed with entertainment people and Banks thought he recognized a star or two, but he couldn't put names to faces. They certainly looked and acted as if they were stars. After a half-hour of family chat and polite enquiries into Banks's career and well-being over a very expensive shepherd's pie and an even more expensive bottle of burgundy, Roy steered the conversation towards the recent scandals. Nothing was said overtly, but Banks went away with the impression that Roy had been pumping him. Not that he knew anything, but his brother had expressed interest in the way such investigations were done, how the police gathered information, what they thought of informers, exactly where the law stood on the issue, and so on. It was done very well, and it continued over the frozen berries and white-chocolate sauce he had for dessert, but it was definitely a fishing expedition.

There was another thing, too. Banks couldn't be certain, but he had been around drugs enough to recognize the signs, and he was sure Roy was high. Coke, he suspected. After all, that was the drug of choice back then among successful young men about town. At one point in the evening Roy excused himself to go to the toilet and came back slightly flushed and even more animated, sniffling every now and then.

And that, Banks realized, was probably when he first started thinking of his brother as a possible criminal. Before that he had merely been the annoying little brother, the paragon against which Banks was matched and found wanting. Even now, when Banks looked back on their conversation that evening, he still thought he was right, that Roy had been up to something and wanted to run down the odds on his getting caught. Well, he hadn't got caught, and now it seemed he had moved on to other things. But were they more honest?

Banks poured the last of the Château Musar into his glass. Maybe he should have ordered a whole bottle, he thought. But that was too much, and he wanted to keep a reasonably clear head for tomorrow. From what he could see between the clustered diners in the dim light, the street outside was even busier still. The crowd was mostly young and they'd probably be drinking and clubbing until the early hours.

Over coffee and cognac, Banks remembered that he had nowhere to stay tonight. He had forgotten to book a hotel room. Then he felt the pressure of the keys and the mobile in his pocket and he knew that he had decided where he was staying the minute he had pocketed them and left Roy's house. It was useless trying to get a taxi at this hour in the maze of Soho streets, so he walked up to the Charing Cross Road, where he picked one up in no time and asked the driver to take him to South Kensington.

•

Winsome had been patiently ringing Banks's parents and children on and off for most of the afternoon and early evening without any luck. When it came to Banks's friends, she was at a loss to know who they were. He had left an old address book in his drawer, but there weren't many entries, and some were so old the numbers were no longer in service. It felt odd, searching for her boss, poring over the personal address book of someone she called sir and looked up to, but there was no doubt that he might be able to answer a few questions. Winsome also realized that he might be in danger. After all, a woman apparently on her way to see him had been shot, and his half-renovated cottage had been broken into. Coincidence? She didn't think so.

Consulting the list of family phone numbers, Winsome had first called the daughter, Tracy, in Leeds. When she had finally got through to her around teatime, Tracy said she had no idea where her father was. The son Brian wasn't answering his mobile, so she left a message. When she phoned Banks's parents for the third time, early in the evening, a woman answered.

'Mrs Banks?' Winsome said.

'Yes. Who is this?'

'My name's DC Jackman. I work with your son DCI Banks. I've been trying to get in touch with you all afternoon.'

'Sorry, love, we've been to visit my brother and his wife in Ely. Why? What's wrong? Has something happened to Alan?'

'Nothing's happened, Mrs Banks. As far as we know everything's just fine. He's on holiday this week, but I'm sure you know how it is with this job. I'm afraid we need him for something, and it's rather urgent. He seems to have forgotten to take his mobile. I was wondering if you knew where he was.'

'No, dear,' said Mrs Banks. 'He never tells us where he's going these days.'

'I don't suppose he does,' said Winsome, 'but it was worth a try. Have you spoken with him recently?'

'As a matter of fact he rang early this morning.'

'What about, if you don't mind me asking?'

'Oh, I don't mind, dear. It was a little bit odd. See, he was asking about his brother, about Roy, and . . . well, they've never been very close.'

'So it was unusual for DCI Banks to be asking about him?'

'Yes.'

'What did he want to know?'

'He wanted to know if I knew where Roy was, just like you want to know where Alan is. What's going on? Are you sure there's nothing wrong?'

'Nothing to worry about, Mrs Banks. We just need him to help us out with something, that's all. Could you give me his brother's address and phone number if you've got them?'

'Of course,' said Mrs Banks. 'I know his address by heart but I'm no good with numbers. You'll have to wait a moment while I look it up.'

'That's all right,' said Winsome. 'I'll hold.'

She heard the handset laid gently to rest on a hard surface, then the sound of muffled voices. A few seconds later, Mrs Banks came back on the line and gave her the number. 'He's got one of those mobiles. Do you want that number, too?' she asked.

'Might as well.'

'Silly business, people having to stay in touch all the time,' said Mrs Banks. 'Makes you wonder how we managed without all these newfangled gadgets, but we did, didn't we? Listen to me go on. You're probably too young to remember.'

'I remember,' said Winsome, who had grown up in a shack high in Jamaica's Cockpit Country, open to the elements, without telephone or electricity or any of the other myriad things that seemed so essential to life in twenty-first-century Britain.

Mrs Banks gave her the number and Winsome said goodbye. For a moment she sat thinking, tapping her ballpoint on the pad, then she found DI Cabbot's mobile number and picked up the phone again.

•

'Sorry about Blunt and Useless,' said DI Brooke. 'They're a right couple of prize plonkers, but it's hard to get good help these days, and they just happened to be on duty.'

'Blunt and Useless?'

'Sharpe and Handy. Get it?'

Annie laughed. 'It's all right. We've got a few like that ourselves.'

They were sitting in a noisy pub on Brixton Road drinking pints of Director's bitter. David Brooke was about Banks's age, but he looked older and he was much more well-rounded, with a placid moon-shaped red face that always made Annie think of farmers, and only a few tufts of ginger hair still clinging to his freckled skull. His navy-blue suit had seen better days, as had his teeth, and he had taken off his tie because of the heat, which made him look even more like some yokel up from Somerset for a wedding or a football match.

Annie's search of Jennifer Clewes's room had yielded nothing of immediate interest – except that Jennifer collected porcelain figurines, mostly fairytale characters, liked Frank Sinatra, Tony Bennett and Ella Fitzgerald, and read hardly anything that wasn't to do with business and commerce, apart from the occasional Mills & Boon. If her clothes were not for work, they were mostly casual: jeans, denim skirts and jackets, T-shirts, cotton tops. Nothing lacy or flouncy. She had one good frock and two pairs of black high-heeled shoes. The rest of her footwear consisted of trainers and sandals.

Her computer, at first glance, revealed nothing out of the ordinary. There was no diary and no personal papers, only a calendar, the days marked mostly with birthdays to remember. She had a dentist's visit scheduled for the 13th. If there was anything else, it was for the computer experts to find. Annie did, however, acquire a much better photograph of Jennifer – alive and smiling against an ocean backdrop. Kate Nesbit told her it had been taken in Sicily the previous year, when Jennifer had gone there on holiday with Melanie Scott, her old school friend from Shrewsbury.

When she had finished at the flat, Annie phoned and booked a room for two nights at a hotel by Lambeth Bridge, after first ringing Gristhorpe again and clearing it with him. Tomorrow was Sunday, so the Berger-Lennox Centre would most likely be closed. Annie would pay her visit first thing on Monday morning before heading back up north. On Sunday, she would go and talk to Melanie Scott. The local police would inform Jennifer's parents in Shrewsbury of their daughter's death and drive them to Eastvale to make a formal identification of the body.

'So how are things going, Dave?' Annie said. 'It's been a while.'

'Too long, if you ask me. Things are fine, thanks. Actually, the big news is that I'm up for promotion at last. Chief Inspector.'

'Congratulations, Dave,' said Annie. 'Detective Chief Inspector Brooke. Has a sort of ring to it, doesn't it?'

Brooke chuckled. 'It does. How did the interview with the victim's flatmate go?' he asked.

Annie sipped some beer. 'Fine. I didn't find out much, but at least I'm building up some sort of picture of Jennifer, however vague. You know what it's like in the early stages.'

'I do indeed. A slow business.'

'The poor woman, though,' Annie went on, 'Kate Nesbit, the flatmate. She was really upset. I finally managed to persuade her to let me fetch the woman from upstairs to sit with her until her parents can come over. I phoned them and they said they'd be there as soon as possible. What'll happen after that I don't know.'

'I'll have someone keep an eye on her, if you like. Drop by now and then, see how she's doing.'

'Not Blunt and Useless.'

Brooke smiled. 'No, I wouldn't wish them on the poor lass. We've got some good police community-support officers.'

'All right,' said Annie. 'It sounds like a good idea. Thanks.'

'No problem.'

'I don't like to ask,' she went on, 'but do you think you could also spare a couple of DCs to do a house-to-house? I'd do it myself, but I'd like to go out to Hounslow to visit one of the victim's close friends tomorrow.'

'And what would they be asking about?'

'If anyone has noticed anything unusual, or suspicious, strangers hanging about, that sort of thing.'

'I think we can manage that,' said Brooke. 'Wouldn't want our delicate DI's feet getting sore, would we?'

'You're a sweetheart, Dave.'

Annie's mobile rang. She excused herself and walked outside so she could hear properly. When Winsome gave her Banks's brother's address and phone numbers and told her there was a possibility Banks might be there, she had to go back into the pub, take her notebook out of her briefcase and write the information down. She thanked Winsome and hung up.

'Important news?' Brooke asked.

'We may have a lead on our missing DCI,' Annie said.

'Missing DCI?'

'It's a long story.'

Brooke nodded towards Annie's empty glass. 'Another?'

'Why not,' said Annie. 'I'm not driving.'

'What about a bite to eat? Then you can tell me all about your DCI over dinner.'

'Here?'

Brooke looked around and pulled a face. 'You must be joking. Let's have one more drink here, then we'll find somewhere decent over the river, if you're up for it?'

'That'd be fine,' said Annie. 'How are Joan and the kids?'

'Thriving, thank you.' Brooke paused. 'You're not very subtle, you know, Annie.'

'What do you mean?'

'You want to know if I'm still happily married, whether I represent any sort of threat to you. Well, I am, and I don't. Do you behave like that whenever a man offers to buy you dinner?'

'Oh, you're buying. I didn't know that. That's all right, then.'

'Now you're hiding behind flippancy.'

'You're right,' said Annie, 'I'm sorry. I should know better. I've just had some bad experiences recently, that's all.'

'Want to talk about them?'

Annie shook her head. The last thing she wanted to talk about was Phil Keane. Throttle him, maybe; hang, draw and quarter him, even better; but talk about him, no way. Brooke wasn't the type to make a pass, and under ordinary circumstances she would have realized it. He had been married to Joan all those years ago, when Annie was a fresh-faced young DC in Exeter and Brooke was her DS. They had kept in touch sporadically over the years. Anyway, his offer of a shared meal was exactly that and no more, and it bothered her that she reacted as if she could no longer trust an old friend.

'I'm sorry,' Annie said. 'I just wasn't thinking.'

'That's all right. And I'm secretly flattered that you still think I'm a contender.'

Annie tapped him on the arm. 'I'm sure you are,' she said. 'But I'm bloody starving, so how about we skip that other drink here and have one when we get where we're going? Does your offer still stand?'

'The West End awaits us,' said Brooke.

'Any chance we can go via South Kensington?'

•

It was late Saturday night, Kev Templeton thought gloomily, and he was supposed to be shagging that gorgeous new red-headed clerk in records, the one with the big tits and legs right up to her arse, but instead he was driving up the M1 in rain so heavy that his windscreen wipers could barely keep up with it.

Still, this was the next best thing, he told himself, if not even better. The thrill of the chase. Well, not exactly a chase, but at least he was out of the office, on the road, tracking down a lead, driving through the night. This was the life. This was what he had joined the force for.

Water cascaded from the windows, lightning streaked across the sky and he could hear the thunder even over the Chemical Brothers CD he was playing at ear-splitting volume.

He knew they didn't take him seriously back at headquarters, just because he was young and took a bit of pride in his appearance. They all thought he was some sort of club-crazy dandy. Well, he liked clubbing, and he liked to look good, but there was more to him than that. One day, he'd show them all. He'd pass his boards and rise up the ranks like a meteor.

Who did they think they were, anyway? Gristhorpe was due to retire any moment now, and he hadn't done any real detecting in years, if ever. Banks was good, but he wasn't a team player and he seemed to be quickly writing himself out of the script due to personal problems. Annie Cabbot wasn't as hot as she thought she was. Too emotional, Kev thought, like she was always on the rag. The only one that really scared him was Winsome. Awesome, as he called her secretly. She'd go far. He could see her as his sidekick when he made superintendent. Could see shagging her, too. Just the thought of it made him sweat. Those thighs.

He had first driven non-stop to the end of the motorway, then turned around, hitting Toddington and Newport Pagnell service stations on the northbound M1 already, showing Jennifer Clewes's photo around without any success. He hadn't eaten at either of the first two service stations – and now as he approached Watford Gap it was going on for midnight and he was feeling peckish. Needed a piss, too. He might as well stop there at the Road Chef. From what he had learned over the years, motorway cafes were all overpriced, and there wasn't much to choose between them.

All the roadside cafes seemed to have a slightly seedy aura at that time of night, Templeton thought; or maybe Watford Gap services were always like that. It was something to do with the lighting and the clientele. Not many nice middle-class families on the road at that hour. Not many old folks either. Most of them, with the odd exception of a commercial traveller or a businessman on his way home from a late meeting, looked like villains. You probably wouldn't go far wrong, Templeton thought, if you made the occasional swoop on motorway cafes. Bound to net a few faces from the wanted posters, at any rate. Maybe he'd pass on the idea to the brass. Then again, maybe not. They'd only steal the credit themselves.

A man came in to the toilet and stood next to Templeton at the urinal, though there was plenty of free space elsewhere. When he started to open a conversation – the usual line about big knobs hanging out – Templeton zipped up, whipped out his warrant card and shoved it in the man's face so hard he staggered back and lost directional control, pissing all over his shoes and trouser bottoms. 'Fuck off, pervert,' Templeton said. 'And think yourself bloody lucky I can't be bothered to arrest you for soliciting. On your bike. Now!' Templeton clapped once, loudly.

The man turned pale. His hands shook as he zipped himself up and, without even pausing at the basin, ran for the door. Templeton washed his hands with soap under hot water for thirty seconds exactly. He hated poofters, and as far as he was concerned they'd made a bloody big mistake when they made homosexuality legal all those years ago. Opened the floodgates, that did, just like they did with immigration. As far as he was concerned, the government should send all the poofters to jail and all foreigners back home – except Winsome, of course; she could stay.

Up in the restaurant, Templeton ordered a cup of tea and sausage, eggs and beans, figuring you couldn't go wrong with something as basic as that, and carried his tray to the first empty table he saw, trying to ignore the smears of ketchup on the surface. The eggs were overcooked and the tea was stewed, but other than that the meal wasn't too bad. Templeton tucked in with as much enthusiasm as he could muster.

When he had finished, he went up to the counter and spoke to the pimply Asian youth who worked there. His name-tag identified him as Ali.

'Were you working here last night about this time?'

'I was here,' said Ali. 'Sometimes it feels like I'm always bloody here.'

'I'll bet it does,' said Templeton, pulling the photo of Jennifer Clewes from his briefcase. 'By the way, I'm DC Templeton, North Yorkshire Major Crimes. Did you happen to see this woman in here?'

'Bloody hell, is she dead?' Ali asked, paling. 'I've never seen a dead person before.'

'The question is, did you see her?'

'What happened to her?'

Templeton sighed theatrically. 'Look, Ali, we'll get along a lot better if I ask the questions and you answer them, all right?' he said.

'Yeah. All right. Let's have a look, then.' Ali reached out his hand, but Templeton held on to the photograph, keeping it just within Ali's field of vision. He didn't want greasy fingerprints all over it.

Ali screwed up his eyes and looked at the photo longer than Templeton thought he needed to, then said, 'Yeah, she was in here last night. Sat over there.' He pointed to a table.

'What time?'

'Can't remember. It's all the same when you're on nights.'

'Was she alone?'

'Yeah. I remember thinking what's a good-looking bird like that doing all alone on a Friday night, like.'

'Did she seem upset or frightened in any way?'

'Come again?'

'How did she behave?'

'Just normal, like. She ate her sandwich – well, half of it. I can't say I blame her. Those ham and tomatoes do get a bit soggy when they've been sitting—'

'Did anyone approach her at all?'

'No.'

'Speak to her?'

'No. But the bloke at the table opposite was definitely giving her the eye. Looked like a bit of a pervert to me, too.'

'What do perverts look like?' Templeton asked.

'You know. Creepy, like.'

'Right. How long did she stay?'

'Dunno. Not more than ten, fifteen minutes, I suppose. Look, aren't you going to tell me what happened to her? She was all right when she left here.'

'Anybody follow her?'

'The bloke opposite, the pervert, went out not long after her, but I wouldn't say he was following her. I mean, he'd finished his sausage roll. Why would he want to hang around?'

Templeton gazed over the decor. 'Why, indeed?' he said.

'Most people here, they're usually in a hurry, see. Quick turn-over.'

'And no one else took an interest in the woman?'

'No.'

'She make any phone calls?'

'Not that I saw.'

'This pervert, had you ever seen him before?'

'No.'

'Can you describe him for me?'

'He was wearing a dark grey suit, like a businessman, wore glasses with black rims, and he had a long, jowly sort of face, with a long, thin nose. Light brown hair, and not much of it. Oh, yeah, and he had dandruff. Reminded me of someone, but I can't think who. Not the dandruff, I mean, the face.'

'How old would you say he was?'

'Old. Maybe forty or so.'

'Anything else you can tell me?'

'Don't think so. Is this gonna be on *Crimewatch*?'

'Thanks for your help.' Templeton left Ali dreaming of TV stardom and walked back to his car. The rain had stopped and dark puddles reflected the lights. Before setting off back up the motorway, Templeton walked over to the garage and into the night manager's office. There he found a sleepy young man behind the counter and showed his warrant card. The boy seemed to wake up a bit.

'I'm Geoff,' he said. 'What can I do for you?'

'Were you working here last night?'

'Yeah.'

Templeton took out the photograph again. 'Remember her?'

'She looks . . .' He frowned. 'I don't know.'

'She looks dead,' said Templeton. 'Just as well, because she is. Do you remember her?'

'She was here. You don't forget someone who looks like that.'

'Do you remember what time?'

'I can't say for certain, but her credit-card receipt should tell us.'

'She used plastic?'

'Most people do. Petrol's so bloody expensive and cards are convenient. Nowadays you can just swipe the card right by the pump. You don't even have to come into the office. Not everyone likes to do it that way, mind you. Some still prefer the human touch.'

'I don't suppose you've still got last night's receipts?'

'As a matter of fact,' said Geoff, 'I have. There's no pick-up till Monday morning.'

'What are we waiting for? Her name's Jennifer Clewes.'

Geoff located the credit-card receipts and sucked on his lower lip as he made his way through them. 'Just give me a minute. Here, I think this is it.' He held the receipt up for Templeton to see: 12.35 a.m. Which meant she'd get to the junction with the A1 about two and a half hours later. It fitted. Templeton thanked Geoff, and just on the off chance asked him about the 'old' man Ali had described.

'The bloke with the dandruff? Old hatchet-face?'

'That's the one.'

'Yeah, he was here, too. Same time as her, now I come

to think of it. I caught him giving her the eye when she was bending over with the pump. Can't say I blame him, mind you. Like something out of *FHM*. Hey, you don't think that—'

'Seen him before?'

'Not that I recall. But we get so much traffic.'

'I don't suppose there's the remotest chance that he paid by plastic, too?'

Geoff grinned, flicking through the stack again. 'I told you. Most of them do. Here you are, right after hers. A Mr Roger Cropley.'

'Do you have CCTV?'

'As a matter of fact, we do,' said Geoff.

Thunder rumbled in the distance. Geoff held up the slip and Templeton read the details. So there is a God, after all, he thought.

•

Back at Roy's, Banks first checked the phone for messages. There was only one, and to his surprise it was from Annie Cabbot. Even more to his surprise, it was clearly intended for Roy because she addressed him as 'Mr Banks'. She'd called around at the house earlier, she said, but he had been out. Would he please get in touch as soon as possible? Of course Annie had no idea that Roy was missing. She sounded rather chilly and official, Banks thought, wondering what she was doing in London. Could it be something to do with the murder she was investigating in Eastvale? It was after half-past eleven now, though, and he didn't fancy getting into a complicated conversation with Annie so late. He'd give her a ring in the morning.

He brought the open bottle of Amarone upstairs and

watched *A Clockwork Orange* on the widescreen plasma TV. Even with the surround sound turned low so as not to disturb the neighbours, it still filled the room. After that, he fell asleep on the sofa, the bottle still half full.

Banks didn't hear the thunder, nor did he see the lightning, when the storm passed over the London area in the small hours of the morning. What did awaken him, however, at shortly after three, was the distinct melody of 'La donna è mobile' coming from very close by.

As Banks struggled to consciousness, his first thought was that he didn't remember putting a CD of *Rigoletto* on before he went to sleep. Then he remembered Roy's mobile, which sat on the table beside him.

He picked it up and, sure enough, that was the source of the sound. The room was dark, but with the help of the blue back-lighting, he found the right button to push.

'Hello,' he mumbled. 'Who is it?'

At first he heard nothing at all except a slight background hiss, perhaps some sort of static interference. He thought he could hear someone making choking or gagging sounds, as if they were trying to hold back laughter. Then he began to think that perhaps someone had rung by accident, and the sounds came from a television playing in the background.

Something similar had happened to Banks once when he had forgotten to lock his mobile. Somehow or other he had activated one of the numbers in his phone book, and Tracy got to listen to the questioning of a murder witness. Fortunately, she couldn't make out the conversation clearly, and she knew enough to switch off when she realized what must have happened. Still, it made Banks paranoid about locking the device after that.

Or maybe this was kids, someone's idea of a joke?

The muffled shouting went on, followed by a thud and the unmistakable sound of someone laughing. Then, as Banks looked at the display, a picture began to form. It wasn't very sharp, but it looked like a photograph of a man slumped in a chair, asleep perhaps, or unconscious, his head to one side. Banks couldn't see whether there were other people around, but given the sounds, it might have been some sort of wild party.

Banks was still half asleep, not thinking at all clearly, and he put the phone back on the table suspecting one of Roy's friends of playing some sort of practical joke on him. Whatever it was, he would be better equipped to deal with it in the morning.

6

The thunderstorm that swept across the southern half of the country during the night drove out the muggy weather, and Sunday dawned clear and sunny, the streets rinsed and sparkling after the rain. The temperature was still in the mid-twenties, but with the humidity all but gone it was a comfortable heat.

Annie woke late after a refreshing sleep, though her hotel room had been too hot and she had had to lie in her underwear on top of the sheets. She had turned the control on the wall to cold, but after nothing happened she concluded it was only for show. Perhaps if you believed it really worked you would start to feel cooler, but she didn't have that much faith.

After a lukewarm shower and a room-service Continental breakfast, again scouring the papers for any traces of Phil Keane's handiwork and finding none, Annie checked her mobile in case she'd missed a message from Roy Banks, but there was nothing. She rang the number again, and again she got the answerphone. This time she left an even terser message. She tried the mobile number, but had no luck there, either. She didn't bother leaving a message.

Next she rang Melanie Scott to make sure she would be at home, then she checked in with Gristhorpe at his home and found out that Jennifer Clewes's parents were being brought to Eastvale that morning to identify their daughter. Then Annie set off for the tube.

First she had to take the Northern Line to Leicester Square, then change to the Piccadilly Line, which ran all the way out to Heathrow. Given the more clement weather and the relative emptiness of the train, her journey out to Hounslow passed pleasantly enough, some of it above ground, and she gazed on the rows of red-brick houses, playing fields, concrete and glass office blocks.

She found Melanie Scott's house with the help of her *A–Z*, only about five minutes' walk away from the Hounslow West tube station. Cars filled every available parking spot on both sides of the street, sun glinting on their windscreens, so she was glad yet again that she wasn't driving.

The woman who answered the door looked to be in her late twenties, the same age as Jennifer Clewes. She was one of those excessively thin yet nicely shaped women, with small breasts, coat-hanger hips and a narrow waist. She was wearing denim shorts, which showed off her long, tapered legs to advantage. Jet-black hair hung straight down to her shoulders and framed a pale oval face with large brown eyes, button nose and full mouth. The red lipstick stood out in contrast against the paleness of her skin. Annie hadn't told her much over the telephone, but she must have suspected something was wrong, and she seemed nervous, anxious to hear the worst.

'You said it's about Jenn,' she said as she pointed Annie towards an armchair in the cramped living room. The front window was open and they could hear snatches of conversation and laughter as people drifted by. Melanie sat on the edge of her chair and clasped her hands between her knees. 'Is something wrong? What is it?'

'I'm afraid Jennifer Clewes is dead, Ms Scott. I'm sorry I can't think of any easier way to put it.'

Melanie just stared into a far corner of the room and her eyes filled with tears. Then she put her fist to her mouth and bit. Annie went over to her, but Melanie waved her away. 'No, I'm all right. Really. It's just the shock.' She rubbed her eyes and smudged mascara over her cheeks, then took a tissue from a box on the mantel-piece. 'You're a policewoman, so there must be some-thing suspicious about it, right? How did it happen?'

No flies on Melanie, thought Annie, sitting down again. 'She was shot,' she said.

'Oh, my God. It's the woman they found in the car in Yorkshire, isn't it? The one in the papers and on TV. You said you were from Yorkshire.'

'North Yorkshire, yes.'

'They wouldn't give her name out on the TV.'

'No,' said Annie. 'We have to be certain. Her parents haven't identified the body yet.' She thought of showing Melanie the photograph, but there was no point in further distressing her. Kate Nesbit had already identified Jennifer, and by now, Jennifer's parents would have confirmed this.

'I can't believe it,' Melanie said. 'Who'd want to kill Jenn? Was it some pervert? Was she . . . ?'

'There was no sexual assault,' Annie said. 'Do you know of anyone who would want to harm her?'

'Me? No, I can't think of anyone.'

'When did you last talk to Jennifer?'

'A few days ago – Wednesday, I think – on the phone. I haven't actually seen her for two or three weeks. Both too busy. We were going to the pictures next weekend. Chick-flick night. I can't believe it.' She dabbed at her eyes again.

'Do you know if there was anything bothering her, anything on her mind?'

'She did seem a bit preoccupied the last time I talked to her. But I must admit, Jenn goes on about work a bit too much sometimes, and I sort of tune it out.'

'She was worried about work?'

'Not specifically. It was just someone she mentioned. One of the late girls, she said. She worked at a family planning centre.'

'I know,' said Annie.

'Late girls? What are they?'

'I've no idea. That's just what she said.'

'A workmate? Late shift?'

'No, I don't think so. I don't think they worked in shifts. It's not a twenty-four-hour centre. But sometimes she has contact with the clients, through paperwork and billing and what have you, or if there's a problem or something. There was some woman . . .'

That was how Jennifer met Kate Nesbit, Annie remembered, through the centre. 'Can you remember her name?'

'I'm trying. Give me a moment. She spoke it very quickly so I can't be absolutely sure, but it was a rather odd name.' Melanie paused and gazed out of the bay window. A white delivery truck passed by, blocking the sun for a moment. 'Carmen, I think.'

'That was her first name?'

'Yes. Carmen. I remember thinking at the time that it sounded like an actress's name, but that's Cameron, isn't it? Cameron Diaz. Hers was Carmen, like the opera. Her surname was Petri, or something like that. I'm sorry.'

'That's all right.' Annie made a note of the name and put a question mark by 'late girl'. 'Did Jennifer say what she was worried about?'

'No. I'm sorry. Just that it was something this Carmen said.'

'Was this Carmen at the centre to arrange for an abortion?'

'I assumed so,' said Melanie, 'but Jenn didn't say. I mean, that's why people go there, or for advice, you know, if they're undecided, they don't know what to do.'

'Did Jennifer have any particular stand on abortion?'

'What do you mean?'

'Do you think she'd advise clients against it, suggest they keep the child and put it up for adoption instead?'

'Oh, I see. No, not really. Jenn believed it was a woman's choice. It's just that some of the women were . . . you know . . . scared, especially if they were young. Some of them just didn't know what to do. But Jenn wasn't an adviser or counsellor. There are other people to take care of that.'

'But she did have contact with the girls?'

'Sometimes. Yes.'

'But you've no idea *why* Jennifer was concerned about this Carmen?'

'Jenn just had a habit of getting involved in other people's problems, that's all. It can be a bit of a drawback in her line of work. Most of the time she doesn't have any contact with the clients, but sometimes . . . like I said. She's got too sympathetic a nature, and she can't always be objective about things. Or people. Mind you,

it's one of the qualities that makes her so special. Sorry.
Made. My God.'

'Did Jenn ever receive any threats because of her
work?'

'You mean because she dealt with abortions?'

'Yes. There are a number of groups actively against it,
some of them violent.'

'She never mentioned it to me. I mean, I think there
was a small demonstration once, but nothing came of it.
Certainly no violence, anyway. Groups like that would
tend to avoid the centre itself because abortions aren't
actually performed there, and many of the clients go on
to have their babies and give them up for adoption, so I
don't think that's a very real possibility.'

Annie realized that Jenn's workmates at the centre
would probably be better informed on this topic. She
moved on. 'It might be a good idea if you gave me a bit
of background. I understand you knew Jennifer a long
time?'

'Ever since primary school. We only lived two streets
away from one another. And we have the same birthday.
Her poor mum and dad . . .' Melanie picked up a packet
of cigarettes from the arm of her chair and lit one. 'Sorry,
you don't mind, do you?' she asked, blowing out the
smoke.

'It's your house,' said Annie. And your lungs, she
thought to herself. 'What about later? University?'

'We both did our postgraduate degrees at
Birmingham. I took international business, and Jenn
studied management.'

'What about your undergraduate degrees?'

'Jenn read economics at Kent and I went to Essex.
Modern languages.'

'You kept in touch?'

'Of course. We were practically inseparable in the hols.'

'I understand that just last summer the two of you went on holiday together to Sicily?'

'Yes.' Melanie frowned. 'Look, may I ask just what you're getting at? Are you suggesting there was anything . . . unusual . . . about our friendship, because if you are—'

Annie waved her hand. 'No, nothing like that. None of my business, anyway.' Unless it contributed to Jennifer's murder. 'No, it's just that her flatmate Kate didn't seem to know an awful lot about Jennifer's life, didn't really seem to know much about her at all.'

'That's hardly surprising,' said Melanie. 'Jenn's a very private person in a lot of ways. She shared the flat because she had to – London's so expensive – but it didn't mean she had to share her life. Besides . . .'

'What?'

'Well, I got the impression from Jenn that this Kate was a bit of a nosy parker, always asking questions, a busybody, wanting to know where she'd been and who she was with. Jenn said sometimes it was worse than being at home with her parents.'

Annie had had a flatmate like that once in Exeter, a girl called Caroline, who had even gone so far as to question her on what sort of birth control she used, and on what exactly went on those nights Annie didn't return to the flat. And some of Caroline's forays into Annie's sex life smacked of digging for vicarious thrills; she never seemed to have a boyfriend of her own, and Annie guessed that was how she got her jollies. Not that Annie gave much away, or had even been up to anything, most of the time.

'Why didn't she share with you?'

'Hounslow's too far out for her, and I need to be here because of my work. I'd hate to have to drive to Heathrow and back every day from the city.'

'They didn't get along, Kate and Jennifer?'

'I don't mean that. You can get along with someone who's not the same as you, can't you, in general, even if some of their habits annoy you, as long as you keep a bit of distance?'

'True,' said Annie. 'Sometimes it's better that way.'

'That's what they were like. They got along well enough. Kate kept the place clean and tidy, didn't leave food to go rotten in the fridge, remembered to lock the door when she went out, didn't make a lot of noise. That sort of thing. The things that are important when two people are sharing a common living space. They never had rows or anything. It's just that Kate's a bit bossy as well as nosy. Likes things just so. And she's got a bee in her bonnet about smoking. I won't even go to the house. It's her prerogative, of course, but even so, you'd think people could be a bit accommodating once in a while, wouldn't you?'

'I suppose so,' said Annie. 'What about boyfriends?'

'What about them?'

'Any problems there?'

Melanie pushed her hair back. 'I think Kate got sort of put off men. She had a scare a while back. Thought she was pregnant, so Jenn told me. Anyway, I know nothing about her love life, or lack of it.'

'And Jennifer?' Annie remembered what Kate Nesbit

had told her about Jennifer's ex-boyfriend, Victor, and she wanted to find out what Melanie knew about him.

Melanie paused, seemed to come to a decision, then went on. 'Jenn's the serious type when it comes to love,' she said. 'Last year, just before we went on holiday, she split up with someone she'd been seeing for three years and it devastated her. I could have told her it would happen, but you can't do that, can you? I mean, Jenn was pushing him towards commitment, living together, maybe marriage, babies, and it was obvious in the end that she'd scare him off.'

'Is that what happened?'

'Yes.' Melanie laughed. 'The holiday was supposed to be a cure. Get him out of her system. Get rat-arsed and shag lots of good-looking blokes.'

'Is that how it worked out?'

'No. Does it ever? Jenn read a lot of books, and I practised my Italian on the waiters, who were all over fifty. There wasn't one decent-looking bloke in the whole place. Most evenings we spent commiserating with one another over a couple of bottles of cheap Sicilian wine and most mornings we woke up with splitting headaches. Oh, and Jenn got sunburn on the second day. All in all, I'd say it was a bit of a farce.'

'And afterwards?'

'She got over him.'

'And he her?'

'Not quite,' said Melanie with a frown. 'Jenn did mention that he'd pestered her once or twice, said he'd made a big mistake and asked her to give him another chance, that sort of thing. And he kept trying to phone her.'

'At work or home?'

'Both.'

'When you say "pestered" her, do you mean stalked her, threatened her, what?'

'She just said he pestered her.'

'Can you remember his name and address?'

'Not his address, no, but I've got it written down somewhere. Remind me before you go. I do remember he lives out Chalk Farm way. His name is Victor Parsons.'

'Was Jennifer involved with anyone else, after Victor?'

'I think so. Very recently.'

'Past few weeks?'

'Yes. Couple of months at the most. She was moving very cautiously. Anyway, I got the impression that she liked him a lot.'

'Do you know his name?'

'Sorry, she didn't say. I mean she didn't really say very much about it at all; she was being very cagey. It's just that I've known her for so long, you get to sort of recognize the signs, if you know what I mean.'

'Do you think he might be married?'

'Married? Good God, I hope not. I mean, Jenn wouldn't go with a married man, not *knowingly*. I told you. She was serious about love. Believed in meeting Mr Right and settling down together forever. She wasn't casual about that sort of thing.'

Annie wondered if Kate Nesbit's suspicions were at all justified or were simply the result of Jennifer's natural reticence when it came to affairs of the heart. 'Do you know where they met?'

'At work, I should think. She hardly goes anywhere else, except with me.'

'Look, I know this is probably a bit of a cliché,' Annie said, 'but we do have to ask. Is there anyone you can think of who might have wanted to harm Jennifer? Has anyone at all ever made any threats against her?'

Melanie didn't hesitate. 'No,' she said, her eyes filling with tears again. 'Jenn was a *good* soul, one of the truly *good* people.'

'You don't know of any enemies she might have had?'

'She didn't make enemies. If you ask me, this was one of those random attacks you hear about on the news, maybe a serial killer, someone who didn't know her. Like that other girl, in the spring.'

'What about at work? Was everything all right there?'

'You'd have to ask them, but she never said anything to me about any problems. She liked her job.' She started to cry again. 'I'm sorry. I just can't get my head around it.'

Annie could think of no more questions anyway. She consoled Melanie as best she could and suggested she call a friend to come and stay. Melanie didn't want to, said she'd be fine by herself, and despite the tears Annie sensed that she was probably tougher than Kate Nesbit. Besides, her parents still lived in Shrewsbury, so they could hardly get down to London quickly. Annie left her card with her mobile number, telling Melanie she could ring at any time for any reason, and walked back to the tube wondering why someone so sensitive, serious and special as Jennifer Clewes had ended up a murder victim.

•

When Banks woke on Sunday morning to the sound of birdsong, his head was pounding, his mouth was dry, and he had the distinct memory of something very odd having happened during the night.

He stumbled to the bathroom and drank two glasses of water and took three paracetamol tablets, then he returned to the entertainment room, where he had slept on the sofa. He picked up Roy's mobile and found that the image was still there – he had at least had the sense to save it – and it made no more sense in the light of day than it had in the middle of the night. He found the incoming call on the call list. It was listed only as 'unknown'.

Banks examined the photo more closely. The foreground was out of focus, the figure blurred. Behind the slumped figure was what looked like a wall and Banks thought he could see the fuzzy outlines of letters written on it. There were no actual words he could read, but an expert might be able to glean something from it.

Was the man in the chair Roy? He could be, Banks supposed; the features weren't clear, but the hair looked about right. If it was Roy, was this some sort of oblique way of informing Banks that someone had taken – had kidnapped – his brother? Would a ransom demand come soon?

The man in the photo could still be anyone, though, Banks decided in the end. Perhaps Roy himself had sent the photo. It could be a message of some kind, or a warning. On the other hand, it had been sent to *Roy's* mobile, so was it intended for Roy, or did someone know that Banks had the phone? The latter thought didn't do much to quell Banks's fears for his brother. If someone already knew he was staying at Roy's house and had Roy's mobile, then he had better keep his eyes open and his wits about him.

Banks put the mobile aside and went back to the bathroom, where he removed his rumpled clothes and climbed into Roy's luxury power shower, turning it on full. The jets of hot water pummelled his body back into some semblance of humanity.

As he dried himself on a thick, soft towel, Banks realized that he had left his overnight bag in the boot of his car, which was parked outside. He didn't want to dash out and fetch it right now, so he brushed his teeth with Roy's electric toothbrush, which almost ripped his gums to shreds, and borrowed a clean short-sleeved shirt and socks from his brother's wardrobe. He had to wear his own jeans because Roy's were too long for him and too big around the waist.

After he had found Roy's stash of coffee in one of the kitchen cupboards and made himself a decent pot, Banks took it with him upstairs and returned to the entertainment room and the mobile. The phone call and digital image should be traceable, Banks knew, given the police's technical skills. You could also learn an awful lot from a mobile phone's SIM card. Unfortunately, he didn't have the resources at the moment. How important is it? he wondered.

Banks still couldn't let go of the idea that his brother might have been involved in something illegal and that that was why he'd vanished. Things had threatened to catch up with him and he'd had to run away fast and hide out. If that was the case and Banks brought in the local police, then he risked getting Roy into serious trouble. If something terrible came out – drugs or pornography, for example – and Roy went to jail, it could kill their parents.

On the other hand, there wasn't much more he could do alone except work on the leads he already had: the names from Roy's call list and phone book, and from the files Corinne had printed for him. He knew what his duty was, what he would advise anyone else in his position to do, but still he hesitated. At least he had the laptop now, so he could spend a bit more time on the CD and the USB drive, and there was one person he could turn to for help.

First he went into Roy's office. There was another telephone message, he noticed. It must have come in while he was taking his shower. Again it was from Annie Cabbot, and she simply asked Roy to ring her as soon as possible. Banks had forgotten all about last night's message. He still wasn't sure that he wanted Annie involved – she would definitely want him to make Roy's disappearance an official police matter – but he was curious enough to dial her mobile number and find out what she was after. He got no reception. Making a mental note to try again later, he picked up the telephone and rang Corinne, just to make sure. He breathed a sigh of relief when she said she was fine. She sounded sleepy. He apologized for waking her, said he'd be in touch and rang off.

Finally he dialled a number he had committed to memory. As requested he left a message and fifteen minutes later the phone rang. He snatched up the handset.

'Banks here.'

'So what's so urgent you have to disturb a hard-working copper on his only day off?' asked Detective Superintendent Richard 'Dirty Dick' Burgess.

'I need to see you,' said Banks. 'Urgently.'

•

Detective Chief Inspector Alan Banks weighed heavily on Superintendent Gristhorpe's mind, and not only because if Banks was around, Gristhorpe might be able to spend a bit more time on his drystone wall rather than having to drive into Western Area Headquarters so early on a Sunday morning. No doubt there would be a crowd of reporters to deal with, as the issue of guns always touched a nerve. Despite the strictest gun-control laws in the world, enacted in the wake of the Dunblane massacre, the country seemed to be flooded with cheap illegal guns from Ireland and Eastern Europe, as well as with reactivated firearms.

As it was, he still had a little time in hand, so he took his mug of strong tea out to the back garden and rested it on his chair while he studied various stones from the pile to see which one would fit best. The wall went nowhere and fenced nothing in, but for Gristhorpe it had become almost as necessary as breathing. He would never finish it – how could you finish something that went nowhere? – but if he ever did, he would pick it apart and start again. Wall-building was almost a lost art in the modern Dales, and while Gristhorpe had no pretensions to being an expert, of doing the work professionally, it was both his homage and his therapy.

As he weighed his options, Gristhorpe was pleasantly aware of the sun on his face and the light breeze that ruffled through his unruly thatch of hair, delicate as a woman's fingers. He thought of his wife, Mary, and her feather-light touch, and realized it was over twelve years now since the cancer had taken her. He still missed her as he would miss a part of himself, and not a day went by when he didn't think of her, remember some detail of her face, an expression, her gentle voice, her sense of humour, a certain gesture.

The air, he noticed, smelled of wild garlic, with a hint

of tar from the hot road surface. Gristhorpe sipped some tea and decided upon a stone. The one he chose fitted perfectly. Then he dragged his thoughts back to the matter in hand: Banks.

Over the years, Banks had been more than just a junior officer to Gristhorpe. He could remember his first impressions of an edgy, nervous chain-smoking detective on the verge of career burnout and wondered if he had made a mistake in approving the transfer. But Banks had made a journey back to some sort of equilibrium, aided in part by the Yorkshire countryside he had now adopted as his home.

In some ways, Gristhorpe knew that he had been a kind of mentor to the new Banks, not so much in terms of doing the job, but in human terms. Banks was a complex sort, and Gristhorpe wondered if he would ever find the peace and harmony he seemed to be looking for. After the divorce from Sandra, which Gristhorpe knew still hurt Banks deeply, and the messy relationship with Annie Cabbot, Banks seemed to have found a measure of happiness in his isolated cottage, but even that had come to an abrupt and violent end. Where next? Gristhorpe hadn't a clue, and he didn't think Banks had, either.

Gristhorpe drank more tea and looked for another stone. He wanted to know what Banks's connection with the dead woman was before word of it leaked out. At the moment, it was simply a matter of trying to track Banks down through his family, but if that didn't work, then the next step would have to be an official one, and that could harm Banks's career. It would mean using the media. They would have to put his photo in the newspapers, request anyone who thought they had seen him to call the police. And every copper in the country would be on the lookout for him, too. It wasn't only that Gristhorpe wanted to know why the dead woman had Banks's address in her back pocket – the wrong address – but that Annie said the cottage had been broken into, and the builders swore they had locked up as usual after their day's work and left no valuable equipment behind.

Gristhorpe finished his tea and put the stone in place. Too big. He chucked it back on the pile and went indoors. Time to go to work.

●

Banks had a couple of hours to kill before his meeting with Burgess. First he called Julian Harwood and was surprised to get an appointment to meet at Starbucks on the Old Brompton Road at two o'clock that afternoon. Harwood sounded like the kind of person who thought giving you the time of day was doing you a big favour, but the mention that Banks was Roy's brother got his interest.

After that, he had made a written note of the names and numbers in Roy's call list and mobile phone book, just in case. Many of the names on the list matched those in the book, and he found Julian, Rupert and Corinne among them. Others were businesses mentioned in the files Corinne had copied, and then there were services, such as hairdresser, tailor, bank manager, dentist and doctor. None of it told him very much. He rang a few of the numbers, including Rupert's, but nobody knew where Roy was – at least, no one admitted to knowing where he was.

A woman called Jenn figured quite prominently in the last thirty calls – at least ten of them were to or from her – and Banks guessed she was Corinne's replacement. He tried ringing the number but it was unavailable. He wondered if there was any other way he could get in touch with her. The odds were that if she had nothing to do with Roy's disappearance, she would ring his mobile before too long.

As Banks glanced through the stack of memos and accounts, looked at all the company logos and names, he felt frustration set in. None of them meant anything to him, and he didn't have the time or the resources to check them all out. He had no access to the Police National Computer, for a start. He could be looking at the names of dozens of criminals and not even know it. Burgess might help, but he would only tell Banks what he wanted him to know.

Banks spent half an hour having another look around the house and found nothing more of interest. Then he started to examine the JPEG files on the CD he had found yesterday. He sat his new laptop computer on the kitchen table, brewed himself some coffee and managed to follow the instructions and get the machine going. He slipped in the CD and found Windows Explorer tucked away at the bottom of the Accessories menu.

His computer automatically displayed the 1,232 JPEG files as thumbnails. Banks scrolled through these, all images of naked women with file names like Maya, Teresa, April, Mia and Kimmie, or of men and women engaged in sex acts. If he rested his cursor on one of them, information about file dimension, type and size would appear in a little box. Most of the JPEG images were between 25 and 75 kilobytes in size.

When he got to the 980th image, however, Banks noticed that it and the next two were different; all three were numbered with the prefix 'DSC' and showed two men sitting together at what looked to be an outdoor cafe. When he let his cursor rest on one of them, he found that, at 650 kilobytes, it was considerably larger than the earlier images, and that it was taken on Tuesday the 8th of June at 3.15 p.m. by a camera identified as E4300. Roy's Nikon was a 4300 model. According to the 'details' view, the other images were all downloaded the next day, so it looked as if Roy had dragged them in from another folder.

Intrigued, Banks double-clicked on the first image of the two men. He didn't recognize either of them. They were leaning towards one another, in earnest conversation. Both wore white open-necked shirts and light, casual trousers. One was bulkier with curly greying hair, the other younger and thinner with spiky black hair, a goatee and a hunted, watchful expression on his face, as if he was worried about being spied upon.

The following two images were of the same scene, taken in rapid succession. Banks scrolled to the end of the folder, but all he found was more Larissas, Natashas, Nadias and Mitzis.

On Tuesday afternoon, then, Roy had taken three candid photographs of two men in conversation at an outdoor cafe, and on Wednesday he had burned them to a CD, hidden among hundreds of erotic images. He had then placed the CD in the Blue Lamps jewel-case, which stood out like a sore thumb in his music collection.

So who were the men and what, if anything, did they have to do with Roy's disappearance? Banks picked up the laptop and took it upstairs. It was time to learn how to use Roy's printer.

●

DC Kevin Templeton thought he'd died and gone to heaven when he reported to Gristhorpe that morning and the boss said to take Winsome with him and pay Mr Roger Cropley an early visit. The credit-card companies were not exactly forthcoming when it came to providing information, even to the police, but the service station's CCTV cameras showed a number plate beginning with YF, which was the Leeds licensing office. The DVLA offices were closed on Sundays, so Templeton had had to resort to the local telephone directories and electoral rolls. As luck would have it, the name eventually yielded a north Eastvale address, which also meant that Mr Cropley would, in all likelihood, have taken the same road from the A1 as Jennifer Clewes.

Templeton let Winsome drive the short distance to Cropley's, sneaking surreptitious glances at the taut black fabric stretched over her thighs whenever she changed gear. Christ, they could kill a man, he thought with wonder. Then he realized he was so randy that morning because he hadn't shagged the red-headed clerk last night, the way he had intended. She had given him a nasty look, too, when he got to work that morning, one of those looks that said you've had your chance, mate, now on your bike. Still, he knew he could break down her resistance again given the opportunity. He was also tired, he realized, not having slept for more than an hour or so, but that he could deal with.

As the empty Sunday morning streets flashed by, he put his head in detective mode and planned out his interview. He liked Cropley for the killing. There were one or two small glitches, but nothing he couldn't reason his way past: no sexual interference, for a start, which was a bit of a puzzle, and no struggle, either. Then there was

Banks's address in the victim's pocket. But Templeton was sure Cropley had pulled her over and tried it on and something had gone disastrously wrong.

'How was your Saturday night?' he asked Winsome.

She gave him a sideways glance. 'Fine. And yours?'

'You already know about mine, spent sampling the delights of motorway cuisine. What did you get up to, then?'

'Up to? Nothing special. Club social.'

'Club?'

'Yeah, the potholing club.'

Templeton knew that Winsome liked to climb down holes in the ground and explore underground caverns. He couldn't think of anything more boring, or, for that matter, more terrifying, given that he suffered from claustrophobia. 'Where d'you hold it?' he asked. 'Gaping Gill?'

'Very funny,' said Winsome. 'Actually we met in the Cock and Bull. You should come along sometime.'

Was she asking him out? 'The Cock and Bull?'

'No, idiot. Potholing.'

'No way,' said Templeton. 'You'll not get me down one of those black holes.'

'Coward,' she said. 'Here we are.'

She pulled up in front of a neat Georgian semi, an unremarkable house with mullioned windows and beige stone-cladding. The street was on a low rise and offered a magnificent view out west to lower Swainsdale. There was a small limestone church with a squat Norman tower at the end of the street, and people were already filing in for the morning service.

Templeton jabbed at the doorbell, Winsome beside him. Despite, or perhaps because of, his lack of sleep, Templeton felt pepped up, excited, like the one time he had taken Ecstasy at a club. Winsome seemed cheerful enough in that cool and graceful way of hers, and if she had noticed him glancing at her thighs in the car, she hadn't said anything.

The man who answered the door didn't look particularly like a pervert, as far as Templeton could tell, except that he was wearing sandals with white socks, but he did match the description Ali had given him at Watford Gap. About forty, with thinning sandy hair, slim but with a beer belly sagging over his worn brown corduroy trousers, he had a long face with pouch-like cheeks and a rather hangdog expression. He reminded Templeton a bit of that actor who seemed to be in all the old sitcom repeats on telly with Judi Dench and Penelope Keith.

'Mr Cropley?' said Templeton, showing his warrant card. 'We're police officers. We'd like a word, if we may.'

Cropley looked puzzled the way they all did when the police came calling. 'Oh, yes, of course,' he said, moving aside. 'Please, come in. My wife's just . . .' He let the sentence trail, and Templeton and Winsome followed him into a living room that smelled of cinnamon and apples, where Mrs Cropley was putting the finishing touches to a colourful flower arrangement. She was taller than her husband, and bony, with strong, almost masculine, features. She looked a bit severe to Templeton, and he could well imagine her cracking out the leathers and whip for an evening S&M session. The thought made him shudder inside. And maybe it drove Mr Cropley to other things.

'It's your husband we want to talk to,' Templeton said, smiling. 'First off, at any rate.'

Mrs Cropley stood there for a moment before the

penny dropped. When it did, she gave her husband a look, then turned and left the room without a word.

Templeton tried to read significance into that look. There was something there, no doubt about it. One of Cropley's dirty little secrets had come back to haunt him, and his wife knew what it was, was letting him know that she knew, and he was on his own.

'We were just going to get ready for church,' said Cropley.

'I'm afraid the vicar will have to manage without you this morning,' said Templeton.

'What's it about?'

'I think you know. First of all, were you driving up the M1 and the A1 late on Friday evening?'

'Yes. Why?'

'What make of car do you drive?'

'A Honda.'

'Colour?'

'Dark green.'

'Did you stop at the Watford Gap services?'

'Yes. Look, I—'

'While you were there, did you notice a young woman alone?'

'There were a lot of people there. I . . .'

Templeton caught Winsome flashing him a glance. She knew. Cropley was evading the question, the first sign of guilt.

'I'll ask you again,' Templeton went on. 'Did you see a young woman there in the cafe alone. Nice figure, hennaed hair. She'd be hard to miss.'

'I can't remember.'

Templeton made a show of consulting his notebook. 'Thing is,' he went on, 'the bloke behind the counter remembers you sitting opposite the girl, and the petrol-station attendant remembers you filling up at the same time this young woman was there. That's how we found out your name, from the credit-card slip. So we know you were there. Do you remember seeing a young woman at the garage? She was driving a light blue Peugeot 106. Think about it. Take your time.'

'Why? What—'

'Do you remember her?'

'Perhaps,' said Cropley. 'Vaguely. But I can't say I was paying much attention.'

'That's not what I heard.'

'Then you heard wrong.'

'Come off it,' said Templeton. 'You were leering at her, weren't you? The attendant said you looked as if you wanted to stick your nozzle in her tank. You fancied her, didn't you? Wanted a piece.' He was aware of Winsome looking askance at him, but sometimes a direct shock to the system worked better than any amount of gentle questioning.

Cropley reddened. 'That's not how it happened at all.'

'Not how what happened?'

'Nothing. Nothing happened. The situation, that's all. I might have noticed her, but I wasn't "leering", as you put it. I'm a married man, a God-fearing man.'

'That doesn't always stop people.'

'Besides, since when has leering been against the law?'

'So you *were* leering at her.'

'Don't put words into my mouth.'

'What were you doing on the road so late?'

'Coming home. That's not a crime, either, is it? I work in London. I usually spend the week there.'

'A commuter, then. What do you do?'

'Computers. Software development.'

'Are you usually that late coming home?'

'It varies. As a rule, I try to get away by mid-afternoon on a Friday to beat the traffic, or early evening at the latest.'

'What was different about last Friday?'

'There was a meeting. We had a deadline to meet on an important project.'

'And if I called your company they'd verify this?'

'Of course. Why would I lie?'

'For all I know,' said Templeton, 'you drive up and down the motorway looking for young girls to rape and kill.'

'That's ridiculous.'

'Is it? Do you read the papers? Watch the news?'

'I try to keep abreast of current affairs.'

'Oh, you do, do you? Well, I don't suppose you've been following the story about the young woman murdered on the road from the A1 to Eastvale, have you? The same road you took. You were following her, weren't you? Waiting for your opportunity. A dark country lane. You cut her off. What happened next? Wasn't she your type after all? Did she struggle? Why did you shoot her?'

Cropley got to his feet. 'This is absurd. I don't even own a gun. I'm going to call my solicitor.'

'Where's the gun, Roger? Did you throw it away?'

'I told you. I don't own a gun.'

Templeton looked around the room. 'We can get a search warrant. Make a mess.'

'Then get one.'

'It'll be better if you tell us all about it,' said Winsome, in a soothing voice. 'We know these things happen, people lose control. Please sit down again, sir.'

'Nothing of the sort happened,' said Cropley, straightening his tie and glaring at Templeton. He sat down slowly.

'Come on, Mr Cropley,' said Winsome. 'Get it off your chest. There were two of them, weren't there?'

'Two what?'

'Two girls. Claire Potter and Jennifer Clewes. What were you doing on the 23rd of April?'

'I can't remember that far back.'

'Try,' said Templeton. 'It was a Friday. You'd be on your way back from London. Get away late that day, too, did you?'

'How do you expect me to remember one Friday out of all the rest?'

'Always stop at Watford Gap services, do you? Like the food there? Or do you stop at other places? Newport Pagnell? Leicester Forest? Trowell?'

'I stop when I feel the need.'

'What need?'

'It's a long drive. I usually take a break when I feel like it. Just the one. Use the toilets. Have a cup of tea. Maybe a sausage roll, a chocolate biscuit.'

'And look at the girls?'

'There's no crime in looking.'

'So you admit you do look?'

'You're doing it again. I simply said there's no crime in looking. Don't twist my words.'

'Were you at Trowell services on the 23rd of April?'

'I don't remember. I don't think so. I usually stop before then.'

'But you have been there on occasion?'

'On occasion. Yes.'

'And maybe you were there on the 23rd of April?'

'I've told you. I doubt it very much. I don't recall being there at all so far this year.'

'Very convenient.'

'It happens to be the truth.'

Templeton could feel his frustration level rising. Cropley was a cool one and he seemed to have mastered the art of not giving anything away. Why would he need to do that unless he did have a secret?

'Look, Roger,' said Winsome, 'we know you did it. The rest is just a matter of time. We can do it the easy way, like this, in the comfort of your own home, or we can take you down to the station. It's your choice. And believe me, every choice you make now will come back to haunt you down the line.'

'What would you do?' Cropley said to her. 'If you were innocent and someone was trying to say you'd done something terrible. What would you do?'

'I'd tell the truth.'

'Well, I am telling the bloody truth, but a fat lot of good it's doing me, isn't it?'

'Watch your language,' Templeton cut in. 'There's a lady present.'

'I'm sure she's heard worse than that.'

'And you a God-fearing man.'

'I didn't say I was a saint. Or a pushover.'

'Right, let's get back to that, shall we. Your unsaintly acts. We might not be able to prove you killed Claire Potter, but we've got a damn good chance of proving you killed Jennifer Clewes.'

'Then you don't need anything from me, do you?'

'Don't you understand?' Winsome said. 'It would make things easier for you later on if you told us now.'

'And what would it do for me? Knock a year off my sentence? Two years? Three years? If I survived that long.'

'That's good, Roger,' Templeton said. 'You're talking about doing time, now. Jail. Shows you're moving in the right direction. What it might mean is the difference in the quality of care once you're inside. See, people like you are on about the same level as kiddy-diddlers as far as the general prison population is concerned, and the court has some discretion as to whether you're to be isolated or not.'

'That's bollocks,' said Cropley. 'There are strict prison guidelines and it doesn't matter a damn whether I confess or not. Besides, you're both missing the point completely. Read my lips. I didn't do it. I have never, not once in my life, raped or killed anyone. Is that clear enough for you?'

Templeton glanced at Winsome. 'So be it,' he said. 'Like I told you, we'll be able to make out a good case from evidence and witness statements.'

'Circumstantial. It means nothing.'

'People have been convicted on a lot less.'

Cropley said nothing.

'What time did you start out on Friday?'

'About half ten.'

'What time did you get home?'

'About five.'

Templeton paused. There was something wrong here. 'Come off it. It doesn't take that long to drive from London to Eastvale, even with a stop or two. Unless you couldn't go straight home after you'd killed the girl.

What did you do? Drive around until you calmed down, felt able to face your wife?'

'As a matter of fact, my car broke down.'

'Pull the other one.'

'It's true. I had a breakdown just a short distance past Nottingham.'

'That's very convenient.'

'It wasn't convenient at all. I had to wait over a bloody hour for the AA to come. They said it was a busy night.'

'The AA?'

'That's right. I'm a member. Want to see my card?'

Templeton felt his forehead getting hot. He didn't like the direction this conversation was taking. 'Can you prove this, about the breakdown?' he asked.

'Of course I can. Ask the AA. They'll verify what happened. I was stuck on the hard shoulder from about half-past twelve till half-past two. Wait a minute—'

'What was the problem?'

'Fan belt. That's put a spoke in your wheels, hasn't it? You never told me what time this girl was killed. It was while I was waiting for the AA, wasn't it?' Cropley smirked.

Templeton suppressed a sudden urge to break Cropley's nose. He felt himself running out of steam. If Cropley had been stuck on the M1 until well after two o'clock, he could hardly have killed Jennifer Clewes. 'Your mobile phone records will bear this out?'

'Should do. Will that be all?'

'Not quite,' said Templeton, loath to let the bastard gloat for too long. 'Who left the garage first, you or Jennifer Clewes?'

'She did.'

'And you followed her?'

'No. I was just behind her, but another car cut in front of me. Came right out of the shadows. I overtook them both shortly after and I never saw her again. She must have passed me later, when I was stuck by the roadside, but I didn't notice.'

'What about this other car? Why didn't you tell us about it before?'

'Because you were too busy trying to accuse me of rape and murder. You never asked.'

'Well, I'm asking now. What make was it?'

'A Mondeo. Dark colour. Maybe navy blue.'

'How many people in it?'

'Two. One in the front, one in the back.'

'Like a taxi?'

'Yes, but it wasn't a taxi. I mean, it didn't look like one. There was no light on top, for a start.'

'Private hire car, then?'

'Maybe. Look, I hate to tell you how to do your job, especially as you've been doing it so well, but why don't you ask me something useful, like do I remember the number?'

'I was getting to that,' Templeton said. 'Do you?'

'As a matter of fact I do. Well, some of it, anyway. I suppose I noticed because he pulled out a bit sharply and I had to brake.'

'What was it?'

'LA51.'

Templeton couldn't remember offhand what DVLA office and local tag the first two letters represented, but he knew that '51' meant the car had been registered between September 2001 and February 2002. The rest he could look up. It wasn't much to go on, but it was better than nothing.

'What did the occupants look like?'

'I didn't get a good look,' said Cropley. 'But I think they were both men. I really didn't think anything of it at the time, except that I had to brake rather sharply.'

'Try to remember.'

Cropley thought for a moment. 'The one in the back turned and looked at me after they pulled out. I suppose I tooted the horn at them. Just instinct.'

'And?'

'Well, as I said, I didn't get a good look. It was dark and his face was in shadow. But I think he had dark hair, tied back in a ponytail, and I doubt it was a friendly glance he gave me. I remember just feeling rather glad they didn't stop and beat me up. You hear so much about road rage these days.'

'What you get for going around tooting your horn,' said Templeton.

'They cut me off.'

'Popular girl, Ms Clewes,' mused Templeton. 'First you've got your eye on her, then another couple of blokes come cutting in and spoil all your fun. How did that make you feel?'

'What the hell are you talking about?' Cropley said. 'Can you hear yourself speak? You sound like a cheap television psychologist. Look, you already know I didn't do it, and I've had just about enough of this, so why don't you both sod off and check with the AA.'

Templeton reddened and Winsome gave him a sign that they should leave. He paused a moment, locking eyes with Cropley, then did as she suggested.

'Nice one, Kev,' she said, when they got outside. 'You handled that really well.'

He could tell she was still laughing at him when she got in the driver's seat and the anger prickled at his skin from the inside like hot needles.

7

The pub Burgess chose was flanked by a halal butcher and an Indian takeaway on a narrow street between Liverpool Street Station and Spitalfields Market. Banks took the tube and checked constantly to see if he was being followed. He was pretty sure he wasn't. After receiving the image on the mobile, though, he didn't feel like taking any chances.

It was lunchtime and most pubs were offering the traditional roast beef and Yorkshire pud, but at this place the choice was between nachos with sour cream and spicy chicken wings with BBQ dip. Banks didn't fancy either, so he stuck with a pint of Pride and a packet of cheese and onion crisps while Burgess attacked the nachos and washed them down with cheap lager.

There wasn't exactly any sawdust on the floor, but looking at the state of the place, Banks thought perhaps there ought to be. Most of the lunchtime drinkers were older Bangladeshis, Indians and Pakistanis – clearly not devoutly Muslim. A group were watching cricket on the television, a tourist match in which Essex were playing Pakistan, commenting loudly now and then on a particularly good off-spinner or square cut.

Burgess looked much the same as he had when Banks last saw him in January, except today he was informally dressed in jeans and a Hawaiian shirt that dazzled Banks. But the shaved head and slight paunch were still there, and the cynical, world-weary look had returned to his eyes. All that was new was his tan. After many rises and falls in fortune, Burgess had landed on his feet after 9/11, when the service required men who got things done, no questions asked. Banks wasn't sure what outfit he worked for now, but assumed it was something to do with Special Branch.

'Nice place you picked,' said Banks.

'It's anonymous,' Burgess said. 'Everyone here just minds their own business. Besides, most of the buggers can barely understand English.' Outside the window, the sky had darkened and a few splashes of rain ran down the grimy glass. Burgess looked at Banks closely. 'You look like a worried man. Care to tell your Uncle Dicky what's wrong?'

Banks looked around, saw that no one was paying them any attention, then brought up the image on the mobile and slid it over the table. Burgess picked it up, examined it closely and raised his eyebrows. 'It could be anyone,' he said, handing it back to Banks. 'Some drunk asleep at a party.'

'I know that. But what if it's not?'

'Who do you think it is?'

'It might be my brother.'

'Roy?'

'How do you know his name?'

Burgess paused. 'It was a long time ago.'

'When?'

'About five or six years. Last century, at any rate. No reason to bother you with it at the time.'

'So what brought brother Roy under scrutiny?'

'Arms dealing.'

'What?'

'You heard me. Arms dealing. Don't look so surprised. Your brother helped broker a deal between a UK arms manufacturer and some rich Arab sheikh. Greased the wheels, handled the baksheesh, attended galas at the consulate and so on.'

'Roy did that?'

'Roy would do anything to make a bit of extra cash. He has an extraordinary range of contacts and connections and the bugger of it is that he doesn't even know who half them really are.'

'Naive was never a description I'd have used to describe Roy,' said Banks.

'Maybe not,' Burgess argued, 'but he took too many people at face value. Maybe he didn't want to dig any deeper, find out any more. Maybe it was safer that way and easier on his conscience. Pocket the money and turn your back.'

Banks had to admit that sounded like the Roy he knew. More likely than naivety was lack of imagination. When they were kids, Banks remembered, they had had to share a bedroom for a few days for some reason. Banks was ten, Roy about five. Banks had tried to torment his younger brother by telling him gruesome ghost stories at bedtime, about headless corpses and misshapen ogres, hoping to scare him well into the night. But Roy had fallen asleep during Banks's version of *Dracula* and it was Banks himself who was left unable to sleep, jumping at every gust of wind and creak in the woodwork, victim of his own imagination. Perhaps Roy had taken his colleagues and their claims at face value, perhaps he hadn't wanted to dig any deeper, or perhaps he had just lacked the imagination to extrapolate on the bare facts. Banks reached for a Silk Cut.

'Didn't think you'd last long,' said Burgess, lighting one of his own Tom Thumb cigars and offering the flame to Banks, who took it.

'It's only temporary,' Banks said.

'Of course. Another pint?'

'Why not?'

Burgess went to the bar and Banks watched the cricket while he was gone. Nothing exciting happened. A second pint of Pride on the table before him, he asked Burgess exactly what he knew about Roy.

'You've got to understand,' Burgess said, 'that your brother did nothing illegal. People manufacture the damn things and people sell them. Back then you could sell anything to anyone, anywhere: missiles, landmines, submarines, tanks, jet fighters, you name it. The problem is that they had a habit of ending up in the hands of the wrong people, despite all the red tape. Sometimes they got used on the very people who sold them in the first place.'

'So where did these particular shipments go?'

'They were destined for a friendly country in the Middle East but they ended up in the hands of a terrorist splinter-group.'

'And Roy's part?'

'He had no idea. Obviously. He couldn't see the big picture, didn't want to, no more than the arms manufacturers did. All they wanted was a nice fat profit.'

'What happened?'

'It was the bloke who recruited Roy for the job, an old crony of his called Gareth Lambert, who we had our eyes on. He's history now. Left the country.'

Banks didn't recognize the name from Roy's call list or phone book. He could have missed it, as there were so many, or Lambert could be one of the 'unknown' numbers. On the other hand, if, as Burgess said, Gareth Lambert was history, there was no reason for Roy to have his phone number. 'And Roy?' he asked.

'One of our lads had a friendly word in his shell-like.'

'And after that?'

'Not even a blip on our radar,' said Burgess. 'So whatever this means,' he said, 'if it means anything at all, it's nothing to do with us. All of this was over and done with a long time ago.'

'That's comforting to know,' said Banks.

'Why don't you tell me what happened?'

Banks told him, from the strange phone call to the arrival of the digital photograph in the middle of the night. Burgess puffed on his cigar as he listened, eyes narrowed to slits. When Banks had finished, he let the silence hang for a while. Someone scored a six and the cricket-watchers cheered.

'Could be a prank. Kids,' Burgess said finally.

'I've thought of that.'

'Could be someone trying to scare you off. I mean, if you're supposed to think it's your brother and he's been hurt in some way.'

'I've managed to work that out for myself, too.'

'You're not scared?'

'Of course I bloody am. But I want to know what's happened to Roy. What do you expect me to do? Give up and go home?'

Burgess laughed. 'You? I should cocoa. What about kidnapping? Have you considered that? A prelude to a ransom demand?'

'Yes,' said Banks, 'but I've received no demand so far.'

'So what are you going to do now?'

'I thought you might be able to help.'

'How?'

'The mobile,' Banks said. 'A forensic examination might give us all sorts to go on. It might even tell us where the image was sent from, maybe even where it was taken. I'm not exactly up on the technology but I know the computer experts can get a lot out of these things.'

'True enough,' said Burgess. 'What with DNA, computers, the Internet, mobiles and CCTV there's hardly any need for the humble detective any more. We're dinosaurs, Banksy, or fast going that way.'

'A sobering thought. Can you help?'

'Sorry,' said Burgess, 'but this is a lot different from looking up a name or accessing a database. My department doesn't actually have a great deal of contact with the technical-support people. We're closer to the intelligence services, information-gathering. It would look bloody odd if I suddenly turned up at the lab and dropped this on their desk without any explanation. They'd be all over me like a dirty shirt. Sorry, Banksy, but no can do. My advice is take it to the local cop shop. Let them deal with it.'

Banks stared at the phone. Burgess's response was what he had half expected, but even so he felt disappointed, lost. What the hell was he supposed to do now? He couldn't go to the local police. It wasn't only that he was worried Roy might be involved in something criminal, but there was no way he would be given any part in an official investigation into the disappearance of his own brother, and he didn't think he could bear standing on the sidelines with his hands in his pockets, whistling.

'OK,' he said. 'And you're sure you've got absolutely no idea why any of this is happening?'

'Swear on my mother's grave. Your brother fell off our map many years ago and we've had no reason to put him back on.'

'You've been watching him?'

'Not recently. We kept an eye on him for a while. Like I said, he's got some interesting contacts. But as for Roy himself, we soon lost interest. It's not guns or terrorism. Believe me, I'd know.'

'And you'd tell me if it was?'

Burgess smiled. 'Maybe.'

Banks took out the envelope he'd brought and slipped out one of the digital photos for Burgess to examine. 'Do you know who these people are?' he asked.

Burgess picked up the photo and examined it closely. 'Well, bugger me,' he said. 'It can't be. Where did you get this?'

Banks told him.

'When was it taken?'

'According to the computer details it was taken on Tuesday the 8th of June at 3.15 p.m.'

'But that's last Tuesday.'

'Who is it?'

'Gareth Lambert.'

'You said he was history.'

'That's what I thought. But look.' Burgess placed the photo in front of Banks and pointed to the grey-haired man. 'He's put on a bit of weight and his hair's turned grey, but it's him all right.'

'Is he bent?'

'Definitely.'

'What was his line?'

'Import–export. At least it used to be. Fancy word for smuggling, if you ask me. Knows the Balkan route like the back of his hand.'

'Smuggling what?'

'You name it.' Burgess ran his hand over his shaved head. 'Look, you might as well know. In his time, Gareth Lambert was a very nasty piece of work, indeed. I don't mean tough, but nasty, sly. Maybe he's mellowed with old age, though I doubt it.'

'What did he do?'

'It wasn't always so much what he did as who he knew. He rubbed shoulders with some of the nastiest bastards in Europe. Smuggled arms, drugs, people, anything. He had connections with the military down in the Balkans – Kosovo, Bosnia – knew all the generals. He smuggled medical supplies – morphine, antibiotics – sometimes diluted. Bit of a Harry Lime, when you come to think about it, and almost as elusive. Likes to keep on the move, one step ahead. He's a slippery bastard. If he's back, you can be certain he's up to his eyeballs in something dodgy, and if your brother Roy . . . well . . .'

That didn't make Banks feel any easier about the situation at all. 'Who's that with him?'

'I don't know. I don't recognize him. Lambert and his crew aren't really my brief any more. Can I hang on to this? I've still got a few contacts where it counts, and I'll make a few enquiries. There'll be quite a lot of old-timers around the Yard interested to know Gareth Lambert's back in business, if they don't know already.'

'Of course,' said Banks. 'I've got copies. And the mobile?'

'Hang on to it for the moment. You might need it. If

that picture was intended for you, then more messages might follow.'

'I suppose you're right,' said Banks, pocketing the mobile. Maybe Annie would be able to hook him up with a computer expert to enhance the image. That way he wouldn't have to relinquish the phone.

'Right,' said Burgess, 'I'd better be off now.'

Banks wondered if he'd done the right thing in telling all and handing over the photo of the two men to Burgess. Now that he'd made Roy's disappearance semi-official there could be no turning back, whatever happened. He had already gone too far to avoid some sort of disciplinary proceedings by not reporting the first phone call and by living in Roy's house and accessing his computer data. He thought he could rely on Burgess's discretion, but there was a limit to everything.

At least this way he could continue his own investigation. He had already made a list of names and numbers, almost a hundred, and he still couldn't remember seeing any Gareth Lambert. He would have to check again, of course, but if Lambert was back in the picture, maybe there was a reason why neither he nor Roy wanted any records of their communications.

'Look,' he said to Burgess, 'I appreciate your help, but if Roy's in the clear and there's nothing really to link him with any serious criminal business . . .'

'You want me to keep your brother out of it?'

'If you can.'

'No guarantees,' said Burgess. 'Gareth Lambert turning up like this out of the blue changes everything. But I promise I'll do my best.'

'You'll keep me informed? I'd like to know where to find this Lambert, for a start.'

'Like I said, I'll do my best. I'll keep my ear to the ground. I'd ask you to bugger off back to Yorkshire and stay out of the way if I thought it would do any good, but at least try to avoid getting under my feet.'

'I'll think about it,' Banks said. He gave Burgess Roy's telephone numbers and glanced towards the window. 'It's almost stopped raining. I'd better go, too.'

Burgess gave him a stern look. 'Be careful, Banksy,' he said. 'Remember, I know you. And this conversation never took place.'

Banks walked out. His car was still parked near Corinne's flat, so he made his way to Liverpool Street, where he could take the District Line back to Earl's Court and pick up his car before meeting Julian Harwood.

While he was on the concourse of the mainline station, he wandered over to look at the Kindertransport Memorial. A sculpture to commemorate the rescue mission that helped over ten thousand children escape Nazi persecution in Europe during 1938 and 1939, it consisted of a glass case shaped like a large suitcase, which held a selection of objects the children had brought with them and, standing beside it, a bronze sculpture of a young girl.

Through the rain-beaded glass, amongst other things Banks could see school exercise books, pages filled with mannered German writing, letters, articles of clothing, dog-eared family photographs, a pair of old boots with clip-on ice skates, a hand-puppet of a kitten, a book of piano music, a battered suitcase and three coat-hangers. On one was written 'Für das Kind', on the second 'Fürs liebe Kind' and on the third 'Dem braven Kinde'. It made Banks think of Mahler's beautiful 'Kindertotenlieder', 'Songs for the Deaths of Children', though these children hadn't died: they had been saved. He wondered if Roy had the Mahler in his collection; he hadn't noticed it.

Looking at the children's personal belongings arrayed like this before him, Banks thought of all the mementoes he had lost forever when his cottage burned down: the family photographs and videos – wedding, holidays, kids growing up – letters, keepsakes, the poems he had written as a teenager, old diaries and notebooks, school report cards, the records of a life.

But he couldn't feel self-pity in the face of this memorial. He hadn't lost nearly as much as these children, who'd lost their homelands and, in many cases, their whole families. Perhaps they had gained something, too, though. They had at least escaped the concentration camps, been taken in by good, caring families, and had grown up to live their lives in relative freedom.

Banks looked at the bronze statue of the girl in her skirt and jacket. The raindrops looked like tears flowing down her face. He turned away and headed for the underground.

●

Annie was glad DI Brooke had suggested a quick lunch together in her hotel that afternoon. She had heard nothing from Roy Banks and she was beginning to wonder if the two brothers had made up their differences and run away together just to make her job difficult.

Brooke was in his Sunday best, red-faced, collar too tight around his neck, looking like a farmer just come from church. Annie, in jeans and a black V-neck jumper, felt underdressed. Neither felt terribly hungry, so they ordered coffee and cheese-and-pickle sandwiches, which came cut into quarters, neatly arranged in baskets.

'Well, Dave,' said Annie, 'I must say you cut a dashing figure.'

Brooke blushed. 'The suit? I've got a christening to go to this afternoon.' He sat down and pulled at his collar, finally undoing the button. 'There, that's better. Plenty of time to choke myself to death in church later.'

Annie laughed.

'I don't have a lot to report,' Brooke said, 'but I had a couple of lads ask around the victim's neighbourhood. I've also had a word with the uniform who walks the beat there, PC Latham.'

'What does he say?' Annie asked.

'Quiet sort of area. No trouble lately.'

'What about the enquiries your lads made?'

'A bit more interesting. A bloke down the street was looking for a parking spot about ten o'clock on Friday night. Seems he usually managed to park right outside his house, but this time he couldn't because someone was already there. Said it had happened before a couple of times that same week. He was a bit miffed, but there was nothing he could do. After all, it was a free spot. Anyway, he remembered there were two men in the car, one in the front and one in the back. He thought they might be leaving so he hung back for a couple of minutes but they ignored him.'

'What happened?'

'He found another spot nearby and that was that.'

'Does he remember anything else about the car?'

'Only that it was dark blue.'

'No number plate?'

'The car was parked. He couldn't see the front or back.'

'Of course. Anything else?'

'When he went out to walk the dog at eleven, it was gone.'

'Could he describe the men?'

'Not very well. Only that the one in the back had something around his neck, like a thick gold chain. He said they looked a bit thuggish. At least their appearance worried him enough that he didn't approach them and ask if they were going to move.'

'Interesting,' said Annie. 'I've just been on the phone with my SIO and one of our DCs has got a similar description from a man called Roger Cropley. Apparently, this Cropley saw Jennifer Clewes at the Watford Gap service station around half-past twelve on Friday night and a car like the one you just described, with one man in the front and one in the back, cut in front of him and went after her.'

'Then it sounds as if someone was waiting for her outside the flat.'

'It does, indeed,' said Annie. 'If it's the same car. I've thought there were two of them right from the start, one who could get out of the car quickly and do the shooting, the other a driver.' Annie consulted her notebook. 'Have you ever heard of a woman called Carmen Petri?'

Brooke frowned. 'Can't say as I have. Why?'

'It's just a name one of Jennifer Clewes's friends mentioned. One of the "late girls", she called her. Jennifer was worried about her, something she said.'

'Late girls?'

'Yes. Why? Do you know what that means?'

'Haven't a clue,' said Brooke. 'It just sounds odd, that's all.'

Given the context – a family planning centre – Annie had come up with a couple of possibilities: either 'late girls' were late with their periods, which was sort of self-evident when you were dealing with pregnancy, or they were 'late' in their pregnancies, beyond the time when terminations could be performed, which according to the law was the twenty-fourth week.

'I'll check our files for you, see if we've any record of this Carmen, but the name doesn't ring a bell.'

'No reason why it should. But thanks anyway. And, Dave? Check mispers and recent deaths, too, if you can.' If someone had been performing late terminations and something had gone wrong, Annie thought, then Jennifer Clewes might have stumbled across something very nasty indeed.

•

'I haven't seen Roy in over a month,' said Julian Harwood, 'so I don't see how I can help you.'

'You never know,' said Banks. 'It's good of you to spare me the time.'

'Nonsense. Roy's a good friend. Has been for years, even if we don't see enough of one another these days. Anything I can do, I'm only too willing.'

Harwood didn't seem out to impress, as far as Banks could tell. He didn't need to; he was a powerful, wealthy businessman, used to getting his own way. Corinne's impression had been different, but then perhaps Harwood behaved differently around women. Many men do. Also, she was Roy's girlfriend, an extremely attractive young woman, and he might have felt the need to compete, to impress her.

The sun was out again and they were sitting outside at Starbucks drinking grande lattes. Before meeting Harwood, Banks had shown a copy of the digital photo to Malcolm Farrow, Roy's neighbour across the street. Farrow had said that the bulky man with the grey curly hair might just have been the one Roy left with at nine-thirty on Friday, but he couldn't be absolutely certain.

Banks could smell Chinese food from somewhere nearby, but he couldn't see a Chinese restaurant. The street was crowded with shoppers, a mix of tourists and locals out for a drink and a stroll. Two pretty young girls in shorts and tank tops were sitting at the next table talking French and smoking Gauloises.

Harwood was younger than Banks had expected, mid-forties most likely, about Roy's age, and completely bald apart from a couple of thick strips of black above his ears. He had a healthy tan and the lean physique of a regular tennis or squash player. His clothes were casual but expensive: a blue denim shirt, open at the collar, and khaki chinos with a razor crease. Only the Nike trainers looked a bit out of character, but they weren't cheap, either.

Banks lit a cigarette – one of the advantages of sitting outside – and said, 'I don't suppose you know where he is?'

'What do you mean?'

Banks explained about Roy's phone call and the unlocked house. Harwood's brow furrowed as he listened, and when Banks had finished, he said, 'Roy could be anywhere. He travels quite a bit, you know. Have you thought of that?'

'Yes,' said Banks. 'But his message was *urgent*, and it seems odd that he hasn't told anyone where he was going. No one I've spoken with so far has any idea where he might be. Is he usually that secretive about his movements?'

'Not usually,' said Harwood. 'It depends. I mean, if there's some sensitive overseas deal in the offing . . .'

'Is that likely?'

'I'm saying it's possible, that's all.'

'Anyway, you're a business associate. You might know if he had any trips scheduled.'

'He didn't as far as I know,' said Harwood. 'But I'm not his personal assistant. Roy has plenty of irons in the fire that have nothing to do with me.'

'Do you think he might have done a runner?'

Harwood thought for a moment. 'Possible, I suppose, if things got too much for him. Tax, debts, that sort of thing. But surely he'd lock his house and take his mobile?'

'Maybe he wanted it to look as if it had happened some other way. I wouldn't put it past him. I don't know,' said Banks. 'I'm just clutching at straws.'

Harwood cleared his throat. 'I know you're a police-man,' he said. 'Have you reported this?'

'No,' said Banks. 'I'm conducting my own investigation so far.'

Harwood nodded. 'Probably wise, given Roy's pen-chant for – how shall I put it? – sailing a little close to the wind.'

'How long have you known him?' Banks asked.

'Years. We met at university.'

'Have you been involved in business ventures together ever since then?'

'On and off.'

'What about arms deals?'

'What arms deals?'

'Roy was involved in one a few years back. I was won-dering if you knew anything about it, as a close friend.'

'I'm afraid that's not my area of expertise,' Harwood said in a tight voice. 'Roy would have known better than to come to me about it, if indeed he was involved.'

'Oh, he was involved, all right. What about insider trading?'

'What about it?'

'It's something else my brother was involved in. I just wondered if you played a part.'

Harwood shrugged. 'There was a time . . . it wasn't uncommon.'

'So you did?'

'I'm not saying that.'

'But you knew Roy did?'

Harwood scraped his chair back and made to get up. 'Is this meant to be some sort of interrogation? Because if it is, I'm going right now.'

'I have questions to ask you,' said Banks. 'Does that constitute an interrogation?'

'Depends on what they are and how you go about it.'

'Then I'll be as gentle as I can if you'll be as frank as you can.'

Harwood moved his chair back to the table. 'Then I'm here to help,' he said. 'But let's leave arms deals and insider trading behind us, shall we? I'm not saying both of them don't still go on – you only have to read the papers to know that – but if Roy or I had any involvement, we left it behind us along with the nineties. You can take my word on that.'

'All right,' said Banks. 'From what I can gather, Roy has been investing in private healthcare recently, and you're a big player in that game.'

'It was me who brought him in. There are a lot of opportunities. I'm the managing director and CEO of a chain of private health centres and clinics offering various procedures and levels of care, all carried out by highly qualified doctors and nursing staff. Roy's one of our major shareholders.'

'What kind of procedures?'

'Pretty wide range, really, from hernia operations to terminal-cancer care.'

'Can you think of any reason why anyone would want to harm him?'

'Anyone connected with our business ventures, you mean?'

'Yes.'

'No,' said Harwood. 'It doesn't make sense. I can assure you that everything is completely in accordance with the law. Why do you ask?'

'Because I'm really stuck here, Mr Harwood, so I'm just casting around in the dark. As far as I can make out, Roy was last seen leaving his house and getting into a big light-coloured car, probably an expensive model, with another man. As far as I know there were no signs of coercion, but it's not out of the question, if the man was carrying a hidden gun or something. Later, possibly during the night, his computer was taken from his house, which was left unlocked. His mobile phone was lying on the kitchen table. There were no signs of a struggle. I've considered kidnapping, and it might still be a possibility, though there's been no ransom demand yet. Roy's a wealthy man.'

Harwood stroked his chin. 'Not *that* wealthy, I wouldn't have thought.'

'It's all relative,' said Banks. 'People have been kidnapped for less, I should imagine.'

'True enough. But wouldn't there have been some sort

of communication by now? When did you say this happened?'

'Friday night. Yes, it's been nearly two days and I've heard nothing so far. Which leads me to think it's something else. It just doesn't look like a bunch of thugs, that's all. More like . . . I don't know.'

'Organized crime?'

'It's a possibility,' said Banks. 'But what connection could Roy possibly have to organized crime?'

'I've no idea,' said Harwood. 'Just an idea I was tossing out. I mean, I don't even know what those people do. It's not as if it's just the Mafia any more, is it? One reads about Russians and Yardies and Vietnamese gangs. People who'd cut your throat as soon as look at you. Who knows?'

Banks took a copy of one of Roy's digital photos out of his briefcase and set it on the table. 'Do you know either of these men?'

Harwood pointed to Lambert. 'Well, I know *him*. That's Gareth. But I can't say I know the other one.'

'You know Lambert?'

'Oh, yes. Roy and I have done a bit of business with him in our time. Not for a while, mind you. He sort of disappeared from the scene.'

'He's back.'

Harwood frowned. 'I didn't know that.'

'Interesting,' said Banks, putting the photo away. 'I mean that Roy would know, but not you.'

'Gareth Lambert and I had a disagreement some years ago,' said Harwood. 'We haven't communicated since.'

'What about?'

'A private business matter.'

'I see. Do you know how I can get in touch with him?'

'As far as I know, he moved to Spain.'

'Big country. You don't have his address?'

'No. As I said, we had a falling out. I no longer have any interest in where Mr Lambert is or what he does.'

Banks would have liked to know more about that falling out, but Harwood was a shrewd businessman, good at keeping secrets, at holding his cards close to his chest. 'Did Roy ever mention anything that led you to believe he was up to something dodgy?'

'No. Not that he would have told me. Sometimes, in the business world, ignorance is bliss.'

'Is it possible he stumbled across something? Maybe someone was stealing and he found out about it?'

'From one of the centres?'

'Wherever.'

'I have nothing to do with the day-to-day running of the health centres or clinics.'

'What about Roy?'

'Your brother's a hands-on sort of investor. He likes to know how the businesses operate, likes to put faces to names. I imagine he's been doing the rounds.'

'So it's likely he visited the centres?'

'I should think so. Some of them.'

'Could he have stumbled on some sort of fraud or something?'

'We keep a pretty close eye on the figures. I think we'd know if anyone was bleeding the company.'

'What about stuff going missing? Drugs, for example.'

'They're strictly controlled.' Harwood looked at his watch. 'Look,' he said, standing up to leave, leaning over the table with his palms spread on its surface, 'I have to go now. I don't know whether you consider me a suspect in whatever you think is going on, but I want you to know that Roy's a valued friend. If I can help you in any way, please don't hesitate to get in touch again.'

'Very well,' said Banks. 'Thank you for your time.'

Harwood walked off. Banks finished his cigarette then stubbed it out and set off along the Old Brompton Road. He turned through the narrow arch into the mews and reached for Roy's key. Just as he put it in the lock someone grabbed his arm and a familiar voice said, 'You're nicked.'

8

'**You look like** death warmed over.'

'Thanks. You know, you shouldn't go around creeping up on people like that doing your *Sweeney* imperson-ation. You might get hurt.'

'You do seem very jumpy.'

'Maybe I've got good reason to be.'

'Care to tell me about it?'

Banks gave her a look she'd seen before. It meant he'd get her to play out her hand first and then decide how much to share with her. So be it.

'All right,' Annie said. 'How about a drink?'

They were sitting in Roy's kitchen, afternoon sunlight pouring in through the open window. Banks picked a bottle of Château Kirwan from the wine rack and Annie watched him attack it with an expensive and compli-cated opener. A simple corkscrew would have taken less time, she thought. After Banks poured, they sat opposite one another in silence.

'Who's going first?' Annie asked.

'How did you find me?'

'That doesn't matter. The point is that I *have* found you.'

'No,' said Banks. 'The point is, why were you looking for me? Why come all the way down here when I'm sure you've got more important things to do?'

'You really don't know?'

'I've got no idea. As far as you're concerned, I'm on holiday. Do you know something I don't?'

'Lots of things, probably.'

'No need to be sarcastic.'

Annie flushed. She hadn't meant to be sarcastic, but he was driving her to it. She knew she used sarcasm to hide behind when she was feeling vulnerable or confused, the way others hide behind smoking or bad jokes. She realized it probably wasn't the right time, but she didn't think she could go on talking to Banks unless she cleared the air. He would have to meet her halfway. The last time she had tried to reach out to him and heal the rift he had dismissed her. She polished off her glass and held it out for a refill. Dutch courage. Banks narrowed his eyes and poured.

'I'm sorry,' Annie said. 'I don't mean to be sarcastic. After everything that's happened things just seem to come out wrong.'

Banks caught her eye for a moment, then gazed past her out of the window. There were flowering shrubs outside in the backyard and Annie could hear bees buzzing from one to another behind her. Impulsively, she reached across the table and put her hand on his arm. 'What is it, Alan? We can't go on like this. *You* can't go on like this.'

Banks didn't flinch when she touched him, but he didn't say anything at first, just kept staring over her shoulder, through the window. Finally, he turned his eyes back to her.

'You're right,' he said. 'I feel as if I've been a long, long way from everything that used to matter, but I'm getting closer again.'

'Light at the end of the tunnel?'

'And all the other clichés. Yes.'

'I'm glad,' Annie said, feeling herself choke up. There was so much more to say but she sensed that now was not the time. Besides, there were other things of more immediate concern that they needed to talk about. She took another sip of wine. Definitely not your everyday quaffing plonk. Banks lit a cigarette.

'I thought you'd stopped that,' Annie said.

'I had,' said Banks. 'It's only temporary.'

'I hope so.'

'So why do you want to see me?'

'Have you heard about the woman found dead in the car near Eastvale?'

'I've read about it in the paper,' Banks said, 'but they haven't really given out much information.'

'Her name is Jennifer Clewes. Do you know anyone by that name?'

'No,' said Banks.

'Guess what we found in the back pocket of her jeans?'

'I've no idea.'

'An address.'

'Whose address?'

'Yours.'

Banks's jaw dropped. 'What? I can't . . . What's her name again?'

'Jennifer Clewes.'

'I've never heard of her. What's it all about?'

'We don't know yet. She had your address and directions written on a slip of paper in her back pocket, in her own handwriting,' Annie went on. 'The directions were to the damaged cottage. It looks as if it has been broken into. You can imagine what a flap it created up there, finding your name and address on a victim's person. Superintendent Gristhorpe decided to sit on it until Monday.' Annie could see that Banks was thinking furiously, trying to make things connect. 'Come on, Alan, give. You know something. What is it?'

'I don't know anything. I'm telling the truth. I've never heard of the girl.'

'But you know *something*. I can tell.'

'It's complicated.'

'I've got time.' Annie was feeling a little tipsy from the wine, but what the hell, she thought, in for a penny in for a pound. 'Maybe you can start,' she went on, 'by telling me what you're doing here. Last I heard, you and your brother were hardly on the best of terms.'

'He's disappeared,' Banks said.

'What?'

Banks told her about Roy's phone call, and the empty, unlocked house.

'Have you reported this?'

Banks said nothing. His gaze shifted back to the window.

'You haven't, have you?'

'Why does everyone keep going on about it so?' said Banks, with a sudden flash of anger. 'You know as well as I do how much effort we put into looking for a missing adult when he's been gone less than forty-eight hours. I've probably done more myself than the locals would have.'

'Who are you trying to convince? Listen to yourself. There are suspicious circumstances and you know it. You told me he said it was a matter of life and death.'

'*Might* be a matter of life and death.'

'Fair enough, you want to split hairs. I'll say no more

right now, but don't forget it might be your brother's life you're playing fast and loose with. For Christ's sake, Alan, you shouldn't even *be* here.'

'Thanks for reminding me.'

'Oh, sometimes I just wish you'd grow up. You might be able to see the light at the end of the tunnel but, quite frankly, you're still a mess. You've done nothing but paperwork for the past few months, you've barely spoken to a soul, you rarely bother to shave, you need a haircut, and you're half pissed most of the time. I was in your flat. I've seen how you live.' There was no point going on at him, Annie knew. She just had to let her frustration out from time to time.

'What put you in such a good mood?' Banks said.

Annie just shook her head. 'Look, I know you're concerned,' she went on in a softer tone. 'I know you're worried about your brother, but you've got to stop being so stubborn. For his sake as well as your own.'

'You're probably right,' Banks said, 'but look at it from my point of view. I'm worried they might find out a few things about Roy our parents would rather not know, and I know there's no way they'll let me work on the case if it becomes official. Besides, how can I know the job's being done properly if I don't do it myself?'

'Sometimes I wonder how you made DCI,' Annie said. 'Such skills of delegation.'

Banks laughed. Annie was surprised, and it broke the tension.

'Are you sure you've never heard of Jennifer Clewes?' she went on. 'You've no idea why she should have your address in her pocket?'

'There's a Jenn in Roy's mobile call list.'

'That's what her friends called her.'

'Wait here a minute.' Banks disappeared upstairs. Annie sipped more wine and looked around the kitchen. Expensive, she thought, especially for a room that didn't get used much. Banks soon returned with a bulging folder under his arm, sat back down and started flipping through pages.

'Do you have her phone number?' he asked.

'Her mobile's missing, but I got the number from her flatmate.' Annie read out the number from her notebook. It was the same one Banks had on Roy's call list.

'My God,' said Annie. 'So there definitely *is* a connection between Jennifer Clewes and your brother Roy.'

'Corinne was right. He did have a new girlfriend.'

'Corinne?'

'Roy's fiancée. Ex-fiancée.'

'From now on this is official,' Annie said. 'I'm going to have a word with DI Brooke about your brother's disappearance. He won't be happy.'

'Suit yourself,' said Banks.

'Look,' Annie went on, trying to placate him. 'You know you're too personally involved to be assigned to the case – either case – but that doesn't mean you can't be of some use.'

'On whose terms?'

Annie managed a thin smile. 'Well, it's not as if anyone's going to be keeping tabs on you twenty-four hours a day, is it? As long as we stay on the same page.'

Banks nodded. 'I suppose that's the best I can hope for.'

'All I ask is that you share with me. Any sign of a Carmen Petri on that list, by the way?'

'Carmen? I don't remember one. It's an unusual name.

Let me have a look.' Banks glanced through the list of names. 'No,' he said. 'Why? Who is she?'

'I don't know,' said Annie. 'The name just turned up in one of my interviews. So how do you think it all connects?'

'Let's review what we know.'

'The way it looks is that someone was watching Jennifer's house in Kennington on Friday evening,' said Annie. 'Maybe other evenings, too, that week. Waiting for her. We don't know why. One witness has already confirmed there was a dark blue car parked near her flat with two men inside around the time she set off, one in the front and one in the back, and he'd seen it there before. The same car – or at least we think it's the same car – was seen at the Watford Gap service station, where Jennifer stopped to eat and fill up with petrol. It cut off another driver pulling in right behind her when she left. The only half-decent description we have is of the man in the back – muscular, with a ponytail.'

'Is that the man who killed her?'

'We don't know, but it's the best lead we've got so far. Stefan's working overtime on the scene. Unfortunately the pursuing car wasn't scratched or anything so we've no paint chips to go on.'

'But why would Roy send this woman to see me? Why not come himself?'

'I don't know. Her flatmate said Jennifer received a phone call around a quarter to eleven that Friday and left right after. Said it shook her up a bit. Did your brother sound worried when he heard the doorbell?' Annie asked.

'No,' said Banks. 'I've thought a lot about that, and he sounded fine. I mean, if he'd been worried it was someone come to do him harm he wouldn't have answered it, would he? He'd probably have tried to scarper out of the back window. Besides, the bloke across the street said Roy just locked his door and got into the car with his visitor as if things were quite normal.'

'So what do you think happened?'

'I've been trying to piece together the events of that day,' Banks said. 'The way I see it is that Roy comes home just before half past nine, from where I don't know, but something has upset him. He puts his mobile on the kitchen table, or it's already there, pours himself a glass of wine and goes up to his office to check phone messages, e-mail, or whatever. He takes the wine with him. Maybe he sits and mulls things over for a minute or two, then he decides that whatever it is he's found out is worth calling his estranged policeman brother about. Maybe he even senses that he's in danger because of something he knows. Anyway, he phones me and tells me he needs my help. While he's on the phone the door-bell rings. He answers it and goes off in a car with whoever it is. Willingly, it appears. And he forgets his mobile, even though he's given me the number. I'd say that means he's more than a little distracted.'

'Maybe it was Roy who rang Jennifer later, then?' Annie suggested.

'And gave her directions to my cottage and told her to set off right there and then because he couldn't come himself? Maybe it was. But why? What happened between half past nine and a quarter to eleven?'

'That we don't know.' Annie paused. 'Poor lass,' she said. 'Everything I've found out about Jennifer tells me she was a decent, hard-working, caring person, perhaps a bit naive and idealistic.'

'So what got her killed?'

'I wish I knew.' Annie sipped her wine. The light changed and she could tell that clouds were gathering, the world darkening around them. 'What are you going to do next?'

'Carry on my own personal covert operation,' said Banks.

Annie smiled. 'What can I say?'

'Nothing. You?'

'I'll talk to Dave Brooke as soon as I can and I'm pretty sure he'll want to see you. I mean it, Alan. Our cases have crossed and I'm not leaving any loose ends. Besides, given what happened to Jennifer Clewes, Roy could be in danger. Have you thought about that?'

'I haven't thought about much else,' said Banks. 'Mostly I've been thinking that he's done a runner, with kidnapping a distant second. Your connecting him with the murdered girl puts a different complexion on things.'

'I'm glad you see it that way. If you'd bothered to keep in touch, we might have got to this point ages ago.'

'How was I to know you were looking for me?'

'You know what I mean. Anyway, I've still got a couple of things to do tomorrow. Jennifer was killed on our patch but her life was down here. It makes things awkward.'

'So what do you have to do?'

'Visit Jennifer's workplace, for a start. She worked at a family planning centre in Knightsbridge. It—'

'What's it called?' Banks asked.

'The Berger-Lennox Centre. Why?'

Banks opened the folder again and started turning

over sheets of paper, some of them covered with his own spidery scrawl. Finally he pointed to a printed sheet. 'I thought I remembered the name,' he said. 'It's one of the centres Roy invested in. One of Julian Harwood's companies. Are you sure that's where Jennifer Clewes worked?'

'Yes.'

'Perhaps that's where they met, then. Harwood told me that Roy's a hands-on sort of investor, likes to check out his assets. And if Jennifer Clewes was a good-looking young woman . . .'

'Which she was,' said Annie.

'Bingo.'

'It doesn't necessarily mean anything.'

'Maybe not,' said Banks. 'But it's another connection. One person murdered, another disappeared. Her phone number is in his book, my address is in her back pocket, and they have this family planning centre in common. I don't know about you, but that's way too many coincidences for me. Maybe I'll go with you tomorrow. Find out for certain. Someone must remember if Roy's been there.'

Annie paused. She wanted to be diplomatic but didn't quite know how to do it. In the end, she threw caution to the wind. 'You can't,' she said. 'You know you can't. It's not your case. I've already made it clear I'm making your brother's disappearance official and I'm giving you a bit of room to manoeuvre, but you can't just come muscling in. You have no official standing in the Jennifer Clewes investigation whatsoever.'

'But what if there's a connection with what's happened to Roy?'

'Look, Alan, you've got no official standing there, either. I'm not taking you with me and that's that.'

'Fine,' said Banks. 'OK. I understand.'

'Don't sulk. It doesn't suit you.' Annie stood up. She felt a little wobbly, but it was nothing she couldn't handle. 'And stick around. DI Brooke will be wanting to take your statement.' Annie heard a light tapping sound on the leaves behind her. It quickly grew louder and faster. The rain had started again.

•

It was early evening and Banks was sitting in Roy's office reading through the files Corinne had printed out when he heard someone at the door. At first he thought it might be Roy, but why would he be knocking at his own door? Then he thought it might be DI Brooke come to interview him, and decided it would be best to get it over with. Even so, he looked for some sort of weapon, just in case. All he could find was a set of golf clubs in the landing cupboard, so he grasped one of the irons and answered the door. The man who stood there was about Banks's age. He was wearing a dark suit, had a neat side parting in his greying black hair and a serious, intelligent look in his eyes. He could have been a policeman, Banks thought, except that he was wearing a clerical collar.

'Hello,' he said, reaching his hand out. 'Hunt's the name. Ian Hunt. Roy home?'

Banks shook his hand. It felt damp and cool. 'No,' he said. 'I'm his brother, Alan. What's it about?'

'He's mentioned you,' said Hunt. 'The policeman. But I didn't think . . . Never mind.'

Banks had a good idea what Ian Hunt didn't think, but he kept quiet. He needed all the information he could get, and a defensive attitude from the outset wouldn't help matters much. He wondered what the hell the vicar was doing calling around at Roy's house. 'Would you like to come in?'

'Yes. Yes, please, if it's all right.'

Banks propped the golf club by the front door and led the way to the kitchen at the back, where he had recently sat with Annie, and offered Hunt a chair. Hunt made no comment about the club. Banks didn't want to seem as if he was interrogating the man, but he realized he had practically forgotten the simple art of conversation after all his years in the force. His job affected the way he saw and dealt with everyone. He had even been brusque with Corinne. 'Why did you want to see Roy?' he asked.

'No real reason,' Hunt said. 'Only he didn't turn up at church this morning, and that's not like him.'

Banks nearly fell off his chair. 'Church?' Wonders never cease.

'Yes. Why? What's so strange about that?'

'Nothing,' said Banks, who hadn't set foot inside a church since his childhood, except for weddings and funerals. He and Roy hadn't been given a particularly religious upbringing, and neither of their parents had been regular churchgoers. At school, back in those days, there were prayers and a hymn every morning, of course, but apart from a few years of Sunday school and a brief stint in the Lifeboys and Boys' Brigade, that had been it as far as Banks was concerned. Now this.

'Normally, I wouldn't bother dropping by,' said Hunt, 'but there was a meeting of the restoration-fund committee after the service and Roy has always been a keen contributor. Not only financially, you understand, but also in terms of ideas. Very creative mind, Roy.'

'Cup of tea, Vicar?'

'Please. And call me Ian. Unless you want me to call you Chief Inspector?'

'Ian it is.' Banks put the kettle on. Tea with the vicar on a Sunday evening, he thought. How very genteel. This wasn't a world he would ever have suspected Roy of inhabiting. He found the teabags next to the coffee and put two in the flower-patterned teapot.

'If you don't mind me asking,' said Banks as the kettle was coming to a boil, 'when did Roy start going to church?'

'I don't mind at all,' said Hunt. 'He started attending services on the 16th of September 2001.'

'I didn't expect you to remember the exact date,' Banks said.

'But how could I forget? You'd be surprised how many people returned to the church, or first started attending, around that time.'

Banks had to think for a moment before he realized the significance of the date. It must have been the first Sunday after the attack on the World Trade Center. But why should that affect Roy so much? He poured boiling water into the pot. 'What drew him there?' he asked.

Hunt paused. 'You really don't know much about your brother, do you?'

'No,' said Banks. 'And the more I find out, the less I know.'

'That's the universal paradox of knowledge.'

'Maybe so,' said Banks, 'but at the moment I'm interested in more practical knowledge. I don't suppose you have any idea where Roy might be?'

Hunt blinked. 'I was the one who came here looking for him, remember?'

'Even so.'

Hunt looked at Banks with curiosity in his eyes. 'I can see you've been trained not to take anything at face value,' he said. 'No, I have no idea where he is.'

'Why did you come here?'

'I told you. The meeting. It's not like Roy not to even leave a message.'

'When did you last see him?'

'Last Sunday.'

'Did you talk to him?'

'We chatted briefly after the service.'

'How did he seem?'

'Fine. Quite normal.'

Banks got the milk from the fridge, giving it a quick sniff to see if it was still all right, poured the tea then sat down opposite Hunt. 'I don't mean to seem so abrupt,' he said, 'but I'm concerned. Roy left a rather disturbing message on my answerphone and when I came down here to see him he'd disappeared and the front door was unlocked.'

'I can see why you would be concerned,' said Hunt.

'So the two of you chatted often?'

'Yes,' said Hunt. 'We'd often spend an hour or two together, usually at the vicarage, sometimes over lunch.'

Lunching at the vicarage was an image Banks found very hard to visualize. 'Did Roy open up to you? I mean, did he . . .'

'I know what you mean.' Hunt shifted in his chair. 'Yes, I'd say he opened up about his feelings. At least to some extent.'

'Feelings about what?'

'Many things.'

'I'm afraid that's a bit vague for me,' said Banks. 'Do you think you could be more specific? It's not as if you took his confession or anything.' Banks realized that he hadn't ascertained what denomination Hunt represented. 'I mean, you're not Catholic, are you?'

'C. of E. But I don't know how much I can help you. Roy never went into great detail about anything he did.'

'I don't suppose he would,' said Banks. 'But did you get any sense of why he started attending church on the 16th of September 2001, other than some vague sense of unease about the way the world was going?'

'It wasn't that.' Hunt took a deep breath. 'It's my feeling that your brother had lost his moral compass, had become so engrossed in the making of money that how he made it no longer mattered to him.'

'He's not unusual in that,' said Banks.

'No. But it's my guess that what happened in New York and Washington on the 11th brought it home to him in no uncertain terms.'

'You're not saying he was somehow connected to the attacks, are you?'

'Oh, no,' said Hunt. 'No, you're missing the point entirely.'

'What, then?'

'Didn't he tell you? He was there.'

Banks had to pause a moment to take this in. 'Roy was in New York when the attacks took place?'

Ian Hunt nodded. 'According to what he told me, he had an appointment with a banker in the second tower. He was running late and his taxi got caught up in traffic. The next thing he knew, everyone was coming to a halt and getting out of their cars, some of them pointing up.

Roy got out, too, and he couldn't believe what he was seeing. The smoke and flames. People jumping out of windows. It took him three days to get on a flight home.'

'Jesus Christ,' said Banks. 'Sorry. He never told me this.'

'But you're not close, are you?'

'No.'

'Anyway, it gave him pause for thought – the enormity of it all, fate, how everything was connected, what unimaginable consequences could arise from seemingly unimportant, unrelated actions. These were all things he wanted to talk about. I had no answers, but he seemed to find something of what he wanted in the church, in prayer, holy communion, and in our discussions.'

Banks remembered what Burgess had said about the arms deal. Roy had found out that a shipment he had brokered had found its way into the wrong hands. Had Roy really been so naive as to think that arms dealing was just a business like any other? He probably hadn't given it too much thought, Banks decided, lured by the money and the excitement. Warned off by Special Branch, he had backed away from that line of work immediately, but he had witnessed the attacks on the World Trade Center and he was stricken by conscience, by the fact that guns or missiles he had exported *could have* been used in something like this. Roy realized he had crossed a line and he didn't like what he saw on the other side.

Suicide bombers in distant desert places are one thing, but being there, in New York on September 11th 2001 and witnessing what happened must have been devastating. It certainly made it impossible for Roy to remain wilfully ignorant of the kind of things terrorists intended to do to the West, given the means and opportunity. And, unknowingly or not, Roy had once helped out with the means. Hence the guilt. Roy had turned to the Church for absolution.

This was a new perspective on his brother, and one that would take Banks a little time to get used to. It certainly didn't match the Roy he remembered from the last time he had seen him just eight months ago, but then that had been Roy-at-home, a careful image he projected for his parents. Had Roy even told their parents what he had seen? Banks doubted it. Despite his religion, though, Roy had continued to make money; he had hardly given it all to charity and taken a vow of poverty, or chastity, for that matter. Clearly guilt only went so far and cut so deep.

So what had happened to him? Had he lost his moral compass again? The making of money, perhaps even more than the money itself, was an addiction to some people, like gambling, heroin or cigarettes. Banks had given up smoking the previous summer when he found out that an old schoolfriend had died from lung cancer, but he had started again after a fire took his home, his possessions and, almost, his life. Where was the logic in that? But such is the nature of addiction.

'Has anything in your recent conversations given you any reason to think Roy might have got into some sort of dangerous grey area again?' Banks asked.

'No,' said Hunt. 'Nothing.'

'He didn't mention his business activities?'

'We didn't talk about business. Our conversations were mostly of a philosophical and spiritual nature. Look, I know Roy's not a natural man of religion, and I very much doubt that he's a saint, even after what happened, but he does have a conscience and sometimes it troubles him. He's still a hard-nosed businessman, the kind of person you'd expect to cut a corner or two and not always ask too many questions, but I'd say he's a lot more careful these days. He's drawn his own lines.' Hunt paused. 'He's always looked up to you, you know.'

'You could have fooled me.' Growing up, Banks had done everything wrong. He had stayed out too late, got caught shoplifting and smoking, got into fights, neglected his schoolwork, and the final insult, he had turned away from business studies and chosen a career of which neither of his parents approved. Roy, on the other hand, from five years behind, had watched his brother's progress and learned what not to do.

'It's true,' said Ian Hunt. 'He did look up to you, especially when you were children. You just never paid him any attention. You ignored him. He felt neglected, rejected, as if he always let you down.'

'He was my little brother,' said Banks.

Hunt nodded. 'And always in the way.'

Banks remembered when he was going out with Kay Summerville, his first serious girlfriend. Roy was about twelve at the time, and whenever their parents went out for a night at the local pub and Banks invited Kay over to listen to records, among other things, he would always have to pay Roy to stay in his room. So maybe Roy was always in the way, Banks thought, but he found the means to profit from it.

'Anyway,' Banks said, 'I wasn't aware that he looked up to me in any way. He certainly never let it show.'

'I'm not saying Roy isn't competitive. You were good at sports, for example. He wasn't, so he worked hard at what he did best. He compensated.'

Good? Banks had been a tolerable fly-half then, fast and slippery. At cricket he hadn't been much of a batsman but had been a decent mid-pace bowler. Roy had been an overweight, bespectacled and unattractive child, not at all athletic, and at school the other kids teased him and called him a swot. Once the bullying got serious enough that Banks stepped in and put an end to it, so no one could say he never did anything for Roy. But he certainly hadn't done enough.

'Even now he looks up to you,' Hunt went on.

'That I find even harder to believe,' said Banks, wondering what there was to look up to: a failed marriage and a thankless job. Especially when Roy had it all: the flash car, women falling at his feet, the mews house. But they were all *things*, Banks realized, all material possessions. Even the women, to some extent, were status symbols. *Look at me with a beautiful young woman on my arm.* All for show. Roy's three marriages had ended in divorce, and not one of them had produced any children. He had even broken off his engagement to Corinne. Banks at least had Brian and Tracy.

He saw that Hunt was standing, ready to leave. 'Sorry,' said Banks. 'Just thinking about what you said.'

'That's all right,' said Hunt. 'I should go. I'm just sorry I couldn't be of more practical help. If there's anything you need, don't hesitate. It's St Jude's, just down the street.'

'Thanks. Oh, hang on a minute.' Banks fetched one of the digital photos and showed it to Hunt. 'Do you recognize either of those men?'

Hunt shook his head.

'You've never seen Roy with either of them?'

'No, never.'

They shook hands again and Ian Hunt left.

Maybe the mistake Banks had made in trying to figure Roy out was to dismiss his spiritual and emotional sides. Now he had discovered that Roy had become a regular churchgoer, it changed things, added a dimension he hadn't suspected. Did it help him figure out what had happened to Roy? Perhaps not, but it might affect the way in which he conducted his investigation. Previously, he'd been looking for something dodgy that Roy had been connected to, something he had perhaps run away from; now, though, the field was wide open. Possibly Roy had stumbled over something he shouldn't have done, or perhaps he had become a threat to people he had once worked closely with, and instead of turning a blind eye he had planned on blowing the whistle? But on what, on who?

•

Gaps in the cloud let through bright lances of light and the western sky turned vermilion and violet. The crowds queuing for the sunset ride on the London Eye shifted rest-lessly in the downpour and people on Westminster Bridge watched on from under their umbrellas and rain hoods.

Eight-year-old Michaela Toth had been excited all day about the promised ride. It was to be the highlight of her first ever weekend in London – even better than Madame Tussaud's and the zoo – and her mum and dad were let-ting her stay up late especially. Even the rain didn't dampen her spirits as she stood in the queue hopping from foot to foot, clutching her yellow plastic handbag with the pink flower on it. It seemed as if they would never get there, edging forward at a snail's pace like this. Michaela could hardly believe that the Eye was so much bigger than she had imagined, or that it never stopped turning, even when you got on and off. The thought made her just a little bit scared, but nicely so.

Slowly, inch by inch, they moved forward. As soon as the cars emptied, they filled up again. A squat red tugboat chugged down the river leaving its arrowhead wake in the darkening water. It was still light enough to see the men standing on the deck and Michaela noticed one of them point in her direction. At first she thought he was just pointing at the Eye, but more men joined him and the tug changed direction, heading for the bank.

Michaela pulled on her father's hand and asked him to take her to the wall to see what the men were pointing at. At first she thought he wasn't going to, but then she could tell he got curious too because he asked her mother to keep their place in the queue and said they'd be back in just a moment.

The tug was getting closer to the embankment as they got to the railings beside the Eye. The people on Westminster Bridge were pointing their way now, too, and Michaela wondered if they'd seen a dolphin, or even a whale, though she didn't really believe there were any whales or dolphins living in the River Thames. Maybe one had escaped from an aquarium. Or maybe someone had fallen in the river and the men on the tugboat were going to rescue him.

Holding her father's hand, Michaela strained to see over the embankment wall. She was just tall enough to manage it. The tide was very low and a shingle bank stuck out of the water like a whale's back just below the wall. Lying on the shingles was the dark shape of a man. A sprawled figure, he was lying on his stomach and his arms were stretched out in front of him, his lower half in the water. Michaela's father pulled her away quickly.

'What is it, Daddy?' she asked, frightened. 'What's that man doing there?'

Her father didn't answer; he simply led her away. When they rejoined her mother in the queue, her father spoke and Michaela heard the words 'dead body'. Soon, others started drifting towards the wall. One woman screamed. Michaela worried she might not get her ride after all. If there was a dead body down there, perhaps the London Eye would even stop turning.

•

After the Reverend Ian Hunt had left, Banks put away the golf club, feeling rather foolish, locked up the house and went upstairs with the remains of his wine. He rang Julian Harwood, who confirmed that he was managing director of the Berger-Lennox Centre but said he had never actually been to the place and had never heard of Jennifer Clewes. Banks had no reason to disbelieve him.

Banks felt a sudden urge to listen to some music. He found a CD he had never heard before: Lorraine Hunt Lieberson singing two Bach cantatas. Roy's top-of-the-line stereo system brought out the rich timbre of the strings, and when he closed his eyes Banks could imagine himself in a room surrounded by the small ensemble. And the voice was sublime, almost enough to make you believe in God. He thought of Penny Cartwright singing 'Strange Affair'. Different, but another wonderful voice.

Banks sipped wine, feeling a pleasant buzz, let the music roll over him and thought about Annie, Roy, Jennifer Clewes and the Berger-Lennox Centre. He would like to have been invited to go along with Annie in the morning, but she was right – it wasn't his case, and he was a bit of a mess. When he examined his feelings, it was curious how little her comments really hurt. At the time, they had stung, but they had quickly sunk in, and he knew they were true. He had let things go. If he wasn't as bad as the hapless fellow in one of his favourite Nick Lowe songs, he had been getting there.

Perhaps a few months ago, before the Phil Keane business, Annie would have welcomed his company, but now she didn't quite seem to trust him. And she was right not to do so. The last thing he had on his mind was going back up to Yorkshire.

The CD finished and Banks looked for something else to put on. Roy didn't have the Mahler songs, but he did have Strauss's 'Four Last Songs', one of Banks's favourite pieces of music, so he put that on. As it turned out, he didn't get far into the second song before he heard the phone ring in Roy's office. Putting his glass down, he hurried across the landing to answer it.

•

The London Eye towered over the scene, a huge dark semicircle against the moonlit clouds. It was closed for the night now, but still turning slowly, always turning. Nearby, on the stone steps that led down to the hump of shingle bared by the ebbing tide, the SOCOs came and went like ghosts in their protective clothing. It was a ballet in which every dancer knew his steps. Despite the occasional shout and chatter or static over police radios, there was an odd hush about the scene, and no sense of hurry, as if the mighty heart of the city were lying still. Arc lamps lit rough slimy stone, shingle and greasy water alike, and a video camera recorded everything. The rain had stopped, and from Westminster Bridge a few curious onlookers watched over it all, silhouettes against the light dying in the west.

When Banks arrived at the taped-off area, Burgess was already waiting for him, a grim look on his face. He had explained to Banks over the telephone that when he saw on the news that the body of a white male about Roy's age had washed up by the London Eye, his alarm bells had automatically gone off. They had found no identification on the body, so there was no evidence yet that it *was* Roy, and indeed he hoped it wasn't, but it might be worth Banks's coming along and having a look.

Banks hadn't needed asking twice.

Burgess took him by the arm and led him over to a thickset man with a red moon-shaped face. 'DI Brooke, Lambeth North,' said Burgess. 'Meet DCI Banks, North Yorkshire Major Crimes.'

The two men nodded at one another. 'DI Brooke?' said Banks. 'You'll be the chap Annie Cabbot's working with on the Jennifer Clewes case?'

'Annie and I go back a long way.'

Banks gestured towards the river. 'Is he still down there?'

'The police surgeon's pronounced death, but the SOCOs haven't finished yet. They'll have to move fast, though, because the tide's coming in.' Brooke paused and looked down at his feet. 'Look, Superintendent Burgess here told me he thinks there's a possibility it might be your brother down there?'

'I hope to God it's not,' said Banks, 'but it's a possibility, yes. He's missing.'

'Sorry to have to put you through this.'

'Better than not knowing,' said Banks. 'Can we go down?'

'There's some extra overalls in the SOCOs' van. And mind your step, those old stone stairs are worn and slippery.'

Kitted out in protective clothing, Banks and Burgess showed their identification to the officer guarding the scene, ducked under the tape and approached the steps. The landing at the bottom didn't quite reach as far as the exposed shingle, so the SOCOs had already set up a makeshift bridge made of planks. It wobbled a little as Banks and Burgess crossed. Once, Banks almost lost his footing and he became suddenly aware of how much he had had to drink that day. Water lapped gently against the stone wall.

Banks felt a tightness in his chest as he approached the shingle and breathing became an effort. Burgess gave a nod and one of the SOCOs gently turned the top half so that the face was visible. Banks squatted, feeling his knees crack, and looked into Roy's dead eyes. There was a little hole in his left temple, close to the childhood scar Banks had accidentally inflicted with a toy sword. Banks felt himself sway on his haunches and stood up so fast it made him dizzy. Burgess grabbed his elbow.

'I'm all right,' said Banks, disengaging himself.

'Well, is it him?'

'It's him,' Banks said, and the only thing he could think as he tried to rein in his surging emotions was, *What the hell am I going to say to my parents?*

'Let's get back up on shore,' Burgess said.

Banks followed him back over the planks and up the steps. DI Brooke and his DS were waiting for confirmation. The sooner you identified the body, Banks knew, the sooner you put the machinery of a major investigation in motion. He nodded to Brooke.

'I'm sorry,' Brooke said.

'Look,' said Banks, 'do you think you could keep it under wraps? His identity, that is. I'd like to be the one who tells our parents, in person, but not tonight. It's too late.'

Brooke looked at the crowd on the bridge and the reporters and camera operators behind the crime-scene tape. 'We can tell them we're still awaiting official iden-tification of the body,' he said. 'That should hold them off for a while.'

'First thing tomorrow,' said Banks. Just not tonight, he prayed. He couldn't stand the idea of going over to Peterborough right now and waking his parents up and spending the night comforting them in their grief, know-ing they would probably prefer it was him rather than Roy. Daylight would make it easier, he thought. Let them have just one more night of peace; there would soon be enough dreadful nights to come. 'Can you tell Annie for me, please?' he asked.

'Of course. In the morning.'

'Thanks.'

Brooke paused. 'I'm sure you know I was intending to visit you, anyway,' he said. 'In fact, DI Cabbot and I had a little word about you earlier this evening.'

'I thought you might,' said Banks.

'This changes everything, of course, but I've still got a few questions for you,' Brooke went on. 'When you're up to it, that is.'

'I'm up to it now,' said Banks.

'Right. Superintendent Burgess tells me you've been staying at your brother's house. How about we go there?'

'Fine,' said Banks, fumbling in his jacket pocket for his cigarettes. 'Let's go.'

9

The Berger-Lennox Centre opened at nine o'clock on Monday morning and Annie was there on the dot. The centre took up the first two floors of a four-storey Georgian crescent house in Knightsbridge, which looked like something out of *Upstairs, Downstairs.* Still, when you paid through the nose for the service, Annie reflected, you didn't expect some bog-standard NHS prefab concrete-and-glass block.

As soon as she got through the front door, the impression of elegant age gave way to one of muted modernity. The walls were painted in pastel hues of blue and green, and there was the kind of hissing hush about the place that made her ears feel stuffed-up, as if she were in an aeroplane. It took her a moment to notice the music playing softly in the background: something classical and soothing, something Banks would probably recognize.

The scent of sandalwood in the air materialized into a sudden vision of Annie's mother leaning over her, smiling. The image shocked her, as her mother had died when she was six and she didn't remember much about her. But now she could almost feel the long soft hair tickling her face. Jane had been something of a hippie, and Annie remembered that sandalwood incense had often been burning in the artists' commune where she had grown up. The memory also made her realize how far she had moved away over the past few years from so many of the ideals of her youth, and she resolved to spend more time on yoga and meditation; she hadn't practised at all since the business with Phil Keane.

The blonde behind the polished-wood reception desk looked up from her computer monitor and smiled as Annie approached. A brass plate said her name was Carol Prescott. Behind her, in the open-plan office space, a young woman stood at an open filing cabinet.

Annie showed her warrant card and explained she was investigating Jennifer Clewes' murder. Carol's public smile dropped and was replaced by sadness. Her eyes moistened slightly.

'Poor Jennifer,' she said. 'It was in the papers this morning. She was really sweet. I can't imagine why anyone would want to do something like that to her. I don't know what the world's coming to.'

'Did you know her well?'

'She was my boss. We didn't socialize outside the centre or anything, but she was always ready with a hello and a smile.'

'How was her state of mind recently?'

'Fine,' said Carol. 'Though come to think of it she did seem a bit scatter-brained last week.'

'Any idea why?'

'No. She just seemed sort of on edge.'

'Was she happy working here?'

'She always seemed to be, but I didn't know her well enough for her to confide in me. Anyway, how can you tell if someone is *really* happy? I mean you read in the papers about people killing themselves when their friends think they've got everything to live for, don't you?'

'Sometimes,' Annie said. 'But Jennifer didn't kill herself.'

'No. I know that. I'm sorry.'

'No need to be. Look, I want to speak to a few people here, people who knew her, but maybe you can give me a bit of background on the place first.'

The phone rang and Carol excused herself. She adopted her professional voice and made a consultation appointment for a new patient.

'Sorry,' she said when she'd hung up. 'Of course, I'll fill you in on what I can.'

'How many people work here?'

'Seven,' said Carol. 'That's including Jennifer. She was administrative director of the centre. Then there's her assistant Lucy behind me there in the office. Andy and Georgina are our two consultation advisers, counsellors, then there's Dr Alex Lukas, the medical director, and Nurse Louise Griffiths.'

'What's Julian Harwood's role?'

'Mr Harwood? He's managing director of the whole group. But we never see him. I mean, he doesn't really have anything to do with the day-to-day running of the centre, or with the clinics.'

'Clinics?'

'Yes. We don't carry out terminations here. If a client decides that's the route she wants to go, we make an appointment at whichever of our clinics is most convenient for her.'

'I see,' said Annie. 'So this centre would hardly be a magnet for anti-abortion activists?'

'Hardly,' said Carol. 'We've had one or two small demonstrations, you know, when there's something in the news, but nothing violent. We offer advice on all aspects of family planning, not just abortion.'

'How does the system work?'

Carol sat back in her chair. 'Well,' she said, 'first they come to me, or phone, and I explain what our services and charges are and give them some pamphlets to read then send them to Lucy, who handles all the basic paperwork. Usually at that point Louise runs a proper pregnancy test, just to make sure. We usually tell them to bring a urine sample with them, but there are facilities here if they forget. Anyway, then they'll go to the waiting room where they can read through the brochures until Andrea or Georgina is ready to see them.'

'Then what?'

'It's up to them, really. Our counsellors will ask a few personal questions, and they'll also answer any questions the client has at that point. You'd be surprised how many are confused by their pregnancies, poor things.'

No, I wouldn't, thought Annie. She had become pregnant after a rape and while there was no doubt that she was going to have an abortion, she could remember the inner turmoil and the guilt she felt. And Annie thought of herself as a modern, forward-thinking woman. Very few women, if any, approached termination lightly.

'After that they'll discuss the choices available,' Carol went on, 'give guidance and advice if necessary. They're specially trained. Then the client sees Dr Lukas, who asks them about their medical history and examines them to confirm the gestation of the pregnancy, then Nurse Griffiths takes a blood sample. There's more paperwork – consent forms and so on – and the doctor will discuss the different methods available and help them decide on the type of procedure most suitable.'

'What if the client decides against abortion?'

'Then Andrea or Georgina will give her information about adoption agencies and so on. She'll still see the doctor, though, to determine her general health and so on.'

'Do you offer antenatal care?'

'No. Not here, at any rate. We usually refer.'

'You say Jennifer was administrative director. What exactly was she responsible for?'

'Everything to do with the running of the place except the medical side. That's an awful lot of work,' said Carol. 'Sometimes she had to work late just to keep up.'

'That reminds me,' said Annie. 'Have you ever heard the term "late girls"?'

Carol frowned. '"Late girls"? No. Why, what does it mean?'

'That's what I'm trying to find out.'

'I'm sorry, but it's not familiar to me.'

'Do you remember ever having a client here called Carmen Petri, or Peters?'

'No.'

'You're sure.'

'You can ask Lucy to check the records, but I think I would remember a name like that.'

'Probably,' said Annie. 'Lucy and Jennifer were close, were they?'

'They worked together. Jennifer was Lucy's boss, too, so that always puts a bit of wedge between you, doesn't it? Not that Jennifer was one to play the high and mighty.'

'Who was closest to her?'

Carol thought for a moment, then said, 'Georgina, I'd say. They'd talk about the centre, some of the clients, and I think they even went out for a drink a couple of times after work if Jennifer didn't have to stay late.'

'Thanks,' said Annie. 'Is Georgina in this morning?'

'Yes, she's in her office.' Carol picked up her phone. 'I don't think there's anyone with her right now. Would you like me to let her know you want to see her?'

'That's all right,' said Annie, who preferred the element of surprise. 'You can just show me where her office is.'

Carol's hand faltered. Clearly this went against standard procedure. 'OK,' she said, putting the phone back. 'It's up the stairs, second door on the right. It's got her name on it: Georgina Roberts.'

'Did you ever have any trouble with a man called Victor Parsons?' Annie asked. 'He's an ex-boyfriend of Jennifer's.'

'Oh, *him*. I remember him all right. Had to get security to throw him out.'

'What was he doing?'

'Making a fuss. Upsetting our clients.'

'About what?'

'He demanded to see Jennifer, but she'd given me instructions not to let him in.'

'What happened?'

'He went away in the end.'

'Did this happen more than once?'

'The first time he went without too much fuss. It was the second time I had to get security.'

Twice, then. 'Did he make any threats?'

'Not that I heard. He just said he'd be back.'

'When was this?'

'Couple of weeks ago.'

That recently, Annie thought. Yet Jennifer and Victor

had split up over a year ago. Anyone who could maintain a fixation for that long was definitely worth looking at.

'One more thing,' said Annie. 'Have you ever seen anyone by the name of Roy Banks here at the centre. Or Gareth Lambert?'

Carol's face brightened, then reddened a little. 'Mr Banks? Yes, of course. He and Jennifer were . . . you know, an item. I know she's a bit young for him but he really is quite tasty. I don't blame her at all.' Her face fell. 'Oh. Poor Mr Banks. He'll be just devastated. Does he know?'

'Not yet,' said Annie. 'So he came here quite often?'

'Quite. He'd pick Jennifer up after work sometimes and we'd chat if he had to wait.'

'What about?'

'Oh, nothing in particular. Films, the weather, just small talk. And Arsenal. We're both big Arsenal fans.'

'Was he ever here at the same time as Victor Parsons?'

'No.'

'You know he was an investor in the centres?'

'Yes, he mentioned it once. But he didn't have any airs or graces.'

'Is that why he came here the first time, when he met Jennifer?'

'Oh, no,' said Carol. 'No, he was here as a client. *Accompanying* a client, I should say.'

Now it was Annie's turn to feel surprised. 'Accompanying a client?'

'Yes,' said Carol. 'His daughter. She was pregnant.'

•

Long before Annie paid her visit to the Berger-Lennox Centre, Banks was ploughing his way through the

Monday morning rush-hour traffic on his way to Peterborough. He felt curiously numb after grappling with the demons of fear and loss most of the night, but he also felt apprehensive about what was to come. His parents doted on Roy; something like this could push his father's heart over the edge. But he had to tell them himself: he couldn't let the news come from some anonymous copper knocking on the door.

Brooke had gone out of his way to protect the identity of the victim from the media. As soon as Banks had told his parents, he had to ring Brooke and tell him it was done; the rest would follow. He remembered he had also promised to keep Corinne and Roy's neighbour, Malcolm Farrow, up to date, but they would have to wait their turns.

After some relatively gentle questioning by DI Brooke – *very* gentle, given the circumstances – Banks had handed over Roy's mobile, the USB drive and the CD to Brooke and tried to get some sleep. The effects of the wine were fast wearing off, leaving him with a throbbing head, and sleep had refused to come. Luckily, there wasn't much of the night left by then, and the dawn came early in June. At six o'clock, Banks was in the shower, then it was time to go and pick up his car from where he had left it the night before, near Waterloo Station, grab a coffee for the road, and head for home.

Progress was slower than he remembered, or expected, and a journey that should have taken under two hours took almost three. Every time the news came on the radio, no matter what station he tuned into, there was the story about the mystery body fished out of the River Thames just below the London Eye last night. In the end, Banks turned it off.

When he finally pulled up outside his parents' house on the Hazels estate in Peterborough, it was close to ten o'clock. Back in London, the murder investigation would be following its natural course: the technical-support-unit experts would be going over Roy's mobile and the SOCOs would be tracking every piece of evidence retrieved from the crime scene. DCs would be out on the streets asking questions and DI Brooke would be sifting through it all, looking for that promising line of enquiry.

The front door was painted green, Banks noticed, which was surely different from his last visit. The tiny lawn looked a little overgrown and some of the flowers in the bed didn't look in peak condition. That wasn't like his mother. He knocked and waited. His mother answered and was, naturally, surprised to see him. She had lost weight, and looked tired and drawn, with dark crescents under her eyes. God only knew what the news of Roy's murder would do to her.

He could tell she knew something was wrong by her ceaseless nervous chatter as she led him into the living room, where his father sat in his usual armchair, newspaper on his lap.

'Look who it is, Arthur. It's our Alan come to call.'

Maybe it was Banks's imagination, but he thought he sensed just the slightest air of neglect about the place; a patina of dust on the TV screen, a picture frame out of alignment, a teacup and saucer on the floor beside the settee, a slight bunching of the rug in front of the fire.

'Hello, son,' said Arthur Banks. 'Just happened to be passing, did you?'

'Not exactly,' said Banks, perching on the edge of the sofa. His mother fussed about, heading for the kitchen to put on the kettle for that great English cure-all, tea.

Banks called her back. There would be time and need enough later for copious quantities of tea. On his way he had rehearsed over and over what he was going to say, how he was going to handle it, but now the time had come he couldn't remember what he had decided would be best.

'It's about Roy,' he began.

'Did you find him?' Ida Banks asked.

'In a way.' Banks leaned forward and took his mother's hand. This was even harder than he had imagined it might be; the words seemed stuck deep inside him and when he spoke he felt them come out as little more than a whisper. 'He wasn't at home and I looked for him all weekend. I did my best, Mum, honestly I did, but I was too late.' He felt the tears brim in his eyes and let them course down his cheeks.

'Too late? What do you mean, too late? Where's he gone?'

'Roy's dead, Mum.' There, he'd said it. 'I'm afraid he's gone.'

'Are you sure?' Ida Banks asked. 'Maybe he's only joking.'

Banks thought he'd misheard. 'What?' he asked, wiping his face with the back of his hand.

Ida Banks laughed and touched her hair. 'Don't you understand?' she said. 'It's a joke. Our Roy's a great practical joker, isn't he, Arthur? He's playing a joke on us.'

Arthur Banks said nothing. Banks noticed he had turned pale and seemed to be clutching the newspaper tightly by its edges. It was already ripped. 'Dad, can I get you anything? Do you need a pill or something?'

'No,' Arthur Banks managed. 'Nothing. I'm all right. Go on.'

'There's not much more to say,' Banks went on, turning to his mother again. 'They found him last night in the river.'

'Swimming in the river?' Ida Banks said. 'But surely the water's too dirty to swim in? I always told him he had to be careful. You can get terrible diseases from dirty water, you know.'

'He wasn't swimming, Mother,' said Banks. 'He was dead.'

His mother took a sharp breath. 'Don't say that,' she said. 'You shouldn't say things like that. Tell him, Arthur. You're only trying to upset me. You never did like Roy. If this is supposed to be some sort of joke then it isn't very funny.'

'It's not a joke.'

Arthur Banks stood up with some difficulty and shuffled over to his wife. 'I think we'd better have that tea now, love,' he said, 'then our Alan can explain it all over a nice cuppa.'

Ida Banks nodded, happy to have a purpose in life. 'Yes, she said, 'that'll be best. I'll make some tea.'

When she had gone to the kitchen, Arthur Banks turned to his son. 'There's no mistake, then?'

'Sorry, Dad.'

His father grunted and glanced towards the kitchen. 'She's not been well. She's got to go in for tests and stuff. We didn't want to worry you. Doctors haven't figured out what's wrong with her yet, but she's not been well. She's not eating properly. She gets confused.' Arthur Banks pointed to his newspaper. 'It's that story in the paper, isn't it? The body pulled out of the Thames. It's on the front page. That's our Roy, isn't it?'

'Yes,' said Banks. 'We've managed to keep his

identity from the media so far, but it'll have to come out. It's going to get worse, Dad. Our Roy was shot. We don't know why yet. But it's a big story. Reporters will be around.'

'Don't you worry, son, I'll soon send that lot packing.'

'It might not be as easy as you think. I'll get in touch with the local police, if you like.' Banks knew his father's attitude to the police, had suffered it all his life, but the need to protect his parents was stronger even than his respect for the old man's opinion.

Arthur Banks shook his head in resignation. 'Whatever you think best. I just don't know. I can't seem to think straight. Our Roy . . . dead. It's a terrible thing when your children die before you do. Shot? No. I can hardly believe it.'

Banks felt a sudden chill, a premonition of what he would feel like if anything happened to Tracy or Brian, and it gave him a stronger sense of empathy with what his parents were suffering. For him it was the loss of a brother, perhaps one he never particularly liked and never really knew, but family nonetheless, and it hurt. For his parents, it was the loss of their favourite son.

'I know, Dad,' he said. 'And I'm sorry to be the one to have to tell you, but I just didn't want you to find out any other way.'

'I appreciate that,' said Arthur Banks, looking at his son. 'It can't have been easy. Will we have to identify the body?'

'It's been done.'

'What about the funeral?'

'I'll deal with all that, Dad, don't worry yourself.'

'What was he . . . I mean, would it have been quick?'

'Yes,' said Banks. 'He wouldn't have felt a thing.'

Except the fear, the anticipation, he thought, but didn't say.

'The paper said he was in the river.'

'Yes. He was spotted on a shingle bank just below the London Eye.'

'You don't know where he went in?'

'Not yet. The tides and currents are pretty strong, especially with the rain we've been having. It's for the experts to figure out.'

'Do you know anything about why? Was he in trouble?'

'I think he was,' said Banks.

'Roy always sailed a bit close to the wind.'

'Yes, he did,' Banks agreed. 'But somehow this time I don't think that's what it was.'

'Why's that?'

'Just a feeling. There's been another murder, a young woman. They might be connected.'

Arthur Banks rubbed his face. 'Not that girl he brought around last year, Corinne?'

'No, Dad. Corinne's fine. It's someone else. Her name's Jennifer Clewes. Did Roy ever mention her to you?'

'No.'

'Look, I'll help around here all I can,' said Banks, 'but I might be more use back in London trying to find out what happened. That's what I do, after all. Right now, though, I'm just worried about you and Mum. Is there someone you'd like me to call? Uncle Frank, perhaps?'

'Bloody hell, no. He'd be more a hindrance than a help, would Frank. No, you leave it to me. I'll handle your mother. Maybe if she wants, I'll ask Mrs Green to pop over later.'

'That's a good idea. I'm sure—'

At that moment Banks and his father heard a cup break on the kitchen floor, followed by a long wail of anguish that froze their blood.

•

Annie mulled over the information she'd got from Carol Prescott as she made her way upstairs to Georgina's office after a quick word with Lucy, who had nothing much to say except that Jennifer was a good boss and a 'nice' person. Annie certainly hadn't known that Roy Banks had a daughter. It had been in April, Carol said, and the girl, eleven weeks pregnant, had opted for an abortion, which had cost Roy Banks about £500 in all. Roy had met Jennifer then. Carol remembered them chatting while the daughter went through her meetings with the counsellor and doctor. Since then, he had been by a number of times to meet her after work or take her for lunch.

The name Carol gave Annie rang a bell: Corinne. Banks had mentioned that Roy had a girlfriend called Corinne, so either he had passed her off as his daughter for reasons of his, or her, own, or the people at the centre had simply assumed she was his daughter because of the age difference. But wouldn't they have seen her name on the forms? Still, for all they knew, she could have been divorced, yet kept her married name, Annie supposed. Perhaps this was a different Corinne? When Annie asked Carol if Roy had specifically mentioned the girl being his daughter, she couldn't recall, and she said she didn't really pay attention to the girl's name.

Well, Annie told herself, it probably meant nothing. She already knew that Roy Banks and Jennifer Clewes were seeing one another, no matter how they first met. It didn't show Roy Banks in a particularly good light, Annie thought, chatting up his next girlfriend while bringing in last year's model for an abortion, but worse things happened. He probably got a discount for being a shareholder, too. And what had Jennifer thought about it? By all accounts she was a 'nice' girl, decent, caring, hardworking. She had never mentioned the 'daughter' at work. Roy Banks must have a hell of a smooth tongue on him, Annie thought, to explain that one away.

Annie knocked on Georgina's office door.

'Come in,' called a voice from inside.

Annie entered and found a pleasantly plump woman with dark curly hair and the hint of a double chin sitting behind a desk. She looked as if her normal expression was a smile. Today, though, it was banished in favour of a frown. Annie introduced herself and the frown lines deepened.

'I understand the two of you were quite close?' she said.

'Yes,' Georgina agreed. 'I'd like to think we were friends. I'm simply devastated by what's happened. I know that sounds like a cliché, but I just can't articulate my feelings any more clearly.'

'I'm very sorry,' said Annie.

'Would you like me to get us some coffee?' Georgina suggested. 'It's really not that bad.'

'No, thanks. I've had my ration for today.'

Georgina stood up. 'Would you mind if I . . . It's not far. I won't be a minute. Sit down. Make yourself at home.'

'Go ahead.' Left alone, Annie first walked over to the open window, which looked out on the hustle and bustle of the street below. Delivery vans came and went. Taxis stopped to pick up or drop off fares. Men and women in business suits dashed across the roads before the lights changed.

Annie sat down. The room was painted a soothing shade of blue, and it reminded her immediately of Bank's old living room at the cottage. Various framed certificates hung on the walls, along with a Monet *Waterlilies* print. There were no family photographs on Georgina's desk. The room was sparsely decorated – no filing cabinets, bookcases or computer – and Annie guessed its primary purpose was to put people at ease. Georgina no doubt had her files and books stored elsewhere.

Moments later Georgina reappeared with a mug of milky coffee.

'I've asked Carol to hold all the calls, so we're not disturbed,' she said. 'Though I don't see how I can help you.'

'That's what everybody thinks,' said Annie, 'but you'd be surprised. First of all, how long did you know Jennifer?'

'About two years. I was here when she started.'

'What was she like?'

'In what way?'

'Whatever comes to mind.'

'She was good at her job. It was important to her, that's why I mention it. She was considerate, cared about people. Maybe a bit too much.'

'What do you mean?'

'Well, as a counsellor you come into touch with a lot of grief, a lot of people with problems. You learn to sort of separate it out of your normal life, distance yourself a little bit. I don't think Jenn could have done that so easily. That's probably why she was in administration.'

'Did she get friendly with the clients here?'

'I wouldn't say "friendly", but she did take an interest. We run a very open office here, as you might have noticed. Everybody pitches in. You know, one day some poor girl would have a crying jag and Jenn would be the first one over to comfort her with tissues and a few kind words. That sort of thing.'

'But she didn't socialize with clients?'

'Not that I know of. Oh, I suppose you mean that girl she shares the flat with, Kate? But that was different. Kate wasn't pregnant. She just had a pregnancy test and that was that.'

'What about Roy Banks?' said Annie. 'She met him here, didn't she, when he was bringing his daughter in.'

'I wouldn't know about that.'

'She never mentioned how they met?'

'No. Jenn didn't like to discuss her private life, not in any detail.'

'Didn't you counsel Corinne?'

'Is that her name? No, it must have been Andrea. I'm afraid she's on holiday at the moment.'

'Never mind,' said Annie, making a note to ask Banks about how things were between Roy and Corinne. 'How had Jennifer been behaving during the past week or so? Did she seem worried, upset, depressed?'

'She certainly had something on her mind last week.'

'But she didn't tell you what it was?'

'No. I didn't see much of her. I was worked off my feet, so we didn't get to have our little chats.'

'She didn't confide in you about anything that was bothering her?'

'No.'

'What about Victor Parsons?'

'That waste of space. What about him?'

'I heard he caused a bit of trouble here at the centre.'

'Yes, but he's all bluster. I mean, he's obnoxious enough, but I can't imagine him doing . . . you know.'

'What happened between them?'

'Search me. I think Jenn wanted to settle down, have a family, but he wasn't interested. To be quite honest, from what I could gather he's a bit of a layabout, a sponger. She was well shut of him.'

'Do you know if he ever hit her?'

'I don't think so. At least she never said, and I never saw any evidence of it. The break-up hit her hard, though. She didn't say much, but you could tell she was under a lot of stress, poor thing. She lost weight, let herself go, as you do.'

'But this was before Roy Banks?'

'Oh, yes. She'd bounced back by then. Even tried one or two dates. They didn't lead anywhere.'

'But Victor Parsons turned up again, as recently as two weeks ago, I understand?'

'Yes, made a terrible scene. I was down in reception at the time.'

'What did he say?'

'He begged her to go back with him. Said he couldn't live without her.' Georgina's lip curled in distaste. 'Pathetic little shit.'

'Did he and Roy Banks ever bump into one another?'

'Not that I know of.'

'But you think that's what might have been upsetting Jennifer this last week? Victor? Or Roy?'

'Maybe they'd had a row or something. Bear in mind,

though, I'm only guessing. It could have been something else entirely.'

'You said she had a tendency for getting involved, trying to help people.'

'Yes.'

'Did she have any particular causes lately?'

'I don't think so. None that she mentioned to me, anyway.'

'Did she ever mention someone called Carmen Petri?'

'No, not to my knowledge.'

'What about the "late girls"? Do you know what that means?'

'I'm afraid I don't. What was the context?'

'It was just something Jennifer said to a friend, to describe this Carmen person. "One of the late girls." It still doesn't ring a bell?'

'No, not at all. I mean, it could be someone late with her period, or late in her pregnancy. As you know the law only allows abortions up to the twenty-fourth week.'

'Yes,' said Annie, 'I'd thought of that. Apart from Roy Banks and this Victor, did Jennifer have any other visitors here, or any other friends you know about?'

'Not that I know of.'

'Do you know anyone who drives a dark Mondeo, either black or navy blue?'

'My father does, but I doubt it's him you're interested in.'

Annie smiled. 'I doubt it. No one else?'

'No. Sorry.'

'Do you think Jennifer would have confided in you if there was anything seriously wrong?'

'Wrong?'

'Say at the centre. Something going on.'

'I can't imagine what you mean, but she might have done. The thing is, though, if there was anything untoward going on here, Jenn would have been in the best position to know about it as she practically ran the place single-handed. She and Alex Lukas, at any rate.'

'Dr Lukas?'

'Alex doesn't stand on ceremony.'

'Is he in today?'

'She. It's Alexandra. You might have noticed that the centre prefers to employ women. It's not some sort of positive-discrimination thing. It's just that we've noticed that the kind of clients we get here respond better to dealing with another woman.'

Annie understood. She had felt the same when she went for her NHS abortion. She certainly wouldn't have wanted a man asking her questions or poking about inside her.

'Look,' Georgina went on, leaning forward so her ample bosom rested on the desk, 'I can't imagine who would want to kill Jennifer, or why, but I think you're barking up the wrong tree if you think it was anything to do with this place. She had no enemies here.'

'I'm just trying to cover all the angles. That's all a lot of police work is, Ms Roberts, covering the angles so you don't look stupid for missing something obvious.'

'A bit like counselling.'

'How?'

'Well, it seems a bit of a cliché asking people how they get on with their parents, how they feel about their father, but if it turned out there was an incestuous relationship you'd look pretty damn silly for not even probing the area, wouldn't you?'

'I see what you mean. Can you think of anything else that might help me?'

'I'm sorry, no.' Georgina paused. 'Look, Jenn wasn't raped or anything, was she?'

'No.'

'Because I thought that might be something the police were holding back, like they do.'

'Sometimes it's important to keep key pieces of information from the public, but not that. Jennifer was shot in the head, pure and simple.' Annie noticed Georgina flinch at the brutality of the remark.

'But what I can't understand,' Georgina said, 'is why on earth someone would want to kill her like that. Don't get me wrong, I'm glad for her it was quick. It's just that I might be able to get my head around some pervert raping her and killing her to gratify his own filthy lust, but this . . . ? It doesn't make sense. It's almost as if someone actually had a *reason* for killing her.'

'We'll do our best to make sense of it,' said Annie, standing up to leave. 'In the meantime, if you can think of anything else at all – and I do mean anything, something Jennifer might have said, done, not done, whatever – then please get in touch with me. Here's my card.'

'Thank you.' Georgina took the card and looked at it.

On her way to Dr Lukas's office, Annie's mobile rang. She went into the stairwell, took it out of her pocket and put it to her ear.

'Hello?'

'Annie, it's Dave here. Dave Brooke.'

'What is it, Dave? Have you got something for me?'

'In a way,' Brooke said. 'Brace yourself. It's not good news.'

'Go on.'

'We found Roy Banks's body last night. Pulled him out of the Thames near the Eye.'

'My God. That story in the paper this morning? That was Roy Banks?'

'Yes. Shot. A .22 by the looks of it.'

'Alan . . . ?'

'He identified the body. Asked us to sit on the identity until he told his parents. He was pretty shaken up.'

'I can imagine. Poor Alan,' said Annie. 'Is there anything I can do?'

'Not right now. He's gone off to Peterborough. I just heard from him. He's going to stay with his parents for a while. I just thought you should know.'

'Yes. Thanks, Dave. Bloody hell, what's going on?'

'I wish I knew.'

10

The Banks family had been seeing Dr Grenville down at the local health centre for more than twenty years, since back when he had his own practice, and he was only too willing to pay a house call when Banks rang him and told him what had happened. A fussily neat man near retirement age, with salt-and-pepper hair and a matching moustache, he tut-tutted over Ida Banks before giving her a sedative and issuing a prescription for more, which Banks rushed down to the chemist's to fill. He felt like taking one or two himself on his way back but resisted the temptation. He'd need a clear head over the next few days.

Ida lay on the sofa, a small, lost figure covered with a blanket. She was mumbling, but she wasn't making much sense, and after a while she drifted off. Banks offered a pill to his father, who gave him a look of distaste and declined. It had always been his way to face life's harshness head on, without a mask, and he wasn't going to change.

'What do we do now?' he asked. 'I mean, aren't there forms to fill in and such like?'

'Don't worry, Dad. I'll take care of it all down in London. Do you know if Roy left a will?'

'Will? Don't know. He never said.'

'I'll talk to his solicitor. He's in Roy's phone book. Can I just make a couple of calls right now? It's important.'

'Go ahead. Make as many as you want.'

First Banks rang Tracy's mobile. The last thing he wanted was his children finding out about their uncle's murder from the television or newspapers.

'Dad, what's up?'

'How are things going?'

'Fine. What's wrong?'

'Does something have to be wrong for me to ring my own daughter?'

'You just sound funny, that's all.'

'Well, you're right this time. It is bad news, I'm afraid,' said Banks.

'What's happened? Are you all right?'

'I'm fine,' said Banks. 'It's your Uncle Roy.'

'What about him? Is he in jail?'

'Tracy!'

'Well, you always seemed to think he'd end up there.'

'I'm sorry to have to be the one to tell you, but he's dead.'

There was a moment's silence at the other end, then Tracy's voice came back on again, shaking a little. 'Uncle Roy? Dead? Are you serious? An accident?'

'No. I'm sorry, love, but he was killed. I don't know how to put it any better.'

'Killed how?'

There was no point trying to save her from the knowledge, Banks realized. She would soon find out from the newspapers. 'He was shot. Murdered.'

'My God,' said Tracy. 'Uncle Roy. Murdered.'

'It'll be in the papers and on the TV,' Banks said. 'I just wanted you to know first.'

'Is there anything I can do?'

'It's under control. Just don't talk to any reporters, if they track you down.'

'Do Grandma and Granddad want me to come and stay with them?'

'You get on with your studying. I'll take care of them and I'll try to come and see you soon. You can do me a small favour, though.'

'What?'

'Will you tell your mother?'

'Dad!'

'Please. Look, normally, I wouldn't bother. They weren't close or anything and she has her own life now. But it'll be high-profile. Maybe the reporters will trace her, too. I don't want it to come as too much of a shock to her.'

'Oh, all right. But this is silly. You've got to talk . . . Oh, never mind. I'm really sorry about Uncle Roy. I know . . . I mean, I know we didn't see him often but he always sent really cool presents.'

'Yes,' said Banks. 'I've got to go now. Keep in touch.'

'I will. I love you, Dad.'

Next Banks rang Brian, who didn't answer. Banks left a message for him to ring as soon as he could, then phoned DI Brooke to thank him for his patience and give him the go-ahead to release Roy's identity. Finally he rang Corinne. She sounded devastated after her initial stunned silence, and he wished he could be there for her, but all he could do was murmur useless words of comfort over the telephone as she cried. He promised to drop by next time he was in London, which he said would probably be soon.

He didn't have Malcolm Farrow's phone number, so that call would have to wait until he went back to Roy's house. Then he realized he probably couldn't go back there, as the whole place would be sealed off by the police investigating Roy's murder. He hesitated, then he called Annie Cabbot on her mobile. She was on the line. DI Brooke would have already told her about Roy, so Banks just left a message asking her to give him a ring at Peterborough as soon as she could, then he went back to his mother and father.

'Would you close the upstairs curtains, son?' Arthur Banks asked. 'Your mother would want it that way.'

'Of course.' Banks remembered how, when he was younger, if someone in the family died his mother would always close the upstairs curtains.

Up in his old room again, Banks looked out over the backyards and the deserted alley to find that the housing estate the builders had been working on during his last visit was now almost finished. Most of the houses were as yet unoccupied, and some were still without windows, but rows of them, all the same, filled the stretch of waste-ground where he used to play football and cricket as a child, where he had his first kiss and first furtive feel of a girl's breast as a teenager. He tried to remember whether Roy, too, had had such formative experiences there, but he didn't know. Most likely, if he had, it had all happened after Banks had left home, when they hardly communicated.

He did remember one incident. When he was about thirteen and Roy eight, he saw an older, bigger boy of about ten or eleven bullying Roy out in the field. Poor Roy was in tears as the bigger boy punched him repeatedly in the stomach and jeered at him for being a weakling. Banks rushed over to stop it, and even though he knew that he was now the bully, he couldn't hold himself back from giving the bastard a bloody nose and a split lip.

It came back to haunt him, too, when the boy's parents called at his house that night. Only because Roy corroborated his story in every detail did Banks get off with a mere admonishment to pick on people his own age in future. It could have been much worse. So he had stood up for Roy, and Roy had stood up for him. What had happened then? What had come between them?

As he usually did on his infrequent visits home, Banks looked in the wardrobe where the boxes of his adolescence were stored. The last couple of times he had been back he had discovered a treasure trove of old records, comics, diaries, books and toys. There were even more boxes he hadn't got around to yet, and he found himself wondering if any of them were Roy's.

The toy box with the lock was long gone, but he did eventually manage to dig out a small cardboard box full of things that definitely weren't his: Corgi toys – better than Dinkys, he remembered Roy arguing, because they had plastic windows and more realistic detail – a stamp album full of bright but worthless stamps, a portable chess set that folded into a box, a Scalextric set that he was never allowed to play with, and several of those tiny submarines that came out of a cornflakes box, the kind you stuffed with baking soda to make them submerge and surface. There were no diaries or old school reports, nothing to flesh out the vague sense of Roy that the toys implied, but down at the bottom was a Junior Driver, a toy steering wheel. Banks remembered Roy used to stick it on the dashboard on the passenger side of their father's Morris Traveller whenever they went anywhere and pretend he was driving. Even back then Roy had been car mad.

Banks held the plastic steering wheel in his hands for a moment, then he put it back, returned the box to the wardrobe and closed the curtains.

•

By mid-morning the whole of Western Area Headquarters in Eastvale knew about the murder of Banks's brother. Gristhorpe went into conference with ACC McLaughlin, and a hush fell over the Major Crimes squad room. Even the telephone conversations seemed to take place in whispers. If it wasn't exactly one of their own who had fallen in the line of duty, it was too damn close for comfort.

'Did you ever meet him?' Winsome asked Jim Hatchley, who had known Banks the longest of all of them.

'No,' said Hatchley. 'I got the idea he was a bit of a black sheep. Alan didn't have much to do with him.'

'Still,' said Winsome. 'It's family.' She thought of her own younger brother Wayne, a school teacher in Birmingham, and how rarely she saw him. She would ring him tonight, she resolved.

'Aye, it is that, lass,' said Hatchley.

Winsome chewed on her lower lip and got back to the telephone. She had had a bit of luck tracking down the Mondeo, first through the DVLA Wimbledon office and then through the Police National Computer database of stolen cars. A car matching the description, with a '51' registration number plate, had been stolen from a cheap long-stay parking facility near Heathrow Airport shortly before Jennifer Clewes's murder. When the car's owner, who had been on a business trip to Rome since Thursday, arrived back on Sunday evening and found his car missing, he had immediately informed the local police. Winsome had rung Heathrow, who would be the first to hear if the car turned up, and asked them to let her know as soon as possible.

If all the leads in this case led to London, as they seemed to be doing so far, it could be a while before DI Cabbot got back to Yorkshire. Winsome envied her. A nice little shopping trip down Oxford Street or Regent Street wouldn't go amiss right now. Not that Winsome was a clothes junkie, but she liked to look fashionable and she liked to look good, even if it meant creeps like Kev Templeton ogling her. She did it for herself, not for anyone else.

Winsome was just about ready to head down to the canteen for lunch when her phone rang.

'DC Jackman?' the unfamiliar voice enquired.

'That's me.'

'PC Owen here, Heathrow.'

'Yes.'

'We just got a report in about a stolen vehicle, a dark-blue Mondeo. I understand you were enquiring about it?'

'That's right,' said Winsome, pencil in her hand. 'Any news?'

'It's not good, I'm afraid.'

'Go ahead.'

'The long version or the short one?'

'The short first.'

'It turned up in the early hours of Sunday morning on the A13 just outside of Basildon.'

'Where's that?'

'Essex.'

'Excellent,' said Winsome. 'Can we get a SOCO team over there?'

'Hold on a minute,' said Owen. 'I haven't finished yet. I said it had turned up, but what I didn't get a chance to tell you was it was involved in an accident.'

'Accident?'

'Yes, the driver lost control and wrapped it around a telegraph pole. By all accounts he was going way too fast.'

'Do you have him in custody?'

'He's in the mortuary.'

'Damn,' said Winsome. 'Any identification on him?'

'Oh, we know who he was all right. His name's Wesley Hughes. The bugger of it is he was only fifteen.'

'Jesus Christ,' whispered Winsome. 'Just a kid. But what happened to our two men? The descriptions we have put them at way over fifteen.'

'I'm afraid I don't know anything about that. We did get one lucky break, mind you: there was a passenger, and he was uninjured. Well, he got a few cuts and bruises, but the doc's checked him out and he's basically OK. A little shaken, though, as you can imagine.'

'How old is he?'

'Sixteen.'

'Have the local police questioned him?'

'I don't know. It's out of my hands now. If I were you I'd give them a ring. I've got the number. Sergeant Singh is handling it. Traffic.' He gave Winsome the number. She thanked him and hung up.

Next she rang Sergeant Singh of the Essex Police at Basildon Divisional Headquarters. He answered immediately.

'Ah, yes, I've been expecting your call,' he said. 'Just

hold on a minute.' Winsome heard some muffled words, then Singh came back on the line. 'Sorry about that. It gets a bit noisy in here.'

'That's all right. What have you got?'

'A real mess is what.'

'Are we sure it's the right Mondeo?' Singh gave her the number. It matched what she'd got from the DVLA and the police computer. 'PC Owen gave me the basics,' Winsome said. 'Have you talked to the surviving boy yet?'

'Just. It took forever to track down his parents, and even when we found them they seemed more interested in opening another bottle of cheap wine than coming down to the station. No wonder the kids run wild. Anyway, he's a cocky young bastard, name of Daryl Gooch, but the crash took some of the wind out of his sails and DI Sefton took the rest.'

'What's his story?'

'According to him, he and his mate Wesley Hughes saw the car in Tower Hamlets, off Mile End Road, when they were coming home from a party at about half-past three on Sunday morning.'

'Tower Hamlets?'

'Yeah, the East End.'

'I know where it is. I'm just surprised and confused, that's all. I thought the car had been stolen from Heathrow on Friday by two men in their early forties who drove it up to Yorkshire to commit a murder in the early hours of Saturday morning. Now I find it was stolen from Tower Hamlets in the early hours of Sunday morning by two teenage joyriders. None of this makes any sense.'

'Well,' Singh went on, 'I wouldn't know about that,

but this is how Daryl Gooch says it happened. Young Daryl said the driver's door was open, the key was in the ignition and there was no one around, so him and his mate thought they'd have a little ride in the country. Pity his friend wasn't a better driver. Witnesses say he was doing close to a hundred when he lost control. As far as I can gather from Daryl they were still pissed and stoned from the party.'

'Do you believe him?'

'I don't know,' said Singh, 'but there's not much advantage to him lying at this point, is there?'

'With some kids it's habitual,' said Winsome.

'I suppose so. Anyway, both kids are from Tower Hamlets, so they'd have had no reason to be out at Heathrow. They're not exactly your jet-setting types. Any idea exactly when the car was stolen from the car park there?'

'Not really,' said Winsome. 'Sometime between Thursday and Friday evening, I suppose.'

'Sorry I can't be any more help,' said Singh. 'Ring me if you have any more questions.'

'Thanks,' said Winsome. 'I will.'

She hung up and nibbled on the end of her pencil as she thought things out. Assuming it *was* the same Mondeo that had been spotted near Jennifer Clewes's flat on Friday night and the one Roger Cropley had seen at Watford Gap, then after killing Jennifer and breaking into Banks's cottage, the two men had probably driven back to London through the night, kept the car out of sight for a day then dumped it in a decidedly dodgy neighbourhood where it was likely to go AWOL very quickly indeed, and hoofed it back home, wherever that might be. It didn't tell her much, but it did tell her one thing about them: they weren't scared of visiting dangerous neighbourhoods at night.

It was a good move to steal a car from a long-stay because the odds were good it wouldn't be reported stolen for a while. If it was, there was always a chance that it might be picked up by a camera on the Automatic Number Plate Recognition system that reads them against the database of stolen vehicles. But that hadn't happened; the car's owner didn't report it stolen until Sunday evening, by which time it was wrapped around a telegraph pole outside Basildon.

Well, Winsome thought, even if there wasn't much chance of finding trace evidence in the Mondeo now, at least they could check the tyres, and there was always a chance that someone in Tower Hamlets had seen the men who dumped the car there. Time to get on the phone again.

●

Dr Lukas's office boasted the same non-threatening decor as the rest of the Berger-Lennox Centre. The seats were padded and comfortable, colourful still-lifes hung on the aquamarine walls and there were no surgical instruments in sight, not even a hypodermic. Still, Annie realized, Dr Lukas didn't perform abortions, at least not here, so there was hardly any need for such things. There was, however, an examination room, and Annie imagined that behind the door would be the table, the instruments, the stirrups.

'It's tragic about Jennifer,' said Dr Lukas, before Annie could start with her questions. 'She was so young and vital.' The doctor had a slight accent, which Annie couldn't place. Eastern European, at any rate.

'Yes,' Annie agreed. 'Were the two of you very close?'

'Not really. We worked together, that's all. Our jobs are very different, of course, but we obviously had to meet regularly to ensure the smooth running of the centre.'

'But you didn't know her socially?'

Dr Lukas managed a weak smile. 'I don't have much of a social life,' she said. 'But, no, we didn't meet socially, only at work.'

Annie looked around the room. 'It's a nice place,' she said. 'Nice centre altogether. It can't be cheap to maintain. I suppose it must be doing rather well?'

'As far as I know,' said Dr Lukas. 'The finances were Jennifer's domain. I stick to what I know best.'

'Everyone tells me that Jennifer wasn't her usual self the week before her murder. They say she was anxious, edgy, worried. Did you notice this?'

'We had one of our regular meetings last Wednesday,' Dr Lukas said, 'and come to think of it, she did seem a little on edge.'

'But you've no idea why?'

'I assumed it was man trouble, but as I said, I know nothing about her private life.'

'Why did you assume man trouble, then?'

The doctor smiled. She was a slight, thin figure, around forty, short dark hair sprinkled with grey, hollow cheeks and a tired look about her eyes. Her body language seemed tense, too tightly strung. 'I shouldn't jump to conclusions, I know,' she said, 'but I have seen her leave here with a man on a number of occasions.'

That would be Roy, Banks's brother. 'Yes, we know about him,' Annie said. 'But we don't think that's what was bothering her.'

The doctor spread her hands on the table, palms up. 'Then I can't help you,' she said.

'What about her previous boyfriend, Victor Parsons? Have you ever met him?'

'Not that I know of.'

'Apparently he's turned up at the centre and created a fuss once or twice.'

'I'm a bit isolated up here,' Dr Lukas said. 'I probably wouldn't have noticed.'

'When Jennifer met her present boyfriend here, he was accompanying a young woman everyone assumed to be his daughter. Her name is Corinne and I don't believe she is his daughter. Did you examine her?'

'When would this be?'

'About two months ago. April.'

Dr Lukas turned to the laptop on her desk and pressed a few keys. 'Corinne Welland?'

'I assume that's the one,' Annie said. 'I don't know her surname.'

'It's the only Corinne I had.'

'Then it must be her.'

'Then yes, I did,' said Dr Lukas. 'And I had no idea whether she was this man's daughter or not. I never met him and she never said anything about him. It was just a straightforward consultation.'

'What happened to her?'

'She had her termination, and I assume she got on with her life.'

'Have you ever heard of Carmen Petri?'

'No,' said Dr Lukas, just a little too quickly for Annie's liking.

'Do you know what "late girls" are?'

'Girls who are late with their periods? Girls who are dead? I have no idea.'

Annie hadn't thought of that one, and she knew that she should have done. Dead. Was Carmen dead? Is that why she was one of the late girls? If so, how many others were there?

'What about girls who are pregnant and too late to have an abortion?'

'Then there would be no abortion. For one thing, it's illegal and for another, it's dangerous.'

'Except if the mother or the foetus is at risk?'

'Exactly. In that case surgery may be performed. But it is not, strictly speaking, an abortion; it is a surgical procedure performed in order to save a life, or lives. Emergency surgery.'

'Yes, I understand the distinction,' said Annie. 'Has the centre ever been involved in such surgery?'

'Not to my knowledge.'

'And you, as medical director, should know?'

'Well, you could check with the individual clinics where the terminations are actually carried out, but I very much doubt it. We're essentially a family planning centre, though we offer a broader range of services than many other such organizations. Anyone requiring a termination after twenty-four weeks would automatically be referred to a hospital. It becomes a medical problem, not a matter of individual choice.'

'I see,' said Annie. She wasn't going to get much further with this. If the centre was a party to illegal abortions, Dr Lukas certainly wasn't going to admit it, but Annie wasn't entirely convinced by her saying that she had never heard of Carmen, or by her evasion of the 'late girls' issue. Perhaps she would come back to

Dr Lukas again later, she thought, as she stood up and made her polite farewell. After she'd seen Victor Parsons, at any rate. But the next time she would make sure they didn't meet in the sterile domain of the Berger-Lennox Centre, where Dr Lukas was clearly used to being in control.

•

DC Kev Templeton soon got fed up sitting around talking on the telephone. He was a man of action; he liked to rattle a few doors and feel a few collars. Now it was Monday and the world was on the move again, he was in his element. With Gristhorpe's approval, he had set up a meeting with a DS Susan Browne, who was still working the Claire Potter case. They had agreed on a late lunch at a pub just off the motorway about halfway between Eastvale and Derby, and Templeton pulled into the car park at half-past two thinking if this Susan Browne was a bit of all right he might even get his end away before the day was done.

He walked through the dim, cavernous bar, where a few regulars sat quietly smoking and watching cricket on the TV, and went out of the back door into the garden. Templeton didn't know if he looked like a detective or not in his jeans, T-shirt and trainers, Ray-Bans covering his eyes.

He scanned the tables for a likely looking woman. There was only one, and when he approached her and she stood up to shake hands, Templeton's heart sank. She was short and a bit thick around the middle, not his type at all. He liked the Keira Knightley type, coltish girls, long-legged and limber. Still, she had nice eyes, he thought, and her manner seemed pleasant enough. She also had a thin gold ring on the third finger of her left hand. A glass of fizzy water sat on the white table in front of her beside the menu, one of those colourful laminated types you usually find in chain pubs, which were the only sort of pubs where you were likely to get lunch at half-past two on a Monday afternoon.

'Let's get the ordering out of the way first, shall we?' she said, sliding the menu over to him. 'I've already decided.'

Templeton scanned the colourful images of burgers, curries and fish and chips and decided that all he felt like was a prawn sandwich. Susan said she wanted a cheese-burger and chips. He almost warned her against it, given her waistline, but decided that probably wasn't the most diplomatic way of starting off the meeting.

He ordered at the bar, bought himself a Coke and went back to the garden. Their table was in the shade of a large copper beech, and a light breeze came and went, ruffling Susan's tight blonde curls and susurrating through the leaves. At the other end of the garden a few children played on the swings and roundabout while their parents sat at nearby tables enjoying the sunshine. Templeton put his Ray-Bans on the table and gave Susan the full benefit of his heart-melting brown eyes.

'You're from Western Area Headquarters, then?' she asked.

'Yeah,' said Templeton.

'Eastvale?'

'You know it?'

'Used to work there. How's DCI Banks? Still around, I suppose?'

Templeton grinned. 'We haven't got rid of all the dinosaurs yet.'

'As I remember, he got results, and he was a pretty good boss.'

'Yeah, well . . . When were you there?'

'A few years back. I left just after I passed my sergeant's boards. Did a year in uniform in Avon and Somerset, then transferred to CID in Derby. How is Alan doing? I heard about the fire. Sent him a card and all.'

'All right, I suppose,' said Templeton, realizing he had to be a bit more circumspect about what he said now that Susan had shown her true colours. 'Actually, he's probably not doing so well right at the moment. They just pulled his brother Roy's body out of the Thames last night.'

'Jesus,' said Susan. 'That's terrible. Look, give him my condolences when you see him, will you?'

'Sure.'

'What happened?'

'Looks as if he was killed. Shot. Did you know him?'

'No. But that's still terrible news. Poor Alan. Do tell him I'm sorry. My name was Susan Gay back then. He'll remember. Browne's my married name.'

There was something in her tone that stopped Templeton from making the obvious comment. Imagine going through life with a name like Gay, he thought. No wonder she changed it when she got married.

'And give my regards to Superintendent Gristhorpe and Jim Hatchley, if they're still around.'

'Oh, they're still around.'

'Right.' DS Browne waved a fly away from the rim of her glass. 'Down to business, then.'

'Claire Potter,' said Templeton. 'Like anyone for it?'

'We've got no suspects at all. Except . . .'

'Yes?'

'Well, can you imagine how many times he must have done practice runs, how many times he must have followed someone, only for her to get home before he could strike? For something like this to work out you need so many things to go right. A woman turning off on to a dark country road, nobody around, an unlocked driver's door. Anyway, we checked around and it seems that a couple of months earlier, the 20th of February to be exact, a woman turning off the M1 north of Sheffield was attacked in a similar way, only she had her doors locked. Paula Chandler.'

'What happened?'

'She managed to start up and drive off. He didn't pursue her.'

'Description?'

'Nothing useful. It was dark and she was scared. She didn't really get a look at his face because she was desperately trying to get the car started again while he was tugging at her door. He was wearing a dark suit, she said, and he had a wedding ring on. She saw his hand go to the door handle.'

'No gloves?'

'No. She said she could see the ring clearly.'

'Prints?'

'Nothing but blurs.'

'Make of car?'

'She couldn't say. Only that it was dark in colour, blue or green. And compact. Maybe Japanese.'

Roger Cropley drove a dark green Honda, Templeton

remembered, with a little shiver of excitement. And he wore a wedding ring. 'Not a lot of use, is it?' he said.

'Very frustrating. And there are others, equally vague. One girl thought a car was following her, another reported someone giving her a funny look at a service station. That sort of thing. We followed them all up but got nowhere.'

'But you still think it's the same man?'

'Yes. Like I said, he'd have to practise, and he'd need to get lucky. And Paula Chandler had stopped at Newport Pagnell services.'

'You think that's where he trawls for his victims, the motorway cafes?'

'Yes. It makes sense. Find a woman alone, follow her and see if she turns off on a quiet stretch of road late at night. Both attacks we know about happened late on a Friday, and both happened after the victim had stopped at a service station.'

'Tell me about Claire Potter.'

'Her car was found in a ditch and the SOCOs found evidence that she'd been driven off the road.'

'Tyre tracks?'

'Nothing we could use.'

'Where did the assault take place?'

'There was a wooded area nearby.'

'And nobody reported seeing the cars?'

'No. Either nobody passed them or someone just didn't want to get involved. It wasn't till the next morning when a chap driving a local delivery van got curious and reported the car in the ditch. When our blokes did a quick search of the area they found her.' She paused and sipped some water. 'I was there. It was bad. One of the worst.'

'What did he do to her?'

Templeton noticed that Susan didn't look him in the eye as she talked. 'Everything. Clothes ripped off. Rape, both vaginal and anal. He also used some sort of sharp object for penetration. We found a bloody stick nearby. Then he stabbed her and she bled to death. Fifteen stab wounds. Breast, abdomen, pubic area. I've never seen such anger.'

'DNA?'

'No. Either he used a condom or he didn't ejaculate.'

'Did the lab find any traces of lubricant?'

'No.'

'I take it they examined the earth around her.'

'Of course. No seminal fluid. No DNA. He'd also subdued her with chloroform so she couldn't struggle or scratch.'

'No hair or skin, then?'

'No. He was very careful, this one, and it looks as if he cleaned up after himself.'

'They usually miss *something*.'

'Not this time. There was a stream nearby. He even washed the body and laid it out properly. Her torn clothes were found beside her. He'd covered her face with her own underwear.'

'For Christ's sake. The knife?'

'Ordinary sheath knife. The kind you can buy just about anywhere.'

'Claire was last seen at Trowell services, right?'

'Right. She stopped for a coffee and a Penguin biscuit. The woman behind the counter at the cafe remembered her.'

'But nobody was taking any undue interest?'

'That's the way it seems. And she didn't need petrol,

the tank was more than half full, so she didn't stop at the pumps.'

'Any marks on the car? Paint scrapings, broken headlights, that sort of thing?'

'No. It was untouched. Whoever did it must have just pulled in front of her and she swerved into the ditch to avoid a collision.'

Their meals arrived and the day's warmth had made them both thirsty, so Templeton went and got another fizzy water for Susan and another Coke for himself. 'This case you're working on,' Susan said when he got back, already halfway through her cheeseburger. 'Do you seriously think there's any connection?'

'I don't know. It's a strange one. Look, this might seem like an odd question, but do you think there's any chance that there were two of them killed Claire Potter?'

'It wasn't a scenario we considered seriously. I mean, usually these things, the degree of rage, the location of the wounds, it all indicates a sexual predator, and they usually act alone.'

'What about Fred and Rose West?'

'I said usually. We've considered other possibilities but we're pretty sure it was just one man. It must have happened quickly, like yours did, only Claire wasn't shot. She suffered much more and for much longer.' She sipped her water. 'It's hard to say whether the differences outnumber the similarities. Probably, if you look at it realistically, they do. I mean, even if you can account for the difference between weapons, our killer went for overkill, showed a remarkable degree of anger. Your killer just coldly shot the victim and drove away. It sounds more like an execution than a botched sex crime to me.'

'You're probably right,' said Templeton, 'but we had to follow up on it. Don't these sorts of killers usually strike more than once, though?'

'Sexual predators? Yes, sometimes. I mean, you can't really predict, but it's doubtful he'll be satisfied for long. We've had the profilers in and run some pretty sharp computer programs and they all seem to indicate a strong likelihood of his striking again. After all, it's been nearly two months since Claire Potter.' She paused. 'There's something that never made it to the papers.'

'What's that?'

'He took a souvenir.'

'What?'

'A nipple. The left one, to be precise.'

'Jesus Christ,' said Templeton. He looked at his prawn sandwich and felt sick. He sipped some Coke.

'Sorry,' said Susan. 'Just thought we should get it all out in the open. I don't suppose that happened with Jennifer Clewes, did it?'

'No,' said Templeton.

Susan had finished her meal. She pushed her plate aside. 'Is there anything else you want to tell me?'

Templeton thought of Sunday's interview. 'We did have a bloke looked likely. For Jennifer Clewes, that is.'

'Oh?'

'Yes. Chap by the name of Cropley. Roger Cropley. Apparently he was paying her quite a bit of attention in the motorway cafe and at the petrol pumps, and he followed her back onto the motorway. Trouble is, he's got an alibi.'

'Does it hold up?'

'Watertight. He was on the hard shoulder with a

broken fan belt. Called the AA. They confirm the time. He couldn't possibly have killed Jennifer Clewes.'

'Pity.'

'But it doesn't mean he didn't want to, does it? Thing is,' Templeton went on, 'he's a funny sort of chap. Thought it was all a bit of a game, then got really stroppy. Seems he works in London and commutes every week. Every Friday, as a matter of fact. And he usually stops for a break. Probably wears a dark suit. Drives a dark green Honda. Married. Wears a ring. Like I said, he's on the M1 most Fridays. Not always that late, he told us, but sometimes. I was just thinking . . . you know.'

'Well, it wouldn't do any harm to have another little chat with him, would it?' DS Browne said. 'And if your suspicions continue, perhaps I could come up and have a word, too? I trust your SIO would OK it?'

'I should think so. It's not a lot to go on, I admit,' said Templeton, 'but there was something about him.'

'A hunch?'

'Call it that if you like. I happen to believe that hunches are made up of hundreds of little observations we're not directly aware of. Body language. Tone of voice. Little things. They all add up to a hunch.'

'Maybe you're right,' said Susan, smiling. 'In my case they usually call it women's intuition.' She looked at her watch. Nice gold band, Templeton noticed. Her husband must have a bob or two. Probably not a policeman, then. 'I'd better be off,' she said. 'Thanks for the tip. You'll keep me posted about Cropley?'

'Absolutely,' said Templeton.

'And do give my best to everyone at the station, and my condolences to Alan Banks.'

'Of course.'

Templeton watched her walk away. Her legs weren't bad at all. If only she could trim down that waistline a bit she might be worth a crack, husband or no. He swatted a wasp away from his prawn sandwich and it buzzed him a few times before zigzagging off into the trees. Time to head back to Eastvale, he thought, and see if anything new had turned up.

11

Late on Monday afternoon, the rain came down again, out of nowhere, splashing against the windscreen of Dave Brooke's Citroën as he drove Annie through the rush-hour traffic to Tower Hamlets, not exactly the kind of place you'd find in a tourist's guide to London. They were in Bow, and the house they wanted stood in a row of run-down terraced houses that had survived both bombing and slum clearance. Across the street lay a couple of acres of tarmacked waste ground with weeds growing through the cracks, surrounded by a six-foot wire-mesh fence with barbed wire on the top. Who was protecting it, and from what, Annie had no idea. She guessed it was earmarked for development. Beyond the waste ground, through the slanting rain, stood more grimy terraced houses, slate roofs dark, and beyond them tower blocks rose bleak as monoliths against an iron-grey sky.

'Pretty, isn't it?' said Brooke, as if reading her mind.

Annie laughed. 'If you like that sort of thing.'

'It's a piece of history. Enjoy it while you can. In a year or so it'll probably be all new tower blocks or an entertainment complex.'

'You sound as if you'd be sorry to see it go.'

'Maybe I would. Here we are.' He pulled up at the kerb and they looked at number forty-six. The front door, Annie thought, could definitely use another coat of paint to cover the cracks and gouges time and, perhaps, would-be burglars had inflicted.

Alf Seaton, a retired ship's carpenter, had not only seen Wesley Hughes and Daryl Gooch drive away in the Mondeo, but he had also seen it arrive in the early hours of Sunday morning, and this was what interested Annie and Brooke. Annie was beginning to wonder if she would ever get home again, the way things were going. She had hoped to be off that afternoon after her visit to the Berger-Lennox Centre, but Brooke called. All roads seemed to lead to London.

Alf Seaton was expecting them, and Annie noticed the edge of the lace curtain twitch just a little when their car pulled up. Before they reached the door, it opened, and a plump, grey-haired man with a broken nose beckoned them in out of the rain.

'Miserable day, isn't it?' he said, in an unmistakable cockney accent. Well, Annie thought, he was in the right area, probably even within the sound of Bow Bells, come to think of it. 'Make yourselves comfy. I'll put the kettle on. Got some chocolate digestives, too, if you're interested.'

Annie looked around the small living room while Alf Seaton busied himself in the kitchen. There was an old-fashioned look and feel to the place, she thought, visible in the ornate pipe rack, the dark wood bureau and the low bookcase under the window, filled mostly with nautical tales, she noticed: Alexander Kent, Douglas Reeman, Patrick O'Brian, some old Hornblower editions. On the wall above the fireplace was a romantic seascape depicting Lord Nelson's fleet engaging the French in rough waters, cannons blazing. The armchairs were old but still firm, and there wasn't a speck of dust in sight.

When Seaton came back in with the tea and biscuits, Annie complimented him on the house.

'I do my best,' he said. 'Just because you're poor doesn't mean you have to be slovenly, does it? That's what my mother always used to say.'

'Are you married?'

'Fran died a couple of years ago. Cancer.'

'I'm sorry.'

'No reason for you to be, love. Life goes on.' He looked around the room. 'We had nearly fifty happy years, me and Fran. Moved here in 1954, our first home. Only one as it turned out. Course, I was just a young lad then, still wet behind the ears. And things have changed a lot. Not all for the best, either.'

'I'm sure not,' said Annie.

'Still you won't be wanting to hear an old man's reminiscences, will you?' he said, winking at Annie. 'You'll be wanting to know what it was I saw.'

'That's why we're here, Mr Seaton,' said Brooke.

'Alf, please.'

Alf was a name you didn't hear much these days, Annie thought, and if you did you could guarantee it belonged to someone of Mr Seaton's generation.

'Alf, then.'

'I'm not sure I can tell you anything I didn't already tell the uniformed bloke.'

'Let's start with what you were doing.'

'Doing? I was sitting here in this very armchair reading. I don't sleep very well, so I've taken to getting up, making myself a cup of tea and settling down for a good read. Beats lying there thinking about all your problems the way you do at that time of night.'

'Yes, it does,' said Annie. 'So what was it that happened first? Did you see or hear the car?'

'Heard it first. I mean, we do get a bit of traffic down here throughout the night, but not that much. It's not a main road, or even the quickest way to one. And as you can see, it doesn't have a great deal of natural charm. Anyway, at three on a Sunday morning it does tend to be quiet apart from the odd group of kids stumbling home from a party.'

'Do you remember the exact time?' Annie asked.

Alf Seaton glanced at the solid, ancient clock on the mantelpiece. 'Ten past three,' he said. 'I remember looking, wondering if it was later. Anyway, first I heard it, then I saw the lights. It parked just across the street there, by the wasteground. Then another car pulled up behind it.'

'And you saw the driver?'

'Yes. Quite clearly. There's a street light and my eyesight's still pretty good for distances.'

'What can you tell us about him?' Annie asked, glancing at Brooke, who nodded, indicating that she should carry on asking the questions. Alf seemed comfortable talking to her.

'I was a bit nervous, I suppose. I mean, there's been quite a lot of crime in the neighbourhood and when you're old and frail in your health like I am, you do worry a bit, don't you. Twenty years ago I'd have given anyone a good run for his money, armed or no, but these days . . .'

'I understand,' said Annie. 'But you did get a look, didn't you?'

'I wasn't *that* scared. I like to know what's going on in my street. Anyway, I didn't want to draw attention to myself, so I turned the light off. I'm glad I did because I saw him look over at the house for a moment and pause, as if he was trying to decide whether there was anyone watching him. He seemed to look right at me, but he must have decided there wasn't.'

'What did he look like?'

'He was a big fellow, hard-looking, as if he lifted weights. He was wearing a dark-coloured tracksuit, the sort with a white stripe down the arm and the outside leg. His hair was a bit long, tied in a ponytail at the back like a right poofter. Black, it was, and shiny, as if he sloshed axle grease on it. And he had a heavy gold chain around his neck.'

It sounded like a better description of the man who Roger Cropley had seen in the back of the Mondeo at Watford Gap, and who the neighbour had noticed on Jennifer's street around the time she set off for Banks's cottage. 'What happened next?' Annie asked.

'That's when I saw him get in the other car.'

'Can you remember anything more about the second car?'

'No, except it was lighter than the first one, maybe cream or silver, something like that. There wasn't really enough light to show up the colour properly, everything was a sort of monochrome, but it was a bit more . . . I don't really know cars . . . but it looked maybe more expensive, more flashy.'

'Did you notice any logos, ornaments, that sort of thing?'

'Sorry, no.'

'It's OK. You're doing fine. I don't suppose you got the number, did you?

'No.'

'Did you get a good look at the driver?'

'Just a glimpse when the door opened and the inside light came on for a second. It was further back, out of the range of the street lamp.'

'Can you describe him?'

'All I could really see was that he had short fair hair. Really short. Cropped. Then the door shut, the light went off and they drove away.'

'What direction?'

'South. Towards the river. Not long after that I heard the kids talking and the car door slam. I just caught a glimpse of them, then they were gone. I know I should have called the police right there and then. Maybe then that poor boy wouldn't have died. But I didn't know what was going on and it doesn't pay to get too involved unless you really have to.'

'It's not your fault,' said Annie.

'Even so, I feel bad.'

'Mr Seaton. Alf,' Brooke cut in, 'do you think you would be able to work with a police artist on a sketch of the man you got a good look at?'

'I think so,' said Seaton. 'I mean, I've got a fairly clear picture of him in my mind. It's just a matter of getting it down.'

'That's what the artist's for. With a bit of luck, we might be able to get him here by tomorrow morning. Would that be all right?'

'I'm not going anywhere.'

'Good. I'll make the arrangements. Is there anything else you can tell us?'

Seaton thought for a moment, then said, 'No, I don't think so. It all happened very quickly, and as I said, I didn't know what was going on. Why would a man abandon a nice car like that and leave it unlocked in a neighbourhood like this unless he *wanted* it to be stolen?'

'Exactly,' said Annie.

•

Banks fetched fish and chips from the Chinese chippie over the road for lunch, but his father just picked at them. He didn't even complain the way he usually did that they tasted of chop suey, his only notion of Chinese food. After a cup of tea Banks was seriously thinking of heading back to London, but he sensed that he should stay. Not that his father asked him, or ever would, but it seemed the thing to do. The family should be together, at least for now.

He felt restless, though, cooped up, so he drove into town and wandered around Cathedral Square and the Queensgate Centre. While he was there he remembered that he had left his mobile back in Gratly and he had given Roy's to Brooke. If he was planning on heading back to London, which he was, he might need one. He went into the first electronics shop he saw and bought a cheap pay-as-you-go mobile and a £10 card. Once he'd got the battery charged back at his parents' house it would be ready to use, but he bought an in-car charger as well.

It was a cloudy afternoon, holding the threat of rain. A group of buskers were playing jigs and reels in the square, a small crowd gathered around them. A steady stream of tourists entered the Cathedral precincts.

When Banks found himself wandering by the Rivergate Centre flats he thought of Michelle Hart, who used to live there, on Viersen Platz. On the opposite side of the river was Charters Bar, an old iron barge moored near Town Bridge, and Banks remembered the blues music he'd heard issuing from it on weekends he had stayed with her.

Banks stared into the murky water and wondered if he should have tried harder with Michelle. He had let her slip away far too easily. But what could he do? Her career was important to her, and when the opportunity in Bristol came up he could hardly plead with her not to go. Besides, there had been problems with the relationship well before the move, so many that he had often thought the new job was at least partly an attempt to put more distance between them.

He walked back to his car and just sat there for a while with the windows open, smoking. How bloody ironic it was, he thought, that he had only come to know his brother after his disappearance. If Roy had died two, three years ago, Banks would have grieved, of course, but he wouldn't have felt the loss in such a personal way. Now, though, it actually hurt, squeezed at his heart. Now there was someone to miss, not just a distant memory.

It wasn't so much that he had revised his opinion of Roy as that he had put it in a larger context. Roy was a rogue, no doubt about it; he had about as much sense of business ethics as a flea and he was a bastard to women. That he'd made a fortune, driven a Porsche and had women falling over him was only a testament to one of those grim truths of life, that the bastards thrive. Maybe they get their just deserts in the afterlife, maybe they come back as cockroaches, but in this life, they thrive.

Roy's crisis of conscience after witnessing the horror of 9/11, his turning to the Church, had probably sharpened what moral instinct he had to some degree. Had he stumbled across something in that last week that offended his sense of right and wrong? Had he gone through a struggle of conscience before ringing his policeman brother? Or had it been business much as usual? Throughout his life Roy had probably stolen, cheated and lied without giving a damn for the consequences, or a moment to worry over those he had hurt. Had he changed that much? Banks wouldn't find out in Peterborough, he knew that, so tomorrow he would have to head back to London and start digging again.

Banks thought it might be a good idea to let a few people, especially his children, know he had a new mobile number, so he turned on the engine, plugged the phone in the car-charger and rang to leave messages. To his great surprise, Brian actually answered in person.

'Dad. Nice to hear from you. We're on a break. Sorry I didn't get back to you sooner but we were in the studio. I was going to ring tonight.'

'It's OK,' said Banks. 'I've been out a lot. Look, it's a long story, but I've got a new mobile. Want the number?'

Brian sounded puzzled. 'Sure, if you like.'

Banks gave it to him. 'How's it going?'

'Well. Slowly, but well.'

'And how's Dublin?'

'Great.'

'Tried the Guinness yet?'

'A pint or two. Look, what is it, Dad? Why did you want to talk to me? Nothing's wrong, is it?'

'I'm afraid it is,' said Banks, thinking, 'Here we go again,' then taking a deep breath and plunging in. 'Your Uncle Roy's been killed. It'll be all over the news in a while, so I wanted you to know.'

'Uncle Roy? No. I mean, I never really knew him, but . . . he always sent cards and stuff. I can't believe it. Why? What happened? Did he have some sort of accident?'

'I'm trying to find out what happened,' said Banks. 'But, no, it wasn't an accident. He was shot.'

'Jesus Christ!'

'Look, I'm sorry, Brian, really. I can't think of an easier way to break the news. Anyway, there's nothing you can do. I've told Tracy, and she's going to tell your mother. Just get on with your recording.'

'You sure?'

'Yes. And be prepared for reporters.'

'When's the funeral?'

'We don't know yet.'

'You'll let me know how it goes? Keep me informed?'

'I'll let you know,' said Banks. 'I'll be back in London in a day or so, probably staying at Roy's house if the police have finished with it. Do you want the address and phone number there?'

'Sure. Might as well. Shot . . . Jesus.'

Banks gave him Roy's address.

'Thanks, Dad,' Brian said. 'And I'm really sorry.'

'Take care,' said Banks, then he broke the connection.

He sat there for a moment longer, thinking he'd probably gone and ruined his son's big recording session, then he stubbed out his cigarette and set off back to the Hazels estate.

●

Victor Parsons shared a flat with two other young men in Chalk Farm. When Annie called around teatime he was sitting in the living room reading a film magazine.

Annie's first impression was of a nice-enough-looking bloke with a bland and unassuming personality, quite a contrast to the chic, successful and dynamic Roy Banks.

Parsons clearly hadn't shaved for a couple of days, and it looked as if he'd been wearing the same T-shirt and jeans for much longer. There was a snail-like lethargy about him that hinted at lack of ambition. Yet, Annie had to remind herself, he had turned up at Jennifer Clewes's place of work and caused a scene. Quite frankly, he didn't look as if he had it in him.

Annie didn't like to make snap judgements, but all she had seen and heard of Jennifer, admittedly only after her death, indicated that she outclassed Victor by far. Had she had such low self-esteem, then, had she been so insecure that she had really seen something of value in him? Still, she thought, there was no accounting for taste and no explanation for many of the strange couplings in life.

The room itself seemed clean and tidy enough, which pleased and surprised Annie. Knowing she had been about to visit a bachelor pad, she had mentally girded herself for dirty laundry over chair backs and posters of Kelly Brook and Jordan in lacy black lingerie plastered to the walls. As it turned out, the only poster in view was for *Kill Bill I*.

'I suppose it's about Jenn?' Victor said, without offering Annie a seat, let alone a cup of tea or coffee. As he was slouching on the sofa, she took an armchair and sat. 'I suppose that bitch Melanie Scott's been talking?'

'Among others,' said Annie. 'You're not exactly popular among Jennifer's friends and acquaintances.'

'I don't care what people think about me. They don't

really know me, anyway. They're just a bunch of superficial losers.'

'Oh, it's like that is, it? Poor, hard-done-by misunderstood genius takes on the world.'

He gave her a look of scorn. 'What do you know? You wouldn't understand.'

'You're right,' said Annie, 'so why don't I ask the questions and you answer them? I find this sort of thing works best that way.'

'Whatever.'

'Good. I'm glad we've got that sorted. Now let's get down to business. Where were you last Friday night?'

'Here.'

'Doing what?'

'Watching TV.'

'What were you watching?'

'*Coronation Street*, *EastEnders*, Lenny Henry, *Have I Got News For You*, then Jools Holland and a late film. It was a horror film called *Session 9*.'

'Any good?'

'It had its moments.'

'That's pretty impressive, Victor, remembering all that.'

'I've just got a good memory, that's all, and it's pretty much the same every Friday. Different film, of course.'

'Anyone else with you?'

'Gavin was out till about one o'clock, but Ravi was here most of the time. You can ask him.'

'Thanks. I will.'

'Look, I'm gutted, you know. By what's happened. I loved her.'

'So I hear. Can be a nasty thing, unrequited love.'

'She loved me, too. She just didn't realize it. She would've, if . . .'

'If?'

'Given time.'

Annie sighed. 'Victor, it sounds to me as if somewhere along the line you lost touch with reality. Jennifer wasn't in love with you. She'd moved on, found someone else.'

'You don't know her.'

'What do you do?'

'Do? What do you mean?'

'Your job. Work.'

'I'm an actor.'

'Resting?'

'At the moment, yes. It's true, though. I've had roles. I've even done TV. Only adverts, and one non-speaking part, but it's a start.'

'Earn much money?'

'Not a lot, no.'

If Annie had held out any hopes that it was Victor who hired someone to kill Jennifer, they were soon dashed. He obviously couldn't afford it.

'Why did you pester her?' she asked. 'You went to her place of work and caused a scene. Why did you do that if you loved her?'

'I'm not proud of that. I was pissed. I'd been drinking with Ravi at lunchtime and I'm not used to it. The booze went to my head, that's all, and I got overexcited. I was sorry about it afterwards. I even rang her to apologize but she wouldn't talk to me.'

'Did you talk at all after you split up?'

'No. I couldn't get near her at work and she always hung up the phone if I tried her at home. Or the other girl did.'

'Kate Nesbit?'

'Is that her name? I don't know.'

'But you knew where she lived, where she'd moved to?'

'Yes. I made it my business to find out.'

'Have you any idea if anything, or anyone, was bothering her over the past while?'

'No. Like I said, she shut me out of her life completely.'

'Did you ever hang around outside her house?'

'I walked by once in a while, yes. I was hoping I might see her in the street.'

'Once in a while?'

'Well, not every day, but regular, like.'

'And did you see her?'

'No. Never.'

'When were you last there?'

'Couple of weeks ago.'

'Did you notice anyone else hanging around?'

'No.'

Of course he didn't, Annie thought. He wouldn't even notice if Godzilla stamped on the house next door. All he had eyes for was Jennifer. 'What about her place of work?'

'She worked late sometimes. I used to wait across the street. Just to see her.'

'Did you ever approach her when she left?'

'No. I didn't have the bottle. I'd just watch her. I told you, it was only because I was pissed that I made a scene.'

'When was the last time?'

'Last week. Monday.'

'And did you see her leave?'

'Yeah, but she was with someone.'

'Who?'

'It wasn't anyone I knew, just some girl, by the looks of her.'

'A young girl?'

'Yeah. Probably one of the rich pregnant teenagers they deal with there. Only this one didn't look particularly rich.'

'What time was this?'

'About eight o'clock.'

'Wasn't the centre closed by then?'

'Yeah. They close at five. I think everyone else had gone home, but Jenn worked late a lot.'

'Can you describe the girl?'

'Long dark hair. Bit skinny, but a nice figure, apart from the bump. She was just wearing ordinary clothes. You know, a flowery dress, sandals. I didn't get a really good look at her face.'

'I take it by the "bump" you mean her pregnancy was showing?'

'Yes.'

'Where did they go?'

'Nowhere.'

'Why not?'

'A bloke got out of a car parked in front, had a word in her ear, and she got in the car with him.'

'Who, Jennifer or the girl?'

'The girl.'

'What did Jennifer do?'

'Walked towards the tube station.'

'Did you follow her?'

'No. I just went for a drink.'

'What did the man look like?'

'Like he lifted weights. You know, big, broad shoulders, no neck. And he had a ponytail.'

'And the car?'

'Didn't notice.'

'Dark or light?'

'Light, I think. Maybe silver.'

'Was there anyone else in it?'

'I didn't see.'

'Did he force the girl into the car?'

Parsons frowned. 'No. But it was like he was in charge and he was saying that's enough, time to go.'

'She didn't resist?'

'No.'

'OK,' said Annie. 'Were you outside Jennifer's house or place of work last Friday?'

'No. I already told you, I stayed in. I do most nights.'

Did Victor Parsons kill Jennifer or have anything to do with her death? Annie doubted it. Stalkers could turn violent, true, but more often than not they didn't. Most of the time they were sad, pathetic pillocks like Victor, or like peeping Toms, irritating and upsetting, but ultimately harmless.

'Tell me something,' she asked, 'just out of interest. Why did you split up with Jennifer?'

'It was all a misunderstanding. That's it, you see. I thought we wanted different things. You know, Jenn wanted marriage, family, all that, and I wanted to pursue my acting career. But I was wrong.'

'So you chucked her?'

'No. It wasn't like that. All I said was that we should give one another a bit more space and get clear about what we wanted, that's all. And I did. I decided I wanted her, no matter what, that I'd even give up my career, she meant that much to me.'

'Generous of you.' No doubt, Annie guessed, as soon as Jennifer had got over the immediate shock of the break-up and got pissed with Melanie Scott a few times in Sicily, she had probably realized just how lucky she was to get out of the relationship.

There was nothing more to be gained talking to Victor Parsons, Annie decided; she would get someone else to check his alibi with his flatmate and cross him off her list. It was only early evening, but it had been a long day, and Annie felt tired, felt like simply going back to her hotel, ordering room service and vegging out in front of the TV. She had rung Peterborough earlier in the afternoon, but Banks was out. Maybe she would try ringing again later.

'What am I going to do now?' Victor asked as Annie opened the door. 'What am I going to do?'

'Maybe you should get out of the house a bit more often and try to get an audition?' Annie suggested, and left.

•

'How is she?' Banks asked when he got back from town.

'No different,' said his father. 'I told you, she wasn't well even before all this. It's only made her worse. Anyway, she's still in bed. Doesn't seem to want to get up.'

'I'll go up and see her in a while. I've decided to stay tonight.'

'You've no need to,' said his father. 'Not for our sake. We can manage.'

'I'd like to.' One thing Banks knew that his father

might not have thought of was that Roy's identity would now be public knowledge and there was a good chance that the phone would be ringing off the hook. He wanted to be there to field the calls for them.

'Suit yourself. Your room's always here, you know that.'

'I know,' said Banks.

'I still can't believe our Roy's dead. Murdered.'

'Me neither. I wish there was something I could do.'

'You can't bring him back.'

'No. Any signs of reporters while I was out?'

'No.'

'Thank the Lord for small mercies, then. Look, Dad, I don't suppose Roy ever talked to you about his business interests, did he? What he was up to, that sort of thing?'

'Me? You must be joking. He knew I'd about as much understanding of business as I have about rocket science.'

'And that you might not approve of how he made his money?'

'I'm not a bloody communist. All I've ever asked for is a fair share for the working man. What's so wrong about that?'

'Nothing,' said Banks, who didn't want to get into that old argument again. Not here, not now. Besides, he agreed. His father had been given a raw deal, made redundant from his job as a sheet-metal worker during the Thatcher years. He had seen the riot police taunting the striking coal miners, and as a result he had come to see the police as the right hand of the oppressor. Banks knew that could happen, had done in some countries, and there was a certain feeling, not entirely unjustified, that it had happened during the Thatcher years. But most of Banks's attempts to explain to his father that he simply put in a long day's work trying to catch criminals fell on deaf ears.

'Anyway,' said his father, 'Roy was always generous to us.'

The implied barb wasn't lost on Banks, but he managed to bite his tongue before asking his father whether it mattered where the money came from. 'So he never mentioned any names?'

'Not as I remember.'

'The Berger-Lennox Centre, Gareth Lambert, Julian Harwood?'

'Never heard of them.'

'What about his girlfriends?'

'Only that young lass he brought over last year, for the anniversary.'

'Corinne. Yes, I've talked to her. He never mentioned anyone called Jennifer Clewes?'

'That girl that got shot up in Yorkshire? You mentioned her earlier. No, I'm certain he never mentioned her to us.'

Arthur Banks sagged back in his favourite armchair. The television was turned off, which was unusual, and there was no sign of a newspaper. Even in the short while Banks had been absent, he noticed more signs of neglect. And his father was clearly as much in the dark about Roy's activities as he was. He picked up two empty cups from the floor beside the armchair. 'Fancy a cup of tea?'

'If you like,' said his father.

'What about dinner?'

'Doesn't matter as long as it's not from that place over the road.'

Banks put the kettle on and found the tea bags. Never an easy task, as his mother kept moving them around like a shell game. This time they were in a jar in the pantry marked cocoa. While the kettle boiled, he washed the few dishes that had been used and stacked them in the rack to dry. He found some bread, tomatoes, cheese and boiled ham and made some sandwiches. They would have to do for dinner.

'Any more idea when the funeral will be?' his father asked when Banks brought in the tea and sandwiches.

'I can't say,' said Banks. 'It depends when they release the body.'

'What do they want to hang on to it for?'

'Sometimes, if someone's arrested and charged, they can ask for a second, independent post-mortem. I don't think that's likely in this case, but it's not my decision. Believe me, Dad, I'll stay on top of it. I don't want you and Mum worrying about the details.'

'Don't we have to register the death?'

'You can't do that until the coroner's released the body. I'll take care of it all when the time comes.'

'What else are we going to do except sit around and mope?'

'Just try to get through it day by day. It'll take time.'

His father sat forward. 'But that's just it. We haven't got time.'

Banks felt a shiver at the back of his neck.

'What do you mean? Has your heart been giving you more problems?'

'My heart's fine. A touch of angina, that's all. It's not me. It's your mother.'

'What about her?' Banks remembered his mother's tired and listless appearance when he first arrived, before he had even told her about Roy, and again he took in the air of neglect about the house. 'Is it something to do with these tests she's been having?'

'They think she's got cancer. That's why they want her in hospital to do some more tests.'

'When?'

'They say they can't fit her in until next week.'

Banks felt the need for a cigarette, but he didn't give in to it, not there and then. He wished he could afford private cover for his parents, then they wouldn't have to wait. 'Christ,' he said. 'It never rains but it pours.'

'You can say that again.'

'What does the doctor think?'

'You know doctors. Won't commit themselves without the test results. Anyway, it's her colon they're worried about. I can tell you what I think, though. The life's slowly going out of her. I've been watching it drain away for weeks.'

'But even if it is cancer, there are treatments. Especially colon cancer. As far as I know the cure rate's pretty good.'

'Depends how far it's spread, doesn't it, how soon they catch it?'

'Look, Dad,' said Banks, 'there's no point being pessimistic. You've got enough on your plate with our Roy. See her through this. That has to be your priority right now. We'll deal with the other thing when we know more about it.'

'You're right, but . . . it's just so bloody hard, all the time thinking I might lose her. Now Roy.'

Banks could see that his father was close to tears, and he remembered that he had never seen him cry. His mother, yes, but not his father. He wanted to spare him the embarrassment, knowing he was a proud man, so he went upstairs to see his mother. She was lying in bed with the sheets pulled up to her neck, but her eyes were open.

'Roy?' she said when he first entered the room. 'Is it really you?'

'No, Mum,' said Banks. 'It's me, Alan.'

He could swear he saw the disappointment register in her face. 'Oh,' she said. 'Where's our Roy?'

Banks sat at the edge of the bed and grasped her hand. It felt dry and thin. 'He's gone, Mum. Our Roy's gone.'

'Oh, yes,' she said. 'I remember now. In the water.' She closed her eyes and seemed to drift off.

Banks leaned forward and kissed her quickly on the cheek, then said goodnight and went back downstairs.

'She's in and out,' he told his father.

Arthur Banks had pulled himself together. 'Yes,' he said. 'It's probably those tablets the doctor gave her.' He looked at Banks. 'You said before you wished there was something you could do, and there is, you know. I've been thinking while you were up with your mother.'

'What's that, Dad?'

'You're supposed to be a detective, aren't you? You can do your job and go back to London and catch the bastard that killed our Roy.'

Banks sat down, picked up his mug of tea and reached for a sandwich. 'Yes,' he said. 'You're right. And that's exactly what I intend to do first thing tomorrow.'

12

Late on Tuesday morning, after breakfast and a brief meeting with Brooke to review their progress so far, Annie went back to her room, packed her meagre belongings and checked out. She was looking forward to getting home, digging out some clean clothes and sleeping in her own bed again, if only for one night. She knew she would have to come back, especially as she planned on visiting Dr Lukas at home in the near future. For the meantime, though, Brooke was leading the Roy Banks investigation, and Annie needed to show her face to the troops back up in Eastvale, talk to Stefan Nowak and Gristhorpe, see how Winsome and Kev Templeton were getting on.

She wondered what Banks was up to as she waited for a taxi. She hadn't tried to ring him again the previous evening, deciding it was probably best to leave him and his parents in peace. From what she could remember Banks telling her, they had doted on Roy. And even though he and Roy hadn't been close, she knew he must be distraught. Though she wasn't unduly worried about him, he had been depressed lately, and something like this could push him over the edge. She would like to talk to him, anyway, to see him, if only to reassure herself and offer her condolences. A taxi pulled up and Annie got in.

'King's Cross, please,' she told the driver.

They had hardly got over Lambeth Bridge when her mobile rang.

'Annie, it's Dave Brooke here.'

'Dave. What is it?'

'Thought you might be interested. I've just got the pathologist's report on Roy Banks. Can you talk?'

'It's OK,' said Annie, 'I'm in a taxi on my way to the station.' The driver was listening to an interview on BBC London, and there was a Plexiglas window between the front and the back.

'Fair enough. Bottom line is, the shot to the head killed him outright. It's a .22 calibre bullet, just like the one that killed Jennifer Clewes.'

'Anything on time of death?'

'He'd been in the water about forty hours. Had to have been to get in the state he was and fetch up on that patch of shingle, so the tide experts tell me.'

'So it can't have been the same killers.'

'No. They couldn't possibly have got back from Yorkshire in time.' Brooke paused. 'DCI Banks isn't going to like hearing this, but it also appears that his brother was tortured before he was shot.'

'Tortured?'

'Yes. There's evidence of serious bruising to the body and cigarette burns on the arms and soles of the feet. Some of the fingernails have been pulled out, too.'

'Jesus,' said Annie. 'Someone wanted something from him?'

'Or wanted to know how much he knew, or had given away.'

'Either way, you're right. Alan won't like that at all. The press—'

'They're not going to find out.'

'Are you sure?'

'Not from us. We're keeping this to ourselves. All the press will be told is that he was shot. That will be enough for them. I can see the gun-crime editorials right now.'

'True enough,' said Annie. 'They're already having a field day with the Jennifer Clewes shooting. Anything else?'

'Just a couple of things,' said Brooke. 'Remember the digital photo that came through on Roy Banks's mobile?'

'Yes. Alan mentioned it to me.'

'As we suspected, it came from a stolen phone. Technical support didn't have much trouble enhancing the image. They've got all sorts of fancy software that can filter and stretch and make predictions based on pixel statistics. The upshot is, though, that it doesn't tell us a hell of a lot. We still can't be absolutely certain whether the man in the chair is Roy Banks. They did manage to get something from the wall in the background.'

'What?'

'It looks as if there were two rows of letters, or words, stencilled on the rough brick. The first ends in NGS and the second in IFE. We've no idea how long the lines were or how many words. We're getting a list of all abandoned factories in the Greater London area, and the experts are working on identifying some of the rusted machines. It might help figure out what sort of a factory it was. If the tide experts can come up with a general idea of where Roy Banks might have been dropped in the river, we should be able to put it all together and pinpoint where the murder took place.'

'That sounds promising,' said Annie. 'Any leads on who might have wanted Roy Banks dead?'

'We've turned up a couple of iffy names from his business correspondence. Oliver Drummond and William Gilmore. Ever heard of them?'

'No,' said Annie.

'Well, they're definitely in our bad books. The first one's been involved in a couple of frauds and we think the second's been running a chop shop. High end. Mostly Jags and Beemers for rich Russians and Arabs. Never managed to track it down, though, and Gilmore always seems to turn out squeaky clean. We've managed to get him on a few minor charges, which is why he's on our books, but nothing big.'

'What about the men in the photograph DCI Banks gave you?'

Brooke paused. 'Gareth Lambert,' he said. 'He's got no form. The other one we don't know.'

'Doesn't it seem important, though? Roy Banks did think it necessary to take and then hide the photo. Maybe blackmail was involved?'

'Give us time, Annie,' Brooke snapped. 'You know damn well how it is with manpower and budgets. And half the bloody team's on holiday right now. We'll get there, eventually.'

'OK, Dave. Hold your horses. I was only trying to be helpful.'

'I'm sorry. I know. Only we're stretched to the limit.'

'I understand. Best of luck, then, and thanks for bringing me up to date. I'll see what's happening up north and probably be back in a day or so. Keep in touch?'

'Absolutely. Oh, by the way, our artist's finished with

Seaton now. The impression doesn't look bad. Want a copy?'

'Thanks. It might be useful.'

'I'll get it faxed to you.'

The traffic slowed to a crawl as the taxi got closer to the chaotic and seemingly endless construction of the Channel Tunnel Rail Link around King's Cross. Annie didn't have a lot of time and worried she might miss her train, but the driver found a gap in the traffic and pulled up at the side with fifteen minutes to spare. Annie paid him, picked up a couple of magazines for the journey at W.H. Smith's then checked the platform number on the board and headed out to the train. The station was bustling with people and it smelled of warm engines, diesel oil and smoke. Annie found her coach and seat, popped her small bag on the rack and sat down to make herself comfortable.

About three minutes before the train was due to set off, a decidedly nervous announcement came over the PA system: 'Would all passengers calmly leave the train and exit the station.'

Everyone sat there for a moment, stunned, wondering if they'd heard correctly. Then it came again, not sounding calm at all: 'Would all passengers calmly leave the train and exit the station.'

That was enough. Everyone grabbed their bags, dashed for the door and ran down the platform to the street.

•

Banks had hoped to be back in London by late morning, early afternoon at the latest, but it wasn't to be. For a start, he slept in. Lying there in his old bed, he hadn't been able to get to sleep for thinking about Roy and worrying about his parents, and only after the light started to grow and the birds started singing did he finally doze off until 9.30. Even then, he was the first one up.

If that had been the only problem, he could probably still have made fairly good time, but after he had made a pot of tea, checked his new mobile was fully charged and walked across the road for a copy of the *Independent*, his mother was up and fussing. Whether the fact of Roy's death had really sunk in yet, he couldn't tell, but she seemed unnaturally calm, alert and in command.

'Your father's having a lie-in,' she said. 'He's tired.'

'That's OK,' said Banks. 'You could have rested a while longer yourself.'

'I rested quite enough yesterday, thank you. Now . . .'

And then she launched into the most extraordinary litany of 'things to do', the upshot of which was that Banks spent a good part of the day driving her around the various relatives who lived close enough to visit, the ones in Ely, Stamford and Huntingdon, at any rate. Many had already phoned the previous evening after hearing about Roy on the news, but Banks had taken care of the telephone – including the reporters – and made sure neither his mother nor his father were disturbed.

Now Ida Banks told each one, calmly, that Roy had died and she didn't know when the funeral would be, but they should be on the lookout for a notice in the paper. Banks's father was up when they got back from the first visit, just sitting in his armchair staring into space. He said he was OK, but Banks worried about him; he seemed to have no energy, no will.

Banks had already seen a piece about the murder in the *Independent*, which referred to Roy as the 'wealthy entrepreneur brother of North Yorkshire policeman Alan Banks, who almost lost his life in a fire earlier this year.' Uncle Frank told him it had been on the television, too, and there had been a picture of Banks and some old footage of his cottage after the fire. Banks was glad he hadn't seen it. God only knew what stories the tabloids were telling. Were they implying a link between the fire and Roy's murder?

By the time he saw his mother settled back at home and fed her another of Dr Grenville's pills, it was mid-afternoon. Mrs Green, a neighbour, came over to sit with them for a while and Banks was finally able to say his goodbyes and set off back to London. Before he left, he rang Burgess, gave him his new mobile number, and arranged to meet in a pub in Soho around five o'clock. It was time to pick up the threads of the investigation again.

Lacking CDs, the best he could do was turn on the car radio. Classic FM was playing Beethoven's 'Moonlight' sonata and Radio Three had Tippett's 'Concerto for Double String Orchestra'. Banks chose the Tippett because he didn't know it as well as he did the Beethoven.

On the A1(M) somewhere around Stevenage, Banks noticed that a red Vectra had been following him for some time. He slowed down; the Vectra slowed. He speeded up; the Vectra kept pace. It was the middle of a warm summer afternoon on a busy road, but still Banks felt the chill of fear. He played cat and mouse with the Vectra for a while longer, then it shot past him. He couldn't get a really good look, but he could tell there were two people in the car, one in the front and one in the back. The one in the back had a ponytail, and when the car was passing Banks's Renault, he turned sideways and smiled, miming a shooting gun with his left hand, thumb signifying the hammer, then he tilted his hand up and blew over the tops of his first two fingers, smiling. It was a split-second vignette, then they were streaking ahead.

Banks tried to keep up with them, but it was no good. The driver was skilful and managed to weave in and out of the lanes of traffic until they had left Banks far behind. Not before he had memorized the number, though.

As he approached Welwyn Garden City, where it started to rain again, Banks wondered what the hell all that had been about. Then he realized with a sudden chill that they must have followed him from Peterborough. *They were letting him know that they knew where his parents lived.*

•

'You again,' said Roger Cropley, when Kev Templeton turned up at his front door again. 'You've got a bloody nerve. What the hell do you want?'

'Just a few more questions,' said Templeton. 'I'm by myself this time. As a matter of fact, I'm very surprised to see you here. I thought you'd be down in London. It was your wife I was planning on talking to.'

'I'm off sick,' said Cropley. 'Summer cold. What do you want to talk to Eileen about?'

'Oh, this and that. But now that you're here, too, let's have a party, shall we?' Templeton edged his way into the hall. Eileen Cropley was standing at the bottom of the stairs. 'Ah, Mrs Cropley. Good afternoon. I don't believe we had a proper chance to get acquainted on my last visit.'

'That's because you were so rude, if I remember correctly. Roger, what does this man want? What have you been up to?'

'I haven't been up to anything. It's all right, dear.' Cropley sighed. 'You'd better come through,' he said.

'Don't mind if I do.'

The living room still smelled of lavender, but the flowers had wilted and shed a few petals. 'I might have been a little hasty last time,' said Templeton, when both Mr and Mrs Cropley had sat down. They sat on the sofa, Templeton noticed, one at each end, like bookends. Mrs Cropley was definitely frosty. Cropley himself seemed resigned. 'I hadn't got all my ducks in a row.'

'You can say that again,' said Cropley.

'But that's water under the bridge, isn't it? No hard feelings?'

Cropley regarded him suspiciously.

'Anyway,' Templeton went on, 'I'm glad I found both of you in. Gives me a chance to make up for bad first impressions. We've talked to the AA, Mr Cropley, and they verify that you were indeed at the time in question stuck on the hard shoulder of the M1 just south of the Derby turn-off.'

'As I told you.'

'Indeed. And I apologize for any . . . disbelief . . . I might have shown at the time. We tend to get quite wrapped up in our search for justice, and sometimes we trample on people's finer feelings.'

'So what do you want this time?'

'Well, we've got a bit more information than we had before, and it looks as if these two men you saw in the dark Mondeo followed Jennifer Clewes – that was the victim's name – off the A1 on the road to Eastvale, where they ran her into a drystone wall and shot her. They then returned to wherever they came from and the following night they dumped the Mondeo in the East End of London, where it was immediately stolen and became involved in a serious accident. Now, we've got some tyre tracks the car made in a private lane in Gratly and some fingerprints that might possibly belong to one of the men. Our forensic scientists are checking the Mondeo for fingerprints to compare, but as you can imagine, after a crash like that, well . . .'

'This is all very interesting,' said Cropley, 'but I still don't see how my wife or I can help.'

'Hear the man out, Roger,' said Mrs Cropley, who seemed interested despite herself.

'Thank you, Mrs Cropley. Anyway, we got a description of the man who dropped off the car in London and a colleague down there faxed me an artist's impression. I was wondering if you'd have a look at it and see if you can identify him.'

'I told you,' said Cropley, 'I didn't get a good look. I'm not very good at describing people.'

'Most of us aren't,' said Templeton. 'That's why looking at a picture helps.' He lifted his briefcase. 'May I?'

'Of course,' said Cropley.

Templeton showed him the sketch.

Cropley stared at it for a while, then he said, 'It could be him.'

'Only could be?'

'As I said, I didn't get a good look.'

'But he did turn to look at you when the driver pulled right in front, didn't he? You told me that.'

'Yes, but it was dark.'

'The petrol station was well lit.'

'I'm still not certain. I mean, I wouldn't want to swear to it in court. Is that what you want?'

'Not yet. We just want to find him.'

'Well, it definitely looks like him. The hair, the general shape of the head, but it was too dark to make out his features.'

'I understand that. Was he well built?'

'He did have rather broad shoulders, now I come to think of it, and not much of a neck. And he seemed tall, high in the seat.'

'Fine,' said Templeton, putting the drawing away. 'Many thanks.'

'You're welcome,' said Cropley. 'But you said you came to talk to my wife. She wouldn't have been able to identify this man as she wasn't with me.'

'Just seizing the opportunity, Mr Cropley. Saved me a trip to London, this has.' Templeton took out his notebook.

'So what did you want to ask *me*?' Mrs Cropley said.

Templeton scratched the side of his nose. 'That's another matter entirely, Mrs Cropley. At least we think it is. On 23rd of April this year, a young woman named Claire Potter was raped and stabbed just off the M1 north of Chesterfield. She was last seen at the Trowell services a short time earlier.'

'You mentioned this the last time you were here,' said Cropley. 'It meant nothing to me then and it means nothing now.'

Templeton ignored him and faced Mrs Cropley. 'We've now got quite a bit more information about that crime,' he said, 'and believe me, whoever did it must have picked up quite a bit of blood. I was just wondering if you had ever noticed anything about your husband's clothing around that time – you know, unusual stains, that sort of thing. Devilishly hard to get rid of, blood. You do the washing around here, don't you?'

'I can't believe you're asking me this,' said Mrs Cropley. 'The sheer nerve of it.'

'Well, I've never been faulted for my lack of nerve,' said Templeton. 'Nothing ventured, nothing gained. That's my motto. So if there's anything you'd like to get off your chest . . .'

'I saw nothing out of the ordinary.'

'Well, the clothes might have been beyond salvation, I suppose,' said Templeton. 'Have any of your husband's clothes gone missing over the past few months?'

'No.'

'Still,' Templeton mused aloud, 'the killer washed the victim's body, so the odds are he managed to deal with his own clothes. Very fastidious, he was. Are you a fastidious man, Mr Cropley?'

'I like to think so,' said Cropley, 'but it doesn't make me a killer, and I resent these accusations.'

'Of course you do. It's only natural. But I have to ask. I'd be a pretty useless detective if I didn't, wouldn't I?'

'Quite frankly I don't care what kind of bloody detective you are,' said Cropley. 'One thing I do know is that you're a very offensive person and I'd appreciate it if you'd leave my house immediately.'

'Just one more question, please, then I'll be out of your hair.'

Eileen Cropley glared at him.

'How often has your husband been unusually late home from work on a Friday? Say after midnight.'

'I don't know.'

'Surely you ought to be able to remember something like that? Don't you wait up for him?'

'No. I usually take a sleeping pill at eleven o'clock and go to bed. I'm fast asleep before midnight.'

'So he usually gets back after eleven then, can we say?'

She looked at her husband. 'I suppose so.'

Templeton turned to Roger Cropley. 'Nearly done now, sir. I remember the last time I was here with DC Jackman that you distinctly told me you usually tried to get away by mid-afternoon to beat the rush-hour traffic.'

'If I could. I didn't always succeed.'

'How often?'

'I don't know. I don't keep track.'

'I think I'd remember,' said Templeton.

'I'm not you.'

'No, you're right about that.' Templeton put his notebook back in his inside pocket. 'Well, I'll be off now. Thanks for your time. No need to see me out. I know the way.'

Templeton walked towards the door, but just before he opened it, he turned to face Cropley again. 'One more thing.' He took out his notebook again, frowned and consulted it. 'The 20th of February. Were you on your way home late that Friday, do you remember? Did you stop at Newport Pagnell?'

'I don't remember.'

'Only a young girl called Paula Chandler was driven off the road and an attempt was made at assaulting her. It failed. Her car doors were locked. There's a chance she might be able to identify her assailant.'

'Am I under arrest?' Cropley said.

'Of course not,' said Templeton, 'I'm only—'

'Then I want you to leave now or I'm calling my solic-itor,' said Cropley, getting to his feet. 'Go on, get out!'

For a moment, Templeton thought Cropley was going to hit him, but he merely grabbed his shoulder and steered him towards the front door. Templeton didn't resist. When the door slammed behind him, he stood for a few moments enjoying the fresh, wet smell of the late afternoon air. It had stopped raining but the sky was still overcast and the streets were glistening. To the west, the low hills were faint grey outlines against a darker grey background. He could hear the sound of flowing water nearby, probably a beck, and a bird was singing in one of the trees. All in all, he thought, it had been a much more successful interview than the previous one.

As he got in his car, Templeton noticed a few flakes of Cropley's dandruff on the sleeve of his jacket and moved to brush it off. Then he had a better idea. If Roger Cropley was their man, he thought, he was damned if DS Susan Browne was going to get *all* the glory.

•

Annie stood in the rain among the massed crowds held back by barricades at the far side of Euston Road. The entire area had been blocked to traffic and all the station exits sealed, the underground shut down. People had swarmed out of the nearby offices, shops and cafes to stand at a safe distance and see what was going on, and their presence only served to swell the crowds. Annie began to feel uncomfortably penned in. Across the road, police in protective clothing moved about like shadows inside the station itself. Obviously the words that were on most people's lips were terrorists, bomb-threat, a fact of life in London. Annie had asked one of the officers on crowd control how long it would be before the trains started running, but he didn't know. Could be a couple of hours, could be longer, was all he would say. Annie saw her trip home quickly slipping away. There was no point going if she didn't get back until evening.

She made her way through the crowds, narrowly avoiding a poke in the eye from one of the many umbrellas raised. She didn't care where she was walking as long as she was getting away from the people. Eventually, when she got off Euston Road and took her bearings, she found herself winding her way via the back streets towards Bloomsbury.

When she got to Russell Square, she remembered the small hotel she and Banks had stayed at a few years ago, when their relationship had been just beginning and seemed full of possibility. She couldn't stay there by herself. It would be far too depressing. She would go back to her faceless, modern, efficient chain hotel; they would be sure to have a room available, perhaps even the same one she had just vacated, though they all looked so much the same that it didn't matter.

If she found herself stuck in London for another night, so be it. She took out her mobile and rang Brooke. He had already faxed the artist's impression up to Eastvale, but said he'd be more than happy to fax it to her hotel right away. Annie then rang the hotel, made a reservation and told them she was expecting a fax. They said they would take care of everything.

In the evening she would go and visit Dr Lukas at her home, but before that, Annie knew she couldn't spend another day and night in London without some new clothes, so she headed for Oxford Street. A bit of retail therapy would help dispel the gloom that seemed to have descended on her with the rain.

•

The pub was on Frith Street and at five o'clock it was already crowded. Burgess was there ahead of Banks, sitting on a wooden stool at a small table in the far corner, and he gestured to Banks, holding up an empty pint glass. Banks bought himself an orange juice and Burgess a pint of lager.

'Not drinking?' Burgess said, when Banks made his way back from the bar.

'Not right at the moment. Tell me,' said Banks, 'why do you always want to meet me in pubs? I don't believe I've ever seen your office. I'm not even entirely convinced that you have one.'

'They'd never let you in. Besides, if they did, they'd probably have to kill you. Best this way. Easier all round.'

'Are you ashamed of me or something?'

Burgess laughed, then turned serious. 'How are you doing?'

'Not bad. It's . . . I don't know. Roy and I weren't close or anything, but it still feels like a piece of me's died.'

'It's family.'

'I suppose so. That's what everyone says. I feel as if I've only just started getting to know him and he's been snatched from me.'

'I had a sister die a few years back,' Burgess said. 'She lived in South Africa. Durban. Hadn't seen her in years, not since we were kids. She was murdered during a robbery. Shot. I felt the same way, though, and I just couldn't stop thinking about her for ages, what it must have been like when she knew she was going to die. Still, it was quick.'

'Roy, too.'

'Nothing like a bullet for that. So what are you up to?'

Banks told him about the men who followed him on the A1(M), the shooting gesture through the window.

'What have you done about it?'

'I almost turned back, but that's probably what they wanted me to do. I called the locals in Peterborough and asked them to keep an eye open. They said they'd post surveillance on the estate.'

'Anything I can do?'

'Can you still run down a number plate?'

'Nothing could be easier.'

Banks gave him the Vectra's number.

'You realize it's probably stolen, don't you?' Burgess said.

'Attention to detail,' said Banks. 'Sometimes they make little mistakes.'

'True enough.'

'Ever heard of the Berger-Lennox Centre?'

'What's that when it's at home?'

'A private family planning centre. They deal with the whole lot. Abortions, adoption, whatever you want.'

'No,' said Burgess, 'I can't say I've heard of them, but then I wouldn't have any need for such a place, would I?'

'I suppose not. But Roy was an investor and Jennifer Clewes worked there, in administration.'

'Sounds interesting, but I still don't know anything about it. What are you going to do next?'

'I want to find out who killed Roy and why.'

'Why doesn't that surprise me? The caped crusader rides again.'

'Aren't you mixing your metaphors?'

'Probably. I don't suppose it's any use telling you to leave it to the locals?'

'No.'

'Thought not. What is it you want from me?'

'You've already told me a bit about Roy's chequered past.'

'The arms thing?'

'Yes.'

'That was years ago. I told you, as far as we know your brother's been clean for the past while. Forget about it.'

'So why is he dead?'

'Some of the nicest people end up dead.' Burgess lit a Tom Thumb cigar and added to the general fug.

'Any idea who the bloke in the photo sitting at a cafe with Lambert is yet?'

'Nope. I'm working on it, though. It's still doing the rounds. Believe me, I want to know as much as you do. Trouble is, this time of year, a lot of blokes are on holiday. And quite a few have retired since back then. Anyway, be patient. Remember it's not the local nick you're dealing with here. I promise you'll be among the first to know.'

'Tell me more about Gareth Lambert.'

'I told you. He was a business associate of your brother's and an all-round nasty piece of work. Charming enough on the surface. Like I said, Harry Lime. I take it you have seen *The Third Man*?'

'It's one of my favourite films. Look, according to Julian Harwood, Lambert's been living in Spain.'

'My, my, you have been a busy boy, haven't you?'

'Why come back?'

'I suppose he got bored with paella. He also got married to some beautiful Spanish actress. Centrefold material. England's quite sexy these days, or didn't you know? Madonna, Gwyneth Paltrow, Liv Tyler and all the rest. They all want to live here. Anyway, he's back, and apparently he's in the travel business.'

'Legit?'

'I didn't say that. But there's no evidence to the contrary. Like I said, Lambert's elusive. He's got no form, never once been arrested. Not in this country, at any rate. Not yet. Always manages to keep one step ahead. Sure you won't have a real drink?'

'No, thanks. I need to keep my head clear.'

'For what?'

'For Roy.'

'OK.' Burgess went up to the bar and bought himself another pint. Banks noticed that the pub was filling up even more with the after-work crowd. There had been a blackboard outside advertising hand-pulled 'real' ale, so perhaps that was what brought them in. Most of the newcomers had to stand and the crush at the bar was getting to be three deep. Some people took advantage of the break in the rain and stood outside drinking, but from what Banks could see through the open door, the sky was darkening again and they'd all be dashing back inside soon.

Burgess came back and squeezed through the bodies to his stool without spilling a drop. 'Are there any other leads on Roy's murder?' he asked.

'I don't know,' said Banks. 'I'll have a word with Annie Cabbot later and see if I find out what's going on with DI Brooke's investigation.'

'Still shagging the lovely DI Cabbot, are you, or have you moved on to pastures new?'

Banks ignored him. Burgess was always looking for buttons to push. Usually he succeeded, but not this time. 'Tell me,' Banks said, 'honestly, do you think Roy could have got involved in something crooked with Lambert again?'

'Anything's possible. But what I'm telling you is that I, we, have no knowledge of it. If they were into something together, it's a smooth operation. You're dealing with pros here. At least, Lambert's a pro.'

'And you'd know if there was something?'

'Maybe. If it was big enough and nasty enough. We spend a lot of time just watching and thinking, but we're not omniscient. We don't know everything, just most things. Besides, it's not my brief any more. And Lambert hasn't been back here very long. Only a couple of months if my sources are right, which they usually are. So if there is anything, it's either new or it's something international and he was working it from Spain, too. Let me ask around. I've still got a few contacts. There's a bloke from Interpol, Dieter Ganz, I know is interested, if I can get in touch with him. I'll see what I can do.'

'I want to know where Lambert lives.'

'I was wondering when you'd get around to asking me that.'

'I'd have got around to it a lot sooner if I hadn't had my parents to cope with. Are you going to tell me?'

'Can't see why not.' Burgess gave him an address in Chelsea. 'You'd only find out some other way. He's got a place out in the country somewhere, too, where he keeps 'her indoors', but this flat's his pied-à-terre when he's in town. He still travels a fair bit. And he runs his business

out of an office above a dry-cleaning shop on the
Edgware Road, the Marble Arch end. But watch him,
Banks. He's slippery. Remember Harry Lime.'

Banks finished his orange juice. 'Tell me something,'
he said. 'You always put up a show of resistance, but in
the end you usually tell me what I want to know. Why?'

'Entertainment value,' said Burgess. 'Besides, I like
you. I like to watch you work. It interests me. I see you
getting more and more like I used to be. You want something, you go after it, and bugger the consequences.
Bugger the law, if necessary.'

'Used to be?'

Burgess sipped some beer. 'I've mellowed, Banksy.
Grown up.'

'Bollocks.'

'It's true. Anyway, let's just say that DI Brooke's interests and mine don't always coincide. Brooke's a plodder.
I know the type. No imagination. No breadth of vision.
He's only interested in short-term results, another tick on
his report card for his next promotion.'

'And you?'

'I'm more interested in the big picture, the long-term
view. And I like to know what's going on. Information's
my stock in trade these days, after all. I don't get out on
the street much.'

'Miss it?'

Burgess looked away. 'Sometimes.' He laughed and
raised his glass. 'Now bugger off. And good luck with
Lambert.'

It had started raining again and Banks had to fight
against the influx of people trying to get back inside. He
found a sheltered doorway and dialled Annie's number
on his mobile. She answered on the fourth ring.

'Annie, it's me, Alan.'

'Where are you? I've been wanting to speak to you ever since I heard. I'm really sorry about what happened to your brother.'

'Thanks, I appreciate it. I'm back in London. Where are you?'

'As a matter of fact,' Annie said, 'I'm in Liberty's at the moment, in one of the changing rooms. You might not have heard, but they've closed King's Cross. Bomb threat. Anyway, it means I'm stuck here for another night. I need something to wear. I'm just about to head back to the hotel. Look, Alan, we have to talk again.'

'I know, but it'll have to wait. Couple of quick questions. Have Brooke's blokes talked to Gareth Lambert yet?'

'I don't think so,' said Annie. 'Last time I talked to him Dave didn't seem all that interested. They're concentrating on a couple of local low-lifes called Oliver Drummond and William Gilmore. Their names came up in your brother's business correspondence and phone records.' Banks remembered the names, but they didn't mean anything to him.

Then Annie told him about her visit to Alf Seaton's that morning, the description of the man with the pony tail and what had become of the Mondeo. Banks knew immediately that it was one of the men who had followed him from Peterborough, the one who had made the gesture.

'Another thing you might as well know,' Annie said. 'It looks as if your brother's girlfriend had an abortion, arranged through the Berger-Lennox Centre. That's when he met Jennifer Clewes.'

'Jesus,' said Banks. 'That'll be Corinne you're talking about?'

'Are there any others?'

'Probably,' said Banks, 'but I think she was the most recent model, the one before Jennifer. Thanks for telling me.'

'Can we meet up? We really should talk about all this.'

'Maybe tomorrow,' said Banks. 'Breakfast? I've still got a couple of people to talk to tonight. How about I give you a bell when I'm finished?' He rang off before she could protest.

The rain was really pelting down now and all Banks had for protection was his light raincoat. He stood in the doorway looking at the people drifting back and forth between the curtains of rain then stepped out and headed as fast as he could for Tottenham Court Road tube station.

13

'How did you get my address?' Dr Alex Lukas asked Annie as she stood under her umbrella on the front step of the Belsize Park house shortly after seven o'clock that evening. 'I'm not in the telephone directory.'

'We have our sources,' said Annie, who had taken a peek at the personnel records when she made a quick, and otherwise fruitless, search of Jennifer Clewes's office at the Berger-Lennox. 'Can I come in?'

'What do you want? It's not a police state yet, is it?'

'Not the last time I checked,' said Annie with a smile. 'But it is raining fast.'

Dr Lukas took the chain off the door and stepped back. Annie folded up her umbrella, took off her raincoat and hung it on the coat stand. She followed Dr Lukas down the thick carpet into a cosy and comfortable living room. The curtains were still open and rain streaked the windowpanes. The radio was playing quietly, an orchestral concert of some sort. Dr Lukas excused herself for a moment and went upstairs. While she waited, Annie looked around the room.

What looked to her like original works of art hung on the wall, mostly abstract expressionist and cubist pieces, and various knick-knacks and framed photographs stood on most available surfaces. The crowded dark-wood bookcase boasted a colourful array of spines, none of them medical. There were novels, mostly Tolstoy and

Dostoevsky, poetry by Mandelstam, Akhnatova, Yevtushenko, Tsvetayeva, and a few biographies, Shostakovich, Gorbachev, Pasternak. Annie could see by the lettering that some of the books were in Russian. Taking into account the matryoshka doll on the mantelpiece, and remembering the hint of an accent, it didn't take much to surmise that Dr Lukas hailed from Russia, or somewhere in the former Soviet republics.

Beside the doll stood a black-and-white photograph of a family group in a wooded area: parents and three children. Annie walked over to have a closer look at it. They were all wearing overcoats and no one was smiling; they had that hard, pinched look you get when there isn't enough food on the table or coal on the fire. Beside it stood another photo of what Annie took to be the parents, more recent and in colour. This time they were smiling into the camera, standing beside a large lake in the sunshine.

'On holiday,' said Dr Lukas, behind her.

'I'm sorry, I didn't mean to be nosy,' said Annie. 'Is that your parents?'

'Yes. It was taken two years ago.'

'So you come from Russia?'

'Ukraine. A city called L'viv, in the west, not far from the Polish border. Do you know it?'

'Sorry,' said Annie, whose geography was terrible.

'It doesn't matter.'

'Do they still live there?'

Dr Lukas paused before answering with a tentative 'Yes.'

'How long have you been here?'

'Thirteen years. I was twenty-five when the Soviet Union broke up. I was lucky. I got into medical school in

Edinburgh. I'd had some training in L'viv, of course, but this country didn't recognize my qualifications. Do you know how many foreign-trained doctors there are over here driving minicabs and working in restaurants and hotels?'

'No,' said Annie.

'It's a shame, a terrible waste,' said Dr Lukas, with a hint of tragic fatalism in her voice.

'You don't have a very strong accent,' Annie said.

'I worked hard to get rid of it. Foreign accents don't work in your favour here. But all this is beside the point. What have you come to see me about?'

Dr Lukas was perching uncomfortably at the edge of an armchair, Annie noticed, body hunched forward and tense, hands clasped in her lap. She was wearing faded jeans and a man's white casual shirt, no make-up. She looked tired and drawn, as she had in her office.

'You're right,' said Annie. 'It's not a social call.' She paused and searched for the right way to begin. 'Look, in a murder investigation, people sometimes hide things, mask the truth. Not because they're guilty, but because they've maybe committed some minor crime and they're afraid we'll uncover it and prosecute them. Do you understand?'

'I'm listening.'

'When that happens, it makes a difficult job even harder. We don't know what's important and what isn't, so how can we know where to focus our line of enquiry?'

'All jobs have their difficulties,' said Dr Lukas. 'Mine included. I don't see what point there is in you telling me how hard yours is.'

'I thought if you understood, then you'd see reason and tell me the truth.'

'Pardon?'

'I think you heard me.'

'But I'm not sure I heard you correctly. Are you suggesting I lied?'

'I'm saying that you might be hiding something because you think it reflects badly on you. I don't think you're lying so much as you're obscuring the truth. Now it may or may not be important, or it may not seem important to you, but I'd like to know what it is, and I think you'd like to tell me.'

'What makes you think that?'

'You get to know people in this job. I think you're a decent person and I think you're under a tremendous amount of pressure. Now that could simply be a matter of your work, or it could be due to personal problems which are nothing at all to do with this investigation. But the feeling I get is that there's something else, and that it is connected.'

'I see.' Dr Lukas stood up and walked to the cocktail cabinet. 'I think I need a drink,' she said, and took out a tumbler and a bottle of Southern Comfort. 'What about you?'

'Nothing, thanks,' said Annie.

'As you wish.' She poured herself a large measure and sat down again. This time she seemed to relax a little more into the armchair and the strain that etched the lines on her forehead and around her eyes and mouth seemed to ease. The concert ended and Annie heard the radio audience applaud before the announcer's voice cut in. Dr Lukas switched it off, took a sip of Southern Comfort and regarded Annie closely with her serious brown eyes. Annie got the sense that she was trying to come to some sort of decision and realized that she might well end up with a partial truth, if anything, as was so often the case.

The clock ticked and rain tapped against the window. Still Dr Lukas thought and sipped. Finally, when Annie could almost bear it no longer, she said, 'You're right.'

'About what?'

'About people withholding the truth. Do you think it doesn't happen in my profession, too? People lie to me all the time. How much they drink. Whether they smoke. What drugs they take. How often they exercise. As if by lying they'd make themselves healthy. But I haven't done anything wrong.'

'Sometimes people use a different standard to measure themselves by,' said Annie. 'You might not think you have done anything morally or ethically wrong, but you might have broken the law. Or vice versa.'

Dr Lukas managed a flicker of a smile. 'A fine distinction.'

'I'm not after getting you struck off.'

'I'm happy to hear it.'

'But I do want the truth. What are late girls?'

Dr Lukas sipped some more Southern Comfort before answering, then she ran a finger around the rim of her glass. 'It's really very simple,' she said. 'They are girls who come late to the centre.'

'In what sense? Late in their pregnancies?'

'No. There you are quite wrong.'

'Well, I've hardly been steered in the right direction. This isn't supposed to be a guessing game.'

'Now I am telling you. There have been no surgical procedures performed on girls beyond the twenty-four-week legal limit.'

'OK,' said Annie, 'so what *is* it all about?'

'Girls who come late to the centre, after regular hours. In the evening.'

'When you're working late?'

'I have a lot of paperwork. You wouldn't believe it, even a doctor . . . but I do.'

'So why do these girls come after hours?'

'Why do you think?'

'They want to bypass the system for some reason, and you help them to do it?'

'These girls are prostitutes, for the most part, and many of them are illegal immigrants or asylum-seekers. They can't go through the National Health and they can't afford our fees.'

'Pro bono work, then?'

'You could say that.'

'What exactly do you do for them?'

'I handle the forms, the papers necessary to secure an abortion, if that's what they want. If another doctor's signature is needed I get that too from someone at one of the clinics. They don't ask me too many questions. It's very easy and it harms no one.'

'Do you perform the abortions?'

'No, they are done elsewhere, at one of the clinics.'

'What do you do, then?'

'I examine them, make sure they are in good general health. There are sexually transmitted infections to worry about. And Aids, of course. Some girls have drug and alcohol problems. Many of the foetuses would be born with severe handicaps, if they lived.'

'Do you supply drugs?'

Dr Lukas looked directly at Annie. 'No,' she said. 'I understand why they might want to take drugs, the life they are living, but I won't supply them. They seem to have no problem getting drugs elsewhere, though.'

'So if we were to check the drugs at the centre against records, they would match?'

'If they don't, it's not me who's been taking them. But, yes, I think they would. Besides, we have no need for the kind of drugs you're talking about at the centre.'

'How often does this happen?'

'Not very often. Maybe once, sometimes twice a month.'

'Why do these girls come to you? How do they know about you?'

'Many of them are from Eastern Europe,' Dr Lukas said, with a shrug. 'I'm known in the community.'

That sounded a bit vague, Annie thought – Eastern Europe covered a large area – but she let it go. Now Dr Lukas was on a roll it was better to get as much as possible out of her than labour one point. 'What about Jennifer Clewes? Did she know about this?'

'Yes.'

'When did she find out?'

'She's known for a month or two. I didn't realize she worked late sometimes, too. I thought I was alone there. You've seen how isolated my office is. The girls usually buzz the front door and I let them in myself. This time Jennifer got there first. She didn't say anything but later she asked me what was going on.'

'What did you tell her?'

'What I'm telling you.'

'And what was her reaction?'

'She became interested.' Dr Lukas swirled the remains of her drink in her glass. 'Jennifer was a truly decent human being,' she said. 'When I explained to her about

the girls and the situation they were in, nowhere to turn
to for help, she understood.'

'It didn't disturb her, upset her?'

'No. She was a bit uncomfortable about it at first,
but . . .'

'But what?'

'Well, she was the administrator. She helped to protect
me. Paperwork got lost, that sort of thing. I told her it
would be best if she didn't tell anyone, that not everyone
would understand.'

'We think she must have told her boyfriend.'

Dr Lukas shrugged. 'That was for her judgement
alone.'

'So Jennifer became involved in it with you?'

'We were both trying to help unfortunate girls. It's not
that this happened often, you understand. It wasn't a
regular thing. These girls would not have been able to
come if they'd had to pay. And remember, they couldn't
just walk into the nearest NHS clinic. What do you think
would happen to them? Do you think there are no longer
back-street abortionists using rusty coat hangers?'

'So what went wrong?'

'Nothing went wrong.'

'Jennifer Clewes is dead.'

'I know nothing about that. I've told you what I was
keeping from you, who the late girls are and how and
why I helped them. I've told you Jennifer's part in all
this. There is nothing more. Once in a while a girl who
needed help would come to me and I provided it. That's
all there is to it.'

'Did anyone else know? Georgina, for example?'

'No. At first it was only me, then Jennifer. She was the
only other person who ever stayed late.'

Somehow it didn't all add up, Annie thought. There were too many pieces missing and the ones she had didn't fit together properly. 'What about Carmen Petri? Was she one of the late girls? What was so special about her?'

Dr Lukas seemed to tense up again, the lines on her forehead deepening, her posture stiffening. 'I don't know the name.'

'She was one of the late girls, wasn't she? What happened to her?'

'I told you I've never heard of her.'

'Did something go wrong? Is that it?'

'I've told you, I don't know anyone called Carmen.'

Annie took out the sketch that Brooke's police artist had coaxed from Alf Seaton. 'Do you recognize this man?' she asked.

'No,' said Dr Lukas. Annie couldn't be certain that she was telling the truth.

'About a week ago, Jennifer was seen leaving this building with a young girl. The person who saw them said that the girl looked pregnant. They were talking, then a man who looked very much like this one came over and the girl went away with him in a car. Do you know what that was about?'

Annie could have sworn that Dr Lukas turned a shade paler. 'No,' she said. 'I told you, Jennifer sometimes worked late, too, saw the girls. Sometimes she talked to them. She was a very caring person and it's a tragedy what happened to her.'

'It is,' said Annie, standing up to leave. 'And I'm going to find out what was behind it, with or without your help.'

'Please, you don't know . . .'

'Don't know what?'

Dr Lukas paused, rubbing her hands together. 'Please. I'm telling you the truth.'

'I think you're telling me part of the truth,' Annie said, 'and I'm going to leave you to think over your position. When you've made your mind up you can call me at this number.' Annie scribbled her mobile number on the back of her card and left it on the coffee table. 'I'll show myself out.'

Well, you can't win them all, Banks thought, after a wasted trip to Chelsea. One of the problems with paying surprise visits was that sometimes the object of your visit wasn't at home, and such was the case with Gareth Lambert that wet Tuesday evening, though Banks had even hung around in a shop doorway over the street for about an hour, waiting. Burgess had said that Lambert was elusive.

The humidity and damp clothing made the crowded underground carriage smell like a wet dog, and Banks was glad to get off at Green Park for the Piccadilly Line. The second carriage was half empty and he passed the short trip reading the adverts and trying to work out the language of the newspaper that the person opposite him was reading. The letters were Roman, but it definitely wasn't anything he recognized. Sometimes the depths of his own ignorance appalled him.

When he got to Corinne's flat he was soaked and she gave him a towel for his hair and made him take off his raincoat and his jacket and hung them up in the bathroom under an electric fire to dry them out. His trousers were stuck to his thighs and shins and he thought of asking her to dry those, too, but she might get the wrong idea. Besides, what would he wear? It would be rather undignified carrying out an interview, albeit a friendly one, sitting around in his underpants.

'Warm drink?'

'Tea, if you've got any. No milk or sugar for me.'

'I think I can manage that.'

Despite, or perhaps because of, the rain, it was a close, muggy evening. Sweat filmed Corinne's upper lip and forehead, and she looked as if she hadn't been sleeping well. Her hair was tangled and her eyes had dark circles under them. So Roy had the power to make a woman feel this way, no matter what he'd done to her. What the hell was it about him? Sandra wouldn't give Banks the time of day, and even Annie couldn't get away quick enough if he talked about anything other than the case at hand. He thought of Penny Cartwright again and her revulsion at the idea of dinner with him. She would probably have jumped at the chance if Roy had asked her.

'I'm sorry I haven't been able to get here before,' Banks said, when he had a cup of tea in his hand. 'You can guess what it's been like.'

'Have you seen your parents? How are they? Your mother was very nice to me. Not that your father wasn't . . . but you know what I mean.'

Banks remembered that last October, much to his surprise, his mother had taken Corinne into the kitchen to help her prepare the anniversary spread and in no time they had been chatting away to one another like old friends.

Thinking of his parents, he also remembered the message that the thug in the red Vectra had given him. *We know where your parents live.* How did they know? From Roy? When it came right down to it, though, it wasn't that difficult to find out such things. Most likely they had followed Banks to Peterborough the day before and he hadn't spotted them. He would ring his father before it got too late and make sure everything was all right there. He would also ring the Peterborough police again to make sure they had someone watching the house at all times. If this man with the ponytail had killed Jennifer Clewes, as Annie seemed to think he had, then he and his friends didn't make idle threats. Banks wished he could arrange for his parents to go away for a while, but they would never agree to it. Not at a time like this.

'They're coping,' he said finally. 'My mother took it rather hard, as you can imagine. Dad's trying to be a rock but the strain's beginning to show.'

'I hope they get through it. Do you think I should give them a ring?'

'It wouldn't do any harm,' Banks said. 'Maybe in a couple of days.' He sipped his tea – a pleasant, scented Earl Grey – then leaned forward and set the cup and saucer down on the low table. 'Look, Corinne, this probably isn't anything to do with what happened to Roy but in a murder investigation you have to follow up all the loose ends.'

'I understand.'

'A couple of months ago, you went with Roy to the Berger–Lennox Centre.'

Corinne looked away. 'That's right. It was a private matter.'

'I'm not here to judge you, either of you. Whose idea was it?'

'Was what?'

'To go to the Berger-Lennox.'

'Oh, Roy's. He'd invested in it. He'd also visited the centre before, checked it out. He said it was a good place.'

So Roy had probably already met, or at least seen, Jennifer Clewes. 'And was it?'

'They treated me well enough.'

'The woman on reception thought you were Roy's daughter.'

'Well, I used my own name. I wasn't trying to pretend or anything.'

'There's plenty of reasons these days for a girl having a different name from her father.'

'I suppose so.'

'So you went through with the procedure?'

Now she looked directly at him. 'Yes. I had an abortion. OK?'

'I assume you're sure it was Roy's baby?'

'Yes, of course. What do you think I am?'

'Why didn't you want to keep it?'

'I . . . I didn't feel ready.'

'What about Roy?'

'He'd already made it clear he wasn't interested. He wasn't much interested in me, either. He thinks I didn't see him chatting up that redhead in the reception area, but I did.'

'Jennifer Clewes?'

Corinne put her hand to her mouth. 'Oh, my God. Is that who it was? The girl who got shot? I've read about her in the papers. What happened?'

'That's where he met her, perhaps even before the visit with you. Perhaps you can see now why I'm asking all these questions. There are too many connections and similarities here, but I'm missing something.'

'I don't think I can help you. I mean, I saw him talking to her, but he's always like that, flirting with girls. And I knew there was someone. I just didn't put two and two together. Story of my life.'

'No reason why you should, or could. So you and Roy were splitting up when you found out you were pregnant?'

'It happened at the worst possible time.' She gave a harsh laugh. 'Like these things always do.'

'And you discussed it and both agreed abortion was the way to go?'

'Yes. Look, it's nothing to do with what happened. It can't be. It was a private matter. You're not trying to say I killed him because I had an abortion and he found a new girlfriend, are you?'

'Of course not,' said Banks, though the thought had crossed his mind. Rejection and jealousy, coupled with the emotional trauma of abortion, could be a lethal mix. She hadn't done it herself, Banks knew, but maybe she had enough money to hire someone, and maybe she even knew how to find someone to hire. After all, she was an accountant to the entertainment world, and that was full of villains, or celebrities who liked to rub shoulders with them. But Banks had dismissed the idea as quickly as it had come into his head. Wronged lovers usually go for a more direct method, as any cop who has responded to a domestic will tell you.

'Roy was chatting up his new girlfriend while you were in the doctor's office,' Banks said. 'How does that make you feel?'

Tears brimmed in her eyes. 'How do you think it

makes me feel?' she said. 'He always was a bastard. I knew that. But I loved him.'

And this time there was no stopping her. The dam burst and the flood was unloosed. Banks went over and sat beside her on the sofa, putting his arms around her. She didn't resist. She just melted against him, buried her head in his already wet shoulder and let it all pour out. Banks held her and stroked her hair. After a few minutes the tears subsided and she gently extricated herself. Banks went back to the armchair and picked up his tea. It was lukewarm now but it was something to hide behind in the awkward moments that follow an emotional outburst. The cup rattled against the saucer as he picked it up.

Corinne went and fetched some tissues. 'I'm sorry about that,' she said. 'It's the first time . . . I was just bottling it all up. It feels better.'

'I'm glad,' said Banks, 'and I'm sorry if I sounded abrupt or rude.'

'It must be very frustrating for you,' Corinne said. 'And I know you and Roy weren't very close, but you must . . . I mean, he was your brother, after all.'

'This might sound an odd question,' said Banks, 'but did Roy ever tell you he'd witnessed the attacks on the World Trade Center?'

'Yes,' said Corinne. 'I didn't know him back then, of course, but he told me it devastated him. He had nightmares for months. I could only imagine what it must have been like.'

'Did he ever talk to you about religion, about spiritual matters?'

'Not really, no. I mean, I knew he went to church on

Sundays, and he said he liked his local vicar, but it didn't really interfere with our life.'

'You're not interested in spiritual matters yourself?'

'Spiritual matters, as far as I can understand them, yes. But not in organized religion. Look at the misery and bloodshed it's caused throughout history. Still causes.'

'Did the two of you ever argue about this?'

'Yes, but we always reached an impasse, the way you do when you talk about such things. He said that was just an excuse and that it was mankind who caused the bloodshed and misery, and I said his must be a pretty rotten God if he was so all-powerful and he let it all happen anyway. We learned to stay away from the subject in the end. I mean, where do you go from there?'

Where, indeed? wondered Banks, who had been involved in one or two similar arguments himself over the years.

'He didn't push religion on me, or on anyone else for that matter, if that's what you're getting at. And he obviously didn't use it to try to talk me out of having an abortion.'

'I just wondered how big a role it played in his life, that's all.'

'Like I said, he went to church on Sunday and had a philosophical chat with the vicar every now and then.'

'OK. Fair enough. Did he ever mention someone called Gareth Lambert, an old friend?'

'Yes, I remember him mentioning the name.'

'Did you ever meet him?'

She pulled out a tissue and blew her nose. It looked raw when she'd finished. 'No,' she said. 'But I heard his name.'

'Do you remember the context?'

'Roy was just talking about an old friend of his who was back in the country. They hadn't seen each other in a long time.'

'When was this?'

'A couple of months ago. Around the time of the abortion. He said he was going to meet him for a drink at some club or other they belonged to on the Strand, talk about old times and see if there were any business opportunities. He was always on the lookout for a new angle. I'm afraid I suspected something else. I asked him who he was going out with and that's what he told me. I didn't believe him, though.'

'Did Roy go for that drink?'

'Yes.'

'Do you remember the name of the club?'

'Sorry, no.'

'Well, if it's any consolation, he was probably telling the truth. Did he say anything about it afterwards?'

'No, not really. He was vague, as usual, and a little tipsy. He just said that he'd had an interesting time. He seemed excited about more business possibilities.'

'Did he say what?'

'No, he was very vague.'

Something dodgy, then, Banks thought. Not arms, in all likelihood, but something crooked if Lambert was involved. He had nothing more to ask Corinne but thought he would stay for a while, anyway, just to keep her company, talk about Roy. It was after nine o'clock; it had been a long day and he was feeling pleasantly tired. He could ring Annie and ask her to meet him in the morning, if that was OK with her.

As if she was reading his mind, Corinne said, 'Look, I've got a nice bottle of white wine in the fridge. I've got red, if you want it, too. I don't want to drink by myself. I don't want to be alone just now. Would you care to keep me company for a while longer? I mean, if there isn't anywhere you have to go. Where are you staying?'

Banks realized that he had completely forgotten about finding somewhere to stay. He had driven to London without making any arrangements and the incident on the motorway had pushed all such practical thoughts from his mind. There was always Roy's – he still had a key – but there was a chance the police weren't finished there yet.

'Don't know,' he said. 'I thought I'd just check into a hotel.'

She looked away and reddened a little. 'You can stay here if you like. I mean, there's a spare room, all made up and everything.'

The idea made Banks nervous. He knew the offer was entirely innocent. The poor girl was alone and devastated by the murder of her lover, and Banks would no more think of letting anything sexual happen than he would with his own sister, if he had one. Then again, she was a very attractive young woman and he was just a man, after all. What if she cried out in the night? What if Banks went to comfort her and she was naked under the sheet? What would they do then?

What really made up his mind, though, was that right at the moment he was so weary he could hardly lift himself out of the armchair, let alone hit the wet streets looking for a cheap hotel, so he said, 'Thanks, that's very good of you. That'll be great. And I prefer red, if that's OK?'

14

Annie woke early on Wednesday morning, and when she opened her curtains she was happy to see that the sun was shining again and the sky was robin's egg blue. She managed twenty minutes of meditation and a short yoga session – ten salutes to the sun, cobra, locust and peacock – then she dressed in her new white cotton slacks, red short-sleeved top and light denim jacket and went down to the restaurant for breakfast with Banks, her wavy brown hair still damp from the shower.

The meditation and yoga hadn't made her feel as calm as she had hoped, and she felt anxious and tense about meeting Banks again, especially after the way he had phoned and so casually put her off late the previous evening. Their last meeting had gone well enough, but nothing had been resolved and Annie still felt as if she was bursting with questions and insecurities.

The stories in the morning paper upset her, too, brought back too many bad memories. Because the reporter was trying to link Banks's fire with his brother's murder, they had also raked up all the stuff about Phil Keane and his hapless policewoman girlfriend. Where they had got it all from in the first place, she didn't know, but there's always a leak somewhere.

Banks didn't look in too bad shape, she thought, when she saw him already sitting at a cloth-covered table drinking coffee. In fact, he looked a lot more like his old self than he had in ages. All he really needed now was a decent haircut and a few more good nights' sleep to get rid of the bags under his eyes. And maybe some fresh clothes. The pallor had all but gone, and there was a certain edginess back in his body language instead of that infuriating languor. There was also a brightness in his dark-blue eyes that she hadn't seen in a long time. Perhaps, she thought, his brother's death had made him realize how lucky *he* was. Or more likely it had just given him something he cared about, a sense of purpose. For there was no denying that he was on the case, officially or not.

She sat down opposite him and noticed that he smelled just a little of original Old Spice. It was a smell she liked, something she remembered from their intimate time together. It had taken her a while to throw out the deodorant stick he had left in her bathroom cabinet, but she had done so eventually, along with the razor, shaving cream and toothbrush.

'So what were you up to last night that you couldn't meet up with me then?' Annie asked.

'Social duties,' said Banks.

'Pull the other one.'

'I went to see Corinne,' he said.

'How is she?'

'She's suffering plenty,' said Banks. 'I don't know about you,' he went on, 'but whenever I'm having breakfast in a hotel, it has to be the bacon and eggs. Don't know why. I'd never have that at home.'

'It's because you don't have to cook it yourself and wash the dishes after,' said Annie.

'And because I never have time to sit around and eat it.'

'How are things going?'

'Not so bad, considering,' said Banks. 'My dad's just worn down by the whole thing but my mother's acting strange.'

'Strange how?'

'As if it's just another family event, like the anniversary party. She's already talking about sandwiches for the funeral tea.'

'Might not be a bad idea,' said Annie. 'The post-mortem's over. Given cause of death I shouldn't imagine they'll be holding on to the body for too long. I'm really sorry about your brother, Alan. I know Dave Brooke will do his best. He's a good copper.'

A waitress came over. Banks ordered the full English, and Annie decided on a cheese and mushroom omelette. She felt a twinge of guilt – her first morning she'd had only a Continental, and the next day muesli – but if you didn't treat yourself once in a while what was the point?

'Anyway,' Banks asked, 'how are things progressing up north?'

Annie ran her hand over her hair. 'I've only been in touch over the phone but they seem to be moving along nicely. Mostly it's forensics on the tyre tracks and finger-prints we found at your cottage and on the door of Jennifer's car. We've also got people asking around, you know, did anyone see anything, that sort of thing. But we don't expect much to come from that. It was late and in a remote place. Anyway, Winsome's on the case, and I know I can trust her.'

'What about Templeton and Rickerd?'

'They're on it, too. You know as well as I do Rickerd's a born office manager. And Kev might be a bit of an arse-hole, but he's got good instincts. He's off on a tangent, but it's not a bad idea to give him some space. Anyway, it's in good hands. I'm hoping to get back up there today, if only for a flying visit to bring everything up to speed. The telephone has its limitations.'

'Indeed it does.'

'What about you?' Annie asked. 'What have you been up to?'

'Me? Apart from keeping my parents company, and Corinne, nothing much, really,' said Banks. 'I doubt that I've discovered anything you'd be interested in hearing.'

'Try me. What is it you usually say to witnesses or suspects? "Let me be the judge of that"?'

'Touché,' said Banks. 'OK. I've found out that Gareth Lambert is back from self-imposed exile in Spain and that one evening a few weeks ago he had drinks with Roy. That mean anything to you?'

'No.'

'They're old pals, known one another for years. No doubt they were mixed up in all sorts of criminal enterprises before the arms deal put the wind up them. Up Roy, at least. Lambert we're not so sure about. Anyway, it's a bit too much of a coincidence for my liking, the two reunited and one of them dead.'

'I suppose you got all this from Burgess, didn't you? That man's a walking disaster area.'

'Dirty Dick has his good points, but I don't know why you should think I got any of it from him.'

'I can't imagine where else, that's all.'

The waitress delivered their breakfasts. Banks asked for more coffee, Annie for tea.

'Anyway,' Banks said, when the waitress had gone, 'DI Brooke's got everything I found: the mobile, the CD and

USB drive, even the digital photos I'd printed from the CD. Everything.'

Annie's eyes narrowed. 'But you kept copies.'

'It's not illegal. I didn't withhold or tamper with anything.'

'Damn it, Alan, you broke into a murder victim's house, you went through his stuff, you used his mobile phone, you found and copied personal information. Don't tell me you haven't tampered.'

Banks rested his knife and fork at the sides of his plate. 'In the first place, I didn't know he was a murder victim at the time. He was simply missing and had been gone for less than twenty-four hours. What would we have done if a call like that had come in? If he'd been a child or a teenager, then perhaps we might just have set the wheels in motion. But a healthy man in his late forties? Come on, Annie, you know as well as I do what would happen. Nothing. And he was my brother. Family. I think that gave me a right to enter his home. What is it that really upsets you?'

'It's that you keep going off all on your own like some kind of maverick,' Annie said. 'You don't tell anyone what's going on. You think you're the only one who can work it all out. You think you can handle everything by yourself. But you don't know everything. You can't do it all yourself. For God's sake, Alan, you nearly got yourself killed.'

When one of the nearby diners looked over, Annie realized she'd let her voice get too loud. The thing was, it had come out spontaneously. She hadn't known what she was going to say when Banks asked her what her problem was because she hadn't really known. Perhaps the stories in the newspaper had stirred it all up, but now she did know. It went back to Phil Keane and the way Banks had suspected him but said nothing, gone and tried to build his own case against Phil on the quiet.

When she thought about it, though, she realized that it went even further back than the Phil Keane case. Banks had been just the same when he went off looking for Chief Constable Riddle's wayward daughter, Emily, and he'd held back so much information from Annie during that case that her hands had been tied. At one point she had even suspected him of being sexually involved with the girl's mother, if not the girl herself. That was what happened when you held things back; the truth got warped and twisted in people's minds. Lacking the facts, they made up stories based on fancy, like stories in the tabloids.

Now she'd said it, though, she felt embarrassed, and she sneaked a look at Banks as she took a bite of her omelette. He seemed to be eating his breakfast again quite placidly. The waitress came with more coffee and tea. Annie thanked her.

'Listen to us,' said Banks, 'bickering over breakfast like an old married couple.'

'We're not bickering,' said Annie. 'It takes two to bicker. Aren't you going to respond?'

'What can I say? I'm glad you got it off your chest.'

'Simple as that, is it?'

Banks looked at her directly, his eyes clear and bright. 'It's a start. If we're going to go on working together, we have to get one or two things sorted.'

'On whose terms?'

'That's not the point. I'm not going to change my ways. Nor are you.'

'Then maybe we *shouldn't* go on working together.'

'Up to you.'

'Not entirely. What do *you* want?'

'I want to carry on working with you. Believe it or not, I like you, and I think you're damn good at your job.'

Annie felt absurdly pleased at the compliment, but she hoped it didn't show in her face. 'But you're still going to leave me in the dark half the time?'

'I don't deliberately hide things from you. If I had told you all my suspicions about Phil Keane as soon as I had them – and God knows I tried to hint – you'd have thrown me out on my ear, accused me of being jealous – which you did anyway – and never talked to me again. All I had to go on was a feeling, at first, some sense that all wasn't what it seemed with him.'

'But I might not have had to run into a burning house and drag you out.'

'So it's that, is it?'

'No, it's not even that, when you come right down to it . . . If you really want to know, it's the way you treated me afterwards.'

'What do you mean?'

'Nothing.' But Annie had gone too far now to hold back. She put her knife and fork down.

'Come on, Annie,' said Banks. 'We've got this far. Let's clear the air. See if we can't come up with a chance of working this out.'

'That's a change of tune.' This was more difficult than Annie thought it would be, especially given the context, the hotel restaurant with its trees and potted plants, waitresses carrying trays, the businessmen in their pinstriped suits planning their days, some of them already on their mobiles and PDAs. 'It's just that you seemed to brush me off,' she said, 'push me aside as if my feelings didn't matter. God knows, I felt bad enough about making the mistake I did over Phil. I mean, can you imagine, sharing your bed with a fucking serial killer?' She shook her head. 'But you. I'd have expected . . . I don't know . . . support . . . comfort, maybe. You went to Corinne last night, didn't you, but you weren't there for me. I know we have our history and it hasn't always been easy, but you should have been there for me and you weren't. I was hurting as much as you, if not more.'

There, she'd said it, said more than enough. Christ, he was staying silent an awfully long time. *Say something. Say something.*

At last Banks spoke. 'You're right,' he said. 'And if it means anything, I'm sorry.'

'Why did you do it? Why did you abandon me? Was it her?'

'Who?'

'Michelle, or whatever her name is.'

Banks looked surprised. 'No, it wasn't Michelle. It's just that Michelle didn't have anything to do with what happened, seeing her didn't make me think about it. She took me away from it, distracted me. It was thinking about it that was doing my head in. I couldn't remember a thing between answering the door and waking up in hospital. Still can't. All I know is what you've told me, and the smell of whisky still gives me panic attacks. Christ, for a while, for weeks, I didn't even want to get out of bed in the morning, let alone have a serious heart-to-heart about what happened. What's the point? It's like these interminable daytime chat programmes, people talking on and on about their bloody feelings and problems and it gets them nowhere. It's just talk, talk, talk, blather, blather, blather.'

'Some people think that might be better than keeping it bottled up inside.'

Banks ran his hand over his hair. 'Look, Annie, I feel like I'm crawling out of a deep trough. By all rights, Roy's murder should have pushed me back in, but it hasn't. Cut me a little slack here.'

'Maybe you're fuelled by anger?'

'Maybe I am, but at least I'm fuelled.'

Annie looked at him for a while over her tea and let his words sink in. Maybe he was right. Maybe it was time to put it all behind them and move on, and maybe part of doing that was allowing Banks some leeway in the investigation of his brother's murder. After all, it wasn't as if she could stop him.

'OK, let's imagine you were investigating the case,' she said. 'Hypothetically, of course. What would your next move be?'

'What's the official line of enquiry?'

'Basically, they're working their way through Roy's mobile phone book and his business contacts listed on that USB drive you handed over. Oliver Drummond and William Gilmore, the names I mentioned last night, are DI Brooke's priorities because their names are on his computer. Chop shop and fraud. Do they sound like enterprises your brother might have been interested in?'

'Probably,' said Banks. 'Though I'd say fraud was the more likely of the two. I can't see Roy in the stolen-car racket. Has Brooke got anywhere with either of them so far?'

'I don't know,' said Annie. 'I haven't talked to him yet this morning.'

'He should be going after Lambert,' Banks said. 'He knows as much as I do, that Roy had taken a photo of

Lambert and an unidentified man and hidden it away shortly before he disappeared. That ought to set off a few alarm bells, don't you think?'

'I'm sure Dave has his reasons. Does Lambert have a record?'

'No.'

'And is his name in the mobile call list or address book?'

'No.'

'There you are, then. Drummond and Gilmore both have form and they appear in the call list.'

'Even so . . .' said Banks. 'What have you been up to?'

'I've been pursuing leads of my own in the Jennifer Clewes murder.'

'They're linked. Roy and Jennifer were lovers.'

'I know that. But they can't both have been killed by the man with the ponytail. The timing's way off. Which is why Dave thinks it's worth looking elsewhere for Roy's killer. And like I said, both Drummond and Gilmore have criminal records. Brooke also has a man trying to find anyone who knows about Roy's movements on the day he disappeared. Apparently the mobile isn't much use there as he only used it once that day. To call his hair-dresser.'

'I know that,' said Banks.

'Of course you do. You got to the mobile first. They've also enhanced the photo you received. Brooke's not convinced yet that the man is Roy, but I'd say it seems likely. Anyway, they think it might lead them to the spot where it happened.'

Banks nodded.

'Any idea who Roy went off with yet?' Annie asked.

'I'm not sure, but I think it might have been Gareth

Lambert. Roy's known him for years. I'd still like to know who that other man in the photo is.'

'Any leads?'

'Nothing yet, but I'm working on it.' He smiled. 'Obviously, I don't have the manpower to follow up every name in Roy's life, the way you and DI Brooke do, so I plan to go straight to Lambert, when I can find the slippery bastard. It still surprises me that Brooke hasn't been there already.'

'I've told you why,' Annie said. 'And his team's over-stretched, anyway.' She paused. 'Look, I shouldn't be telling you this, but there was something going on at the Berger-Lennox Centre. Dr Lukas told me she was helping young Eastern European prostitutes who got pregnant – mostly illegal immigrants, she said – to get free abortions on the quiet. She called them "late girls". Jennifer Clewes found out about it, but instead of blowing the whistle she helped bury some of the paperwork. I don't think that's everything Dr Lukas knows, but it's a start. And don't even think of going to see her. She's on the edge and a visit from a stranger would alienate her completely.'

'Don't worry,' said Banks. 'I'm not altogether stupid. I'll leave her to you. You don't believe her story?'

'Most of it,' Annie said. 'I think she might be willing to tell me more, but she'll only do it in her own time, on her own terms.'

'How long has this been going on?'

'About a year.'

'How much money is involved?'

'The centre charges between four hundred and a thousand pounds for consultation, termination and post-operative care, depending on how advanced the preg-nancy is.'

'So it could add up to quite a tidy sum over time?'

'Yes. But not worth killing over.'

'I suppose not,' said Banks. 'Did Roy know about it?'

'Jennifer knew, and I'll bet she told Roy. The problem is that Dr Lukas says Jennifer had known about it for a couple of months, but it was only in the last few days that people noticed any difference in her behaviour.'

'So perhaps she found out something else?' Banks suggested. 'Something we don't know. How did the girls find Dr Lukas?'

'That's what seems a bit vague about it all. She's from Ukraine. She said she's known in the community. It's possible, I suppose. Some of these communities are very close-knit. Word gets around.'

'But you don't think so?'

'I think she's holding something back. And I think she's scared.'

'I'm not surprised,' said Banks. 'Two people have been murdered.'

'I think there might be three.'

'Oh?'

'Jennifer mentioned a girl called Carmen Petri – one of the late girls – to her close friend Melanie Scott shortly before she was killed. Her ex-boyfriend Victor Parsons was sort of stalking Jennifer. Ironically enough, it's the first time a stalker's actually been any practical use to us. He saw Jennifer come out of the centre last Monday evening with a young girl who looked pregnant. A man immediately came out of the shadows and the girl went off with him in a car.'

'And you think that girl was this Carmen?'

'Yes. And I think she's dead, too. The man she went off with was a muscle-bound lump with a ponytail, the one I told you about before, and he sounds remarkably like the man we think shot Jennifer Clewes and broke into your cottage.'

'And followed me back here from Peterborough,' said Banks.

Annie's eyes widened. 'What?'

Banks told her what happened on the A1(M) the previous day and what measures he had taken to protect his parents.

'Did you get the number?' Annie asked.

'What do you take me for?'

'Give it to me. I'll trace it.'

'It's already being done.'

'Burgess?'

Banks said nothing.

Annie sighed. 'Give it to me anyway.'

Banks did as she asked.

'I take it you haven't told Dave Brooke about this yet?'

'I told you. I rang the Peterborough police. It's their manor. I checked with them again this morning and nothing out of the ordinary happened during the night.'

'Fine,' said Annie. 'I'll tell him myself.'

'Ponytail might well have killed Jennifer and tried to scare me off, but we know he can't have killed Roy.'

'So there's someone else involved.'

'Well, if ponytail is the muscle and prostitution is the business, I'd say there's a pimp somewhere at the top of it all, wouldn't you?'

'Possibly,' Annie agreed. 'Lambert?'

'Maybe.' Banks stood up. 'Anyway, we won't find out the answer by sitting around here, however pleasant it is. Thanks for breakfast, Annie, and for clearing the air.'

'Where are you going?'

Banks smiled. 'Well, if I told you that, you'd really be in trouble, wouldn't you?'

Annie put her hand on Banks's arm. 'I know I can't stop you,' she said, 'but promise me a few things?'

'Go on.'

'Keep in touch, let me know what you find out.'

'OK. You, too.'

'Stay away from Dr Lukas. She'll come around in her own time You'll only scare her away.'

'No problem.'

'And be careful, Alan. This isn't a game.'

'Believe me, I know that.' Banks bent forward, kissed her lightly on the cheek, and left. Annie watched him go, then she hurried back up to her room to pack. This morning, after checking in with Brooke, she was going back to Eastvale come hell or high water.

•

'You wouldn't believe it. It was like a bloody three-ring circus here the last couple of days,' said Malcolm Farrow as he settled in his armchair with a stiff gin and tonic in his hand. Banks had declined the offer of gin as it was only ten o'clock in the morning, but he accepted the tonic water gratefully. Farrow had looked puzzled but poured it anyway. 'As you can see, things have settled down a bit now.'

Banks looked out of Farrow's window at Roy's house. The detectives must have finished their search and removed everything they thought pertinent to their investigation, because the place was unguarded.

They would have gone through Roy's stuff for any evidence related to the crime and also for information about his lifestyle, his habits and his associates that might give them a lead to follow. Banks knew what they would find because he had already made a thorough search himself and handed over everything to Brooke. Now the formalities were done with, the house would be turned over to Roy's next of kin – their parents, Banks assumed.

'I can imagine what it was like,' said Banks. 'Look, I'm sorry I didn't ring you straight away, but I had to go and take care of my parents and I didn't have your number handy.'

'That's all right. I was really shocked to hear the news. It's been all over the papers, and the television. We've had reporters around. They've gone now the police seem to have moved on.'

'There's nothing left for them here,' said Banks.

'Anyway, it's nice of you to remember me and drop by.'

'No problem. Did the police want to talk to you?'

'The police? Oh, yes. They were all over the street.'

'What did you tell them?'

'Just what I told you. It's all I know.'

'What about the reporters?'

His face reddened. 'Sent them packing. Bunch of scavengers.'

'Have you thought any more about that photo I showed you?' asked Banks, slipping the envelope out of his briefcase.

Farrow looked at it again through his reading glasses, which were wedged tightly to his bulbous, purple-veined nose. 'Look, I'm not going to have to say anything in court, am I?'

'This is just between you and me,' said Banks. As Farrow squinted at the photos, Banks sipped some tonic water. The fizziness made him burp and he could still taste the bacon and eggs he'd eaten for breakfast.

'Well,' said Farrow, 'it certainly could be him. The more I look, the more I see the resemblance. As I said, my eyesight's not so good on detail, but there are street lights and the man's size and the grey hair look about right.' He passed the photo back to Banks. 'A bit vague, I know, but it's the best I can do.'

'I appreciate that.'

'Who is he, anyway? He's surely not the one who . . . ?'

'I don't think so,' said Banks. 'If it really is him, he's an old business partner of Roy's.' Someone Roy would probably open the door to and accompany for a drink or whatever, which was the way it seemed to have happened. Someone he trusted.

Banks thanked Farrow for his help, made his excuses and left.

There were no signs of activity around Roy's house on Wednesday morning, not even a police seal across the door. Banks used his key and walked inside. The only sound he could hear was the humming of the refrigerator. There was a deep silence at the core of the house, the silence of Roy's absence, and it felt heavier now than it had when Banks first arrived.

First he checked the kitchen. The laptop he had left on the table there was missing, and he assumed the police had taken it. There was nothing he could do about that right now, but he would have to let Brooke know that he wanted it back when they had finished with it.

Next he went upstairs to look at Roy's office. Whoever had searched the room had made a neat and tidy job of it. Nothing looked out of place.

Banks went into the entertainment room and flopped on the sofa. He thought about the CD he had found. Roy must have known that he was involved in something dodgy by Wednesday, when he buried the photos of Lambert and friend among the pornographic images. And perhaps he knew that the something dodgy – whether it was prostitution or illegal immigrants or something else – was fast reaching critical mass. Did he know that his life was in danger? Banks doubted it. If Roy was used to skirting the edges of the law and mixing with bad company, as he seemed to be, then he was probably cocky enough to think there was nothing he couldn't handle. But something had changed all that, and it had happened between Wednesday and Friday evening – or even a couple of days earlier, if Jennifer Clewes's behaviour was anything to go by.

What had Roy's movements been during those crucial days? Where had he been? Who had he talked to? If Banks could get the answer to those questions, he thought, then he might be able to answer the riddle of Roy's death. And Jennifer's.

He thought about what Annie had told him over breakfast, the doctor helping out prostitutes. Had Jennifer Clewes told Roy? Most likely she had. What had his reaction been? Was it anything to do with their deaths? But Banks failed to see how helping out a few unfortunate illegal immigrants could lead to murder. Unless, of course, the people who brought them in were involved and were beginning to feel threatened by something.

Banks also hadn't forgotten that Burgess had told him Gareth Lambert was a smuggler with a large network of underworld connections. Burgess had also said that

Lambert knew the Balkan route like the back of his hand, and now Annie was telling Banks about Eastern European prostitutes using the Berger-Lennox Centre. At least a vague picture was beginning to form in his mind, but he still didn't know Roy's place in it, or why he had been killed.

Banks thought back to his chat with Corinne the previous evening. He had found out a lot about his brother through talking to her. Roy loved *The Goon Show* and *Monty Python*; he did a hilarious Ministry of Silly Walks impression and quite a decent version of the Four Yorkshiremen sketch; New York was still his favourite city, Italy his favourite country; he had recently taken up digital photography and all the photos on his walls were his; he played golf and tennis regularly; he supported Arsenal (typical, Banks thought, who lumped Arsenal in the same category as Manchester United, the best teams money could buy); his favourite colour was purple; his favourite food was wild-mushroom risotto, his favourite wine Amarone; he loved opera and often took Corinne to Covent Garden (though she admitted that she never quite *got* opera); and they both enjoyed going to see Hollywood musicals and old foreign films with subtitles – Bergman, Visconti, Renoir, Fellini.

Roy gave money to beggars in the street but complained when he thought he was being overcharged in shops and restaurants. He could be moody, and Corinne had to confess that she never quite knew what was going on in his mind. But she loved him, as she told Banks when her tears flowed for the second time, after the third glass of wine, no matter that she hadn't known where she stood with him for weeks, no matter that he had left her largely alone to deal with the trauma of her abortion.

She had still hoped, somehow, that he would tire of his new conquest and come back to her.

There was only one family photograph in Roy's entertainment room. It was taken on the prom at Blackpool, Banks remembered, in August 1965, and you could see the Tower in the background.

There they stood, all four of them, parents on the inside and Roy, freckled then, his hair a lot fairer than it was when he got older, and Banks at fourteen looking moody and what he had supposed passed for cool back then, in his black drainpipe trousers and polo-neck Beatles jumper. He hadn't really looked at the photo closely before, but now he did he realized that it must have been taken by Graham Marshall, who had accompanied the Banks family on that holiday only a week or so before he disappeared during his Sunday morning paper round.

This was the holiday when Banks had fallen for the beautiful Linda, who worked behind the counter at the local coffee bar. She was far too old for him, but he had fallen nonetheless. Then he and Graham had picked up a couple of girls at the Pleasure Beach, Tina and Sharon, and taken them under the pier for a bit of hanky-panky. He didn't remember having the photograph taken, but that was no surprise. He hardly remembered Roy being on that holiday, either. What fourteen-year-old would waste his time hanging around with his nine-year-old brother?

Graham Marshall was dead, another murder victim, and now Roy. Banks looked at his father in an old grey V-necked pullover, shirt sleeves rolled up, cigarette dangling from the corner of his mouth, hair swept back with Brylcreem. Then he looked at his mother, hardly a dolly bird, but surprisingly young and pretty, with a full-bodied perm and a summer dress showing off her trim waist, smiling into the camera. What would they find when they explored her insides next week, Banks wondered. Would she survive? And his father, after all this trauma? Banks was beginning to feel as if everyone he came into contact with was cursed, that all his companions became hostage to death, like the wraiths that haunted 'Strange Affair'.

Then he told himself to stop being so maudlin. He had solved Graham Marshall's murder more than thirty-five years after it had been committed, his mother would suffer the inconvenience of a small operation at worst, and his father's heart would go on beating for a long time yet. Roy was dead and Banks would find out who killed him. And that was that.

As Banks headed out to try Gareth Lambert again, his mobile rang.

'Alan, it's Annie.'

'Thought you were on your way home.'

'So did I, but something's come up.'

Banks gripped the phone tighter. 'What?'

'Technical support have worked out where the digital photo on your brother's mobile was taken.'

'How on earth did they manage that?'

'From the list of abandoned factories,' Annie said. 'There were some letters visible on a wall in the background: NGS and IFE. One of the factories listed was Midgeley's Castings, and one of the older detectives on the team remembered he used to pass by the place on his way to school and they had a sign that read MIDGELEY'S CASTINGS: CAST FOR LIFE. The place shut down in 1989 and nobody's done anything with it since.'

'Where is it?'

'By the river, down Battersea way. I'm sorry to be so brutal, Alan, but the tide experts also agree that it's very likely the area where your brother's body was dumped in the river, so it's looking more and more as if it was Roy in the foreground of the picture. We're heading out there now. Want to come?'

'You know I do. What does Brooke have to say?'

'He's OK with it. Meet us there?'

'Fine.'

Annie gave him an address and directions and Banks hurried out to his car.

•

'DS Browne?'

'Speaking.'

'This is DC Templeton from Eastvale. How are things down your way?'

'Fine, thanks. Anything new?'

'Maybe,' said Templeton, fingering the plastic bag on the desk in front of him. 'I went to talk to Roger Cropley's wife and found him at home. Says he's got a summer cold but I didn't notice any sniffles. Anyway, I think I rattled him a bit more. He seemed nervous when I told him the surviving woman thought she might be able to recognize her attacker.'

'But that's not true,' Susan said.

'Cropley doesn't know that. And I think his wife might know a lot more than she's letting on, too. Anyway, I've got an idea. Did your SOCOs do a thorough trace-evidence search of the victim's car?'

'I'm sure they did,' said Susan. 'But there was no

evidence that he was ever in the car. He clearly dragged her out and into the bushes.'

'But he'd have to lean in to apply the chloroform.'

'True. What are you getting at?'

'You've still got all the collected samples, I assume? Hair? Skin?'

'Of course.'

'And the car?'

'That, too. Look, what's going on? What are you getting at?'

'Can you check if they found any dandruff on the seat back?'

'Dandruff?'

'Yes.'

'I'll check. What do you have in mind?'

'I've been on the Web, and it all sounds a bit complicated, but as far as I can gather you can get DNA from dandruff. I mean it is just skin, isn't it?'

'It won't do us much good,' said Susan, 'unless we have a sample for comparison.'

'Er . . . well, as a matter of fact, we might have.'

'What do you mean?'

'I've got a sample of Cropley's dandruff. Can I send it down to you?'

'I trust you didn't ask Mr Cropley for this?'

Templeton laughed. 'No. Believe me, he gave it quite freely, though.'

'That's not the point,' Susan said. 'I'm sure you know as well as I do that you have to get the suspect's written permission even for a non-intimate sample, unless you've detained him for a serious offence and the super gives permission to take one.'

'I know my PACE regulations,' said Templeton. 'What

I'm saying is that this could confirm my suspicions. If you knew it was him, if *we* knew it was him, then it would make a difference and we could start to build a real case. He wouldn't even have to know about the previous sample. Nobody does except you and me. Right now we've got no real grounds to arrest him and demand a sample, but if the sample I took matches any of the dandruff found in the car, then we'd know where to look and you can be damn sure we'd come up with something to arrest him for. After that . . . well, then we'd get an official sample, of course.'

'What if it's not him?'

'Then he's off the hook.'

'But there'd be records, paperwork relating to the first test. These things are expensive.'

'I know that, but so what? It needn't come out. Surely you must know *someone* at the lab with a bit of discretion? How is anybody going to know?'

'A good defence lawyer would use it as ammunition against our case.'

'Only if they found out. Besides, it wouldn't matter. By that point we'd have *officially* matching DNA which we'd have no trouble getting admitted, all by the book. You can't argue with that. Christ, I'll even pay for the test myself if that's your problem.'

'That's not the problem. And I doubt you could afford it, anyway. The point is that if it does turn out to be Cropley, the real evidence could be thrown out because of what you're asking. It's iffy. No, I don't like this at all.'

Templeton sighed. He hadn't realized what a stickler DS Browne was. 'Look,' he said, 'do you want this guy or not? Maybe it'll rule him out. I don't know. But we should at least keep an eye on him. If I'm right – and the

DNA would prove that one way or another – he's done it before and he'll do it again. What do you think? Wouldn't you like to *know*?'

Templeton felt himself tense during the silence that followed.

Finally, Susan Browne said, 'Send it down. I'll talk to my SIO, see what I can do. I'm not promising anything, though.'

'Great,' said Templeton. 'It's already on the way.'

•

Banks felt more trepidation than he could ever have imagined as he walked with Brooke and Annie over the weeds and stony ground towards the dirty brick factory, its ugly facade covered in graffiti. Was he now going to see the exact spot where his brother had been shot and killed? Little Roy, whom he'd saved from a bully and scarred with a toy sword. He gritted his teeth and felt his neck and arm muscles tense up.

The doors looked forbidding, but they were easily opened, and the three were soon crossing the vast shop floor, footsteps echoing. There was something about abandoned factories, with the gaping holes in their roofs, rusted old machines, drums, pallets and weeds growing through cracks in the walls and floor, that always disturbed Banks. He thought it had something to do with a dream that had scared him when he was young, but he couldn't remember the details. He also thought it had something to do with the ball-bearing factory across the road from where he grew up, though it had been in operation during his time there and he had no unpleasant experiences associated with it. There had always been derelict houses, workshops and factories, though, and he had explored most of them with his friends, tracking down imaginary monsters. Whatever the reason, places like that still gave him the shivers, and this one was no exception.

'You do take me to the nicest places, Dave,' said Annie. 'This is almost as cheerful as that street in Bow.'

'At least it's not raining today,' Brooke said.

A rat scuttled out from under a rusted sheet of metal and practically ran over Annie's feet on its way out. She pulled a face but made no sound. Sunlight lanced through missing sections of roof, illuminating the dust motes the three of them kicked up as they walked. The large windows behind their protective grilles were all broken, and shattered glass was strewn all over the floor, sparkling in the rays of light. Here and there were oily puddles and damp patches from the previous night's rain.

At the centre of the shop floor, almost hidden by rusty machines, Banks saw a wooden chair. On the floor beside it lay snake-like lengths of cord.

'Better stand back,' said Brooke as they approached it. 'The SOCOs will be here soon and they won't appreciate it if we trample all over their scene.'

Banks stood and looked. He thought he could see spots of blood on the cord and splatters on the ground near the chair. For a moment, he pictured Roy tied there, felt his terror as he knew he was going to die in this filthy place, then his policeman's instinct kicked in and he tried to interpret what he was seeing.

'Roy was shot in the head with a .22, like Jennifer Clewes, right?' he said.

'That's right,' said Brooke.

'And there was no exit wound?'

'No.'

'So where did all the blood come from?'

Banks noticed Brooke exchange a glance with Annie.

'Come on,' said Banks. 'I'm not a fool.'

'The pathologist found some evidence that he was beaten,' Brooke admitted.

'So they tortured him, the bastards.'

Brooke stared down at his shoes. 'It looks that way. But we don't know for certain that your brother was even here yet. You can't really tell who it is from the photograph.'

'And just who else do you think it would be?' Banks said. 'Anyway, now you've got all the blood samples you could possibly need to make a match.'

'I suppose we have,' said Brooke.

'But why torture him?' Banks asked.

'We don't know,' Annie said. 'Obviously to make him tell them something. Or to find out how much he knew about something or how much he'd already told.'

'I don't think it would have taken long to get Roy to talk,' Banks said. The image of the boy bullying Roy flashed though his mind, Roy crying and holding his stomach in pain. Banks's intervention. But this time he hadn't come to the rescue. He hadn't been there for him. And this time Roy had been killed. Banks could only hope that his parents never found out about the torture. He didn't blame Annie and Brooke for trying to keep it from him – he'd probably have done the same if it was one of their relatives – but now he had the job of protecting his own mother and father from the truth.

'They didn't bother tidying up after themselves,' said Annie, pointing to a single shell casing on the floor close to the chair.

'Probably thought no one would ever find the place,' said Brooke.

'Some kids would have found it eventually,' Banks said. 'Kids love places like this.'

Pigeons flew in and out through the holes in the roof and walls, perching on the rafters and ruffling their feathers. Their white droppings speckled sections of floor, and even the chair itself. Despite its partial openness to the elements, the factory smelled of dead animals and stale grease.

'I'll see if I can get some uniforms to canvass the neighbourhood,' Brooke said. 'Who knows? Someone might have noticed unusual activity around the place.'

The wind made a mournful sound as it blew through the broken windows, harmonizing strangely with the cooing pigeons. Banks gave a little shiver, despite the warmth of the day. He'd seen all he wanted, the god-forsaken place where Roy had spent his last few hours being tortured, then shot. No matter how long he lived, he knew he would never get the image out of his mind. For now, though, he had other things to do. He told Brooke and Annie he was leaving, and neither asked him where he was going. As he was getting in his car, the technical-support van turned into the factory yard. They would scrutinize the place where Roy had died, scrape blood, search for fingerprints, fibres, hair, skin, any traces that the murderers left behind. With any luck, they would turn up enough to secure a conviction, should the police ever find a viable suspect. Banks left them to it.

15

After dropping his car off outside Roy's – he didn't
fancy spending the day driving in London traffic, trying
to find parking spots, and the tube was much faster –
Banks tried Lambert's travel operation on the Edgware
Road first but was told that Mr Lambert was unavailable.
Next he went back to the Chelsea flat and found to his
surprise that Gareth Lambert was just on his way out of
the front door.

'Going somewhere, Gareth?' he said.

'Who the fuck are you?' Lambert tried to push past
him.

Banks stood his ground. 'My name's Banks. Detective
Chief Inspector Alan Banks.'

'You're Roy's brother.' Lambert stood back and eyed
Banks up and down. 'Well, fuck a duck. The old killjoy
himself.'

'Can we go back inside?'

'I'm busy. I've got to get to the office.'

'It won't take long.' Banks stared Lambert down.
Finally Lambert shrugged and led Banks upstairs to a first-
floor flat. The interior was functional enough but lacked
the personal touch, as if Lambert's real life lay elsewhere.
The man himself looked just the same as he did in Roy's
photo: bearish, a bit overweight, with a red complexion –
part sun and part hypertension, Banks guessed – and a
thick head of curly grey hair. He was dressed in ice-blue

jeans and an oversized, baggy white shirt. Burgess had made a comparison with Harry Lime, but as far as Banks could remember, Lime was suave and charming on the surface, more like Phil Keane. Lambert was rougher around the edges and clearly didn't seem to rely on charm to get by. They sat down opposite one another like a pair of chess players, and Lambert regarded Banks with a vaguely amused look in his eyes.

'So you're Roy's big brother, the detective.'

'That's right. I understand the two of you go back a long way?'

'Indeed we do. I met Roy just after he'd graduated from university. We were a bit wet behind the ears back then. 1978. As I remember it, all the kids were wearing torn T-shirts and safety pins in their ears, listening to the Sex Pistols and The Clash, and there we were in our business suits sitting in some square hotel bar planning our next venture. Which was probably marketing torn jeans and safety pins to the kids.' He laughed. 'They were good days. I was very sorry to hear about what happened to Roy, by the way.'

'Were you?'

'Of course. Look, I really am a busy man. If you're just going to sit there and—'

'Because you really don't seem to be grieving very deeply for someone you'd known for so long.'

'How do you know how much I'm grieving?'

'Fair enough. Did your ventures together involve arms dealing?'

Lambert's eyes narrowed. 'Why bring that up?' he said. 'It's ancient history. Yes, we were involved in what we thought was a perfectly legitimate weapons sale, but we were hoodwinked and the shipment was misdirected.

Well, that was enough for me. What do they say? Once bitten, twice shy.'

'So you stuck with less risky ventures after that?'

'I wouldn't say any of our ventures were without risk, but let's just say the risk was of a more monetary kind, not the sort of risk where you could end up in jail if you weren't careful.'

'Or dead.'

'Quite.'

'Insider trading can carry a hefty penalty.'

'Hah! Everybody was doing it. Still are. Have you never had a hot tip from the horse's mouth and made a few bob on it?'

'No,' said Banks.

'So if I said right now such and such a company is making an important merger next week and their share prices will double, you can honestly say you wouldn't run right out and buy as many shares as you could get your hands on?'

Banks had to think about that one. It sounded easy, and perhaps just a little bit naughty, put that way. Hardly criminal. But he didn't understand the stock market, and that was why he didn't play it. Besides, he never felt that he had the money to spare for such gambles. 'I might splurge on a couple,' he said in the end.

Lambert clapped his hands. 'There you are!' he said. 'I thought so.' It sounded as if he was welcoming Banks to a club he had no desire to join.

'I've also heard rumours that you have been involved in smuggling,' Banks said.

'That's interesting. Where did you hear them?'

'Are they true?'

'Of course not. The word has such negative connotations,

don't you think? *Smuggling.* It's so emotive. I regard what I've done more as a matter of practical geography. I move things from one place to another. With great efficiency, I might add.'

'I'm glad you've got no time for false modesty. What things?'

'Just things.'

'Arms? Drugs? People? I hear you know the Balkan route.'

Lambert raised an eyebrow. 'You do have your ears to the ground, don't you? Roy never told me how sharp you were. The Balkan route? Well, I might have known it once, but these days . . . those borders change faster than you can draw them. And you'd better stop accusing me of breaking the law right now or I'll have my solicitor on you, Roy's brother or no. I've never been convicted of anything in my life.'

'So you've been lucky. Still lots of opportunities for entrepreneurs in the Balkans, though. Or the ex-Soviet republics.'

'Much too dangerous. I'm afraid I'm too old for all that. I'm semi-retired. I have a wife I happen to love very much and a travel agency to run.'

'When did you last see Roy?'

'Friday night.'

Banks tried not to let his excitement show. 'What time?'

'About half-past twelve or one o'clock in the morning. Why?'

'Are you sure it was Friday night?'

'Of course I am.'

Lambert was playing with him, Banks sensed. He could see it in the man's restless, teasing eyes. Lambert knew that the neighbour had seen him getting into his car with Roy, and that Banks had no doubt talked to the neighbour and got his description. But that was at half-past nine. What were they doing until half-past twelve or one o'clock?

Lambert picked up a box of cigars from the table and offered one to Banks. 'Cuban?'

'No, thanks.'

'Suit yourself.' Lambert fiddled with a cutter and matches and finally got the thing lit. He looked at Banks through the smoke. 'You seem surprised that I said I saw Roy on Friday evening. Why's that?'

'I think you know why,' said Banks.

'Indulge me.'

'Because that's when he went missing. He hasn't been seen alive since half-past nine on Friday.'

'I can most sincerely assure you that he has. By me and countless other members of the Albion Club.'

'The Albion Club?'

'On the Strand. It's a rather exclusive club. Membership by invitation only.'

Banks remembered that Corinne had told him Roy went to a club on the Strand with Lambert a few weeks ago. 'What goes on there?'

Lambert laughed. 'Nothing illegal, if that's what you're thinking. The club has a gaming licence. It also has a top-class restaurant and an exceedingly comfortable bar. Roy and I are both members. Have been for years. Even when I was living abroad I'd drop by if I happened to be in town.' He puffed on his cigar, eyes narrowed to calculating slits, as if daring Banks to challenge him.

'Let's backtrack, then,' said Banks.

'Of course.'

'What time did you first see Roy on Friday night?'

'About half-past nine,' said Lambert. 'I dropped by his place and picked him up.'

'Was this a regular arrangement?'

'I wouldn't say regular, but we'd done it before, yes. Roy prefers to leave the car when he goes out drinking, and I hardly touch the stuff these days, so I don't mind driving. It's not far out of my way.'

'And you'd arranged to pick him up and take him to the Albion Club on Friday?'

'Yes.' The cigar had gone out. Lambert lit it again. Banks got the impression that it was more of a prop than anything else.

'What happened when you got there?'

Lambert shrugged. 'The usual. We went into the bar and got a couple of stiff brandies and chatted for a while. No, I tell a lie. I had a brandy – my only drink of the night – and Roy had wine. The club does a decent house claret.'

'Who did you talk to?'

'A few of the other members.'

'Names?'

'Look, these are important people. Influential people. They won't take too kindly to being harassed by the police, nor to knowing it was me who set you on them.'

'Maybe you haven't quite grasped the seriousness of this,' Banks said. 'A man has been murdered. My brother. Your friend. You were one of the last people to see him alive. We need to trace his movements and activities on the evening he disappeared.'

'This puts me in a difficult position.'

'I don't bloody care what position it puts you in. I

want names.' Banks locked eyes with him. Eventually Lambert reeled off a string of names and Banks wrote them down. He didn't recognize any of them.

'How did Roy seem?' Banks asked. 'Was he depressed, worried, on edge?'

'He seemed fine to me.'

'Did he confide in you about any problems or anything?'

'No.'

'What did he talk about?'

'Business, golf, cricket, wine, women. You know, the usual man talk.'

'Did he mention me?'

Lambert gave a tight little smile. 'I'm afraid he didn't, no.'

Banks found that hard to believe, given that Roy had just phoned him out of the blue with an urgent problem, a 'matter of life and death', but he let it go for the time being. 'Did Roy ever mention a girl called Carmen Petri?'

It was over in a second, but it was definitely there, the shock, the slight hesitation before answering, a refusal to look Banks in the eye. 'No,' Lambert said.

'Have you ever heard the name before?'

'There's an actress, Carmen Electra, but I doubt that it's her you're thinking of.'

'No,' said Banks. 'There's also an opera called *Carmen* but it's not her, either.' Casually, he slipped a copy of the photograph he had printed from Roy's CD out of his briefcase and set it on the low table. 'Who's the other man sitting with you in this photo?' he asked.

Lambert peered closely at the photograph then looked at Banks sideways. 'Where did you get this?' He gestured at the photo with his cigar.

'Roy took it.'

Lambert sat back in his chair. 'How strange. He never told me.'

'I assume you do know who the man you're sitting with is?'

'Of course I do. It's Max. Max Broda. He's a business colleague. I can't imagine why Roy would want to take a photo of us together.'

'What business would that be?'

'Travel. Max puts tours together, recruits guides, works out itineraries, hotels, suggests destinations of interest.'

'Where?'

'Mostly around the Adriatic and Mediterranean.'

'Including the Balkan countries?'

'Some, yes. If and when they're safe to visit.'

'I'd like to talk to him,' said Banks.

Lambert scrutinized the end of his cigar and took another puff before answering. 'I'm afraid that will be rather difficult,' he said. 'He's gone home.'

'Where's that?'

'Prague.'

'Do you have an address?'

'Are you thinking of going there? It's a beautiful city. I know someone who can fix you up with the best guided tour.'

'Maybe,' said Banks. 'I would like his address, though.'

'I might have it somewhere.' Lambert scrolled through the files on his PDA and finally spelled out an address for Banks, who copied it down. 'What time did you leave the club?' he asked.

'Roy left sometime between half-past twelve and one o'clock.'

'You weren't still together at that time?'

'No. We weren't joined at the hip, you know. Roy likes to play the roulette tables. I prefer poker, myself.'

'Did he leave alone?'

'As far as I know.'

'Where did he go?'

'I've no idea.'

'What time did you leave?'

'About three. I was knackered by then. Not to mention broke.'

'Where did you go?'

'Back here.'

'Not home to your wife?'

Lambert leaned forward, face thrust forward, and stabbed the air with his cigar. 'You leave her out of this.'

'Very understanding, is she?'

'I told you. Leave her out of it.' Lambert relit his cigar and his tone softened. 'Look,' he said, running his free hand through his curly grey hair, 'I was tired, I came back here. I don't know what you suspect me of, but Roy was a good friend and a colleague of many years' standing. I didn't kill him. Why would I? What possible motive could I have?'

'Are you sure he didn't say where he was going?'

'No. I assumed he was going home.'

'Was he drunk?'

Lambert tipped his head to one side and thought for a moment. 'He'd had a few,' he said. 'Mostly wine. But he wasn't staggering or slurring his speech. Not fit to drive, I'd say, but fit enough to get a taxi.'

'Is that what he did?'

'I've no idea what happened once he got outside.'

'And you didn't see him again?'

'No.'

'OK,' said Banks, standing to leave. 'I suppose we could always ask around the taxi drivers.'

'One thing,' said Lambert, as he walked Banks to the door. 'You already know about the arms deal years back. You mentioned it earlier.'

'Yes?'

'I think he wanted to get involved in that sort of thing again. At least, it might be a direction worth looking in. I mean, Roy had been making a few noises, you know, sounding me out, asking about old contacts and such.'

'On Friday?'

'Yes. In the club.'

'And?'

'I told him I'd lost touch. Which is true. The world has changed, Mr Banks, in case you haven't noticed. And I warned him off.'

'How did he respond?'

Lambert clapped a hand on Banks's shoulder as they stood near the door. 'You know Roy,' he said. 'Or maybe you don't. Anyway, once he's on the trail of something, he's not easily deterred. He persisted, got a bit pissed off with me, as a matter of fact, thought I was holding out on him, depriving him of a business opportunity.'

'So you ended the evening on a sour note?'

'He'd have got over it.'

'If he hadn't been killed?'

'Yes.'

'Why did you fall out with Julian Harwood, by the way?'

Lambert looked surprised. 'You know about that?'

'Yes.'

'It was years ago. Storm in a teacup. Harwood insisted I'd cheated him out of some money in a land sale, that I knew the new motorway was going to run right by it.'

'And did you?'

Lambert did his best to look innocent and outraged but it came out like a poor parody. 'Me? Of course not. I wouldn't do a thing like that.'

'Of course not,' Banks echoed. 'Is there anything more you can tell me?'

'I'm afraid not. Except . . .'

'What?'

Lambert stood by the door and scratched his temple. 'Don't take this amiss,' he said. 'Just a piece of friendly advice. Roy's dead. I can't change that. I don't know anything about it, and I certainly don't know who did it, but don't you think you should think twice, take heed of what you're getting into, and perhaps be a bit more careful lest you disturb a nest of vipers?'

'Is that a warning, Mr Lambert?'

'Take it as you will.' Lambert looked at his watch. 'Now I'm afraid I really must head for the office. I've got business to take care of.'

•

Annie hardly had time to call at her cottage in Harkside and water the wilting potted plants before heading to Eastvale for the three o'clock team meeting. It was another beautiful Dales day, a little cooler than it had been, with one or two fluffy white clouds scudding across the pale blue sky, but she didn't have time to pause and enjoy any of it. Sometimes she wondered what the point of living in the country was, given her job and the hours she put in.

They were all waiting in the boardroom: Gristhorpe, Hatchley, Winsome, Rickerd, Templeton and Stefan Nowak, crime-scene coordinator. The long table was so highly polished you could see your reflection in it, and a whiteboard hung on the wall at one end of the room surrounded by cork boards where Stefan had pinned the crime-scene photographs. They made quite a contrast to the paintings of the wool barons on the other walls.

After Annie had brought everyone up to speed on the Berger-Lennox Centre, Roy Banks, Carmen Petri and their possible connection with Jennifer Clewes's murder, Gristhorpe handed the floor over to Stefan Nowak.

Stefan stood by the boards and the photographs and cleared his throat. Not for the first time Annie wondered what sort of life Stefan led outside of work. He was one of the most charming and elegant men she had ever known, and his life was a complete mystery to her.

'First of all,' said Stefan, 'we have fingerprints from DCI Banks's door that don't match the builders', we have tyre tracks from his drive and . . .' Here he paused dramatically and lifted up a plastic bag. 'We also have a cigarette end found near the beck on DCI Banks's property, fortunately before the rain came. From this we have been able to get the saliva necessary for DNA.'

'What about the tyre tracks?' Annie asked.

'They're Michelins, of a type consistent with tyres often used on a Mondeo,' said Stefan. 'I've sent the necessary information to Essex for comparison with what's left of the Mondeo that crashed outside Basildon. I'm still awaiting results.'

'So,' Gristhorpe said, 'you've got prints, tyre tracks

and DNA from the scene of DCI Banks's cottage, and if and when we find a suspect, these will tie him to the murders of Jennifer Clewes and Roy Banks?'

'Well,' said Stefan, 'they'll tie him to DCI Banks's cottage.'

'Exactly,' said Gristhorpe. 'And no crime was committed there.'

'That's not strictly true, sir,' said Annie. 'Someone definitely broke in.'

Gristhorpe gave her a withering look and shook his head. 'Not enough.'

'We've got Jennifer Clewes's mobile records from the network,' Winsome said. 'Not that they tell us a great deal. As far as I can gather the calls are all to and from friends and family.'

'What about the last call?' Annie asked. 'The one Kate Nesbit remembered on Friday evening.'

'Yes, I was coming to that,' said Winsome. 'Jennifer received a phone call at 10.43 p.m. on Friday the 11th of June, duration three minutes. The problem is that it's an "unknown" number. I've got the mobile company working on it, but they're not offering a lot of hope.'

'Thanks for trying,' said Annie.

Gristhorpe looked at his watch. 'I've got to go,' he said. 'I've got ACC McLaughlin and the press breathing down my neck. I appreciate your progress so far, but it's not enough. We need results, and we need them fast. Annie, you'd better get back down to London tomorrow and keep pushing the Berger-Lennox connection. The rest of you keep at it up here. Winsome, get back to the mobile company and see if they can come up with a number for us. Get them to cross-check with Jennifer's outgoing calls. That's it for now.'

When he left the room, everyone breathed a sigh of relief.

'He's in a bit of a grumpy mood this morning, isn't he?' said Stefan to Annie as they all filed out a few moments later.

'I think he's had the chief constable as well as ACC McLaughlin on his case,' said Annie. 'And it's my guess that however enlightened he thinks he is, he still doesn't like being given a bollocking by a woman.'

Stefan smiled. 'Ouch,' he said.

'Ma'am, can I have a word?'

It was DC Templeton. 'Of course, Kev,' said Annie, waving goodbye to Stefan. 'Let's grab a coffee in the canteen.'

Templeton pulled a face. 'With all due respect, ma'am . . .'

'I know,' said Annie. 'It tastes like cat's piss. You're right. We'll go to the Golden Grill.'

They threaded their way through the crowd of tourists on Market Street and were lucky to find a free table. The poor waitress was rushed off her feet but she managed to bring them each a cup of filter coffee quickly enough. 'What is it, Kev?' Annie asked.

'It's this Roger Cropley business,' Templeton said. 'I haven't bothered you with it much so far because, well, you've been down south and you've had lots of other things on your plate. I mean, it might be a bit tangential, but I really think we're onto something here.'

'What?'

'The Claire Potter murder.'

'I don't know,' said Annie. 'Seems like a bit of a coincidence, doesn't it?'

'That's what I thought at first,' said Templeton, warming to the subject, 'but if you really think about it, if Cropley has been preying on young women alone on the motorway on Friday nights, then the only coincidence is that he was at the Watford Gap services at the same time as Jennifer Clewes, and that's exactly the kind of coincidence he'd always be hoping for. He trolls those places: Watford Gap, Leicester Forest, Newport Pagnell, Trowell. Claire Potter and Jennifer Clewes were exactly what he was looking for.'

'I see your point,' said Annie. 'But I mean a coincidence that this time he picked on a girl who was already singled out by someone else to die.'

'OK, but strange things happen sometimes. It still doesn't mean Cropley's harmless.'

'You don't need to tell *me* that, Kev,' said Annie.

'There was another woman, too: Paula Chandler. Someone drove her off the road late on a Friday night in February and tried to open her car door, only it was locked and she managed to get away.'

'Did she get a good look at him?'

'Just his hand.'

Annie thought for a moment. 'It still doesn't mean Cropley's the killer.'

'Maybe there's a way we can find out.'

'Go on.'

Templeton leaned forward, the excitement clear in his eyes. 'I met DS Browne from Derby,' he went on, 'and she agrees it's worth a shot. I've talked with Cropley and his wife again since then and I'm still convinced there's something there. Anyway . . .' He went on to tell Annie about the dandruff.

'I must say,' Annie commented when he'd finished,

'that's very clever of you, Kev. I didn't know they could get DNA from dandruff.'

'They can,' said Templeton. 'I checked with Stefan and DS Browne confirmed it when she phoned to tell me she put a rush on it. They can also process DNA pretty quickly these days when they've a mind to.'

'Leaving aside the problem of its being inadmissible,' Annie went on, 'what do you expect to happen next?'

'It doesn't need to be admissible,' Templeton explained, as he had done to DS Browne. 'We just need some concrete evidence that we've got the right guy, then we can pull out all the stops and nail him the right way. We get legitimate DNA samples. We interview him again. We get him to account for every minute of every Friday night he's ever spent on the motorway. We get his colleagues and his employers to tell us what they know about him and his movements. We interview people at all the motorway garages and cafes again. All the late-night lorry drivers. *Someone* has to have seen *something*.'

Templeton was looking at her with such keenness that she felt it would be churlish to disappoint him, despite her misgivings. And if Derby CID was involved, too, at least he couldn't go too far off the rails. Templeton was beginning to show all the signs of becoming a bit like Banks, Annie thought, and two of them she didn't need. But he had at least talked to her, told her about his thoughts, which was more than Banks did most of the time.

'OK,' she said finally. 'But I want you to work directly with Derby CID on this. If you talk to Cropley, I want this DS Browne or someone else from Derby with you. I don't want you going off on your own with this, Kev. Understood?'

Templeton nodded, still looking like the dog who'd got the bone. 'Yes, ma'am. Don't worry. It'll be a solid case, by the book.'

Annie smiled. 'Don't make promises you can't keep,' she said. 'But when it comes to it, I do expect a case that the CPS will be willing to take to court.'

'That's a tall order.'

Annie laughed. The Crown Prosecution Service were notoriously reluctant to take on anything they didn't feel gave them 100 per cent chance of getting a conviction. 'Do your best,' she said. 'Let's get back to the office.'

They finished their coffees, paid and set off back across Market Street. Annie had no sooner got inside the station doorway than her mobile rang. She gestured for Templeton to go on ahead of her.

'Detective Inspector Cabbot?' a familiar voice asked.

'Yes, Dr Lukas.'

'I'd like to talk to you.'

'Go ahead.'

'Not on the telephone. Can we meet?'

Well, thought Annie, there went her evening at home relaxing in the tub with a good book. It had better be worth it. 'I'm up north,' she said, glancing at her watch. 'It's twenty to four now. Depending on the trains I should be able to get down there by about eight.'

'That will be fine.'

'At the house, then?'

'No.' Dr Lukas named a French restaurant in Covent Garden. 'I will wait for you there,' she said, and hung up.

•

After his talk with Gareth Lambert, Banks took the tube to Charing Cross and headed for the Albion Club. It didn't open until late evening and the doors were locked. He tried knocking a few times, then he rattled them, but no one answered. A few passers-by gave him disapproving glances, as if he was an alcoholic desperate for a drink. In the end he gave the door a hard kick, then walked to Trafalgar Square and wandered among the hordes of tourists for a while, trying to rid himself of the sense of frustration and anxiety that had been building up in him ever since he had seen Roy's body laid out on the shingle.

It was mid-afternoon, and he felt hungry despite the full English breakfast at Annie's hotel that morning. He found an American-style burger joint near the top of Old Compton Street, just across from a body-piercing studio, and ordered a cheeseburger and a Coke.

As he sat eating and watching the world go by outside, he thought about his talk with Gareth Lambert: the theatrics with the cigar, the joke about Carmen Electra, the reference to Roy's being interested in arms deals again, the garbled warning as he was leaving – none of these things had been necessary, but Lambert hadn't been able to resist. Innocence? Arrogance? It wasn't always easy to tell them apart.

But there was something else that left him feeling very unsatisfied indeed. Banks, perhaps more than anybody, felt that Roy might have been less than legal in his business dealings over the years, and as Corinne had pointed out, Banks had always been ready to think the worst of his brother. It wasn't something he was proud of, but he thought he was right.

After the talk with Ian Hunt, though, not to mention after looking a bit deeper into Roy's life, he had come to believe that Roy really had learned a lesson from the foolhardy arms deal he had been involved in once. What he had seen in New York on September 11th 2001 had shaken him to the core and brought home to him the stark reality of terrorism. It was no longer a bus full of strangers in Basra or Tel Aviv, but people just like him going about their daily routine, some of whom he knew, dying right in front of his eyes.

Banks was starting to think that perhaps Gareth Lambert had overplayed his hand. He didn't believe that Roy wanted to get into arms dealing again and had been asking Lambert about old contacts. Unless he intended to seek retribution, which was unlikely at this late stage in the game. If Roy had any old scores he wanted to settle he would have done so years ago in the white heat of his rage after 9/11. But he hadn't. Which made Banks think that Lambert was lying. And there was only one clear explanation of that – to put Banks off the scent, divert him from the real business. More and more he was beginning to believe that that had something to do with the goings on at the Berger-Lennox Centre, with Jennifer Clewes and Roy, with Dr Lukas, with the mysterious Carmen Petri and the late girls. But how Lambert himself fitted in, Banks still didn't know. So what was the missing piece?

He doubted that Lambert would give it up. He was far too shrewd for that. He had enjoyed toying with Banks, telling him he had seen Roy on Friday when he no doubt already knew that was the day Roy disappeared. But he had done that because he knew Banks had got a description from Malcolm Farrow and because he thought there was nothing in his actions that night to incriminate him. No doubt it was true that Roy had left the Albion Club between half-past twelve and one o'clock, and that

Lambert hadn't left till three. Banks would go back to the club and check later that evening.

He finished his burger and took the tube back to South Kensington with a view to nosing around Roy's files again to see if there was anything there relating to the Albion Club or any of the members' names Lambert had given him. Perhaps he could phone some of them and see if they would verify Lambert's story. He also wanted to get in touch with his parents and the Peterborough police again and make sure everything was all right on the Hazels estate.

All was still quiet inside Roy's house. Banks locked the door behind him, slipped the keys in his pocket and headed for the kitchen. When he got there, he was surprised to see a man sitting at the kitchen table. He was even more surprised when the man turned and pointed a gun at him.

16

'Sit down slowly,' the man said, 'and keep your hands in sight.'

Banks did as he was told.

'Who are you?' the man asked.

'I might well ask the same.'

'I asked first. And I've got the gun.'

'My name's Alan Banks.'

'Do you have any identification?'

Banks put his hand slowly in his inside pocket and brought out his warrant card. He shoved it across the table to the man, who examined it carefully then pushed it back and slipped his gun inside a shoulder holster hidden by his jacket.

'What the fuck was all that about?' said Banks, feeling a rush of anger as the adrenalin surged back.

'I had to be sure,' said the man. 'Dieter Ganz, Interpol.' He offered his own card, which Banks studied, then stuck out his hand. Banks didn't feel like shaking it; he felt more like thumping him. Ganz shrugged. 'I'm sorry,' he went on. 'Detective Superintendent Burgess told me you might be here, but I had to make certain.' He didn't have much of an accent, but it was there, if you listened, in his speech patterns and careful diction.

'How did you get in?'

'It wasn't difficult,' said Ganz, glancing towards the back window. Banks saw that a circle of glass about the size of a man's fist had been cut out of it just below the catch.

'Well, I don't know about you,' said Banks, 'but after that little scare I could do with a drink.'

'No, thank you,' said Ganz. 'Nothing for me.'

'Suit yourself.' Banks opened a bottle of Roy's Côte de Nuits and poured himself a generous glass. His hand was still shaking. 'So Burgess sent you, did he?'

Ganz nodded. 'He told me where you would be. I'm sorry it took so long but he had a little difficulty finding me. I've been out of the country. It seems that we have interests in common.'

'First of all, you'd better tell me what yours are.'

'At the moment, my interest is in people-smuggling, more specifically the smuggling of young women for the purposes of sexual exploitation.'

Ganz looked undercover, Banks thought. He was young, early thirties at most. His blonde hair was a bit too long and greasy, and he clearly hadn't shaved for four or five days. The linen jacket he wore over his shirt was creased and stained, and his jeans needed a wash.

'And what interests do we have in common?' Banks asked.

Ganz took a piece of paper from his side pocket and unfolded it on the table. It was the photo Banks had given to Burgess. 'You've been asking questions about who this man with Gareth Lambert is,' he said.

'Lambert told me his name is Max Broda.'

'That is correct,' said Ganz. 'Max Broda. He's an Albanian travelling on an Israeli passport.'

'Why would he do that?'

Ganz smiled, showing a missing front tooth. 'No troublesome visas to worry about.'

'What's his business?' Gareth Lambert had told Banks that Max worked in the travel business, organizing tours and cruises, but somehow or other Banks didn't think Ganz would be here if that were the case.

'Broda's a trader,' said Ganz. 'Do you know what that is?'

'A trader in what?'

'Have you ever heard of the Arizona Market?'

'No.'

'It's in Bosnia, between Sarajevo and Zagreb. It's like those old markets you see in movies, you know, the Kasbah, so romantic with its stalls of colourful goods and its narrow winding streets. During the day many people go there to buy pirated CDs and DVDs and knock-off Rolexes and Chanel perfume. But at night it becomes a market of a different kind. At night you can buy stolen cars, guns, drugs. And young women. They are sold there like sheep and cattle are sold at your country shows. Sometimes they are auctioned off, made to parade naked holding numbers while the traders touch them and caress them before they make their bids, look in their mouths like you would if you were buying a horse. When they've been bought, many of them end up working in clubs and brothels in Bosnia, servicing the international peace-keeping forces, but many are also smuggled into other countries to work in peep-shows and massage parlours.'

'I suppose that's where Lambert comes in?' Banks said. 'The Balkan route.'

'That's one way,' Ganz agreed. 'Serbia, Croatia, Albania, Macedonia, Bosnia-Herzegovina, Montenegro and Kosovo. But there are others, and they are always changing. They cross wherever the border is unguarded.

Many women from Russia, Ukraine and Romania are smuggled through the eastern route, through Poland to Germany, or through Hungary. From Serbia to Italy many smugglers prefer to use Albanian seaports and ship the women over on rubber dinghies. But however they get here, once they are inside the EU, they can be moved around more freely.'

'So Lambert and Broda are in business together?'

'Yes. But not just England. That's why it is difficult to pin them down. We are trying to build up dossiers on similar operations in Paris, Berlin and Rome. It's a widespread problem.' He paused. 'I have seen these women, Mr Banks, talked to them. To call them "women" is not strictly accurate in the first place. They are no more than girls, some as young as fourteen or fifteen. They are lured from their homes by promises of jobs overseas as nannies and models, maids and waitresses. Sometimes they are smuggled out and sold straight away, sometimes they are taken to breaking-houses in Belgrade. There they are forced to live in filthy conditions. They are humiliated, beaten, starved, denied even the most basic human decencies, raped repeatedly, drugged, made to be compliant. When their spirits are broken, they are taken to the markets and sold to the highest bidder. After that, even if they are smuggled to Rome, Tel Aviv, Paris or London, they are forced to live in terrible conditions and service ten, twenty, even thirty men a night. If they don't play the game and pretend they are enjoying what is done to them, they are beaten and threatened. They are told that if they try to escape they will be hunted down and killed along with their families back home.'

'I've heard something of this,' said Banks shaken by

the images Ganz was offering up, 'but not . . . the extent.' He shook his head.

'Most people do not know,' Ganz said. 'Many prefer not to know. People like to think that girls who end up as prostitutes deserve no less, that they *chose* what they do, but many didn't. You can buy a young girl for as little as a thousand pounds and make over a hundred thousand pounds a year from her. Once she is worn out, you buy a new one. It makes good business sense, does it not?'

'I can't believe my brother was involved in this.'

'He wasn't, as far as I know,' said Ganz. 'From what Superintendent Burgess has told me, it is my guess that your brother and his girlfriend found out what was going on.'

'Through the Berger-Lennox Centre?'

'And through Dr Lukas, yes.'

'What's her part in all this?'

'She is trying to help the girls who get pregnant. That is all. She asks no questions. They are lucky they have someone like her, otherwise . . .'

'But what's her connection?'

'That we do not know for sure. This investigation here is very new. Most of the work we have been doing has been in Bosnia, Romania and Serbia.'

'Was Carmen one of the girls she was trying to help? Carmen Petri?'

Ganz frowned. 'I'm sorry, I do not know the name.'

'Are you certain?'

'Yes. Petri, you say?'

'Something like that.'

'It sounds Romanian.'

'But you haven't heard of her?'

'No.'

'OK,' said Banks. 'Go on.'

'Anyway,' Ganz went on. 'No matter what Dr Lukas does or does not know, there's a pimp involved somewhere, and Lambert and Broda supply him with girls smuggled from Eastern Europe. He probably keeps them in more than one house, depending on how many girls he owns. Perhaps there is even more than one pimp. I do not know. We have been waiting for Broda or Lambert to lead us there.'

'But they haven't?'

'Not yet. We were worried they might be onto us. Lambert's moving between the flat and the travel office, and he spends most weekends playing the local squire in his country manor.'

'Where's that?' Banks asked.

'A village called Quainton, near Buckingham. That's where he leads his exemplary life. Anyway, where there are pimps and smugglers you will usually find organized crime, too, and that is always dangerous.'

'The Russian Mafia?'

'Most likely.'

Banks told him what he had heard from Annie about the two men suspected of killing Jennifer and, perhaps, Roy.

Ganz nodded slowly. 'Sounds like their style.'

'So what next?'

'We think these recent murders might bring things to a boil. Someone might make a mistake.'

'Are you here to warn me off?'

Ganz laughed. 'Warn you off? Superintendent Burgess told me you would probably say something like that.'

'Oh? What else did he tell you?'

'That it would do no good. Some people we can warn off easily, but not you. He said you're nobody's man.'

'He's right.'

Ganz waved his hand in a dismissive gesture. 'No, I don't want to warn you off. I want to use you in a way I can't use the police who are investigating the case. I want you to keep on doing right what you're doing. I just want you to know that you're involved in stirring up a wasps' nest.'

'Go on.'

'I'm not saying that you're not in danger – they might have killed you if you had been at the address your brother gave his girlfriend – but I think with all the trouble caused by the two murders they have already committed, they would think twice right now about killing a policeman. When you came down here they no doubt kept an eye on you, just for form's sake, but they had other things to occupy them, and they knew your brother hadn't had time to tell you anything, or you wouldn't have been floundering around in the dark the way you were. They also tortured him before they killed him and he told them you knew nothing. He also told them where you lived, and they rang the men in the car. Fortunately, your brother gave them the wrong address. They sent the digital image on the mobile, too. Perhaps they didn't know you had it, but they knew your brother didn't. That's just their style, a sick joke. Max Broda himself, most likely. If you hadn't got it, whoever had the phone at the time would have. Even the police. It didn't matter to them. It couldn't be traced. It was stolen and they threw it away as soon as they had used it. After that, they let you know that they know where your parents live. That is also very much their style. And don't worry, your parents are safe. It wasn't something we could leave for the locals to deal with alone.'

'You have men there, too?'

'One. Armed. Anyway, now that you have actually been to see Gareth Lambert, and probably got him worried, things might be a bit different, I'm not sure.'

'You know I've seen Lambert?'

'Superintendent Burgess said he'd told you where to find him. I didn't think you would just sit around and not act on that information. What did you think?'

'I didn't believe him, didn't trust him.'

'In that, you were right. From now on, we'll try to watch your back as best we can, but for obvious reasons I can hardly show my hand. It is a shame you English police are unarmed.'

'I'm not too sure about that,' said Banks, thinking that there weren't many times in his career when he had felt the need for a gun, though now might be one of them. 'And by the way, do you have a licence for that one you're carrying?'

Ganz laughed. 'I have your government's permission, if that's what you mean. Do you want one? I'm sure I can get one for you.'

'I'd probably shoot myself in the foot,' said Banks. 'But thanks for the offer.'

'I almost forgot,' Ganz said. 'Mr Burgess told me to tell you he checked the number and the red Vectra was stolen from a multistorey car park in Putney. Does that mean anything to you?'

'Yes, thank you,' said Banks. It meant the car that had followed him from his parents' house was stolen, as he had expected.

'What are you going to do now?'

Banks looked at his watch. 'I'm going to have another glass of wine and think over what you've said.' Later, when it was open, he planned to visit the Albion Club on the Strand and see if he could find out more about Roy's final hours, but he didn't see any reason for telling Dieter Ganz that. If Interpol were keeping an eye on him, they'd find out soon enough, anyway.

•

DS Browne arrived in Eastvale from Derby at four o'clock, just after Annie had left for the station, bearing the positive fruits of the very discreet DNA comparison, and more.

She told Templeton on their way to Roger Cropley's house that DI Gifford had made enquiries at Cropley's software firm in London and found that he regularly left late on Fridays and that he had left late on Friday 23 April as there had been an office party that evening to celebrate a lucrative new contract.

Cropley was clearly not thrilled to see the two detectives on his doorstep late that afternoon. He tried to shut the door, but Templeton got a foot in. 'It's better if you let us in,' he said. 'Otherwise I'll stay here while DS Browne goes for a warrant.'

Cropley relaxed the pressure on the door and they entered, following him into the living room. 'I don't know why you won't leave me alone,' he said. 'I've told you time after time I know nothing about any murders.'

'You mean you've lied time after time,' said Templeton. 'By the way, this is DS Browne. She's come all the way from Derby just to talk to you. Say hello.'

Cropley said nothing, just stared at Susan Browne.

She sat down and smoothed her skirt. 'Mr Cropley,' she said, 'I'll come right to the point. When DC Templeton here first came to me with his suspicions I was sceptical. Now I've had time to think about it and make a few enquiries, I'm not too certain.'

'What enquiries?'

Susan slipped a folder out of her briefcase and opened it. 'According to my information, you left your office in Holborn at about eight o'clock on Friday the 23rd of April this year.'

'How do you know that?'

'Is it true?'

'I don't remember. How can you expect me to remember that far back?'

'It's true according to our evidence. That would put you at Trowell services around the same time as Claire Potter.'

'Look, this is absurd. It's nothing but circumstantial.'

'On two other occasions you left late,' Susan went on reading, 'two other women were either followed or assaulted shortly after leaving the M1.'

'I haven't assaulted anyone.'

'What we're going to do, Mr Cropley,' Susan went on, 'is take you down to the police station for further questioning. There you will be fingerprinted and photographed and a sample of your DNA will be taken. Once we have—'

The door opened and Mrs Cropley walked in. 'What's going on, Roger?' she demanded.

'They're harassing me again,' Cropley said.

His wife looked at Susan and Templeton, then back at her husband, an expression of scorn on her face. 'Maybe you deserve it,' she said.

'Do you know something, Mrs Cropley?' Templeton asked.

'He's my husband,' Mrs Cropley said.

'A woman has been murdered,' Susan said. 'Raped and stabbed.'

Mrs Cropley folded her arms.

Susan and Templeton looked at one another and Susan turned back to Cropley, who was now ashen. 'Once we have the photographs we'll be showing them to every worker in every cafe and petrol station on the motorway. Once we have your DNA we'll be comparing it with traces found at the scene of Claire Potter's murder. You might have thought you were thorough, Mr Cropley, but there's always something. In your case it's dandruff.'

'Dandruff?'

'Yes. Didn't you know we can get DNA from dandruff? If you even left one flake at the scene, we'll have it in the evidence room and we'll be testing it.'

Cropley looked stunned.

'Anything to say?' Susan went on.

Cropley just shook his head.

'Right.' Susan stood up. 'Roger Cropley, you're under arrest for suspicion of the murder of Claire Potter. You do not have to say anything, but it may harm your defence if you do not mention when questioned something which you later rely on in court. Anything you do say may be given in evidence.'

When Cropley left between Susan and Templeton, head hung, his wife turned her back and stood in the centre of the room rigid as a statue, arms still folded.

●

Annie was half an hour late as she made her way through the crowded pavements of Covent Garden to the restaurant Dr Lukas had mentioned on Tavistock Street. She had just missed the 4.25 and as the 5.05 was a slow train she had to catch the 5.25, which arrived on time at 8.13. On the train, she rang Dr Lukas at the centre, but was told the doctor wasn't there that day. She left a message, which she couldn't be sure Dr Lukas had received, and then she had phoned the restaurant to leave a message there, too. She also rang her usual hotel to book a room for the night. The desk clerk recognized her name and voice and got so chatty it was embarrassing.

Well, Annie thought as she dashed into the crowded restaurant, Dr Lukas had said she would be waiting, and there were worse places to wait. She spotted the doctor at a corner table and made her way over. It was a small restaurant with intimate lighting and white linen table-cloths. A blackboard on the wall listed specials and wine suggestions. There was music playing, but it was so faint Annie couldn't make out what it was. It sounded French, though.

'Did you get my message?' she asked, sitting down and catching her breath.

Dr Lukas nodded. 'It's all right,' she said, tapping the paperback she was reading. 'I have my book. I was prepared to wait. They know me here. They are very understanding.'

Annie browsed the menu, which was decidedly traditional, and decided on coq au vin. Dr Lukas had already settled on bouillabaisse. Once they'd got their orders in, the doctor poured Annie a glass of Chablis and topped up her own.

'I'm sorry I made you come all this way,' she said, 'but I couldn't possibly tell you over the telephone.'

'It's all right,' said Annie. 'I had to come back anyway. You're going to tell me everything?'

'Everything I know.'

'Why not tell me before?'

'Because the situation has changed. And things have gone too far.'

The waiter appeared with a basket of bread and Annie broke off a chunk and buttered it. She hadn't eaten on the train and realized she was starving. 'I'm listening.'

'It's very difficult for me,' Dr Lukas began. 'It's not something I'm proud of.'

'Helping the girls?'

'Not that so much. If I hadn't done, who would?'

'Is it about Carmen Petri?'

'Only partly. To understand what I have to say, you have to know where I come from. L'viv is a very old city, a very beautiful city in many ways, with many fine ancient buildings and churches. My mother was a seamstress until arthritis made her fingers no more use. My father was a mining engineer. My parents remember when Jews were rounded up and killed by the Germans in the war. You hear about the massacre at Babi Yar, near Kiev, but there were many smaller massacres elsewhere, including L'viv. My parents were lucky. They were children then and they hid and were not found. When I lived there, Ukraine was still part of the Soviet Union. I grew up in a modern part of the city, ugly Stalinist blocks. We were poor and ill-fed, but there was a strong sense of community, and sometimes you could even believe in the ideals behind the reality of Soviet life. When Ukraine became an independent state in August

1991, things were chaotic for a while. Nobody knew what was going to happen. That was when I left.'

Annie listened, interested in Dr Lukas's story but curious as to where it was leading. Before long, their food was served and Dr Lukas poured more wine. As if reading Annie's mind, she smiled and said, 'You might be wondering where all this is going, but please indulge me.' She talked more about her childhood, the state school, unsanitary living conditions, her ambition to become a doctor. 'And here I am,' she said. 'Ambition fulfilled.'

'You must be very proud.'

Dr Lukas frowned. 'Proud? Yes. Most days. About a year ago a man came to see me at my home. I remembered him from school, from the building in L'viv where his family lived, close to mine. He said he had heard I was here through his parents, who had read an article about me in the local newspaper. It's true. Many people left Ukraine but their stories continue to be of interest to those who have not experienced the world outside.'

'What did he want?'

'When he was at school he was a bully. When he got older he and his gang terrorized the building we lived in, extorting money, burgling units, selling black-market goods. Nobody was safe from him. Then suddenly he was gone. You can imagine how relieved we all were.'

'But he turned up here, in London?'

'Yes, he told me he travelled all around Europe, learning the ways of the free world, the free economy, and his training in L'viv served him well.'

'He's the man who sends the late girls to you, isn't he?'

Dr Lukas said nothing for a moment. She had turned

pale as she was talking, Annie noticed, and her bouillabaisse sat mostly uneaten in front of her. Finally, she
whispered, 'Yes. That's what he is now. A pimp. When
he first came to see me it was because one of his girls
had problems with her periods that made her unreliable.
Then he realized what a good idea it would be for me to
be their unofficial doctor, so to speak. And that was the
start of it all.'

'And this has been going on for a year?'

'Yes.'

'And how many girls have you seen during that time?'

'Maybe fifteen, sixteen.'

'All pregnant?'

'Most. Some had sexually transmitted infections. One
had a bad rash in her pubic area. One girl was bleeding
from her anus. Whatever it was, he brought them to me
at the centre after it was closed for the day. I would get
a phone call telling me to stay late.'

'Why did you help him?' Annie thought she knew the
answer to the question as she was asking it, but she
needed to hear it from Dr Lukas. A noisy party across
the room broke into gales of laughter.

Dr Lukas looked over at them, then turned to face
Annie, her expression sombre. 'He told me he would kill
my parents back in L'viv if I didn't do as he said or if
I told anyone. I know he can do it. He still has contacts
there.'

'What's changed?'

'My parents are no longer in L'viv. They have left for
America to live with my brother in San Francisco. I was
waiting to hear confirmation. They telephoned me today.'

'What about you?'

'I don't care about me,' said Dr Lukas. 'Besides, he's not going to hurt me. I'm far too useful to him alive.'

'If it's any consolation,' Annie said, 'he'll be in jail.'

Dr Lukas laughed. 'Yes,' she said. 'Running his empire from a cell. And on the outside someone will replace him. Another monster. The world has no shortage of monsters.' She shook her head. 'But it's gone far enough. Poor Jennifer . . . that man . . .'

'Roy Banks was his name. What about Carmen Petri?'

Dr Lukas gave Annie a curious look. 'That was the beginning of the end, really. Carmen.'

'What do you mean?'

'Until Carmen, I could turn a blind eye, could even believe that what I was doing was good and that the girls had better lives as prostitutes here than they would in their war-torn villages and towns back home. I didn't know the truth. Like everyone, I thought they chose what they did, that there must be something wrong with them to start with, something bad about them. I was naive.'

'How did Carmen change this?'

'The girls wouldn't talk. I asked them about their lives but they refused to tell me anything. They were too scared. Carmen . . . she was a bit more confident, more intelligent . . . I don't know. Perhaps it was even Jennifer, the way she was kind to her. Whatever the reason, Carmen did let something slip.'

'What was that?'

'She told me that one of the new girls had been locked in a small room and beaten because she refused to perform some vile sex act. She also told me that the girl had been on her way home from school in a small village in Bosnia when two men abducted her at knifepoint and forced her into prostitution. She was fifteen. That was the first time I realized that these girls didn't start out one step from prostitution, that there was nothing "bad" about them. They were normal girls, like you and me, and they were forced to do what they do. Like me, they fear for their families back home. Those who have families. These poor girls . . . He has them smuggled from Bosnia, Moldavia, Romania and Kosovo. Many are orphans because of the wars. When they have to leave the orphanages at sixteen they often have no money and nowhere to go. His men are waiting for them on the doorstep. The girls are terrified of him. They won't talk about what happens, but I've seen bruises, cuts sometimes. I didn't ask questions, and I am not proud of that, but I saw. Then Carmen . . . she spoke out.'

'When was this?'

'A week last Monday.'

'What happened to her?'

'Nothing, as far as I know.'

'She's not dead?'

'I don't think so. I can't see why she would be.'

'But if they thought she told you and Jennifer what was really going on . . . ?'

'I don't think they knew what she told us, and she's too valuable to them.'

'But they must have found out something,' Annie said. 'Jennifer and Roy Banks are dead. When Jennifer told Roy, he must have started digging, asking questions. He had contact with people who . . . well, let's just say he knew criminals.'

'Perhaps I am wrong, then. I don't know. All I know about Carmen is what she told me. She got pregnant, so he sent her to me. I suppose the only unusual thing is that Carmen has decided to have the baby. She's a devout Catholic and she refused to have a termination.'

'That's permitted?'

'In some circumstances,' said Dr Lukas. 'It would depend on the loss of income. Carmen is one of the special girls, blessed with good looks and a fine figure. She is also a very intelligent girl and she speaks English very well. She was never a street prostitute, more what you would term a call girl.'

'So how is he going to make up for his loss of income?'

'I can only guess,' said Dr Lukas. 'There are some men who like to have sex with pregnant women and are willing to pay extra for it. That way she would have fewer customers but make as much, or more, money.'

Annie's stomach turned. She could understand why Dr Lukas wasn't eating. She'd lost her appetite as well. 'And the baby?'

'Adoption. She spoke about the way they were taking care of her and feeding her well for a Mr Garrett, who I assume is paying good money for Carmen's baby.'

'Will you tell me the pimp's name?'

'His real name is Hadeon Mazuryk. He calls himself Harry. His nickname is "Happy Harry" because he looks eternally sad. He is not, of course, it's just a freak of physiognomy.'

'Do you know where he keeps the girls?'

Dr Lukas nodded. 'There's a house near King's Cross. I went there once. An emergency. You must be careful, though.'

'Why?'

'He has a gun. I've seen it.'

•

Banks had raided Roy's wardrobe again for suitable attire. He didn't think he would get far in the Albion Club wearing jeans and a casual shirt. Trousers were a problem. Roy's didn't fit him and he had only brought one pair with him, which didn't match any of Roy's jackets. In the end he just had to hope the place was poorly lit so that black and navy blue didn't look too bad together.

The man on the door, looking rather like a cross between a butler and a bouncer, asked him for his membership. Banks flashed his warrant card.

'Police? I hope there's no trouble, sir?' he said.

'None at all,' said Banks. 'Just a few questions and I'll be out of your hair.'

'Questions?'

'Yes. Were you on duty here last Friday?'

'Yes, sir.'

'Do you remember Roy Banks arriving with Gareth Lambert?'

'Such a tragedy about Mr Banks. The perfect gentleman. Who could do such a thing?'

'Who indeed? But did you see them arrive?'

'Yes. It would have been about a quarter, maybe twenty, past ten.'

'And were you here when they left?'

'They didn't leave together, sir. Mr Banks left first, at about twelve thirty, and Mr Lambert stayed much later. Perhaps three o'clock, something like that.'

So Lambert was telling the truth about that much, at least. 'Did they leave alone?'

'Yes, sir.'

'Do you know where Mr Banks went after he left?'

'Mr Banks didn't say. He just bade me goodnight as usual.'

'You didn't call a minicab for him?'

'There are always plenty of taxis on the Strand, and there's a taxi-rank at Charing Cross.'

'Right,' said Banks. 'OK to go inside?'

'Please try not to upset the members.'

'I only want to talk to the staff.'

'Very well.'

Banks was surprised when he got inside the club. The door opened into a spacious, low-ceilinged bar, and where he had been expecting dark wainscoting, chandeliers and waiters in burgundy bum-freezers, he found tubular fittings, muted pastel lighting and waitresses in pinstripe suits, with trousers rather than skirts. Fan-shaped splashes of colour from well-hidden lights decorated the walls in shades of blue, pink, green, red and orange. The chrome tables were high, with matching leather-topped stools. This definitely wasn't one of those old gentlemen's clubs where the right sort of people stay over when they are down in the city for the weekend; it was primarily an upmarket casino with bar and restaurants facilities, the sort of place you might have found James Bond in fifty years ago. Now it played host to a hipper, younger crowd of stockbrokers, investment bankers and the occasional old smuggler like Gareth Lambert.

As it turned out, the dress code was also a lot more relaxed than Banks had expected – he had never been to a club before and he still thought in terms of Lord Peter Wimsey and Bertie Wooster – and he was surprised to see that not everyone was wearing a tie or a suit. Business casual was in. The place wasn't very busy, but a few people sat around drinking and chatting, and a group of Japanese businessmen had the one large table by the far wall, where they were entertaining some expensive-looking women. Most of the people in the place seemed to be in their thirties, which made Roy and Lambert slightly older than the average member. Still, from what Banks had learned, Roy was certainly young at heart. Nobody paid Banks any undue attention. There was no music.

Banks took one of the stools at the bar and ordered a bottle of Stella. The price was every bit as outrageous as he had expected. The bartender was a woman in her late twenties, by the look of her, about the same age as Corinne and Jennifer. She had very fine short hair dyed pink and blonde. She smiled at Banks when she took his order. She had a nice smile, dimples too.

Banks showed her his card. 'Do you work here every night?' he asked.

'Most nights,' she said, scrutinizing the card more closely than the doorman had. 'Yorkshire? What brings you down here?'

'Cases can take you all over the place,' Banks said. 'People move around a lot more than they used to.'

'You can say that again.'

'Actually, I'm making a few enquiries about Roy Banks. I understand he was a member.'

'Poor Mr Banks,' she said. 'He was a real sweetheart.'

'You knew him?'

'Not really "knew". I mean, not outside of work. But we talked from time to time. You tend to do that, in this job. He always had time for the bar staff, not like some of our more stuck-up members.'

'Did he sit at the bar and tell you his troubles?'

She laughed. 'Oh, no. That only happens in films.'

'What's your name, by the way?'

'Maria.'

'Pleased to meet you, Maria.'

'What relation are you?'

'What do you mean?'

'Your name's Banks, too. I saw it on that card. Are you his brother?'

'Yes,' Banks said.

'You must be gutted.'

'I am. But I'm also trying to find out what happened. Did you talk to him last Friday?'

'Yes. He and Mr Lambert were sitting at that table just over there.' She pointed to a discreet corner table. 'Mr Banks always made a point of coming over and saying hello and asking me how I was doing. And he always made sure he left a decent tip.'

'Did he have anything to say that night?'

A waitress appeared asking for drinks. Maria excused herself for a moment and filled the order with graceful efficiency. 'What was it you wanted to know?' she asked when she came back.

'Just if Roy had said anything out of the ordinary to you.'

'No. Nothing. Not that that I remember.'

'Did he seem worried?'

'Not at first. A bit preoccupied, maybe.'

'Later?'

'After he'd been talking to Mr Lambert for a while he seemed to be getting uncomfortable, if you know what I mean. I don't know how to describe it, but you could sort of feel the tension, even from over here.'

'Others noticed?'

'I wouldn't say that. I've always been very sensitive to the vibes people give off.'

'And these were bad?'

'Yes, I think so.'

'Were they arguing?'

'No. They never raised their voices or anything like that. It was just a sort of tense negotiation.'

Lambert had told Banks that Roy had been pressing him for contacts in the arms business, but he didn't believe that. 'What happened next?'

'After he used the telephone, Mr Banks went through to the casino and I didn't see him again.'

'Mr Lambert?'

'He sat by himself for a while, then he went into the casino, too.'

'You say Roy used the telephone?'

'Yes.'

'Where is it?'

'There's a public telephone in the corridor by the toilets,' she said. 'Down there.' She pointed directly across the room. Banks turned and saw the phone on the wall. From where Lambert had been sitting, he couldn't possibly have seen Roy make the call. 'Not a lot of people use it because everyone's got a mobile these days, haven't they, but he must have forgotten his or the battery was dead or something.'

Banks thought of the mobile sitting on Roy's kitchen table. 'Was it a long phone call?'

'No. Just two or three minutes.'

'How long had he been here when he made it?'

'Not long. Maybe half an hour or so, a bit longer.'

That must have been the call he made to Jennifer,

Banks thought, sending her up to Yorkshire, and to her death. 'And how did he seem after that?'

'Like I said, he went into the casino. He didn't say goodbye, though, and that's not like him.'

'Did Mr Lambert make any phone calls?'

'Not that I saw.'

'Could he have done?'

'Oh, yes. I mean, he went to the toilet. He could have used his mobile there, if he had one with him. But I didn't see him make any calls, that's all I meant.'

'Thanks very much, Maria,' said Banks. 'You've been a great help.'

'I have?'

Banks made sure to leave her a decent tip and wandered out onto the Strand. He glanced about him to see if there was anyone watching for him, but if there was, he didn't notice. According to the doorman and Maria, Roy had left the club around half-past twelve. There were plenty of taxis passing by, Banks could see. So what had Roy done? Got in a taxi? Or had someone offered him a lift? It couldn't have been Lambert, because he was still in the casino. So who?

17

The sun was up by the time the operation had been approved by the brass in SO19, the Metropolitan Police Force Firearms Unit at Scotland Yard, and the team had been assembled and briefed. Annie and Brooke gathered with the specialist firearms officers outside the house near King's Cross station, in the narrow streets around Wharfdale Road. The house was part of a terrace, and the SO19 team leader had acquired a set of plans. There were eight officers, all wearing protective headgear and body armour and carrying Glock handguns and Heckler and Koch MP5 carbines. Each man had been told what section he was to secure. Three more men watched the back of the house.

It was an eerie sight, Annie thought, and there was something slightly unreal about it. One or two onlookers had gathered at the street corners, held back by uniformed officers stationed there. It was a humid morning and a light mist hung in the air. There was little traffic in the immediate area but Annie could hear horns and engines in the distance. Another day in the big city was beginning.

In a way, Annie wished that Banks had been granted permission to attend; she would have liked him by her side. But these operations were strictly regulated and there was no way they were letting Roy Banks's brother be a part of it. She had talked to him on the phone late the previous evening, and he had told her about his visit to the Albion Club. In exchange, she had told him what Dr Lukas told her about the late girls and Carmen Petri.

On the prearranged signal, the SO19 team battered down the front door and stormed into the house. Annie and Brooke, unarmed, had instructions to wait outside until the place was secured, then they would be allowed in to question any witnesses or suspects. Brooke was unusually quiet. Annie felt herself tense up as she heard sounds from inside the house, shouts, commands, a woman's scream, something thudding on the floor.

But there were no shots, and she took that as a good sign.

She had no idea how long it took, but eventually the team leader emerged and told them the house was secured. There had been one guard armed with a baseball bat and three other men, none of them armed. The rest of the occupants were young women. They had best take a look for themselves, he told them, shaking his head in disbelief.

Annie and Brooke went inside. It was a shabby place, in poor repair, with old wallpaper stained and peeling off in places, no stair carpet and only dirty linoleum on the ground floor. The smells of stale sex and cigarette smoke permeated the air. Little light got in through the windows, so the officers had turned on all the lights they could find, mostly bare bulbs, and they hardly flattered the scene, just gave it an extra harsh edge.

The seven girls were all in a small room upstairs. Probably more lived there, Annie guessed, but they would be out working the streets around King's Cross. No matter what the time of day, business never stopped. The area had had a bad reputation for years, and Annie remembered how the girls were once called Maggie's Children because they came down on the trains from the north when all the jobs disappeared up there. These days they might be known as Putin's Children, Iliescu's or Terzic's.

The SO19 officers wandered around as Annie and Brooke went over to the girls. The sparsely furnished room smelled of sweat and cheap perfume and the girls were all dressed in skimpy clothing, tight hot pants, micro skirts, thigh-highs, see-through tops, and their faces were garish with lipstick and eye make-up. Some of them looked high; none looked much older than fifteen. Beyond the fear in their expressions Annie could see only resignation and despair. This was truly the generation of lost girls Dr Lukas had described, she thought. Christ, she wanted to take them home and scrub the make-up off and feed them a decent meal. Most of them were skinny, and some had sores on their lips. Several of them were smoking and that added to the cloying atmosphere of the room.

Other rooms in the house were equipped with beds and washbasins for the girls to entertain clients, but this seemed to be a general sitting room. The four men the SO19 team had found had all been handcuffed and bundled out into the van. The girls had been checked for weapons as a matter of routine, then left alone, a guard on the door.

'Ma'am?' One of the team stood at the door and beckoned Annie. 'I think you should see this.'

He led Annie to a room no bigger than a cupboard. Inside was a young girl, naked but for the thin sheet another officer was wrapping around her. She was painfully thin and blood crusted the cleft between her nose and upper lip. She was alive, but her eyes looked dead. The only other thing in the room was a bucket, its stench abominable.

'Get an ambulance,' Annie said. She helped the girl to her feet, keeping the sheet wrapped around her and slowly took her back to the others. One of the girls ran forward and took the newcomer in her arms, mumbling endearments, and helped her sit in an armchair, perching on the arm beside her.

'Can you speak English?'

The girl nodded. 'A little.'

'What happened to her?'

'She's new,' the girl told her, in heavily accented English, still stroking her friend's hair. 'She would not do what they tell her so they lock her up and beat her. She has not eaten for three days.'

Brooke was trying to talk to the other girls but it didn't appear they spoke English. Whatever the reason, they all seemed afraid of him and no one would say a word. Most of them wouldn't even look at him. Annie thought she understood why. She took him aside.

'Look, Dave,' she said, seeing his crestfallen expression. 'It's not your fault, but they don't know you're a decent man. They don't know any decent men. It might be best if you went down and questioned the men.'

Brooke nodded. 'You'll be OK?'

'I'll manage,' said Annie. She touched him gently on the shoulder and he left.

'What will happen to us?' asked the girl on the chair arm, who seemed to have taken charge. She had dark hair down to her shoulders, thin arms and a pale complexion.

It was a good question and Annie wasn't sure she knew the answer. The object of the raid had been to take

Happy Harry Mazuryk and, with any luck, find Carmen
Petri. Annie didn't know if Harry had been one of the
men arrested, though from what she had seen in passing,
none of them matched his description.

'You'll all be taken care of,' she said. 'What's your
name?'

'Veronika.'

'Right, Veronika. I'd like to ask you a few questions.'

'I can't tell you anything. He will kill me.'

'No, he won't,' said Annie. 'We'll put him in jail.'

'You don't understand. *He* wasn't here, only his stupid
guard. Those men are here for . . .' She made an obscene
gesture with her hips.

'Where is Hadeon Mazuryk?'

She flinched at the sound of his name. 'I don't know.'

'OK,' said Annie. 'What about Carmen? Do you know
Carmen Petri?' She looked around at the frightened girls.
'Is she here?'

They all shook their heads. One started crying. Annie
turned back to Veronika. 'Do you know Carmen?'

Veronika nodded.

'Where is she?'

'She is not here. Carmen is one of the special girls.'

'What do you mean?'

'She is very beautiful. She speaks very good English.
She does not have to go out to the street. Men come to
her. Pay more.'

This was what Annie had heard from Dr Lukas. Still
she wondered whether Carmen had been killed. 'Do
you know where she is, Veronika? I really need to talk to
her.'

Veronika turned to the girl in the sheet and stroked
her hair again, then she looked back at Annie, her face

stern. 'There is another house,' she said. 'I have talked to Carmen. She has told me. She is there.'

•

Banks didn't regret too much being barred from the King's Cross raid. He had been on such operations before and generally found the paramilitary elements quite tedious. He did, however, want to know the results, which was why he was sitting anxiously at the kitchen table early with his morning coffee and newspaper, mobile beside him at the ready.

He was still puzzling over what had happened between Roy and Lambert at the Albion Club that Friday, and the best he could come up with was that Lambert had proposed something Roy didn't approve of and became worried he'd give the game away. Their friendship went back to university days and they had got up to all sorts of things together. They had been out of touch for a long time, though, and Lambert probably didn't know that Roy had redrawn his moral lines.

If Lambert wanted him to come in on importing abducted teenage girls for the sex trade, as Annie suggested was happening, then Roy would probably have balked at that, Banks thought. If he had been ignorant of the true way in which the girls were forced into prostitution, as Dr Lukas had told Annie she was, then he would have found out via Jennifer, who had talked with Carmen Petri and learned something of the truth on the Monday of the week she died. The timing was important here. Roy might have been on the verge of getting involved when he found out the truth after Carmen told Jennifer, and Lambert spent the next few days trying to convince him it was OK. Then something else must have tipped the balance, something Roy found out the day he disappeared.

Banks guessed that when Roy left the bar for the casino, Lambert went into the toilet and phoned someone – maybe Max Broda – and told him the situation was critical. After that, Broda took control and had a car ready to pick Roy up outside the club and take him to the abandoned factory in Battersea. Ponytail and his crony must also have been working for Broda, and they had been assigned to watch Jennifer and keep an eye on her movements. Banks could imagine the mobile conversations back and forth between the Mondeo, following Jennifer, and the factory, where Roy had been taken, culminating in the order to kill her. Perhaps Roy had also intended to head up to Banks's cottage when he realized things had gone too far, but he hadn't had the chance. They'd got to him first.

As Banks thought about it all, a number of things came together in his mind, the way it sometimes happened when he felt most lost. Annie had told him that Dr Lukas had said the baby was being adopted by a 'Mr Garrett'. He remembered Dieter Ganz saying 'Gareth' with his slight accent yesterday, and imagined that the men Carmen Petri had heard saying it also had accents, as she no doubt did herself. In Ganz's case, it had come out sounding like 'Garrett' and that was exactly what Dr Lukas had said, that the men were taking good care of Carmen and her baby for 'Mr Garrett'.

Was that it, then, the new thing that Roy had discovered? Was Lambert himself adopting Carmen's baby, buying it, and was that why it was so important for him to stop Roy blowing the whistle? There was one way to find out, one person he could ask.

Banks went up to Roy's office, where he thought he had seen an atlas. He pulled it down and found that Quainton was in Buckinghamshire, not too far from Aylesbury. It was a nice day for a drive in the country, he thought, and it would be interesting to meet the elusive Mrs Lambert. He grabbed his jacket and his mobile and set off for the car.

•

The second house was about a mile away, in Islington, but light years away in comfort. It was a detached house with a small garden, the curtains all shut tight against the morning light. If the SO19 team leader hadn't verified that it belonged to Mr Hadeon Mazuryk, Annie would have thought it the home of a perfectly normal family with a couple of kids, a dog, and a people carrier.

The team had had to move fast, before Mazuryk found out about the King's Cross raid, and the SO19 team had reassembled in the van for a quick briefing. The layout of the house was similar to many others in the area, including the house one of the men lived in, and between them, the officers were able to sketch out a likely floor plan. Then they quietly evacuated the houses on either side and sealed off the street at both ends.

Annie sat across the street in the car with DI Brooke, who had got nowhere talking to the men at King's Cross, and watched. She could hear faint music from one of the downstairs rooms, a bass line of some pop song she didn't recognize. Then she heard a man cough and someone laugh.

'You're very quiet, Dave,' she said, turning to Brooke, who was staring down the street.

'I was warned off,' he said, without looking at her.

'What?'

'I was warned off, Annie.' Now he looked her in the eye and she could see his self-disgust. 'Orders from the top. Gareth Lambert's part of an international investigation. If the police swarmed over him, all the major players would disappear into the woodwork for years. That's what I was told. If I valued my promotion . . . well, I think you can fill in the rest. Oliver Drummond and William Gilmore seemed likely leads.'

'I'm sorry, Dave,' Annie said, feeling embarrassed for him. 'You were only following orders.'

He gave her an ironic glance. 'Isn't that what the Germans said?'

'This is different. What else could you do?'

Brooke shrugged. 'I don't know. I just don't like the feeling, that's all. I doubt they'd warn off your pal Banks so easily.'

Annie smiled. 'DCI Banks is a law unto himself,' she said. 'Partly because he doesn't feel he has anything to lose. It's not necessarily a position to envy.' She gestured to the SO19 officers in the street. 'Anyway, for better or for worse we're getting some action now.'

Brooke nodded. 'It's gone too far. Even the brass couldn't justify leaving vulnerable underage girls in captivity like that for one night longer than they had to. Besides, we still don't know if or how Lambert is connected. Maybe it's something completely different.'

'Whatever it is, we'll find out soon,' said Annie. 'They're going in.'

Half the men went around the back and the rest prepared to enter through the front door. Annie held her breath as one of them slammed the battering ram and the wood splintered, then they were in. She heard similar sounds from the back.

This time, in addition to the shouting and screaming, Annie heard shots. So did the neighbours further down the street, who soon appeared at windows and in doorways, only to be kept at bay by the uniformed officers deployed on crowd duties. After an agonizing period of silence, the team leader stepped out and waved Annie and Brooke inside.

'Everybody all right?' Annie asked.

'We are,' he said. 'Eddie took one on the chest but the body armour worked fine. He's feeling a bit sore, that's all. Look, we're waiting for the ambulance and for the brass to get here. You know what it's like whenever shots are fired. Forms in triplicate. Questions. You feel more like a criminal than a copper.'

Annie and Brooke followed the grumbling team leader into the front room. Four men had been sitting around playing cards at a folding table. Two of them were handcuffed and two of them were slumped against the wall with holes in their chests, covered in dark bibs of blood. Blood had also sprayed on the walls and carpeting. Annie felt a bit sick. She hadn't seen many gunshot victims before and hadn't been prepared for the smell of the exploded ammunition mingled with fresh blood in the room.

One of the dead men resembled the description she had heard of Hadeon 'Happy Harry' Mazuryk, and the other one had a body builder's physique, with long greasy hair tied back in a ponytail and a thick gold chain around his neck. One of the bullets must have severed the chain because it snaked in one long piece down his bloody chest.

Annie didn't recognize the other two men. Both were looking sullen, handcuffed and guarded by SO19 officers with their Heckler and Kochs at the ready. One of the men might have been the driver of the Mondeo, but all the descriptions she had of him were vague. The more she looked at the other one, the more he seemed familiar: spiky hair, goatee. Then she remembered: the photograph Banks had showed her, the one his brother apparently took just days before he died. This was the man who had been sitting with Gareth Lambert at an outdoor cafe. Now there was a connection, whatever it meant.

An ambulance arrived and men filled the room. Annie and Brooke followed one of the officers upstairs. There were three bedrooms, all of them occupied by beautiful young girls, who were all more than a little unnerved by the shooting. SO19 officers dealt with the other two and Brooke hung back as Annie entered the room and walked over to the only pregnant girl, who was lying on the bed looking frightened.

'Carmen?' she said. 'Carmen Petri?'

The girl nodded, seeming surprised that Annie knew her name. She looked a little older than the girls in the King's Cross house, perhaps as old as nineteen or twenty, and she wore much less make-up. It was difficult to tell what her figure had been like because she was about six months pregnant, but she had a beautiful face: full lips with a Bardot pout, a perfectly proportioned nose, flawless complexion – apart from a beauty spot by the side of her mouth – and deep dark-blue eyes damp with tears. Annie couldn't read her expression and guessed that Carmen was a girl who had become adept at hiding her feelings and thoughts for the purposes of self-preservation.

'What happened?' Carmen asked.

'I'll explain it all later,' Annie said. 'I'm happy to meet you at last. I'm Annie Cabbot. Will you answer some questions?'

'Where's Hadeon?'

'Dead.'

'Good. And Artyom?'

'Who's he?'

'Big man. Ponytail.'

'He's dead, too.'

'That is good, too,' she said, shifting on the bed slightly. Annie could see an expression of discomfort cross her features as she moved. Probably the baby kicking.

'What happened to you?' Annie asked. 'How did you get here?'

'Is a long story,' she said. 'And a long time ago. I was taken from the street when I was a young girl.'

'How young?'

'Sixteen.'

'By who?'

She shrugged. 'A man.'

'Where.'

'A village near Craiova, in Romania. You will not have heard of it.'

'You went to see Dr Lukas at the Berger-Lennox Centre?'

'Yes. She was good to me.' Carmen reached for a cigarette. 'She wanted me to stop smoking, but I tell her a girl must have one vice. I don't drink and I don't take drugs.' Her English was remarkably good, Annie thought, and she could see what Veronika meant about her being beautiful. There was a sophistication about her beyond her years, and Carmen had the kind of class you don't usually associate with people in her profession.

Annie wondered how on earth she could stand the life without some form of escape, but what did she know? And what could she presume to know about someone who had been through what Carmen had been through?

'Do you remember Jennifer Clewes?'

'Yes. She works with Dr Lukas.'

'She's dead, too, Carmen. Someone killed her.'

Carmen looked alarmed. 'Why?'

'We don't know. We think it might have to do with something you told her. Jennifer and her boyfriend seemed to know something about what was going on here. Did you say anything to her when you were talking last week?'

Carmen looked down at her swollen belly. 'The doctor think we do this because we want to,' she said. 'I tell her she does not know how bad things are, that none of us are here because we want. I tell Jennifer, too. Some stories of what happen to girls. I should not have said that. But I think I was feeling brave because they were treating me well, different from the others.'

'When did you tell her this?'

'Last time I go to clinic. Not long. Monday, I think.'

'Did Artyom know you'd been talking?'

'He took me back in the car and told Hadeon. They could not hurt me to make me tell them anything. I knew that. But . . .'

'I think I know,' said Annie. 'They threatened to harm your parents back home, didn't they?'

'Yes,' Carmen whispered.

'So you told them.'

'Yes.'

Annie nodded. 'That house in King's Cross,' she said. 'We've just come from there. Those girls were treated terribly. I've never seen anything like it.'

'I have been there. Hadeon always tells me I have been very lucky. For me men pay hundreds of pounds a night, for those girls they must have many men to make such money. Hadeon makes his girls work very hard. He tells me if I am not good he will send me there, too. I am happy he is dead.'

'Do you think he would have people killed who found out what he was doing?'

Carmen nodded. 'Harry once killed a girl with his bare hands for refusing to have sex with him.'

'Did Artyom work for him?'

'Yes. And Boris.'

'With the cropped blonde hair?'

'That is Boris.'

The driver, Annie thought. 'There was another man downstairs.' Annie described him. 'Do you know who he is?'

'All I know is that his name is Max and that he brings new girls for Harry. He is not always here. I have never talked to him.'

Annie imagined that when Mazuryk knew Carmen had talked, he or Max had brought Lambert in to handle damage control, and that was what had been going on all week. Mazuryk had also set Artyom and the driver to keep an eye on Jennifer, watch where she went. Perhaps Lambert had talked to Roy and managed to assure Mazuryk that no one would be ringing the police, but negotiations were tense, then something else happened, something that changed it all.

'Do you know a man called Lambert?' Annie asked.

'Lambert? No,' said Carmen.

Annie gestured towards her stomach. 'What's going to happen to you?'

'I'm going to have my baby. It makes them take good care of me. I get food and they leave me alone. I get bored sometimes. The only times I can go out is to see Dr Lukas, and then Artyom usually takes me. But it is much better than before.'

'Do you know who the father is?'

Carmen gave her a scornful look.

'And what about the baby? Dr Lukas told me it was going to be adopted.'

'Yes. They want to sell the baby to a rich man. She will go to a good family and have a good life. That is why they treat me well, to keep the baby healthy. Harry always jokes when he sees me, how he must keep me healthy for Mr Garrett.' A sudden anxiety came into her voice. 'But Harry is dead. What is going to happen to me now?'

'I don't know,' said Annie. 'I really don't know.'

•

Banks remembered something on his way out and opened the door to Roy's garage. The Porsche still stood there, gleaming and immaculate. He opened the driver's door and sat down, reaching into the side pocket for the AA road atlas. It was still open to the same page, and this time Banks spotted Quainton somewhere towards the top right. Well, he thought, it was hardly conclusive, but a bit of a coincidence nonetheless. Perhaps Quainton had been Roy's port of call before he got home, rang Banks and went off to the Albion Club with Lambert. What had he found out there that disturbed him so?

Banks took the AA atlas, locked up the car, garage and house behind him and headed for the M41 and Quainton. As far as he could gather, after a number of diversionary manoeuvres, there was no one on his tail. He had his mobile on the seat beside him and just beyond Berkhamsted Annie rang and told him about the raids, the deaths of Hadeon Mazuryk and Artyom, and about her interview with Carmen Petri. It put a few things in perspective and persuaded him that he was certainly heading in the right direction.

An hour and a half after leaving London, he was there.

Quainton stood at the bottom of a hill, a straggling sort of place scattered around a village green. Banks parked there, near the George and Dragon. He paused a moment and glanced at the brick windmill at the top of the hill, then went into the pub. He hadn't got an address from Ganz, just the village name, but he guessed the place was small enough that they would probably know Lambert and his Spanish wife at the local.

It looked like a good place to eat. Blackboards offered steak and Stilton pie, French country chicken and Thai red curry. Maybe he'd call back after talking to Lambert and his wife. The barman knew the Lamberts and told him they lived in a big house on the Denham Road, and he couldn't miss it. Banks thanked him and set off.

He found the house easily enough on the outskirts of the village. It looked the sort of place that had had a few additions over the years – gables, an extra wing, a garage – so it was hard to tell in what period the original building had been erected. Banks pulled into the drive, parked at the front and went to ring the doorbell.

In no time at all a young woman answered, smiled at

him and asked what he wanted. Banks didn't want to alarm her, so he showed her his warrant card but told her that he was Roy Banks's brother.

The woman made a sympathetic face. 'Poor Mr Banks,' she said. 'Please come in. Gareth is still in London at the moment but you are welcome to a cup of tea. I know you English love your tea. I am Mercedes Lambert.' She held out her hand and Banks shook it lightly.

Her accent matched her sultry Mediterranean looks and Banks could indeed believe that she had been a Spanish actress and pin-up. She still had a fine figure, shown to advantage in the shorts and sleeveless top she was wearing, and her olive skin stretched taut over exquisite bone structure and her long chestnut hair fell in waves over her shoulders.

When they got inside she led Banks to a large living room, big enough to hold a grand piano along with a damask three-piece suite. Every inch the English country lady, she called the maid and asked her to bring tea. Banks should have known she wouldn't be taking care of a place as big as this by herself. He wondered if she was bored stuck out in the country and whether she often stayed at the St John's Wood flat with her husband. She looked a good few years younger than Lambert, but not as young as Corinne or Jennifer. Banks pegged her at mid- to late thirties.

'I understand you were an actress in Spain?' he said, sitting in a chair with carved wooden arms.

She blushed. 'Not very good. I was in . . . what do you call them, films where monsters come after me and I scream a lot?'

'Horror films?'

'Yes. Horror films.' She shrugged. 'I do not miss it.'

I'll bet you don't, thought Banks, glancing around the room. French windows opened on a patio beyond the piano, and Banks could see sunlight shimmering on the blue surface of a swimming pool like a Hockney painting. 'Did you know Roy well?' he asked.

'No,' she said. 'I met him only once, last week, when he came here, but Gareth told me what happened. It is terrible.'

She pronounced the name 'Garrett', too.

'When did you meet him?' Banks asked.

'I think it was last Friday.' She smiled. 'But sometimes the days all seem the same here.'

'What did he want?'

At that moment, the maid came in with the tea and set the tray down on the table between Banks and Mercedes Lambert. After she had added milk and poured, she left as soundlessly as she had entered. Banks didn't usually take milk, but it didn't bother him.

Mercedes frowned. 'I don't really know why he came,' she said. 'He wanted to talk to me about a girl called Carmen, but I said I didn't know her. Carmen sounds very Spanish, I know, but you also find it in other countries.'

'What did he say next?'

'He told me this Carmen was pregnant and that she was selling her baby to me for adoption.' Mercedes frowned. 'He said Gareth told him this was so.'

'*Are* you adopting Carmen Petri's baby, Mrs Lambert?'

'No, of course not. That's what your brother asked me. I didn't understand why he would think such a thing.'

'Are you sure?'

'Yes, as I told your brother. Then a very strange thing happened.'

'What?'

'Little Nina cried, and I showed her to him and told him all about her, and Mr Banks said he was sorry he'd made a mistake, and he left very quickly.'

'I'm sorry,' said Banks. 'I don't understand. Who's little Nina?'

And then he heard it himself. A baby crying upstairs. Mercedes Lambert smiled. A few moments later, a nanny brought the baby down. She couldn't have been more than a few months old, and Mercedes held the tiny bundle, tears in her eyes.

'She is sick,' she explained to Banks. 'This is what I told your brother. There is a problem with her heart. It is, what do you say? Con . . . con . . .'

'Congenital?'

'Yes. Congenital. And if she does not get a new one very soon she will die.' Then her expression brightened. 'But Gareth says we are high on the list. He has arranged with a clinic in Switzerland – the best in the world, he says – to be ready at a moment's notice. So maybe my Nina will be lucky, yes?'

'Are you sure you have no intention of adopting another baby?' Banks asked, feeling his blood start to turn cold.

Mercedes smiled. 'No. Of course not. Nina will have her new heart and she will become strong. I know it. Do you not think so?'

Banks looked at Mercedes Lambert, saw the desperate hope in her face, and he looked at the pale face buried in the blankets and said, 'Yes. Yes, maybe you will.'

•

The train ride did Annie good and when she got back to Eastvale around lunchtime she didn't feel quite so depressed as she had after the raids. Before leaving, she had tried to console Brooke over what he perceived to be a lack of backbone in giving in to 'orders from above', but in the long run she knew it was something he would have to live with and get over by himself. For reasons of their own, the powers that be, maybe through Burgess, had hampered the official police investigation and encouraged Banks to go stirring things up by himself, no doubt in the hope of luring more players out into the open rather than causing them to disappear. And no one had given a damn whether Banks got killed in the process.

When Annie got to the station, Gristhorpe, Stefan, Winsome and Rickerd were all in the squad room and there was an air of celebration around the place. It seemed appropriate. After all, Jennifer Clewes's killer was dead, along with his boss, and the accomplices were in custody. Case solved.

'I hear you've been in the wars,' Gristhorpe said, looking up as she entered.

Annie sat at her desk and automatically turned on the computer. 'More like doing battlefield triage,' she said. 'Anyway, DI Brooke and the SO19 guys have got it all under control now. My job's done down there.'

'Congratulations,' said Gristhorpe.

'Anything new, Stefan?' Annie asked.

'I was just telling the superintendent here that we got a quick match on the fingerprints found on DCI Banks's door: Artyom Charkov. He doesn't have a record but the prints match the body in the mortuary in London, the one who was shot this morning in the second raid. And they also match the partial we found on the door of Jennifer Clewes's car. London say they found a gun on Charkov, too, a .22. It's being checked out.'

'That's what got him shot,' said Annie. 'Opening fire on an armed police officer.'

'Well, I'd have used something with a bit more stopping power than a .22.'

'Just as well for the officer concerned he didn't. Anyway, it's all a bit academic now he's dead, isn't it?' said Annie.

Stefan looked disappointed.

'Oh, Stefan, I'm sorry. I didn't mean to belittle your efforts. There's always the other one, Boris, the driver.'

'Essex technical support got his print from the Mondeo,' said Stefan, suppressing a smile. 'From inside the glovebox.'

'Excellent. Things have been happening, then.'

'How's Alan?' asked Gristhorpe.

'He's doing OK, as far as I know, sir,' said Annie. 'I think he'll be heading back to Peterborough later today to spend more time with his parents. At least he'll be able to tell them some sort of justice has been done.'

The door opened behind Annie and she saw Gristhorpe get to his feet, a big grin on his face. 'Well, if it isn't Susan Gay,' he said, advancing towards the slightly stocky woman with the tight blonde curls who stood in the doorway, Kev Templeton beaming beside her. 'Come on in, lass. Join the party.'

'We've got him,' Susan said. 'Cropley. He's down in the custody suite. All by the book. We've taken a DNA swab and it's on its way to Derby. We're also getting three DCs to do the motorway service stations with his photo. But the DNA itself will be enough.'

Templeton was beaming, too, Annie noticed. 'Congratulations, Kev,' she said. 'Good one.'

Templeton grinned. 'Thank you, ma'am.'

'Right, then,' said Gristhorpe. 'Seeing as we've got two reasons to celebrate, who's going for the beer?'

•

Banks worked most of it out on his drive back from Quainton, but he still needed some answers. He tracked Gareth Lambert down at the travel agency on the Edgware Road, leaving his Renault parked outside. Lambert seemed surprised and more than a bit put out at being practically manhandled into the street as his staff looked on open-mouthed, but he went without putting up a struggle.

Banks opened the passenger door and shoved him in. 'Buckle up.'

'Where are we going?'

'I've got something to show you.' Banks made his way through the traffic down the side of Hyde Park to Chelsea Bridge, then across the river and along to the old Midgeley's casting factory. If Lambert realized where they were going or recognized the place when they arrived, he didn't show it.

Banks pulled up on the weed-cracked concrete in front of the door and got out. He opened Lambert's door and almost dragged him out. Lambert was heavier, but he was in poor shape, and Banks's wiry strength was enough to push him towards the factory door.

'What the hell's going on?' Lambert protested.

'There's no need to rough-handle me this way. Roy's brother or no, I'll bloody report you.'

Banks pushed Lambert through the door and into the factory. Birds took off through the holes in the roof. The police had finished with the scene, and the chair and ropes were gone, but there were still bloodstains visible on the floor. Roy's. The lab had confirmed it. Banks stopped and shoved Lambert down onto a heap of broken pallets and rusty, twisted scrap metal. Lambert groaned as something sharp stuck into his back.

'I'll have your fucking job for this,' he yelled, red-faced, struggling to get up.

Banks put a foot on his chest and pushed him back. 'Stay there,' he said. 'And listen. This is where they brought Roy. You can still see his bloodstains here.' He pointed. 'Look at that, Gareth, that's my brother's blood.'

'That's nothing to do with me,' said Lambert, sitting up now and rubbing his back. 'I've never seen this place before. You don't know what you're talking about. You're rambling.'

'That's a good one,' said Banks. 'Let me be perfectly clear about it, Gareth. After you and Roy had your little talk in the Albion Club, you rang Hadeon Mazuryk or Max Broda on your mobile from the club's toilet and asked for help. I'm sure your mobile records will bear this out. You needed to get Roy out of the way. Mazuryk came himself or sent someone else, and they got him in a car outside the club and brought him here. They tortured him, you know, Gareth, to find out how much he knew, what my address was and what I knew. Maybe they even got our parents' address out of him, because they've made threats in that direction, too. He was tied up on a chair just over there, bleeding, knowing he was

probably going to die at the end of it all.' Banks felt close
to tears of rage as he talked and it was all he could do to
hold himself back from thrashing Lambert. He found an
iron bar on the floor, picked it up and slapped it against
his palm.

Lambert cringed. 'I told you,' he said. 'It's nothing to
do with me. Why would I do that? The girl and your
brother were a danger to Mazuryk, not to me.'

'But you're connected with Mazuryk. You arranged
to get the girls to him after Max Broda bought them at
markets in the Balkans.'

'You'll never find any evidence of anything like that.'

'It doesn't matter,' said Banks, 'because that wasn't
what it was really all about. At first I thought it was
about the girls you and Max Broda conspired to smuggle
in for Mazuryk. Girls who had been lured by false job
offers or abducted from the street. You wanted Roy in it
with you, didn't you, just like old times, and you'd been
talking about it for a while, a couple of months. Roy
didn't know the whole story at first, and he might even
have shown a flicker of interest if there was enough
money in it for him. Lord knows, Church or no, my
brother was no saint.

'Then Carmen Petri let slip to Roy's girlfriend that
these girls were not willing participants. Jennifer told
Roy and that changed things for him. I'd guess at that
point he wanted nothing to do with it. I imagine he gave
you a chance, though, for old times' sake. I think on the
Tuesday, the day after Carmen told Jennifer, Roy had
lunch with you and Max Broda and you both tried to
convince him everything was above board. But he wasn't
convinced. That's when he took the photograph of the
two of you. He left the cafe first, didn't he?'

Lambert said nothing.

'Maybe he wouldn't have turned you in to the police,' Banks went on, 'no matter how much what you were doing sickened him. I doubt that my brother had a very healthy regard for the boys in blue, given his track record. But there was his girlfriend to consider, too, wasn't there? And she was even more outraged, being a woman. Roy must have told you at lunch on Tuesday that he'd persuaded her to keep quiet for the time being, not to contact the police, and that you needn't harm her. But Mazuryk set Artyom and Boris to watch her just in case, to see where she went and who came to see her. If she had rung the police, they wouldn't be content with just some anonymous voice over the phone; they'd want to visit her, or have her visit their station. That's what Artyom and Boris were looking out for. Then, when things came to a head that Friday night in the Albion Club and Roy told Jennifer to drive up to see me, they followed her and killed her on a quiet country road.'

'This is ridiculous,' said Lambert, a condescending smirk on his face. 'If only you could hear yourself. You can't prove any of this. When I get out of here I'm going to—'

Banks kicked him hard in the stomach. Lambert groaned and rolled over, clutching his mid-section and retching. 'Bastard,' he hissed.

Banks swung the iron bar and hit him on the shoulder. Lambert screamed. 'But it wasn't even about the girls, was it?' Banks went on. 'That was just the start of it. Oh, I'm sure you tried to convince Roy how they had a better life here, away from their war-torn countries, away from the poverty and disease and death. Maybe he even wanted to believe it. Then, in a final bid to enlist his sympathy, you told him that you were adopting Carmen Petri's baby yourself. You probably gave him some sob story about how your wife couldn't bear children and desperately wanted a family. You told him you'd give the child a much better life than it could have hoped for in Romania, or as the child of a prostitute in London. That was supposed to be the clincher. How benevolent of you. He'd hardly stand in the way of his old mate adopting a child privately, would he? It might not be strictly legal, but people do it all the time, don't they? How can it be that much of a crime, to give a child hope? And even Roy had to see that any child you adopted had far more advantages than most. Financial advantages, that is.'

'So what?' Lambert argued. 'So what if I was adopting her child. It's true. The kid *would* have a much better life with us. Any fool can see that.'

'Maybe so,' said Banks. 'But that wasn't the real intention, was it?'

'What do you mean?'

'I know why Roy had to die,' said Banks.

'What are you talking about?' Lambert's voice was scarcely more than a whisper.

'Because of where he went earlier that day, before you came to call on him. He found out the truth.'

'I don't understand.'

'It's where I've just been. Quainton.'

Lambert said nothing. He seemed to shrink into himself.

'Roy went to see your wife to ask her about the adoption,' Banks went on. 'They'd never met before. If it was true, he would probably have agreed to keep quiet about it all and keep Jennifer quiet, too. But Roy found out what I found out. That you and your wife have a baby girl called Nina and she needs a new heart. And the only heart that can help a baby in need of a transplant is the heart of another baby. You know what the chances are of getting your hands on one by normal routes, so when you found out one of Mazuryk's girls was pregnant – not just any girl, mind you, but Carmen, intelligent, healthy and clean – you struck a deal. You'd pay Mazuryk for the privilege of adopting Carmen's baby. That way he wouldn't be out of pocket when she couldn't work during her pregnancy. But you weren't adopting the baby, were you? You were buying the baby's heart. I don't know if Mazuryk was in on it with you, but one way or another, as soon as that baby was born, it was going to be on its way to Switzerland. Were you going to kill it yourself or have you paid a crooked doctor to do that for you?'

'Don't be absurd. This is pure fantasy.'

'Is it? My guess is that you had someone lined up, a crooked doctor from your Balkan days, probably. You wouldn't have the stomach to do it yourself. And then there's the Swiss clinic, all ready to go at a moment's notice, no questions asked. Got it all organized, haven't you?'

Lambert squirmed like a toad on his bed of broken wood and twisted metal. At some point he had cut his lip and the blood welled up as he spoke. 'Look, you're obviously off your rocker, Banks. Let me go and we'll say no more about this.'

He made to get up again but Banks kicked him down and swung the bar dangerously close to his head.

'Stay where you are. Don't you realize, it's over? Do

you think that even your wife will want to know you after what you had planned?'

'She doesn't know,' said Lambert. 'If you've—'

'I haven't. Not yet. Tell me the truth, Gareth. How could you be sure you had a match? Who did the tests?'

'What tests?' Lambert paused and rubbed his shoulder.

'Come on, Gareth. Humour me. Tell me all about it.' Banks swung the bar again and caught it with a smack in his palm.

Lambert was quiet for several moments, then he spoke. 'The blood groups matched,' he said. 'That's the best you can hope for with babies, and even the blood group doesn't matter if they're newborn. Do you think I haven't researched it? The heart only survives six hours outside the body, so you do the transplant first and ask questions later. A chance. It was all I asked for.'

Though Banks had pieced it all together after seeing Mercedes and Nina, he could still hardly believe it, now that he was actually hearing it, that this man had cold-bloodedly bought a baby and planned to use its heart to save his daughter's life.

'Do you have even the slightest idea what you're saying?' he said.

'Look,' said Lambert. 'What chance did it have with a mother like that? Huh? Tell me? Look at her. A common prostitute. A slut. This way at least the baby could serve some *purpose* in being born. These people give birth in fields and think nothing of it. You haven't seen them, Banks. You haven't been there. I have. I know them. I've lived with them. They're animals. Their filthy children wander the streets and beg and steal and grow up to be criminals and prostitutes, just like their parents. The orphanages are full of abandoned children and none of them have a chance. My child *will* have a chance. She can make a difference in life. Achieve something. Contribute something.'

Banks shook his head in disgust. 'I wondered where Roy drew the line,' he said, 'and now I know. He'd turn a blind eye to most things for the sake of money and an old friendship. To the girls. To the illegal adoption. But not to this, not to the murder of an innocent baby for its heart. What did you do on Friday at the Albion Club? Offer him money to keep quiet or try to convince him you were morally right?'

'We'd been talking all week about the girls, the adoption. Seeing Mercedes and finding out . . . well, that was the last straw for him.'

'Why not tell the police straight away? Why did he bother to meet with you?'

'He wasn't going to tell the police. He was going to tell you.'

'What? But I am the police,' said Banks.

Lambert shook his head. 'You don't understand. You're his big brother. He expected you to handle it.'

Banks felt stunned. He hadn't realized Roy had been calling on him as much, if not more, as a brother than as a policeman: the brother who defended him from bullies. It made a difference. Roy always shied away from the police and he would expect Banks to sort the situation without letting it become official. Banks didn't know if he could have done that even if they hadn't killed Roy and Jennifer, even if he'd wanted to. Things had probably gone too far already.

'So what happened at the club?' Banks asked.

'He said he'd give me an hour to think about it, for

friendship's sake. He'd be in the casino if I wanted to talk. He also told me that he already had someone on her way to see you, but he could ring her mobile and bring her back if I agreed to drop my plans.'

'What did you say after the hour was up?'

'Nothing.'

'You could have lied, told him you'd drop the plans.'

'He would still have known. Do you think he'd have let it go, not kept checking?'

'I suppose not,' said Banks. 'So you sent him to his death?'

'I had to. What else could I do? I couldn't abandon Nina and Mercedes. He was going to ruin everything. Mazuryk's business, my Nina's life. Mercedes's life. Everything. Don't you understand? I *couldn't* give in to him. Without a new heart my daughter will die.'

Blood dribbled over Lambert's lower lip and bubbled as he spoke. Banks felt like hitting him again but he knew if he started he might never stop.

'So you had Roy killed.'

'Not me. Mazuryk.'

'Did Mazuryk know what you planned to do with Carmen's baby?'

'Are you crazy? Nobody knew except me and the doctor I was paying. And the doctor owed me. I helped him out of a jam once. You can't prove anything, you know. I'll deny it all. I'll tell them you beat me up and made me admit to things I haven't done. Look at me, I'm all bruised and bleeding.'

'Not nearly enough,' said Banks. 'You made a call to Mazuryk from the Albion Club about Roy being a loose cannon, and Mazuryk came himself, or sent Broda to pick up Roy outside and bring him here.'

'I told him Roy was threatening to tell everything. All Mazuryk cared about was the girls, the profits they made for him.'

'So Mazuryk protected his interests, and you protected yours?'

'What else could I do? What would you do if it was your daughter?'

Banks didn't want to think about that one. 'Why did they go back and take Roy's computer? Who did that? There couldn't be anything on it about the baby because he'd only just got back from seeing Mercedes when you arrived.'

'Mazuryk's men. Not Artyom and Boris. Others. Not very bright. We thought he might have information on it. About me. About Mazuryk's operation, the girls. We had talked a lot that week. I really thought he was interested at one time. I told him things. Roy used his computer a lot.'

And they hadn't taken the mobile because they hadn't been in the kitchen, hadn't even known it was there, Banks guessed. Not that it mattered. Roy and Lambert had been careful not to use mobiles in their communications. They knew how wide open and incriminating such phone use could be. That was why most criminals used stolen ones. And Banks doubted that Roy had ever been in direct telephone contact with Mazuryk or Broda. Later, of course, Broda had used the mobile to send his calling card, his sick joke.

'What changed things in the first place?'

'If that stupid whore hadn't told Roy's girlfriend that some girls had been abducted and badly treated, I don't think any of this would have happened,' said Lambert, 'and your brother and me would have been partners. I spent that week trying to convince Roy it was still the right thing to do but he didn't like the idea that the girls were working against their will. That's when I told him about the adoption. I thought he would see what a good thing it was.'

'And did he?'

'He wasn't convinced. Obviously. But it softened him a bit. Until he went to see Mercedes.'

Roy a pimp, or procurer? Banks found it hard to imagine. He would probably have described himself as an investor in an escort agency, or perhaps as a travel consultant. At least his spiritual and moral conversion hadn't cut into his desire to make a profit from just about anything, short of illegal body parts. 'And to threaten my parents? Whose idea was that?'

'Mazuryk's. When the digital photo they sent didn't scare you off, they had to try stronger measures. They could have killed you, but I told them the last thing they needed right then was a dead policeman hot on the heels of his brother. I told them that, Banks. I saved your life. These people are not always reasonable, but I have spent time with them. I can talk to them. They followed you home and back and showed themselves on the road, to frighten you off.'

'I don't frighten that easily. And Jennifer Clewes?'

'They were already worried about her. At first she was happy enough to help Dr Lukas take care of the girls, but she got too friendly and Mazuryk was worried someone might actually let something slip about how they really came to be there. They thought Carmen was getting too cocky because she didn't have to turn tricks any more and when Artyom saw them talking together, Carmen and Jennifer Clewes, he got suspicious and told Mazuryk. They made Carmen tell them what she had said. Without hurting her physically, you understand. They couldn't risk harming the baby.'

'Don't tell me. They threatened to harm *her* parents back home.'

'Possibly. But Artyom and Boris had been keeping an eye on Roy's girl for a few days, then when she took off like that at the same time I told Mazuryk that Roy was out of control . . . Look, I wasn't there . . . I don't know for sure how it happened. But it wasn't me.'

'But you know *what* happened. You set it in motion.'

'Max told me after it was done. They found out where she was going. Roy told Mazuryk when they were beating him and he phoned Artyom in the car. As soon as she got to a quiet spot on the road they killed her. Artyom was going to kill you, too, just in case, but you weren't there. He's not very bright.'

'It's a pity he didn't,' said Banks, 'because now Mazuryk is dead, Artyom is dead and the rest are going to jail. And you . . .'

'What about me?'

'I can't decide whether to kill you or turn you in.'

And it was true. Banks had never in his life felt like killing someone as much as he felt like killing Gareth Lambert at that moment. If he'd had a gun, he might have done it. He hefted the iron bar, heavy in his hand, and smacked it against his palm. That would do it. One swift blow. Crush his skull like an eggshell. Lambert was looking at him, fear in his eyes.

'No!' he said, holding his hands out to protect his face. 'Don't. Don't kill me.'

It wasn't just revenge for Roy, but also because he had never come across anyone so loathsome he'd even contemplate doing what Lambert was doing, let alone defend it and justify it. He could not have imagined such a thing if he hadn't gone to see Mercedes Lambert, as Roy had, and heard poor Nina cry. Mercedes Lambert obviously knew nothing about her husband's unholy scheme. The disgust Banks felt churned the bile in his stomach and he could bear to look at Lambert no longer.

'What are you going to do? Are you going to hurt me?' Lambert whined.

Banks hurled the iron bar. It clanged into the tangled metal about two inches above Lambert's head. Then Banks walked away, bent over and vomited on the floor. When he had finished, he took a few deep breaths, hands on his knees, wiped his mouth with the back of his hand and took out his mobile.

●

A few days later, Banks crossed the old packhorse bridge at the western end of Helmthorpe High Street and turned right on the riverside path. It was a walk he had often enjoyed before. Flat and easy, between the trees and water, no hills to climb, and he'd end up back in Helmthorpe, where there were three pubs to choose from.

As he walked he thought about the events of the past month, how it had all started that night he saw Penny Cartwright in the Dog and Gun singing 'Strange Affair'. He thought about Roy, Jennifer Clewes, Carmen Petri, Dieter Ganz and the rest.

And Gareth Lambert.

Now it was just about over. Artyom and Mazuryk were dead. Gareth Lambert was in custody, along with Boris and Max Broda, and the odds were good that they would get very long sentences. Banks's actions had forced his hand, but Dieter Ganz seemed to think his team had enough evidence to convict them on charges of trafficking in underage girls across international borders for the purposes of prostitution. Unfortunately, raids on similar houses in Paris, Berlin and Rome had netted only minor players, as word of what happened in London had spread fast. In the Balkans, guides, drivers, kidnappers and traders had scattered. They would be back, though, Dieter had told Banks, and he would be waiting for them.

Whether Lambert would be tied to the conspiracy to kill Roy Banks and Jennifer Clewes was another matter. Lambert's more sinister intentions couldn't be proved. And as he had said, only he and the doctor knew what they intended to do with Carmen's baby, and neither was talking. Banks had received a reprimand for his treatment of Lambert at the abandoned factory, which would also tend to discredit anything he claimed Lambert had told him. Still, there was a good chance that Max Broda would implicate him in the conspiracy rather than take the fall alone. And Lambert's mobile phone records for that Friday, 11th June, at the Albion Club, showed a call to Mazuryk's number at about eleven o'clock.

As for the rest, Banks wasn't quite sure how things would turn out. Mazuryk's girls would eventually be processed and sent home, but who was going to repair their lives, heal their broken spirits? Perhaps some would recover in time and move on, but others would drift back into the only life they knew. Carmen Petri, Annie had told Banks, was to be reunited with her parents in Romania, where contrary to what Gareth Lambert thought, there was a good chance that her baby might end up with a decent crack at life. Carmen had been abducted from the street three years ago and in all that time her parents hadn't given up hoping she was still alive.

Of all of them, perhaps Mercedes Lambert had come out of it worst of all, and Banks felt deeply for her. Not only was her husband probably going to jail for a long time, but in all likelihood, short of a miracle, her baby Nina was going to die soon. The police were investigating Banks's accusation and had questioned her about it, so now she also had to live with the knowledge of what her husband had been about to do. Banks could only imagine how knowledge like that might tear a mother apart and haunt her dreams forever. What might have been. The nameless, faceless issue of a Romanian prostitute she had never met measured against the life of her daughter.

His mind turned to other thoughts. He had just got back from Roy's funeral in Peterborough. Needless to say, it had been a sad and tearful affair, but at least he had spent some time with Brian and Tracy, who had come in for the occasion, and it had given his parents some sense of that closure they valued so much. Banks never really got it. For him there was no closure.

The good news was that his mother had managed to get speedy results on the medical tests. Her colon cancer was operable and her chances of making a full recovery were excellent. She also seemed to be coping a bit better with the loss of her son, though Banks knew she would never fully recover from it, never be her old self again.

Brilliant green dragonflies hovered above the water's surface and clouds of gnats and midges gathered above the path. The sun had almost set and the water was dark blue, the sky streaked with blood orange. Banks could hear the calls of night birds from the trees and the sounds of small animals scuttling through the under-growth. Across the river he could see the backs of the shops and houses on Helmthorpe High Street. People were sitting outside in the beer garden of the Dog and Gun and he could hear muffled conversations and music from the jukebox. It should have been Delius's 'Summer Night on the River', he thought, breathing in the per-fumed air, but it wasn't even 'Strange Affair', it was Elvis Costello's 'Watching the Detectives'.

Banks paused to light a cigarette and saw a figure walking towards him from the other direction. He couldn't make out any more than a dark shape but when it got closer he saw it was Penny Cartwright. He stood aside to let her pass. The overhanging leaves brushed the back of his neck and made him shiver. It felt like a spider had slipped under his collar and was making its way down his back.

As she passed, Banks nodded politely and said hello, making to hurry along, but her voice came from behind him. 'Wait a minute.'

Banks turned. 'Yes?'

'Got a light?'

As Banks flicked his lighter she leaned in towards him, cigarette in her mouth, and her eyes were on his as she inhaled. 'Thanks,' she said. 'Fancy meeting you here.'

'Yes. Fancy. Good night, then.'

'Don't go. I mean, wait a sec. OK?'

She sounded nervous and edgy. Banks wondered what was wrong. They stood and faced one another on the narrow path. An owl hooted deep in the woods. Elvis continued to watch the detectives. It was almost dark now, only a few streaks of purple and crimson in the sky like some great god's robes.

'I was sorry to read about your brother,' she said.

'Thank you.'

Penny pointed to the beer garden. 'Do you remember that night?' she said. 'All those years ago?'

Banks remembered. He had sat in the garden with his wife Sandra, Penny and her boyfriend Jack Barker, explaining the Harry Steadman murder. It had been a warm summer evening, just like tonight.

'How's Jack?' he asked.

Penny smiled. She wasn't a woman who smiled easily, and it was worthwhile when she did. 'I'm sure Jack's doing fine,' she said. 'I haven't seen him in ages. He went off to live in Los Angeles. Does a bit of TV writing. You even see his name on the screen sometimes.'

'I thought you two were . . . ?'

'We were. But it was a long time ago. Things change. You ought to know that.'

'I suppose so,' said Banks.

'Kath behind the bar told me about the fire, about what happened to your cottage, after she saw us talking. I'm really sorry.'

'Water under the bridge,' said Banks. 'Besides, I'm having it restored.'

'Still . . . Anyway,' she went on, not looking at him. 'I was rude that night, and I'm sorry. There, I've said it.'

'Why did you react the way you did?'

'It wasn't deliberate, if that's what you mean.'

'What, then?'

Penny paused and stared into the river. 'You really don't know, do you? All those years ago,' she said finally, 'the way I felt. It was like some sort of violation. I know you saved my life and I should thank you for that, but you treated me like a criminal. You actually believed that I killed my best friend.'

At one point, that was probably true, Banks thought. It was just a part of his job, and he had never stopped to think how it might have made Penny feel. Everyone gets tainted by a murder investigation. Roy had wanted his big brother, Banks remembered, not a policeman. But where did the one end and the other begin?

'And there you were,' she went on, 'asking me out to dinner, casual as anything, as if none of it had ever happened.'

'People aren't always what they seem,' he said. 'When the police come around asking questions, people lie. Everyone's got something to hide.'

'So you suspect everyone?'

'More or less. Anyone who might have motive, means and opportunity.'

'Like me?'

'Like you.'

'But I cared about Harry Steadman. He was my best friend.'

'That's what you told us.'

'I could have been lying?'

'As I remember it, that case was full of lies.'

Penny took one last drag on her cigarette and flicked the stub into the river. 'Oops,' she said. 'I shouldn't have done that. The river police will be after me.'

'Don't worry,' said Banks. 'I'll put in a good word for you.'

She favoured him with another flicker of a smile. 'I'd better be going,' she said, edging away. 'It's getting late.'

'All right.'

She started along the path, paused and half turned to face him. 'Good night, then, Mr Policeman. And I'm sorry I reacted so badly. I just wanted to tell you why.'

'Good night,' said Banks. He felt a tightness in his chest, but it was now or never. 'Look,' he went on, calling after her, 'maybe I'm being insensitive again, and I'm sorry I got off on the wrong foot, but is it at all within the bounds of possibility, you know, what I asked you about the other night, maybe the possibility of us, of you and me, you know . . . having dinner some time?'

She turned briefly. 'I don't think so,' she said, shaking her head slowly. 'You still don't get it, do you?' And she walked off into the shadows.

Acknowledgements

I would like to thank the following people for the time and care they have put into helping this book into its final shape: Sarah Turner, Maria Rejt and Nicholas Blake at Pan Macmillan; Dan Conaway and Jill Schwarzman at William Morrow; and Dinah Forbes at McClelland & Stewart. I would also like to thank Michael Morrison, Lisa Gallagher, Sharyn Rosenblum, Angela Tedesco, Dominick Abel, David Grossman, David North, Katie James, Ellen Seligman and Parmjit Parmar for all their ongoing hard work and support.

I also want to thank Commander Philip Gormley, head of SO19, the Metropolitan Force Firearms Unit, and Detective Inspector Claire Stevens of the Thames Valley Police. As usual, any mistakes are my own and are made entirely in the interests of the story.

I also owe a debt of thanks to the music of Richard Thompson and to Victor Malarek for his book, *The Natashas*.

PLAYING WITH FIRE

For Sheila

19 July

I was on my third sleeping pill and my second glass of whisky when he knocked on my door. Why I bothered to answer it, I don't know. I had resigned myself to my fate and arranged matters so that I would leave the world as peacefully and comfortably as possible, and nobody would mourn my passing.

Beethoven's 'Pastoral' symphony was playing on the stereo mostly because I had once seen a film about a futuristic society, in which a man goes to be put to sleep in a hospital and there are projections of brooks, water-falls and forests on the walls, and the 'Pastoral' is playing. I can't say it was doing much for me, but it was nice to have something to go along with the incessant tapping of rain on my flimsy roof.

I suppose answering the door was an instinctive reaction, like a nervous tic. When the phone rings you answer it. When someone knocks at your door – especially as it was such a rare occurrence in my isolated world – you go and see who it is. Anyway, I did.

And there he stood, immaculate as ever in his Hugo Boss suit, under a black umbrella, a bottle in his free hand. Though I hadn't seen him for twenty years, and the light was dim, I recognized him immediately.

'Can I come in?' he said, with that characteristic,

sheepish smile of his. 'It's raining fit to start the second flood out here.'

I think I just stood aside dumbfounded as he folded his umbrella. I might have swayed a little. Of all the people I never expected to see again, if indeed I ever expected to see anyone, it was him.

He stooped and walked in, and I could see his eyes register everything immediately, the way they always did. It was another characteristic of his I remembered, that instant absorption and interpretation. The minute he saw you his eyes were everywhere, even in your very soul, and within seconds he had you completely pegged. It used to scare the hell out of me, while it fascinated me at the same time.

Of course, I hadn't bothered hiding the whisky and the pills – everything happened too quickly – but he didn't say anything. Not then. He propped his umbrella against the wall, where it dripped on the threadbare carpet, and sat down. I sat opposite him, but my brain was already fogging up and I couldn't think of anything to say. It was a hot summer evening and the heavy shower only served to increase the humidity in the air. I felt sweat prickling in my pores and nausea churning in my stomach. But he looked as cool and relaxed as ever. Not a bead of sweat on him.

'You look like hell,' he said. 'Fallen on hard times?'

'Something like that,' I mumbled. He was going in and out of focus now, and the room was swirling, the floor undulating like a stormy ocean.

'Well, it's your lucky day,' he went on. 'I've got a little job for you, and it should be a profitable one. Low risk, high yield. I think you'll like it, but I can see you're in no shape to talk about it right now. It can wait a while.'

I think I nodded. Mistake. The room was spinning out of control, and I felt the contents of my stomach starting to heave up into my throat. I saw him lurching across the room to me. How he could even stand, when the floor was tilting and throbbing so much, I had no idea. Then the waves of nausea and oblivion engulfed me at last, and I felt his strong grasp on my arm as I started to keel out of my chair.

He stayed for two days and I spilled out my guts to him. He listened to it all patiently, without comment. In the meantime, he took care of my every need with the uncomplaining competence of a trained nurse. When I could eat, he fed me; when I was sick, he cleaned up after me; when I slept, I am sure he watched over me.

And then he told me what he wanted me to do.

1

'**The barge she** sat in, like a burnish'd throne, burn'd on the water,' Banks whispered. As he spoke, his breath formed plumes of mist in the chill January air.

Detective Inspector Annie Cabbot, standing beside him, must have heard because she said, 'You what? Come again.'

'A quotation,' said Banks. 'From *Antony and Cleopatra*.'

'You don't usually go around quoting Shakespeare like a copper in a book,' Annie commented.

'Just something I remember from school. It seemed appropriate.'

They were standing on a canal bank close to dawn, watching two barges smoulder. Not usually the sort of job for a detective chief inspector like Banks, especially so early on a Friday morning, but as soon as it had been safe enough for the firefighters to board the barges, they had done so and found one body on each. One of the firefighters had recently completed a course on fire investigation, and he had noticed possible evidence of accelerant use when he boarded the barge. He had called the local constable, who in turn had called Western Area Headquarters, Major Crimes, so here was Banks, quoting Shakespeare and waiting for the fire investigation officer to arrive.

'Were you in it, then?' Annie asked.

'In what?'

'*Antony and Cleopatra.*'

'Good Lord, no. Third spear-carrier in *Julius Caesar* was the triumph of my school acting career. We did it for O Level English, and I had to memorize the speech.'

Banks held the lapels of his overcoat over his throat. Even with the Leeds United scarf his son Brian had bought him for his birthday, he still felt the chill. Annie sneezed and Banks felt guilty for dragging her out in the early hours. The poor lass had been battling with a cold for the last few days. But his sergeant, Jim Hatchley, was even worse: he had been off sick with flu most of the week.

They had just arrived at the dead-end branch of the canal, which lay three miles south of Eastvale, linking the River Swain to the Leeds–Liverpool Canal, and hence to the whole network of waterways that criss-crossed the country. The canal ran through some beautiful countryside, and tonight the usually quiet rural area was floodlit and buzzing with activity, noisy with the shouts of firefighters and the crackle of personal radios. The smell of burned wood, plastic and rubber hung in the air and scratched at the back of Banks's throat when he breathed in. All around the lit-up area, the darkness of a pre-dawn winter night pressed in, starless and cold. The media had already arrived, mostly TV crews because fires made for good visuals even after they had gone out, but the firefighters and police officers kept them well at bay and the scene was secure.

As far as Banks had been able to ascertain, the branch ran straight north for about a hundred yards before it ended in a tangle of shrubbery that eventually became dry land. Nobody at the scene remembered whether it had ever led anywhere or had simply been used as a mooring, or for easier access to the local limestone for which the region was famous. It was possible, someone suggested, that the branch had been started as a link to the centre of Eastvale itself, then abandoned due to lack of funds or the steepness of the gradient.

'Christ, it's cold,' moaned Annie, stamping from foot to foot. She was mostly obscured by an old army greatcoat she had thrown on over her jeans and polo-neck sweater. She was also wearing matching maroon woolly hat, scarf and gloves, along with black knee-high leather boots. Her nose was red.

'You'd better go and talk to the firefighters,' Banks said. 'Get their stories while events are still fresh in their minds. You never know, maybe one of them will warm you up a bit.'

'Cheeky bastard.' Annie sneezed, blew her nose and wandered off, reaching in her deep pocket for her notebook. Banks watched her go and wondered again whether his suspicions were correct. It was nothing concrete, just a slight change in her manner and appearance, but he couldn't help feeling that she was seeing someone and had been for the past while. Not that it was any of his business. Annie had broken off their relationship ages ago, but – he didn't like to admit this – he was feeling pangs of jealousy. Stupid, really, as he had been seeing DI Michelle Hart on and off since the previous summer. But he couldn't deny the feeling.

The young constable, who had been talking to the leading firefighter, walked over to Banks and introduced himself: PC Smythe, from the nearest village, Molesby.

'So you're the one responsible for waking me up at this ungodly hour in the morning,' said Banks.

PC Smythe paled. 'Well, sir, it seemed . . . I . . .'

'It's OK. You did the right thing. Can you fill me in?'

'There's not much to add, really, sir.' Smythe looked tired and drawn, as well he might. He hardly seemed older than twelve and this was probably his first major incident.

'Who called it in?' Banks asked.

'Bloke called Hurst. Andrew Hurst. Lives in the old lock keeper's house about a mile away. He says he was just going to bed shortly after one o'clock and he saw the fire from his bedroom window. He knew roughly where it was coming from, so he rode over to check it out.'

'Rode?'

'Bicycle, sir.'

'OK. Go on.'

'That's about it. When he saw the fire, he phoned it in on his mobile and the fire brigade arrived. They had a bit of trouble gaining access, as you can see. They had to run long hoses.'

Banks could see the fire engines parked about a hundred yards away through the woods, where a narrow lane turned sharply right as it neared the canal. 'Anyone get out alive?' he asked.

'We don't know, sir. If they did, they didn't hang around. We don't even know how many people live there or what their names are. All we know is there are two casualties.'

'Wonderful,' said Banks. It wasn't anywhere near enough information. Arson was often used to cover up other crimes, to destroy evidence, or to hide the identity of a victim and, if that were the case here, Banks needed to know as much about the people who lived on the barges as possible. That would be difficult if they were all dead. 'This lock keeper, is he still around?'

'He's not actually a lock keeper, sir,' said PC Smythe. 'We don't use them any more. The boat crews operate the locks themselves. He just lived in the old lock keeper's house. I took a brief statement and sent him home. Did I do wrong?'

'It's all right,' Banks said. 'We'll talk to him later.' But it wasn't all right. PC Smythe was clearly too inexperienced to know that some arsonists delight in reporting their own fires and enjoy being involved in the fire-fighting. Hurst would now have had plenty of time to get rid of any evidence if he had been involved. 'Heard anything from Geoff Hamilton yet?' Banks asked.

'He's on his way, sir.'

Banks had worked with Hamilton once before on a warehouse fire in Eastvale which turned out to have been an insurance fraud. Though he hadn't warmed to the man's gruff, taciturn personality, he respected Hamilton's expertise and the quiet, painstaking way in which he worked. You didn't rush things with Geoff Hamilton; nor did you jump to conclusions. And if you had any sense, you never used the words 'arson' or 'malicious' around him. He had been browbeaten too many times in court.

Annie Cabbot joined Banks and Smythe. 'The station received the call at one thirty-one a.m.,' she said, 'and the firefighters arrived here at one forty-four.'

'That sounds about right.'

'It's actually a very good rural response time,' Annie said. 'We're lucky the station wasn't staffed by retained men.'

Many rural stations, Banks knew, used 'retained' men, or trained part-timers, and that would have meant a longer wait – at least five minutes for them to respond to their personal alerters and get to the station. 'We're lucky they weren't on strike tonight, too,' he said, 'or we'd probably still be waiting for the army to come and piss on the flames.'

They watched the firefighters pack up their gear in silence as the darkness brightened to grey and a morning mist appeared seemingly from nowhere, swirling on the murky water and shrouding the spindly trees. In spite of the smoke stinging his lungs, Banks felt an intense craving for a cigarette rush through his system. He thrust his hands deeper into his pockets. It had been nearly six months since he had smoked a cigarette and he was damned if he was going to give in now.

As he fought off the desire, he caught a movement in the trees out of the corner of his eye. Someone was standing there, watching them. Banks whispered to Annie and Smythe, who walked along the bank in opposite directions to circle around and cut the interloper off. Banks edged back towards the trees. When he thought he was within decent range he turned and ran towards the intruder. As he felt the cold, bare twigs whipping and scratching his face, he saw someone running about twenty yards ahead of him. Smythe and Annie were flanking the figure, crashing through the dark undergrowth, catching up quickly.

Smythe and Annie were by far the fittest of the three pursuers, and even though he'd stopped smoking Banks soon felt out of breath. When he saw Smythe closing the gap and Annie nearing from the north, he slowed down and arrived panting in time to see the two wrestle a young man to the ground. In seconds he was handcuffed and pulled, struggling, to his feet.

They all stood still for a few moments to catch their breath and Banks looked at the youth. He was in his early twenties, about Banks's height, five foot nine, wiry as a pipe-cleaner, with a shaved head and hollow cheeks. He was wearing jeans and a scuffed leather jacket over a black T-shirt. He struggled with PC Smythe, but was no match for the burly constable.

'Right,' said Banks. 'Who the hell are you, and what are you doing here?'

The boy struggled. 'Nothing. Let me go! I haven't done anything. Let me go!'

'Name!'

'Mark. Now let me go.'

'You're not going anywhere until you give me a reasonable explanation why you were hiding in the woods watching the fire.'

'I wasn't watching the fire. I was . . .'

'You were what?'

'Nothing. Let me go.' He wriggled again, but Smythe kept a firm grasp.

'Shall I take him to the station, sir?' Smythe asked.

'Not yet. I want to talk to him first,' said Banks. 'Come on, let's go back to the canal.'

The four of them made their way through the woods back to the smouldering barges. Smythe kept a firm grasp on Mark, who was shivering now.

'See if you can scrounge up some tea or coffee, would you?' Banks said to Smythe. 'One of the fire crew's bound to have a flask.' Then he turned to Mark, who was staring at the ground shaking his head. Mark looked up. He had pale, acne'd skin, and the fear showed in his eyes, fear mixed with defiance. 'Why won't you let me go?'

'Because I want to know what you're doing here.'

'I'm not doing anything.'

'Why don't I believe you?'

'I don't know. That's your problem.'

Banks sighed and rubbed his hands together. As usual

he had forgotten his gloves. The firefighters were resting now, most of them in silence, sipping tea or coffee, smoking and contemplating the wreckage before them, perhaps offering a silent prayer of thanks that none of them had perished. The smell of damp ash was starting to predominate and steam drifted from the ruined barges, mingling with the early morning mist.

As soon as Geoff Hamilton arrived, Banks would accompany him in his investigation of the scene, just as he had done on that previous occasion. The fire service had no statutory powers to investigate the *cause* of a fire, so Hamilton was used to working closely with the police and their scenes-of-crime officers. It was his job to produce a report for the coroner. There had been no one hurt in the warehouse fire, but this was different. Banks didn't relish the sight of burned bodies; he had seen enough of them before, enough to make fire one of the things he feared and respected more than anything. If he had to choose a floater over a fire victim, he'd probably choose the bloated misshapen bulk of the former rather than the charred and flaking remains of the latter. But it was a tough choice. Fire or water?

And there was another reason to feel miserable. It was now early on Friday morning and Banks could see his planned weekend with Michelle Hart quickly slipping away. If, indeed, the fire had been deliberately set and if two people had been killed, then it would mean cancelled leave and overtime all round. He'd have to ring Michelle. At least she would understand. She was used to the vagaries of police life, being a DI with the Cambridgeshire Constabulary, still living and working in Peterborough, despite the controversial outcome of the case she and Banks had worked on there the previous summer.

PC Smythe came back with a vacuum flask and four plastic cups. It was instant coffee, and weak at that, but at least it was still hot, and the steam that rose when Smythe poured it helped dispel some of the dawn's chill. Banks took a silver hip flask from his pocket – a birthday present from his father – and offered it around. Only he and Annie indulged. The flask was full of Laphroaig, and although Banks knew what a terrible waste of fine single malt it was to tip it into a plastic cup of watery Nescafé, the occasion seemed to demand it. As it happened, the wee nip improved the coffee enough to make the sacrifice worthwhile.

'Take the cuffs off him, would you?' Banks asked Smythe.

'But sir . . .'

'Just do it. He's not going anywhere, are you, Mark?'

Mark said nothing. After Smythe had removed the handcuffs, Mark rubbed his wrists and clasped both hands around the cup of coffee, as if its warmth were sustaining him.

'How old are you, Mark?' Banks asked.

'Twenty-one.' Mark pulled a dented packet of Embassy Regal out of his pocket and lit one with a disposable lighter, sucking the smoke in deeply. Seeing him do that made Banks realize they would have to have the boy's hands and clothing checked for any signs of accelerant as soon as possible. Such traces didn't last for ever.

'Now look, Mark,' said Banks, 'what you have to realize first of all is that you're the closest we have to a suspect for this fire. You were hanging about the scene like a textbook arsonist. You're going to have to give us some explanation of what you're doing here, and why you ran when we approached you. You can either do it here and now, without the handcuffs, or you can do it in a formal interview at Eastvale nick and spend the night in a cell. Your choice.'

'At least a cell would be warm,' Mark said. 'I've nowhere else to go.'

'Where do you live?'

Mark paused for a moment, tears in his eyes, then pointed a shaking hand towards the northernmost barge. 'There,' he said.

Banks looked at the smoking remains. 'You lived on that barge?'

Mark nodded, then whispered something Banks couldn't catch.

'What?' Banks asked, remembering that the firefighters had found a body on that barge. 'What is it? Do you know something?'

'Tina . . . Did she get off? I haven't seen her.'

'Is that why you were hiding?'

'I was watching for Tina. That's what I was doing. Did they get her off?'

'Did Tina live with you on the barge?'

'Yes.'

'Was there anyone else?'

Mark's eyes burned with shame. 'Yes,' he said. 'That's where I was. A girl. In Eastvale. Tina and I had a row.'

That wasn't what Banks had meant, but he absorbed the unsolicited information about Mark's infidelity. That would be a tough one to live with; you're screwing another woman and your wife or girlfriend burns to death in a fire. If, that is, Mark hadn't set it himself before he left. Banks knew that Tina's was probably one of the two bodies the firefighters had found, but he couldn't be certain and he was damned if he was going to tell Mark that

Tina was dead before finding out what he'd been doing when the fire broke out, and before verifying the identity of the bodies.

'I meant was there anyone else living with you on the barge?'

'Just me and Tina.'

'And you haven't seen her?'

Mark shook his head and rubbed his nose with the back of his hand.

'How long had you lived there?'

'About three months.'

'Where were you tonight, Mark?'

'I told you. I was with someone else.'

'We'll need her name and address.'

'Mandy. I don't know her last name. She lives in Eastvale.' He gave an address and Annie wrote it down.

'What time did you get there?'

'I got to the pub where she works – the George and Dragon, near the college – a bit before closing time. About quarter to eleven. Then we went back to her flat.'

'How did you get to Eastvale? Do you have a car?'

'You must be joking. There's a late bus you can catch up on the road. It leaves at half-past ten.'

If Mark was telling the truth – and his alibi would have to be carefully checked with the bus driver and the girlfriend – then he couldn't possibly have started the fire. If it had been set before half-past ten, there would have been nothing left of the barges by half-past one, when Andrew Hurst reported the blaze. 'When did you get back here?' Banks asked.

'I don't know. I don't have a watch.'

Banks glanced at his wrist. He was telling the truth. 'How late. Twelve? One? Two?'

'Later. I left Mandy's place at about three o'clock by her alarm clock.'

'How did you get back? Surely there are no buses running that late?'

'I walked.'

'Why didn't you stay the night?'

'I got worried. About Tina. Afterwards, you know, sometimes things start to go around in your mind, not always good things. I couldn't sleep. I felt bad. Guilty. I should never have left her.'

'How long did it take you to get back here?'

'Maybe an hour or so. A bit less. I couldn't believe the scene. All those people. I hid in the woods and watched until you found me.'

'That was a long time.'

'I wasn't keeping track.'

'Did you see anyone else in the woods?'

'Only the firemen.'

'Mark, I know this is hard for you right now,' Banks went on, 'but do you know anything about the people on the other barge? We need all the information we can get.'

'There's just the one bloke.'

'What's his name?'

'Tom.'

'Tom what?'

'Just Tom.'

'How long has he been living there?'

'Dunno. He was there when me and Tina came.'

'What does he do?'

'No idea. He doesn't go out much, keeps himself to himself.'

'Do you know if he was home last night?'

'I don't know. It's likely, though. Like I said, he hardly ever went out.'

'Seen any strangers hanging about?'

'No.'

'Any threats made?'

'Only by British Waterways.'

'Come again?'

Mark gave Banks a defiant look. 'You must have worked out that we're not your typical middle-class folk.' He gestured to the burned boats. 'Those were clapped-out hulks, hadn't been anywhere in years, just sitting there, rotting away. Nobody knows who owns them, so we just moved in.' Mark glanced at the barge again. Tears came to his eyes and he gave his head a little shake.

Banks allowed him a moment to collect himself before continuing. 'Are you saying you're squatters?'

Mark wiped his eyes with the backs of his hands. 'That's right. And British Waterways have been trying to get rid of us for weeks.'

'Was Tom squatting too?'

'Dunno. I suppose so.'

'Was there any electricity on the boats?'

'That's a laugh.'

'What did you do for heat and light?'

'Candles. And we had an old wood stove for heat. It was in pretty bad shape, but I managed to get it working.'

'What about Tom?'

'Same, I suppose. They were both the same kind of barge, anyway, even if he had done his up a bit, slap of paint here and there.'

Banks looked back at the burned-out barges. An accident with the stove was certainly one possible explanation of the fire. Or Tom might have been using a dangerous heating fuel – paraffin, diesel or Coleman fuel, for example. But all that would be mere speculation until Geoff Hamilton and the pathologist had done their jobs. *Patience*, Banks told himself.

Were there any motives immediately apparent? Mark and Tina had had a row – maybe he had lashed out and run off after starting the fire. Certainly possible, if his alibi was untrue. Banks turned to PC Smythe. 'Constable, would you put the cuffs back on and take Mark here up to headquarters? Turn him over to the custody officer.'

Mark jerked his eyes towards Banks, scared. 'You can't do that.'

'As a matter of fact, we can. For twenty-four hours, at least. You're still a suspect and you've got no fixed abode. Look at it this way,' he added, 'you'll be well treated, warm and well fed. And if everything you've told me is true, then you've nothing to be afraid of. Do you have a criminal record?'

'No.'

'Never got caught, eh?' Banks turned to Smythe. 'See that his hands and clothing are checked for any signs of accelerant. Just mention it to the custody officer. He'll know what to do.'

'But you can't believe I did this!' Mark protested. 'What about Tina? I love her. I would never hurt her.'

'It's routine,' said Banks. 'For purposes of elimination. This way we find out you're innocent, so we don't have to waste our time and yours asking pointless questions.' Or we find out you're guilty, Banks thought, which is another kettle of fish entirely.

'Come on, lad.'

Mark hung his head and Smythe put the handcuffs on again, took his arm and led him to the patrol car. Banks sighed. It had already been a long night and he had a feeling it was going to be an even longer day as he saw Geoff Hamilton walking along the canal bank towards him.

•

Mist clung to the blackened ruins of the two barges as Banks, crime-scene photographer Peter Darby, SOCO Terry Bradford, and FIO Geoff Hamilton climbed into their protective clothing, having been given the green light to inspect the scene by the station officer, who was officially in charge. Annie stood watching them, wrapped tightly in her greatcoat.

'This isn't too difficult or dangerous a scene,' Hamilton said. 'There's no ceiling left to fall on us and we're not likely to sink or fall in. Watch how you go, though. The floor is wooden boards over a steel shell, and the wood may have burned through in places. It's not a closed space, so there should be no problem with air quality, but you'll still have to wear particle masks. There's nasty stuff in that ash. We'll be stirring some of it up and you don't want it in your lungs.' Banks thought about all the tobacco smoke he'd put in his lungs over the years and reached for the mask.

'Got a film in your camera?' Hamilton asked Peter Darby.

Darby managed a smile. 'Thirty-five mm colour. OK?'

'Fine. And remember, keep the video running and take photos from all angles. The bodies will probably be covered with debris and I want photos taken before and after I remove it. Also, photograph all possible exits, and I want you to pay particular attention to any hot spots or possible sources when I tell you. OK?'

'Basically every square foot, at least twice, while video-taping the entire search.'

'You've got it. Let's go.'

Darby shouldered his equipment.

'And I don't want any of you under my feet,' Hamilton grumbled. 'There's already too many of us going over this scene.'

Banks had heard the complaint before. The fire investigation officer wanted as few people as possible on the boats to lessen the chance of destroying evidence already in a fragile state, but he needed police and SOCO presence, someone to bag the evidence. Not to mention the photographer.

Banks adjusted his particle mask. Terry Bradford picked up his bulky accessory bag and they entered the scene, starting with Tom's barge. Banks felt a surge of absolute fear as he stepped on to the charred wood. One thing he had never told anyone was that he was terrified of fire. Ever since one particular scene back when he was on the Met, he'd had recurring nightmares about being trapped on a high floor of a burning building. This time it wasn't so bad, he told himself, as there were no flames only soggy debris, but even so the mere thought of the flames licking up the walls and crackling as they burned everything in their way still frightened him.

'Go carefully,' Hamilton said. 'It's easy to destroy evidence at a fire scene because you can't see that it *is* evidence. Fortunately, most of the water the fire hoses sprayed has drained over the side, so you won't be ankle deep in cold water.'

All Banks knew, as he forced himself to be detached and concentrate on the job at hand, was that a fire scene was unique and presented a number of problems he simply didn't encounter at other crime scenes. Not only was fire itself incredibly destructive, but the act of putting out a fire was destructive too. Before Banks and Hamilton could examine the barges, the firefighters had been there first and had probably trampled valuable evidence in their attempts to save lives. The damage might have been minimized this time because the firefighter who spotted possible signs of arson had some knowledge of fire-investigation techniques, and he knew they had to preserve the scene as best they could.

But of everything, Banks thought, it was probably the sheer level of destruction caused by fire that was the most disturbing and problematic. Fire totally destroys many things and renders others unrecognizable. Banks remembered from the warehouse fire how burned and twisted objects, which looked like nothing he had ever seen before – like those old contests where you're supposed to identify an everyday object photographed from an unusual angle – had definite shape and identity to Hamilton, who could pick up a black, shapeless object, like something from a Dali painting, and identify it as an empty tin, a cigarette lighter or even a melted wine glass.

The barge was about thirty or thirty-five feet long. Most of the wooden roof and sides were burned away now, exposing the innards as a maze of blackened and distorted debris – sofas, shelving, bed, chest of drawers, ceiling – all charred by the flames and waterlogged from the firefighters' hoses. One part of the room looked as if it had been dominated by a bookcase and Banks could see soggy volumes lying on the floor. He couldn't smell the place now through his mask, but he'd smelled it from the canal side, and the acrid odour of burned plastic, rubber and cloth still stuck in his memory. As most of the windows had exploded and the stairs and doors had burned away, it was impossible to tell if anyone had forced access.

Banks walked carefully behind Hamilton, who would stop every now and then to make a quick sketch or examine something, instructing Terry Bradford to pop it into one of his evidence bags. The three of them moved slowly through the ruins. Banks could hear the whir of the camcorder, which he held while Peter Darby took still photographs on Hamilton's instructions.

'This looks to be where it started,' said Hamilton as soon as they got to the centre of the living quarters.

Banks could see that the fire damage here was greater and the charring went deeper in certain areas than anywhere else they had seen yet, in places running in deep channels, pooling. They had to go slowly to make their way through all the debris littering the floor. Hamilton's voice was muffled by his mask, but Banks could make out the words clearly enough. 'This is the main seat. You can see that the burning on the floor is more severe than that on the underside of this piece of roofing.' He held up a piece of partially burned wood. 'Fire moves upwards, so the odds are that it started at the lowest point with the worst degree of burning. This is it.' Hamilton took off his mask and instructed Banks to do the same. Banks did so.

'Smell anything?' Hamilton asked.

Amidst the mingled odours of ash and rubber, Banks thought he could smell something familiar. 'Turps,' he said.

Hamilton took a small gadget from his accessory bag, bent and pointed a tube at the floor. 'It's a hydrocarbon detector, technically known as a "sniffer",' he explained. 'It should tell us whether accelerant has been used and –' he flicked a switch – 'indeed it has.'

Hamilton instructed Terry Bradford to use his trowel and shovel two or three litres of debris into a doubled nylon bag and seal it tight. 'For the gas chromatograph,' he said, sending Bradford to other parts of the room to do the same thing. 'It looks as if it's multi-seated,' he explained. 'If you look at the pattern of burning closely, you can see more than one fire occurred in this room, linked by those deeply charred narrow channels, or "streamers", as they're called.'

Banks knew that a multi-seated fire was an indication of arson, but he also knew he wouldn't get Hamilton to admit it yet. Peter Darby handed him back the camcorder and clicked away with his Pentax. 'Hasn't the water the firefighters used got rid of any traces of accelerant?' Darby asked.

'Contrary to what you might imagine,' said Hamilton, 'water cools and slows the process down. It actually pre-serves traces of accelerant. Believe me, if any was used, and the sniffer indicates that it was, then it'll be present in these bits of carpet and floorboard.'

Terry Bradford bent to remove some debris and uncov-ered the mostly blackened human shape that lay twisted on its stomach on the floor. It was impossible to tell whether it was a man or a woman at first, but Banks assumed it was most likely the man known to Mark only as 'Tom'. Though he looked quite short in stature, Banks knew that fires did strange and unpredictable things to the human body. A few tufts of reddish hair still clung to the cracked skull, and in some places the fire had burned away all the flesh, leaving the bone exposed. It was still possible to make out patches of a blue denim shirt on the victim's back, and he was clearly wearing jeans. Banks felt slightly sick behind his particle mask. 'That's odd,' said Hamilton, stooping to look at the body more closely.

'What?' said Banks.

'People usually fall on their backs when they're overcome by flames or smoke inhalation,' Hamilton explained. 'That's why you often see the knees and fists raised in the "pugilistic" attitude. It's caused by the contraction of the muscles in the sudden heat of the blaze. Look, you can see the pooling where the accelerant trickled into the cracks of the floor around the body. Probably under it, too. The charring's much deeper around there and there's far more general destruction.'

'Tell me something,' said Banks. 'Would he have had time to escape if he'd been conscious and alert when the fire started?'

'Hard to say,' said Hamilton. 'He's on his stomach and his head is pointing towards the source of the fire. If he'd been trying to escape, he'd most likely have been running or crawling *away*, towards the exit.'

'But *could* he have got out if he'd seen it coming?'

'We know a part of the ceiling fell on him. Maybe that happened before he could escape. Maybe he was drugged, or drunk. Who knows? You'll not get me speculating on this. I'm afraid you'll have to wait till the post-mortem and toxicology screens for answers to your questions.'

'Any signs of a container or igniter?'

'There are plenty of possible containers,' said Hamilton, 'but not one with ACCELERANT written in capital letters on it. They'll all have to be tested. Odds are he used a match as an igniter and sadly there won't be anything left of that by now.'

'Deliberate, then?'

'I'm not committing myself yet, but I don't like the

looks of it. It's hard to predict what happens with fires. Maybe he was drunk and spilled some accelerant on his clothes and set fire to himself and panicked. People do, you know. I've seen it before. And smoke inhalation can cause disorientation and confusion. Sometimes it looks as if people have run into the flames rather than away from them. Let's just call it *doubtful* origin for now, OK?'

Banks looked at the blackened figure. 'If the doctor can tell us anything from what's left of him.'

'You'd be surprised,' said Hamilton. 'Rarely is a body so badly damaged by fire that a good pathologist can't get something out of it. You'll be having Dr Glendenning, I imagine?'

Banks nodded.

'One of the best.' Hamilton instructed Terry Bradford to take more samples, then they moved towards the bow of the barge, to the point where it almost touched its neighbour's stern. They waited while Peter Darby changed the film in his camera and the cassette in the camcorder.

'Look at this,' Hamilton said, pointing to a clearly discernible strip of deeply charred wood that started in the living quarters, near the main seat, and continued to the bow, then over to the stern and living quarters of the other boat. 'Another streamer,' he said. 'A line of accelerant to spread a fire from one place to another. In this case, from one *barge* to another.'

'So whoever did this wanted to burn *both* barges?'

'It looks like it.' Hamilton frowned. 'But it's not very much. Just one narrow streamer. It's like . . . I don't know . . . a flick of the wrist. Not enough. An afterthought.'

'What are you getting at?'

'I don't know. But if someone had *really* wanted to

make sure of destroying the second boat and anyone on it – and I'm not saying that's what happened – then he could have done a more thorough job.'

'Maybe he didn't have time?' said Banks.

'Possible.'

'Or he ran out of accelerant.'

'Again, it's a possible explanation,' said Hamilton. 'Or maybe he simply wanted to confuse the issue. Either way, it cost another life.'

The body on the other barge lay wrapped in a charred sleeping bag. Despite some blistering on her face, Banks could see that it was the body of a young girl. Her expression was peaceful enough, and if she had died of smoke inhalation, she would never have felt the fire scorching her cheeks and burning her sleeping bag. She had a metal stud just below her lower lip, and Banks imagined that would have heated up in the fire too, explaining the more deeply burned skin radiating in a circle around it. He hoped she hadn't felt that either. One charred arm lay outside the sleeping bag beside what looked like the remains of a portable CD player.

'The body should be fairly well preserved inside the sleeping bag,' Hamilton said. 'They're usually made of flame-resistant material. And look at those blisters on the face.'

'What do they mean?' Banks asked.

'Blistering is usually a sign that the victim was alive when the fire started.' Making sure that Peter Darby had already videotaped and photographed the entire scene, Hamilton bent and picked up two objects from the floor beside her.

'What are they?' Banks asked.

'Can't say for certain,' he said, 'but I think one's a

syringe and the other's a spoon.' He handed them to Terry Bradford, who put them into evidence bags, taking a cork from his accessory bag first, and sticking it over the needle's point. 'The fire's sure to have sterilized it,' he said, 'but you can't be too careful handling needles.'

Hamilton bent and scraped something from the floor beside the sleeping bag and Bradford put it in another bag. 'Looks like she was using a candle,' Hamilton said. 'Probably to heat up whatever it was she injected. If I wasn't so certain the fire started on the other barge, I'd say that it could have been a possible cause. I've seen it more than once, a junkie nodding off and a candle starting a fire. Or it could even have been used as a crude timing device.'

'But that's not what happened here?'

'No. The seats of the fire are definitely next door. It'd be just too much of a coincidence if the two fires started simultaneously from separate causes. And this one caused so much less damage.'

Banks felt a headache coming on. He glanced at the young girl's body again, nipped the bridge of his nose above the mask between his thumb and index finger until his eyes prickled with tears, then he looked away, into the fog, just in time to see Dr Burns, the police surgeon, walking towards the barges with his black bag.

2

Andrew Hurst lived in a small, nondescript lock keeper's cottage beside the canal, about a mile east of the dead-end branch where the fire had occurred. The house was high and narrow, built of red brick with a slate roof and a satellite dish attached high up, where the walls met the roof. It was still early in the morning, but Hurst was already up and about. In his forties, tall and skinny, with thinning, dry, brown hair, he was wearing jeans and a red zippered sweatshirt.

'Ah, I've been expecting you,' he said when Banks and Annie showed their warrant cards, his pale grey eyes lingering on Annie for just a beat too long. 'It'll be about that fire.'

'That's right,' said Banks. 'Mind if we come in?'

'No, not at all. Your timing is immaculate. I've just finished my breakfast.' He stood aside and let Banks and Annie pass. 'First on the left. Let me take your coats.'

They gave him their overcoats and walked into a room lined with wooden shelves. On the shelves were hundreds, perhaps thousands, of long-playing records, 45 rpm singles and EPs, all in neat rows. Banks exchanged a glance with Annie before they sat in the armchairs to which Hurst gestured.

'Impressive, aren't they?' Hurst said, smiling. 'I've been collecting sixties' vinyl since I was twelve years old.

It's my great passion. Along with canals and their history, of course.'

'Of course,' said Banks, still overwhelmed by the immense collection. On any other occasion he would have been down on his hands and knees scanning the titles.

'And I'll bet I can lay my hands on any one I want. I know where they all are. Kathy Kirby, Matt Monro, Vince Hill, Helen Shapiro, Joe Brown, Vicki Carr. Try me. Go on, try me.'

Christ, thought Banks, an anorak. Just what they needed. 'Mr Hurst,' he said, 'I'd be more than happy to test your system, and to explore your record collection, but do you think we could talk about the fire first? Two people died on those barges.'

Hurst looked disappointed, like a child denied a new toy, and went on tentatively, not sure if he still held his audience. 'They're not filed alphabetically but by date of release, you see. That's my secret.'

'Mr Hurst.' Annie echoed Banks. 'Please. Later. We've got some important questions for you.'

He looked at her, hurt and sulky, but seemed at last to grasp the situation. He ran his hand over his head. 'Yes, I know. Pardon me for jabbering on. Must be the shock. I always jabber when I'm nervous. I'm really sorry about what happened. How did . . . ?'

'We don't know the cause of the fire yet,' said Banks, 'but we're definitely treating it as suspicious.' *Doubtful* was Geoff Hamilton's word. He knew as well as Banks that the fire hadn't started on its own. 'Do you know the area well?' he asked.

Hurst nodded. 'I think of this as *my* stretch of the canal, as my responsibility.'

'Including the dead-end branch?'

'Yes.'

'What can you tell me about the people who lived on the barges?'

Hurst lifted up his black-rimmed glasses and rubbed his right eye. 'Strictly speaking, they're not barges, you know.'

'Oh?'

'No, they're narrowboats. Barges are wider and can't cruise on this canal.'

'I see,' said Banks. 'But I'd still like to know what you can tell me about the squatters.'

'Not much, really. The girl was nice enough. Pale, thin, young thing, didn't look well at all, but she had a sweet smile and she always said hello. Quite pretty, too. When I saw her, of course. Which wasn't often.'

That would be Tina, Banks thought, remembering the blistered body in the charred sleeping bag, the blackened arm, into which she had injected her last fix. 'And her boyfriend, Mark?'

'Is that his name? Always seemed a bit furtive to me. As if he'd been up to something, or was about to get up to something.'

In Banks's experience, a lot of kids Mark's age and younger had that look about them. 'What about the fellow on the other boat?' he asked.

'Ah, the artist.'

Banks glanced at Annie, who raised her eyebrows. 'How do you know he was an artist?'

'Shortly after he moved there, he installed a skylight and gave the exterior of his boat a lick of paint, and I thought maybe he'd actually rented or bought the boat and was intending to fix it up, so I paid him a courtesy visit.'

'What happened?'

'I didn't get beyond the door. He clearly didn't appreciate my coming to see him. Not very courteous at all.'

'But he told you he was an artist?'

'No, of course not. I said I didn't get past the door, but I could *see* past it, couldn't I?'

'So what did you see?'

'Well, artist's equipment, of course. Easel, tubes of paint, palettes, pencils, charcoal sticks, old rags, stacks of canvas and paper, a lot of books. The place was a bloody mess, quite frankly, and it stank to high heaven.'

'What of?'

'I don't know. Turpentine. Paint. Glue. Maybe he was a glue-sniffer. Have you thought of that?'

'I hadn't until now, but thank you very much for the idea. How long had he been living there?'

'About six months. Since summer.'

'Ever see him before that?'

'Once or twice. He used to wander up and down the towpath with a sketchbook.'

A local, perhaps, Banks thought, which might make it easier to find out something about him. Banks's ex-wife Sandra used to work at the Eastvale Community Centre art gallery and he still had a contact there. The idea of meeting up with Maria Phillips again had about as much appeal as a dinner date with Cilla Black, but she would probably be able to help. There wasn't much Maria didn't know about the local art scene, including the gossip. There was also Leslie Whitaker, who owned Eastvale's only antiquarian bookshop and who was a minor art dealer.

'What else can you tell us about him?' he asked Hurst.

'Nothing. Hardly ever saw him after that. Must have

been in his cabin painting away. Lost in his own world, that one. Or on drugs. But you'd expect that from an artist, wouldn't you? I don't know what kind of rubbish he painted. In my opinion, just about all modern—'

Banks noticed Annie roll her eyes and sniffle before turning the page in her notebook. 'We know his first name was Tom,' Banks said, 'but do you know his surname?'

Hurst was clearly not pleased at being interrupted in his critical assessment of modern art. 'No,' he said.

'Do you happen to know who owns the boats?'

'No idea,' said Hurst, 'but someone should have fixed them up. They weren't completely beyond repair, you know. It's a crying shame leaving them like that.'

'So why didn't the owner do something?'

'Short of money, I should imagine.'

'Then he could have sold them,' said Banks. 'There must be money in canal boats these days. They're very popular with the holiday crowd.'

'Even so,' said Hurst, 'whoever bought them would have had to go to a great deal of extra expense to make them appeal to tourists. They were horse-drawn boats, you see, and there's not much call for them these days. He'd have had to install engines, central heating, electricity, running water. Costly business. Tourists might enjoy boating along the canals, but they like to do it in comfort.'

'Let's get back to Tom, the artist,' said Banks. 'Did you ever see any of his work?'

'Like I said, it's all rubbish, isn't it, this modern art? Damien Hirst and all that crap. I mean, take that Turner Prize—'

'Even so,' Annie interjected, 'some people are willing to pay a fortune for rubbish. Did you actually *see* any of his paintings? It might help us find out who he was, if we can get some sense of the sort of thing he produced.'

'Well, there's no accounting for taste, is there? But no, I didn't actually see any of them. The easel was empty when I paid my visit. Maybe he was some sort of eccentric. The tortured genius. Maybe he kept a fortune under his mattress and someone killed him for it.'

'What makes you think he was killed?' Banks asked.

'I don't. I was just tossing out ideas, that's all.'

'The area looks pretty inaccessible to me,' Banks said. 'What would be the best approach?'

'From the towpath,' Hurst said. 'But the nearest bridge is east of here, so anyone who came that way would have had to pass the cottage.'

'Did you see anyone that night? Anyone on the towpath heading towards the branch?'

'No, but I was watching television. I could easily have missed it if someone walked by.'

'What would be the next best approach?'

Hurst frowned for a moment as he thought. 'Well,' he said finally, 'short of swimming across the canal, which no one in their right mind would want to do, especially at this time of year, I'd say from the lane through the woods directly to the west. There's a lay-by, if my memory serves me well. And it's only about a hundred yards from there to the boats, whereas it's nearly half a mile up to where the lane meets the B road at the top.'

The fire engines had parked where the lane turned sharply right to follow the canal, Banks remembered, and he and Annie had parked behind them. He hoped they hadn't obliterated any evidence that might still be there. He would ask DS Stefan Nowak and the SOCOs to examine that particular area thoroughly. 'Ever see any strangers hanging around?' he asked.

'In summer, plenty, but it's generally quiet this time of year.'

'What about around the branch? Any strangers there?'

'I live a mile away. I don't spy on them. I sometimes saw them when I cycled by on the towpath, that's all.'

'But you saw the fire?'

'Could hardly miss it, could I?'

'How not?'

Hurst stood up. 'Follow me.' He looked at Annie and smiled. 'I apologize for the mess in advance. It's one of the advantages of the bachelor life, not having to keep everything neat and tidy.'

Annie blew her nose. Banks was hardly surprised to hear that Hurst was a bachelor. 'Except your record collection,' he said.

Hurst turned and looked at Banks as if he were mad. 'But that's *different*, isn't it?'

Banks and Annie exchanged glances and followed him up the narrow, creaky stairs into a room on the left. He was right about the mess. Piles of clothes waiting to be washed, a tottering stack of books by the side of the unmade bed, many of them about the history of canals but with a few cheap paperback blockbusters mixed in, Banks noticed: Tom Clancy, Frederick Forsyth, Ken Follett. The smell of unwashed socks and stale sweat permeated the air. Annie was lucky she was stuffed up with a cold, Banks thought.

But Hurst was right. From his bedroom window you could see clearly along the canal side, west, in the direction of the dead-end branch. It was impossible to see very far now because of the fog, but last night had been clear until early morning. Hurst wouldn't have been able to see the branch itself because of the trees, but Banks had no doubt at all that it would have been impossible for him to miss the flames as he went to draw the curtains at bed-time.

'What were you wearing?' Banks asked.

'Wearing?'

'Yes. Your clothes. When you cycled out to the fire.'

'Oh, I see. Jeans, shirt and a thick woolly jumper. And an anorak.'

'Are those the jeans you're wearing now?'

'No. I changed.'

'Where are they?'

'My clothes?'

'Yes, Mr Hurst. We'll need them for testing.'

'But surely you can't think . . . ?'

'The clothes?'

'I had to wash them,' said Hurst. 'They smelled so bad, with the smoke and all.'

Banks looked again at the pile of laundry waiting to be washed, then he looked back at Hurst. 'You're telling me you've already washed the clothes you were wearing last night?'

'Well, yes . . . When I got home. I know it might seem a bit strange, but how was I to know you'd want them for testing?'

'What about your anorak?'

'That, too.'

'You *washed* your anorak?'

Hurst swallowed. 'The label said it was machine wash-able.'

Banks sighed. Traces of accelerant might well survive the firefighters' hoses, but they used only cold water. He doubted that anything would survive washing powder and hot water. 'We'll take them anyway,' he said. 'What about your shoes? I suppose you put them in the washing machine as well?'

'Don't be absurd.'

'Let's be thankful for small mercies, then,' Banks said as they set off downstairs. 'What time do you usually go to bed?'

'Whenever I want. Another advantage of the bachelor life. On Friday I happened to be watching rather a good film.'

'What was it?'

'Ah, the old police trick to see if I'm lying, is it? Well I don't have an alibi, it's true. I was by myself all evening. All day, in fact. But I did watch *A Bridge too Far* on Sky Cinema. War films are another passion of mine.'

Hurst led them into the tiny kitchen, which smelled vaguely of sour milk. The anorak lay over the back of a chair, still a little damp, and the rest of his clothes were in the dryer. Hurst dug out a carrier bag and Banks bundled the lot inside, along with the shoes from a mat in the hallway.

'What time did the film finish?' he asked, as they returned to the living room.

'One o'clock. Or five past one, or something. They never seem to end quite on the hour, do they?'

'So when you looked out of your bedroom window around one o'clock—'

'It would have been perhaps one fifteen by the time I'd locked up and done my ablutions.'

Ablutions. Banks hadn't heard that word in years. 'OK,' he went on, 'at one fifteen, when you looked out of your bedroom window, what did you see?'

'Why, flames, of course.'

'And you knew where they were coming from?'

'Immediately. Those wooden boats are death traps. The wood above the waterline's as dry as tinder.'

'So you knew exactly what was happening?'

'Yes, of course.'

'What did you do?'

'I got on my bike and rode down the towpath.'

'How long did it take?'

'I don't know. I wasn't timing myself.'

'Roughly? Five minutes? Ten minutes?'

'Well, I'm not that fast a cyclist. It's not as if I was going in for the Tour de France or something.'

'Say ten minutes, then?'

'If you like.'

'What did you do next?'

'I rang the fire brigade, of course.'

'From where?'

He tapped his pocket. 'My mobile. I always carry it with me. Just in case . . . well, the Waterways people like to know what's going on.'

'Do you work for British Waterways?'

'Not technically. I mean, I'm not officially employed by them. I just try to be of use. If those narrowboats hadn't been in such sorry shape, and if they hadn't been moored in such an out-of-the-way place, I'm sure BW would have done something about them by now.'

'What time did you make the call?'

'I don't remember.'

'Would it surprise you to know that your call was logged at one thirty-one a.m.?'

'If you say so.'

'I do. That's fifteen minutes after you first saw the flames and cycled to the boats.'

Hurst blinked. 'Yes.'

'And what did you do after you rang them?'

'I waited for them to come.'

'You didn't try to do anything in the meantime?'

'Like what?'

'See if there was anyone still on the boats.'

'Do you think I'm insane? Even the firefighters couldn't risk boarding either of the boats until they'd sprayed water on them, and they were wearing protective clothing.'

'And it was too late by then.'

'What do you mean?'

'Everybody was dead.'

'Yes . . . well, I tried to tell them how dangerous it was, living there. I suspect one of them must have had a dodgy heater of some sort, too, as well as the turpentine. I know it's been a mild winter, but still . . . it *is* January.'

'Mr Hurst,' Annie asked, 'what were you thinking when you saw the fire's glow above the treeline and got on your bike?'

Hurst looked at her, a puzzled expression on his face. 'That I had to find out what was happening, of course.'

'But you said you already *knew* at once what was happening.'

'I had to be certain, though, didn't I? I couldn't just go off half-cocked.'

'What else did you think might have been causing the orange glow?'

'I don't know. I wasn't thinking logically. I just knew that I had to get down there.'

'Yet you didn't *do* anything when you did get down there.'

'It was too late already. I told you. There was nothing I could do.' Hurst sat forward, chin jutting aggressively. He looked at Banks. 'Look, I don't know what she's getting at here, but I—'

'It's simple, really,' said Banks. 'DI Cabbot is puzzled why you decided to cycle a mile – slowly – down to the canal branch, when you already knew the boats were on fire and that the wood they were made of was so dry they'd go up in no time. I'm puzzled too. And I'm also wondering why you didn't just do what any normal person would have done and call the bloody fire brigade straight away. From here.'

'Now there's no need to get stroppy. I wasn't thinking clearly. Like I said, you don't when . . . when something like that . . . The shock. Maybe you're right. Looking back, maybe I should have phoned first. But . . .' He shook his head slowly.

'I was waiting for you to say you hurried down there to see if there was anything you could do,' Banks said. 'To see if you could help in any way.'

Hurst just stared at him, lower jaw hanging, and adjusted his glasses.

'But you didn't say that,' Banks went on. 'You didn't even lie.'

'What does that mean?'

'I don't know, Andrew. You tell me. All I can think of is that you wanted those narrowboats and the people who lived on them gone, that you didn't call the fire brigade the minute you knew they were on fire, and that as soon as you got home you put your clothes in the washing machine. Perhaps nobody can fault you for not jumping on board a burning boat, but the fifteen minutes it took you to cycle down the towpath and make the call could have made all the difference in the world. And I'm wondering if you were aware of that at the time, too.' Banks looked at Annie, and they stood up, Banks grabbing the bag of clothes. 'Don't get up,' he said to Hurst. 'We'll see ourselves out. And don't wander too far from home. We'll be wanting to talk to you again soon.'

•

Banks wasn't the only one who saw his weekend fast slipping away. As Annie pulled up outside the Victorian terraced house on Blackmore Street, in south Eastvale, blew her raw nose and squinted at the numbers, she realized that the fire on the barges, or narrowboats, as Andrew Hurst had insisted they were called, was probably going to keep her well occupied for the next few days. She had been hoping that Phil Keane, the man she had been seeing for the past few months – when work and business allowed, which wasn't all that often – would be coming up from London for the weekend. Phil had inherited a cottage in Fortford from his grandparents, though he had grown up down south, and he liked to spend time there no matter what the season. If Phil didn't make it, Annie had planned to spend her free time getting over her cold.

Annie got out of the car and looked around. Most of the houses in the area were occupied by students at the College of Further Education. The area had been tarted up a lot since Annie had started working in Eastvale. What was once a stretch of marshy waste ground between the last straggling rows of houses and the squat college buildings was now a park named after an obscure African revolutionary, complete with flowerbeds that rivalled Harrogate's in spring. A number of cafes and a couple of fancy restaurants had sprung up there over the past few years, too. Students weren't as poor as they used to be, Annie guessed; especially the foreign students. Many of the old houses had been renovated and the flats and bed-sits were quite comfortable. Like the rest of Eastvale, the college had grown and its board knew they had to work to attract new students.

This morning, though, in the clinging January fog, the area took on a creepy, surreal air, the tall houses looking like a Gothic effect in a horror film, rising out of the mist with their steeply pointed slate roofs and elaborate gables. Through the bare trees across the park, Annie could see the lonely, illuminated red sign of the Blue Moon Cafe and Bakery offering cheap breakfasts. For a moment she considered going in and ordering fried eggs, mushrooms and beans on toast – skipping the sausage and bacon because she was a vegetarian – but she decided against it. She'd grab something more healthy later, back in the town centre. Besides, she thought, looking up at the looming house, she had an alibi to check.

She walked up the steps and peered at the names on the intercom box. Mandy Patterson. That was the person she wanted. She pressed the bell. It seemed to take for ever, but eventually a sleepy voice answered. 'Yes? Who is it?'

Annie introduced herself.

'Police?' Mandy sounded alarmed. 'Why? What is it? What do you want?'

Annie was used to that reaction from members of the public, who either felt guilty about some driving or park-ing offence or didn't want to get involved. 'I just want to talk to you, that's all,' she said in as convincing a friendly voice as she could manage. 'It's about Mark.'

'First landing, flat three, on your left.'

Annie heard the door release click and pushed it open. Inside, the place was far less gloomy than out. The thick-piled stair carpets looked new, the hallway was clean and well kept, the interior well lit. Better than the student digs of her days, Annie thought, even though those days were only about fifteen years ago.

Annie climbed the steep stairs and knocked on the door to flat three. Fit as she was, she was glad Mandy didn't live all the way up at the top. The damn cold was sapping her energy, making her feel dizzy when she exerted herself. She couldn't meditate, either. All she experienced when she sat in the lotus position and tried to concentrate on the breath coming and going, as it passed the point between her eyebrows, was either a stuffed-up nose or a thick, phlegmy sniffle.

The girl who opened the door looked as if she had just been woken up, which was probably the case. She rubbed her eyes and squinted at Annie. 'So you're the police?' she said, looking at Annie's open greatcoat, long scarf and high boots.

'Afraid so.'

Annie followed her into the room. Perhaps because Mandy had heard over the intercom that Annie was female, or perhaps because semi-nudity didn't concern her, she hadn't bothered putting anything on other than a long white T-shirt with a George and Dragon logo on the front. Annie thought it was too cold for such scanty clothing, but she could soon feel that the bedsit was centrally heated. Another change from her own student days, when she had braved a dash from the piled blankets to the gas fire and hoped to hell her five pence from last night hadn't run out. She took off her overcoat and found that she was warm enough without it.

'You woke me up, you know,' Mandy said over her shoulder.

'Sorry about that,' Annie said. 'Part of the job.' The messed-up sheets on the mattress under the window testified to what Mandy said.

'Cup of tea? I'm having one myself. Can't think in the morning without a cup of tea.'

'Fine,' said Annie. 'If you're brewing up anyway.' Mandy had a posh accent, she noticed. What had she been doing with Mark, then? Slumming it? A bit of rough?

The kitchenette was separated from the rest of the bedsit by a thin green curtain, which Mandy left open as she filled the electric kettle. Annie sat in one of the two small armchairs, which were arranged around an old fireplace filled by a vase full of dried purple and yellow flowers and peacock feathers. There was a poster of Van Gogh's Sunflowers on the wall, and the radio was playing quietly in the background. Annie recognized an old Pet Shop Boys number, 'Always on My Mind'. That had been a hit back in her own student days in Exeter. She had liked the Pet Shop Boys. A vivid memory of Rick Stenson, her boyfriend at the time, came to her as the music played. A handsome, fair-haired, media-studies student, he had always put her down for her musical tastes, being into Joy Division, Elvis Costello, Dire Straits and Tracy Chapman. He thought he was a cut above the Pet Shop Boys, Enya and Fleetwood Mac fans. He even used to go on about the original Fleetwood Mac, when Peter Green played with them. What had she seen in him? Annie wondered now. He'd been nothing but a bloody arrogant snob, and he hadn't been an awful lot of good in bed, either, showing a slight flair for the obvious and no imagination whatsoever beyond. Ah, the mistakes of your youth.

Mandy came in with the tea and sat in the other armchair, legs curled up, the hem of her T-shirt barely covering the tops of her slim, smooth thighs. Curly brown hair, messy from sleep, framed a heart-shaped face with thin lips, a small nose and loam-brown eyes. She had beautiful Brooke Shields eyebrows, Annie thought with envy, her own being definitely on the thin and skimpy side.

'What did you do last night?' Annie asked.

'Do? What do you mean? Why do you want to know?'

'Would you just let me ask the questions?' Annie didn't know why she was becoming testy with Mandy, but she was; she could feel the irritation building at the girl's voice, the thighs, the eyebrows. She took out a paper handkerchief and blew her nose. The room felt hot now; she could feel the sweat prickling under her arms. Or maybe it was a fever that came with her cold.

Mandy sulked and sipped some tea; then she said, 'OK. Ask away.'

'Was Mark here with you?'

'Mark? Of course not. That's ridiculous. What's he supposed to have done? If he said—'

'You do *know* him, don't you?'

Mandy toyed with a strand of hair, straightening and curling. 'If you mean Mark Siddons, yes, of course I know him. He comes by the pub sometimes when he's working on the building site.'

'Which building site?'

'Over the park. They're putting up a new sports centre for the college.'

'And are you friendly with Mark?'

'Sort of.'

Annie leaned forward. 'Mandy, this could be important. Was Mark here with you last night?'

'What kind of girl do you think I am?'

'Oh, for crying out loud,' Annie said, feeling her head spin with the fever and the irritation. 'This is supposed to be a simple job. I ask you the questions and you give me honest answers. I'm not here to judge you. I don't care what kind of girl you are. I don't care if you just fancied a bit of rough and Mark—'

Mandy reddened. 'It wasn't like that!'

'Then tell me what it *was* like.'

'What's this all about? What has Mark done?'

Annie didn't want to give Mandy any reason for prevarication and she knew that every piece of information altered the equation. 'You answer my questions first,' she said, 'then I'll tell you why I'm asking them.'

'That's not fair.'

'It's the only deal you'll get. Take it or leave it.'

Mandy glared at her, then settled down to playing with her curls again. She let the silence stretch before answering. 'Mark came to the pub a few times, at lunchtime, like I said. It was the holiday period, so I was working extra shifts. I liked him. He wasn't a bit of rough.' She gave Annie a harsh glance. 'Maybe he seems like that on the surface, but underneath, he's . . . well, he's a nice bloke and you don't get to meet many of those.'

So cynical so young, Annie thought, but Mandy had a point. Annie thought of Banks. He was a nice bloke, but she had split up with him. Maybe she should have hung onto him instead. He had another girlfriend now, she knew, even though he didn't like to talk about her. Annie was surprised at the flash of jealousy she felt whenever she knew he was going away for the weekend. Was she younger than Annie? Prettier? Better in bed? Or just less difficult? Well, she had her reasons for doing what she did, she told herself, so leave it be.

'He'd flirt a bit and we'd chat,' Mandy went on. 'You know what it's like.'

'What about last night?'

'He came to the pub late. He seemed a bit upset.'

'Why?'

'He didn't say. He just seemed depressed, like he had a lot on his mind.'

'What time was this?'

'About a quarter to eleven. Nearly closing time. He only had the one pint.'

'Then what?'

'I invited him back here for a coffee.'

'So he *was* here?'

'Yes.'

'Why did you lie to me?'

'Because I didn't want you to think I was a tramp or a slag or anything. It wasn't like that at all. I only asked him up for a coffee because I felt sorry for him.'

'What happened?' Annie asked.

'We talked, mostly.'

'Mostly?'

Mandy looked down, examining her thumbnail. 'Well, you know . . . One thing led to another. Look, I don't have to spell it out, do I?'

'What did you talk about?'

'Life.'

'That's a big subject. Can you narrow it down a bit for me?'

'You know, relationships, hopes for the future, that sort of thing. We'd never really talked like that before.' She frowned. 'Nothing's happened to him, has it? Please tell me he's all right.'

'He's fine,' said Annie. 'Did he tell you about Tina?'

'Tina? Who's that?'

'Never mind,' said Annie. 'What did he talk about?'

'Does he have a girlfriend? He never told me. The two-timing bastard.'

'Mandy, can you remember what he talked about?'

It took Mandy a few moments to control her anger and answer. 'The boat. Living on the boat. How he was only working on a building site, but he wanted to get into masonry and church restoration work. He told me he had a sister on drugs and he wanted to help her. That sort of thing. Like I said, relationships, dreams. Wait a minute! Was that Tina? His sister?'

'I don't know,' said Annie. 'Did he say anything about someone called Tom?'

'Tom? No. Who's that?'

'A neighbour. An artist who lived on the boat next to Mark's.'

Mandy shook her head. Her curls bounced. 'No,' she said. 'He never mentioned any Tom. Apart from saying how he liked it there and how peaceful it was, he just complained about some interfering old anorak who kept trying to get him to move.'

That would be Andrew Hurst, Annie thought, smiling to herself at the description. 'What time did he leave here?'

'I don't know. Late. I was half asleep. I hardly noticed him go.'

'How late?' Annie persisted. 'One o'clock? Two o'clock?'

'Oh no. Later than that. I mean we really *did* talk for hours, until two at least. It was only *after* that . . .'

'What?'

'You know. Anyway, he seemed edgy later, said he couldn't sleep. I told him to go because I needed my sleep for work.'

'So it was after two?'

'Yes. Maybe around three.'

'OK,' said Annie, standing to leave.

'Your turn now,' said Mandy, at the door.

'What?'

'You were going to tell me why you're asking these questions.'

'Oh,' said Annie. 'That. You can read all about it in the papers,' she said and headed down the stairs. Then she added over her shoulder, 'Or if you can't wait, just turn up your radio.'

●

It was late morning by the time Banks had put in motion the complex machinery of a murder investigation. There was a team to set up, actions to be assigned, and they would need a mobile unit parked down by the canal. Banks had already arranged for a dozen constables to search the immediate area around the narrowboats, including the handiest point of access and the woods where Mark had been hiding. If they found anything, they would tape it off for the SOCOs. Unfortunately, the closest house to the boats was Andrew Hurst's, and the village of Molesby lay half a mile south of that, across the canal in a hollow, so he didn't expect much from house-to-house enquiries in the village. They still had to be carried out, though. Someone might have seen or heard something.

Banks went to his office. His left cheek still stung from where the twigs had cut him as he'd chased Mark through the woods, and his clothes and hair all smelled of damp ash. His chest felt tight, as if he'd smoked a whole packet of cigarettes. There was nothing he wanted more than to go home, take a long shower and have a nap before getting back to work, but he couldn't. The pressure was on now.

Geoff Hamilton was still at the fire scene and had already put a rush on forensics to find out what accelerant had been used. The gas chromatograph ought to provide speedy results. Dr Glendenning, the Home Office pathologist, would conduct the post-mortems later that afternoon, starting with Tom, the artist, as it was his boat where the fire had started.

Banks knew he was being premature in treating the incident as a double murder before Geoff Hamilton or Dr Glendenning gave him the supporting evidence necessary for such a decision, but he had seen enough on the boats. It was important to act quickly. The first twenty-four hours after a major crime are of vital significance and trails quickly go cold after that. He would take the heat from Assistant Chief Constable McLaughlin later, if he turned out to be wrong and to have wasted valuable budget funds, but Area Commander Kathleen Finlay and Detective Superintendent Gristhorpe had agreed with him on the necessity of an early start, so things were in motion. Banks was senior investigating officer and Annie his deputy.

There was one more thing that Banks had to do before he could even think of lunch. He rang down to the custody officer and asked him to send up Mark – whose full name, it turned out, was Mark David Siddons – to his office, not to an interview room. Mark's hands had checked out negative for accelerants. His clothes were at the lab waiting in line for the gas chromatograph, and would take a bit longer. He wasn't out of the running yet, not by a long chalk.

While he waited, Banks found a chamber music concert on Radio 3. He didn't recognize the piece that was playing, but it sounded appropriately soothing in the background. He didn't imagine that Mark would be a fan of classical music, but that didn't matter. Mark wouldn't be listening to the music. Banks remembered an article he'd read recently about playing classical music in underground stations to discourage mobs of youths from gathering and causing trouble. Apparently it drove the yobs away. Maybe they should blare Bach and Mozart out of city-centre loudspeakers, especially around closing time.

Banks glanced at his *Dalesman* calendar. January's picture was of a snow-covered hillside in Swaledale dotted with black-faced sheep.

Finally a constable knocked on the door and Mark walked over the threshold.

'Sit down,' Banks said.

Mark looked around the room apprehensively and sat on the edge of a chair. 'What's going on?' he asked. 'You know something, don't you? It's about Tina.'

'I'm sorry, Mark,' Banks said.

The loud wail that rang out of Mark's small body took Banks by surprise. As did the violence with which he picked up his chair and threw it at the door, then stood there, chest heaving, racked with sobs.

The door opened, and the constable poked his head around it. Banks gestured for him to leave. For a long time, Mark just stood there, his back to Banks, head down, fists clenched, body heaving. Banks let him be. The music played softly in the background and now Banks thought he recognized the adagio of one of Beethoven's late string quartets. Finally, Mark wiped his arms across his face, picked up the chair and sat down again, staring at his knees. 'I'm sorry,' he mumbled.

'It's all right,' said Banks.

'It's just . . . I suppose I knew. All along I knew, soon as I saw it, she couldn't have got away.'

'It didn't look as if she suffered, if that's any help.'

Mark ran the back of his hand under his running nose. Banks passed him the box of tissues that had been languishing on his desk since his December cold had cleared up.

'Well, at least she won't suffer any more,' Mark said, sniffling. He looked up at Banks. 'Are you sure she didn't? I've heard terrible things about fires.'

'The way it looked,' said Banks, 'is that she probably died in her sleep of smoke inhalation before she even knew there was a fire.' He hoped he was right. 'Look, Mark, we've still got a long way to go. If there's anything else you can tell me, do it now.'

Mark shot him a glance. 'There's nothing else,' he said. 'I was telling you the truth about where I was. I only wish to God I hadn't been.'

'So you were gone from ten-thirty to four in the morning?'

'About that, yes. Look, surely the tests . . .'

'I need to hear it from you.' Banks felt sorry for the kid, but procedures had to be followed. 'We're looking at murder here,' he said, 'two murders, and I need a lot more information from you.'

'Someone *murdered* Tina? Why would anyone want to do that?' Mark's eyes filled with tears again.

'She probably wasn't the intended victim, but it amounts to the same thing, yes.'

'Tom?'

'It looks that way. But there's something else, another criminal matter.'

Mark wiped his eyes. 'What?'

'Are you a user, Mark?'

'What?'

'A drug addict, a junkie.'

'I know what it means.'

'Are you?'

'No.'

'Was Tina?'

'Tina was . . .'

'What?'

'Nothing.'

'Look, Mark, we found a syringe beside her on the boat. I'm not looking to bust you for anything, but you've got to tell me. It could be important.'

Mark looked down at his shoes.

'Mark,' Banks repeated.

Finally, Mark gave a long sigh and said, 'She wasn't an addict. She could take it or leave it.'

'But mostly she took it?'

'Yes.'

'What?'

'Whatever. Heroin, if it was around. Morphine. Methadone. Demerol. Valium. Downers. Anything to make her oblivious. Not uppers. She said those only made her too alert, and alertness made her paranoid. And she stayed away from pot, acid and E. They made her see things she didn't want to see. You have to understand. She was just so helpless. She couldn't take care of herself. I should have stayed with her. She was so scared.'

'What was she scared of?'

'Everything. Life. The dark. Men. She's had a hard life, has Tina. That's why she . . . it was her escape.'

'Did Tina have any drugs when you left?'

'She had some heroin. She was just fixing up.' Mark started to cry again. Banks noticed his hands had curled into tight fists as he talked. He had tattoos on his fingers. They didn't read LOVE and HATE like Robert Mitchum's in *The Night of the Hunter*, but TINA on the left and MARK on the right.

'Where did she get the heroin?'

'Dealer in Eastvale.'

'His name, Mark?'

Mark hesitated. Banks could tell he was troubled by the idea of informing on someone, even a drug dealer, and the inner struggle was plain on his features. Finally, his feelings for Tina won out. 'Danny,' he said. 'Danny Corcoran.'

Banks knew of Danny 'Boy' Corcoran. He was strictly a small-time street dealer, and the drugs squad had been watching him for weeks, hoping he might lead them to a large supplier. He hadn't done yet.

'How did you know about Danny Corcoran?'

'A contact in Leeds, someone from the squat where we used to live.'

'How long had Tina been using?'

'Since before I met her.'

'When was that?'

'About six months ago.'

'How did you meet?'

'At the squat in Leeds.'

'How did you end up on the boat?'

'We didn't like the squat. There were some really ugly characters living there and one of the bastards kept putting his hands on her. We got into a fight. And the place was always dirty. Nobody bothered cleaning up after themselves. Think what you like of Tina and me, but we're decent people, and we don't like living in filth. Anyway, the boat needed a lot of work, but we made it nice.'

'How did you find the boat?'

'I knew about it. I'd seen them before. I used to go for walks on the towpath and sometimes I'd stop and wonder what it would be like, living on the water like that.'

'When was that?'

'A year or so back.'

'So you're from around here? From Eastvale.'

Mark gave a quick shake of his head. Banks didn't pursue the matter. 'Carry on,' he said.

'We just wanted to be together, by ourselves, without anyone to rip us off or fuck up our lives. I was trying to get Tina off drugs. I loved her. I don't care if you believe me or not. I did. I looked out for her. She needed me and I let her down.'

'What about her parents? We'll need to contact them. Someone will have to identify the body.'

Mark glanced sharply at Banks. 'I'll do it,' he said.

'It needs to be a relative. Next of kin.'

'I said I'll do it.' Mark folded his arms.

'Mark, we'll find out one way or another. You're not doing anybody any favours here.'

'She wouldn't want those bastards anywhere near her,' he said.

'Why not?'

'You know.'

'Was she abused?'

He nodded. 'Him. Her stepfather. He used to do it to her regularly and her mother did nothing. Too frightened of losing the miserable bastard. I swear I'll kill him if I ever see him again. I mean it.'

'You won't see him, Mark. And you don't want to go talking about killing anyone. Even in grief. Now, where do they live?'

'Adel.'

'La-di-dah,' said Banks. Adel was a wealthy north Leeds suburb with a fine Norman church and a lot of green.

Mark noticed Banks's surprise. 'He's a doctor,' he said.

'Tina's stepfather?'

'Uh-huh. That's how she first got addicted. She used to nick morphine from his surgery when he'd . . . you know. It helped her get over the shame and the pain. He must have known about it, but he didn't say anything.'

'Did he know where she lived, on the boat?'

'He knew.'

'Did he ever visit you there?'

'Yes. To try to take Tina back. I wouldn't let him.'

Mark probably weighed no more than eight or nine stone, but he looked wiry and strong. People like him often made deceptively tough scrappers, Banks knew, because he'd been like that himself at Mark's age. He was still on the wiry side, despite all the beer and junk food. A matter of metabolism, he supposed. Jim Hatchley, on the other hand, seemed to show every pint he supped right in his gut.

'So Tina's father knew about you?'

'Yes.'

'When was the last time he paid you a visit?'

'About a week ago.'

'You sure he didn't come yesterday?'

'I don't know. I was at work. On the building site. Tina didn't say anything.'

'Would she have?'

'Maybe. But she was . . . you know . . . a bit out of it.'

A little chat with Tina's stepfather was definitely on the cards. 'What's his name?' Banks asked.

'Aspern,' Mark spat out. 'Patrick Aspern.'

'You might as well give me his address.'

Mark gave it to him.

'And stay away,' Banks warned him.

Mark looked sullen, but he said nothing.

'Is there anything else you can tell me about Tom on the next boat? What did he look like?'

'Ordinary, really. Short bloke, barrel-chested. He had long fingers, though. You couldn't help but notice them. He didn't shave very often, but he didn't really have a beard. Didn't wash his hair much either.'

'What colour was it?'

'Brown. Sort of long and greasy.'

Maybe the victim wasn't 'Tom' after all. Banks remembered the tufts of red hair that had somehow escaped the flames and made a note to talk to Geoff Hamilton about the discrepancy.

'Did he have any visitors?'

'Just a couple, as far as I know.'

'At the same time?'

'No. Separate. I saw one of them two or three times, the other only once.'

'What did he look like, the one you saw a few times?'

'Hard to say, really. It was always after dark.'

'Try.'

'Well, the only glimpse I got of him was when Tom opened his door and some light came out. He was thin, tallish, maybe six foot or more. A bit stooped.'

'See his face?'

'Not really. I only saw him in the shadows.'

'What about his hair?'

'Short. And dark, I think. Or that could have just been the light.'

'Clothes?'

'Can't say, really. Maybe jeans and trainers.'

'Would you recognize him if you saw him again?'

'Dunno. I don't think so. There was one thing, though.'

'What's that?'

'He carried one of those big cases. You know, like art students have.'

'An artist's briefcase?'

'I suppose that's what you'd call it.'

So if Tom was an artist, Banks thought, then this was probably his dealer or agent. Worth looking into. 'When did you last see him?' he asked.

'Yesterday.'

'Yesterday when?'

'Just after dark. I hadn't been home from work long.'

'How long did he stay?'

'I don't know. I went back inside before he left. I was having a smoke and Tina doesn't like me smoking indoors. It was cold.'

'So he could have still been there after you left for the pub?'

'He could've been, I suppose. I didn't hear him leave. We did have the music on, though.'

'What about the other visitor?'

'I can't really say. It was just the once, maybe two, three weeks ago. It was dark that time, too.'

'Can you remember anything at all about him?'

'Only that he was shorter than the other bloke and a bit fatter. I mean, not really fat, but not skinny, if you know what I mean.'

'Did you see his face?'

'Only when Tom opened the door. I can tell you his nose was a bit big. And hooked, like an eagle. But I only saw it from the side.'

'Did you ever see any cars parked in the lay-by through the woods?'

'Once or twice.'

'What cars?'

'I remember seeing one of those jeep things. Dark blue.'

'Jeep Cherokee? Range Rover?'

'I don't know. Just a dark blue jeep. Or black.'

'Anything else?'

'No.'

'But you never saw anyone getting in or out of it?'

'No.'

'Was it there yesterday, when the man came?'

'I didn't see it, but I didn't look. I mean, it was dark, I'd have had to have been walking that way. I'd seen it there before when he visited, though. The tall bloke.'

'Can you remember anything else that happened before you went out yesterday?' Banks asked.

'That sad bastard from the lock keeper's cottage was round again on his bike.'

'Andrew Hurst? What was he doing there?'

'Same as always. Spying. He thinks I can't see him in the woods, but I can see him all right.'

Just like we saw you, Banks thought. 'Who is he spying on?'

'Dunno. If you ask me, though, he's after seeing Tina without her clothes on.'

'Why do you say that?'

'The way he ogles her whenever he's around. He just looks like a perv to me, that's all, and he's always lurking, spying. Why else would he do that?'

Good question, Banks thought. And it was interesting that Andrew Hurst had specifically mentioned that he *didn't* spy on the people on the boats. He also hadn't told Banks and Annie about his earlier visit during their conversation that morning. Banks would have to have another chat with the self-styled lock keeper.

'What's going to happen to Tina now?' Mark asked.

Banks didn't want to go into the gory details of the post-mortem, so he just said, 'We'll be hanging onto her until we've got this sorted.'

'And after? I mean there'll be a funeral, won't there?'

'Of course,' said Banks. 'Don't worry. Nobody's going to abandon her.'

'Only once we were talking, like you do, and she said when she died she wanted "Stolen Car" played at her funeral. Beth Orton. It was her favourite. She wanted to be a singer.'

'I'm sure that can be arranged. But that's a while off yet. What are you going to do in the meantime?'

'Find somewhere to live, I suppose.'

'The social will help out. With your clothes and money and accommodation and all. Talking about that, have you got any money?'

'I've got about ten quid in my wallet. There was some money we'd saved on the boat, a couple of hundred. But that's gone now, along with everything else. I'm not a sponger. I've got a job. I'm not afraid of hard work.'

Banks remembered what Annie had told him about her interview with Mandy Patterson, about Mark's dreams. 'Someone said you wanted to be a stonemason, do church restoration work. Is that right?'

Mark looked away, embarrassed. 'Well, I don't have the qualifications, but I'd like to have a go. I just like old churches, that's all. I'm not religious or anything, so I don't know why. I just do. They're beautiful buildings.'

'What about clothes?'

'The clothes you took are all I've got,' he said. 'Everything else went up with the boat.'

'We're about the same size,' said Banks. 'I can let you have some old jeans and stuff till you get yourself sorted.'

'Thanks,' said Mark, looking down at the red low-cost suspect overalls he had been issued with. 'Anything would be better than this.'

'Can you go home for a while? To your parents?'

Mark gave a sharp shake of his head. Again Banks knew better than to pursue the subject, no matter how curious he was to know what made Mark react in such a frightened manner at the mention of his parents. Same as Tina, most likely. There was too much of it about, and most of it still didn't get reported.

'What about mates? Someone from the building site, perhaps?'

'I suppose there's Lenny.'

'Do you know his address?'

'No, but he's in the George most lunchtimes. Besides, the people at the site know him.'

'Do you think he'd be willing to put you up for a couple of nights until you find a flat, get on your feet again?'

'Maybe. Look, don't worry about me,' Mark said. 'I'll be all right. I'm used to taking care of myself. Can I go back to my cell now? I didn't sleep and I'm dog tired.'

Banks glanced at his watch. 'It's lunchtime. I hear they do a decent burger and chips.'

Mark stood up. The two of them walked downstairs, where Banks handed Mark over to one of the constables on duty, who would escort him down to the basement custody facilities. Then Banks walked out into the market square and headed for the Queen's Arms. He fancied beefburger and chips, too, but he'd have to miss out on his usual lunchtime pint. He was going to Adel to talk to Tina's parents, and he didn't want the smell of beer on his breath when he spoke to Dr Patrick Aspern.

3

After stopping off at home for a quick shower and a change of clothes, Banks headed down to Adel early that afternoon, listening to the same Beethoven string quartet that had been playing on the radio during his talk with Mark: No. 12 in E flat.

The fog had thinned to a mere gauze, except in patches, so it wasn't a difficult drive, and the temperature was heading towards double figures. One or two hardy souls were out playing on the golf course near Harrogate, dressed in sweaters and jeans.

Banks turned off the Leeds ring road onto Otley Road and stopped by the imposing gates of Lawnswood Crematorium to consult his map. A little further along the main road he turned right and drove into the affluent community of winding streets that was Adel.

He soon found the large, detached corner house, which also doubled as the doctor's surgery. This wasn't going to be an easy job, Banks reflected as he got out of his car. Mark's allegations against Dr Patrick Aspern might be groundless, and Banks was there to tell the parents that their daughter was dead and ask them to identify the body, not to interrogate the stepfather over sexual abuse. That might come later though, Banks knew, so he would have to be alert for anything out of the ordinary in Aspern's reactions to his questions.

Banks took a deep breath and pushed the doorbell. The

woman who answered looked younger than he expected. About Annie's age, early thirties, with short, layered blonde hair, pale, flawless skin and a nervous, elfin look about her. 'Mrs Aspern?' he asked.

The woman nodded, looking puzzled, and put her hand to her cheek.

'It's about your daughter, Tina. I'm a policeman. May I come in for a moment?'

'Christine?' Mrs Aspern fingered the loose neck of her cable-knit sweater. 'She doesn't live here any more. What is it?'

'If I might come in, please?'

She stood aside and Banks stepped onto the highly polished hardwood floor. 'First on the right,' said Mrs Aspern.

He followed her direction and found himself in a small sitting room with a dark blue three-piece suite and cream walls. A couple of framed paintings hung there, one over the decorative, but functional, stone fireplace, and the other on the opposite wall. Both were landscapes in simple black frames.

'Is your husband home?' Banks asked.

'Patrick? He's taking afternoon surgery.'

'Can you fetch him for me, please?'

'Fetch him?' She looked alarmed. 'But . . . the patients.'

'I want to talk to you both together. It's important,' Banks said.

Shaking her head, Mrs Aspern left the room. Banks took the opportunity to stand up and examine the two paintings more closely. Both were watercolours, painted in misty morning light, by the looks of them. One showed the church of St John the Baptist just down the street, which Banks happened to have visited once with his ex-wife Sandra during his early days in Yorkshire. He knew it was the oldest Norman church in Leeds, built around the middle of the twelfth century. Sandra had taken some striking photographs. A plain building, it was most famous for the elaborate stone carvings on the porch and chancel arch, at which the painting merely hinted.

The other painting was a woodland scene, which Banks assumed to be Adel Woods, again with that wispy, fey, early-morning light about it, making the glade look like the magical forest of *A Midsummer Night's Dream.* The signature 'Keith Peverell' was clear enough on both. No connection to 'Tom' there, not that he had expected any.

Mrs Aspern returned some minutes later, along with her clearly perturbed husband. 'Look,' he said, before any introductions had been made, 'I can't just leave my patients in the lurch like this. Can't you come back at five o'clock?'

'I'm afraid not,' said Banks, offering his warrant card.

Aspern scrutinized it, and a small, unpleasant smile tugged at the corners of his lips. He glanced at his wife. 'Why didn't you say, darling? A detective chief inspector, no less,' he said. 'Well, it must be important if they sent the organ-grinder. Please, sit down.'

Banks sat. Now that Aspern was pleased he'd been sent someone he thought commensurate with his social standing, though probably a chief constable would have been preferable, the patients were quickly forgotten. Things were likely to go a bit more easily. If Banks let them.

Aspern was a good fifteen years or so older than his wife, Banks guessed. Around fifty, with thinning sandy hair, he was handsome in a sharp-angled way, though

Banks was put off by the cynical look in his eyes and the lips perpetually on the verge of that nasty little superior smile. He had the slim, athletic figure of a man who plays tennis and golf and goes to the gym regularly. Being a doctor, of course, he'd know all about the benefits of exercise, though Banks knew more than one or two doctors, the Home Office pathologist Dr Glendenning among them, who smoked and drank and didn't give a damn about fitness.

'I'm afraid it's bad news,' he said, as Dr and Mrs Aspern faced him from the sofa. Mrs Aspern was chewing on a fingernail already, looking as if she was expecting the worst. 'It's about your daughter, Tina.'

'We always call her Christine. Please.'

'Out with it, man,' Aspern prodded. 'Has there been an accident?'

'Not quite,' Banks said. 'Christine's dead. I'm sorry, there's no easier way to say it. And we'll need one or both of you to come and identify the body.'

They sat in silence, not looking at one another, not even touching. Finally Aspern found his voice. 'Dead? How? What happened?'

'There was a fire. You knew she was living on a canal boat just outside Eastvale?'

'Yes. Another foolish idea of hers.' At last Aspern looked at his wife. Tears were running from her eyes as if she'd been peeling an onion, but she made no sound. Her husband got up and fetched her a box of tissues. 'Here you are, dear,' he said, putting them down on her knees. She didn't even look at them, just kept staring ahead into whatever abyss she was seeing, the tears dripping off the edges of her jaw on to her skirt, making little stains where they landed on the pale green material.

'I appreciate your coming yourself to tell us,' said Aspern. 'You can see my wife's upset. It's been quite a shock. Is that all?'

'I'm afraid not, sir,' Banks said. 'The fire was of doubtful origin. I have some questions I need to ask you as soon as possible. Now, in fact.'

'It's all right, Patrick,' Mrs Aspern said, coming back from a great distance. 'Let the man do his job.'

A little flustered by her command of the situation, or so it seemed to Banks, Aspern settled back onto the sofa. 'If you're sure . . .' he said.

'I'm sure.' She looked at Banks. 'Please tell us what happened.'

'Christine was living with a boy, a young man, rather, called Mark Siddons on an abandoned narrowboat.'

'Siddons,' said Aspern, lip twisting. 'We know all about him. Did he do this? Was he responsible?'

'We have no evidence that Mark Siddons had anything to do with the fire,' said Banks.

'Where was he? Did he survive?'

'He was out at the time of the fire,' Banks said. 'And he's unharmed. I gather there was no love lost between you?'

'He turned our daughter against us,' said Aspern. 'Took her away from home and stopped her from seeing us. It's as if he took control of her mind like one of those religious cults you read about.'

'That's not what he told me,' Banks said, careful now he knew he was walking on heavily mined land. 'And it's not the impression I got of him.'

'Well, you wouldn't expect him to admit it, would you? I can only imagine the lies he told you.'

'What lies?'

'Never you mind. I'm just warning you, that's all. The boy's no good. Don't believe a word he says.'

'I'll bear that in mind,' said Banks. 'How old was Christine?'

'Seventeen,' said Aspern.

'And how old was she when she left home?'

'She was sixteen,' Mrs Aspern answered. 'She went the day after her sixteenth birthday. As if she just couldn't wait to get away.'

'Did either of you know that Christine was a drug user?'

'It doesn't surprise me,' said Aspern. 'The crowd she was hanging around with. What was it? Pot? Ecstasy?'

'Apparently she preferred drugs that brought her oblivion rather than awareness,' Banks said softly, watching Patrick Aspern's face closely for any signs of a reaction. All it showed was puzzlement. 'It was heroin,' Banks continued. 'Other narcotics, if she couldn't get that, but mostly heroin.'

'Oh, dear God,' said Mrs Aspern. 'What have we done?'

Banks turned to her. 'What do you mean?'

'Fran,' her husband said, 'we can't blame ourselves for this. We gave her every opportunity. Every advantage.'

Banks had heard this before on so many occasions that it slipped in one ear and out the other. Nobody had a clue what their kids really needed – and how could they, for teenagers are hardly the most communicative species on earth – but so many parents assumed that the advantages of wealth or status were enough in themselves. Even Banks's own parents, working class as they were, thought he had let them down by joining the police force instead of pursuing a career in business. But wealth and status rarely were enough, in Banks's experience, though he knew that most kids from wealthy families went on to do quite well for themselves. Others, like Tina, and like Emily Riddle and Luke Armitage, cases he had dealt with in the recent past, fell by the wayside.

'Apparently,' Banks went on, cutting through the husband–wife tension he was sensing, 'Christine used to steal morphine from your surgery.'

Aspern reddened. 'That's a lie! Did Siddons tell you that? Any narcotics in my surgery are safely under lock and key in absolute compliance with the law. If you don't believe it, come and have a look for yourself right now. I'll show you. Come on.'

'That won't be necessary,' said Banks. 'This isn't about Christine's drug supplies. We know she got her last score from a dealer in Eastvale.'

'It's just a damn shame you can't put these people away *before* they do the damage,' said Aspern.

'That would assume we know who the criminals are going to be before they commit their crimes,' said Banks, thinking of the film *Minority Report*, which he had seen with Michelle a few weeks ago.

'If you ask me, it's pretty bloody obvious in most cases,' said Aspern. 'Even if this Siddons didn't start the fire, you can be damn sure he did *something*. He's got criminal written all over him, that one.'

More than once Banks, like his colleagues, had acted on the premise that if the person they had in custody hadn't committed the particular crime he was charged with, it didn't matter because the police *knew* he had committed other crimes, and had no evidence to charge him with them. In police logic the crime they were convicted for, the one they didn't commit, made up for all the crimes they had committed and got away with. It was easier in the old days, of course, before the Police and Criminal Evidence Act gave the criminals more rights than the police and the Crown Prosecution Service wouldn't touch anything with less than 100 per cent possibility of conviction, but it still happened if you could get away with it. 'We'd have to overhaul the legal system,' he said, 'if we wanted to put people who haven't done anything away without a trial. But let's get back to the matter in hand. Did you know of anyone who'd want to hurt Christine, Mrs Aspern?'

'We didn't know her . . . the friends she made after she left,' she answered. 'But I can't imagine anyone would want to harm her, no.'

'Dr Aspern?'

'Me neither.'

'There was an artist on the adjacent boat. All we know is that his name was Tom. Do you know anything about him?'

'Never heard of him,' said Patrick Aspern.

'What about Andrew Hurst? He lives nearby.'

'I never saw anyone.'

'When did you last visit the boat?' Banks asked him.

'Last week. Thursday, I believe.'

'Why?'

'What do you mean why?' Aspern said. 'She's my stepdaughter. I was concerned. I wanted to persuade her to come home.'

'Did you ever see the neighbour on one of your visits?'

'Look, you're making it sound as if I was a regular visitor. I only went up there a couple of times to try to persuade Christine to come home and that . . . thug she was with threatened me.'

'With what?'

'Violence, of course. I mean, I'm not a coward or a weakling or anything, but I wouldn't put it past someone like him to have a knife or even a gun.'

'You didn't go there yesterday?'

'Of course not.'

'What kind of car do you drive?'

'A Jaguar XJ8.'

'Did you ever visit the boat, Mrs Aspern?' Banks asked.

Before Frances Aspern could answer, her husband jumped in. 'I went by myself,' he said. 'Frances has a nervous disposition. Confrontations upset her. Besides, she couldn't bear to see how Christine was living.'

'Is this true, Mrs Aspern?' Banks asked.

Frances Aspern nodded.

'Look,' said Dr Aspern, 'you can see we're upset over the news. Can't you just go away and leave us in peace for a while, to grieve?'

'I'm afraid you'll have to save that for later,' said Banks. 'When I've finished here, I'd like one or both of you to follow me up to Eastvale and identify the body.'

Mrs Aspern touched her chalk-like cheek. 'You said it was a fire.'

'Yes,' said Banks. 'I'm sorry. There is some disfiguration. Not much, but some.'

'I'll go, darling,' said Aspern, resting his hand on her knee. 'I can cancel surgery. I'm sure everyone will understand.'

She shook him off. 'No. *I'll* go.'

'But you're upset, dear. I'm a doctor. I can deal with these things. I've been trained.'

She shot him a scornful glance. '*Deal with*? Is that all this means to you? I said I'll go. Mr Banks, can you take me and have someone bring me back? I'm afraid I'm far too upset to drive myself.'

'At least let me drive you,' her husband pleaded.

'I don't want you there,' she said. 'Christine was *my* daughter.'

There. It was said. And it lay heavily between them like an undigested meal. 'As you wish,' said Patrick Aspern.

'Are you certain it couldn't have been an accident?' Mrs Aspern asked, turning to Banks. 'I still can't believe that anyone would want to harm Christine.'

'Anything can happen when drugs enter the equation,' said Banks. 'And that's another angle we'll be looking at. There's also a strong possibility that Christine wasn't the intended victim.'

'What do you mean?' asked Aspern.

'I can't say much more at this point,' said Banks. 'We still have a lot of forensic tests to do and a lot of questions to ask. At the moment we're simply trying to get as much information as possible about the people who lived on the boats. When we know more, we'll know where to focus our investigation, which line of enquiry to follow.'

'I can't believe this is happening,' said Aspern.

His wife stood up. 'I'm ready to go,' she said to Banks, then added, looking at her husband, 'you can get back to your patients now, Patrick.'

He started to say something, but she turned her back and walked out of the room.

•

Mark's cell was small and basic, but comfortable enough. It smelled a bit – a hint of urine, vomit and stale alcohol – but they were old smells. At least it was clean and he wasn't shut in with a gang of sexually frustrated bikers with fourteen-inch penises. There were a couple of drunks down the corridor even at that time in the afternoon. One of them kept singing 'Your Cheatin' Heart' over and over again until one of the officers made him shut up. After that, Mark could hear them snoring or calling out in their sleep from time to time, but other than those few irritations things remained fairly quiet. All in all, it wasn't so bad. The only thing was, he couldn't go out when he wanted. It was like home, until he plucked up the courage to take on his mother and Crazy Nick and made his final break.

Mark tried, but sleep just wouldn't come. Most of his thoughts centred on Tina and the news the policeman had given him of her death. Of course, he had known it, known as soon as he got to the woods and saw the firemen and the smouldering barges that she had to be dead. But he had tried to deny it to himself; now he had to face it and accept it: he would never see Tina again.

And it was *his* fault.

Tina. So gentle, so frail and so birdlike: it broke his heart that he had been unfaithful to her and hurt her and would never get the chance to put things right, to tell her he was sorry and that he loved her, only her, not Mandy or anyone else. Tina trusted him, needed him and depended on him. He got her through the bad times and when there were good times – which there were – they laughed together, and sometimes went on walks in the country and drank screw-top wine and ate cheese-slice sandwiches beside a crystal stream.

Sometimes they seemed to live an almost normal life, the kind of life Mark wanted for them. In his dreams he got a steady job in Eastvale, maybe working on church restoration, got Tina straight, then they rented a little flat.

When the first baby came, they had saved enough for a small semi, maybe by the sea. At least that was how he saw their life developing. He knew he'd be taking care of Tina for ever, because she would always need that, even if she got straight – she was so badly scarred inside – but he could do it, he wanted to do it, and once she kicked the habit she couldn't help but get stronger. She was intelligent, too, much brighter than him; maybe she could get into the college like Mandy and get a job as a secretary or something. He bet she could work with computers if she put her mind to it.

Sometimes they even made love, but that was hard for Tina; she was never far from the hunger and the darkness at the centre of her being. The wrong word or gesture and she was burrowing deep inside herself again, scrunching up in the foetal position with her thumb in her mouth, on the nod. And when she was like that, it didn't matter if he was there or not. Which was why he hadn't been there last night.

Tina wasn't much interested in sex, partly because drugs do weird things to your sex drive, but mostly because of her stepfather. When Mark thought of Patrick Aspern his stomach knotted and rage surged through him. One day he'd . . .

Despite what the policeman had said, Mark wondered if Tina could have started the fire accidentally. She heated her spoon over a candle to prepare her fix and she'd been careless once or twice in the past. But he'd been there then, not like this time.

But no, he realized; it couldn't have happened that way. He remembered that he had been careful to snuff out the candle himself before leaving her on the nod, in a sleeping bag, her eyes glazed, pupils dilated, to all intents and purposes lost to the world, wrapped in a warm cocoon of safety and oblivion, without a care, until it started to wear off and she started to itch and her stomach knotted up and her every pore oozed with craving for more. He'd been through it all with her so many times, and he knew he'd have gone through it again when he got home, if it hadn't been for the fire.

He'd told Tina he was sick of her and her junkie ways, and if she didn't get into some sort of rehabilitation centre or methadone programme he was leaving her. She didn't care when he said it because the heroin was kicking in and flooding her veins and that rush, that golden warmth, was the only thing she cared about in the whole world when it spread through her like an orgasm. So he stormed out. Out to Mandy and her tantalizing, lithe young body. Tina didn't know where he was going, of course, and she never would now. But *he* knew, and that was more than enough.

At least he knew the fire couldn't have started on their boat. Did she know it was happening, that the flames were creeping closer, the smoke enveloping her? Even if she had come round when she smelled the smoke or saw the flames, would she have had time to get her head together and jump for land? Or water. Perhaps then she would have drowned. Tina couldn't swim.

Mark curled up on the hard bunk, and the thoughts and fears tumbled around in his tired brain. When the drunk started up again with 'Your Cheatin' Heart', he put his hands over his ears and cried.

•

'Is the music all right?' Banks asked Frances Aspern.

'Pardon?'

'The music. Is it OK?'

They were entering the Dales landscape beyond Ripon, and the distant shapes of the hills rose out of the mist in shades of grey, like whales breaking the water's surface. Banks was playing Mariza's *Fado em Mim*, traditional Portuguese songs, accompanied by classical guitar and bass, and he realized they might not be to everyone's taste. Frances Aspern had been staring out of the window in silence the whole way so far, and he had almost given up trying to start a conversation. He couldn't help but be aware of the weight of her grief beside him. Grief or guilt, he wasn't certain which.

'Yes,' said Mrs Aspern. 'It's fine. She sounds very sad.'

Indeed she did. Banks didn't understand a word of the songs without the translations on the CD booklet, the print of which was daily getting too small for him to read without glasses, but there was no mistaking the sense of loss, sadness and the cruelty of fate in Mariza's voice. You didn't need to know what the words meant to feel that.

'I didn't want to ask you while your husband was present,' Banks said, 'but is Christine's birth father still around?'

She shook her head. 'I was very young. We didn't marry. My parents . . . they were good to me. I lived with them in Roundhay until Patrick and I married.'

'We'll still need to talk to him,' said Banks.

'He's back home. In America. We met when he was travelling in Europe.'

'Can you give me the details?'

She looked out of the window, away from Banks, as she spoke, so that he could barely hear her. 'His name is Paul Ryder. He lives in Cincinnati, Ohio. I don't have his address or telephone number. We haven't been in contact since . . . well . . .'

Banks made a mental note of the name and city. It might be hard to track down this Paul Ryder after so long, but they'd have to try. 'How did you and Dr Aspern meet?' he asked.

'Patrick was a colleague of my father's, a frequent visitor to our house when I was at home when Christine was only a baby. My father is also a doctor. I suppose, in a way, he was Patrick's mentor. He's retired now, of course.'

Banks wondered how well that marriage had gone down with Mrs Aspern's family. 'Were you both at home last night?' he asked.

She turned to look at him. 'What do you expect me to say to that?'

'I expect you to tell me the truth,' Banks said.

'Ah, the truth. Yes, of course we were both at home.' She turned to look out of the window again.

'Did your husband go out at all yesterday?'

Mrs Aspern didn't reply.

'Is there anything else you want to say?' Banks asked. 'Anything at all you want to tell me?'

Mrs Aspern glanced at him again. He couldn't make out the expression on her face. Then she turned back to look out of the window. 'No,' she said, after a long pause. 'No, I don't think so.'

Banks gave up and drove on, Mariza singing against a backdrop of the misty Dales landscape, a song about sorrow, longing, pity, punishment and despair.

•

The scene looked different in the late afternoon, Annie thought, as she walked through the woods to the canal branch. The area was still taped off and she had to show her warrant card and sign in before entering, but the firefighters and their equipment were gone and in their stead was an eerie silence shrouding the two burned-out narrowboats and the scattering of men in hooded white overalls patiently searching the banks. The smell of ashes still hung in the damp air.

She found Detective Sergeant Stefan Nowak poking through debris on the artist's boat. Stefan was their crime-scene coordinator, and it was his job to supervise the collection of possible crime-scene evidence by his highly trained team and to liaise between the special analysts in the lab and Banks's team.

Stefan looked up as Annie approached. He was a hand-some, elegant man – no doubt a prince, Annie thought, as so many exiled Poles were – and he looked aristocratic, even in his protective clothing. There was a certain remoteness about him, which stopped on just the polite side of aloofness and made him seem regal in some way. He had a faint Polish accent, too, which served to heighten the mysterious effect. He was friendly enough to be on a first-name basis with both Annie and Banks, but he didn't hang out in the Queen's Arms with the rest of the lads and nobody knew much about his private life.

Annie sniffled. 'Found anything?' she asked.

Stefan gestured towards the murky water. 'One of the frogmen found an empty turps container in there,' he said. 'Probably the one used to start the fire. No prints or anything, though. Just your regular, commercial turps container. Anyway, I'm finished here,' he said. 'Come on, I'll show you what we've found so far.'

Annie wrapped her scarf more tightly around her sore throat as they took the narrow path through the woods. Wraiths of fog still drifted between the trees like elaborate spiders' webs, and here and there they had to step around a patch of muddy ground or a shallow puddle.

About halfway to the lane Annie saw the plastic retaining frames around faint imprints in the mud, each with a ruler lying next to it. 'Luckily, the ground was just muddy enough in places,' Stefan said. 'Probably protected by the trees. Anyway, we got reasonably fresh shoe impressions, but they could be anybody's.'

'How many?'

'Just the one person, by the looks of it.'

'Did the firefighters use this path?'

Stefan pointed. 'No, down there. This is the path you'd take from the lay-by. They parked further down, closer to the canal. This part of the woods is riddled with paths. I gather it's a popular spot in summer.'

Annie looked down at the markings. 'So they could be our man's?'

'Yes, but don't get your hopes up. Anyway, they've all been carefully photographed and casts have been made. They're drying out right now, but tomorrow we'll run them through SICAR.'

SICAR was an acronym for Shoeprint Image Capture and Retrieval, which combines a number of scanned databases to match footwear files with specimens, primarily the 'Solemate' database of over 300 common brands of shoe and 2,000 different sole patterns. Stefan's expert would have sprayed the muddy impression with shellac or acrylic lacquer, then he would have made a cast in dental stone. Back at headquarters he would enter the details of the shoe impression on the computer, coding by common patterns such as bars, polygons and zigzags, and by manufacturers' logos, if any were present. From these reference databases they could find out what type and brand of shoe caused the imprint, and they could also search the crime and suspect databases to see if it matched the shoe of a person taken into custody or a footprint left at a previous crime scene.

Of course, what everyone really hoped for was something more than just class characteristics – some sort of unique markings, the kind that come from wear and tear, a nice drawing-pin embedded in the sole, for example, something that could be matched with a specific shoe. Then, once you have your suspect and his shoe, you have solid evidence that links him to the scene.

They got to the lay-by, beside which the police mobile unit was parked, completely blocking the lane. It didn't matter much, though, as the track was hardly ever used and it led only towards a narrow bridge over the canal about two miles west. Anyone wanting to get there was advised to take the next turning by a diversion sign posted at the junction of the lane and the B road half a mile north.

Annie noticed more retaining frames, measures and markers on the lay-by itself.

'Impressive,' she said. 'You have been busy.'

'We'll see,' said Stefan. 'Trying to process a crime scene like this is like peeling the layers off the onion, and you don't know which layer is the important one.' He pointed to one of the imprints. 'Here we've got parallel tyre tracks,' he said. 'And that should be enough to tell us who the manufacturer was. From these we can also get the track width and wheelbase measurements, which might even help us identify the make of car. If there are a number of individual characteristics present in the tyre impressions, which may be the case, then we should be able to match them to the specific tyre and vehicle too.'

'If and when we find it,' said Annie.

'Naturally. We've also collected soil samples from the entire area. No rare wild flowers at this time of year, of course, but there are some unique mineral features, and they should also help us tie in the shoes and tyre to the scene, should we find them.'

'And should they still be dirty?'

Stefan narrowed his eyes. 'Trace evidence can be microscopic sometimes. You ought to know that. You'd be surprised how little we can work with.'

'I'm sorry,' said Annie. 'I don't mean to be negative. It's just . . . I have a feeling we're not dealing with an amateur here.'

'And we're not amateurs, either. Besides, we don't know *what* we're dealing with here yet.'

'True enough,' Annie agreed. 'I'm just suggesting that he'll have done his best to cover his tracks, and the longer it takes us to find him . . .'

'The more tracks he'll manage to cover. OK, I'll grant you that. But it'll take more than a car wash and a good polishing to get rid of every atom of soil he might have picked up here. Besides, don't forget, we've got the tyre impression to go on. There's an oil stain, too, by the looks of it.' He pointed to another protected area on the lay-by. 'We'll have that back for analysis by the end of the day. It's certainly beginning to look as if *someone* parked here recently, and if it wasn't you or the fire brigade . . .'

Annie knew that it was neither her nor Banks. They had been concerned to preserve as much of the scene as they could when they arrived, almost by instinct, so they had left their cars further up the lane and made their way through the woods without benefit of using a marked path. All in all, then, things were looking promising. Even if the evidence that Stefan and his team painstakingly collected didn't lead them directly to the arsonist, it would come in useful in court when they did find him.

'Any chance it was a Jeep Cherokee?' Annie asked, remembering what Banks had told her Mark said he'd seen. 'Or something similar?'

Stefan blinked. 'Know something I don't?'

'Just that something resembling a Jeep Cherokee has been reported seen in the area. Not last night, but recently.'

Stefan looked down at the tyre tracks. 'Well, he said, 'it's something to go on. We can certainly compare wheelbase and track width. Anyway,' Stefan said, opening the door of the mobile unit with a flourish, 'it's not exactly the Ritz, but the heater works. How about coming in for a cuppa?'

Annie smiled, her body leaning towards the source of heat the way a sunflower leans towards the sun. 'You must be a mind-reader,' she said and followed him in.

•

By the time Banks and Frances Aspern got to Western Area Headquarters after Mrs Aspern's positive identification of Christine at the mortuary of Eastvale General Infirmary, Annie had already left to talk to the SOCOs at the canal. Banks arranged for a uniformed constable to drive Mrs Aspern back home, and he had just settled down to review the findings so far, with Gil Evans's Jimi Hendrix orchestrations playing quietly in the background, when Geoff Hamilton appeared at his office door. Banks invited him in and Hamilton sat down, glancing around.

'Cosy,' he said.

'It'll do,' said Banks. 'Tea? Coffee?'

'Coffee, if you've got some. Black, plenty of sugar.'

'I'll ring down.' Banks ordered two black coffees. 'Anything new?'

'I've just come from the lab,' Hamilton said. 'We carried out gas chromatograph tests this afternoon.'

'And?'

Hamilton took two sheets of paper and a videotape from his briefcase and laid them out on Banks's desk. The sheets of paper looked like graphs, with peaks and valleys. 'As you know,' he said, looking at Banks, 'I took debris samples from a number of places, especially on boat one, Tom's boat, the main seat of the fire. I don't know how much you know about it,' he went on, 'but gas chromatography is a relatively simple and quick process. In this case, we put the debris in large cans, heated them and used a syringe to draw off the headspace, the gases given off, and we then injected that into the chromatograph. This –' he pointed to the left graph – 'is the chromatogram we got from the point of origin.' He then pointed to the graph beside it, which, to Banks, looked almost identical. Both showed a series of low to medium peaks with one enormous spike in the middle. 'And this is the chromatographic representation of turpentine.'

'So we were right,' Banks said, studying the chromatograms. 'What about the other boat?'

'Apart from the streamers I noted on my initial examination,' Hamilton said, 'there are no other signs of accelerant. Anyway, that's the physical evidence so far. Turpentine is your primary accelerant. Its ignition temperature is four hundred and eighty-eight degrees Fahrenheit, which is quite low. As we found no evidence of timing or incendiary devices, I'd say someone used a match.'

'Deliberate, then?'

Hamilton looked around, as if worried that the room was bugged, then he let slip a rare smile. 'Just between you and me and these four walls,' he said, 'not a shred of doubt.'

The coffee arrived and both remained silent until the PC who delivered it had left the office. Hamilton took a sip and lifted up the videotape. 'Want to watch a movie?' he asked.

Videotaped evidence and interviews were so common these days that Banks had a small TV/video combination in his office. Hamilton slipped the tape in and they both got a driver's seat view as the fire engine raced to the scene.

Most engines, or 'appliances' as the firefighters called them, were fitted with a 'silent witness', a video recorder that taped the journey to the source of the call. It could come in useful if you happened to be really quick off the mark and spotted a getaway vehicle, or arrived at the scene and got a picture of the arsonist hanging about enjoying his handiwork. This time there was nothing. The fire engine passed a couple of cars going the other way, and it would probably be possible to isolate the images and enhance the number plates. But Banks didn't hold out much hope they would lead anywhere. The fire was well under way by the time Hurst called it in and the arsonist would be well away too. It was an exhilarating journey, though, and Hamilton ejected the tape when the appliance came to a halt at the bend in the lane.

'There's one thing that bothers me,' Banks said. 'The boy, Mark, described the artist's hair as brown, but what little of it we saw on the boat was more like red.'

'Fire does that,' said Hamilton.

'Changes hair colour?'

'Yes. Sometimes. Grey turns blond and brown turns red.'

'Interesting,' said Banks. 'What about Tina? Could she have survived?'

'If she'd been awake and aware, yes, but the state she was in . . . not a chance.'

'The way it looks, then,' said Banks, 'is that the artist on boat one was the primary victim, yet some small effort had been made to see that the fire spread to boat two, where Mark and Tina lived. But why Mark and Tina?'

'I'm afraid that's your job to find out, not mine.'

'Just tossing ideas around. Elimination of a witness?'

'Witness to what?'

'If the arsonist was someone who'd visited the victim before, then he might have been seen, or worried he'd been seen.'

'But the young man survived.'

'Yes, and Mark *did* see two people visit Tom on different occasions. Maybe one of them was the killer and he had no idea that Mark was out at the time. He probably thought he was getting them both, but he was in a hurry to get away. Which means . . .'

'What?'

'Never mind,' said Banks. 'As you said, it's my job to work that out. At the moment I feel as if we've got nothing but assumptions.'

Hamilton tapped the graphs and stood up. 'Not true,' he said. 'You've got confirmation of accelerant usage in a multi-seated fire.'

Hamilton was right, Banks realized. Until a few minutes ago, all he'd had to go on were appearances and gut instincts, but now he had solid scientific evidence that the fire had been deliberately set.

He looked at his watch and sighed. 'Dr Glendenning's conducting the post-mortem on the male victim soon,' he said. 'Want to come?'

'What the hell,' said Hamilton. 'It's Friday evening. The weekend starts here.'

4

'**Do you know** that it takes about an hour or an hour and a half at between sixteen and eighteen hundred degrees Fahrenheit to cremate a human body?' Dr Glendenning asked, apropos of nothing in particular. 'And that the ordinary house – or in this case, boat – fire rarely exceeds twelve hundred? That, ladies and gentlemen, is why we have so much material left to work with.'

The post-mortem lab in the basement of Eastvale General Infirmary was hardly hi-tech, but Dr Glendenning's experience more than made up for that. To Banks, the blackened shape laid out on the stainless-steel table looked more like one of those Iron Age bodies preserved in peat bogs than someone who had been a living, breathing human being less than twenty-four hours ago. Already the remnants of clothing had been removed to be tested for traces of accelerant, blood samples had been sent for analysis, and the body had been X-rayed for any signs of gunshot wounds and internal injuries. None had been found, only a belt buckle, £3.65 in loose change and a signet ring without initials engraved on it.

'Thought you wouldn't know that,' Glendenning went on, casting an eye over his audience: Banks, Geoff Hamilton and Annie Cabbot, fresh from the scene. 'And I hope you appreciate my working on a Friday evening,' he went on as he examined the body's exterior with the help of his new assistant, Wendy Gauge, all kitted out in blue scrubs and a hairnet. Glendenning looked at his watch. 'This could take a long time, and you also probably don't know that I have an important dinner engagement.'

'We realize you're a very important man,' said Banks, 'and we're eternally grateful to you. Aren't we, Annie?' He nudged Annie gently.

'We are, indeed,' said Annie.

Glendenning scowled. 'Enough of your lip, laddie. Do we know who he is?'

Banks shook his head. 'All we know was in the report I sent you. His name's probably Tom and he was an artist.'

'It would help if I knew something about his medical history,' Dr Glendenning complained.

'Afraid we can't help you,' said Banks.

'I mean, if he was a drug addict or a drunk or on some sort of dodgy medication . . . Why do you always make my job so much more bloody difficult than it needs to be, Banks? Can you tell me that?'

'Search me.'

'One day I probably will,' Glendenning said. 'Inside and out.' He scowled, lit a cigarette, though it was strictly forbidden, and went back to work. Banks envied him the cigarette. He had always smoked at post-mortems. It helped to mask the smell of the bodies. And they always smelled. Even this one would smell when Dr Glendenning opened him up. He'd be like one of those fancy, expensive steaks: charred on the outside and pink in the middle, and if he'd got enough carbon monoxide in his system, his blood would look like cherryade.

'Anyway,' Glendenning went on, 'if he was an artist, he was probably a boozer. Usually are in my experience.'

Annie said nothing, though her father Ray was an artist and a boozer. She stood beside Banks, eyes fixed on the doctor, already looking a little pale. Banks knew she didn't like post-mortems – nobody really did except, arguably, the pathologist – but the more she attended, the sooner she'd get used to them.

'He's got burns over about seventy-five per cent of the body's surface area. The most severe burning, the greatest combination of third- and fourth-degree burning occurs in the upper-body area.'

'That would be the area closest to the point of origin,' said Geoff Hamilton, cool and glum-looking as ever.

Dr Glendenning nodded. 'Makes sense. Mostly what we've got is full-thickness burning on the front upper body. You can see where the surface looks black and charred. That's caused by boiling subcutaneous fat. The human body keeps on burning long after the fire's been put out. Sort of like a candle, burning in its own fat.'

Banks noticed Annie make an expression of distaste.

'Further down,' Glendenning continued, 'on the legs and feet, for example, you can see the skin is pink and mottled in places, covered with blisters. That indicates brief exposure and lower temperature.'

When Dr Glendenning got to the external examination of the victim's head, Banks noticed what looked like skull fractures. 'Found something, Doc?' he asked.

'Look, I've told you before not to call me Doc. It's lacking in respect.'

'But have you found evidence of blows to the head?'

Glendenning bent over and probed the wounds, examining them carefully. 'I don't think so,' he said.

'But that's what they look like to me,' Annie said.

'To you, lassie, maybe. But to *me* they look like fractures caused by the heat.'

'The heat causes fractures?' Annie said.

Dr Glendenning sighed. Banks could imagine the sort of teacher he'd be and how he'd terrify the poor medical students.

'Of course it does,' he said. 'Heat contracts the skin and causes splits that may easily be interpreted as cuts inflicted during life. It can also cause fractures in the long bones of the arms and legs, or make them so bloody brittle that they're fractured while the body is being moved. Remember, we're sixty-six per cent water and fire is a great dehydrator.'

'But what about the skull?' Annie asked.

Glendenning looked at her, a glint in his eye. 'The fractures are caused by pressure. The brain and the blood start to boil, and the steam needs an outlet, so it blows a hole in the skull. Pop. Just like a bottle of champagne.'

Annie shuddered. Even Banks felt a little queasy. Dr Glendenning went back to work, a mischievous grin on his face.

'Anyway,' he went on, 'skull fractures caused by fire often radiate along suture lines, the weakest point in the skull's surface, and that's the case here. Also, the skull splinters haven't been driven *into* the brain matter, which would most likely be the case if blunt-instrument trauma were present. They've been forced outwards.'

'So you're saying he *wasn't* hit over the head?'

'I'm saying nothing of the kind,' Glendenning said, 'I'm only saying it seems unlikely. That's typical of you, Banks, jumping to conclusions when you've got only part of the evidence, going off half-cocked. What about a bit of scientific method, laddie? Haven't you been reading your Sherlock Holmes lately?'

'I know that when you have eliminated the impossible,

whatever remains, however improbable, must be the truth. Or something like that.'

'Well, in this case,' said Glendenning, 'almost anything's still possible. Your report mentioned that the body was covered by debris and I've seen the crime-scene photos and sketches. The damage might have been caused by a section of the ceiling falling on the deceased after his death.'

'I suppose it could have happened that way,' said Banks.

'Definitely possible,' said Geoff Hamilton.

'I'm glad you both agree,' Glendenning said.

'On the other hand, though,' Banks argued, 'wouldn't you expect to find skull splinters in the brain if that were the case?'

Glendenning graced him with a rare smile. 'You're learning, laddie. Anyway, we don't even know whether the injury was post- or ante-mortem yet. That's my point.'

'Do you think you could find out?'

Glendenning rolled his eyes. 'Do I think I could find out?' he mimicked, then went back to the body. 'Well, why don't we start by looking for signs of smoke inhalation?' He held out his hand theatrically. 'Scalpel.'

Wendy Gauge suppressed a smile as she handed him the required instrument and the pathologist bent over the corpse. The nose had burned away, along with enough skin and flesh to allow the chin and jawbone to show through in places. Glendenning worked away at exposing the tracheal area and bronchial passage, parts of which Banks could see were black with soot or charring, then he bent over the body again. 'There's definitely some thermal injury to the mouth, nose and upper airways,' he said, 'but that's not unusual and it doesn't tell us much.' He poked around some more. 'There's soot present, but not a great deal. In fact, in this case, there's little enough to conclude that he was still breathing but shallowly.'

'Was he unconscious?' Banks asked.

'Very likely.'

'So that blow to the head might have been administered prior to the starting of the fire? It might have *caused* the unconsciousness?'

'Hold your horses.' Dr Glendenning bent over the body again. 'I've already told you – that blow was more likely caused by the fire or falling debris than by human force. Deposition of soot on the tongue, in the nares, the oropharynx and the nāropharynx, all of which we have here, cannot be held to imply life during the fire.'

'So he could have been already dead?'

Glendenning gave Banks a nasty look and went on. 'Traces of soot below the larynx would indicate that the victim was alive at the start of the fire.'

'And is there any?' Banks asked.

'A little. Right now, we need to dig deeper.' Glendenning gave the go-ahead and Wendy Gauge wielded her own scalpel and made the customary Y-shaped incision. The blackened skin, which had been dried by the fire and then wetted by the firefighters' hoses, peeled back like burned paper. And there it was, the sickly smell of death. Cooked or raw, it amounted to the same thing. 'Hmm,' said Glendenning. 'You can see how deep the burning goes in some places. It's never uniform, for a number of reasons, including the fact that your skin's thicker in some places than in others.'

'Needs to be around you,' said Banks.

Glendenning pointedly ignored him. 'There's some exaggerated redness of the blood,' he said, 'which indicates the presence of carbon monoxide. We'll know the exact amounts when that incompetent pillock Billings brings the results back from the lab.'

Banks remembered the day he found his old chief constable, Jimmy Riddle, dead in his garage from carbon monoxide poisoning. Suicide. His face had been cherry red. 'How much carbon monoxide does it take to cause death?' he asked.

'Anything over forty per cent is likely to cause impaired judgement, unconsciousness and death, but it depends on the person's state of health. The generally accepted fatal level is fifty per cent. All right Wendy, you can go on now.'

'Yes, Doctor.' Wendy Gauge pulled up the chest flap and took a bone-cutter to the ribcage, which she cracked open to expose the inner organs.

At that moment, the door opened and Billings appeared from the lab. The scene of carnage being played out on the stainless-steel post-mortem table didn't faze him, but he was clearly terrified of Dr Glendenning and developed a stutter whenever he had to deal with him. 'H-here it is, Doctor,' he said. 'The c-carbon monoxide results.'

Glendenning glared at him and studied the report. 'Do you want the short answer or the long one?' he said to Banks, after dismissing Billings with an abrupt jerk of his head.

'The short one will do for now.'

'He has a CO level of twenty-eight per cent,' Glendenning said. 'That's enough to cause dizziness, a nasty headache, nausea and fatigue.'

'But not death?'

'Not unless he had some serious respiratory or heart disease. Which we'd know about if we had his medical history. In general terms, though, no, it's not enough to cause death. And given the levels of soot and particulate matter in the airways, I'd say he was alive but most likely unconscious when the fire started, in which case the cause is probably asphyxia caused by smoke inhalation. And don't forget there are plenty of other nasty gases released during fires, including ammonia and cyanide. A full analysis will take more time.'

'What about tox screening?'

'Don't try to tell me my job, laddie,' Dr Glendenning growled. 'It's being done.'

'And dental records?'

'We can certainly get impressions,' said Glendenning, 'but you can hardly check his chart against every bloody dentist in the country.'

'There's a chance he may have been local,' said Banks, 'so we'll start with the Eastvale area.'

'Aye, well, that's *your* job.' Glendenning glanced at the clock and turned back to the body. 'There's still a lot to be done here,' he said, 'and I'm afraid I can't promise you I'll get to the second victim tonight. I might even miss my dinner engagement as it is.'

Wendy Gauge removed the inner organs en bloc and placed them on the dissecting table.

'Well,' said Banks, looking at Hamilton and Annie, 'whether our victim was hit on the head, whether his brains blew out through his skull, or whether he had a bad heart and died of low-level carbon monoxide inhalation, we know from the evidence so far that *someone* set the fire, so we're looking at murder. The best thing we can do now is try to find out just who the hell he was.' Banks glanced again at the loathsome hulk on the table, the charred and leathery skin, the exposed intestines and dribbles of reddish-pink blood. 'And,' he added, 'let's hope we're not dealing with a serial arsonist. I wouldn't want to be attending any more of these post-mortems if I could help it.'

•

'Isn't this intimate?' said Maria Phillips, settling into her chair at a dimpled, copper-topped table in a quiet corner of the Queen's Arms. 'Go on, then, I'll be a devil and have a Campari and soda, please.'

Banks hadn't asked her if she wanted a drink yet, but that didn't seem to bother Maria as she set her faux-fur coat on the chair next to her, patted her bottle-blonde curls, then reached into her handbag for her compact and lipstick, with which she busied herself while Banks went to the bar. He had given her a ring at the community centre that afternoon and discovered she was working late, which suited him fine. He was glad to be in a friendly pub after the ordeal of the post-mortem and wanted nothing more than to be surrounded by ordinary, living people and to flush the taste of death by fire out of his system with a stiff drink or two.

'Evening, Cyril,' he said to the landlord. 'Pint of bitter and a large Laphroaig for me and a Campari and soda for the lady, please.'

Cyril raised his eyebrows.

'Don't ask,' Banks said.

'You know me. The soul of discretion.' Cyril started pumping the beer. 'Wouldn't have said she was your type, though.'

Banks gave him a look.

'Nasty fire down Molesby way.'

'Tell me about it,' said Banks.

'You involved already?'

'From the start. It's been a long day.'

Cyril looked at the scratch on Banks's cheek. 'You look as if you've been in the wars, too,' he said.

Banks put his hand up and touched the scratch. 'It's nothing. Just a disagreement with a sharp twig.'

'Pull the other one,' said Cyril.

'It's true,' said Banks.

'But you can't talk about the case, I know.'

'Nothing much to say, even if I could. We don't know anything yet except two people died. Cheers.' Banks paid and carried the drinks back to the table, where Maria sat expectantly, perfectly manicured hands resting on the table in front of her, scarlet nails as long as a cat's claws. She was an unfashionably buxom and curvaceous woman in her early thirties, and she would look far more attractive, Banks had always thought, if she got rid of all the warpaint and dressed for comfort rather than effect. And the perfume. Especially the perfume. It rolled over him in heavy, acrid waves and soured his beer. He took a sip of Laphroaig and felt it burn pleasantly all the way down. He didn't usually drink shorts in the Queen's Arms, but this evening was an exception justified by a particularly nasty post-mortem and Maria Phillips both within the space of a couple of hours.

Maria made it clear that she noticed the scratch on Banks's cheek, but that she wasn't going to ask about it, not yet. 'How's Sandra doing?' she asked instead. 'We do so miss her at the centre. Such energy and devotion.'

Banks shrugged. 'She's fine, far as I know.'

'And the baby? It must be very strange for her, becoming a mother all over again. And at her age.'

'We don't talk much these days,' said Banks. He did know, though, through his daughter Tracy, that Sandra had given birth to a healthy seven-pound girl on 3 December, not much more than a month ago, and that she had named her Sinéad, not after the bald pop singer, but after Sean's mother. Well, good luck to her. With a name like that, she'd need it. As far as he knew, via Tracy, both mother and daughter were doing fine. The whole business churned his guts and changed everything, especially the way he related to his past, their shared life together. In a strange way, it was almost as if none of their twenty-plus years together had happened, that it had all been a dream or some sort of previous existence. He didn't know this woman, this child. It even made him feel differently about Tracy and his son, Brian. He didn't know exactly why, how, or in what way, but it did. And how did they feel about their new half-sister?

'Of course not,' Maria said. 'How insensitive of me. It must be very painful for you. Someone you spent so many years with, the mother of your children, and now she's had a baby with another man.'

'About this artist, Tom,' Banks said.

Maria waved a finger at him. 'Clever, clever. Trying to change the subject. Well, I can't say I blame you.'

'This *is* the subject. At least it's the one I intended to talk about when I asked you for a drink.'

'And here's silly old me thinking you just wanted to talk.'

'I do. About Tom.'

'You know what I mean.'

'Have you ever encountered or heard of a local artist whose first name is Tom?'

Maria put her hand to the gold necklace around her throat. 'Is this what you're like when you interrogate suspects?' she said. 'You must terrify them.'

Banks managed a weak smile. He hadn't been lying when he told Cyril it had been a long day and it was getting longer. Every minute spent with Maria felt like an hour. 'It's not an interrogation, Maria,' he said, 'but I *am* tired, I don't want to play games and I really do need any information you might have.' He felt like adding that he had just seen the charred remains of a corpse, watched Dr Glendenning peel away the blackened flesh and pull out the shiny organs, but that would only make things worse. Patience. That was what he needed. And plenty of it. Problem was, where could he get it?

Maria pouted, or pretended to pout, for a moment, then said. 'Is that all you know about him? That his name was Tom?'

'So far, yes.'

'What did he look like?'

Banks paused, again recalling the ruined face, melted eyes, exposed jawbone and neck cartilage. 'We only have a vague description,' he said, 'but he was fairly short, thickset, with long greasy brown hair. And he didn't shave very often.'

Maria laughed. 'Sounds like every artist I've ever met. You'd think someone capable of creating a thing of beauty might take a little more pride in his appearance, wouldn't you?'

'Oh, I don't know,' said Banks. 'It must be nice to be able to wear what you want, not to have to put a suit on and worry about shaving every morning when you go to work.'

Maria looked at him, her blue eyes twinkling. 'I don't suppose you'd have to wear anything at all, would you, if it was really warm?'

'I suppose not,' said Banks, gulping more Laphroaig,

followed by a deep draught of beer. 'But does that description ring any bells?'

She gazed at him indulgently, as if he were a wayward schoolboy, then frowned. 'That *could* be Thomas McMahon,' she said. 'He's certainly the shortest artist I've ever met. I suppose Toulouse-Lautrec was shorter, but he was before my time.' She smiled.

Banks's ears pricked up. 'But he fits the description, this Thomas McMahon?'

'Sort of. I mean, he was short and squat, a bit toadish, really. He had a beard back then, but his hair wasn't really long. One thing I do remember, though . . .'

'What?'

'He had beautiful fingers.' She held out her own hand, as if to demonstrate. 'Long, tapered fingers. Very delicate. Not what you'd expect for such a small man.'

Wasn't that what Mark had said about Tom? That he had long fingers? It wasn't a lot to base an identification on, but it was the best they had so far. 'Tell me more,' Banks said.

Maria waved her empty glass. 'Well, I could be bribed,' she said.

Banks had finished his Laphroaig and he still had half a pint left, but he wasn't having any more as he had to drive home. He went to the bar and bought Maria another Campari and soda. The pub was filling up now and he had to wait a couple of minutes to get served. Someone put an old Oasis song on the jukebox. The Queen's Arms was certainly a lot different from the previous summer, Banks thought, when foot and mouth had emptied the Dales, keeping even the locals away, and Cyril hardly had a customer from one day to the next. And this was only January, most of the people here local. Maybe the coming summer would be a boom time for the Dales businesses. They certainly needed it. Back at the table he handed Maria her drink and said, 'Well?'

He was surprised when she opened her handbag and brought out a packet of Silk Cut and a slim gold lighter. He didn't remember her as a smoker. 'Do you mind?' she asked, lighting up.

It wouldn't have mattered if he did mind; the smoke was already drifting his way, along with the perfume. 'No,' he said, surprised to find that, instead of a craving, for the first time he felt revulsion. Was he going to turn into one of those obnoxious, rabid anti-smokers? He hoped to hell not. He sipped some beer. It helped a little.

'I can't tell you much about him,' Maria said. 'If indeed he is the one you think he is.'

'Let's assume that he is, for the sake of argument,' said Banks.

'I mean, I wouldn't want to be responsible for sending you off in the wrong direction, wasting police time.'

Banks smiled again. 'Don't worry about that. I won't arrest you for it. Just tell me what you know and leave the rest to us.'

'It must have been about five years ago,' Maria said. 'Sandra was still with us at the time. She used to talk to him quite a bit, you know. I'm sure she'd remember even better than me.'

Wonderful! Banks thought. Was he going to have to go and talk to his ex-wife to get information about a case? Maybe he'd send Annie. No, that would be cruel. Jim Hatchley, then? Or Winsome? But he knew, if it came to it, that he'd have to go himself. It would be rude and cowardly not to. No doubt he'd get to see the new baby, bounce little Sinéad on his knee. Maybe Sean would be there, too, and they'd ask him to stay for dinner. Happy families. Or he might end up babysitting while they went out to the cinema or the theatre for the evening. On the other hand, maybe it could be avoided altogether if he pressed Maria just a little harder. 'Let's start with what you remember,' he said.

'Well, as I said, it was a long time ago. McMahon was a local artist, lived on the eastern edge of town, as I recall. It was part of our job to encourage local artists – not financially, you understand, but by giving them a venue to exhibit their work.'

'So Thomas McMahon had an exhibition of his work at the community gallery?'

'Yes.'

'And there'd be records of this? A catalogue, perhaps? A photograph of him?'

'I suppose so. Down in the archives.'

'Was he any good?'

Maria wrinkled her nose. 'I won't pretend to be an expert on these matters, but I'd say not. There was nothing distinguished about his work, as far as I could see. It was mostly derivative.'

'So he'd have a hard time making a career of it?'

'I imagine he would. He sneaked a couple of ghastly abstracts in too, at the last moment. I have a feeling they were what he really wanted to paint, but you can't make a living from that sort of thing unless you have real talent. On the other hand, you can make a fair bit from selling local landscapes to tourists, which he did.'

'Any chance that his death might affect the value of his work?'

Maria's eyes widened. 'My, my, you do have a devious

mind, don't you? What a delicious motive. Kill the artist to increase the value of his paintings.'

'Well?'

'Not in his case, I shouldn't think. A bad watercolour of Eastvale Castle is a bad watercolour of Eastvale Castle, whether the painter is alive or dead. Perhaps a dealer might know more than I do, but I think you'll have to look elsewhere for your motive.'

'Was he a drinker?'

'He liked his drink, but I wouldn't say he was a drunk.'

'Drugs?'

'I wouldn't know. I saw no signs, heard no rumours.'

'And you've neither seen nor heard anything of him since?'

'Oh, yes. He's dropped by a couple of times, for other artists' openings, that sort of thing. And he was at the Turner reception, of course.'

'I see,' Banks said. The Turner. By far the most valuable and famous painting ever to be housed in the modest community-centre gallery, a Turner watercolour of Richmond Castle, Yorkshire, believed lost for many years, had spent two days there after being discovered under some old insulation during a cottage renovation. Nobody knew how it had got there, but the speculation was that the original owner died and whoever had the insulation put in didn't know the value of the small painting. There had been a private reception for local bigwigs and arty types. Annie had been involved in the security, Banks remembered. It had happened last summer, while Banks had been in Greece, and he had missed all the excitement.

'Other than that?'

'No. He dropped out of the local scene shortly after the exhibition, five years ago. I understand that his dealer had trouble selling his work and that McMahon went through some sort of personal crisis. I don't know the details. Leslie Whitaker might be able to help. I know they were friends and he tried to sell some of McMahon's serious paintings as well as the junk he painted for the tourist trade.'

'So Whitaker was McMahon's agent?'

'Sort of, I suppose.'

'Recently, too?'

'Yes. I've seen Thomas McMahon coming out of Leslie Whitaker's shop once or twice this month. He looked as if he'd been buying some books. He was carrying a package, at any rate.'

'Did you talk to him?'

'Only to say hello.'

'How did he seem?'

'Remarkably fit, actually. Though, as you mentioned earlier, his hair was a bit long and it could have done with a wash. He also hadn't shaved for a few days, by the look of him.'

'Do you think you could dig out a catalogue and give me the names of the artists whose openings he attended?'

'Why?'

'The catalogue might help identify any of his works that show up, and we'd like to talk to anyone who might have known him. A photograph would help, too.'

'I can try. I'd have to look at the centre's records, though.'

'Could you do it first thing?'

Maria eyed him for a moment and sipped some Campari and soda. Her glass was almost empty again. 'I suppose I could. You do realize it's Saturday tomorrow, though, don't you?'

'The centre's open.'

'Yes, but it's my day off.'

'I'll send one of my DCs along then,' said Banks. 'It might take him a bit longer, but . . .'

'I didn't say I *wouldn't* do it.'

'Then you will?'

'All right, yes. If you want.'

'And you'll ring me at the station, send anything you find down there?'

'Yes.' She held out her glass. 'You never know; I might even deliver it myself.'

'You want another drink?' Banks asked.

'Please.'

'All right. But I'm afraid you'll have to drink this one by yourself. I've got a long drive home.'

Maria looked disappointed. 'Oh, well, in that case I won't bother . . . But I thought . . .'

'What?'

'Well, I don't live that far away. Maybe you'd like to come for a nightcap, or just a coffee or something?' She wrinkled her nose. 'It might perk you up a bit.'

'Thanks for asking,' Banks said, hurriedly finishing his beer. 'But perking up's the last thing I need right now. I really do have to get some sleep.'

'Never mind, then. Some other time.' Maria gathered her things together and stood up to put on her coat. 'I'll ring you in the morning,' she said and made a hasty exit.

Oh, shit, thought Banks, embarrassed by the looks he was getting from others in the pub. Surely he had never given Maria Phillips any reason to think he wanted more from her than information about the artist? He had only seen her two or three times since Sandra had left, and on those occasions they had simply bumped into one another on the street, or he had visited the community centre for one reason or another and had seen her there. They had done nothing but exchange small talk. Still, she had always been a strange one, he remembered, always superficially flirtatious, even when he was married to Sandra. He had thought it was just her way of relating and had never taken her seriously. And maybe that's all it was, even now. He picked up his overcoat and briefcase. At least she was going to ring him with the information he wanted in the morning, information that might take him a bit closer to the mystery that was Tom.

•

Annie drove her aching bones home after the post-mortem, on Banks's advice. There was nothing more to be done tonight, he had told her, so best get some rest. That was exactly what she intended to do, she thought, as she locked the door of her small Harkside cottage behind her, the cottage that seemed to be at the centre of a labyrinth of narrow, winding streets, as Banks had once pointed out. She would have a glass of Chilean cabernet and a long hot bath, then take a couple of night-time cold-relief capsules and hope for a peaceful night's sleep. Maybe she'd feel better in the morning.

There was one message waiting for her on her answering machine, and she was absurdly pleased to hear that it was from Phil. He would definitely be coming up to Swainsdale tomorrow and would be staying a few days at his cottage in Fortford. Would Annie care to have dinner with him one evening over the weekend, perhaps, or even early next week, if she wasn't too busy?

Well, she would, but she didn't know if she could commit herself right now, what with a big new case on the go and this damn cold dragging on. Still, being a DI gave her some perks, even if it did mean no overtime, and her evenings should be free, barring the necessity to head out somewhere overnight. If she felt well enough, there was no reason why she shouldn't tentatively agree to dinner tomorrow.

Annie dropped her keys on the table, poured herself a glass of wine and picked up the telephone.

•

When Banks arrived home after his drink with Maria Phillips, he also found one message waiting for him. It was from Michelle Hart, whom he realized he had forgotten to call. She just wanted to tell him that she wouldn't be able to see him this weekend as they were all working overtime on a missing child case. Banks could well understand that. Missing children were the worst, every policeman's nightmare. It was while Michelle was looking into the disappearance of Banks's childhood friend, Graham Marshall, whose bones had been discovered the previous summer over thirty-five years since he had disappeared, that they had met.

Even though he couldn't get away either, he still felt disappointed. This sort of thing was happening more and more often lately, so much so that they felt and acted like strangers for the first few hours every time they did meet. It was no way to sustain a relationship. First the distance, the long, winter drives in fog, rain or hail; then the job, the unpredictable hours. Sometimes he wondered if it was possible for a copper to have anything but the most superficial and undemanding of relationships.

He had also wondered more than once over the past few months where things were going with Michelle. They met up when they could, usually managed to have a good time, and the sex was great. But she always seemed to hold a part of herself back. Most people did, Banks realized, including himself, but with Michelle it was different, as if she were carrying around some great weight she couldn't, or wouldn't, share and in a way it made their relationship feel superficial.

With Annie, Banks had developed a deeper relationship. That was the problem, what had made Annie run: the intimacy, and Banks's residual feelings for Sandra. And the kids, of course. The idea of Banks's two children seemed to scare Annie to death. Michelle never talked about children. Banks wondered if she had been deeply wounded by her past in some way. Annie had been raped and they had talked about that, got it out in the open, but with Michelle . . . she just wouldn't open up.

Banks sorted through his post, pleased to see that his copies of *Gramophone* and *Mojo* had both arrived, and poured a wee dram of ten-year-old cask-strength Laphroaig, which DS Hatchley had bought him at a duty-free shop. Talk about a drink with teeth; it bit deep into your tongue, throat and gut and didn't let go. The aroma alone was enough to make you feel pissed.

Banks thought about Michelle again. Was he attracted only to wounded women? he wondered. Did he see himself as some sort of healer, a Travis McGee figure, remembering the books he'd read with prurient interest as an adolescent, along with James Bond, the Saint, Sexton Blake and Modesty Blaise? *Just a few days on the* Busted Flush *with old Travis and you'll be right as rain.* Well, if he did see himself that way, he wasn't making a very good job of it, was he? And you didn't get to his age, or Michelle's, without taking a hefty emotional, even physical, knock or two along the way. Especially if you happened to be a copper. Banks laughed at himself, tilted his head back and tipped his glass.

He phoned back, but Michelle was out, so he left a message of regret on her answering machine. Maybe next weekend, he said, though he doubted either of their cases would have wound down by then.

At least he had had one bit of good news when he called back at the station after his little chat with Maria Phillips: their body was *definitely* Thomas McMahon. There was only one dentist in the village of Molesby, the nearest settlement to the narrowboats, and DC Templeton had had the good sense to check there first with the dental impression. Thomas McMahon had been there for a filling less than a week before.

Sometimes it was that easy.

It was cold in the cottage and Banks considered lighting a peat fire. Then he decided it wasn't worth it; he was sure he wouldn't be able to stay awake long enough to enjoy it. Besides, after today, there was something about the idea of even the most innocent domestic fire that frightened him. He checked the smoke detectors to see if they were both still working. They were. Then he turned on two bars of the electric fire and poured himself another drink.

He thought of watching a movie on DVD. He had recently bought a player and it had revitalized his interest in movies. He was starting to collect them the way he did CDs. In the end he decided that it was too late; he knew he would fall asleep on the sofa halfway through. Instead he put on Cassandra Wilson's *Belly of the Sun* CD and browsed through the *Gramophone* reviews. God what a deep, rich sensuous voice Cassandra had, he thought, like melting chocolate as she worked each syllable for all she could get, stretched them out until you thought they'd break, dropped on them from high or crept up underneath them and licked and chewed them out of shape.

The whisky tasted good, sharp, peaty and a little bit medicinal, and he wished he could go outside and stand by Gratly Falls and look down the daleside to the lights of Helmthorpe the way he did when the weather was good, but it was too cold. Oh, certainly it was mild enough for January, but after dark a chill came to the air that defied even the properties of a fine single malt whisky to warm the cockles of your heart. A wind had sprung up, too, and he felt as if he were marooned in his little cottage, straining against its ropes to stay on the ground.

As he put the magazine aside and settled back with his feet up, only a dim table light on, Cassandra singing Dylan's 'Shelter from the Storm', his mind drifted over the day's events as it often did at times like this. He wasn't so much thinking as just riffing, improvising on a theme, the way a jazz player did or the way Elgar had written his *Enigma* variations.

Enigma was a good place to start. Everything about today's events seemed infused by that very quality. Elusive, inchoate, equivocal. On the one hand, it appeared as if Thomas McMahon was the intended victim, but there were no signs of external injury other than the fire damage and they knew nothing about any possible motive. On the other hand, Mark Siddons had had a row with his drug-addict girlfriend Tina and stormed off, but his alibi held tight and the physical evidence exonerated him.

Tina, or Mark, had also bought drugs from Danny Boy Corcoran, and wherever drugs are concerned you have to look closely at everyone involved. Then there was Tina's stepfather, Dr Patrick Aspern. Banks hadn't particularly liked him, but that didn't mean much in itself. He had disliked innocent people before. But if what Mark said about Aspern and his stepdaughter were true, that was enough to give the doctor a strong motive. And both Aspern and his wife had been evasive, to say the least, when it came to alibis. On the other hand, perhaps something in Mark's own background had made him only too eager to believe Tina's story without question. That background might well be worth looking into, he thought, making a mental note to put DS Hatchley on it in the morning.

Andrew Hurst was another problem. Hurst haunted the canal side, he had lied about his activities, he had washed his clothes and he had no alibi. But what motive did he have? Perhaps he didn't need one. He had first approached the scene, then he had rung the fire brigade. Maybe he was an arsonist who just liked to start fires, a pyromaniac. From what Banks knew of the basic psychology of pyromaniacs, many of them liked not only to report, hang around and watch their own handiwork, but they liked to take part in the firefighting operation, too, and help the police. Banks would see just how helpful Andrew Hurst wanted to be.

Banks thought about a third Laphroaig as the CD came to an end, but decided against it. Instead he took himself off to bed.

5

Danny Boy Corcoran lived in a small flat off South Market Street, on the fringes of the student area. He had once been a business student at Eastvale College, but he had discovered a more lucrative career in selling drugs and dropped out before finishing his diploma. His flat had been under surveillance all night, and Danny and his girl-friend hadn't arrived home until eight in the morning, so Banks and Annie had the advantage. Banks felt surprisingly well rested after his early night, and even Annie looked and sounded more cheerful than she had in days. The cold still lingered, Banks could tell, by her red nose and the occasional sneeze, but it was on the wane.

Danny Boy, on the other hand, looked like crap. He had clearly just gone to bed and was wearing only a red sweat-shirt with a Montego Bay logo and Y-fronts, his scrawny hairy legs sticking out below. Danny was a wannabe bad boy Jamaican drug dealer, but unfortunately for him, in reality, he had been born to white middle-class parents in Blandford Forum. His dreadlocked hair stuck out in all directions, and his bloodless face seemed paler than a vampire's in a time of famine. 'Can we come in, Danny?' Banks asked, as they showed their warrant cards.

'Why? Whaddya want?'

'I'll tell you if you let us come in.'

Danny's lanky frame still blocked the doorway. 'Gorra-warrant?'

'We don't need one. We just want to talk.'

A figure appeared behind Danny, framed by his outstretched arm and the doorpost, similarly thin, and pale enough to make her flesh-toned bra and panties look like a suntan. Banks could see she had goose bumps on her arms. And needle marks. 'Danny, who is it? Tell them to go away and come back to bed.'

'Fuck off, Nadia,' Danny said, without turning round. 'It's business.'

Nadia made a face at his back, turned and shambled away.

'Look, I don't know what you've come here disturbing my rest for,' he said. 'I've not done anything wrong.'

'Spare us the poor, wronged-youth act, Danny. You spent last night peddling your wares in the pubs on York Road and South Market Street, then you ended up at a party on the East Side Estate.'

Danny first looked puzzled, then affronted. 'You've been *watching* me?'

'Someone else has. I wouldn't waste my time. Listen, Danny, how about if I tell you we're not drugs squad and this isn't about drugs? Not really. We don't *have* to search the flat, but we can if you like.'

'Look, you told me . . .'

'I told you what, Danny?'

'Never mind.'

'I've never spoken to you before in my life,' Banks said, gently easing Danny's arm out of the way and walking into the flat. The living room was a mess, with clothes and CD cases strewn around the place, but at least it was clean and didn't smell of smoke, or worse. There was a big poster of Bob Marley smoking a spliff on one wall, probably the closest Danny Boy had ever got to Jamaica, and a few sad-looking potted plants on the window sill, none of them marijuana.

'Just a few questions, Danny, that's all.'

'I've always cooperated with you in the past, haven't I?'

'Like I said, I've never clapped eyes on you before in my life, but I'm sure your conduct has been exemplary,' Banks said. 'Let's keep it that way. Perhaps you might answer one or two little questions. Mind if we sit down?'

Danny looked suspicious, as well he might, and nodded towards two winged armchairs. He scratched his head. 'You're not going to trick me, you know,' he said. 'I wasn't born yesterday.'

'No,' said Annie, making herself comfortable. 'You were born on the ninth of August, nineteen-eighty-two. We know that. We know plenty about you, Danny.'

Danny was still standing, hopping from foot to foot. 'Look,' he said, 'it's cold. Can I put the fire on and get dressed?'

'Course you can,' said Banks. 'It *is* a bit nippy in here.'

Danny turned on the gas fire and headed to the bedroom to get dressed. Banks followed him. 'What you doing?' Danny asked.

'Just routine,' said Banks. 'We've sort of developed a habit of not letting suspects out of our sight.'

'*Suspect*? You said this wasn't about drugs.'

'Get dressed, Danny.'

Nadia lay in bed in the half-dark with the sheets and blanket pulled right up to her chin. 'What's going on, Danny?' she asked in a whiny voice. 'Come back to bed. Please.'

'Go to sleep, Nadia. This won't take long.' Danny pulled on a pair of jeans.

'What were you wearing on Thursday night?' Banks asked.

'Thursday? Dunno. Why?'

'I'd like to see.'

'Whatever it was, it'll likely still be in the laundry basket over there. Nadia takes care of all that shit.' He glared over at Nadia. 'When she can be bothered.'

'Oh, Danny . . .'

The laundry basket was only half full. 'Got a plastic bag, Danny?' Banks asked. 'A bit bigger than the ones you use for the stuff you sell.'

'Very funny.' Danny reached into the wardrobe and found a bin liner. 'This do?'

'Nicely.' Banks filled it with the clothes from the laundry basket, then followed Danny back into the living room, which was warming up a treat now.

When they had all sat down, Banks asked, 'Did you hear about the boat fire just south of town?'

'I might have heard something in the pub last night. Why?'

'Two people died in that fire,' said Annie.

'That's a tragedy, but it's nothing to do with me.'

'You think not?' Annie took a folder from her briefcase and opened it on her knees. 'We have a statement here from a young lad called Mark Siddons to the effect that you supplied him with heroin for his girlfriend, Tina Aspern. What do you have to say about that, Danny?'

Danny looked mystified. 'Look, you *know* I do people little favours like that once in a while. Like I do for you. You know I'm not some big-time drug dealer. I don't understand this. What's going on? You say you're not drugs squad. You said this wasn't about drugs.'

'It isn't, Danny,' Banks explained. 'Not exactly. I think

I know what you've been trying to say. You're not sure about us, about DI Cabbot and me, so you're being very shy about it, but you've got a nice little deal going with the drugs squad, haven't you? In exchange for information about the big guys from time to time, they leave you alone. You've got protection. You're immune. It's a dangerous game, Danny. Those big guys always seem to find out where the leak is in the end and they're not forgiving types. But that's your business. I'm sure you know the risks already. Thing is, you're not immune from me and DI Cabbot here. We've got nothing to do with the drugs squad. We're Major Crimes. What we're concerned about is the fire. It's murder we're investigating, Danny. That's why we want your clothes. Arson, not drugs. Unless there's a connection?'

'That fire was nothing to do with me. I wasn't even near the place. Nadia and me was down in Leeds till yesterday evening.'

'Picking up more smack to sell this weekend?'

Danny scratched one of his underarms. 'Seeing some friends.'

'Getting the itch, are you?' Banks asked.

'You don't think I use that shit myself, do you?'

'Look,' Annie said, 'did you supply Mark Siddons with heroin for his girlfriend, Tina Aspern?'

'I don't know who it was, do I? Wait a minute.' He looked from one to the other. 'There was nothing wrong with that shit. Nobody overdosed on that stuff. It was well cut.'

'So you did?'

'Where's this going?'

Annie looked at Banks and raised her eyebrows. Banks took over. 'It's serious, Danny,' he said. 'You see, Tina Aspern was one of the people who died in that boat fire.'

'I didn't know that. I mean I hardly even knew her. Poor kid.'

'But if you supplied the heroin, Danny . . . You see, if she hadn't been under the influence, she might have survived.'

'You're not sticking me with that. No way.' He folded his arms.

'It's a matter of culpability, Danny,' said Banks, stretching the truth and the law quite a bit. 'See, if you sold her that stuff and it resulted in her death, even indirectly, then you're responsible. You don't think we'd bring you in just for selling a bag here and there, do you? This is serious business, Danny. Serious jail time.'

'That's a load of bollocks and you know it,' said Danny. 'You must think I'm stupid or something. I didn't make her shoot the stuff. I didn't even sell it to her. It was him who bought it from me, the boyfriend. He probably stuck the needle in her too. How does that make me guilty of anything?'

'It's the law.'

'Yeah, well, we'll wait to hear what my brief has to say about that, won't we?' He picked up a mobile phone from the coffee table. Before he could dial a number Banks slapped it out of his hand and it bounced on the hardwood floor into the corner by the stereo.

'Hey, if you've broken that—' Danny started to rise from his chair, but Banks leaned forward, put his hand on the boy's chest and pushed him back. 'I haven't finished yet.'

'Now, you wait—'

'No. *You* wait a minute, Danny. Hear me out. What happened? Did Mark and Tina rip you off, or did you figure they had more money stashed away on the boat and you'd go over there and help yourself while they were on the nod? You weren't to know Mark wasn't a user.'

'I never—'

'Did you go down there last night while Tina was stoned and steal the money? Did the man from the next boat see you? Did you get into a scuffle and knock him out? What made you think of the fire, Danny? Was it the bottle of turpentine just sitting there, so inviting? It was very clever of you, by the way, leading us to think the other bloke was the victim. Very clever.'

Danny just sat there shaking his head, jaw open.

'Or maybe it was one of the big guys who found out about your deal with the drugs squad? Was that it? A warning to you, Danny? "You'll be next"?'

Banks knew he was winging it, just throwing out the line and hoping for a bite, and the further he went the more he could see that he wasn't going to get one. Danny Boy Corcoran hadn't been near the boats; he hadn't killed Tina Aspern or Thomas McMahon. All he'd done was what he usually did, sell a few quids' worth of low-grade smack to weekend thrill seekers and, in this case, the boyfriend of a more serious addict. But there was still a chance that he might know *something*.

'What kind of car do you drive?' Banks asked.

'Red Mondeo. Why?'

'Ever heard of an artist called Thomas McMahon? He lived on the next boat.'

'I've never been down there. I don't like water.'

'You didn't sell McMahon heroin, too?'

'No way.'

'How did Mark and Tina find you in the first place?'

'It's not difficult, if you want what they wanted. Word

of mouth usually works just fine. Anyway, as it happens, there's this mate in Leeds, said they're all right.'

That was what Mark had told him, Banks remembered. 'What's his name?'

'Come off it!'

'His name,' Annie said. 'If you don't tell us, Mark Siddons will. His girlfriend's been killed, remember?'

Danny looked from Annie to Banks, then down at the floor. 'Benjamin Scott,' he whispered. 'And don't tell him I told you. He can be a nasty piece of work, can Benjy.' Danny clutched his stomach. 'My guts hurt. Are you nearly finished?'

'Address?' Annie asked.

Danny gave her an address in Gipton. Banks would phone DI Ken Blackstone at Millgarth in Leeds and ask him to check out Mr Benjamin Scott.

'One more thing, Danny,' Banks said as they stood up to leave.

'What?'

'As of now, you're out of business.'

'What do you mean?'

'You heard.'

'You can't—'

'I can do what I want, Danny. And I will. Let me put it simply: I don't like drug dealers. You'll be watched. Not by me, and not by the drugs squad, but by people I trust. And if anyone sees you dealing smack again you'll be pulled in before your feet can touch the ground. Got it?'

'I don't—'

'And if that doesn't work, pretty soon Benjy and his friends will find out you've been two-timing them with the drugs squad. Is *that* clear enough?'

Danny paled.

'Is it?' Banks pressed.

Danny swallowed and nodded.

At that moment Nadia walked in again and stood over Danny, rubbing her pale, thin arms. 'Danny,' she said, 'please hurry up. I need something. I need it bad.'

Danny rolled his eyes. 'Oh, for fuck's sake.'

Banks and Annie left with their bag of laundry.

•

Mark signed for his belongings: money, penknife, keys and the portable CD player he'd had stuck in his pocket with an old David Bowie CD in it, the only CD he had left now. He liked Bowie; the man never stood still long enough for anyone to pigeonhole him; he was always changing, moving on. Ziggy Stardust. The Thin White Duke. Maybe Mark would be like that now. When Tina was around there was someone worth working for, worth settling down with. But now . . . what was the point in going on without her?

'What about my clothes?' he asked.

'Not back from the lab yet,' said the custody officer.

'But they've done the tests. They've proved I didn't set the fire. It's cold out there. I'll need my jacket.'

'It's the weekend. These things take time. Try coming back next week. In the meantime . . .' With obvious disapproval, the officer brought out a carrier bag from under the desk and handed it over to Mark. 'DCI Banks said to give you this.' He gestured with his thumb. 'You can change in there.'

Mark went into the room they used for fingerprinting and photographing suspects and took off his red overalls. Banks's jeans fitted him OK around the waist, but they were a bit long, so he rolled up the bottoms. The sleeves of the old three-quarter-length suede overcoat with the worn fleece lining were also too long, and it was hardly top of the line as far as youth fashion was concerned. Still, it looked warm enough, and it was decent of the copper to remember his promise, Mark thought.

This was all he had now, what he was wearing, borrowed as it was, and what had been in his pockets. He didn't even have any cigarettes left, and given how expensive they were, he probably shouldn't go spending what little money he had left on them. So this was it, then. Oh, there was stuff back at home, of course, if Crazy Nick hadn't destroyed it all. Old clothes, toys, some CDs. But he'd never be going back there. Certainly not now his mum had died of lung cancer, as his Auntie Grace had told him, and there was only Crazy Nick left.

At last he walked through the front doors of the police station to freedom, though it was a freedom blighted by loss and uncertainty. To be honest, Mark wouldn't have complained if they'd locked him up for a bit longer. He'd been warm and well fed in the nick and no one had mistreated him. Outside, in the grey Tina-less world, who knew what lay ahead?

A couple of passers-by edged around him and looked down their noses, as if they knew exactly where he'd just come from. Well, sod them, he thought, taking a deep breath of cool air. Sod them all.

The copper, Banks, had just come out of the Golden Grill and was walking across Market Street towards him. 'Mark,' he said. 'How do they fit?'

'All right,' said Mark. 'They'll do for now. I mean, thanks.'

'You're welcome. Just a quick word.'

'What?'

'It might be nothing,' Banks said, 'but I've been thinking about the fire, the way it was spread to your boat.'

'And?'

'Well, I don't want to alarm you, but it might have been a sort of shot across the bows, so to speak, a warning shot.'

'What do you mean?'

'Maybe whoever did it didn't know whether you could identify him or not. Maybe he didn't even know Tina was there, but he was just sending you a message.'

'What message?'

'Not to say anything, or else.'

'But I don't know anything.'

'Are you sure, Mark? Are you certain you didn't get a better look at Tom's visitors?'

'No. I told you the truth.'

'All right,' said Banks. 'I believe you. Like I said, I don't want to alarm you, but if he thinks you know who he is, you could be in danger. Go carefully. Keep your eyes open.'

'I can take care of myself,' said Mark.

'Good,' said Banks. 'I'm glad to hear it. Just watch your back, that's all.' He gave Mark a card. 'And here's my number if you think of anything. Mobile, too.'

Mark took the card and Banks disappeared inside the police station.

It was market day and the canvas-covered stalls were all set up in the cobbled square, chock-a-block with cheap clothes, car accessories, washing-up liquid, batteries, the cheese van, the butcher, the greengrocer, crockery, cutlery, toys, used books and videos. The older, cloth-capped, waxed-jacketed punters milled around with the younger leather and denim crowd, fingering the goods while

barkers shouted out the virtues of their unbreakable table-
ware or infallible electric bottle openers.

There was nothing Mark wanted at the market, so he set
off down the street, hands thrust deep in his pockets, head
down, thinking about what Banks had just told him. He'd
never realized that *he* might be in danger. Now, though, he
looked at everyone with a keener eye, though he didn't
really know who he was looking for. Still, if what Banks
said was right, and if the killer did believe that Mark might
have seen him, then he'd better watch himself.

Mark felt something in one of the pockets of Banks's
suede overcoat. He pulled it out. A packet of Silk Cut, with
two left, and a disposable lighter. What a piece of luck.
Mark lit up. At least he had a fag, old and dry as it tasted.

He went through the other pockets to see if Banks had
left any money, but all he found were a couple of old
parking stubs and a note with 'Schoenberg – Gurrelieder
– del Mar/Sinopoli' written on it, which meant bugger all
to him. Mark had always admitted he wasn't much when
it came to the brains department. He was a hard worker,
good with his hands, and he'd tackle anything within
reason, but when it came to brains and spelling, leave
him out of it. The copper must be a brainy fellow if he'd
written that, Mark thought. It didn't even look like English. Maybe it was somewhere he went on his holidays.
Mark had never been abroad, but he'd probably do that
one day, too, he thought. Somewhere really weird like
Mongolia. Ulan Bator. He'd seen it on a map in the squat
and liked the sound of it. *Ulan Bator*. See, he wasn't so
stupid after all.

He put the headphones over his ears and turned on
the CD player as he made his way among the Saturday-
morning shoppers on South Market Street. Bowie came on

singing 'Five Years', one of Mark's favourites. It was nice to have real music again, better than that fucking drunk singing 'Your Cheatin' Heart'. Even so, he felt numb and aimless, as if the music was coming down a long tube from far away. Everything had seemed like that since he knew Tina was dead. He was going through the motions, but really he wasn't going anywhere.

After walking for about half an hour, Mark arrived at the construction site. The outside of the new gym complex was mostly completed, but there was a lot to be done inside – laying the floors, plasterboarding, fixtures and fittings, plumbing, electrics, painting – and it could all be done in winter, even if the weather was bad. The door was open and Mark went in. Things weren't going full tilt because it was a Saturday, but a lot of blokes worked weekends, Saturdays at any rate, to get their jobs done by the deadline.

Inside, the place had the smell of newness about it. Not paint because that hadn't been applied yet, but just a melange of various things, from new-cut wood to the slightly damp cardboard boxes that things came in, to the sawdust that scattered the floors. Mark used to like the smell, the way he liked the smell of cut stone, but he couldn't say why, only that it sparked something instinctive in him, something beyond words, beyond brains. There was a music to all the activity, too, a unity. Not David Bowie's music, but hammers, drills and electric saws. To some it was noise, but to Mark it used to have pattern and meaning, the pattern and meaning of something being made. A symphony. It made him feel the same way as the music of the sea, which formed the background to some of his only happy childhood memories. He thought he must have been there when he was very young with his mother, before the drinking, before Crazy Nick. He thought it was Scarborough, had a vague memory of the castle on the hill, the waves crashing over the promenade. But he couldn't remember for certain. None of it mattered now, anyway.

Lenny Knox was a subcontractor, a big, burly Liverpudlian with a face like red sandpaper, who usually worked every day God sent until the job was done. Sure enough, he was having a smoke by what was to be the showers and locker rooms when Mark came over. Vinnie Daly, one of his other workmates, put down his spanner when he saw Mark.

'Where you been, mate?' Lenny asked. 'We was worried sick when we heard about the fire, weren't we, Vinnie? They wouldn't say on the news who got hurt, like. You all right?'

'I'm all right,' said Mark. 'Police took me in, didn't they? Kept me overnight.'

'The bastards.'

'It wasn't so bad.'

'What about your young lass?'

Mark looked down at the unfinished floor. 'She's dead, Lenny.'

'Oh, no,' said Lenny, touching Mark on the shoulder. 'Poor wee devil. I'm sorry, son, really I am. She were a nice lass.'

Mark looked at him, holding back the tears. 'I wasn't there, Lenny. I wasn't there for her.'

'It's not your fault, what happened. Look, if you need somewhere to kip, you know, for a couple of days, like, I'm sure my Sal won't mind.'

'You sure, Lenny? 'Cos I've got nowhere else to go right now.'

'Yeah, it's OK. Look, you don't want to be here today. Take yourself off, if you like, and come round to ours later.'

'No. I want to work. What else would I do? Where would I go? Besides, it'll take my mind off things for a while at least. And I need the money.' The last was certainly true, but whether work would take his mind off his problems Mark didn't know. How could anything stop him from thinking about Tina?

Lenny looked down at him. 'Of course,' he said. 'Of course. Right. Look, why don't you pick up those shower heads over there and come with me?'

•

Late Saturday morning, after warning Mark Siddons and setting a slowly recovering DS Hatchley the task of digging into the boy's background, Banks headed for Adel again. Maria Phillips, true to her word, had left him the catalogue and the names of three local artists whose openings Thomas McMahon had attended in Eastvale over the past five years. Unfortunately, there was no photograph of McMahon in the catalogue. Apparently, people were not particularly interested in what artists looked like unless they painted self-portraits.

Banks wanted another crack at Patrick Aspern, without his wife present this time if possible, and with the gloves off.

As Banks drove, he listened to Bob Dylan singing about being in Mississippi for a day too long and thought he knew the feeling. Not so much being in Yorkshire too long – he was still happy there – but staying with something or someone until long after you should have left, let go, when it all falls to pieces and the real damage gets done.

He pulled up outside the Tudor-style house, and this

time Patrick Aspern himself answered the door, casually dressed in grey trousers, white shirt and a mauve V-neck sweater. He looked as if he were dressed for a round of golf, and he probably was. Banks suspected there would be no surgery at weekends.

'My wife's lying down,' said Dr Aspern, clearly surprised to see Banks back so soon. 'This has all been a great shock to her, you know, especially seeing Christine, the state the body was in. If only she'd listened to me, at least she might have been spared that.'

'A shock to you, too, I should imagine,' said Banks. 'I mean Christine's death.'

'Yes, of course. But we men realize we have to get on with our jobs, don't we? Can't afford to dwell on our emotions the way women do. Anyway, I can't imagine how I can help you, but do come in.'

Banks followed him into the same room he had been in the previous day. The clock ticking on the mantelpiece was the only sound.

'Have you found anything out yet?' Aspern asked.

'Not much, I'm afraid,' said Banks. 'We do know that the man on the other boat was an artist called Thomas McMahon, and that he was most likely the intended victim. Have you ever met him or heard of him?'

'McMahon? Can't say as I have.'

'I'd like to talk to you about Mark Siddons a bit more,' Banks said.

Aspern's expression darkened. 'If anyone's responsible for what happened to Christine, it's him,' he said. 'I've been thinking about it. If he'd been with her, as he should have been, she'd be alive today. He knew she was ill, for crying out loud, knew she needed taking care of.'

'I thought you didn't like the idea of their being together?'

'That's not the point. If he was supposed to be with her, he should have been there. He knew she wasn't capable of looking after herself properly. Where was he, anyway?'

Banks was damned if he was going to tell Patrick Aspern that Mark had been in bed with Mandy Patterson at the time of the fire. 'His alibi's been checked,' was all he said. 'I take it your surgery is attached to the house?'

Aspern looked surprised by the abrupt change of subject. 'Yes. Actually it was two houses knocked into one. I know it's rather old-fashioned, but people around here like it. It's so much more civilized than some anonymous clinic. That's one of the reasons we bought the houses in the first place.'

'Pretty expensive proposition.'

'Not that it's any of your business, but Fran's father helped us out.'

'I see. Very nice of him. Anyway, what I'm getting at is that Christine *could* have had access to drugs here, couldn't she? They were in the house, after all.'

Aspern crossed his legs and tugged at the crease of his trousers. 'As I told you last time, I keep everything in my surgery under lock and key. The surgery itself is also securely locked when I'm not there.'

'Yes, but presumably the keys are somewhere around?'

'On my key chain. In my pocket.'

'So they're always with you?'

'Well, almost always. I mean . . . not when I'm asleep or in the bath . . .'

'So Christine could have got access, for example, while you were asleep or out somewhere.'

'I'd have my keys with me if I was out.'

'But there is a possibility, isn't there? She could even have had copies made.'

'I suppose there's the possibility. But it didn't happen.'

'Did you ever notice any drugs missing from your surgery? Specifically morphine?'

'No. And, believe me, I would have noticed.'

'Didn't you ever notice anything unusual about Christine's behaviour while she was living at home?'

'No, not particularly. She seemed tired, listless, spent a lot of time alone in bed. You know teenagers. They seem to need sixteen hours' sleep a day. To be honest, I didn't even see that much of her.'

'But you're a *doctor*. You're trained to spot signs other people might miss.'

Aspern gave a grim smile. 'We're not infallible, you know, despite what some people think.'

'So you had no idea that Christine was taking drugs?'

'None at all. Like I said, she was a teenager. Teenagers are surly and uncommunicative, whether they're on drugs or not.'

'What about her eyes? Didn't you notice pinpoint pupils?'

'I might have done, but I wouldn't necessarily jump to the conclusion that my stepdaughter was a drug addict. Would you?'

Banks wondered. What would he think if he noticed those signs in Tracy or Brian? As a policeman, he had certainly been trained to look for them. But if he challenged either of his children and the explanation was innocent, such a challenge could cause irreparable damage to their relationship. They'd never trust him again. On the other hand, if he were right . . . Fortunately, he had never been put to the test. Brian played in a rock band, so he was probably the one with the best access to drugs. Banks didn't doubt that his son had tried marijuana, perhaps even Ecstasy. Banks could live with that. Maybe Brian had also taken the odd upper on the road to stay awake. But nothing stronger, surely? Not heroin. And Tracy? No, she was far too sensible and conventional, wasn't she?

'Didn't you ever notice needle marks on her arms?' Banks paused. 'Or in other places, perhaps?'

Aspern stared at him. His expression was hard to read: cold but quizzical. 'That's a strange question,' he said finally. 'If I had, then I would have known what was going on. I said I didn't know, ergo I can't have noticed anything.'

'I suppose she must have worn long-sleeved tops,' Banks said.

Aspern got up, walked over and leaned on the mantelpiece by the watercolour of Adel woods. He looked as if he were posing for a photograph. 'Indeed she must have,' he said. 'Look, I understand you have your job to do and all that, and I think I've been more than patient with you. But I've just lost my stepdaughter, and I'm beginning to get a very suspicious feeling about this conversation. If this artist on the other boat was the intended victim, why are you asking so many questions about Christine? She was merely an innocent bystander.'

'Oh, nothing's obvious yet,' Banks said. 'It's still early days. Believe me, we're gathering as much information as we can about Thomas McMahon, but we have to follow every lead we have and avoid jumping to conclusions. I said it *looked* as if Christine wasn't the intended victim, but criminals can be very clever at misdirecting investigations, especially if they've had a chance to think out and plan their crimes ahead of time.'

'You think that's how this happened? It was planned?'

'It's beginning to look that way to me.'

'I still don't understand why you're questioning *me* this way. You can't think I had anything to do with it, surely?'

'Where were you on Thursday night?'

Aspern laughed. 'I don't believe this.'

'Humour me.'

'I was here, of course. With my wife. Just like I told you the last time you asked.'

'Nobody else? No dinner guests?'

'No. We ate by ourselves, then we watched television. It was a quiet evening at home.'

'What time did you go to bed?'

'Eleven o'clock, as usual.'

'You always go to bed at eleven o'clock?'

'Weeknights, yes. We sometimes stay up a bit later at weekends, or we may go to the opera, dine with friends. Believe it or not, my job can be rather tiring and I do need my wits about me.'

'Of course. Wouldn't want the hand that holds the needle to be shaking, would we?' Banks was wondering how he could get around to Mark's accusation that Aspern had sexually abused Christine. If there was an easy way, he couldn't think of it. He decided to jump right in. 'Mark Siddons had something else to say about Christine,' he said.

'Oh?'

'He said that one of the reasons she left home was that you were sexually abusing her.'

At least Aspern didn't act outraged, Banks noticed. He seemed to take the accusation calmly and consider it. 'And you believe him?'

'I didn't say that.'

'Then why mention it? Especially at a time like this. Can't you see how upsetting an accusation like that can be to a grieving relative, however groundless?'

Banks stood up and looked Aspern in the eye. 'Dr Aspern, this is a murder investigation. We might not know exactly who the intended victim was, or victims were, but we do know that two people died. One of them was your stepdaughter. Now, I'm very sorry for your loss, but as you said earlier, we men have to get on with our jobs, don't we? That's what I'm doing. And anything that I think might be relevant to the investigation, I ask questions about. That's not unreasonable, is it?'

'Put that way,' Aspern said, 'I suppose not.'

'So will you answer my question?'

'It's hardly worth dignifying with a denial.'

Banks looked into his eyes. 'Try anyway.'

'Very well. The accusation is absurd. I never touched my stepdaughter. Will that do?'

He was lying, Banks knew it. In that instant, he knew that Tina and Mark Siddons had been telling the truth. But who would believe him? And how could it be proved? What could he do about it?

So intent was he on registering his awareness of Patrick Aspern's body language and facial signals that he didn't notice the figure in the doorway until she spoke.

'What is it?' Frances Aspern asked, her face still soft and puffy from sleep. 'What's going on?'

They both turned to face her. Patrick Aspern looked at his wife and said, 'It's nothing, darling. Just a few more questions, that's all.'

The look that passed between them said more than enough.

6

Banks had loved the smell of old bookshops ever since he was a child and Leslie Whitaker's Antiquarian Books and Prints, in the maze of cobbled alleys at the back of the police station, was no exception. It stood in a row of particularly ancient shops with low, crooked beams and mullioned bay windows thick as magnifying glass. On one side was a tobacconist's, with its wooden bowls of exotic pipe tobaccos, and on the other, J.W. Allen, apothecary, with the antique blue, green and red bottles in the window. Purely for the tourists, of course.

The bell jangled over the door as Banks entered. It was hard to define the smell, a mix of dust, leather and paper, even a spot of mildew, perhaps, but its effect was as comforting to Banks as that of freshly mown hay or bread straight from the baker's oven. Something to do with a childhood spent in the children's library and many days as a teenager browsing in second-hand bookshops. He paused on the threshold to inhale and savour the sensation, then presented his warrant card to the man shelving books across the room.

'A chief inspector, indeed,' Whitaker said. 'And on a Saturday afternoon, too. I am honoured.'

'We're short staffed,' Banks said. While this was partly true, it was not the real reason he often made such routine calls himself. Most chief inspectors spent their careers behind desks piled high with paper, or in meetings thrashing out details of budget and manpower, paper clips and databases, cost-effective policing, flow charts and value assessments. While Banks had plenty of that to do, he also liked to keep his hand in, liked to stay close to the street policing he had grown up with. It was partly a matter of solidarity with the troops, who appreciated that their boss would often carry out the same tedious, dead-end tasks as they did, even get his hands dirty, and partly selfishness because Banks hated paperwork and loved getting out there and sniffing out the lie or the possible lead. Some of the young turks who had come up through accelerated promotion schemes didn't understand why he just wouldn't settle down to 'administrative' duties, which was what many of them aspired to in the long run.

Banks's instincts as a working detective had developed enough over the years, and his success rate was high enough, that neither Detective Superintendent Gristhorpe nor Assistant Chief Constable Ron McLaughlin stood in his way. And if Banks also chose to interview a suspect – a task usually carried out by a lowly DC, or DS at the highest, and one which most people above the rank of inspector had forgotten how to do – then that was fine with his bosses, too, as he had a knack for the thrust and parry, or the subtle persuasiveness of a good interrogation.

All Banks knew so far was that Leslie Whitaker had taken over the business from his father, Ernest, who had died two years ago. There was a framed photograph of what Banks took to be the two of them on Whitaker's desk. He didn't correspond with Banks's mental image of an antiquarian book dealer, though the picture of the wispy-haired man in the ill-fitting sweater was a bit of a stereotype. Whitaker was in his early forties, dressed in a light-grey suit, white shirt and maroon tie. His short dark hair was thinning a bit at the temples, but the look suited him. He looked fit and well muscled. Banks supposed that, with his strong chin and clear blue eyes, women, and perhaps even men, found him handsome. He had no criminal record, and DS Hatchley, who knew everything about these matters, hadn't been able to unearth any gossip about him.

'What can I do for you?' Whitaker asked. 'Do please sit down.'

He sat behind his ancient polished desk at the rear of the shop and gestured Banks to a hard-backed chair. Banks sat. 'It's information I'm after, really,' he said.

'Some crime in the book world?'

'Art world, actually. Or so it appears.'

'Well, that would certainly make more sense. The art world's rife with crime.'

'I suppose you've heard about the fire on the canal boats?'

'Yes. Tragic. Terrible business.'

'We have reason to believe that one of the victims was an artist called Thomas McMahon. I believe you knew him?'

'Tom McMahon? Good Lord. I had no idea.'

'So you did know him?'

'Tom? Well, yes, vaguely. I mean, I'd no idea where he was living or what he was up to, but I know him – knew him – yes.'

'From what context?'

'I sell his work. Or rather, I liaise between Tom and the various craft markets, shops and boutiques throughout the Dales that sell the landscapes he paints. And a few years ago, when he was regarded as an up-and-coming artist, I collected a couple of his paintings and even managed to sell a few.'

'What happened?'

'He just never took off. It happens more often than you'd think. The art world's brutal and it's very difficult to break into. He had a big exhibition at the community centre and I thought maybe he had a chance, but . . . in the end he just didn't make the grade.'

'Was he talented?'

'Talented?' Whitaker frowned. 'Yes, of course. But what does that have to do with anything?'

Banks laughed. 'Well, I've seen enough squiggles on blank canvases selling for thousands to know what you mean, but it was a genuine question.'

Whitaker pursed his lips. 'Tom's technique was excellent,' he said, 'but derivative. When it came right down to it, he just wasn't very original.'

That was exactly what Maria Phillips had said. 'Derivative of whom?'

'He was all over the map, really. Romantic landscapes. Pre-Raphaelites. Impressionism. Surrealism. Cubism. That was the problem with Tom; he didn't have any particular distinctive style, nothing you could point to with any amount of certainty and say *that's* a Thomas McMahon.'

'So the paintings you bought . . . ?'

'Worthless.'

'Doesn't his death change that?'

Whitaker laughed. 'I see what you're getting at. Many artists didn't get famous until after they were dead. Van Gogh, for one. But he *was* an original. I don't think death is going to make Thomas McMahon's works immortal, or valuable. No, Mr Banks, I'm afraid I have no motive for

Tom McMahon, and I didn't exactly pay a
he paintings in the first place.'

was much the same as Maria had told him. 'I
plying that you had a motive,' said Banks. 'I'm
simpl, ying to get at who might benefit from his death.'

'Nobody I can think of. It can't have been easy for him,
though,' mused Whitaker.

'Why not?'

'Failure's never easy to handle, is it?'

Banks, who had missed nabbing more than one
obvious villain in his career, knew how true that was.
He remembered the failures more than the successes and
every one of them galled him. 'I suppose not,' he said.

'I mean you head out of a successful exhibition thinking you're Pablo Picasso and the next day people don't
even bother reading your name in the bottom right-hand
corner of the canvas. Then all you've got left to give them
is nothing more than a sort of glorified photograph to
remind them of their holiday in the Dales. So much for
artistic vision and truth.'

'Is that how McMahon felt?'

'I can't say for certain. He never talked about it. But I
know it's how I'd feel. Forgive me, I'm just extrapolating.'

'But you sell these "glorified photographs" – or at least
you help to.'

'For a commission, yes. It's a business.'

'I understand McMahon was also a customer of yours?'

Whitaker shifted in his chair and glanced at the top
shelf of books. 'He dropped by the shop from time to time.'

'What did he buy?' Banks looked around at the leather-
bound books and the bins of unframed prints and
drawings. 'I'd have thought your fare was a bit pricey for
the likes of Thomas McMahon,' he said.

'They're not all expensive. Many books and prints, even old ones, are hardly worth more than the paper they were printed on. It's actually quite rare to come across the sort of find that makes your pulse race.'

'So McMahon bought cheap old books and prints?'

'Inexpensive ones.'

'Why?'

'I've no idea. I suppose he must have liked them.'

'What did he buy the last time you saw him?'

'An early nineteenth-century volume of natural history. Nothing special. And the binding was in very poor shape.'

'How much did it cost.'

'Forty pounds. A steal, really.'

Yes, Banks thought, but what was a man squatting on a narrowboat doing spending forty pounds on an old book? He remembered the wet, charred pages he'd seen on the boat with Geoff Hamilton. Well, McMahon *was* an artist, and perhaps he just loved old books and prints. 'Can you tell me anything about his state of mind?'

'He seemed fine whenever I saw him. In very good spirits, really. He even so much as hinted that things might be on the up for him.'

'Was he specific?'

'No. It was just when I asked him how he was, you know, as you do. Well, you don't really expect much more than "Fine, thanks" as a reply, do you? But he said he was thriving and that they might think they could grind old Tom down, but he'd still got a trick or two up his sleeve. He often referred to himself in the third person.'

'Who are "they"?'

Whitaker shrugged. 'Didn't say. The world in general, I assumed. The ones who refused to recognize his talent and buy his masterpieces.'

'And what trick did he have to show them?'

'No idea. I'm merely reporting what he said. Tom always tended to talk a good game, as they say.'

'You think there was any truth to it – that his fortunes were improving?'

'Who can say? Not from sales to the tourists, they weren't.'

'So you hadn't noticed any decline in him? In his appearance or mental state?'

'Quite the opposite, really. I mean, Tom was never the model of sartorial elegance – he was always a bit paint-stained and dishevelled – but his clothes sense seemed to have improved. He'd also lost a bit of weight. And mentally, I'd say he was in good spirits.'

'Was he ever married?'

'I think he might have been once upon a time, but if he was, it was long before he fetched up here in Eastvale.'

'Womanizer?'

'No, not really.'

'Men? Little boys?'

'No, don't get me wrong. Tom wasn't that way inclined. He liked women, even had the occasional girl-friend, but nothing lasted. There was only one love for him and that was art. It was always his art that came first – came even before such mundane matters as punctual-ity and thoughtfulness, if you see what I mean. And it was such a damn shame that his art wasn't really worth much to anyone else.'

Banks nodded. Whitaker might as well have been describing a policeman's lot. He'd forgotten his share of dates and anniversaries because he'd been too involved in a case. That was partly why his marriage had ended. The miracle was, he realized only later, that it had lasted so long in the first place. He had assumed everything was fine because Sandra was an independent spirit and got on with her own life. And so she did – ultimately to the extent of taking up with Sean, dumping Banks and getting pregnant in her mid-forties. And now she was a mother again. 'Any particular girlfriends you remember?' he asked.

'Well, he was rather taken by young Heather. Can't remember her second name. Worked in the artists' supplies shop down York Road. I can't say I blame him. She was quite a stunner. Real page-three material. I don't think she's there any more, though the owner might know where she is. Much too young for Tom, of course. He was asking for grief, there.'

'How old was he?'

'It was about five years back, so he'd have been in his late thirties.'

'And Heather?'

'Early twenties.'

'Serious?'

'On his part. He was quite broken up when she traded him in for a more successful artist. That was one of the few times I saw him pissed. I think it really depressed him, you know, feeling all washed up as an artist, and then his girl chucks him for someone more successful. That was about as low as I ever saw him.'

Well, that would do it, thought Banks. 'Who did she leave him for?'

'Jake Harley. Glib bastard, I must say. Up-and-comer at the time, but I'm happy to report that he went nowhere, too. He didn't have the guts to live with his failure, though. He committed suicide about eighteen months ago down in London. Of course, he'd split with Heather ages before then.'

'And you don't know where she is now?'

'Sorry. Haven't clapped eyes on her in about three years. Sam Prescott might know, though. He still runs the shop.'

'You don't know of any more recent girlfriends?'

Whitaker shook his head.

'Was he ever with anyone when he came in here, male or female?'

'No. He was always alone.'

'Did he ever mention anyone, any names at all?'

'No, not that I can recall. But he was always a bit of a loner, especially after Heather.'

Banks stood up and stretched out his hand. 'Well, thanks very much, Mr Whitaker. You've been a great help.'

'I can't see how, but you're welcome, I'm sure.'

'Can you think of anyone else we might talk to about McMahon?'

Whitaker thought for a moment. 'Not really.' He mentioned a couple of artists whose names Banks had already heard from Maria Phillips. It sounded to Banks as if McMahon had shed his earlier life and friends and cut off all contact with the old world, the world that had burned him, had refused to recognize his talent. Whether he had found new friends or adopted the life of a recluse, the way it seemed, remained to be seen. And why had he been buying worthless old books and prints from Leslie Whitaker?

•

Annie had been around enough artists in her time to recognize the type. Baz Hayward had adopted the persona of the suffering, world-weary, misunderstood, dissolute genius, justifying all his excesses and his total lack of talent and social graces by his devotion to art – right down to the beard, the ragged clothes and the body odour. Whether he really did have any talent or not, she didn't know. Some of the most obnoxious people she had ever known possessed immense talent, though many of them squandered it.

Hayward bid her wait for a moment while he finished off some essential brush strokes to a painting he was working on. Smiling to herself over the pathetic arrogance of his need to seem important, Annie wandered over and looked out of the window. She knew she could play the heavy if she wanted, but luckily she was in a good mood because she was going to dinner with Phil tonight, all being well.

Hayward lived in a converted barn on the high road between Lyndgarth and Helmthorpe. It was an isolated spot with a spectacular view down the slope past the stubby ruins of Devraulx Abbey to the drizzle-darkened flagstone roofs of Fortford, where Phil's cottage was. Smoke from chimneys drifted slowly eastwards on the faint breeze, bringing a hint of peat to the air. On the steeply rising slopes of the south daleside, beyond the clustered cottages of Mortsett and Relton, Annie could see the imposing symmetry of Swainsdale Hall.

It was odd to see the hall from this perspective, she realized. Only last summer, she had spent some time there, heading the search for a missing boy. Today no smoke came from the high chimneys. Annie guessed that ex-footballer Martin Armitage was in Florida or the West Indies with his wife, ex-model Robin Fetherling. Well, good for them. There wasn't much left for them at Swainsdale Hall now.

Hayward's loft was chilly and Annie kept her greatcoat

on. The cold didn't seem to bother Hayward himself, though, who was prancing around waving his paintbrush, wearing torn jeans and a dirty white T-shirt. If he'd been at the Turner reception, Annie didn't remember him.

She had been surprised to hear from Banks that Thomas McMahon had also been there, and when she cast her mind back she thought she remembered a short, burly fellow with a glass of wine in his hand chatting to some of the centre's committee members. It had been a crowded room, though, and she had been there partly to keep an eye on the painting in the adjoining room, so she could easily have missed both McMahon and Hayward.

Annie had met Phil Keane at the reception. He was there in his professional capacity as an art researcher to help authenticate the find. They hadn't talked much that evening, but Phil had phoned her a few weeks later and asked her out to dinner. She'd been busy – it wasn't an excuse – but he had phoned again a week later as she suggested. That time she accepted. They had seen one another only four or five times since then, because of the pressures of their work, but each time Annie found herself becoming more and more attracted to his charm, his consideration and his intellect – not to mention his graceful and finely honed body. She was also inordinately pleased to find that Phil had heard of her father's work.

Finally, she heard Hayward throw down the brush and play himself a brief fanfare. 'Finished.'

'It's a wonderful view,' Annie said, gesturing towards the window.

'What?' Hayward looked confused. 'Oh, yes,' he said, catching on, 'I suppose it is, if you like that sort of thing. Personally I think landscapes are vastly overrated, and landscape painting died with the invention of the camera.

It just hasn't had the decency to roll over and accept the fact. A good digital camera can do anything the Impressionists ever did.'

'That's an interesting way of looking at it,' said Annie, sitting on the only uncluttered chair. Discarded clothes littered the floor and mould grew in a half-empty coffee cup on the low table. She was glad he didn't offer her tea or coffee. But it was the walls that disturbed Annie most of all. They were covered with what she could only assume to be Hayward's own sketches and paintings, all looking like Rorschach tests painted by Francis Bacon on drugs. The whole effect was dizzying and disturbing, and it made her vaguely queasy, though she wasn't at first sure why. Still, they must sell, she thought, or he wouldn't be able to afford this place.

'It is, isn't it?' said Hayward, waving his hand dismissively. 'I try to break free from conventional ways of thinking and living. Anyway, it's the isolation I like. I keep the curtains closed most of the time.'

'Good idea,' said Annie. 'Thomas McMahon. You were friends once. What happened?'

'Tom? Friends?' He ran his hand through his lank, greasy hair. 'Yes, I suppose we were, in a way.'

'Did you have a falling out?'

'I disagreed with his artistic direction, or lack of one – the kind of abstract effects he was working on went out with the Cubists, and then there were those dreadful landscapes he churned out for the tourist trade.'

'To pay the rent?'

'I suppose so. But rent's not that important in the grand scheme of things, is it?'

Annie felt glad she wasn't Hayward's landlord. 'When did you last see him?'

'Must have been four, five years ago.'

'Not since?'

'No. He just sort of dropped out of the scene. What scene there is.' Hayward scratched his crotch. 'I saw less of him. He became more distant and moody. In the end I didn't even know where he was living. I thought he'd left town.'

'You didn't bump into him at the Turner reception last summer, then?'

Hayward pulled a face. 'Do me a favour. *Turner*? You think I'd waste my time with that sort of tripe?'

'Of course,' Annie said. 'Forgive me. I should have known. Despite the fact that you didn't approve of McMahon's art, did you have any sort of personal falling out?'

'No. We were always on good terms. Polite terms, at any rate. And whatever it was he did, it wasn't art.'

'But you've no idea what he was up to more recently?'

'None at all.'

'His work hasn't appeared anywhere?'

'Thank God, no.'

'Would it surprise you to hear that we think he was squatting on a boat on the canal, a boat that was set on fire on Thursday night, killing him and the girl on the neighbouring boat?'

If Annie had any hopes of shocking Hayward into some sort of decent human reaction, they were soon dashed. 'No,' he said. 'Nothing really surprises me any more. Except art. And even that doesn't surprise me as often as it used to. As Diaghilev said to Jean Cocteau, "*Etonne moi.*" Ha! If only.'

'Do you have any idea why anyone would want to kill Tom McMahon?'

'For painting bad pictures?'

'Mr Hayward.'

Hayward grinned. 'A bit too brutal for you, that, was it? Too close to the bone?'

'You seem to be very aware of the effects you're striving for,' Annie said. 'I'd be careful that it doesn't give a sort of stiff, wooden aspect to your art. That kind of arrogant, straining self-consciousness can be quite counter-productive, you know.'

'What would you know about it?'

'Nothing. Just an opinion.'

'Uninformed opinion is about as interesting as a Constable landscape.'

'Ah,' said Annie, who thought Constable landscapes quite interesting. More interesting than what was on Hayward's walls, anyway. She was getting nowhere here, and Hayward was clearly far too wrapped up in himself to be capable of noticing anyone else's existence, let alone killing anyone. It was time to go.

'Look,' said Hayward, when Annie got up to walk to the door. 'I'm sorry I can't be of more help to you, but I really haven't seen Tom in years and I've no idea what he did with his life. He just wasn't a very original painter, that's all.'

'That's OK,' said Annie. 'Thanks for your time.'

Hayward stood in the doorway, leaning on the jamb and blocking the exit. 'Maybe your visit wasn't entirely wasted, though,' he said.

Annie felt her breath tighten in her throat. 'Oh?' she said.

'No. I mean, there are often other purposes, aren't there? Hidden purposes. You do something for one reason, at least on the surface, but it turns out there's an underlying, deeper reason you just weren't conscious of. A more important reason. Fate, perhaps.'

'Speak English, Baz. And get out of my way.'

Hayward stood his ground. 'I'd like to paint you,' he announced, beaming, as if offering her a place on the queen's honours list.

'Paint me?'

'Yes. We could start now, if you like. Perhaps some preliminary sketches?'

Annie looked around at the walls. She knew now what it was that disturbed her about the artwork hanging there. Every piece, either charcoal sketch or colour painting, was of a gaping vagina. It was hardly an original idea – the flower-like symmetry and individuality of female genitals had excited artists for years – and Annie was open minded as far as most things were concerned. But being in this room, surrounded by garish paintings of them, and knowing that the odious Baz Hayward was now quite openly staring at the inverted V of her jeans between her legs, where her greatcoat gaped open, gave her the creeps.

She grabbed his wrist so quickly he had no time to stop her, twisted his arm behind his back and pushed him into the room. He stumbled into the easel, knocking the painting he had been working on to the floor. Then Annie pulled her coat tight around her waist, fastened the belt, said, 'Fuck off, Baz,' and left.

•

When Banks walked down the front steps of Eastvale General Infirmary, it was already dark, and the drizzle had turned into a late afternoon mist that blurred the shop lights on King Street. For some reason, he was overcome with a vivid memory of a similar afternoon when he was fifteen or sixteen, when he'd been upstairs on a bus coming home from town, a copy of the *Fresh Cream* album and the latest *Melody Maker* tucked under his arm. Looking out at the yellow halos of the streetlights and the hazy neon signs, he had lit a cigarette and it had tasted magnificent, by far the best cigarette he had ever smoked. He could taste it now and he automatically reached in his pocket. Of course, there were no cigarettes in his pocket. He looked across King Street at the light in the newsagent's window, bleary in the late afternoon mist, strongly tempted to dash over and buy a packet. Just ten. He'd smoke only the ten and then no more. But he got a grip on himself, turned his collar up and trudged up the hill to the station.

Christine Aspern's body had been in far better shape than Tom McMahon's. In fact the skin that had been covered by the sleeping bag was not charred, but pale and waxy, like that of most corpses. It was only her face and hands, where she had suffered second-degree burns, that had been at all blackened or blistered by the fire. The blisters were also a sign, Dr Glendenning said, that the victim was probably alive when the fire began, though a small amount of blistering can occur after death. Given the other evidence, though, he would surmise that the blistering in Tina's case was post-mortem.

Dr Glendenning had approached the autopsy with his usual concern for detail and confirmed that, pending toxicology results that probably wouldn't be in until Monday afternoon at the earliest, this being the weekend, she had died, like Thomas McMahon, of asphyxiation due to smoke inhalation and most likely not from a heroin overdose.

As in the case of McMahon, Glendenning had also

found thermal injury to the mouth and nose but not lower down, in the tracheal area. He had found only trace amounts of soot below the larynx, indicating that Christine was most likely unconscious when the fire started.

There was always the chance that Danny Boy's heroin had been unusually pure and that she had died of an overdose before or during the fire, but Banks was willing to bet she was probably just on the nod. Mark had already told him that she had injected herself that evening. She wouldn't have been the first junkie to lie there in the cocoon of safety and emptiness she had created for herself while the flames consumed her flesh. Either way, there was no evidence of foul play other than the starting of the fire itself, and going by the splash patterns and accelerant tests Geoff Hamilton had carried out, the arsonist had probably not even set foot on Mark and Christine's boat.

It was late Saturday afternoon and the duty constables were bringing in a couple of drunken Eastvale United supporters when Banks got to the station. Eastvale was hardly a premier division team, but that didn't stop some fans from acting as if they were at a Leeds–Manchester United match. Banks edged around the wobbly group and headed upstairs to the relative peace of his office, grabbing the handful of completed actions from his pigeonhole on the way. He slipped off his raincoat, kicked the heater to get it started and turned on his radio to a Radio 3 special about Bud Powell on *Jazz Line Up*.

As he listened to 'A Night in Tunisia', he flipped through the actions and found only one of immediate interest.

According to her ex-employer Sam Prescott, Heather Burnett, the girl from the art supplies shop who had left

Thomas McMahon for Jake Harley, had later left Harley himself for an American installation specialist called Nate Ulrich, and they now lived in Palo Alto, California. Well, it had been a long shot in the first place, Banks thought.

Because it was the weekend, things were slow. Banks didn't expect any preliminary forensic results, including analysis of clothing samples and toxicology, until early Tuesday. He still needed to know who had owned the boats, but as yet DC Templeton hadn't got very far with his enquiries. There was a good chance he might have to wait until Monday or later to find someone who knew, maybe someone from British Waterways.

Then there was the car to consider, the dark blue Jeep Cherokee, or Range Rover, whatever it was, that had been seen parked in the lay-by nearest the boats. It was probably a waste of time as there would be so many of them to check out, but Banks issued the actions anyway. He also ordered a survey of all the car-rental agencies in the area. There was a good chance that if someone was out to break the law, he might not want to use his own car when visiting McMahon in case he was spotted. Also, if he knew the roads in the immediate area of the boats, he would know that a Jeep was a much better option than an ordinary car, especially in winter.

Banks had no sooner issued the action than his phone rang.

'Alan, it's Ken.' DI Ken Blackstone, phoning from Leeds. 'We sent a couple of lads over to interview that dealer you mentioned, Benjamin Scott.'

'That was quick. Must be a slow day down there.'

'United's away this week. Anyway, we leaned on him a bit – seems there were small amounts of suspicious substances in his flat – and he's got a watertight alibi. He was in Paris with his girlfriend when the fire started.'

'How the other half lives. You're sure?'

'She verified it, and they showed us used tickets, credit-card receipts, gave us the number of the hotel. Want me to phone?'

'No, it's all right, Ken. It was only a vague possibility. Look, do you happen to know anything about a bloke called Aspern, a Dr Patrick Aspern?'

'I can't say I do, not off the top of my head. Why?'

'He's the dead girl's stepfather and her boyfriend's made a rather serious accusation. There might be something in it. Think you could check around, see if there's anything on him?'

'Can do.'

'And there's no need to be *too* discreet about your enquiries.'

'Understood. Where's he live?'

'Adel.'

'That'll be Weetwood station. I know a DI there. I'll get back to you after the weekend. It's been a while. How's things?'

'Not bad,' said Banks.

'Sandra?'

'A distant memory.'

'She's had the baby?'

'She's had the baby. Sinéad. Nice of you to ask, Ken. Mother and child are doing fine.'

'Sorry, I didn't know it was still such a touchy point. Any chance you'll be down in my neck of the woods again soon?'

'Depends on how the case goes. And what you dig up on Aspern, of course.'

'Well, if you've got time, give me a bell. We can go out for a curry and a piss-up. My sofa's yours any time. You know that.'

'Thanks, Ken. I'll likely take you up on that soon. Talk to you later.'

'Bye.'

Banks tapped his ballpoint on the desk. He didn't really expect anything to come of enquiries into Patrick Aspern. If Mark's accusation was to be believed, whatever went on was a family matter, in more ways than one, and they might never be able to find any evidence. Frances Aspern knew something, Banks was certain, but she didn't seem likely to talk. Whatever the reason, her relationship with Aspern was important to her; she needed him enough to sacrifice her daughter to him, if, indeed, that was what had happened.

Banks did, however, want Aspern to know that the local police were on his case, which was why he had told Ken Blackstone not to worry about discretion. It would be interesting to see how the good doctor reacted to that. He glanced at his watch. Time to get a few more actions issued, have a chat with Annie about progress so far, then go home. And what would he do there? Well, it wasn't always Laphroaig and *La Cenerentola* for Banks. He did, at times, give in to his baser instincts, and tonight he felt like an evening alone with a Chinese takeaway, a James Bond DVD – Sean Connery, of course – and a few cans of lager. Ah, the lush life.

•

Lenny Knox and his wife Sally lived on Eastvale's notorious East Side estate, a living testament to the fact that it wasn't only big cities that had problem areas. But like all

the big-city estates, the East Side estate also had its share
of decent people just trying to make the best of a bad situation, and Lenny was one of them. He was a founding
member of the local neighbourhood watch, keeping an
eye out for drug dealers and vandalism. He'd had his own
problems when he was a teenager, Mark knew from their
conversations, but a short prison sentence in his early
twenties had turned him around.

They'd done a fair day's work when Lenny pulled his
rusty old Nissan up outside the terraced house on the
estate's central artery. Street parking wasn't especially
safe in the area, but everyone knew Lenny's car and no
one dared touch it. Lenny probably thought that was
because everyone was scared of him, but Mark thought it
was more likely because the car was a piece of crap no
respectable thief would waste a second glance on. Mark
looked around warily as he got out of the car, and it wasn't
because of what Banks had warned him about. He had
bad memories of the East Side estate, and even though he
didn't think Crazy Nick was around any more, it still paid
to be careful. He knew that Nick would kill him if he
found him. That was why the boat had been safe. Nick
would never think to look anywhere rural like that; if anything, he had even less upstairs than Mark himself.

Mark followed Lenny inside and saw Sal's look of surprise when he entered. She welcomed her husband with
a perfunctory kiss on the cheek and disappeared into the
kitchen to make tea. A black cat with half its left ear missing rubbed up against Mark's leg then slunk off upstairs.

'Make yourself at home,' Lenny said, pointing to a
threadbare armchair.

'Are you sure it's all right?' Mark asked. 'I don't want
to be a bother.'

'Oh, don't worry about Sal,' he said. 'She'll come around. She always does.'

Mark had seen the expression on Sal's face and he wasn't too certain about that.

Lenny offered Mark a cigarette. 'We'll have a cuppa first,' he said, 'just to wash the dust out, then I'll go get us all some fish and chips and a few cans of lager. OK?'

Mark reached in his pocket. 'I've got some money . . .'

Lenny waved it away. 'Don't be daft. My treat.'

'But—'

'No arguments. You can buy us pizza on pay day, all right?'

'OK.'

Lenny tuned the television set to a snooker game and settled back in his chair. The house smelled faintly of burnt bacon and cat's piss. Mark couldn't concentrate on the game; he'd never been a big snooker fan, anyway. He couldn't stop thinking of Tina, couldn't quite get his head around the fact that she was dead, gone, kaput, and that they'd never again be able to snuggle up to one another against the winter chill in their sleeping bag. His home was gone too. It might not have been much, but it had meant a lot to them. It was their very own place, an escape from the miserable squat in Leeds, and they'd added a little personal touch here and there – a nice candlestick, a primus to boil water and cook tinned foods on, a framed photo of the two of them on the wall, a mini CD player and a few of their favourite CDs: Beth Orton, David Bowie, Coldplay, System of a Down, Radiohead, Ben Harper.

Tears pricked Mark's eyes. He couldn't cry, not in front of Lenny, but he felt like it. What would he do now without Tina to look after? What was the point of it all? Until he'd met her, his life had been nothing but an aimless mess, and that's what it would turn into again. He knew people looked at the way they lived and judged them, but he didn't care what people thought. One day he and Tina were going to get it all together: home, kids, the lot. Let them laugh. But now . . . And it was all his fault.

The snooker game droned on. Sal poked her head around the door and said, 'Tea's ready. Can I talk to you a minute, Len?'

Len pulled a long-suffering face for Mark's benefit, as if to say, *Women!* Then he dragged himself away from the TV set and went into the kitchen.

When Mark thought of Tina's stepdad, he felt the voiceless anger boil in him until his hands shook. He had no doubt that Aspern was responsible for Tina's drug addiction. She had told him that she started doing morphine to dull the pain and humiliation of his sexual advances, and when Aspern caught her at it one day he started using the drugs as a reward for sexual favours. He'd already given her sedatives before, to make her easier to handle. And him supposed to be a doctor. The mother knew more than she let on, but she was scared shitless of Aspern, Tina had told him. A mouse. If he so much as raised his voice at her, her lower lip would start to tremble and she'd run away in tears. Tina had nobody to stand up for her. Nobody but Mark. But now it didn't matter anyway.

'What the hell do you think you're doing?' he heard Sal saying in the kitchen. 'Bringing him here. The kid's just come out of jail, for Christ's sake. It's been all over the news. I knew it was him when I first heard about that fire.'

'I've been in jail myself, love,' Lenny said, 'but it doesn't make me a criminal.'

'That's different. That was years ago. *We* can't be responsible for him.'

'Have a heart. The poor kid's just lost his girlfriend and his home.'

'Home! A clapped-out boat. Lenny, what's got into you? You're not usually such a soft touch.'

'What do you mean?'

'Oh, no doubt he's spun you a sob story of some sort. Got you thinking he's the son you never had—'

'Now, wait a minute!'

'No! *You* wait a minute. You bring him here without asking, without even ringing first to let me know, and you expect me to cook for him, clean up after him? What do you think I am, Lenny, a skivvy? Is that all I am to you? A bloody skivvy?'

'Come on, love.'

'Don't you "love" me.'

'Sal . . .'

'Have you thought for just one moment, has it even crossed that tiny little brain of yours, that *he* might have been the one who set the fire? Have you thought of that?'

'For crying out loud, Sal, Mark wouldn't do anything like that. Besides, the police let him go.'

'The police are always letting murderers go. Just because they don't have enough evidence. But it doesn't mean they don't know *someone* did it.'

'Oh, come on. He's a good kid.'

'Good kid! You won't be saying that when the bloody house is burning down around you, will you!'

'Sal, I'm not—'

But Mark didn't hear any more. Tears finally blurring his vision and anger seething inside him, he snatched up his overcoat and dashed out of the door. He was halfway down the street before he heard Lenny shouting after him, but he ignored the calls and ran on, under the railway bridge, away from the town.

•

The Angel was reputed to have the finest chef east of the Pennines and he was even rumoured to have something of a flair for vegetarian dishes. Thoughtful of Phil to take that into account. Annie had dressed accordingly, toning down her sartorial flamboyance a bit with her little black number in deference to Phil's decidedly more conserva-tive-but-casual look. She hadn't worn the frock in ages and felt a bit self-conscious in it. She was pleased to find that it still fitted. The last time she wore it, she remem-bered, was on one of her dinner dates with Banks. And that reminded her: something he'd said in their brief meeting a short while earlier had rung a bell somewhere and she wanted to ask Phil about it.

She had also done the best she could to hide her red nose with cunningly applied make-up and had taken Nurofen so she didn't have to reach for her hankie all evening, although she could still feel that irritating tickle at the back of her throat. From experience, she knew that it responded best to red wine, but they were driving to the restaurant separately and she would have to take it easy on the alcohol. Before she left, she made sure she had her beeper and mobile, though she hoped to hell she wouldn't have to use either.

Phil was already waiting at the bar, a half pint in front of him, and he waved her over. 'They're just preparing the table,' he said. 'Won't be a minute. Drink?'

'Mmm, I think I'll just have a grapefruit juice for now,

thanks.' That way, Annie thought, she'd be able to have a couple of glasses of wine with dinner.

Phil ordered the drinks without comment. That was one of the things she liked about him. He never questioned you or made a snarky comment the way some people did when you didn't order real booze, or if you happened to be a vegetarian. All he'd asked her the first time they went out to dinner was whether her reasons for not eating meat were humanitarian or health. A bit of both, she had replied.

'Busy day?' he said.

Annie nodded. 'The boat fire. You must have heard about it by now.'

'Yes, of course. Any leads yet, or shouldn't I ask?'

'Probably best not to,' Annie said with a smile, 'but no, nothing really.'

The maître d' came over and led them to their table. It was in a quiet corner of the restaurant, a table with a scarlet cloth, lit by a shaded lamp, polished silverware gleaming. Wallpaper music piped softly in the background, Beatles via Mantovani, not loud enough to interfere with conversation, but audible enough to create an atmosphere of soporific calm. Cosy and intimate.

Annie watched Phil as he studied the menu: the small, boyish mouth, slightly receding dark hair, just showing a tinge of grey here and there, the watchful and intelligent grey eyes. He must be seven or eight years older than her, she thought, probably in his early forties. Banks was older than her, too. Why was it she went for older men? Did she feel safer with them? Was she looking for a father figure? She almost laughed out loud, thinking what Ray, her dad, would have to say about that.

In some ways, Annie thought, Phil was actually quite

similar to Banks: a little traditional, conservative even, on the surface, but broad-minded and free-spirited underneath it all. Besides, it wasn't so much age that mattered to her, but intelligence, maturity and a sense of culture. Not that career and money didn't matter, but most of the mobile-flaunting men she had dated of her own age had been interested in them to the exclusion of other things, and it was the other things that interested Annie most.

She decided on a salad with pears, walnuts and crumbled blue cheese to start with and a wild mushroom risotto as her main course, then put the menu aside. Phil was still studying his.

'Problem?' Annie asked.

'Just can't decide between the venison and the guineafowl.'

'Sorry, can't help you there.'

Phil laughed and put his menu down. 'I don't suppose you can.' He took out a coin from his pocket, spun it in the air and caught it. 'Heads,' he said, looking at the way it had landed. 'Venison.'

'How do I know you didn't cheat?'

'Actually, I did,' he confessed. 'It was supposed to be heads for the guineafowl, but I realized at the last moment I really wanted venison. Wine?'

'Please.'

Phil chose a bottle of 1998 Chianti Classico. Not too ostentatious, Annie thought, but not cheap, either.

'How's the Turner?' she asked when they had given their orders.

'Still resting comfortably. It should be up for auction soon. The Tate's interested, naturally, but so are the V&A and several private collectors.'

'It's definitely genuine, then?'

'Oh, yes. So the team of experts attest.'

'It wasn't just your opinion?'

'You must be kidding. Not a chance. It would be immodest of me to say my voice doesn't carry some weight, but a discovery like that comes under incredible scrutiny. Any art forger worth his salt wouldn't pick a big-name artist like Turner or Constable to copy. Forgers with any sense stick to less famous artists. Turner's a national treasure. You might as well try and pass off a da Vinci or a Van Gogh.'

'It has been done, though, hasn't it?'

'Oh, yes. It has been done. Tom Keating, for one, comes to mind. He did Rembrandt, among others. And Eric Hebborn did all right with Corot and Augustus John. But that was in the fifties and sixties. These days there are far more forensic tests and, as I said, a battery of experts to get past. This one's been verified through fingerprints among other things.'

'Fingerprints?'

'I thought that might interest you. They can last a very long time, you know. Prints have even been found on prehistoric cave paintings and pottery unearthed at archaeological digs.'

'But how can you verify them? Turner's been dead for years.'

'Painting can be a messy business. You get your hands dirty, and as often as not an artist applies his fingers to the paint and the paper or canvas during the process of painting. Especially oils, but even with watercolours like this one. If you examine the surface carefully with a magnifying glass – a bit like Sherlock Holmes, I suppose – you can often find very good fingerprints.'

'But how do you check against the artist's original?'

'That's the problem. It's not always possible and the results are sometimes dubious, but in the case of Turner it actually works very well.'

'Why?'

'His prints are on file in the Tate archives.'

'Of course,' said Annie.

'Naturally, you need an impeccable source. A painting with credible provenance leading right back to the artist. But not many other people would have been in a position to get their fingerprints in the paint on a Turner canvas. He was known to work alone, without assistants.'

Annie nodded.

'And it's been done before,' Phil went on. 'A Canadian called Peter Paul Biro pioneered the whole technique some years ago. He worked with the West Yorkshire police to identify a Turner called *Landscape with Rainbow* in 1995. I'm surprised you didn't hear about it.'

'In 1995 I was a mere DC in Somerset and Avon.'

'Well, that explains it.'

'We tend not to notice that much outside our immediate areas,' Annie explained. 'You get focused on the job in hand and . . .'

'I understand,' said Phil.

'How much do you reckon it will go for?'

Phil pursed his lips and thought for a moment, then said, 'About three hundred thousand. Maybe a bit more, seeing as it's part of a set.'

The wine came and the waiter first showed off the bottle, then presented the cork and a tiny splash in Phil's glass. 'Just pour it,' said Phil. 'I'm sure if it's corked you'll bring us another bottle.'

'Of course, sir,' said the waiter. Annie wasn't used to such deference in Yorkshire restaurants, or restaurants anywhere, for that matter. But there was something about Phil that seemed to bring it out in people. Maybe he looked like someone famous, though Annie couldn't think who. Stefan Nowak was the only other person she could think of who had the same sort of aura. She could imagine waiters being deferential around Stefan too.

Phil sipped some wine and looked around. 'Turner actually dined here once,' he said, 'on the same tour he did the sketches for that watercolour.'

'Really? I knew the place was old but . . .'

'Well, I don't think it was the same chef. Mostly he complained about the weather. Bit of a miserable bugger, was J. M. W. Bit of a miser, too.'

'He'd fit in well up here, then.'

'I've never found Yorkshire folk to be anything less than generous.'

'I agree, actually. It's just one of the myths around these parts and people sometimes seem quite proud of it, the parsimony.'

'They're canny with their money, I'll give them that. But there's no harm in not being a wastrel as my grandfather always used to say.'

Annie almost asked him about his Yorkshire grandparents, but she held herself back. She didn't feel like getting into family histories and reminiscences tonight. There was something about other people's families that always disturbed her a bit.

The starters arrived and both ate in silence for a while. 'One thing I never got around to asking you is why this painting went missing for so long,' Annie said, when she had finished the last walnut. 'I mean, seeing as it was a Turner and part of a set.'

'There are plenty of Turners unaccounted for,' said Phil.

'As you know, this one was part of a series of twenty watercolours Turner painted for the *History of Richmond-shire*. He delivered the first twelve to the publisher for engraving in spring, 1817, and the other eight in December the same year. After that, the originals were sold to various buyers. The one we saw, *Richmond Castle and Town*, was one of six that the publishers of the history were selling off at cost. Twenty-five guineas. Can you believe it? Previously the only record of it seems to have been at an exhibition of the Northern Society in Leeds in 1822. After that, nothing. Anyway, three of the twenty went missing, two untraced – until last summer – and one was destroyed in a fire.'

Annie's ears pricked up. 'A fire?'

'Ah, I see. You're thinking about the boat fire you're investigating, aren't you? Well, I hate to disappoint you, but this was decades ago. There's no connection.'

'But there's still one more missing from the set?'

'Yes. *Ingleborough from Hornby Castle Terrace*. Hasn't been seen since the turn of the last century. It fetched a record price when it was sold at Christie's in 1881 to a certain W. Law Esq. Two thousand guineas, in fact. It would be nice to find it and complete the set, of course, but it's not as if they're all collected in one place.'

'Real *Antiques Roadshow*.'

'You may well laugh, but it happens more often than you think. That dusty old frame in the attic. The ugly landscape old Aunt Eunice's grandad hid away in the cellar.'

Annie laughed. 'You could hardly call the Turner ugly.'

'Of course not. But somebody thought little enough of it to bury it under a couple of layers of insulation.'

As they ate their meals, they talked about paintings and

films they liked, and Annie discovered that they were both fans of Alec Guinness in the old Ealing comedies, though Phil preferred *The Captain's Paradise* to Annie's favourite, *The Lavender Hill Mob*. They both loved *The Horse's Mouth*, though.

When it was time for dessert, Annie decided to hell with her diet – not that she was really on one, but she was always full of good intentions – and went for the crème brûlée. She resisted the cognac, though, and chose café au lait. She was pleased that she had managed to restrict herself to only one glass of wine.

'Have you ever heard of a local artist called Thomas McMahon?' she asked Phil after her first mouth-watering spoonful.

Phil frowned. 'McMahon? Can't say I have, no. Why? He any good?'

'I probably shouldn't be telling you,' she said, 'but it'll be in the papers tomorrow, and probably on the radio and TV tonight. He's most likely the victim in the boat fires. One of the victims. I just wondered if you'd heard of him at all, come across him in your line of business.'

'I don't come across many living artists, I'm afraid,' said Phil.

'From all accounts, after a promising start he dropped out of the scene some years ago, made a living painting landscapes for tourists.'

'Then I'd have even less reason to have heard of him. Always the detective, eh, Annie?'

Annie blushed. There was some truth in that. She was slowly and indirectly getting around to what she had wanted to sound him out on. 'One thing we found out – my boss discovered it, actually – was that he frequented an antiquarian bookshop on Market Street and that he bought a number of old books and prints.'

'Nothing unusual in that, surely?'

'We don't think he was very well off and, besides, most of the stuff he bought was worthless. Worthless but old.'

Phil looked at her, and she saw the beginnings of understanding in his eyes. 'I was just thinking,' she went on, 'that—' Right then her beeper went off. The station. One or two of the other diners gave her dirty looks. 'Oh, shit,' she said. 'Sorry. I mean, I'd better . . . I won't be long.'

'OK. Don't worry. I'll be waiting.'

Annie hustled outside and fumbled with her mobile. 'Yes?'

'DI Cabbot?'

'Yes.'

'DCI Banks said to tell you there's been another one – another fire, that is – and he wants you to get out to Jennings Field asap. You know where it is?'

'I know it,' said Annie. 'Thanks. I'm on my way.'

Bollocks, she thought, putting her phone away and re-entering the restaurant. Inconsiderate arsonist, spoiling her evening. She just had time to make a quick apology to Phil before heading out.

'Can I give you a lift?' he asked.

'No thanks,' said Annie. 'I'll go in my own car.' She could just imagine the expression on Banks's face if she turned up at a crime scene in Phil's BMW. She wasn't even dressed for standing around in an open field on a cold night, she realized, as she threw on her elegant but lightweight black overcoat.

Just to end their evening together on a perfect note, Annie found herself unable to get her handkerchief to her mouth fast enough to stop a sneeze and ended up spraying the entire table with germs. Phil just smiled and gestured for her to go. Red-faced now, as well as red-nosed, Annie went.

7

Jennings Field lay on the eastern outskirts of Eastvale, beyond the East Side estate and the railway lines, where the landscape flattened out towards the fertile vale that lay between the Yorkshire Dales and the North York Moors. It was a clear, cold night; the day's light mist had completely dissipated. The stars shone icily bright and lights twinkled from distant villages, where the good citizens would all be sitting nice and warm in front of their tellies watching Des Lynam. A half moon dripped its milky light on the far woods, silvering the bare lattices of the treetops.

The call had disturbed Banks part way through *Goldfinger* – the bit where the laser is slowly creeping up towards Bond's privates – a takeaway chicken with fried rice and his second can of lager. He stood with his hands in his pockets, breathing out plumes of air, and watched Annie get out of her car and sign in with the uniformed officer at the perimeter. A couple of reporters shouted questions at her, but she ignored them. One of them whistled as she ducked under the police tape, and Annie froze for just a moment, then carried on walking. She was nicely dressed, Banks noticed, when she got in range of the lights the fire department had erected, and was she wearing a bit more make-up than usual? Out with her new boyfriend, then? Well, it *was* Saturday night, after all.

She caught him looking and blushed. 'What?'

'Nothing,' Banks said. 'You look nice.'

Annie rolled her eyes. 'So what have we got?'

The remains of a caravan, the sole dwelling in the field, parked at the far end, just under the shelter of a couple of beech trees, still smouldered, and an acrid stink of burned rubber and plastic wafted their way. There was nothing left of the roof and sides, only a skeleton of soot-blackened metal struts remained, and the innards lay open to the elements. Water from the fire hoses dripped to the ground and puddled.

'Anyone inside?' Annie asked.

'We've got one body,' Banks told her. 'And luckily this time we think we know who it is.'

Annie blew on her bare hands. She was wearing simple black court shoes, tan tights and a long black coat, elegant rather than practical, Banks noticed. Going-out-for-a-meal clothes. Her feet must be cold.

Banks pointed to a man talking to DC Winsome Jackman over by the group of parked cars and two gleaming red fire appliances. 'That's Jack Mellor. He's a regular at the Fox and Hounds, about half a mile down the road in the nearest village, and he reported the fire. He's still pretty shaken. He says he saw the flames as he was walking his dog down the road at about nine o'clock for a couple of pints and a chat with his mates as usual.' Banks pointed away from the village lights. 'He lives in Ash Cottage, about two hundred yards in that direction. Says the chap who lived in the caravan was another Fox and Hounds regular. Quiet bloke, by all accounts. Harmless. Name of Roland Gardiner.'

'He lived alone in the caravan?'

'Yes. Been there at least a couple of years now, according to our Mr Mellor. There's no car in evidence. Not even any wheels on the caravan. See the way it's propped up on blocks? Anyway, this field's common land despite its name. Nobody knows who the hell Jennings was. I'm sure the local council's been trying to squeeze Gardiner out, just like British Waterways was trying to get rid of the barge squatters, but for better or for worse . . . this was Gardiner's home.'

'What the hell's going on?' Annie said. 'Is someone trying to set fire to all the eyesores and down-and-outs in the area?'

'It certainly looks that way, doesn't it?' said Banks. 'But let's not jump to conclusions. We've no evidence yet that there's any connection between the fires. And they weren't down-and-outs, despite their living conditions. Don't forget that Thomas McMahon was an artist who managed to make a living painting local landscapes for the tourist trade. I think he *chose* to live the way he did. Even Mark Siddons works at the Eastvale College building site. None of the victims were really spongers or bums.'

'The girl was a junkie, though.'

'Well,' said Banks, watching Geoff Hamilton guide the SOCO in packaging debris from the caravan, 'there might be any number of reasons for that.' He was thinking, as Mark had been thinking earlier that evening, about Patrick Aspern, with whom he was far from finished. 'Besides, in my book, that makes her ill, not criminal.'

'You know what I mean,' Annie said. 'And you also know that I agree with you. All I'm suggesting is that a junkie loses a certain . . . strength of will, that someone who needs something so much will do whatever it takes to get it, sponging being the least of it.'

'Point taken,' said Banks.

The local constable, PC Locke, came over to them. 'Mr Mellor wants to know if he can go to the Fox and Hounds,' he said. 'Says the dog's freezing its balls off – if you'll pardon my language, Ma'am – and he needs a pick-me-up.'

'I can understand that,' said Banks. 'Look, this isn't exactly kosher,' he went on, taking Locke aside and lowering his voice. 'Strictly speaking, we have to consider Mellor a suspect, but why don't you accompany him to the Fox and Hounds and wait for us? We've got to talk to him somewhere and it might as well be there. At least I suppose it'll be warm.'

'Yes, sir.'

'And keep a sharp eye on his alcohol intake. He's allowed one, a small one, for the shock, but no more. I don't want him pissed when we get there to question him, OK?'

'Understood, sir.'

'And one more thing.'

'Sir?'

Banks gestured over to the road, where the phalanx of media people jostled for space and pointed cameras. 'Avoid them. Mum's the word, OK?'

'I think I can manage that, sir. We'll go the back way.'

PC Locke walked over to Mellor and they headed towards the back lane, the dog on its leash trotting along beside them, and before they had got very far they vanished over a stile into the darkness. Banks hoped that no bright spark of a reporter decided to go and check out the local pub. They'd get there eventually, he knew, but they wouldn't leave the scene yet, not while there was still some action.

'Are you sure that was wise?' Annie asked.

'Probably not, but I don't think Mellor started the fire. Let's have a look at the damage.'

They walked closer to the burned-out caravan. In the bright artificial light, it was easy to spot the pooling at the centre of the floor, one sign of accelerant use, and Banks fancied he could even smell a whiff of petrol on the air. Geoff Hamilton's electronic 'sniffer' had already detected something and confirmed that some sort of accelerant had been used. The damage to the caravan was far worse than that to the boats. It was also such a small scene, and the remains of the floor were so unstable, that Hamilton and DS Stefan Nowak were trying to do the best they could by working their ways in from the outside edges, not trampling on the flimsy caravan floor at all. Peter Darby was videotaping their progress, occasionally swapping his camcorder for his trusty Pentax and taking a flurry of stills.

At the centre of it all, by the pooling that marked the seat of the blaze, lay a blackened body, this one on its side, curled in the familiar pugilistic pose. It had been hard to spot at first among the charred furniture and fixtures, but once you managed to separate it from its context, you couldn't miss it. Hamilton said that the warped and cracked object beside the body was a glass. There had been a glass lying beside Tom McMahon's body too, Banks remembered, wondering if it was relevant. He noticed Annie give a little shiver and he didn't think it was caused by the cold.

Hamilton and Stefan Nowak came walking towards them.

'Anything?' Banks asked.

'Pooling, traces of accelerant,' said Hamilton.

'Same as before?'

'Looks like it.'

'Anything to connect the two?'

Hamilton shifted from foot to foot. 'Well,' he said, 'apart from the fact that we've had two suspicious fires in out-of-the-way places in two days, when we're usually only unlucky enough to get two a year, I'd say no.'

It was an important point. Banks needed to know whether they were now running two separate arson investigations or just one. 'How long would it take for a caravan that size to be reduced to that state?' he asked.

'Half an hour or so. Whatever caused it was hot and fast.'

'What about the accelerant used?'

'This one smells like petrol to me – you can smell it yourself – though I'd rather wait for the chromatograph results and the spectral analysis, just to be certain.'

'The previous victim, or one of them, was an artist,' Banks mused aloud. 'So it was reasonable to assume that he'd have turpentine somewhere around. We don't know what Mr Gardiner was yet, but the killer clearly brought his own accelerant this time. Maybe he *knew* both victims, knew that McMahon would have turps handy to start the fire, but also knew that he had to bring his own to Gardiner's caravan. But why bring petrol instead of turps?'

'Probably had some on hand,' said Hamilton. 'Most people do, if they've got a car. It'd be easy enough to siphon a little off. And safer than going to a shop to buy turps. Someone might have remembered him.'

'Good point,' said Banks. 'What about the victim?'

'What about him?'

'Well, he didn't just lie there and let himself burn to death, did he?'

'How the hell would I know what he did?'

'Speculate. Use your imagination.'

Hamilton snorted. 'That's not my job. I'll wait for the test results and the post-mortem, thank you very much.'

Banks sighed. 'OK,' he said. 'If the victim had been conscious, and capable, might he have been able to escape this fire?'

'He might have been,' Hamilton conceded, 'unless he was overcome by smoke or fumes. They can disorient a person very quickly.'

'Whoever set the fire had to be inside the caravan at the time, didn't he?'

'It looks that way from the pattern of pooling. If he'd poured it through the window or tossed it through the door, for example, you'd see evidence of that in the trail, and in the charring.'

'And there isn't any?'

'Not that I can see.'

'And whoever set the fire got out?'

'Well, there's only one body.'

'What about access, escape route?'

'There's a lane runs by the back, behind the trees and the wall.'

'OK,' said Banks. He turned from Hamilton and looked at the charred, smoking caravan again. There wasn't much more they could do at the scene. Best leave it to Stefan and his team, see what they could turn up, if anything.

Banks turned to Annie. 'Let's go and talk to Mr Mellor,' he said. 'I could do with a bloody stiff drink.'

Annie looked at her watch. 'It's after closing time,' she said.

Banks smiled. 'Well, I think being a copper ought to have *some* advantages, don't you?'

•

Mark ran fast, away from the fire, until he was exhausted, and then slowed to walking speed. All the time his mind was filled with echoes and rage. The voices of Lenny and Sal became those of his mother and Crazy Nick as they argued about him drunkenly downstairs, getting louder and louder until they ended in blows and screams. *Get rid of him! Get rid of him! Get rid of him! He should have been drowned at birth!*

Mark put his hands over his ears as he ran, but it didn't do any good. The voices went on, from inside. *Always in the bloody way. Can't you do something about him?* He remembered the nights spent locked in the dank, spidery cellar alone, with no light, no warmth, no human company. And he remembered the time when he was sixteen and got brave enough to fight back, how he had smacked Crazy Nick right in the mouth and how both of them were too stunned to do anything when they saw the blood start to flow.

You little fucker! Look what you did.

Mark knew right there and then that he was fighting for his life, so he laid into Crazy Nick with all he'd got, punching and kicking until Nick was on the floor gargling blood, and Mark's mother was beating on his back with her hard little fists. He smashed a chair over Crazy Nick's head and that was it, the last night he spent at home, the night he ran, with his mother's screams of revenge and hatred burning in his ears. Just like he was running now.

He stopped for breath and looked around, realized he didn't have a clue where he was. He had headed east from

Lenny's, he knew that much, beyond the town limits, so he was out in the country now. If he looked behind him, he could see the lights of Eastvale, even hear a distant train going by. He wished he had enough money to take a train somewhere. Or a plane. That would be even better. *Ulan Bator.* But then he realized he didn't even have a passport, so he was stuck here. Stuck here for ever. But not in Eastvale. He was never going back there. Not if he could help it.

He was on a dark country road with trees and drystone walls on either side. The flames were well behind him now and he thought he could hear the sirens of fire engines. Good luck to them. They didn't do Tina much good. He thought of her fragile, pretty face, her slight form. Tina hadn't had a chance. Tears stained Mark's face as he felt the waves of guilt tearing him apart for the hundredth time. If only he hadn't gone chasing after Mandy, if only, if only, if only . . .

Dark winter fields stretched away from him on both sides of the road, bare branches clawing like talons at the starlit sky, and now and then he could make out the lonely glow of a distant farmhouse or clustered lights in a small village. For a moment, Banks's words of warning came back to him, that he might be in danger, that he might be the next victim, and he felt a tremor of fear. Shadows moved and rustling sounds came from behind him. But it was only the wind in the trees. Why would anybody want to kill him? He didn't know anything. But Tina hadn't known anything either.

Mark didn't know where he was going; all he could do was keep walking. If he kept going on, eventually he'd end up at the seaside. Maybe he'd live there. It was easy enough to get a job at the seaside, no questions asked, with all those tourists to take care of. Drake from the squat had told him that. Drake had lived in Blackpool and worked at the Pleasure Beach on one of the rides. Made a fucking pile, he said, and pulled plenty of talent too. But not in January. Blackpool was a cold and lonely place in January. Still, maybe there'd be some building work. There was always building. And there was the sea. Mark loved the sea.

Running had warmed him up, but now, as he slowed his pace, he realized he was cold, cold as the night he'd watched the fire on the boats. Was it only the other day? It seemed like years ago. Tina had only been dead for two days. And was the rest of his lifetime without her going to be as miserable as it was now? Maybe he should just do away with himself. That would serve them all right, wouldn't it? His mother – bless her miserable little soul and may she rot in hell – Crazy Nick, Lenny, Sal, the police, the lot of them. That's what he'd do; he'd top himself. Join Tina. Even save the bloke who'd killed her from having to kill him, too. But he knew he didn't really have the guts to do it. Besides, no matter what the religious people said, Mark didn't believe in reunions beyond the grave.

He pulled the fleece-lined coat tight around him, tightened up the collar around his neck. Wearing a copper's clothes. That was one for the books. It would serve them all right if he did die, though, wouldn't it? He wasn't even sure any more whether he cared or not, whether it wasn't such a good idea after all. Everything inside was going numb, like his feet, and he realized he didn't even need to do anything painful to die. It would be easy. All he had to do was find an out-of-the-way spot – plenty of them around here – and lie down in the cold. They said it was just like falling asleep. You got cold, then numb, so you couldn't feel it, then you went into a coma and died. Especially as he was halfway there already. He saw a stile and the silhouette of a ruined barn in the next field, a little moonlight shining through the empty windows. That would do, he thought, at least for the night. That would do just fine. And if he died there . . . well, that would serve the bastards right, wouldn't it?

•

It was well after official closing time when Banks and Annie joined Jack Mellor at the table nearest the fireplace in the Fox and Hounds, but the landlord was not in any hurry to lock up as long as the police were drinking there.

Banks dismissed PC Locke, who had been babysitting Mellor since his initial questioning at the scene, and ordered three double brandies, breaking any number of laws and police rules in doing so. He didn't give a damn. It was bloody freezing out there and he needed something to warm him up. Annie seemed glad of the fire, too, and sat as close as she could. She didn't seem to mind the brandy, either, judging by the way she knocked back her first sip. Only Mellor, the dog sleeping curled on the floor by his side, let his glass sit without touching it, but he'd had one already, and his moon-shaped face was looking a little less pale than it had at the scene. The landlord tossed a couple more logs on the fire. They crackled and spat, throwing out enough heat for Banks to take off his overcoat. Annie crossed her legs and took her notebook out, giving Banks a look when she caught him glancing at the gold chain on her ankle.

'Can you start by telling us exactly what happened tonight?' Banks asked.

Mellor stared into the flames. 'It's still quite a shock,' he said. 'Seeing something like that . . . even from a distance . . . someone you know.'

Thank God he hadn't seen the body close up, Banks thought. 'I'm sure it is,' he said. 'Take your time.'

Mellor nodded. His cheeks wobbled. 'I was walking Sandy here as usual. We always dropped by the Fox for a couple of jars of an evening, ever since my wife died.'

'I'm sorry to hear it,' said Banks.

'Well, these things happen.' Mellor reached forward and took a sip of brandy. 'Anyway, as I said, it was habit. Creatures of routine. Boring sort of life, I suppose.'

'And tonight?'

'I saw the fire through the trees. I think Sandy must have smelled it first because he was acting strange.' He leaned over and stroked the dog's glossy ruff. Banks could see from the light ginger fur how he had got his name. Sandy stirred, opening one brown eye and cocking an ear, then drifted off again. 'Anyway, we hurried over there, but . . . I could see immediately there was nothing I could do.'

'What time was this?'

'I usually set off at nine, pretty much on the dot, and it's about ten minutes from home, so . . .'

'Ten past nine, then?'

'About that, yes.'

Banks knew that the emergency call had been logged in at 9.13 p.m. 'Where did you call from?'

'Phone box down the road. It's only a short distance. I hurried as best I could, but . . .' He patted his stomach. 'I'm afraid I'm not built for speed.'

Banks had seen the phone box and estimated that Mellor's timing was pretty much accurate.

'I don't have a mobile phone,' he explained. 'No need

for one, really. No one to call and no one who'd want to ring me.'

That didn't stop most people owning a mobile, Banks thought, remembering the sad, pointless conversations he'd overheard during the last few years: 'It's me. I'm on the train. We're just leaving the station now. It's raining up here.' And so on and so on.

'I take it you were by yourself at home?'

'Yes. I live alone now – apart from Sandy, of course.'

'What did you do after you'd rung the fire brigade?'

'I just waited.'

'Where?'

'By the gate.'

'You didn't approach the caravan?'

Mellor sniffed and wiped his eyes with the back of his hand. 'I knew there was nothing I could do by then,' he said. 'Just watch it burn. I felt so useless. The firemen were very fast getting here.'

'It's all right, Mr Mellor,' Banks assured him. 'Nobody could have done anything by then.' Geoff Hamilton had said the fire would have taken less than half an hour to do the damage it did, and it was well under way by the time Mellor saw it. That would mean that it had probably been set between about eight forty-five and nine o'clock. 'Did you see anyone in the area?' he asked.

'Nobody.'

'Nobody passed you on the road?'

'No. I didn't see a soul. Never do at that time of night.'

'Any cars?'

'One or two. We get a fair bit of traffic, especially on a Saturday night. It's the main road between Eastvale and Thirsk.'

'Remember anything about them?'

'I'm afraid not.'

'Anything suspicious or unusual happen?'

'No.'

Banks took a sip of fiery brandy. His knees were getting hot from the fire and he noticed Annie's shins turning red under her tights. 'All right, Mr Mellor,' he went on, 'what can you tell us about the victim?'

'Roland? Not much. He was rather a reserved sort of man.'

'But you drank with him regularly?'

'Well, neither of us is a big drinker. We'd pass the time of evening over a couple of halves, maybe.'

'How often?'

'Two or three times a week. Though sometimes I didn't see him for days.'

'Did he ever say where he was on those occasions?'

'No.'

'But the two of you must have talked quite a bit?'

'Oh, yes. Current events. Politics. Sports. That sort of thing. Roland was very well informed.'

'Did he ever tell you anything about himself?'

'A little, I suppose. It's . . .'

'Mr Mellor,' Banks said, sensing some sort of generic regard for the confidences of a dead friend, 'it looks very much as if Mr Gardiner is dead. And anything you tell us would be in the strictest confidence, of course.'

'What do you mean it looks as if Roland is dead? Is he or isn't he?'

'There was a body found inside the caravan,' Banks said carefully. 'It's dead. Unfortunately, we haven't been able to identify it yet, so we're being cautious. Can you think of anyone else who might have been in the caravan?'

Mellor shook his head. 'No. Roland valued his privacy and he lived alone, like me.'

'Then we're assuming it's him, just between you and me, but we can't make any official statement until there's been a positive identification. Right now, anything you can tell us will be a great help. What did he look like?'

'Nothing to write home about, really. I suppose he was about five foot seven or eight, a little overweight.' He patted his belly. 'Not quite as much me, though. Receding hair, a touch of grey here and there. Hooked nose. Not really big, but hooked. Pale blue eyes.'

Mark Siddons had seen a man with a hooked nose visiting Tom McMahon's boat on one occasion, Banks remembered. 'How old was he?'

'Early to mid-forties, I'd say.'

'Go on.'

'That's about it, really. Dressed casually most of the time. At least, I never saw him in a suit. Just jeans and a cotton shirt. Soft spoken. Polite. Didn't laugh much.'

'Did he have any living relatives?'

'Not that I know of. He never talked about his family. I think his parents are dead and he never mentioned any brothers or sisters.'

'Was he married?'

'Well, you see, that's just it, that's the problem,' said Mellor. 'Roland was divorced. About two years ago, just around the time he came to Jennings Field.'

'What happened?'

'He lost his job and his wife walked out on him. Another man. All he had left were the caravan and the car, the way he told me, and he drove around until he found somewhere he could stay, and he's been there ever since.'

'How did he survive?'

'He was on the social.'

'Was he from around these parts?'

'Yes. Not broad-spoken, though, but as if he'd travelled a bit. You know, spent time down south or abroad.'

'What happened to the car?'

'Roland just left it there, where he'd parked his caravan. He said he'd no use for it. He'd given up on life. He didn't want to go anywhere. In the end it rusted and fell apart.'

'How long ago?'

'Maybe a year or so.'

'Where is it now?'

'Hauled away for scrap metal and spare parts.'

'Do you know what Mr Gardiner did for a living?'

'Yes. He worked for a small office-supplies company.'

'What happened?'

'Competition got too big and too fierce. They couldn't afford the kind of discounts and delivery the big boys were offering, so they started cutting costs. Roland was quite bitter about it.'

'Do you know where he lived when he was with his wife?'

'They lived in Eastvale, down on that new Daleside estate. I'm sorry, but he never told me the actual address.'

'I know it,' said Banks. The Daleside estate, only three years old, was a mix of council and private housing built on the site of the old Gallows View fields on the western edge of town. There had been a short debate in the council over the name of the place, some suggesting they stick with Gallows View for historical purposes, others arguing that it would put off potential buyers. In the end progress won out and it became officially 'Daleside', but most Eastvalers still called it the Gallows View estate. It was the area where Banks had worked on his first case in Eastvale, although he felt no sentimental attachment. The old row of cottages and the corner shop had all been demolished now to make way for the newer houses.

'Is she still there?'

'He never said otherwise. I assume she stayed on in the house.'

Annie made a note. The ex-wife wouldn't be hard to find, Banks thought.

'How did he feel about his wife?' Banks asked.

'I got the impression that he'd had a hard time supporting her taste for exotic holidays abroad and creature comforts as much as anything else. Then when he loses his job she chucks him and walks out. Talk about kicking a bloke while he's down.'

'Yes, I suppose I'd feel pretty bitter about that myself,' said Banks. It certainly gave Gardiner a good motive for killing his wife, but that was not what had happened.

Annie looked at Banks. His situation wasn't quite the same, but he knew – and he knew that Annie knew – that it was close enough to all intents and purposes. Maybe the only real difference was that Banks hadn't pushed so hard at his career only for Sandra's sake – Lord knows her tastes were pretty modest – but more for his own needs. Still, she had left him – out of the blue, it had seemed at the time – he had almost lost his job and his sanity, and now she was living with Sean and Sinéad in London. Banks certainly understood bitterness and betrayal.

'Did she ever visit him at the caravan?' Banks asked.

'Not that I know of. He never said.'

'Were they actually divorced or just separated?' Banks

was wondering whether the ex Mrs Gardiner needed her husband permanently out of the way for some reason.

'He said divorced. In fact I saw him the day he told me the decree came through and he got quite maudlin at first, then angry. He had a bit too much to drink that night, I remember.'

There went one theory. 'Did he ever have any visitors at all?'

'He never spoke of any and I can't see the caravan from my cottage. I do remember seeing someone leaving the place once while I was walking down the lane, but that's all.'

'When was this?'

'Few months ago. Summer.'

'A man or a woman?'

'A man.'

'What did he look like?'

'Too far away to see and he was walking away from me.'

'Tall or short, black or white?'

Mellor raised his eyebrows. 'White. And maybe a bit taller than you. Not a big man, though. Carried himself well.'

'But you didn't see what he looked like.'

'No, I'm only going on the way he walked. It can tell you more than you think, you know, sometimes, the way a man walks. They do say when you're in the cities to walk as if you know where you're going, no-nonsense and all, and you're less likely to get mugged. That sort of walk.'

'Which direction did he take?'

'Towards the car park off the lane, behind the caravan. It's quite handy, really. There's some waterfalls across

Jennings Field. Not more than a trickle, really, but you know what tourists are like. So the council cleared a small car park. Pay and display.'

It was the area of easiest access to the caravan. The SOCOs had taped it off and would be searching come daylight. 'Did you see him drive away?'

'I'm afraid not. The exit's on the lane behind the field, behind Roland's caravan. It's hidden by the trees and a wall. I must admit, though, I was a little curious as I hadn't seen or heard of a visitor to Roland's place before.'

'Did you ever see a dark-coloured Jeep in the area?'

'No. Sorry.'

'Thanks anyway,' Banks said. 'Did you ask Mr Gardiner about his visitor?'

'Yes, but he just tapped the side of his nose. Said it was an old friend. You know,' Mellor said, swirling the remains of the brandy in his glass, 'when I first got to know Roland I worried about him a lot.'

'Why is that?'

'He seemed prey to fits of depression. Sometimes he wouldn't leave the caravan for days, not even to come here. When he did come and you asked him if he was all right, he'd shrug it off and say something about taking the "black dog" for a walk.'

Black dog. Winston Churchill's term for the depression that hounded him all his life. 'Do you think he might have been suicidal?'

Mellor thought for a moment. 'There were times,' he said. 'Yes. I worried he might do himself harm.'

Fire wasn't a common method of suicide, Banks knew. The last case he'd come across was of a man chaining himself to the steering wheel of his car, pouring petrol all around and setting it alight. He'd left the windows closed, though, and there wasn't enough oxygen in the interior of the car for a fire to take hold, so when the brief flames had consumed it all the man died of asphyxiation, with hardly a mark on him. Still, Banks had to consider every possibility. 'Do you think he might have done this himself?' he asked Mellor.

'Start the fire? Good Lord, no. Roland wouldn't do anything irresponsible like that. Someone else might have got hurt. One of the firemen, for example. And it would certainly be a painful way to go. No. He had some strong pills from the doctor, he told me once. Sleeping pills. I don't know what they were called. Apparently he had terrible trouble sleeping. Nightmares and so on. If he was going to go, that was the way he would have done it.'

Black dog. Nightmares. Roland Gardiner certainly sounded like a troubled man. Was that all down to him losing his job and his wife leaving him, or were there other reasons?

'Besides,' Mellor went on, 'things had been looking up for him recently.'

Banks glanced at Annie. 'Oh?'

'Yes. He seemed a lot more cheerful, a lot more optimistic.'

'Did he say why?'

'Just that he'd met an old friend.'

'What old friend?'

'He didn't elaborate on it. Like I said, Roland was a secretive sort of chap.'

'The same old friend who visited him at the caravan?'

'Might have been. It was about the same time.'

'Last summer?'

'Yes.'

'When was the last time you saw Roland?'

Mellor thought for a moment. 'Last Wednesday, I think it was. He lent me a book.'

'What book was that?'

'Just a history book. We were both interested in Victorian England.'

Banks stood up. 'Thanks very much, Mr Mellor. You've been a great help. Need a ride home?'

'Thank you. Normally I'd walk, but it's late, cold, and I've had a bit of a shock. You've got room for Sandy, too?

'Of course. No trouble.'

Annie's car was still back at Jennings Field, so they all crammed into Banks's Renault, Sandy curling up beside Mellor on the back seat, and headed towards Ash Cottage, the heater on full. In a few minutes the interior of the car was warm and Banks found himself feeling sleepy from the brandy. He knew he wasn't over the limit, just tired. They dropped Mellor and Sandy, and Banks handed over his card, 'In case you remember anything else.' Then Banks drove Annie back to the field. They sat a moment in his car, the engine running and heater still on, watching the activity around the burned-out caravan. Things were definitely on the wane, but Stefan was still there, as were Geoff Hamilton and a group of firefighters. Both appliances had gone.

'Christ, I *hate* fires,' said Banks.

'Why? Have you ever been in one?'

'No, but I have nightmares about it.' He massaged his temples. 'Once, way back when I was on the Met, I got called to an arson scene. Terraced house in Hammersmith. Some sort of arranged marriage gone wrong and the offended family pours petrol through the letter box of the other lot.' He paused. 'Nine people died in that fire. Nine people. Most of the time you couldn't tell the bodies from the debris, except for one bloke who still had a boiling red blister on his skull. And the smell . . . Jesus. But you know what stuck in my mind most?'

'Tell me,' said Annie.

'It was this little girl. She looked as if she was kneeling by her bed with her hands clasped, saying her prayers. Burnt to a crisp, but still there, stuck for ever in that same position. Praying.' Banks shook his head.

Annie touched his arm gently.

'Anyway,' Banks went on, shaking off the memory, 'what do you think?'

'I don't know what to think, really. I've got to admit it seems to be stretching coincidence to have two similar fires so close together. But where's the link?'

'That's what we have to find out,' said Banks. 'Unless we're dealing with a pyromaniac, a serial arsonist who likes starting fires in out-of-the-way places, then there *is* a connection between the victims, and the sooner we find it, the better. We'll get Kevin Templeton on it. He's good at ferreting out background. I'm going back to the station.'

'I'll follow you.'

'OK. It's late, but I want to set a few things in motion while they're fresh in my mind. For a start, I want to know about Mark Siddons's and Andrew Hurst's alibis for tonight. And Leslie Whitaker's. I'm not at all certain about him yet. Then we'll have to track down Gardiner's ex-wife. And let's not forget Patrick Aspern, Tina's stepfather.'

'Surely you can't think he had anything to do with all this?'

'I don't know, Annie. Serious allegations were made, at least as far as his conduct towards his stepdaughter is concerned. And neither he nor his wife have solid alibis for the boat fires. He's not off my list yet. I think I'll send Winsome down to talk to him in the morning, ask him for an alibi. That should be interesting.'

Annie sighed. 'If you think it's necessary. It's your neck.'

'And I want to put a rush on toxicology, too. These people didn't just lie down and let themselves be burned.'

'Alan?'

'Yes?'

'I was talking to a friend of mine earlier, a chap called Philip Keane. He operates a private art-authentication company, the one that was involved in the Turner find up here last July. I think he might be able to help, at least as far as the art angle is concerned. I'm sure he'd be happy to have a chat with you.'

Banks looked at her. He knew she was seeing someone, but not his name. Was this him? Was this why she had dressed up specially tonight and put a little extra make-up on? The timing was right, and he knew she'd helped the local gallery out with security for the brief period the Turner was housed there. 'Did he know McMahon?'

'No, nothing like that. It's just something that crossed my mind earlier and Phil might have some ideas, that's all.'

'All right,' said Banks. 'Tell him to come to the station tomorrow.'

'Oh, come on, Alan. He's a friend, not a suspect. How about the Queen's Arms? Lunch?'

'If we've got time. Tomorrow might be a busy day.'

'If we've got time.'

'OK,' said Banks.

Annie opened the door and when she moved Banks caught a whiff of her Body Shop grapefruit scent, even over the fire smells and the smoke from the pub that lingered in her hair and on her clothes. Annie stepped over to her own car. Banks slipped Tom Waits's *Alice* in the CD player and headed back through the dark lanes to the station, listening to the croaking voice sing about shipwrecks, ice and dead flowers.

8

DC Winsome Jackman hated Yorkshire winters. She didn't think much of the summers either, but she really hated the winters. As she got out of her nice warm car in front of Patrick Aspern's house on Sunday morning, she felt a pang of longing for home, the way she often did when the cold and damp got to her, even through her thick sweater and lined raincoat. She remembered the humid heat back home, way up in Jamaica's Cockpit Country, the lush green foliage, the insects chirping, the bright flame trees, banana leaves click-clacking overhead in the gentle breeze from the ocean; remembered how she used to walk up the steep hill home from the one-room schoolhouse in her neat uniform, laughing and joking with her friends. She missed her mother and father so much she ached for them sometimes. And her friends. Where were they all now? What were they doing?

Then she remembered the shanties, the crippling poverty and hopelessness, the way so many men treated their women as mere possessions, chattels of no real value. Winsome knew she had been lucky to get out. Her father was a police corporal at the Spring Mount station, and her mother worked at the banana-chip factory in Maroon Town, sitting out back in the shade with the other women, gossiping and slicing bananas all day. Winsome had worked for two summers at the Holiday Inn just outside Montego Bay and she had often talked to the tourists there. Their stories of their homelands, of America, Canada and England, had excited her imagination and sharpened her will. She had envied them the money that allowed them to have luxurious holidays in the sun, and the opportunities they must have at home. These countries, she had thought, must indeed be lands of plenty.

And it wasn't only the white folk. There were handsome black men from New York, London and Toronto, with thick gold chains hanging around their wrists and necks, their wives all dressed up in the latest fashions. What a world theirs was, with all the movies, fashions, cars and jewellery they wanted. Of course, the reality fell a long way short of her imagination, but on the whole she was happy in England; she thought she had made the right move. Apart from the winters.

She sensed, rather than saw, a number of curtains twitch as she walked up the path to ring Aspern's doorbell. A six-foot-one black woman ringing your doorbell was probably a rare event in this neighbourhood, she thought. Anyway, winter or not, it was nice to get away from the computer for a while and out of the office. And she was on overtime.

A man answered her ring and she was immediately put off by the arrogant expression on his face. She had seen looks like that before. Other than that, she thought he was probably handsome in a middle-aged English sort of way. Soft strands of sandy hair combed back, unusually good white teeth, a slim, athletic figure, loose-fitting, expensive casual clothes. But the expression ruined everything.

He arched his eyebrows. 'Can I help you?' he asked, looking her up and down, the condescension dripping like treacle from his tongue. 'I'm afraid there's no surgery on Sundays.'

'That's all right, Dr Aspern,' Winsome said, producing her warrant card. 'I'm fit as a fiddle, thank you very much. And I probably couldn't afford you, anyway.'

He looked surprised by her accent, no doubt expecting some sort of incomprehensible patois. The Jamaican lilt was still there, of course, but more as an undertone. Winsome had been in Yorkshire for seven years, though she had only been in Eastvale for two after her transfer from Bradford, and she had unconsciously picked up much of the local idiom and accent.

Aspern examined her warrant card and handed it back to her. 'So first they sent the organ-grinder and now they send the monkey.'

'Excuse me, sir?'

'Never mind,' said Aspern. 'Just a figure of speech. You'd better come in.'

Winsome got the impression that Aspern scanned the street for spies before he shut the door behind them. Was he worried what the neighbours might think? That he was having an affair with a young black woman? Drugs, more likely, Winsome guessed. He was concerned that they would think he was supplying her with drugs.

He showed her into a sitting room with cream wallpaper, a large blazing fire and a couple of nice landscape paintings on the wall. A recent medical journal lay open on the glass-topped coffee table beside a half-empty cup of milky tea.

'What is it this time?' he asked.

Winsome sat in one of the armchairs without being asked and crossed her long legs. Aspern sat on the sofa and finished off the tea.

'Where were you last night, sir?' Winsome asked.

'What?' Aspern's superior expression was replaced by one of puzzlement and anger.

'I think you heard me.'

'Let's say I just didn't believe what I'm hearing.'

'OK,' said Winsome, 'I'll repeat the question. Where were you last night?'

'Has *he* put you up to this?'

'Who?'

'You know damn well who I'm talking about. Banks. Your boss.'

'DCI Banks issues the actions, sir, and I just carry them out. I'm merely a humble DC. I'm not privy to his inner thoughts. As you so accurately put it yourself, the monkey, not the organ-grinder.' She smiled. 'But I *do* need to know where you were last night.'

'Here, of course,' Aspern answered after a short pause. 'Where the hell else do you think I'd be, with my daughter so recently deceased? Out for a night on the town?'

'I understand she was your stepdaughter?' Winsome said.

'I always thought of her as my own.'

'I'm sure you did. No blood relation, though. Probably a good thing.'

Aspern's face darkened. 'Now, look here, if Banks has been putting ideas in your head . . .'

'Sir?'

Aspern took a few calming breaths. 'Right,' he said. 'I see. I understand what you're up to. Well, it won't work. Last night Fran and I both stayed in and watched television, hoping for something to take our minds off what's happened.'

'Did you succeed?'

'What do you think?'

'What did you watch?'

'A film on Channel Four. I'm sorry, but I can't remember the title. I wasn't really paying attention. It was set in Croatia, if that helps.'

'Is your wife here at the moment?'

'She's resting. As you can imagine, this has been very hard on her. Anyway, she'd only corroborate my statement.'

'I'm sure she would,' said Winsome. 'We'll let her rest for now.'

'Very good of you, I'm sure.'

'But you must admit it's not a very strong alibi, is it? It's been my experience that wives will often stand by their husbands, no matter what horrors or atrocities they might be guilty of.'

'Well, I'm not guilty of anything,' said Aspern, getting to his feet. 'So if that's all, I'll bid you goodbye. I don't have to sit around and listen to your filthy insinuations.'

Winsome held her ground. 'What insinuations would those be, sir?'

'You know what I'm talking about. Banks obviously briefed you on his groundless suspicions and you're here to do his dirty work for him. It won't wash. I'll be complaining to my MP about the both of you.'

'That's your prerogative,' said Winsome, 'but you have to understand that our job can be difficult at times, insensitive, even. I really *am* sorry for your loss, Dr Aspern, but I still have questions to ask.'

'Look, I've told you what I was doing. What more do you want?'

'What clothes were you wearing?'

'Come again?'

'You seem a bit hard of hearing this morning, sir. I asked what clothes you were wearing last night.'

'I don't see how that's relevant to anything.'

'If you'd just tell me. Or, better still, fetch them for me.'

Aspern narrowed his eyes, then stomped out of the room. A few moments later he returned and flung a dark-blue cotton shirt and a pair of black casual trousers over the arm of the chair beside her. 'Unless you want my underwear, too?' he said.

'That won't be necessary,' said Winsome. She knew it was a farce, that he could have given her any old clothes and said he'd worn them last night, or that he could have washed and dried them in the meantime, but that wasn't the point of the exercise. The point was to shake him up and in that she thought she was succeeding remarkably well. 'What about your jacket and overcoat?' she asked.

'What jacket and overcoat? I told you we stopped at home last night. Why would I need a jacket and overcoat?'

'Of course, sir. My mistake.' Winsome stood. 'Mind if I take these?'

'Take them where? What for?'

'For forensic testing.'

'And what do you hope to find?'

'I don't *hope* to find anything, sir. It'll just help us eliminate you from our enquiries.'

'I love the language you people use. "Eliminate you from our enquiries." Talk about bureaucratese.'

'That's a very good word for it, sir. Sometimes it does sound a bit overly formal, doesn't it? Anyway, if you could lay your hands on some sort of a bag. Plastic would be best. Bin liner, or something like that.'

Aspern went into the kitchen and found her a white plastic kitchen bag.

'Thanks. That'll do just fine,' Winsome said.

'Eliminate me from *what* enquiries?' Aspern asked.

'What do you mean, sir?'

Aspern sighed. 'You said earlier that this would help eliminate me from your enquiries. I'm asking exactly *what* enquiries you're talking about.'

'I'm surprised you haven't heard,' she said. 'It's been all over the news. There was another fire last night, remarkably similar to the one in which your stepdaughter died, and not too far away.'

'And I'm a suspect?'

'I didn't say that, sir, but we'd look pretty unprofessional if we didn't cover every possibility, wouldn't we?'

'I don't care what you'd look like, this is discrimination, pure and simple.'

'Against what group? Doctors, for a change?'

'Now, look here, you fucking—'

Winsome raised a finger to her lips. 'Don't say it, Doc,' she said. 'You know it'll only get you into trouble in these politically correct times.'

Aspern ran his hand over his hair and regained his composure and his arrogant air. 'Right,' he said, nodding. 'Right. Of course. I apologize.' He spread his hands. 'Take whatever you like.'

'That's all right, sir,' she said, lifting the bag of clothes. 'This is all I need. I'll be on my way now.'

'I'm sorry you've had such a wasted journey. It's a long way to come for so little.'

'Oh, I wouldn't call it wasted,' said Winsome. 'Not at all.'

She felt absurdly pleased with herself as she walked down the path to her car. Curtains twitched again and

Winsome smiled to herself as she hefted the bag onto the seat beside her and drove off.

•

Annie tracked down the ex Mrs Gardiner easily enough – she was now Mrs Alice Mowbray, wife of Eric – and by mid-morning she was knocking on the door of their semi on Arboretum Crescent. The woman who answered the door looked about forty and she had a hard-done-by air about her. The red cashmere jumper and black skirt she was wearing looked a bit Harvey Nicks, the gold necklace wasn't cheap either, and her blonde hair definitely came from a bottle.

'Who is it, Alice?' a voice from inside the house called. 'If it's those bloody Jehovah's Witnesses again tell them to bugger off!'

Annie showed her warrant card and Alice stood back to let her in. 'It's the police,' she called out.

A man came out of the room on the left of the hall, a curious expression on his face. Annie put him at about the woman's age, or maybe five years younger. It was hard to tell. He didn't have a grey hair on his head and was, she supposed, handsome in a way, the sort of bloke who's full of confidence and tries to pick up women in the better class of pub. Well, some women fall for the brash, sleazy charm, Annie realized.

'What do you want?' he asked. 'If it's about that speeding ticket, then—'

'It's your wife I want to see, sir,' said Annie.

'I can't imagine why,' said Alice, 'but let's talk in the conservatory. I know the weather's not very good, but it's a nice view and we've got an electric heater.'

'That'll be fine,' said Annie, aware of Eric Mowbray

breathing down her neck as she followed Alice to the conservatory. Well, it wouldn't do any harm to talk to him, too, she thought. He looked the type who would get nervous easily and blab, if there was anything to blab.

They settled in the conservatory, which was warm enough and did indeed have a magnificent view looking west into Swainsdale, the distant hills shrouded in light mist. Alice Mowbray sat down on a wicker chair and tugged her skirt over her plump knees. The skirt was at least two inches too short for someone with her thighs, Annie thought, and in conjunction with the peroxide blonde hair, it gave her a definite look of mutton dressed as lamb. Her husband, black hair slicked back with a little gel, jeans too tight over the slight paunch he was already beginning to show, looked as if he didn't mind. Unbidden, an image of the two of them disco-dancing under a whirling, glittering globe, Eric waving his hands in the air and doing his best John Travolta imitation, came into her mind and she had to hold back the laughter.

'What is it, then?' Alice Mowbray asked.

'I'm afraid I've got some rather bad news for you,' she said.

Alice put her hand to her necklace. 'Oh?'

'It's about your ex-husband. I don't know if you've seen or heard any news this morning . . . ?'

'Only the Sunday papers,' Alice said.

Annie knew the Jennings Field blaze had been too late to make the national Sunday papers. 'Well, I'm afraid there's been a fire at the caravan where your ex-husband was living.'

'Oh, no,' said Alice. 'Is Roland hurt?'

'There was one person in the caravan at the time. As

yet, we can't be certain if he was Mr Gardiner, but I'm afraid that person is dead, whoever he is.'

'I don't believe it. Not Roland.'

'I'm sorry, Mrs Mowbray, but it's true. If it is him. Are you all right?'

Alice had turned pale, but she nodded. 'Yes, I'll be fine.' She looked at her husband. 'Darling, can you fetch me a glass of water, please?'

Eric didn't look too happy at being asked to fetch and carry in front of another woman, but there wasn't much he could do about it without looking a complete arsehole.

'I'm sorry to spring such a shock on you like this,' Annie said, 'but there are some questions I need to ask.'

'Of course. I understand. We've been apart for over two years now, but it's not as if I don't . . . well, still have some feelings for Roland. Was he . . . you know . . . ?'

Annie knew all about divorced men's feelings for their ex-wives at first hand, through Banks, and they could be complicated. She felt lucky that Phil had never been married. 'I'm afraid the body was badly burned,' she said, 'but if it's any consolation we think he was unconscious before the fire started.'

Alice frowned. 'Unconscious? But how . . . ?'

'Sleeping pills, perhaps. But we don't know anything for certain yet. That's why I need to talk to you.'

Eric came back with a glass of water and a pill and handed them to Alice. 'What's this?' she asked, looking at the pill.

'Your Valium,' he said. 'I just thought you might need it.'

Alice set the pill aside. 'I'm fine,' she said and sipped some water.

'He was a useless pillock,' Eric said.

'Pardon?' Annie said.

'Her ex. Roly-Poly. He was a prize pillock.'

'Eric, don't be so disrespectful.'

'Well, he was. I'm only telling the truth, Allie, and you know it. Why else are you here with me while he was off living in a poky caravan in a godforsaken field somewhere? He was a loser.'

'Mr Mowbray,' Annie said. 'I don't think you've quite grasped the situation here. A man, possibly Roland Gardiner, is dead.'

'I heard you the first time round, love. And I say it doesn't make a scrap of difference. He was a useless pillock while he was alive, and he's a useless pillock dead.'

Annie sighed and turned back to Alice, who was glaring at her husband. 'I don't know what's wrong with him,' she said. 'He's not usually rude like this.'

'Never mind,' said Annie, giving Eric Mowbray a dirty look. 'Maybe he's just trying to hide his grief.' *Or something else*, she thought. She turned back to Alice. 'One problem we do have is with identification. Dental records are often useful in such cases. Could you tell me who your family dentist is? Doctor, too.'

'I don't know if Roland ever went after he left,' said Alice, 'but we went to Grunwell's, on Market Street. Our family doctor's Dr Robertson, at the clinic on the Leaside estate.'

Annie knew the place.

'We don't know much about your ex-husband,' Annie went on. 'Is there anything you can tell us that might be of use?'

'He was just ordinary, really,' said Alice.

'You can say that again,' said Eric Mowbray.

'Shut up, Eric,' said Alice.

Annie was fast starting to think that Eric Mowbray had outstayed any usefulness she might have erroneously attributed to him in the first place. 'Mr Mowbray,' she said, 'perhaps you could leave us for a while? I have some questions to ask your wife.'

Mowbray got up. 'Fine with me. I've got work to do, anyway.'

After he'd left the conservatory, the two women let the silence stretch a few moments, then Alice said, 'He's a good sort, really, Eric. Just got a bit of a sore spot where Roland's concerned.'

'Oh? Why's that?'

'Because he's my ex. Eric's the jealous type.'

'I see,' said Annie. 'Does he have any reason to be?'

'Not of Roland.'

'What does Mr Mowbray do for a living?'

'He's in computers. He makes very good money. Look at this conservatory. It certainly wasn't here when me and Roland were together. Nor the Volvo. And we're having our holidays in Florida in February. We're going to Disneyworld.'

'Very nice. Do you own any other vehicles?'

'Eric used to have a Citroën, but he sold it.'

'No Jeep or Range Rover?'

'No. Why?'

'Was Roland a successful businessman?'

'I often thought he was in the wrong business.' Alice said. 'He just wasn't that much of a salesman. Didn't have the oomph. Didn't have an ounce of ambition in his entire being. No get up and go at all. Sometimes I thought he'd have been far better off as a schoolteacher, maybe. And happier. Still, he wouldn't have earned much money at that, either, would he?'

Money seemed to figure large in Alice Mowbray's view of the universe, Annie gathered, and perhaps in her second husband's, too. Jack Mellor had already hinted as much the previous night. 'Did he not try to get another job?' she asked.

'It would have been a bit difficult for him, wouldn't it?'

'Why? Lots of people get made redundant and find new jobs.'

'Redundant? That's a good one. Where on earth did you get that idea?'

'Your husband *didn't* lose his job?'

'Oh, Roland lost his job, all right, but it wasn't through redundancy. No. He was fired. You could have knocked me over with a feather. I never thought he had it in him.'

'Had what in him?'

'He'd been on the fiddle, hadn't he?'

'Had he?'

'Yes. Something to do with forging orders and cooking the books. Stealing from the company. I must say he didn't have a lot to show for it, but that's typical Roland, that is. Small-time, even as a crook. No ambition.'

'Can you tell me the name of the company he worked for?'

Alice told her. Annie wrote it down.

'Did Roland have any enemies?'

'Enemies? Roland? He was too much of a mouse to make enemies. Never offended a soul. He'd never stand in anyone's way enough to make an enemy. No, Roland was likeable enough, I'll give him that. He had a natural charm. People liked him. Perhaps because he was so passive, so easy-going. He'd do anything for anyone.'

'This forgery business, did he have a partner?'

'Did it all by himself. As I said, you could have knocked me over with a feather.'

'How long were you married?'

'Ten years.'

'Quite late in life, then?'

Alice narrowed her eyes. 'For Roland, yes. He was thirty-two when we married.'

Annie didn't dare ask Alice how old *she* was. 'Had he been married before?'

'Neither of us had. I must admit, he turned my head. He could be a real charmer, could Roland. Until you got to know him, of course, then you saw how empty it all was.'

'Was the divorce amicable?'

'As amicable as these things go. He didn't have anything I wanted, despite his little business on the side, and he seemed quite willing to let me keep the house.'

'You didn't want the caravan?'

'The caravan? I hated the bloody thing! That was typical Roland, though. Soon as we did have a bit of extra cash, off he goes and buys a bloody caravan. That was his idea of a good time: two weeks in a caravan at Primrose Valley or Flamborough Head. I ask you.'

'So there was no unsettled business between you?'

'I got on with my life and he got on with his.'

'Mr Mowbray, your present husband, when did he come on the scene?'

'What do you mean?'

'Did you meet him before or after you split up with Roland?'

Alice paused a few moments before answering.

'Before,' she said, 'but things were already over for Roland and me.'

Annie supposed that Alice needed someone to go off with, an excuse to end her marriage, and somewhere to go. Many people did. They didn't want to stay in a relationship, but they didn't want to go it alone, either.

'What did you do last night?'

If Alice found the question offensive, she didn't let on. 'We were out to dinner at a friend's house.'

'Can you give me the address? Just routine, for the paperwork.'

Alice gave it to her.

'Do you think Roland might have committed suicide?'

'I don't think he had the guts. It might have been something he'd think of, but when it came to it he'd bottle out. And certainly not in a fire. He wasn't exactly the most physically brave man I've ever met. He used to make enough fuss about going to the dentist's, for crying out loud.'

'Can you give me a list of his friends?'

'Friends? Roland? There was no one close. I can probably come up with a few names of people who knew him, mostly from work, but I don't think they'll be able to tell you any more than I can.'

'Was he secretive, then?'

'I suppose so. Just quiet, though, mostly. I don't think he really had much to talk about.'

'Do you happen to have a photograph of him? As recent as possible?'

'I might have one or two,' Alice said. 'Would you excuse me for a moment?'

Annie heard her go upstairs. She also heard her husband question her as she went. Annie sat and admired the view as two sparrows fluttered in the birdbath out in the garden. She thought she could see a hawk circling over distant Tetchley Fell. A couple of minutes later, Alice came back with a handful of photographs.

'These were taken at the last office Christmas party we went to,' she said. 'Three years ago.'

Annie flipped through them and picked one of the few that were actually in focus: Gardiner sitting at a table, a little flushed from the wine, raising his glass to the photographer and smiling. It was good enough for identification purposes.

'Has anyone been around asking for him since he left?' she asked.

'No. But there was a phone call.'

Annie's ears pricked up. 'When?'

'In July, I think.'

'Did the caller identify himself?'

'No. That was the funny thing. When I told him Roland no longer lived here, he just asked me if I knew where he did live.'

'What did you say?'

'I told him. I mean, I knew where Roland was. I had to, with the divorce, the solicitors and everything.'

'Did he ever call back?'

'No. That was all.'

Interesting, Annie thought. July. Around the time Roland Gardiner started being a bit more optimistic, according to Jack Mellor, and the same time Thomas McMahon got a spring in his step. What happened last summer? Annie wondered. She asked Mrs Mowbray a few more questions about Roland's past, where he went to school, where his parents lived, and so on, then she left.

She didn't see Eric Mowbray on her way out, and she couldn't say it bothered her.

•

'One of the main problems an art forger faces,' Phil Keane explained to Banks and Annie that Sunday lunchtime in the Queen's Arms, 'is getting hold of the right period paper or canvas.'

Banks looked at him as he talked. So this was the mysterious man Annie was now seeing. She had referred to Phil merely as a friend, but Banks sensed a bit more chemistry than Platonic friendship between them. Not that they were fawning over one another, playing kissy-face or holding hands, but there was just something in the air – pheromones, most likely – and something in the way she listened as he spoke. Not so much hanging on his every word, but respectful, *involved*.

Banks had noticed that one or two of the women in the pub had cast appraising glances when Phil walked in ten minutes late and insisted on going to the bar to buy a round of drinks. He was handsome, Banks thought, but not outrageously so, well dressed but not showy, and he talked with the easy charm and knowledge of a habitual lecturer. He did, in fact, give occasional lectures, Annie said, so it was hardly surprising that he seemed so confident, even a bit pedantic, in his delivery. What was there not to like about this man? Banks wondered. This man who was probably shagging Annie. Let it go, Banks told himself; they'd moved on ages ago, hadn't they? And he had Michelle.

The trouble was that Michelle was far away right now, and here was Banks sitting in the Queen's Arms with Annie and her new fancy man, desperately looking for things to dislike. In his experience anything or anyone who seemed too good to be true *was* too good to be true. Well, the man was too old for her, for a start, but then so had *he* been too old for her, and Phil Keane was a few years younger than him.

'Anyway,' Phil went on, 'not everyone can do a John Myatt and forge modern masters with emulsion paint on any old scrap of paper he finds lying around, so the typical forger tends to be careful, especially in these days of scientific testing. He has to make sure his materials, and not just his techniques, pass all the requisite requirements. Not always an easy task.'

'You were saying about the paper . . . ?'

'Was I? Oh, yes.' Phil scratched the crease between the side of his nose and his cheek. It was a gesture Banks immediately disliked. It said, *Until I was so rudely interrupted.* The pontificator's irritation at being interrupted in his digressions. He was damned glad he'd found *something* to dislike about the man at last, even though it wasn't much.

'Well, until the end of the eighteenth century all paper was made by hand, usually from rags, and after that it was slowly replaced by machine-made paper, some of it made from wood pulp.'

'What's the difference?' Banks asked.

'Wood pulp makes far inferior paper,' Phil replied. 'It's weaker and discolours more easily.' He leaned forward and tapped the table. 'But the point I'm trying to make is that if you want to forge an artist's work, you'd damn well better make sure you use the same materials he did.'

Banks took a sip of his Theakston's bitter. Phil was working on a half of XP, slowly, and Annie stuck with fruit juice. 'Makes sense,' Banks said. 'Go on. Where do you find that sort of thing?'

'Exactly the problem. There are several places he might look for the paper,' Phil went on, 'and one of the best sources is an antiquarian book and print dealer. Not everything they sell is expensive, but a lot of it is old. The endpapers of old books are especially useful, for example, and books usually have a publication date to guide you as to the age of the paper you're using.'

'What about prints?' Banks asked. 'I mean, wouldn't some old drawings be dated, too?'

'Yes, but that's not always reliable. They could easily be copies of etchings, made posthumously, in another country even, and until you've developed a very good nose for the genuine article you wouldn't want to slip up by believing what you read on an old print.'

'What about canvas?' Banks asked. 'Aren't most paintings done on canvas?'

Here Phil allowed himself a slight smile, which Banks pounced on as not being entirely devoid of condescension. He was starting to like the man less and less moment by moment, and he was enjoying the feeling very much.

'Quite a lot are,' said Phil, 'but the same applies as to paper, except you don't find canvas in books. You try to seek out old worthless canvases. Quite often what you find determines which artist you forge.'

'I see,' said Banks. 'And you think Thomas McMahon was a forger?'

Phil glanced at Annie, a concerned expression flitting across his face.

'Phil only said that could be one possible explanation of McMahon's odd purchases from Whitaker's,' Annie said.

'Yes,' Phil added. 'I'm not making any accusations or anything. I didn't even know the man.'

'Wouldn't matter if you did make accusations,' said Banks. 'McMahon's dead. He can't sue you.'

'Even so . . .'

'The problem is,' Banks went on. 'Does any of this have anything to do with his murder and, if so, how? Shall we order lunch?'

Phil looked around. 'Look, I know a cosy little place out Richmond way that serves the most tender roast lamb you've ever tasted in your life.' He looked at Annie. 'And I hear they do a delicious vegetable curry, too. What say we head out there?'

●

Mark awoke the next day still very much alive and he realized that he probably had the fleece-lined overcoat to thank for that. Even in his favourite leather jacket he would have been too cold in the barn. He didn't know what time it was because he didn't have a watch, but it was daylight and a hell of a lot warmer than it had been during the night.

He had slept surprisingly well, he thought, but exhaustion will do that for you. He must have run and walked well into the night. And it was the first real sleep he'd had since the fire. Rubbing his bleary eyes, he cast a look around his surroundings, a half-demolished barn littered with rubble and sheep droppings. It stank of piss, too. Time to move on. He wished he could have a hot cup of tea and something to eat, some bacon and eggs perhaps. He wouldn't get far on the ten quid in his pocket and a bit of loose change, but at least he could buy himself a couple of small meals. It would be nice to find a proper toilet, too, somewhere he could wash his hands and face. If only he could find a cafe. Hardly likely in the sort of classy villages you got around this part of the world. No greasy spoons or lorry drivers' cafes.

It was nearly one o'clock, he saw by the church clock in the first village he came to. Christ, he hadn't realized he'd slept in *that* long. You could hardly call the place picturesque. This was one the tourists would drive straight through without even slowing down. There was one tarmac main street of squat red-brick houses with the red pantile roofs so common in East Yorkshire, a post office, general store and newsagent's.

The village was dead quiet, apart from some faint pop music coming from the shabby-looking local pub, the Farmer's Inn. There was a blackboard outside advertising bar food, and Mark noticed that he could get a ham and cheese sandwich for £2.99 or a roast beef lunch with Yorkshire pudding, vegetables and roast potatoes for £5.99. What should he do? Go carefully and save enough for another sandwich later, or blow nearly everything on a hearty lunch? Finally, he decided on the latter course, mostly because he was starving. He hadn't eaten since they kicked him out of jail.

Cautiously, he walked inside. It wasn't one of those places where all conversation stops and everyone looks at you when you walk in, like in that werewolf film he'd seen on the telly in the squat, but he still felt exposed in his ill-fitting clothes, no doubt with a twig or two stuck on the hem of his overcoat and a smear of sheep shit on his jeans. He just hoped he didn't smell too bad.

The pub was exactly the slightly down-at-heels local you'd expect in such a village, which was probably why the food was quite cheap. It smelled of last night's beer and cigarette smoke and was mostly full of hard-looking unemployed farmhands, who wouldn't be squeamish about a bit of sheep shit here and there. The landlord was a surly bugger, but he copied down Mark's order and gave him a number, only turning his nose up when Mark ordered a small lemonade to drink. He didn't want to waste his money on beer. With the change in his pocket, he now had a little over four pounds left, and that might buy him a roll and a cup of tea for dinner, if he could find anywhere serving such fare. He'd worry about tomorrow when it came.

He realized he'd have to do something about the money situation soon, and it might mean a bit of burglary. He didn't like it, but he'd done it before, and he'd do it again if he had to. It was the one thing Crazy Nick had taught him, when he had forced Mark to go out on jobs with him. There was hardly a house he couldn't get into. Mark would never beg, but he would thieve if necessary. At least thieving took guts, and you didn't look like you'd just given up and sat down with your hand sticking out permanently.

Mark had one cigarette left, he realized, courtesy of the copper who had given him the clothes. He decided to smoke it *after* his lunch. He sat in a deserted corner by the window and looked out through the greasy glass onto the empty High Street. People would be eating their roasts behind their dusty net curtains, perhaps watching football or racing like Crazy Nick did when he came back from the pub. If his team lost he used to smack Mark around. Mark's mother too, sometimes, though she was a tough old bird and you could tell Crazy Nick had to be really pissed to have a go at her. As often as not, he came out the worse for wear.

The telly was on behind the bar in the pub, sound off,

and Mark was just in time to catch the local news. A tart with a microphone was standing by a burned-out caravan dripping with water the fire hoses had sprayed on it. Was that what he had seen last night, when he was running from Lenny's place? Then the screen displayed a still photograph of a man Mark had never seen before. The tart talked on for a while as the cameras lovingly panned over the scene of desolation, then the film cut to footage of the two boats. Mark felt his breath catch in his throat as looked on his former home again, now in daylight, with men in protective clothing going over the scene.

There was another reporter by the canal side, a man, this time. His name was captioned at the bottom of the screen, but it was too small for Mark to read. He was wearing a heavy overcoat and a scarf wrapped around his neck. He talked and gestured as the others, police officers, Mark supposed, went about their work.

Next came an old picture of Tom in the next boat, the man they said was an artist. He was barely recognizable from the photograph, but it was definitely him.

And then came the picture that grabbed a hold of Mark's heart and squeezed. He'd never seen it before, but it was Tina, maybe taken two or three years ago before they met. Her blonde hair was long, over her shoulders, and it seemed to glow with health. She was smiling at the camera, but Mark could tell it was a bit forced. If you didn't know her well, though, didn't know that telltale clenching of the jaw and shadows behind her eyes, then you'd never know. Time hung suspended. He almost felt as if she could see him, was looking right at him, and he wanted to call out to her, tell her he was sorry he had failed her, sorry he hadn't been there for her.

When the picture vanished as quickly as it had

appeared, and the programme cut back to the reporter by
the canal, Mark stood up so quickly he knocked his drink
over and ran out into the street.

•

Banks bowed out of the excursion to the pub out Richmond way, allowing Annie to go with Phil, which was
probably what she wanted anyway, ate a hurried roast
pork lunch at the Queen's Arms alone and returned to the
station. Because it was a Sunday, things were slow, especially as far as forensics went, but a major investigation
was under way, and Banks's Major Crimes core team was
hard at work.

At this point, while each fire was being investigated
separately for cause and motive, every possible effort was
being made to find the link between them that everyone
suspected was there. When Banks dropped by the incident room, Winsome was back entering the green sheets
into the HOLMES computer system, DC Gavin Rickerd
was making sure everything was in its place, neatly logged
and filed, DC Kevin Templeton was chewing the end of a
pencil as he tried to gather information on any similar
fires, and DS Hatchley was pondering over the bits and
pieces he had dug up on Mark David Siddons. The phones
rang from time to time, computer keyboards clacked and
fax machines hummed. Everything was ticking over
nicely, but just ticking over. Of course, everyone was on
overtime except Banks. A DCI didn't get paid overtime.

Banks hadn't been back in his own office more than a
couple of minutes when Stefan Nowak tapped at the door.

'A moment?'

Banks looked up. 'Good news, I hope?'

'I don't know,' said Stefan, standing at the open door,

'but there's something you might like to see if you've got a minute or two to spare.'

Curious, Banks followed Stefan down the corridor into the 'new' part of the building, which they called the annex. It was just as old, in fact, but it used to be a hotel before Eastvale expanded from divisional HQ into Western Area Headquarters and knocked through the walls. Now it housed fingerprints, photography, scenes-of-crime and computers, among other departments.

Stefan stopped at a lab bench. 'I thought you might be interested in this,' he said, pointing to a blackened cube about the size of a computer monitor. 'We retrieved it from the caravan. Looks as if it was hidden in one of the cupboards.'

'What is it?' Banks asked.

'Well, it looks to me like a fire-resistant safe,' said Stefan.

'A fire-resistant safe? What on earth is a bloke living on his wits in a dilapidated caravan doing with a fire-resistant safe?'

'You tell me,' said Stefan. 'I only found it and identified it.'

'Can you open it?'

'It might take a bit of brute force.'

'Any reason to treat it gently?'

'No. We've already checked for prints. Nothing.'

'So let's do it.'

Stefan had already got his hands on a small crowbar – from the police garage, he told Banks – and he proceeded to wedge it in the lock area and exert pressure. Nothing happened. He looked up at Banks. 'Any safe-crackers down in the cells?'

'I wish,' said Banks. 'Keep at it. Fire-resistant or not, the fire must have weakened the lock a bit, at least.'

Stefan kept at it. Still nothing happened. 'I think we might have to dynamite it,' he said.

Banks laughed. 'Let me have a go.'

Stefan handed him the crowbar and Banks shifted it to the side opposite the lock, where the deep-seated hinges were. It was hard to see exactly what he was doing because of the fire damage, but he thought he had succeeded in inserting the sharp, flat end of the crowbar between the body of the safe and the hinged door. Gently at first he worked the crowbar up and down and managed to get it in another few millimetres. Finally, the first hinge cracked and it was only a matter of time before he broke the second one too.

'Fire proof, but not Banks proof,' he said, pulling open the door. He reached into the dark interior. 'Looks like something's there.'

'What is it?' Stefan asked.

Banks pulled out the safe's contents, wrapped in black plastic bin liner, and placed them on the lab bench. Both men looked down in astonishment. On the table in front of them lay some rolled-up tubes of paper and three bundles of twenty pound notes, fastened with rubber bands, probably five hundred quid or more in each of them. Banks unfolded the tubes and saw a number of sketches of a castle, and a finished watercolour painting, about eleven by sixteen, of a view along a valley from the castle terrace.

'That's Hornby Castle,' said Stefan.

'How do you know?'

He glanced sideways at Banks. 'I've been there. I do a lot of walking. It's near Kirkby Lonsdale. And this,' he pointed to the watercolour, 'is the view from the castle. That's Ingleborough, one of the Three Peaks. I've walked them.'

The Three Peaks walk was a popular one, but it had always seemed just that little bit too eccentric for Banks. Not to mention exhausting. You had to walk over twenty miles in twelve hours, climbing three bloody great hills – Pen-y-Ghent, Whernside and Ingleborough – as often as not in the pouring rain.

Banks looked at the sketches and the watercolour again. They looked old. There was no signature, but it was obvious enough, even to Banks's untrained eye, that he was looking at the work of J. M. W. Turner, or a close facsimile.

'Bloody hell,' he said. 'I'd better ring Annie.'

•

'I don't think your boss likes me very much,' Phil Keane said to Annie that evening. They were at her place and were just finishing a light evening meal of pasta primavera, neither being terribly hungry after their big lunch.

Annie poured them each another glass of Sainsbury's Montepulciano d'Abruzzo. 'What makes you say that?' she asked.

'Oh, I don't know. Just a feeling. Do you think he might be jealous?'

Annie felt herself blush. She hadn't told Phil about her and Banks. 'Why would he be?'

'Maybe he's got designs on you himself?'

'Don't be silly.' Annie drank some wine rather too quickly and it went down the wrong way. Along with her cold, that set her coughing. Phil brought her a glass of water and watched her concernedly as she took a few seconds to get it under control.

'OK?' he said.

'Fine. Look, Alan and I, we . . . well . . .'

Phil looked at her, interested.

'Do I have to spell it out?'

'Of course not,' Phil said. 'And I'm sorry for bringing it up. You could have told me sooner, though. It's not as if I expected you to have lived the life of a nun, you know.'

'You didn't?'

'Well, *I* certainly haven't. The life of a monk, I mean.'

'You haven't?'

'No.'

'Anyway, it was a while ago.'

'It just surprises me, that's all.'

'Why?'

'I don't know,' Phil said. 'I suppose because he doesn't seem your type.'

'What *is* my type?'

'I don't know. He just . . . what's he like?'

'What do you mean?'

'What did you like about him?'

'Alan? Well, he's fun to be with. Most of the time, at any rate. He loves music, likes single malt whisky, has tolerable taste in films apart from an unfortunate fondness for action adventure stuff – you know, James Bond, Arnold Schwarzenegger and dreadful macho stuff like that. Which is odd because he's not really a macho kind of bloke. I mean he's sensitive, kind, compassionate, and he's got a good sense of humour.'

'Did you live together?'

Annie laughed. 'No. I stayed in my little hovel at the centre of the Harkside labyrinth, as he used to put it, and he's got a lovely little cottage near Gratly. He's a bit of a loner, actually, so it suits him quite well.'

'What went wrong?'

'I don't know. It just didn't work out. Too much baggage. Alan's recently divorced and his family's still on his mind a lot. It just didn't work out. Oh, we work well together. That's not a problem. Except . . .'

'What?'

'Well, you know. Sometimes you can't help but be aware of your history. It can make things difficult. But it's manageable. And he's a good boss. Gives me a lot of freedom. Respects my opinions.'

'About those fires?'

'About anything.'

'And what are your opinions?'

'I don't have any yet. Early days.'

'You're not comfortable talking about your work with me, I can see. I'm sorry.'

Annie reached out and squeezed his arm. 'Oh, it's all right,' she said. 'To tell the truth, I was just getting used to having no one to talk to outside the station. I do have to exercise some discretion, but it's not as if I've signed the Official Secrets Act or anything. Anyway, as I said, I don't have any theories yet. Not enough evidence. All we know is that they seem to be the work of an arsonist. Which is hardly a bloody secret.' She wasn't going to tell Phil about the Turner and the money that Banks had phoned her about just yet, not until she had talked to Banks about possibly getting Phil involved as a consultant.

'Not even the tiniest suspicion?'

'I could hardly tell you if I suspected someone, could I?'

'Then you *have* signed the Official Secrets Act?'

Annie laughed and topped up her glass. She felt a little

tipsy, but it had been a long weekend and she was still fighting off the remnants of her cold. 'It's like doctors and patients,' she said.

'Until your suspect is arrested?'

'Ah, then the rules change, yes. Look, you haven't told me how long you're staying up north this time.'

'I don't know,' said Phil. 'It's fairly quiet at the office, but something could come up and I might get called back.'

'A suspicious Sickert, perhaps? Or a dodgy Degas?'

Phil laughed. 'Something like that. Look, do you fancy a weekend in New York?'

'New York!' Annie had never been to America. She and Phil had been to Paris in September, and she'd had a hard time getting him to let her pay her own way. She didn't think she could afford New York and she didn't want him to pay.

'Yes. Next weekend. Business mostly, I'm afraid. I've a few gallery owners and dealers to meet with. But we could take in a Broadway show, dinner later.'

'I'm not sure I'd be able to get away next weekend.'

'The case?'

'Yes. And there's the money . . .'

'Oh, don't worry about that. It's a business trip. On the company.'

'Both of us?'

'Of course. You'd be my security adviser.'

Annie laughed and carried their empty dishes over to the kitchen sink. 'It sounds wonderful, but . . .'

'Tell me you'll at least think about it.'

'I'll think about it.' Annie sensed Phil behind her before she felt his hands on her hips and his lips nuzzle the hollow between her neck and shoulder. She wriggled and he circled his arms around, holding her to him tightly enough so she could feel his erection pressing at the base of her spine. She couldn't help but experience a moment of fear and panic as she felt his hardness against her. Images of the rape of three years ago flashed through her mind and set her nerves on edge. But she had learned to control the emotions and, if not to enjoy sex as fully as she might, at least not to run away from it.

'Leave those dishes for now,' Phil said, loosening his grip.

Annie turned to face him, surprised to feel the panic dissipating so quickly, the warmth spreading like wetness between her legs, her knees weak. It hadn't been like this with Alan, she thought, then felt ashamed for making the comparison. Phil put his arms around her and she smiled up at him. 'OK,' she said. 'Stay the night?'

'I don't have my toothbrush.'

Annie laughed and buried her face in the soft cotton of his shirt. 'Oh, I think I've got an unused one in the bathroom,' she said.

'In that case . . .' Phil said. He let his arms fall by his side, then Annie took him by the hand and led him towards the stairs.

9

Annie looked pleased with herself on Monday morning, and Banks guessed it wasn't entirely to do with her job. She sat down opposite him in his office and crossed her legs. She was wearing tight black jeans and a red shirt made of some silky sort of material, which seemed to whisper when she moved. Her hair looked tousled and her cold seemed to be on the wane. There was a glow about her that Banks wasn't sure he liked.

'Anyway,' she said, 'I talked to Roland Gardiner's ex-employer and it seems as if Roland was playing a minor variation on the long-firm fraud.'

'Was he, indeed?' A long-firm fraud involves setting up a fraudulent company – easy enough to do these days with computer software – and acquiring goods or services without paying. A true long-firm fraud takes a long time to get going – hence its name – and requires a bit of capital. You first have to pay your bills promptly to gain the trust of the companies you purchase from. 'How did he manage that?' Banks asked. 'I thought you told me his ex-wife said he never had a penny to spare.'

'He didn't. That was the beauty of it. He bought from himself.'

'What do you mean?'

'From the company he worked for. Office products. Good market. Easy to get rid of. Gave himself a nice line of credit and took it from there. He didn't need to establish trust over a long period.'

'He can't have made much,' Banks said.

'He didn't. I think that's what bothered his ex-wife, too. I get the impression that if he'd made a bit more money she wouldn't have minded too much where he got it from.'

'What happened when his boss found out?'

'Offered the honourable way out. Pay back and resign. No police. Seems he was well liked enough around the office.'

'So where does this get us?' Banks asked, talking to himself as much as to Annie.

'Well,' Annie answered, 'we've got a dead art forger, and now it seems as if the second victim was a different kind of fraudster. And he had a Turner watercolour and about fifteen hundred quid in a fire-resistant safe. It seems like too much of a coincidence to me. Whatever it was, they must have been in it together.'

'Sounds logical,' said Banks. 'But what? And what's the link between them? How did they know one another?'

'I can't answer those questions yet,' said Annie. 'Not enough information. But if there's a link, we'll find it. What interests me right now is who else was involved.'

'The third man?'

'Yes. Someone killed them.'

'Unless they fell out and Gardiner killed McMahon.'

'Still doesn't explain who killed Gardiner.'

'His ex? Her new husband?'

'Possible,' said Annie.

'But unlikely?'

'In my opinion. What about Leslie Whitaker?'

'He's another possibility,' said Banks. 'I'm not entirely

convinced that he didn't know exactly what McMahon was up to. I think we should have another crack at him, anyway. Let's have him in, this time.'

'Good idea.' Annie paused. 'Alan, about this Turner . . . ?'

'Yes?'

'I was just wondering, before we do anything else, you know, if we should perhaps bring Phil in, let him have a look at it? After all, it is his line of expertise.'

'I think we'd be better going through correct channels,' said Banks, feeling about as stiff and formal as he sounded.

'That's not like you,' Annie said. 'Besides, it could take ages. Phil might be able to tell us something useful right away.'

'Don't forget there's Ken Blackstone,' said Banks. 'He's got a strong background in art forgery.'

'But he's West Yorkshire,' Annie argued. 'And that was ages ago. Phil knows the business and he's here right now.'

'I gathered that,' said Banks.

Annie's mouth tightened. 'What's that supposed to mean?'

'Nothing. Only that I think we should go through official channels.'

'Oh, for crying out loud, we use consultants all the bloody time. What about that psychologist? The redhead who fancies you?'

Banks felt himself flush, partly with anger and partly with embarrassment. 'You mean Dr Fuller? She's a professional psychologist, a trained criminal profiler.'

'Whatever. Phil's a trained art authenticator.'

'We don't know *what* Phil is. You've hardly known him five minutes.'

'You know what your problem is?' Annie said, running her hand through her hair. 'You're bloody jealous, that's what it is. You're playing dog in the manger. What you can't have nobody else should get either, right?'

'He can have you as much and as often as he wants, for all I care,' said Banks, 'but I won't compromise this investigation because of your private life.'

'Oh, pull the carrot out of your arse, Alan. Can you hear yourself? Do you have any idea what you sound like?'

Banks felt as if he'd taken a wrong turn and the brick wall was looming dead ahead. 'Look . . .' he began, but Annie cut in, after a deep breath.

'All I'm saying is let him have a look at the Turners, that's all,' she said, softening her tone. 'If you're worried he's going to run off with them, you can chain them to your wrist.'

'Don't be absurd. I'm not worried about anything of the kind.'

'Then what is your objection? What can it possibly be?'

'He's an unknown quantity.' Banks felt that his objections were inadequate and he knew he was well on the defensive now, partly because he also knew he was acting irrationally, out of jealousy, and he didn't know how to get out of the situation without admitting it.

'I know him,' Annie said. 'And I can vouch for him. He knows his business, Alan. He's no dilettante.'

Banks thought for a moment. He knew he had to give in gracefully, knew that he'd brushed against dangerous ground indeed during their little exchange. Much as he didn't like the idea of bringing Annie's boyfriend into the investigation, it was certainly true that Phil Keane might be able to help them with the art forgery angle, had in fact helped them already in elaborating on the possible reasons why McMahon had bought useless old books and prints from Whitaker. Besides, he *was* objecting because he was jealous and that was unprofessional.

'All right,' he said. 'I'll put it to Detective Superintendent Gristhorpe. I can't be fairer than that.'

'*You'll* put it to him? Are you sure you won't put it to him the way you've just put it to me?'

'Annie, this stops now, OK? I said I'll put it to him. Take it or leave it.'

Annie glared at Banks, then she snatched up her files. 'Fine,' she said. 'I'll take it. You put it to him.'

•

'Look, what's all this about?' said Leslie Whitaker, clearly uncomfortable to find himself on the receiving end of a police interrogation. 'You've kept me waiting over an hour. I've got a business to run.'

'Sorry about that, Mr Whitaker,' said Banks, arranging his folders neatly on the desk in front of him. They were in interview room two, which was hardly any different from interview rooms one and three, except that it let in even less light from the high, grille-covered window. Banks had brought DS Hatchley in to assist. Annie was digging up more background on Roland Gardiner, then she would be going to see Phil Keane with the Turners. Besides, she and Banks were barely speaking, and that was not conducive to the teamwork required for a successful interview.

'Can you get on with it, then?' said Whitaker, tapping his left hand against the desk. His foot was jumping too, Banks noticed. Nervous, then. Something to hide? Or just angry?

Banks glanced at Hatchley, who raised his eyebrows.

'*Get on with it*?' Hatchley repeated. 'It's not often we get someone telling us to get on with it, is it, sir?'

'That's true,' said Banks. 'Still, we'll do as you say, Mr Whitaker, and get on with it. If you've nothing to hide, and if you're truthful with us, you'll be opening up that shop again in no time.'

Whitaker leaned back in the chair. He was wearing a beige jacket over a dark blue polo-neck sweater. Banks tried to match him with the description he had of McMahon's visitor from Mark Siddons, but all he could conclude was that the description was vague enough to fit Whitaker and a hundred or more others.

'When we talked to you the other day,' Banks said, 'you told us that you sold books and prints on occasion to Thomas McMahon.'

'Yes, I did. So what?'

'Do you know why he wanted them?'

'I already told you, I had no idea.'

'I think you do, Mr Whitaker.'

Whitaker's eyes narrowed. 'Oh?'

'Yes,' said Banks. 'Want to know what I think? I think you deliberately sought out certain books and prints for Thomas McMahon at his request.'

Whitaker folded his arms. 'Why would I do that?'

'You're an art dealer, aren't you?'

'In a small way, yes, I suppose so. More of a local agent, really.'

'And you probably know a bit about forgery.'

'Now, hang on a minute. What are you suggesting?'

Banks repeated the lecture he'd first heard from Phil Keane about the re-use of old endpapers and prints. Whitaker listened, making a very bad job of pretending he hadn't a clue what Banks was talking about.

'I still don't see what any of this has to do with me,' he said, when Banks had finished.

'Oh, come off it,' said Hatchley. 'You were in it together. You and McMahon. You supplied him with the right sort of materials, he turned out the forgeries, you sold them and then you split the profits. Only he got greedy, threatened to expose you.'

'That's ridiculous. I did no such thing.'

'Well, you must admit,' said Banks, 'that it all looks a bit dodgy from where I'm sitting.'

'I can't help it if you have a suspicious nature. It must be your job.'

Banks smiled. 'The job. Yes, it does tend to make one a little less ready to accept the sort of bollocks you've been dishing out so far. Why don't you just admit it, Leslie? You had something going with McMahon.'

Whitaker faltered a moment, but kept quiet.

'Maybe you didn't kill him,' Banks went on, 'but you know something. You knew why he wanted those books and prints, and I'll bet he paid *above* the odds for them. Your cut, nicely bypassing the taxman. What was Roland Gardiner's role?'

'I don't know who you're talking about.'

'Come off it, Leslie. Roland Gardiner. He died in a caravan fire in Jennings Field on Saturday night.'

'And you think I . . . ?'

'That's what I'm asking. Because if you didn't kill him, and if you didn't kill McMahon, then maybe you're next.'

Whitaker turned pale. 'You can't mean that. Why would you say that?'

'Stands to reason,' said Hatchley. 'These things happen when thieves fall out.'

'I am *not* a thief.'

'Just a figure of speech,' Hatchley went on. 'See, if you weren't the ringleader, as you swear you weren't, then you were just one of the underlings and two of them are dead. See what I mean? Stands to reason.'

'No,' said Whitaker, regaining his composure. 'It doesn't stand to reason at all. Your whole premise is rubbish, absolute rubbish. I've done nothing.'

'Except supply Thomas McMahon with the paper necessary for his forgeries,' said Banks.

'I didn't know what he was doing with the damn stuff.'

'We think you did.'

Whitaker folded his arms again. 'Well, that's your problem.'

'No. It's yours. What kind of car do you drive?'

'A Jeep. Why?'

'What kind of Jeep?'

'A Cherokee. Four-wheel drive. I live out Lyndgarth way. The roads can be bad.'

A Jeep Cherokee was close enough to a Range Rover or any other kind of four-wheel-drive station wagon for Banks, especially when the cars had only been spotted through the woods by people who had little knowledge of the various shapes and forms the vehicles took. 'Colour?'

'Black.'

Again, close enough to dark blue. 'Where were you last Thursday evening?'

'At home.'

'Where's that?'

'Lyndgarth, as I said.'

'Alone?'

'Yes. I'm recently divorced, if you must know.'

'Not much of an alibi, is it?' Hatchley cut in.

Whitaker looked at him. 'I wasn't aware I'd be need-
ing one.'

'That's what they all say.'

'Now, look—'

'All right, Mr Whitaker,' said Banks, 'you can argue
with my sergeant later. We've got more important matters
to cover right now. Where were you on Saturday evening?'

'Saturday? I . . .'

'Yes?'

Whitaker thought for a moment, then he looked at
Banks, triumphant. 'I was at a dinner in Harrogate. Yorkshire booksellers. We get together every month, about ten
of us. They'll all vouch for me.'

'What time did you arrive?'

'Eight o'clock.'

Banks felt his hopes wane. If Whitaker really was
with nine other people at eight o'clock Saturday, and the
fire started around eight forty-five, it seemed to let him
off. Especially as it took at least an hour to drive from
Lyndgarth to Harrogate. But watertight alibis, in Banks's
experience, were made to be broken.

'We will check, you know.'

'Go ahead,' said Whitaker. 'Do you want their names.
The others?'

'You can give them to Detective Sergeant Hatchley
later.'

'I don't see that we have anything more to talk about,
do you?'

'Plenty,' said Banks. 'I still want to know what role
Gardiner played in all this and why he had to die too.'

'I've told you I never heard of any Gardiner. I'm an
antiquarian bookseller. I occasionally deal in works of art.
That's my only connection with Thomas McMahon. But I

have no knowledge whatsoever of anyone called Gardiner.'

Banks paused for a moment, whispered something in Hatchley's ear, mostly for effect, then turned back to Whitaker. 'The way things look right now, Leslie,' he said, 'I think it's time to move on to the next stage.'

'Next stage? What do you mean?'

'Well, this is just a preliminary interview, you understand. Just to get the lie of the land, so to speak. I'm not satisfied with what I've heard. Not satisfied at all. So now we take it a step further. We go over your finances, your car, your clothes, your business dealings, your life, with a fine-tooth comb, and if we find any of the evidence we're looking for, we haul you back in.'

Whitaker swallowed. 'You can't do that,' he said, without much conviction.

Banks stood up. 'Yes, we can,' he said. 'And we will. Detective Sergeant Hatchley will take down those names now.'

•

On Monday afternoon results started trickling in from the lab. First of all, Andrew Hurst's clothes were clean, as expected, and so were Danny Boy Corcoran's and Patrick Aspern's. None of this surprised Banks; apart from Hurst, who had washed his clothes, they had all been outsiders in the first place.

Banks would like to think that Aspern was involved somehow, but he very much doubted the good doctor had set the fires. Even so, he reminded himself that Patrick Aspern didn't have a decent alibi for either fire, and that he could have gone to see Tina on the day of the boat fires, then returned later. Perhaps she had threatened to tell the world what he'd done to her. He could have started the fire on McMahon's boat to draw the enquiry away from Tina. As yet, nobody had had any luck trying to locate Paul Ryder, Christine Aspern's birth father. Banks didn't imagine he was important to the case, as he had never even known his daughter, but at least he ought to know what had happened to her.

But there were other matters to consider. Banks would have liked to know why Andrew Hurst had washed his clothes in the middle of the night, for a start. As things stood, it just didn't make sense. DC Kevin Templeton was checking into Hurst's background, along with everyone else's, so maybe he would turn up something.

Then there were the Turner, the money, and the possible criminal activities of McMahon and Gardiner. Well, perhaps a closer look at Leslie Whitaker's business dealings would help turn up something there.

Banks sat in his office and browsed through reports and actions, a CD of Soile Isokoski singing Richard Strauss's orchestral songs playing in the background. Just when he was about to wander out for a coffee break, his phone rang. It was the front desk. Someone to see the man in charge of the fires on the boats. Someone called Lenny Knox.

Puzzled, Banks asked the duty officer to have him escorted upstairs, and he appeared at Banks's door, a burly, pock-marked, red-faced fellow, a couple of minutes later.

'Sit down,' Banks said.

Knox sat. The chair creaked under his weight.

'What can I do for you, Mr Knox?' Banks asked, leaning back and linking his hands behind his head.

'I'm worried about Mark, Mark Siddons,' said Knox, traces of a Liverpool accent in his voice.

'Maybe you'd better start at the beginning.'

Knox sighed. 'Mark's a good kid. A pal of mine. He's a good grafter, too. Doesn't mind getting his hands dirty. We were doing a job together at the college – you know about that?'

Banks nodded. He knew about Mark's job.

'Anyway,' Knox went on, 'when you let him out of jail, the poor kid had nowhere to go and he'd just lost his girl-friend, so I invited him home with me.'

'That was a kind gesture,' Banks said.

Knox looked at him and sighed. 'It was meant to be. Backfired, though, didn't it?'

'How?'

'You've got to understand, Sal's a good girl, really, but she's . . . well, she doesn't like to feel put upon. Likes to think she's part of things, decisions and such like. And she likes things planned out, doesn't like surprises.'

'Sounds reasonable.'

'Anyway, it was my fault. I brought Mark home with me, told him he could stay without even consulting her. She hit the roof. Mark must have heard us arguing in the kitchen and the next thing I knew he'd legged it. I yelled after him but he didn't pay it any mind.'

Banks reached for his notepad. 'When did this happen?' he asked.

'Saturday evening.'

'What time?'

'About half-past seven.'

'Which direction did he go?'

'Towards the railway tracks.'

Banks tapped his pencil on his pad. Jennings Field lay

a short distance east of town, beyond the tracks. For a number of reasons, Banks hadn't considered Mark to be a strong candidate for the boat fires, but this put a different complexion on things. Mark could easily have made it to the field by the time the fire started. But why? Was he a pyromaniac? Was there something that triggered him? Anger? Rejection? He had been angry at Tina, too, before he left for Mandy's flat on Thursday night. But the alibi . . . the timing . . . the clothes . . . it just didn't make sense. Still, the important thing now was to find him and bring him in.

'Did Mark say anything to you about the fires?'

'Like what?'

'Anything at all.'

'No. Only that he was cut up about Tina.'

'He didn't voice any suspicions, any ideas about what happened?'

'Not to me, no. Look,' said Knox, going on to echo Banks's own fears, 'I'm not the sort to go blabbing to the police, which is why I didn't come straight here, but I'm worried about Mark. I thought he might have got in touch, but he hasn't, and there's no one else to report him missing. Like I said, at bottom of it all he's a good kid. Not like some you see around these days. And he's had it rough. He doesn't have any money and he's got nowhere to go. You can bet he'll be sleeping rough. I know it's not exactly brass-monkey weather right now, but it's still bloody cold to be sleeping out in the open. And things can change pretty quickly up here.'

'Too true,' said Banks. 'And if Mark himself wasn't responsible for the boat fires, there was a good chance that whoever was wanted him out of the way. So he was out in the cold, possibly being hunted. Definitely not an ideal state of affairs. 'Is there anything else?'

'No,' said Lenny, 'but perhaps you can find him, tell him I'm sorry. Poor Sal was beside herself when she knew he'd heard her. Tell him he can come back to ours any time he likes, she says now. I told you she was a good lass. It was just the shock, that's all, and her not being asked.'

'What was Mark wearing?'

'A ratty old suede coat, fleece lined, and jeans rolled up at the bottoms. Looked like hand-me-downs.'

Banks smiled at the description of the clothes he'd given Mark: his own cast-offs. 'We'll put out a bulletin for him.'

'Don't frighten him, will you?' said Lenny. 'I don't know what he'd do if he felt cornered. He's in a right state.'

'We'll do our best, Mr Knox,' said Banks. 'The important thing is to find him. I don't suppose you have a photograph?'

'Me? No. Didn't you take one when you had him in?'

'We don't do that as a matter of routine, Mr Knox. We need a reason, and permission. In Mark's case it simply wasn't necessary.'

Knox stood up. 'Right, then,' he said. 'You'll let me know?'

'Give me your telephone number. I'll see to it personally.'

Knox gave him the number. 'Thanks,' he said.

When Knox had left Banks walked over to his window. The CD had come to the *Four Last Songs* now, Banks's favourites. He remembered an occasion some years ago, before everything went wrong, when he had arrived home very late after attending the scene of a teenage girl's murder in an Eastvale cemetery. He had sat up smoking, drinking Laphroaig and listening to the *Four Last Songs*, Gundula Janowitz's version that time, and his daughter Tracy had woken up and come down to see what was wrong. They had talked briefly – Banks deliberately not telling her about the murder – then they had shared mugs of cocoa as they cuddled up on the sofa and listened to the Strauss songs. It was a moment forever etched in his memory, all the more so because it could never be repeated. Tracy was gone now, grown up, living her own life. Sandra was gone, too. And Brian.

The day was still grey but fairly warm outside. Lucky for Mark. There were plenty of people crossing the market square, shopping along Market Street and York Road. The church facade was covered in scaffolding, like an exoskeleton, and the weather was good enough for the restorers to get up there and work away at the ancient stonework and lead roofing. He thought of Mark, who said he wanted to do church restoration work. Banks knew Neville Lauder, the stonemason in charge of the project, from the Queen's Arms. Maybe he could put in a word. He had to maintain his objectivity, though. Much as he thought Lenny was right in his assessment of Mark, and much as Banks liked the kid, felt sorry for him, there was still a chance that Mark Siddons was a killer.

'Got a minute, sir?'

Banks looked up. DS Hatchley. 'Come in, Jim,' he said. 'How you doing?'

'Not too badly, thanks.' Jim Hatchley sat down and ran his hand over his untidy straw-coloured hair. He still looked tired, Banks thought, with bags under his eyes and puffy, blotchy skin. Still, not only was he just recovering from a nasty bout of flu, but his youngest was teething. Having babies would do that to you. Would Sandra lose sleep? he wondered. She had looked good when he last saw her, but that could change when little Sinéad started teething.

'What is it?' Banks asked. 'Anything on Whitaker's alibi?'

'Checks out so far,' Hatchley said. 'But it's early days yet. Anyway, that other job you asked me to do. Mark David Siddons.'

'Yes?'

Hatchley shook his head. 'Poor bastard,' he said.

'What can you tell me?'

'His mother's Sharon Siddons, a right slag if ever there was one. I thought the name rang a bell. They lived on the East Side estate, where else? She died a year ago. Lung cancer.'

'Father?'

'Dunno,' said Hatchley. 'Sharon was an alcoholic as well as a slag. Started young. She worked as a prossie for a while, till she got pregnant at seventeen. After that there was a long line of men in her life. Most of them losers, and none of them lasting very long. Last one was a charmer by the name of Nicholas Papadopoulos. Perhaps you've heard of him?'

'Crazy Nick?'

'One and the same.'

Banks had indeed heard of Crazy Nick. You couldn't be a copper in Eastvale for five minutes without hearing of him. Disturbing the peace, breaking and entering, assault, GBH, drunk and disorderly. You name it, and if it took no brains, Crazy Nick had done it. Stopping just short of murder. The last time he'd been arrested it had taken four strapping PCs to hold him down and bring him in. He never stopped swearing and struggling the whole time and once he was in the cell he drove the custody section insane with his non-stop stream of curses and banging.

'Isn't he a guest of Her Majesty at the moment?'

'Indeed he is,' said Hatchley. 'Strangeways. And he won't be out for quite a while. Whacked a nightwatchman with a hammer during a warehouse break-in and fractured his skull.'

'How long was he with the Siddons woman?'

'Until she started to show the cancer symptoms,' said Hatchley. 'Then he was off like a shot. Died alone and in agony, poor cow.'

'Was he around when Mark ran off?'

'Yes. Probably the reason. Believe it or not, Mark gave him a bloody good hiding. Enough to put him in hospital for a couple of days, at any rate. Broken nose. Couple of ribs. Twenty stitches in his scalp. Concussion. Took him by surprise. Went crazy on him, according to the neighbours. Even his mother couldn't drag him off.'

'Good for him,' Banks said. 'And Nick didn't take his revenge? That's not like him.'

'Couldn't find the kid, then he got caught for that warehouse job.'

'But Mark's got no form, himself?'

'No. We've had him in on sus for a couple of housebreakings, and he once got caught shoplifting in HMV. Charges dropped. That's all.'

'Anything important we *haven't* got him for?'

'No. At least I can't find any rumours.'

And if anyone could, Banks knew, it was probably Hatchley, with his long list of snitches and a pair of eyes in practically every pub in Eastvale. 'So he's basically a clean kid?' he said.

'Looks that way,' Hatchley agreed. 'He attended Eastvale Comprehensive, but truanted as often as not. Didn't get into much trouble there, apart from a bit of a shoving match with one teacher, but he didn't exactly shine academically, either. Good at games, though. Want me to keep on digging?'

'Anything to do with fires come up in connection with him?'

'Not that I can find.'

'He didn't try to set fire to the school, or to the house after he beat up Crazy Nick?'

'Just ran off. Never went back.'

'Sensible,' said Banks. Given the sort of background Mark had endured, both with his mother and her earlier men friends, and with Crazy Nick Papadopoulos, it was no surprise that he was willing to believe Tina's tale of woe without question. It didn't mean she wasn't telling the truth, however, and Banks had certainly sensed *something* wrong in the Aspern household. There was another thing, too; from what Hatchley had told Banks Mark certainly had a violent temper, no matter how justifiable his uprising against Crazy Nick had been. The lad needed watching.

'OK, Jim,' Banks said. 'Thanks very much.'

'Cheers,' said Hatchley. 'My pleasure.'

●

By Monday afternoon Mark was close to Sutton Bank and starving. He was glad he had gone back into the pub for his lunch the previous day after the shock of seeing Tina's image on the TV screen. The landlord had given him a dirty look, but other than that his abrupt departure and return hardly raised an eyebrow. That evening he had eaten fish and chips and kipped down in another old barn. He had got up earlier on Monday morning with only enough money for a chocolate bar left in his pocket. After walking a few miles he realized he wasn't trying to do the coast-to-coast walk, that was for anoraks, so he might as well at least try to get a lift.

Just outside Northallerton a man towing a horsebox gave him a lift to Thirsk. All the way he had been aware of the horse shifting nervously behind him, and he thought he could smell manure. The driver hadn't said much, just dropped him off in the High Street, and now he was on the Scarborough Road, hoping for another kind soul to stop for him.

It was a grey afternoon, the clouds so low and the air so moist it was almost, but not quite, raining. 'Mizzling' they called it in Yorkshire, describing that bone-chilling combination of mist and drizzle. There wasn't much traffic and most of the cars and vans that passed just whizzed by without even slowing down. If he got to Scarborough, Mark knew, there was a good chance he'd be able to pick up some casual labouring work. It didn't matter what – ditch-digging, demolition, construction – he could turn his hand to almost anything as long as it didn't involve being educated. School had hardly been more than a mild distraction throughout his childhood and adolescence.

A police patrol car cruised by and seemed to slow down a bit just ahead of him. Mark tensed. He knew the coppers weren't going to give him a lift. Most likely beat the shit out of him and leave him lying bleeding in a field.

He must have been imagining things, though, because the car carried on and disappeared into the distance.

Mark trudged on, hardly bothering to stick out his thumb. He must have walked a couple of miles, the steep edge of Sutton Bank looming before him, when he heard a car coming and remembered to stick out his thumb. The car slowed to a halt about ten yards in front of him. It was quite a posh one, he noticed, an Audi, and shiny, as if it had just been cleaned. It would make a nice change from the horsebox. For a moment Mark worried that it might be the killer, but how could anyone know where he was?

The driver leaned over and opened the passenger window. He was a middle-aged bloke, Mark saw, wearing a camel overcoat and leather driving gloves. Mark didn't recognize him.

'Where you going?' he asked.

'Scarborough,' said Mark.

'Hop in.'

He seemed a pleasant enough bloke. Mark hopped in.

10

Banks grabbed his leather jacket, left by the back door and slipped behind the wheel of his 1997 Renault, thinking it was about time he had a new car, maybe something a bit sportier, if he could afford it. Nothing too flashy and definitely not red. Racing green, perhaps. A convertible wasn't much use in Yorkshire, but maybe a sports car would do. His midlife-crisis car, though he didn't particularly feel as if he were going through a crisis. Sometimes he felt as if his life was on hold indefinitely, but that was hardly a crisis. The only thing he knew for certain was that he was getting older; there was no doubt about that.

A snippet of interesting information about Andrew Hurst had just come to his attention. Annie was showing Roland Gardiner's Turners to Phil Keane, Detective Superintendent Gristhorpe having easily agreed to the consultation, so Banks decided to head out to the canal by himself.

He slipped in an old Van Morrison CD to dispel the January blues – not entirely convinced that they were caused by the weather – and drove off listening to 'Jackie Wilson Said'. It was just over a mile to the edge of town, past the new-look college, and another couple of miles of mostly open countryside to the canal. The road wound by fields of cows and sheep, drystone walls on either side, an occasional wooded area and stiles with signposts pointing the direction for ramblers. Not that it was rambling weather.

You'd soon catch a chill and probably get bogged down in the mud before you got too far in open country. To his right he could see the far-off bulk of the hills, like the swell before the wave, frozen in a grey ocean.

The landscape flattened out towards the canal, which was why the channel had been dug there, of course, and Banks soon found the lane that ran down to the side of the lock keeper's cottage. He parked by the towpath and turned off Van just as he was getting going on 'Listen to the Lion'.

It seemed an age before Hurst answered the doorbell, and when he did he looked surprised to find Banks standing there.

'You again,' he said.

'Afraid so,' said Banks. 'You weren't expecting me?'

Hurst avoided his eyes. 'I told you everything I know.'

'You must think we're stupid. Can I come in?'

'You will anyway.' Hurst opened the door and moved aside. The hallway was quite low and he had to stoop a little as he stood there. Banks walked into the same room they had been in before, the one with Hurst's extensive record collection. Helen Shapiro was singing 'Lipstick on Your Collar'. Hurst turned off the record as soon as he followed Banks into the room, as if it was some sort of private experience or ritual he didn't want to share.

He was fastidious in his movements. He lifted the needle off gently, then stopped the turntable, removed the disc and slipped it lovingly inside its inner sleeve. It was an LP called *'Tops' with Me*, Banks noticed, and on the cover of the outer sleeve was a picture of the smiling singer herself. Banks had forgotten all about Helen Shapiro. Not that he had been much of a fan to start with, not enough to know about her LPs at any rate, but he did remember buying an ex-jukebox copy of 'Walkin' Back to Happiness' at a market stall in Cathedral Square, Peterborough, when he was about ten, before the covered market opened. It was one of those 45s with the middle missing, so you had to buy a plastic thingamajig and fix it in before you could play it.

Banks perched on the edge of an armchair. He didn't take his leather jacket off because the house was cold, the elements of the electric fire dark. Hurst was wearing a thick, grey, woolly polo-neck sweater. Banks wondered if he was too poor to pay the electricity bills.

'You should have told us you had a criminal record,' Banks said. 'You could have saved us a lot of trouble. We find out things like that pretty quickly and it looks a lot worse for you.'

'I didn't go to jail. Besides, it wasn't—'

'I don't want to hear your excuses,' Banks said. 'And I know you didn't go to jail. You got a suspended sentence and probation. You were lucky. The judge took pity on you.'

'I can't see what it has to do with present events.'

'Can't you? I think you can,' said Banks. 'You were charged with conspiracy to torch a warehouse. The only reason you got such a soft sentence was because the person who co-opted you was your boss and he was the one who actually lit the match. But you helped him, you gave him a false alibi and you lied for him throughout the subsequent investigation.'

'It was my job! He was my boss. What else was I supposed to do?'

'Don't ask me to solve your moral dilemmas for you. In any situation there are a number of possible choices. You made the wrong one. You lost your job, anyway, and all you gained was a criminal record. When the insurance company got suspicious and called the police in, the company went bankrupt. Since then you've had a couple of short-term jobs, but mostly you've been on the dole.' Banks looked around. 'Lucky you'd paid off most of your mortgage. Was that with the cash your boss gave you for helping with the arson?'

Hurst said nothing. Banks assumed he was right.

'Was that where you got your taste for fire?'

'I don't have any taste for fire. I don't know what you're talking about.'

'The narrowboats, Andrew. The narrowboats.'

Hurst shot to his feet. 'You can't blame that on me.' He stabbed his chest with his thumb. 'I was the one who called the fire brigade, remember?'

'When it was way too late. You've been seen skulking around in the woods, probably spying on Tina Aspern. You have no alibi. You washed your clothes before we could get a chance to test them. Come on, Andrew. How would it look to you? Why did you do it? Was it for the thrill?'

Hurst sat down again, deflated. 'I didn't do it,' he said. 'Honest, I didn't. Look, I know it *looks* bad, but I'm telling you the truth. I was here by myself all evening watching videos. It's what I do most evenings. Or sit and read a book. I hardly have an active social life and I don't have a job. What else am I supposed to do?'

'Do you feel inadequate, Andrew? Is that what it's all about? Do the anger and rage just build up in you until they get so strong that you just have to go out and burn something?'

'That's ridiculous. You're making out that I'm some sort of pyromaniac or something.'

'Aren't you?'

'No. Of course I'm not. That other fire, which I *didn't* start by the way, was purely a business thing. Nobody got hurt. Nobody got any weird gratification in setting it. It was just a way of dealing with a financial problem.'

'Maybe this one was too.'

'Oh? Now you're changing your approach, are you? Now I'm not a drooling pyromaniac but a cold, practical businessman dealing with a problem.' He folded his arms. 'And what problem might that have been?'

'Maybe Tina Aspern was your problem.'

'I don't know what you mean.'

'Perhaps she was going to tell on you. You used to spy on her, didn't you?'

'No.'

'Where were you on Saturday evening?'

'Saturday? Same place as usual. Here.'

'Watching another war video?'

'*Force Ten from Navarone*, as a matter of fact. Very underrated film.'

'Andrew, get this clear: I don't care about your fucking film reviews. All I care about is that three people are dead and that you might be responsible. Ever heard of a man called Gardiner? Roland Gardiner?'

'No.'

'Leslie Whitaker?'

'No.'

'What kind of car do you drive?'

'I don't. I can't afford to run a car and I don't need one.'

That would have made it very difficult for Hurst to have got to Jennings Field and back on Saturday night, Banks realized, but perhaps there were buses. 'In all your nosing about the area,' he asked, 'have you ever seen a car of any kind parked in the lay-by closest to the boats?'

'A few times. Yes.'

'What kind of car?'

'Different ones. Picnickers in summer, mostly.'

'And more recently?'

'Only once or twice.'

'What make, do you remember?'

'A van of some kind. You know, a Jeep Cherokee, Land Cruiser or a Range Rover, that sort of thing. I'm not very well up on the latest models.'

'But it was definitely that kind of vehicle?'

'Yes.'

'Colour?'

'Dark. Blue or black.'

'Ever see the driver?'

'No.'

'OK. Let's get back to the fires. Why did you hang around the boats so much? Was it the girl?'

Hurst looked away, scanning the rows of his LP collection, lips moving as if he were silently reading the names off the covers to himself. Banks's mobile rang. He excused himself and walked outside to answer. It was DC Templeton calling from headquarters. 'Sir, we've identified the owner of the boats.'

'Good work,' said Banks.

'It's some bigwig in the City. Name's Sir Laurence West. Merchant banker.'

'Can't say I've heard of him,' said Banks, 'but then I don't exactly move in those kinds of circles.'

'Anyway,' Templeton went on, 'I've already been on the phone to him and he's agreed to grant an audience at his office tomorrow, but you'll need to make an appointment.'

'Good of him.'

'Yes,' said Templeton. 'I think he also believed he was being magnanimous about it.'

'I see. OK then, Kev, thanks. I'll go down there myself tomorrow morning, seeing as he's so important.' Besides, thought Banks, it would be nice to get away, if just for a day. He'd take the train if the trains happened to be running. It was actually faster and far less hassle than driving to London, and train journeys could be relaxing if you had a good book to read and some CDs to listen to. 'Make an appointment for one o'clock, would you?'

'Yes, sir.'

'Any first impressions?'

'Only that this is all a terrible intrusion into his valuable time, and he needed reminding he even owned the boats.'

'OK,' said Banks. 'I don't suppose we can expect much from him, then, but it's got to be done.'

'And sir?'

'Yes.'

'A woman called.'

'Which woman?'

'Maria Phillips, from the art gallery. Wants to talk to you again. Says she'll be in the Queen's Arms at half-six. I think maybe she fancies you, sir.'

'I'll deal with her. Anything else?'

'DS Nowak wants to see you as soon as you can make it.'

'Where is he?'

'Here, in his office.'

'Right. Tell him to hang on. I'll be back in half an hour.'

'Will do, sir.'

Banks hung up and went back to Andrew Hurst, who

was in the same chair, chewing on a fingernail. There was no point pursuing the peeping angle. If Hurst had been trying to get a peek at Tina naked, then he wasn't going to admit it. And even if he did, what could Banks do about it? It wasn't as if Tina were still around to press charges. But if she'd noticed and had threatened to tell on him . . . ? No, there was scant enough evidence to link Hurst with the first fire, and none at all with the second. Besides, the fire had definitely been set on McMahon's boat. Why risk tackling a grown, fit man when you could set fire to a junkie on the nod?

Banks thought Hurst was weird, and probably a peeper, but he was quickly coming to the realization that there was nothing he could do about it. The only obvious motive he might have had was revenge at McMahon treating him so badly when he paid his neighbourly visit, but that didn't seem a strong enough motive for murder unless Hurst had more than just one screw loose. Still, there were enough questions about him that needed answers to keep him on the list.

'Why did you wash your clothes, Andrew?' Banks asked. 'Including the anorak. You must admit that looks suspicious.'

Hurst looked at him. 'I know it does. It's just . . .' He shook his head. 'I don't know. Maybe I wasn't thinking straight. I mean, yes, of course I knew you'd find out I'd been arrested in connection with a fire. I don't think you're stupid. I just thought maybe that by the time you did find out about me you'd have caught whoever did it, so you wouldn't need to look at me as a suspect. I'd been close enough to the fire for my clothes to pick up traces. They stank of smoke and turpentine. I've heard how good your forensic tests are these days. I didn't want to spend a night at the police station.'

'You smelled turps?'

'Yes. It was in the air.'

'You didn't tell us at the time.'

'I didn't want to get involved.'

If Banks had a penny for every time he'd heard that from a member of the public, he would be a rich man. He stood up. 'You're bloody lucky you don't get to spend a night in the nick,' he said, 'for wasting police time.' He tossed Hurst a card. 'Don't go on any holidays just yet, and if you think of anything else that might help us, give me a ring.'

Hurst nodded gloomily and put the card on the table.

'You can get back to your Helen Shapiro now,' Banks said and left.

•

Annie was always amazed when she stepped inside Phil's cottage at how spick and span everything was. It wasn't as if all the men she had ever known were slobs – Banks's place was generally quite neat except for the CD cases strewn around the coffee table, usually next to an empty whisky tumbler and an overflowing ashtray when he used to smoke – but Phil's cottage had an almost military sparkle to it, along with the scent of pine air-freshener. Still, it wasn't his main home and he didn't spend all that much time there. She wondered what his London flat looked like. Chelsea, he'd said. Maybe soon they'd have a weekend in London. Expensive as it was, it would be a hell of a lot more affordable than New York, especially if she didn't have to stop in a hotel.

'What a pleasure to see you,' said Phil, closing the door behind her.

'It's not exactly a social call,' said Annie, smiling to soften the words. 'I need your help.' She was still angry at Banks, but Phil didn't need to know about their exchange.

Phil raised his eyebrows. 'Me? A consultation? Official?'

'Approved by the superintendent, no less,' said Annie.

'But what can I possibly do to help you?'

Annie got him to fill out the necessary paperwork, then she unzipped her briefcase and laid out the Turner sketches and the watercolour, now safe inside their labelled and numbered plastic evidence covers.

'Well, well,' said Phil. 'These are a surprise. Where did you find them?'

'In a fire-resistant safe in that caravan that burned down over the weekend. It belonged to a man by the name of Roland Gardiner.'

'The fire you had to leave dinner for?'

'That's right.'

Phil leaned over and studied the drawings closely. Annie could see the concentration furrow his brow. When he had finished, he turned back to Annie. 'Anything else found with them?'

'Only some money. No more drawings, if that's what you mean.'

'No documents, letters, auction catalogues, nothing like that?'

'No.'

'Pity.' Phil took a large magnifying glass from a box on the bookshelf and went back to the sketches, studying them more closely. 'It certainly *looks* like authentic period paper,' he said. 'I might get a better sense if I could touch it, too, though.'

'Sorry,' Annie said. 'It's still to be tested for fingerprints.'

'Whose fingerprints would you expect to find?'

'You never know. We might find the victim's. And Thomas McMahon's, if there's a link between them.'

'You think McMahon forged these?'

'I don't know. That's partly why I came to you.'

'But how would you know it was this McMahon's fingerprints? I mean, I assume if he'd been badly burned – both of them, in fact – then their hands . . .'

'Well, that's true,' said Annie. 'Unless either of them has a criminal record for some reason . . .' Then she remembered the book Jack Mellor said Gardiner had lent him. There was a good chance his fingerprints would be on that. Or perhaps even some object from where he used to live with his wife, on the Daleside estate. Thomas McMahon might be more difficult, but she was sure that if they looked they'd find his fingerprints somewhere. Whitaker's shop, for example. 'We have to try,' she said.

'How do you get fingerprints from paper? I mean, if they're not immediately visible through a magnifying glass.'

'I leave it to the boffins,' said Annie. 'I think they usually use a chemical called ninhydrin, or something similar, but it's not my area of expertise.'

'Isn't that a destructive process? Couldn't it damage the works? If these are genuine Turners . . .'

'I'm sure that's something they'll take into consideration. They can probably use some sort of light source – laser or ultraviolet. I really don't know, Phil. The technology keeps changing. It's hard to keep up with. But don't worry, our fingerprints expert knows what he's doing. The last thing he'd want to do is to damage a work of art, especially if it's a genuine one.'

'That's good,' said Phil. 'Then I assume you brought these to me because you want me to tell you if they're fake or real?'

'That would be a great help,' said Annie. 'In fact, *anything* at all you can tell us about them would be a help.'

'It's not as easy as all that, you know, especially when they're covered in plastic. I mean, I can give an opinion off the cuff, mostly based on the style, but there are tests, other experts to be consulted, that sort of thing. And the provenance, of course. That would go a long way towards establishing whether it's genuine or not.'

'I understand,' said Annie. 'Off the cuff will do fine for now.'

'Well, they're similar to other Turner sketches in the large sketchbook and pocketbook he used on his 1816 Yorkshire tour, so it might also be possible to do a bit of comparison work with some bona fide originals. Later, of course, when you've finished with them.'

'Was it unusual to do more than one sketch of the same sort of thing?'

'Not at all. Turner did dozens of sketches like this for the Richmondshire series. Three sketchbooks full. But that's the interesting thing: he usually worked in the books, not on loose sheets.'

'So that's one mark against authenticity?'

Phil smiled at her. 'It signals caution, that's all,' he said. 'But genuine or not,' he went on, 'this is certainly a beautiful watercolour. Look at that mist swirling around Ingleborough summit. You can almost see it moving. And there's not a soul around, see? It's very early in the morning, just after dawn. You can tell by the quality of the light. Turner was always very keen on reproducing time of day and weather conditions. And do you see that peacock in the right foreground? Marvellous detail.'

Annie had looked at plenty of paintings in her time, many with her father's guidance, and was even a passable landscape artist herself in what little spare time she had, but she lacked the training both in technique and in history and found she always learned something from Phil's point of view. It was one of the things she liked about him, his knowledge of and passion for art.

'May I ask exactly what makes you think it's a forgery?' he asked.

'Well, I'm certainly no expert,' Annie said. 'It'd just be the circumstances of its discovery. In the first place, it seems a bit of a coincidence that this should turn up so soon after the other Turner, don't you think? And what would Roland Gardiner – the victim in the caravan – be doing owning a Turner watercolour, several sketches and about fifteen hundred pounds in cash? When you consider what we talked about yesterday, about McMahon's buying up old eighteenth- and nineteenth-century books for the endpapers from Leslie Whitaker, then . . . I don't know. Perhaps we're trying to make a connection where none exists, but you have to admit it's a bit of a strong coincidence when you put it all together. Two murders in two days – three, if you count the girl – an artist buying old paper, these Turners, the money.'

'You think this Whitaker character might have something to do with it?'

'It's possible,' said Annie.

'Did they know one another, Roland Gardiner and the artist?'

'We don't know. Not yet. But we're trying to link them. I just wanted to get your take on whether we were dealing with the real thing here, the watercolour in particular.'

'Well, it looks genuine enough to me on first examination. If not, then it's a damn good forgery. To be absolutely certain, though, I'd have to hang onto it for a while, perhaps show it to some colleagues, conduct a few tests. Fingerprints examination, as we did with the other one. Radiography. Ultraviolet. Infrared photography. Computer image-processing. Pigment analysis. That sort of thing. I'd also try to track down its provenance, if any exists. And I can't do that, can I?'

'I'm afraid not,' said Annie. 'Not yet, at any rate. As I said, there are fingerprints to be considered. And it may be evidence.'

'Evidence of what?'

'I don't know.' She grinned at him. 'That's just the way the job is sometimes.'

Phil smiled back. 'Mine, too. I suppose you could say we're both detectives, in a way.'

'That's one way of looking at it. Anyway, as soon as we're done with it, I'll ask you to look into its authenticity a bit further, if you'd still be willing to help.'

'Of course. I've signed the Official Secrets Act, haven't I? Look, how rude of me. I never offered you any refreshments. It must have been the excitement of seeing the Turners. Tea, coffee, something stronger?'

'I can't,' said Annie, carefully putting the papers back in her briefcase. 'Too much on right now.'

'Not even a tea break?'

Annie laughed. 'Sometimes I don't even get dinner, as you know quite well.' She leaned forward and kissed him quickly on the lips. He tried to make it into more, but she slipped free. 'No. Really. I have to go.'

He spread his hands. 'OK. I know when I'm beaten. See you tonight?'

'I'll give you a ring,' Annie said, and hurried out to her car before she changed her mind about the tea and whatever else was on offer.

'And be careful with your briefcase,' he called after her.

•

It was DS Stefan Nowak's job to coordinate between the crime scene, the lab and the SIO, making sure that nothing was missed and priorities were dealt with as quickly as possible. He wasn't a forensic scientist by training, though he did have a degree in chemistry and had completed the requisite courses. As a result, he'd picked up a fair bit of scientific knowledge over his three years on the job, along with the ability to present it in layman's terms. Which was just as well. The best Banks had ever done at chemistry and physics was a grade five pass in each at O level.

Though Stefan himself was elegant and always well groomed, his office was a mess, with papers, plastic bags of exhibits and half-full mugs of coffee all over the place. Banks hardly dared move once he had sat down for fear the resulting vibration or disturbance of the air would bring a stack of reports, or beakers full of God knows what, toppling down.

'I trust you've got some positive results?' Banks said as he eased himself onto the chair. Nothing fell.

'Depends on how you look at them,' Stefan said, the Polish accent barely audible in his cultured voice. 'I've been over at the lab most of the afternoon, and we've finally got something on toxicology. I think you'll find it interesting.'

'Do tell,' said Banks.

'Luckily, in all three cases there was still enough fluid present in the bodies for tox analysis. McMahon, the artist, was the worst, but even there Dr Glendenning found blood in the organs and traces of urine in the bladder. Unfortunately, the vitreous fluid in the eyes evaporated in all victims.'

'Go on,' Banks urged him, not wishing to dwell on the evaporation of vitreous fluid.

'Let's take the girl first,' Stefan said. 'Christine Aspern. Because she was a known heroin addict we could be more specific in our search. As you probably know, heroin metabolizes into morphine once injected into the bloodstream and it bonds to the body's carbohydrates. Only a small amount of morphine is secreted unchanged into the urine. Sometimes none at all.'

'So you can't tell whether she injected heroin or morphine?'

'I didn't say that. Only that heroin becomes morphine once it's in the blood. Besides, heroin's a morphine derivative, made through a reaction with acetyl chloride or acetic anhydride. Anyway, spectral analysis indicated traces of heroin. The presence of other substances, such as quinine, bear out the result.'

Banks knew that quinine was often used to pad heroin for sale on the streets. 'It's what we expected,' he said. 'How much?'

'The stuff was around thirty per cent pure, which is pretty much the norm these days. And there wasn't enough to cause death. At least, the lab results make that seem unlikely.'

'So the fire killed her one way or another?'

'Asphyxia did. Yes.'

'What about the other two?'

'Ah, there it gets a little more interesting,' Stefan said. He leaned forward and a pile of books teetered dangerously. 'Alcohol was present in the urine in both cases, though none was present in the girl's system.'

'How much?'

'Not a lot in McMahon's case, maybe between one and two drinks.'

'Not enough to make him pass out, then?'

'Unlikely.'

'And Gardiner?'

'About twice as much. But there's more.'

'I hoped there would be. Go on.'

'During general screening spectral analysis also discovered the presence of flunitrazepam in the systems of Thomas McMahon and Roland Gardiner. Comparisons indicate it's the same drug in both cases.'

'Flunitrazepam?' said Banks, remembering one of the drugs circulars he'd read in the last few months. 'Isn't that Rohypnol?'

'Rohypnol is one form of it, yes. The "date-rape" drug. Recently upgraded from Class C to Class A. It's a form of benzodiazepine, a tranquillizer about ten times stronger than Valium. It causes muscle relaxation, drowsiness, unconsciousness and amnesia, among other things. It also impairs basic motor skills and lowers the blood pressure. It's often used to spike drinks because it's colourless, odourless and tasteless and it dissolves in alcohol. At least it used to do. The problem is that since 1998, La Roche, the chief manufacturer, has added a component that makes any drink you add it to turn bright blue. The drug itself also dissolves more slowly and forms small chunks.'

'Which makes it a lot harder to sneak into people's drinks.'

'Yes. Even dark drinks will turn cloudy. Anyway, if that were the case one or both victims might have noticed.'

'Which means?'

'Which means it's either counterfeit, bootleg Rohypnol, or another member of the benzodiazepine family. Remember, this test took a bit more time because they had to do a general tox screen. They're still working on it to pin down specifics, but I thought you'd like some sort of advance notice of what you're dealing with.'

'Thanks, Stefan,' said Banks. 'Much appreciated. How long does it take to act?'

'Twenty minutes to half an hour.'

'Any ideas what quantities they were given?'

'Certainly enough to be effective. One odd thing.'

'Yes?'

'Gardiner, the caravan victim, also had a significant amount of Tuinol in his system. Tuinol's—'

'I know what Tuinol is, Stefan. It's a form of barbiturate.'

'Yes. It's not prescribed very often these days.'

'We know who Gardiner's doctor is. We can make enquiries. He's the one who had more to drink, too?'

'Yes. Just thought you'd like to know.'

'Interesting,' said Banks. 'I wonder why?'

'Search me. One more thing,' said Stefan as Banks walked towards the door.

Banks paused and turned. 'Yes?'

'The tyre tracks are consistent in all their dimensions with those of a Jeep Cherokee, and if you ever find a suspect he was wearing Nike trainers with a very distinctive pattern of criss-cross abrasions on the right heel.'

As Banks left the office, he had a mental image of McMahon in his cabin and Gardiner in his caravan, each welcoming an old friend, chatting, making plans for whatever it was that was going to make their fortunes, drinking to it, then after a while starting to feel drowsy, finding it hard to move. At which point their faceless killer splashes turpentine or petrol about the place, drops a match and leaves. Couldn't be easier.

Or crueller.

11

'**I'm Clive,**' said the driver.

'Mark.'

'Pleased to meet you, Mark.'

'Likewise. And thanks for the lift.'

'My pleasure.' Clive turned and flashed Mark a quick smile. 'I'd stop a while so we could admire the view when we get to the top, but I'm afraid we wouldn't see much today.'

They were climbing the winding road up Sutton Bank now, the Audi moving easily despite the one-in-five and one-in-four gradients. The higher they got, the mistier it became, as if they were ascending into the very clouds themselves. Mark's ears started to feel funny. He was enjoying the warm, plush interior of the car.

Sutton Bank forms the western edge of the North York Moors, and when you get high up, you can look back over your shoulder and see all the way from the Vale of York to the Dales. Only on a clear day, of course.

When they finally crested the top after about a mile or so, Mark managed a quick look behind and saw nothing but vague shapes through a grey veil. Ahead was mostly rough moorland, similarly mist shrouded. It was an eerie landscape, and the occasional sheep that materialized out of thin air only made it seem eerier. Sheep gave Mark the creeps. He didn't know why, but they did.

'What do you do, Mark?' Clive asked.

'I'm looking for work.'

'What sort of work?'

'Restoration. Old buildings. Churches and stuff.'

'That's interesting. Where do you live?'

'Eastvale,' Mark said. It was the first thing that came to his mind.

'Lovely town,' said Clive. 'Have you got a girlfriend?'

Mark said nothing, thought of Tina, the way she had looked at him from the TV screen. He felt his heart shrivel in his chest.

Clive turned and flashed him another quick smile. Mark didn't like the way he did that. He didn't know why, just a feeling.

'A handsome, strong lad like you surely must have a pretty girlfriend?' Clive went on. He patted Mark's knee and Mark stiffened instinctively.

'It's all right, you know,' Clive said. 'You can be frank with me. I'm a doctor. Look, I know you young people today. You're always at it, aren't you? I do hope you practise safe sex, Mark.'

Mark said nothing. He was thinking of another doctor, Patrick Aspern, and how he'd like to smash the bastard's face in. He was aware of Clive chuntering on beside him, but he wasn't really paying much attention. He just hoped they'd get to Scarborough soon. The sea.

'. . . very important to be circumcised, you know,' Clive went on. 'I know it's not always fashionable, but it's much more hygienic. There are plenty of germs around that part of your body, you know, Mark. Your penis. And smegma. It's nasty stuff. Circumcision is much better all around.'

'What?'

'Weren't you listening?' Clive glanced over at Mark. 'I'm talking about circumcision. It doesn't have to be painful, you know. Look, I've got some cream in the boot that will numb all feeling, like the dentist gives you, only it's not an injection. If you like, we could pull over into a lay-by and I can do it for you right now.'

His hand slid over into Mark's lap, groping for his penis. Mark lashed out with his left fist and caught Clive a hard blow on the side of his head. Clive gasped and the car started to snake along the road. Mark hit him again, this time connecting with soft tissue near his nose and drawing blood. Then he did it again and thought he felt a tooth crack.

Clive barely had control of the wheel now. He was trying to talk, pleading, calling Mark a maniac, blood dribbling with the saliva from his mouth. But Mark couldn't stop. He wasn't even looking to see if there were any cars coming the other way; he just kept on pummelling at Clive, seeing Crazy Nick and Patrick Aspern and everyone who had ever hurt him.

Finally, they came to a sharp bend and Clive had to slow down. He barely managed to change down in time, and as he gave all his attention to keeping control of the wheel, Mark slipped his hand into Clive's inside pocket, grabbed his wallet, then opened the passenger door and leapt out, rolling on the wet mossy grass by the side of the road. A little dazed, he sat up ready to run, but he was just in time to watch Clive reach over and pull the door shut, then speed off into the mist. When the sound of the car's engine had faded, Mark was left with nothing but the occasional baaing of a distant sheep to break the silence in the gathering dark.

●

Banks was pleased to find the mercury pushing nine or ten as he walked down Market Street towards the main Eastvale fire station, where Geoff Hamilton had his office. January had been quite a month for ups and downs in temperature. He unbuttoned his overcoat, but he still felt a little too warm. The whiskey-soaked strains of Cesaria Evora came from the headphones of his portable CD player.

As he walked past the end of the street where he used to live with Sandra, Tracy and Brian, Banks couldn't resist the temptation to walk up to the old house and see how much it had changed. He stood by the low garden wall and looked at the front window. It hadn't changed. Not much. The curtains were closed, but he could see the flickering light of a television set in the living room. The most surprising thing was the 'For Sale' sign on the lawn. So the new owners were selling already. Maybe it wasn't a happy home. But how many innocuous-looking houses on innocent streets ever were? Inner-city slums and tower blocks hadn't cornered the market in human misery yet.

Banks arrived at the fire station, put away his CD player and went inside. Two of the firefighters on shift were working on equipment maintenance, another was doing paperwork and two were playing table tennis.

Banks tapped on Geoff Hamilton's office door and entered. Hamilton ran his hand across his hair and bade Banks sit down. Certificates hung on the wall and an old-fashioned fireman's helmet rested on top of the filing cabinet. Hamilton's desk was tidy except for the papers he was working on.

'Report to the coroner,' he said, noticing Banks looking at the papers. 'What can I do for you?'

'Anything new?'

'Nothing yet.'

'Look, Geoff,' said Banks, 'I know you don't like to commit yourself, but off the record I'd just like to get some sense of motive, whether you think we're dealing with a serial arsonist here, if we can expect more of this sort of thing. Or might there be some other reason for what's happening around here?'

Banks noticed a hint of a smile pass over Hamilton's taciturn features. 'And what would your guess be? Off the record.'

'I don't know. That's why I'm here.'

'You've uncovered no links between the victims yet?'

'We're working on it.'

Hamilton rubbed his eyes. They had dark bags under them, Banks noticed. 'What if you don't find any?'

'Then perhaps we're dealing with someone who just likes to start fires, and he's choosing relatively easy targets. Someone with a grudge against down and outs.' Andrew Hurst came to Banks's mind, partly because of the way he seemed to disapprove of the narrowboat squatters. 'But I'm not sure if that's the case.'

'Why not?' asked Hamilton.

'According to the toxicology results, both Roland Gardiner and Thomas McMahon were dosed with Rohypnol before the fires started.'

'The glasses we found at the scene?'

'Most likely they contained alcohol, into which the drug had been introduced.'

'And the girl?'

'We're pretty sure that Christine Aspern was high on heroin. Anyway, leaving Tina out of it for the moment, it looks as if both male victims admitted the killer to their homes and probably accepted a drink from him. If he didn't want to get rid of them for a reason, then he was doing it just for fun. What can you tell me about motivation in cases like this?'

'Fancy a coffee?'

'Wouldn't mind,' said Banks. He followed Hamilton into the large, well-appointed kitchen, a white-tiled room complete with oven, fridge, microwave and automatic coffee-maker. A cook came in on weekdays and made the firefighters a meal, and the rest of the time they brought their own food or took it in turns to cook.

Hamilton poured the coffees into two large white mugs, adding a heap of sugar to his own, then they went back to his office and sat down. The coffee tasted good to Banks, dark and strong.

'As you know,' Hamilton began, 'there are plenty of motives for arson. Probably the most common is sheer spite, or revenge.'

Banks knew this. About ninety per cent of the arson cases he had been involved in during his career – including the very worst, the one that haunted him whenever the thought of fire raised its ugly head – arose out of one human being's disproportionate malice and rage directed towards another.

'These can vary between simple domestic disputes, such as a lover's quarrel, and problems in the work place or racial or religious confrontations.'

'Is there any kind of profile involved in these sort of fires that compares to ours?'

'Well,' said Hamilton, 'they can be set by any age group, they're usually set at night and they generally involve available combustibles or flammable liquids. Three out of three isn't bad.'

'Aren't most fires set at night?'

'Not necessarily, but more often than not, yes.'

'So what other possibilities do we have?'

'There's always the simple profit motive. You know, insurance frauds, eliminating the competition, that sort of thing. That's probably the next most common motive. But these weren't commercial fires.'

'Not the caravan, certainly. It belonged to Gardiner. But I suppose the boats were commercial properties, to some extent,' Banks said. 'We've traced the owner and I'll be talking to him tomorrow. Even so, I can see someone burning empty boats for the insurance, but not deliberately drugging Thomas McMahon and setting fire to him in order to do so.'

'Lives are often lost in commercial fires,' Hamilton argued. 'Often by accident – the arsonist didn't know there was anyone in the building – but sometimes deliberately. A nosy nightwatchman, say.'

'Point taken,' said Banks. 'And we'll try to keep an open mind. What about pyromania as a motive?'

'Well, first of all you should bear in mind that pyromaniacs are extremely rare, and they're usually between fifteen and twenty.'

'Mark Siddons is twenty-one,' Banks said.

'I wouldn't rule him out, then. Anyway, they generally use whatever combustible comes to hand. I mean, they don't plan their fires. And there's no particular pattern in the kind of places they burn, or even where they strike. They're impulsive and often act for some sort of sexual gratification. The main problem here is that I can't see a pyromaniac doping or knocking someone out *before* starting a fire. They're usually loners and shun social company. Contrary to rumour, they don't usually stay at the scene, either. They'll be long gone by the time the fire brigade arrives. It's starting the fire that gives them their thrill, not watching firefighters put it out.'

'Any chance it was a woman?'

'There *are* female pyromaniacs,' Hamilton said. 'But they're even rarer. Oddly enough, they usually set their fires in daylight. They also set them fairly close to their own homes, often don't use accelerant and they generally start small fires.'

'I suppose we men like to start bigger ones?' said Banks.

'It would seem so.' Hamilton sipped some coffee. 'You know, I don't like to say it, but all these profiles are pretty much . . . well, I won't say a load of bollocks, they have been of some use to us on occasion, but they're pretty vague when you get right down to it.'

'Under twenty-five, loner, bed-wetter, harsh family background, absent father, domineering mother, not too bright, problems at school, problems at work, can't handle relationships.'

'Exactly what I mean. Fits any sociopath you'd care to point out. From all that, you'd think we'd be able to spot them *before* they strike.'

'Oh, we can,' said Banks. 'We just can't do anything about it until they commit a crime. Anyway, I'm inclined to dismiss the pyromaniac in this case. I mean, from what you've seen, would you call these fires impulsive?'

'No. But there are also vanity fires, you know,' Hamilton went on. 'Someone wants to draw attention to himself through an act of heroism. Those are the sort of blokes who stick around and watch, or even help out.'

'There weren't any heroes here, except the firefighters. Andrew Hurst hung around for a while, but he didn't get close enough to be a hero.'

'What about the boy you found at the scene of the first fire?'

'Mark Siddons?'

'Yes.'

'He hung around because his girlfriend was on one of the boats. His alibi held and his clothing and hands checked out clean. He also didn't have anywhere nearby he could have gone and cleaned up or changed. All his belongings, including his clothes, perished in the fire. I don't know, Geoff. I'm inclined to believe his story. Even so, he could have acted out of anger, I suppose, and covered his traces somehow. I just can't see the girl, Mandy, giving him an alibi if he wasn't, in fact, there. Annie said she had a tough enough time getting her to admit to having Mark in her bed in the first place. Didn't want to be known as "that kind of girl". We could talk to her again. I don't suppose you found any trace of a timing device?'

'Not yet, but we're still sifting through the debris. Is it possible that the boy drugged McMahon, if that is indeed what happened, but someone else set the fire?'

'Possible,' said Banks, 'but highly unlikely, wouldn't you say? Don't forget, someone drugged Gardiner too.'

'Could that also have been the boy?'

'He was in the vicinity of Jennings Field at the right time,' Banks admitted, 'but there's no trace of a motive. Don't worry, though, we'll keep him on our list of suspects. I'm hoping to have another chat with him soon, when we find him.'

'You let him go missing?'

'We had no reason to keep him locked up. He had an altercation with a friend and hoofed it. We'll find him. OK?'

Hamilton put up his hands in mock surrender. 'All right. All right.'

Banks smiled. 'So what's left as far as motive is concerned?'

'Well, there are fires started to conceal a crime.'

'Which is also a distinct possibility here,' Banks said. 'Fire destroys evidence. Maybe not as much as the criminal thinks, but often it's enough.'

'Evidence of what, though?' Hamilton asked.

'That's what we don't know yet. It looks as if Thomas McMahon might have been involved in art forgery and Gardiner was fired for fiddling the company he worked for, but that's all we've got so far. We're still digging. First we need to know if there was any connection between the victims. If there was, and if we find it, that might lead us to some enemy they had in common.'

'Sounds fair enough. I'm just hoping to hell there aren't any more fires.'

'Me too,' said Banks.

'There is one ray of hope,' said Hamilton.

'What's that?'

'The use of petrol as an accelerant might be a godsend.'

'How come?'

'Well, you know that different brands of petrol contain different additives, so you can tell, say, Esso from Texaco from Shell through spectral analysis?'

'I've heard about that,' said Banks, 'but it won't do us a lot of good in this case. Millions of people use Esso, Shell or Texaco.'

'Yes, but it doesn't stop there,' Hamilton went on. 'When the petrol is pumped into a station's underground tank, then more contaminants are added unique to that tank.'

'Are you telling me we can discover what *garage* the petrol came from through spectral analysis of the debris at the scene?'

'Not only that,' said Hamilton, 'but when you put the petrol in your fuel tank, another unique blend is created. By checking all local petrol stations and sampling each tank, we can actually determine which station the petrol came from and link it to the scene, or to a specific car's fuel tank.'

'You're not serious?'

'I always take my work seriously, double-o-seven.'

Hamilton didn't crack a smile, so it took Banks a moment to catch on. A Bond reference. Geoff Hamilton clearly had hidden depths.

'But in order to find a possible match,' Banks said, 'we'd have to sample every underground tank in every petrol station in the area?'

'That's right. It helps if you have other information that helps you narrow down the search field.'

'Not yet we don't, but it's something to think about,' Banks said. 'Thanks.'

'My pleasure,' said Hamilton. He glanced at his watch. 'And believe it or not, I'm going home now. My wife's beginning to wonder whether we're still married.'

'I remember the feeling,' said Banks, who planned on spending the evening at home catching up with the Sunday papers, maybe with a dram or two of Laphroaig. After meeting Maria Phillips in the Queen's Arms at half-six, of course.

Later, just after nine, there was a modern version of *Great Expectations* on the BBC, starring Gwyneth Paltrow. Banks liked the original Dickens novel, and he liked

Gwyneth Paltrow, the way she sort of lit up the screen when she walked on.

Besides, he found watching television – *anything* on television – a great way of sorting out his thoughts and coming up with new hypotheses. The TV seemed to numb a part of his mind and leave the rest free to wander and make wild connections without too many inhibitions. At least that was the way it felt to him, and it had worked before.

•

Mark waited by the roadside for five minutes until he was certain Clive had gone, then he opened the wallet. It contained two hundred and fifty pounds in cash, all in nice crisp twenties and tens, fresh from the cashpoint, along with credit cards, photos of a smiling woman and three blonde children – Clive's family, no doubt – and a number of receipts for petrol and meals. Nowhere did it say that Clive was a doctor, and Mark guessed he was probably just a travelling salesman. And a pervert. Worried that the police would be after him after the incident, though, he thought of striking out across open country and avoiding the roads. But there was no way, he realized, that Clive was going to report what had happened. Even if he said Mark just attacked him in order to rob him, Mark could make enough noise to cause problems. And maybe others would come forward. Clive must know this; Mark doubted he was the first victim. And there was that smiling woman with the three blonde children to consider. No, he thought, he was safe for the moment.

It was getting dark and he still had a long way to go. The moors became even eerier as the light faded and mist settled in patches. He knew he'd get lost if he headed for open country, probably die of exposure. Mark thought he could hear a dreadful howling in the distance. Weren't there ghostly hounds on the moors? Or werewolves? He thought about that film again, the one where the American tourist got bitten by a wolf on the moors and turned into a werewolf, and realized he had seen it when he was back with his mum and Crazy Nick, not at the squat. Or seen some of it. When Crazy Nick saw Mark was enjoying the film, he declared it was rubbish and switched to boxing. After that, Mark pretty much lost interest in television. There was no point, as he never got to watch anything he wanted anyway. He shivered and started to walk towards the nearest village, Helmsley, which he didn't think was very far.

When he got to the village, the lights in the houses and pubs were all on. It looked like a twee, tourist sort of place from what Mark could make out as he walked down the main street. He checked for Clive's car in the main car park and by the roadside, but thankfully couldn't see it. He laughed at himself, not sure why he was so paranoid. Clive had taken off like a bat out of hell and he wouldn't stop until he got to Scarborough. Mark had scared the shit out of him. Mark looked around to see that no one was watching, then he stopped and dropped Clive's wallet, minus the cash, down a grating.

There was a newsagent's shop still open at the corner, and Mark went in and bought a packet of cigarettes, twenty Benson & Hedges, seeing he was so flush, and a copy of the evening paper, just to see if there was any news about the fires. He was hungry and the cafes were all closed, the way they always seemed to be at teatime, so he ducked into a friendly looking pub. He went first to the toilet, where he was able at least to clean up his hands

and face and brush some of the muck off the suede overcoat. It was badly stained from his fall on the wet grass,
though, and there was nothing he could do about that.
Other than the overcoat, which he took off and carried
over his arm so no one could see the stains, he reckoned
he didn't look so bad.

Nobody paid him much attention as he sipped his pint
of Guinness and ate the ham and cheese sandwich, which
was all he was able to get there in the evening. The newspaper didn't tell him anything he didn't already know.
The second fire was a caravan and another man had been
killed. Nobody would come right out and say it, but Mark
could tell they thought it was deliberate and that it had
something to do with the fire on the boats.

It was half-past six. The pub was warm and the log fire
crackling in the hearth made him feel drowsy. He didn't
want to move, didn't want to go anywhere. He lit his first
cigarette in ages and inhaled the acrid smoke deep into
his lungs. Heaven.

But what to do next? He knew he was about fourteen
miles from the nearest railway station, back in Thirsk,
but thought maybe he could get a bus from Helmsley to
Scarborough. He'd have to find somewhere to stay when
he got there, though, and that could be a problem if it
was late and dark, especially as he was alone and without luggage or transport. He didn't want to draw attention
to himself, even though he was almost a hundred per cent
certain Clive wouldn't report him to the police. He also
had the killer to worry about, he realized. Somehow or
other he might have found out where Mark was, where
he was going. He would have to be careful.

Then he saw the notice behind the bar: B & B. The
landlord had been friendly enough when he served Mark,

even apologizing for the lack of hot meals, so Mark walked over to the bar and asked if there were any rooms vacant.

The landlord smiled. 'It's not often we're full up at this time of year,' he said. 'I suppose it'll be a single you're wanting?'

'Yes,' said Mark.

'I think we might be able to accommodate you. Rachel.'

The woman helping behind the bar came over.

'Show this young lad the single, would you? Number six.'

Rachel, a pretty young woman with fair hair and a peaches and cream complexion, blushed and said, 'Of course, Mr Ridley.' She turned to Mark. 'Come on.'

Mark followed her up the narrow, creaking staircase. At the top she opened a heavy door. The room looked magnificent to Mark, and he realized he must have been standing on the threshold with his mouth open. Rachel was expecting him to look around and say something.

'How much is it?' he managed to ask.

'Twenty-eight pounds, bed and breakfast,' she said. 'Breakfast's downstairs, between eight and nine o'clock. Well, do you want it?'

'Yes,' said Mark, reaching in his pocket for the money.

'Tomorrow, silly,' Rachel said. 'You pay when you leave.'

'Oh. Right,' Mark said, amazed that someone would trust him not to run off without paying.

Rachel handed him the key and explained about the various locks and how he had to make sure he was in before they closed up the pub. He didn't even think he was going out, so that was no problem.

'Where's your rucksack?' she asked

'Don't have one,' he said.

She looked at him as if she thought he was daft, then shrugged and left, shutting the door behind her.

It was the nicest room Mark had ever been in in his entire life. It wasn't very big, but that was all right: he didn't need much space. The wallpaper was a cheerful flower pattern and the air smelled of lemons and herbs. It had a solid bed and a dresser and drawers for clothes and stuff. There were facilities for making tea and coffee and also a television. But best of all, there was a bathroom/toilet.

It had been difficult managing without running water on the boat. Once a week they went to the public baths in Eastvale, next to the swimming pool, but most days they did the best they could. Mark had found a bucket and a nice big enamel bowl in a junk shop, and usually he would walk half a mile west along the canal bank to the taps installed by the tourist board for the boaters, campers and walkers and get fresh water there, which he would carry back and heat on the stove. It was a hassle, but it was better than being dirty.

But now he had a bath to himself, and soap and shampoo and towels, too. First he turned on the television. It didn't matter what was on; he just wanted the sound for company. Then he started running a hot bath and made himself a cup of tea. When everything was ready he took his tea into the bathroom, climbed in the tub and lit a cigarette. It was wonderful. He could hear *Emmerdale* on the television through the half-open door as he lay back and luxuriated in the steamy warmth. This must be what it was like to be normal, he thought. He only wished Tina could be here with him. He knew it wouldn't all seem so

special to her because she'd grown up with all these lux-
uries, but she would have loved it nonetheless.

He wished he could stay there for ever, with the hot
water enveloping him, the steam rising and the comforting voices on the television, but he knew he couldn't.
Tomorrow he would have to find a way to get to Scarborough and get a job. Clive's money wouldn't last for ever,
especially if he had to pay so much for a room every night.
But maybe he'd find somewhere cheaper in Scarborough.
A little flat, even. And then he'd start putting his life back
together.

•

Banks certainly felt as if he needed a drink when half-past
six came around, but left to his own devices he would
have chosen other company than Maria Phillips. Still, he
thought, pushing open the pub's door, duty calls, and she
was harmless enough if you kept your distance.

The Queen's Arms was busy with the after-work
crowd, most of whom seemed to prefer standing elbow to
elbow at the bar. Banks was the first to arrive, so he managed to get Cyril's attention, bought himself a pint of bitter
and settled by the window to read the paper.

Maria came dashing in ten minutes late, breathless
and full of apologies. Someone hadn't turned up for an
evening shift and she'd had to deal with it. Banks offered
to get her a drink.

'You dear man,' she said unbuttoning her coat and
unwinding her scarf. 'I'll have the usual.'

When he came back with her Campari and soda, she
was composed, smoking a Silk Cut. A momentary pang
of desire – for a cigarette, not for Maria – leapt through
Banks's veins like an electric current, then passed as

quickly as it came, leaving him feeling vaguely uneasy and fidgety.

'Cheers,' Maria said, clinking glasses.

'*Slainte*,' said Banks. 'So what is it you want to see me about?'

Her eyes sparkled with mischievous humour. 'It's all business with you, isn't it?'

'It's been a long day.'

'And I don't suppose there's a dear devoted woman waiting for you at home, ready to massage your neck and shoulders and run a nice warm bath for you, is there?'

'Afraid not,' Banks said, thinking there was only Gwyneth Paltrow in *Great Expectations* and a tumbler of Laphroaig. But Gwyneth wouldn't be massaging him or running him a hot bath. 'There's not even a faithful dog to fetch my slippers. Policing doesn't lend itself to pet-owning, especially when you live alone.'

'Wives, either,' Maria said.

'Well, I'd never claim to have *owned* a woman.'

She slapped him playfully on the forearm. 'Silly. You know what I mean. Your job. It must make relationships difficult.'

Damn near impossible, thought Banks, realizing he hadn't even talked to Michelle in a day or two. He wondered how her missing-child case was going. Better than his triple murder, he hoped. His train would pass through Peterborough on his way to London. Maybe she could come to the station and he could lean out of the window and kiss her like a scene in an old black-and-white film. All that would be missing would be the atmospheric steam from the engine. 'Well,' he said, 'you should probably talk to Sandra about that.'

'I would, except she seems to have deserted all her old friends.'

'She's burned a few bridges, all right,' said Banks. 'So, Maria, what is it?'

'Nothing, really. It's just that after our little tête-à-tête the other day, well, you know how you start thinking back, trying to remember things?'

'Yes,' said Banks. 'That's why I usually give anyone I question my phone number. They often remember something later.'

'You didn't give *me* your phone number.'

'Maria! Stop doing your Miss Moneypenny imitation. You're just down the street.'

'Just down the street. Story of my life. Ah, well.' Maria laughed. 'Oh, don't look so exasperated. I'm only teasing.'

'You were talking about remembering something.'

'So stern. Yes, like I said, I got to thinking, trying to play the scene in my mind's eye, so to speak.'

'Which scene would this be?'

'The Turner reception, of course. There were quite a lot of people there, including that pretty young policewoman I've seen you with on occasion.'

'Annie was involved in the security. As you well know.'

'I'm surprised you two haven't . . .' Then she looked at Banks and opened her eyes wider. 'Well, maybe you have. None of my business, anyway.'

'That's right,' said Banks. 'The reception.'

'I'm getting to that. I was trying to picture Thomas McMahon, what he was doing, who he was talking to. That sort of thing.'

'And?'

'Well, he wasn't talking to anyone most of the time, but I did see him chat with Mr Whitaker from the bookshop.'

That made sense. Whitaker had told Banks that McMahon bought old books from him. For the endpapers, Phil Keane had suggested, perhaps to make forgeries of period sketches. And Banks was still keeping an open mind as to whether Whitaker was involved in some sort of forgery scam with McMahon and Gardiner, especially after Stefàn Nowak had confirmed that the car parked in the lay-by on the night of McMahon's murder was a Jeep Cherokee, the same model Whitaker owned. Thanks to Geoff Hamilton's expert knowledge, they could now check Whitaker's fuel tank against the accelerant used in the Gardiner blaze.

'What was Thomas McMahon doing?'

'Well, his wine glass was rarely empty, I can say that.'

'But he wasn't drunk?'

'No. Maybe a little bit tipsy. But not so's you'd notice that much. I seem to remember he was the kind of chap who could hold his liquor, as they say in the movies. But that's not what I wanted to tell you.'

'What is it, then?'

'Just that at one point he *was* talking to someone who might be able to tell you more about him than I can.'

'Who?'

'That art researcher from London. Well-heeled, yummy-looking fellow. Do you know who I mean?'

Banks felt the hackles rise on the back of his neck. Annie's 'friend' Phil. Philip Keane. 'Yes,' he said. 'I know him. Why do you say well-heeled?'

Maria rolled her eyes. 'Honestly, you *men*. His suit, dearie. You can't get a suit like that off the peg in Marks and Sparks. That was a made-to-measure job, *bespoke*, tailor. Beautifully made, too. Best quality material. Nice bit of schmatter. At a guess I'd say Savile Row.'

'How do you know?'

She winked. 'I've got hidden depths.'

Banks imagined an art researcher probably made a fair income, and if Phil Keane wanted to spend it on Savile Row suits, good for him. 'Go on,' Banks said. 'What were they talking about?'

'I don't know that, do I? I was some distance away doing my hostess routine, seeing that everyone's glass was full. It was just something I noticed, that's all, perhaps because most of the time McMahon *wasn't* talking to anyone.'

'How long were they talking?'

'I don't know that, either. My attention was diverted. Next thing I knew McMahon was studying one of the paintings on the wall and Mr Art Researcher was chatting up Shirley Cameron.'

'Which painting?'

'I can't remember. Just one of the ones we had on display in the reception room. Nothing fancy. Local, most likely.'

'Did you get any sense of what their conversation was about?'

'Not really.'

'I mean, were they arguing?'

'No.'

'Exchanging pleasantries?'

'No.'

'Intimate?'

'Not in *that* sort of way.'

'An animated, passionate discussion?'

'No. More casual than that.'

'Just passing the time of day, then?'

'Well, yes, except . . .'

'Except what?'

'When I was playing it back in my mind last night . . . I don't know if I'm imagining things, you know, embroidering on what I actually saw, but I could swear they were talking as if they *knew* one another.'

'Not as if they'd just met?'

'No, that's it. You can tell, can't you, when there's a history? Even if you don't hear a word.'

'Sometimes,' Banks said, 'body language can actually tell you quite a lot.'

'Body language,' Maria, repeated. 'Yes . . . anyway . . .' She reached into her handbag. 'He gave me his business card and I dug it out of the files, if that's any use.'

Banks looked at the card. Some ornate sort of typeface, black and red. It gave Phil Keane's company name as ArtSearch Ltd, along with an address in Belgravia. 'Can I keep this?' Banks asked.

'Of course. It's no use to me, is it?'

Banks thanked her.

'Well, that's it, then.' Maria spread her hands. 'I've told you all I know. I have nothing left up my sleeve to keep you here with.'

'Oh, I don't know,' said Banks, suddenly feeling magnanimous towards Maria and not in any great hurry to go home. After all, it was not yet seven o'clock and the film didn't start till nine. 'What about the pleasure of your company?'

Maria looked puzzled. 'You don't have to dash off somewhere?'

'No. Not yet, at any rate. As you pointed out, there's no wife waiting to massage my shoulders and neck and run a hot bath. How about another drink?'

Maria narrowed her eyes and looked at him suspiciously. 'Are you sure?'

'Of course.'

Maria blushed, then slid her empty glass towards him. 'I'll have another Campari and soda then, please.'

She actually seemed quite shy when *he* took the lead, Banks thought, as he made his way to the bar. As he stood there waiting for Cyril to pull his pint, he wondered about what he'd just heard. It didn't mean anything, necessarily, even if Maria's intuition was right, but why hadn't Phil told him? Why had he lied about knowing McMahon? And how could Banks go about checking into it without damaging his already fragile relationship with Annie?

12

On the train to London Banks fretted about what Maria Phillips had told him the previous evening and what to do about it. He couldn't even relax and enjoy his John Mayall CD for worrying, and he certainly couldn't concentrate on the Eric Ambler thriller he'd brought along.

There was no denying that Maria had told him Phil Keane was deep in conversation with Thomas McMahon, as if they already knew one another, and Keane had said he didn't know the artist. It could be a simple, honest mistake in identity – after all, it was a few months ago – but Banks didn't think so.

Maybe Keane, like anybody else, wanted to avoid any connection with a police investigation. It was a natural response, after all. Don't get involved. Leave me out of it. Leslie Whitaker had done the same thing and Banks was convinced that he was in a lot deeper than he had admitted.

But Phil Keane *was* involved. As a consultant and as Annie's lover. Which meant he was supposed to be on *their* side, didn't it? The last thing Banks could do was talk to Annie about it. She would immediately turn on him for trying to come between her and Phil out of personal jealousy, making their last little set-to seem like a preliminary round.

Shortly after Grantham, Banks had an idea. He made a call on his mobile to an old colleague on the Met, someone who might be able to help. After that, he had a bit more success in putting the matter out of his mind and listening to *Blues from Laurel Canyon*.

King's Cross was the usual melee. Banks headed straight for the taxi rank and joined the queue. Within a few minutes he was on his way to Sir Laurence West's office in the City. The journey was slow, like most road journeys in London, and the mild weather seemed to have brought more people out onto the streets. Couriers on bicycles wove in and out of the traffic with total disregard for safety – theirs or anybody else's – and pedestrians wandered across the streets no matter where, or what colour, the traffic lights were. Many were wearing only their suits or windcheaters and jeans.

There aren't many skyscrapers in the City, but Sir Laurence's offices were on the twelfth floor of one of them and offered a splendid view south over the river to Southwark, or would have done had the day not been so overcast.

By the time Banks finally made it past the security, receptionists, secretaries, office managers and personal assistants, he was beginning to wish he'd sent someone else instead. He didn't cope well with bureaucracy and soon found himself losing patience. When he was finally ushered into the inner sanctum he was ready to give Sir Laurence a hard time.

The office was about as big as the entire upper floor of Western Area Headquarters and most of it was uncluttered open space. Thick carpets with intricate eastern designs covered most of the floor area, the rest being shiny hardwood, and a big teak desk sat in the centre, a sleek laptop computer the only object on its surface. In one corner a black-leather-upholstered three-piece suite was arranged around a low, glass-topped table, a cocktail cabinet nearby. There was a faint whiff of old cigar smoke in the air.

The man himself was tall and portly, bald-headed and bushy-eyebrowed, with more than a passing resemblance to Robert Morley, probably in his early seventies, but well preserved. He was wearing a slate-grey suit, white shirt and a striped tie, no doubt representing some old school, exclusive club or regiment. He came forward with a genial smile on his face and shook hands, gesturing for Banks to sit in one of the armchairs.

'Drink?' he offered.

'No thank you,' said Banks.

'Hope you don't mind if I do.'

'Not at all.'

West poured himself some amber fluid from a cut-glass decanter and added a splash of soda. Banks got a whiff of brandy.

'I know it's a bit early,' said West, 'but I always make it a point to have a drink before lunch. Just the one, you understand. It helps sharpen the appetite.'

Banks, who might have time to grab a burger at the nearest McDonald's if he was lucky, nodded. 'I'll have a Coke, if you've got any,' he said.

'Of course.' West opened what looked like a filing cabinet. It was a small fridge. He took out a can of Coke, poured it into a crystal tumbler and handed it to Banks, who thanked him and took a sip.

'Now, what can I do for you?' said West, perching on the edge of the chair opposite Banks. He didn't have to explain that he was a busy man; it was evident from his body language. 'The young man on the telephone didn't tell me very much. I do hope those wretched British

Waterways people haven't been bothering you. They've been on at me for years, but I'm afraid I've rather ignored them.'

Anyone else's boats would probably have been towed away long ago, Banks reflected. Wealth and power do have their privileges. Slowly he explained about the fires and the deaths.

'Oh, dear,' said West. 'I hope you won't be holding me legally responsible for their condition?'

'That's not my department,' said Banks. 'All I'm interested in is who set the fire and why.'

'Then I'm afraid I can't help. You say there were squatters living on the boats? Perhaps they started the fire?'

'That's highly unlikely, given that two of them died.'

'I wish I could help.'

'How did you come to be the owner of the boats?'

West swirled his drink in his glass. 'They were my father's,' he said. 'I suppose I inherited them.'

'But you had no interest in his business?'

'No. He lived to be ninety-six years old, Mr Banks. He died just two years ago, though he had been uncommunicative for some time. I know he was in the haulage business, but believe it or not, I didn't even know about those two boats until the Waterways people got in touch with me after his death. I know I should have delegated, put someone on it, had something done, but I had more important things on my mind at the time. I didn't imagine they'd be doing any harm just sitting there.'

'There was no reason you wanted to keep them?'

'Good Lord, no.'

'Or sell them?'

'I suppose I might have got around to that eventually.'

'Were they insured?'

'I imagine so. My father was a thorough man before his illness.'

'But you don't know for how much?'

'I have no idea.'

'Do you know of anybody who might have had a reason to set fire to them?'

'No. Surely you're not suggesting some sort of insurance fraud?'

'I'm not suggesting anything,' said Banks. It was a patently absurd idea, anyway. West probably made a few billion a year and the insurance on the boats wasn't likely to amount to more than twenty or thirty thousand. Still, stranger things had happened. The rich don't get richer by missing opportunities to make even more money. Or West might simply have got someone to torch them to get them off his hands.

'It's funny,' said West, 'but now you bring it up, I actually did receive an offer to buy one of the boats a few months ago. My secretary brought it to my attention, but I'm afraid I didn't take the offer very seriously.'

'I thought you didn't need the money.'

West laughed. 'My dear man, that's no reason to let oneself be taken for a fool.'

'How long ago was it?' Banks asked.

'Oh, not long. October, perhaps.'

'Do you think you could find the letter?'

West called in his secretary, a buxom woman in a no-nonsense pinstriped skirt and matching jacket, who disappeared for a few moments and returned with a buff folder.

'How did the letter come to you?' Banks asked the secretary before she scurried off.

'It was forwarded through British Waterways,' she said.

She looked at Sir Laurence for guidance. He nodded, and she passed the folder to Banks. It contained just one sheet of paper, a letter dated 6 October. It was brief and to the point.

Someone wanted to buy the southernmost narrow-boat – Tom's boat – moored on the dead-end branch off the Eastvale Canal, near Molesby. He was willing to pay ten thousand pounds – such a low sum, he explained, because the boat needed a lot of work – and that some-one was Thomas McMahon himself.

•

Mark could smell and hear the sea as he made his way down the hill to the sands from Scarborough bus station just after eleven o'clock on Tuesday morning. After a breakfast of fried eggs, bacon, sausage, mushrooms and grilled tomatoes, he had paid his bill in Helmsley and wandered towards the bus stops in the square. There he had caught the half-past nine bus and stared out of the window at the bleak, misty moorland landscape to the north, until the bus headed down from the moors near Pickering.

His plan, inasmuch as he had one, was to find a job as soon as possible. The money he had stolen from Clive would enable him to get a roof over his head and food in his belly, for a while at least. But he would need some-thing more dependable in the long term. If there was going to be a long term.

Mark didn't know why, but he felt both apprehension and numbness at the same time. A part of him was numb because he had lost Tina, yet another part of him was afraid of what was around the next corner, who might be lying in wait for him. There was still the guilt, too. If only he'd been on the boat with Tina instead of with that slut Mandy. Anger raged inside him somewhere, unfocused yet growing stronger. He might have killed Clive, he realized, if they hadn't slowed at the bend and he'd been sharp enough to seize his opportunity to grab the money and get away. He remembered what the policeman had said about the fire not being an accident. That meant someone had killed Tina, whether she was the intended victim or not. The only person he could think of who had a reason to kill Tina was Patrick Aspern, and when Mark thought of Aspern he felt his rage surge up again.

A cold wind blew off the North Sea, pushing inland a mass of cloud the colour of dirty dishwater. There was no blue to be seen anywhere on the horizon, no rays of sunshine lancing through to make diamonds dance on the water; the whole world was wrapped in a grey shroud.

Down on the prom all the amusements were closed for the winter, the cafes and fish-and-chip shops shut up, Jimmy Corrigan's, the Parade Snack Bar, the sands deserted except for a man in a hooded overcoat walking his dog, hunched forward against the wind. The tide was high and waves like molten metal crashed on the beach, churning the brown sand. One or two other people were walking along the prom, old couples, a young family. Probably people who lived in town, Mark thought. After all, Scarborough was a big place and the people who lived there had to go on even when the tourist season was over.

A solitary grey Vectra was parked across the street, outside the Ghost Train, with two men in it drinking tea and eating Kit Kats. They both glanced towards Mark and he kept his face averted. He couldn't tell whether he recognized them or not, but there was no sense in falling right into their hands. Maybe two people had set fire to the boats, not just one, and this could be them. Hands in his pockets, he strolled on beside the harbour, where the nets were stacked and the fishing boats were moored.

He tried to light a cigarette, but the wind was too strong and after three matches he gave up. He'd have one later in a warm pub. It felt good to be near the sea. He didn't know why, but the sight of the water stretching out as far as the eye could see, until it met the sky way in the distance, evoked a feeling of awe in him: the way it was always changing, the surface swelling and dipping, the scudding white caps and huge breakers. It put you in your place, put things in perspective. He could watch it for ever.

He imagined sailors years ago in wooden ships with canvas sails bellied out tossing on seas like this, no land in sight, and thought that was what he would have liked to have been if he'd lived then. A sailor on a whaling ship. Not throwing the harpoons because he didn't particularly like the idea of killing whales, but maybe at the wheel, steering, discovering new worlds. Maybe even now he could join the Merchant Navy, if they'd have him, and spend the rest of his days at sea. The ships were more modern, he knew, but they'd still be at the mercy of the waves.

Out of his peripheral vision, he noticed the Vectra start moving just behind him, to his left. He walked past the empty funfair and on to Marine Drive. The car didn't overtake him, but kept up a slow, steady pace about twenty yards behind him. Were they following him? Mark risked a glance back and thought he saw one of them talking into a mobile phone.

Mark felt exposed, out in the open. Marine Drive curved around the base of Castle Hill, with nothing but the steep rocky slope on one side and the cold North Sea on the other. Nowhere to run. The wind howled in his ears and the waves crashed high over the sea wall and the metal railings, and Mark was soaked in no time.

The Vectra remained twenty yards behind him, crawling along, no matter how much he altered his pace. A few other souls were braving the weather, all dressed in waterproof gear. Out in the distance the dark shape of a ship bobbed on the water. Mark wondered what it was doing there, what it felt like, who was on it. Were they in danger? He couldn't see any danger signals flashing, any flares, or SOS lights. Weathering the storm. Just like him.

The car was still following him, no doubt about it. Mark picked up his pace, nearly running now, and it surged forward, pulling over onto his side of the road just a few feet in front of him, blocking the pavement.

Mark turned and ran the other way, back towards town, ignoring the doors slamming and the shouts behind him. He couldn't hear what they were saying anyway because of the wind and the crashing waves. He ran back towards the prom. If he could get into the maze of narrow streets behind the amusements, he might have a chance of losing them, whoever they were.

He hadn't got very far when he felt a hand on his shoulder. He shook it off and kept going, but it was no use. Within seconds, his legs went from under him and he fell onto the hard surface, smashing his cheek against the stone. He felt a knee between his shoulders and his arm twisted up his back. The pain was excruciating and he thought he screamed out, then he lay still. He could hear them talking but still couldn't grasp what they were saying, what they wanted. Mark could taste blood and salt on his lips and his tongue as they hauled him to his feet and back to the car. He cried out, but nobody came to help. One final, magnificent wave smashed against the sea wall and drenched them all from head to toe before they got him inside the Vectra.

•

The garage was a mere stone's throw from the Askham Bar Park and Ride, off the outer ring road just west of York city centre. Owner's name, Charlie Kirk. Handy place for a car-rental agency, Annie thought. You could arrive at the train station and take the bus out, then you never had to worry about the murderous city-centre traffic or the parking.

As it had done so many times before, legwork had paid off once again, and it looked as if this was the place where the killer might have rented his Jeep Cherokee. At least, the same person had rented the same vehicle on several occasions since the previous summer, including the past weekend. They had got lucky because not many local outfits had Cherokees for hire, but Charlie Kirk did. Now Annie was about to question the owner, with Stefan and his impressions expert in tow. They went off to the car park around the back with the mechanic, while Annie went to talk to the clerical staff.

The small office was overheated and stuffy. Three people worked there, one up front to deal with customers and the other two, a young girl and an older man, further back. The office was full of the usual stuff – computers, filing cabinets, phones and fax machines – and the walls were covered with posters of cars.

Annie slipped her overcoat off, laying it on a chair, and offered her warrant card to the woman at the front desk.

'I've been expecting you,' the woman said, standing up to shake hands. 'I'm Karen Talbot, office manager.'

Annie put Karen Talbot at about thirty. She had blonde highlights, glossy red lipstick and eyes so blue they had to be contact lenses, and she was wearing a black silk blouse, showing plenty of cleavage, and a short, tight red skirt. The effect was lost on Annie, but she imagined it wasn't on most of the male customers.

Karen sat down again, pulling her skirt as far over her thighs as it would go, which wasn't far.

'Is the owner around?' Annie asked.

'The captain isn't in today. This isn't his only outpost, you know. Quite the empire-builder, our captain is.'

'Captain?'

'Kirk. Captain Kirk. Our little joke. Only when he's not here, of course.'

'I see,' said Annie. 'We'll talk to him later, then. Maybe you can help me for now?' She sat down opposite Karen.

Karen patted her hair. 'I'll do my best. As a matter of fact, the captain wouldn't be able to tell you much, anyway. It's not as if he actually *works* here, if you know what I mean.'

'So it's you who deals with the public?'

'Mostly, yes.' Karen glanced behind at the other two. 'But we take it in turns. That's Ned and Sylvia.'

Annie said hello. Ned returned her greeting with a broad, salesman's smile and Sylvia smiled shyly at her. Annie wondered how Ned, who must be well the wrong side of forty, felt working for a young upstart like Karen. She also found herself rather uncharitably wondering how Karen had got the job and what her relationship with the owner was. But such thoughts had little to do with the business on hand, so she pushed them aside and got down to business.

'We've been told that you've rented out a dark blue

Jeep Cherokee, or a similar vehicle, to the same person on five different occasions since last summer. Is that correct?'

'Yes,' said Karen. 'Three times it was the Jeep, and twice we had to substitute a Ford Explorer.'

'Did that cause a problem with the customer?'

'Not that I remember. He just wanted the same type of vehicle.'

'Did you deal with this customer yourself?'

'Not every time.'

'I did, twice,' said Ned. 'And Sylvia did once.'

'First off,' said Annie, 'what were the dates?'

Karen went to the filing cabinet by her desk, flipped through the folders for a few seconds and pulled one out. Then she reeled off a string of dates in September, October, November and December, ending with the previous weekend.

'When did he take it out?' Annie asked.

'Thursday morning.'

'And when did he return it?'

'Saturday morning.'

So he had the Cherokee before the narrowboats' fire, but he took it back before the Roland Gardiner fire. Annie wondered why he would do that.

'Ever any problems when he brought it back?'

'No. It was always in excellent condition.'

'Did he return it full or empty?'

'Empty. It costs a bit more, but it saves the customer having to search for a garage himself.'

'You fill the cars here?'

'Yes, of course.'

That was a piece of luck, Annie thought. They could take samples from the garage's tank and from the Cherokee's. Banks had told her that forensics could identify the tank from which the petrol used in the Gardiner fire came. Whoever had rented the Cherokee would most likely not have needed to refill the tank anywhere else. If they came up with a match, that was solid evidence to use in court.

'What's the customer's name?'

'Masefield. William Masefield.'

'What did he look like?'

'Ordinary, really.'

'Let's see if we can improve on that, shall we?' said Annie, with a sigh. She hated trying to get descriptions out of people. Most witnesses, in her experience, were neither observant nor good at expressing themselves in words. This time proved no exception. After about ten minutes the best the three of them could come up with was that he was a little above medium height, generally in good shape though perhaps just a tad overweight, a little stooped, gold-rimmed glasses, greying hair and casual clothes – jeans, blue windcheater. Ned thought he'd been wearing white trainers on at least one occasion, but didn't know if they were Nike or not. At least Annie ought to be grateful there were no glaring contradictions about height or hair colour. It could have been the person Mark Siddons had described visiting Thomas McMahon, but it could have been a thousand other people, too.

'Any closed-circuit TV here?' Annie asked.

'Only out back, where the cars are,' said Karen. 'And it's only turned on at night, when no one's here. Otherwise we'd be changing the tapes every five minutes.'

Too bad, Annie thought. But it was worth a try. 'Was there anything else you remember about him?' Annie asked.

'No,' said Karen.

'How did he pay?'

'Credit card.'

'Can you give me the details?'

Karen quickly made a photocopy of William Masefield's file and passed it to Annie. The address, she noticed, was Studley, a Midlands village in Warwickshire, not far from Redditch.

'Did he have any sort of accent at all?' she asked.

'Just ordinary,' said Karen.

'What do you mean? What's ordinary? Yorkshire? Birmingham?'

'Sort of no accent, really. But nice. Educated.'

Annie understood what she meant. They used to call it 'received pronunciation', and it was what all the radio and television presenters spoke before regional and ethnic accents came into fashion. RP was generally regarded as posh and related to public schools, Oxford and Cambridge, and south-eastern England, the Home Counties. Most accents tell you where a person comes from, RP only tells you social status.

Stefan poked his head around the door and Annie noticed Karen immediately start to preen.

'Any luck?' she asked.

'It looks like the same vehicle,' he said. 'The measurements are the same, as are the tyres, and there's some distinctive cross-hatching on the casts we took from the lay-by that appear to match this specific Jeep Cherokee. Mike's still working on it, and we'll be taking soil and gravel samples, but I thought I'd give you the breaking news.'

'That's great,' Annie said, tapping the sheet of paper in front of her. 'William Masefield. We've got his details here. We've got him.' In her mind she could see them swooping in and making an arrest even before Banks got back from London, unrealistic as that was. Still, she *felt* jubilant. She could even see a possibility of that weekend in New York with Phil. *If* she could afford it, because she would insist on paying her own way.

'There's only one problem,' Stefan said.

'Oh?'

'It's been thoroughly cleaned, inside and out.'

Annie looked at Karen, who shrugged. 'We always get the returns cleaned up as promptly as we can,' she said.

'Shit,' said Annie. 'No forensics.'

'Most likely not,' Stefan agreed. 'Though we can certainly take it in and try. We might pick up a print or a hair the cleaners missed.'

'Wait a minute,' said Karen. 'What do you mean, "take it in"? Take it where?'

'To the police garage,' Annie said.

'But you can't take the Jeep. It's booked.'

'Mr Masefield again?'

'No. But they're good customers. Regular.'

'It's evidence,' said Annie. She turned to Stefan. 'Tell Mike to take it to the police garage, but to make sure he gets that petrol sample first, along with a sample from the underground tank here.'

'But the captain will . . .'

'Don't worry, Karen,' said Annie, picking up a pad from the desk. 'We'll give you a receipt. And you can always rent them the Explorer instead. I'm sure they'll understand.'

•

'*Commander* Burgess? Well, bugger me!'

'Watch it with the vile language, Banks. And why such surprise?'

'The last time I saw you, you were a detective super-intendent in National Criminal Intelligence. I thought they'd put you out to pasture for good.'

'Things change. I'm resilient, me.'

Not only that, Banks remembered, but Burgess had been sent somewhere he could do little harm because he was accused of dragging his feet over a sensitive race-related investigation. The two had known one another for many years, and their relationship had changed significantly over the course of time. At first they had been like chalk and cheese: Burgess brash, right wing, racist, sexist, cutting corners to get results; Banks trying his damnedest to remain a liberal humanist in a heart-breaking job in demoralizing times. Now Banks cut more corners and Burgess toed the line more closely. They both came from working-class backgrounds, and both had worked their way up the hard way, through the streets. Burgess was the son of an East End barrow boy. He had thrived in the Thatcher years, lain low during John Major's reign and now he was thriving again in the Blair era. It just went to show what Banks had always believed: there wasn't much difference between Thatcher and Blair except for gender, and sometimes he wasn't too sure about that.

They were about the same age, too, and had managed to find a certain amount of common ground over the years. It was fragile ground, though, thin ice over a quag-mire. Banks had phoned Burgess from the train, with an idea in mind, and Burgess had suggested that Banks buy him lunch. Thus they stood at the bar of a crowded pub near the Old Bailey, washing down the curry of the day with flat lager and rubbing elbows with barristers, clients and clerks. At least Burgess hadn't changed in one respect; he still drank like a fish and smoked Tom Thumb cigars.

What had changed most, though, was his appearance. Gone were the silver ponytail and the scuffed leather jacket, in their place a shaved head and a dark blue suit, white shirt and paisley tie. Shiny shoes. Burgess had also put on a few pounds, and his complexion was pink, the nose a little redder and more bulbous. The world-weary, seen-it-all look in his eyes had been replaced by one of mild surprise and curiosity.

'I can see you're doing all right for yourself,' Banks said, pushing his plate away. He'd only eaten half of the curry, which wasn't very good. The sign read lamb, but he suspected it was mutton. And the spicing was so bland as to be immaterial.

'Can't complain. Can't complain. My old oppos at Special Branch didn't forget me, after all. I managed to pull off one or two coups that pleased a number of people in high places. I tell you Banksy, this post nine/eleven world is full of opportunities for a man of my talents.'

'On whose side?'

'Ha, ha. Very funny.'

'So where are you now? Back in Special Branch?'

Burgess put his finger to his lips. 'Can't say. If I did, I'd have to kill you. Top secret. Hush-hush. Actually, we're so new we haven't even got our acronym sorted yet. Anyway, what brings you down here? You were all mysterious on the phone.' He offered Banks a Tom Thumb. Banks refused. Burgess's eyes narrowed. 'What is it, Banksy? Have you stopped smoking? I haven't seen you light one up yet. That's not like you. You've quit, haven't you?'

'Six months now.'

'Feel any better?'

'No.'

Burgess laughed. 'How's that lovely wife of yours? Ex, I should say.'

'She's fine,' said Banks. 'Remarried now.'

'And you?'

'Enjoying the bachelor life. Look, there was something I wanted to ask you. In complete confidence, of course.'

'Of course. Why come to me otherwise?'

One thing Banks did know about Burgess was that he could be trusted to keep quiet and be as discreet as necessary. He had a network of informers and information-gatherers second to none, no matter who, or what, it was you wanted to know about. That was why Banks had rung him.

'It's rather delicate,' said Banks.

'What's happened? Your girlfriend's chucked you and you want me to look into her new boyfriend's back-ground, find some dirt on him?'

It was astonishingly close to home, but Banks knew Burgess was only casting stones in the dark to see if he could hit anything. His scatter-shot approach often worked wonders, but Banks was a little wiser to it than he used to be and less inclined to react. He was still in awe of Burgess's uncanny ability to hit the right nerve, though.

'It's probably nothing,' he said, 'but I'd like a back-ground check on a bloke called Philip Keane.'

'Can you be a bit more specific?' Burgess said, thumb-ing through a soft black-leather-covered notebook for a clean page. It wasn't standard issue, Banks noticed. Must be his private notebook. 'I mean, unless he's related to that hothead who plays for Man U.'

'Not as far as I know. Pretty cultured bloke. Oxford or Cambridge. One of the two. Works as an art researcher, checking pedigrees and provenance, mostly for private collectors, but does some work for the Tate and the National. As far as I know, it's his own business. I don't know if he has any employees or partners.'

'Where's the office?'

'Belgravia.' Banks gave him the address he'd got from the business card Maria Phillips gave him.

'Company name?'

'ArtSearch Ltd.'

'Anything else that might help?'

'Not really. He's in his early forties. Also owns a cottage in Fortford, North Yorkshire. Well-dressed, good-looking sort of bloke—'

'He *has* stolen your girlfriend, hasn't he, Banksy?'

'It's nothing like that.'

'That pretty young DS you were bonking. What's her name?'

'If you mean Annie Cabbot, she's a DI now and—'

'Annie Cabbot, that's the one.' Burgess grinned, not a pleasant sight, least of all for the glimpse it gave of his smoke-stained, crooked teeth. He shook his head. 'Tut tut tut, Banksy. Will you never learn?'

'Look,' said Banks, trying hard not to let Burgess's prodding and teasing exasperate him. 'The bloke lied to me about something that might be important in a murder investigation. I want to know why.'

'Why don't you ask him?'

'I'll do that. In the meantime, I want to find out as much about him as I can.'

'You mean you want *me* to find out as much about him as *I* can.'

'OK. Will you do it?'

'You want me to find some dirt on him?'

'If there is any, I'm sure you'll find it. If not . . . I just want the truth.'

'Don't we all? And you don't want Annie Cabbot to know about these discreet enquiries, I take it?'

'I don't want anybody to know. Look, maybe the lie's important and maybe it's not. What you find out, or don't, might help me to decide. It's a serious case.'

'The Eastvale Canal fires?'

'You know about them?'

'Like to keep my finger on the pulse. And another thing, you paid a visit to Sir Laurence West this morning.'

Banks smiled. 'I don't suppose I should be surprised you know that already.'

Burgess winked. 'The walls have ears,' he said. 'Go carefully, Banksy. Sir Laurence has some very powerful connections.'

'He told me what I wanted to know. I don't think I have a problem with him.'

'Make sure you don't. These are difficult times. The world's going to hell in a handbasket. You don't know who you can trust.'

'You always seem to land on your feet.'

'I'm a Weeble, me. Remember those when you were a kid? You could knock them down as many times as you wanted but they always rolled back up.'

'I remember,' said Banks.

'Anyway, how's about another couple of pints? Unless you have to run.'

Banks glanced at his watch. There was somewhere he wanted to go, but he didn't have to run. 'Fine with me,' he said.

'My shout this time.'

●

Winsome was driving the unmarked police car down the M42, weaving in and out the lanes of lorries with natural ease, windscreen wipers flapping like crazy to get rid of all the filthy spray. Annie, no mean driver herself, was surprised she didn't feel in the least bit nervous, considering the speed they were going and the narrow spaces Winsome seemed able to manoeuvre them in and out of.

'Where the hell did you learn to drive like this?' Annie asked.

Winsome flashed her a grin. 'Dunno, Ma'am,' she said. 'Back home, I suppose. I mean I started when I was twelve and I guess I just took to it. Some of those mountain roads . . .'

'But there aren't any motorways in Jamaica, are there?'

'You never been there, Ma'am?'

'No.'

'Well, there aren't. Not really. Not what you'd call motorways. But you can go pretty fast sometimes, and you get a lot of traffic in Montego Bay.'

'What about Kingston?'

'Dunno,' said Winsome. 'Never been there. Mostly I learned driving here, though, on the job. I took a course.'

'I'm glad to hear it. Look, Winsome . . .'

'What, Ma'am?'

'About this ma'am business. It makes me feel like an old woman. Do you think you could call me something else?'

Winsome laughed. 'What do you recommend?'

'Up to you, really.'

'Boss?'

'No. Don't like that.'

'Chief.'

'No.'

'How about Guv?'

Annie thought for a moment. Banks didn't like 'guv', she knew. He said it sounded too much like television. But Annie didn't mind that. And she liked the sound of it. 'OK,' she said. '"Guv" will do fine.'

'Right you are, Guv. What do you think?'

'About William Masefield?'

'Yes.'

'I'm not sure,' said Annie. 'It can't be as easy as this, surely?'

'Sometimes it is. Easy, I mean.'

'Not in my experience. If he's got any brains at all, he must have known we'd track him through the rental and the credit card eventually.'

'Maybe he's not so bright as you think.' Winsome dodged in and out of a convoy of about six articulated juggernauts with Spanish number plates, and Annie looked at the map. 'We're nearly there. Get over in the left-hand lane.'

Winsome flashed her signal and edged over.

'You want junction three. The A435. Here it is.'

Winsome took the exit and slowed down quickly. Annie turned to a more detailed map of the area she had bought before the journey and found the street in Studley. Winsome drove more sedately now and there was little traffic on the road. They turned down a hill then right into a network of streets, Annie looking for the address they had got from the garage.

Finally, Winsome pulled up in front of where the house should have been. The ones around were all detached. Not large, but comfortable enough, with bay windows and garages. The only problem was that where number eleven was supposed to be there was nothing but an empty lot.

They got out of the car, puzzled, and looked at the empty space.

'Help you, love?' said a voice behind them in a slightly nasal Midlands accent.

Annie turned and saw the woman had come out of the house across the street, a grey cardigan wrapped around her shoulders. 'Maybe you can,' she said, flashing her warrant card and introducing Winsome. 'We're looking for a Mr William Masefield.'

'Ah, Mr Masefield,' the woman said. 'I'm afraid you're a bit late, love. And so's he. He's dead.'

'When?'

'Last August.'

'What did he die of? What happened to the house?'

'Burned down.'

'There was a fire?'

'Yes. Whole place went up. Lucky it didn't take the rest of the street.'

Annie's mind raced. 'Did you see it? The fire?'

'No. Gerald and me were in Spain. Go every summer. When we got back it was all over. Just a ruin.'

'What caused it?'

'I don't know all the details, love. You'll have to ask the firemen.'

'Did Mr Masefield live alone?'

'Yes. He was a bachelor.'

'Did he have any visitors?'

'Not that I saw. Bit of a dark horse. Reclusive.'

'What did he look like?'

'About six foot, maybe a bit more. Stooped from bending over all those textbooks at university, I wouldn't be surprised. Going a bit grey.'

'What university?'

'He was a lecturer at Warwick.'

'What subject?'

'Physics, I think. Or chemistry. Some sort of science, anyway.'

'How old was he?'

'Hard to say, really. Early to mid-forties, at a guess. Look, why do you want to know all this?'

'Just a case we're working on up north,' said Annie. 'Thanks, anyway. You've been a great help.'

The woman stood there for a moment until she seemed to realize she'd been dismissed, then she turned, sniffed, and walked back to her house.

'Well,' said Annie, looking at Winsome. 'I think we'd better get cracking and ask a few questions while we're down here, don't you?'

'Yes, Guv,' said Winsome.

•

Banks wondered what the hell he was doing sitting on a park bench in Camden Town on a grey January afternoon. Nothing but a small triangle of grass, a few scrappy trees, swings and a roundabout and a couple of damp green benches. On the face of it he was trying to pluck up the courage to visit Sandra, whose house he could see through the bare branches across the street. But why he wanted to see her was beyond him. Yes, Maria Phillips had told him that Sandra had talked to Thomas McMahon often, but it was unlikely she would be able to tell him anything useful about the dead artist. Banks hadn't seen Sandra in over a year, not since she told him she wanted a divorce, in a cafe not far from the spot where he was sitting. So why now? Was it the baby? Morbid curiosity? And why was it so hard to pluck up the courage?

He stood up and walked towards the gates. This was stupid, he told himself; he might as well head for King's Cross and catch the next train home. He could even phone Michelle. Maybe they could manage a bit more than a quick kiss through the train window. It would be easy to get off at Peterborough if she happened to have the evening free. There was nothing for him here.

Just as he turned the corner towards the tube station, he saw a woman walking towards him, pushing a pram. It was Sandra, no doubt about it. She was still wearing the same arty granny-glasses and short, layered haircut as the last time he saw her, blonde hair and black eyebrows. She also wore a long, beige raincoat and had a black wool scarf wrapped around her neck.

When she saw him, she stopped. 'Alan. What . . . ?'

'I just wanted a word,' said Banks, surprised the words came out so easily with his heart stuck in his throat the way it was.

'I've just been to the shops,' Sandra said. Then she leaned forward and adjusted the blanket in the pram. Banks was still facing her and couldn't see inside. She looked up at him again, her expression unreadable, except he sensed some sort of protection, something primal, unconscious, in the way she tended to the child. It was almost, Banks felt, as if he were perceived as a *threat*, as if he were the *enemy*. He felt like saying, 'There's nothing to be afraid of. It's only me,' but he didn't. Instead, Sandra spoke. Glancing over at the park, she said, 'Walk?'

'Fine,' said Banks. He stepped aside as she started walking again and fell in beside her. They paused to check the traffic carefully before crossing the road, and Banks sneaked his first glance at baby Sinéad. He almost breathed a sigh of relief to discover that she looked pretty much the same as any other month-old child did: like Winston Churchill. Sandra caught him looking, and he noticed her redden before she pushed the pram forward across the street.

'What is it?' she asked.

'What?'

'You wanted to talk to me.'

'Oh, yes. It's nothing, really. Just a case I'm working on. Remember an artist called Thomas McMahon?'

'Tom? Yes, of course. Why?'

'He's dead.'

'Dead?'

'Yes, killed in a fire. He was squatting on a barge down on the canal.'

'I take it he was murdered or you wouldn't be here.'

'Looks that way,' said Banks.

'Poor Tom. He was harmless. He wouldn't hurt a soul.'

'Well, someone hurt him.'

'A fire, you said?'

'Yes. Arson. He was unconscious at the time. He wouldn't have . . . you know.'

Sandra nodded. Her small, pale nose was a little red at the tip, he noticed, as if she had a cold. 'I haven't seen him in five years or more,' she said. 'I don't know how I can help you.'

'I don't know, either,' said Banks, sticking his hands in his overcoat pockets. 'I'm sorry. Perhaps I shouldn't have come.'

They came to a bench and Sandra sat, wheeling the pram close and locking the brake with her foot. Banks sat beside her. He craved a cigarette. It wasn't a sharp, fast, overwhelming urge like he usually felt, but a simple, deep, gnawing need. He tried to ignore it.

'You smell of beer,' Sandra said.

'I'm not pissed.'

'I didn't say you were.'

Banks paused. He'd had a couple of pints with Burgess, true enough. But that was all. And he certainly wasn't going to mention Dirty Dick to Sandra. Red rag to a bull. 'Maria Phillips was asking after you,' he said.

Sandra shot him an amused glance. 'Between trying to get her hands down the front of your trousers?'

'How did you guess?'

'She never was a subtle one was Maria.'

'She's rather sweet, really.'

Sandra rolled her eyes. 'To each his own.'

'I didn't mean it like that,' Banks rushed on. 'I think she's just very insecure underneath it all.'

'Oh, please.'

'She said you spent a lot of time with Tom.'

'And you think she was hinting at an affair?'

'I didn't say that.'

'It's obvious in your tone. For your information, not that it matters any more, but I didn't have any affairs while we were together. Not one.'

Sinéad stirred and made a gurgling sound. Sandra leaned forward and did something with the blanket again, then she put her hand to the side of the baby's face, stroked it and smiled, murmuring nonsense words. It was a gesture Banks remembered her making with both Brian and Tracy when they were very young, and it cut him to the quick. He had forgotten all about it, and there it was, a simple maternal gesture with the power to hurt him so. What the hell was going on? he wondered, breath tight in his chest. This baby was nothing to do with him. If anything, it was an insult to the relationship he thought he had had with Sandra. It wasn't even a particularly beautiful baby. So why did he feel so excluded, so alone? Why did he care?

'So what can you tell me about McMahon?' Banks asked.

'Tom had a lively mind, wandering hands and low self-esteem,' Sandra said.

'Why the low self-esteem?'

'I don't know. Some people are just like that, aren't they?' She rocked the pram gently as she spoke. 'Even when he was moderately successful, getting the odd exhibition and managing to sell a painting or two – and I don't mean just the tourist stuff – he still couldn't seem to believe in himself. You know, he once told me he felt more himself imitating other artists than he did doing his own work.'

'Oh,' said Banks. 'Who did he imitate?'

'Just about anyone.' Sandra laughed. 'He once dashed off a Picasso sketch for me. It took him about five seconds. I don't know if you could have got it by a team of experts but it would have fooled me. Why are you so interested?'

'What about Turner?'

'What about him?'

'Do you think McMahon could have forged Turner sketches and watercolours?'

Sandra swept her hand over her hair. 'Do I think he had the talent for it? Yes. Did I ever see him imitate or even hear him mention Turner? No.'

'Just a thought,' said Banks. 'Some have turned up.'

'Is this connected with his death?'

'It could be,' said Banks.

Sandra shivered and adjusted her scarf.

'Is there anything else?' Banks asked.

'Not that I can think of.'

'You didn't know his circle of friends?'

'Didn't know he had one. I only saw him at the gallery. Sometimes we'd have a coffee there together. That's all.' Sinéad gurgled again and Sandra leaned over.

'She's a lovely child,' Banks said.

Sandra didn't look at him. 'Yes.'

'Well behaved.'

'Yes.' Sandra glanced over at her house. 'Look, I'd better go,' she said. 'It's nearly Sinéad's feeding time and . . .' She held her hand out. 'I think it's starting to rain.'

Banks nodded. 'Goodbye, then.'

Sandra stood up. 'Goodbye,' she said. 'And take care of yourself, Alan.'

Banks watched her push the pram down the path as it started to drizzle. She didn't look back.

13

'**Well, Mark,**' said Banks, leaning back in his chair and linking his hands behind his head, 'why did you run?'

'How was I to know they were plainclothes coppers? You told me I was in danger, to watch out. That's what I did.'

'And what do you have to say about it all now?'

'Just the same as I told those bastards in Scarborough yesterday. The bloke attacked me. I defended myself. What was I supposed to do, let him put his hands all over me?'

Banks scratched the scar beside his right eye. 'I still don't know what you're talking about, Mark,' he said. 'What bloke is this? Who attacked you? Where?'

Mark stared at him. He'd been held overnight at Scarborough for resisting arrest and delivered to Western Area Headquarters that morning. The arresting officer had mentioned some gibberish about an attack and self-defence, but he had no idea what Mark was talking about either. Nor did he want to know. Enough paperwork on his plate already without picking up Eastvale's leftovers. One thing that did bother Banks was the black eye, split lip and bruising on Mark's cheek. He wondered how 'necessary' the force was that the two DCs who arrested him had used. And had they announced that they were police officers first? Mark said not.

'You mean you don't know?' Mark asked.

'Know what?'

'The bloke. The poofter. He didn't report it?'

'Nobody reported anything as far as I know. What are you talking about? Did you get into trouble hitching a lift?'

'Never mind,' said Mark. 'That's what I thought it was all about when I found out there were coppers after me. It doesn't matter now. What am I here for this time, then?'

'Know anything about a fire in Jennings Field last Saturday night? Caravan.'

'I don't even know where Jennings Field is.'

'You'd have passed close by there on your way east from your friend's house.'

'I still don't know. Why are you asking me this?'

'Just seems too much of a coincidence, that's all. Two fires and you pretty much on the scene of both of them.'

'Look, you've already cleared me on the boat fire. Mandy told the truth about where I was and your blokes tested my clothes. They didn't find anything.'

'I know,' said Banks. And he also knew that they couldn't test Mark's clothes for traces of accelerant this time because they'd been given to him by Banks himself. Even if the bloody things were soaked in petrol, that wouldn't make a scrap of difference to the Crown Prosecution Service. 'But that doesn't let you out of the Jennings Field fire. Or out of killing Thomas McMahon.'

'How do you work that out?'

'McMahon was unconscious before the fire. Maybe you drugged him. You certainly seem to be able to lay your hands on any drug you want.'

'Why would I do that?'

'I don't know. Maybe he made a move on Tina. He was an artist. Maybe he offered to pay her for posing nude.'

'He didn't.'

'Only your word.'

'He didn't. And I didn't touch him.'

'OK. Did you see anything when you passed Jennings Field on Saturday?'

Mark looked away, watching the workmen on the scaffolding around the church. 'I thought I saw a fire,' he said, 'in the distance. But I wasn't anywhere near it. And I had other things on my mind.'

'What time was this?'

'I don't remember. No watch.' He turned to face Banks again. 'Look, I'd nothing to do with it. You *know* that. Why don't you ask Dr Patrick fucking Aspern where *he* was? Or is he beyond your reach? A *doctor.*'

'Don't worry, Mark. We'll ask whoever we want. Anyway, what reason do you have to think Dr Aspern had anything to do with the Jennings Field fire?'

'I don't know. But if you think it was the same person set both of them, then I'm saying you should have a good look at him, too.'

'We will. Don't worry. Have you got any other suggestions?'

Mark shook his head and looked back out of the window. Banks wrote down a name, address and phone number on a sheet of paper and passed it to him.

'What's this?' Mark asked.

Banks nodded towards the window. 'Name of the person in charge of the restoration crew out there,' he said. 'He's a friend of mine. Drop by the office or give him a call. Tell him I sent you.'

Mark glanced back and forth from the men on the scaffolding to Banks. Finally, he folded the sheet of paper, and lacking a pocket in the red overalls he'd been issued, held onto it. 'Thanks,' he said.

'No problem. And your pal Lenny says it's all right to go back to his place, if you want.'

'You talked to Lenny?'

'Yes, I talked to him. His wife is really sorry. She doesn't like surprises, that's all. They'd be glad to have you.'

Banks could see doubt cloud Mark's features. He didn't blame the kid. He'd be suspicious himself. Things hadn't worked out especially well for Mark so far this past week or so.

'Up to you,' he said. 'One more thing.'

'What?'

Banks slid the photograph of Roland Gardiner that Annie had got from Alice Mowbray across the desk. 'Recognize him?'

Mark studied the photo. 'Dunno,' he said finally. 'It could be one of the blokes I saw visit Tom. He's got the right sort of nose. But . . .'

'OK,' said Banks. He described Leslie Whitaker. 'That sound anything like the other bloke?'

Mark shrugged. 'Could be,' he said. 'But again . . .'

'I know,' said Banks. 'It's vague.' He thought he should perhaps organize an identity parade, see if Mark could pick out Whitaker from a group of people who looked a bit like him.

'Can I go now?' Mark asked.

'As far as I'm concerned. Where will you be if I need you?'

'Need me? For what?'

'More questions. There's still a chance you can help us find Tina's killer.'

'I'll be at Lenny's,' Mark said.

'I take it you're not pressing charges?'

'What?'

'Police brutality.'

Mark fingered his bruises and grinned. 'The pavement was hard,' he said. 'I fell.' He got up and walked to the door.

'There's a constable outside,' said Banks. 'He'll take you back down to the custody suite and get you sorted.'

'Thanks.'

'And Mark?'

'Yes?'

'When you were arrested you had over two hundred pounds in your pocket, but when you first left here you only had about ten. Where did you get the rest?'

'Found it,' said Mark and nipped out of the door quickly.

There was more to it than that, Banks was convinced, but it didn't concern him now. No doubt there had been a problem with someone who had given him a lift, and Mark had probably nicked his wallet in the scuffle. That the theft hadn't been reported made Banks lean in favour of Mark's garbled explanation, that he'd been assaulted by the man, who needed police attention like he needed a hole in the head. Call the two hundred 'damages', then, and have done with it.

He watched the restorers at work for a few moments, thinking about the kind of life Mark had been living at home, in the squat and on the boat, and what the future might hold for him. It had to be better than the past. His phone rang.

'Alan, it's Ken Blackstone.'

'Good to hear from you. Any news on the doctor?'

'Nothing you'd be interested in hearing, I'm afraid. Clean bill of health, even down to the scrupulously up-to-date shotgun certificate.'

'He's got a shotgun?'

'Likes to shoot small, winged creatures with like-minded people.'

'It takes all sorts. No rumours, gossip?'

'No. Seems he's a capable doctor. Not much of a bed-side manner. Some described him as a bit of a cold fish. There was just one little thing.'

'What's that?' Banks asked.

'One of the neighbours saw a black woman coming out of his house carrying a plastic bag on Monday morning. She thought it might be drugs.'

Banks laughed. 'That would have been our very own DC Winsome Jackman with Dr Aspern's clothing for test-ing. Which came out negative as expected, by the way.'

'Well, at least he's been getting wind there's something going on,' Blackstone said. 'Already put a complaint in to Weetwood about harassment, and he gave one of his neighbours a right chewing out after he saw her talking to one of our men.'

'Good,' said Banks. 'Let's hope it keeps him off balance.'

'Have you thought, Alan, that maybe he hasn't actu-ally done anything?'

'There's something there. Trust me.'

'Instinct?'

'Call it what you will: body language, unspoken com-munication, but there's something there. The girl was screwed up and why should she lie to Mark?'

'Junkies lie habitually. You know that as well as I do. And maybe the boyfriend has his own reasons for believ-ing her.'

'I've thought of that. We did a background check on him, and it's true he had it rough at home. I still think there's something going on, though. And if I get any proof, I'll have the bastard.'

'The fires?'

'Possible. But I don't think so. He did something to Tina, though. I'm certain of it.'

'Well, best of luck, mate. Want me to keep trying?'

'No, it's OK. Thanks, Ken.'

'Cheers. And don't forget, if you're down in my neck of the woods that sofa's always there for you.'

'I won't forget.'

Banks stood at his window after the phone call, thinking and looking out at the people in raincoats down in the market square. He was certain that Patrick Aspern had sexually abused his stepdaughter, and that his wife knew about it. But he had no proof. Nor did he seem to have much hope of getting any now that Tina was dead. Her death was convenient for Aspern, but Banks was almost certain he hadn't started the fire on the boats. That had something to do with Thomas McMahon, he was convinced of it. Tina was incidental, maybe an unwanted witness. Which made the killer an especially nasty piece of work.

Thoughts of McMahon brought Banks back to Phil Keane and his little lie. He would have to contrive to have a chat with Phil without Annie around. He knew exactly how she would behave if she thought he was trying to dig up some dirt on her precious Phil. And maybe she would be right; maybe Maria Phillips's version was exaggerated or even untrue. But until he knew for certain, one way or another, he would distance himself from Phil and Annie, do a bit of discreet digging and wait to hear from Dirty Dick.

•

It felt good to be wearing his own clothes again, Mark thought, as he headed out of Western Area Headquarters for the second time in a week. The old leather jacket felt like a second skin. And it was good to be free again. His face and body still ached from the beating the Scarborough cops had given him, for 'resisting arrest', but, just as he had suspected, Clive hadn't reported the hitchhiking incident and the police had no reason to keep him in custody.

And he still had over two hundred quid in his pocket.

Mark crossed the market square, anonymous among the crowd of shoppers and the occasional out-of-season tourist. He hadn't a clue where to go, but he knew he wasn't going back to Lenny's, no matter what he'd told Banks. That had been a mistake in the first place. Lenny was a decent bloke, but he had enough on his plate without bringing Mark home. Sure, maybe they did both feel all guilty right now after upsetting him, but that would soon wear off. He knew he wouldn't be able to bear Sal's silent resentment of his presence. And when he thought about it he realized that, if it wasn't Clive, then it must have been Lenny who'd set the cops on him. He wouldn't have expected that from him, but there it was. Did Lenny believe he'd started the fires, too? No matter, he wouldn't be seeing Lenny or his bitch of a wife again.

Across the square, he turned left for a short way on York Road and went into the Swainsdale Centre. When he was at Eastvale Comprehensive and wanted to put off going home after school, he had often hung around the centre with his mates, not doing anything, just loitering and smoking, sometimes looking in Dixon's windows at the fancy computers and stereos he couldn't afford. Well, there had been an occasional bit of shoplifting, he remembered, but that was as bad as the gang got. Sometimes, too, he had spent the day there instead of going to school at all.

The centre wasn't very busy; it never was on a Wednesday morning. Just a few young women pushing prams, and kids skiving off school, the way Mark had done. On the upper level, at the top of the escalator opposite HMV, was a food court, and Mark bought himself a Big Mac, fries and Coke and sat at one of the Formica-topped tables to eat. There was something about a shopping centre that numbed your brain, Mark thought. Something to do with the weird lighting and the barely audible music. Maybe it hypnotized you into buying things. Well, there was nothing Mark wanted, except maybe a new CD. He'd grown tired of *Ziggy Stardust* over the past few days and it was the only one he had left. Maybe he'd get something by Beth Orton in memory of Tina. He'd probably need new batteries soon, so he might as well pick some up in Dixon's.

As he sat there munching on his Big Mac, lulled by the bland ambience of the Swainsdale Centre, watching the people who seemed to float around him as insubstantial as ghosts or shadows to the faint, pale music of an orchestral version of 'Eleanor Rigby', Mark mulled over the past few days. The fire had occurred on Thursday night and it was now the following Wednesday. Had it really only been such a short time since Tina had died and Mark had had his adventures on the road? He'd also been assaulted by a queer, been in and out of jail twice, beaten up by the police and spent the most luxurious evening of his life in a B and B in Helmsley. And there was still a chance that someone out there was after him, wanted him dead.

It was hard to think with his brain so numb, but there was something very wrong with the picture he was seeing. What did he think he was trying to achieve? Did he have any control over his life at all? He'd run away from Lenny's more because of echoes of his past than anything else, but had it all happened because he'd been trying to force himself in the wrong direction in the first place?

He had been thinking about putting his life back together. Getting back to work on the building site. Living with Lenny and Sal. Making things normal again. But could they ever be normal again? When he thought about it, he didn't really think so. And what on earth did he think he was up to, running off to Scarborough? It was the same thing, when you got right down to it. A new start. A job. A place to live. The normal life.

But with Tina gone nothing could ever be normal again. He felt that as he sat there in the Swainsdale Centre staring into space.

And all the things he had been aiming for, trying to do – the job, Lenny's, Scarborough – they weren't *meant* to be. That was clear now. They weren't meant to be because there was somewhere he had to go before he could get his own life sorted. Something he had to do. For Tina.

•

In the Queen's Arms that lunchtime, Banks, Annie and Winsome managed to bag a corner table near the window. As usual, one or two heads turned at the sight of Winsome, but Banks could tell she was used to it. She had a model's carriage and managed to handle all the attention with mild amusement and disdain.

'Lunch is on me,' Banks said.

Annie raised her eyebrows. 'Last of the big spenders.' She looked at Winsome, who smiled, but Banks sensed less humour in the remark than Winsome had. Annie was still pissed off with him over Phil, even though she'd got her way in the end.

Banks wasn't very hungry, but he ordered chicken in a basket anyway, while Annie went for a salad and Winsome a beefburger and chips. That settled, drinks in front of them, they got down to business, and Annie first told Banks about the visit to 'Captain' Kirk's garage and the trail leading to the mysterious William Masefield in Studley.

'And there's no doubt this Masefield is dead?' Banks asked, after he'd digested what she had told him.

Annie glanced at Winsome. 'None at all,' she said. 'We checked with the pathologist who conducted the post-mortem. Getting hold of him was one of the reasons it took us so long down there. We had to stay over. He couldn't see us until early this morning. Anyway, Masefield had no living relatives, so DNA was useless, but he was identified by dental records.'

'So someone stole his identity?'

'Looks that way,' Annie said. 'And whoever did it simply had Masefield's post redirected.'

'Where to?'

'A post-office box in central Birmingham.'

'I see,' said Banks. 'And the credit-card company had no way of knowing about this?'

Annie shook her head. 'All they cared about was that the bills were paid on time. It's a common enough form of identity fraud.'

'He used a bank account in Masefield's name?'

'Yes. And he paid all his bills from Masefield's bank account over the Internet, so no signed cheques. There'll be a trail, but these things are complicated.'

'We'll get computers on it,' said Banks. 'Why did no one in the post office spot what was going on?'

'Why should they?' said Annie. 'Whoever arranged for the redirected post went to a busy central office, presented the right sort of identification and signed the forms. Whoever it was must have resembled Masefield enough and been able to forge his signature. Easy. And all above board, as far as the post office was concerned. I mean they're careful, they have their precautions, but the whole thing's pretty routine. Most clerks probably don't even examine the documentation closely.'

'Are we certain it's the same car?'

'Well,' said Annie, 'the tyre impressions are identical to those found on the lay-by near the boats. The SOCOs also managed to find a few soil and gravel samples, and they've gone to the lab for further analysis.'

'Good.'

'But there is one small problem.'

'Oh?'

'The petrol in the Cherokee's tank matches the petrol from the garage – it's Texaco, by the way – but *not* the petrol used to start the Gardiner fire. That's Esso.'

'Interesting,' said Banks. 'Maybe he used his own car, for some reason.'

'I suppose that's possible,' Annie agreed.

'Anyway, whatever the explanation, forensics can tie the Jeep Cherokee that this "Masefield" rented to the scene of the boat fires, right?'

'Yes.'

'Thank heaven for small mercies. We're still in business, then.'

Jenna, the young girl who worked in the kitchen, brought their food. Winsome was the only one who ate with a vengeance. Banks glanced at her. 'I hope you didn't run up your expenses too high in the hotel restaurant last night,' he said.

'No, sir,' said Winsome. 'We ate at McDonald's.'

Banks looked at Annie. 'It's true,' she said. 'And you can imagine what delights they had for a vegetarian like me. I told you we were busy. All we had time for before bed was a couple of drinks in the hotel bar.'

'And those two good-looking salesmen bought us the second round, didn't they, Guv?' Winsome added.

'Yes,' said Annie. 'Connor and Marcus. So you needn't worry about our expenses, skinflint.' She picked at her salad.

'It's ACC McLaughlin gets his underpants in a knot over things like that,' Banks said. 'Not me. Did you find out anything else about Masefield while you were down there?'

Annie and Winsome exchanged glances and Annie said, 'A few things. We asked around about him – neighbours, co-workers at the university – but nobody seemed to know very much.'

'And the fire?'

'Chip pan. There was no accelerant and no reason to treat it as suspicious at the time. The only thing even remotely interesting was that one of the other lecturers at the university where Masefield worked said he'd recently lost some money in a bad investment. I also got the impression that he was in a bit of trouble at the university over his drinking, that he might have stood to lose his job. But you know what academics are like when it comes to giving out information.'

'A bit like us,' Banks said.

'Anyway, there was a lot of alcohol in his system. The

general assumption in the fire investigator's office was that he'd passed out and left the chip pan on. It happens often enough, especially with alcoholics and drug addicts. You come home pissed or high, put the frying pan on, pop another couple of pills or take another stiff drink, and the next thing you know . . .'

'No traces of Rohypnol or Tuinol?'

'No. Just alcohol.'

'So it could have been an accident?'

'Yes.'

'And someone, a colleague, friend, whatever, could have taken advantage of Masefield's demise and stolen his identity?'

'Or helped him along a bit. I mean, nobody saw anyone, but that doesn't mean whoever did it didn't leave Masefield passed out on the sofa with the chip pan on full heat.'

'True,' Banks agreed. 'Did anyone have any ideas at all about exactly who might have taken Masefield's identity?'

'Unfortunately not,' said Annie. 'Nobody knew who he hung around with, if anyone. Apparently, he wasn't the gregarious type. If he did have any friends, he kept them a secret from his colleagues and neighbours.'

'What about this bad investment? Who did he make it with? Was he swindled?'

'Don't know, sir,' said Winsome. 'That was all his colleague could tell us.'

Banks sighed. He knew they could get a forensic accountant to look into Masefield's finances and a computer expert to track down the Internet banking records, but that would all take time. There would no doubt be all kinds of false trails and blind alleys. As it stood right now, they still didn't have very much to go on. The first big lead, the rented Jeep Cherokee, had led them to a dead end. Or so it seemed at the moment.

'How did "Masefield" get to Kirk's garage?' Banks asked.

'I assume he took a bus,' said Annie. 'They run in a constant loop from Askham Bar to the city centre.'

'So he travelled to York by train?'

'Or by bus.'

'What if he didn't?' Winsome said.

'Didn't what?' Banks asked.

'Take a train or a bus, sir. Maybe he's local. What if he *drove* to the garage? I mean, if he only wanted to use a rental car so that his own car wasn't spotted by the canal or by Jennings Field, for whatever reason, then he probably has a car of his own, too.'

'Well,' said Annie, 'there are plenty of residential streets around there he could leave a car for a few days without attracting too much attention.'

'Except he might have got unlucky,' Winsome said.

'The Son of Sam,' Banks said.

Winsome smiled. 'Yes, sir.'

'A parking ticket?' Annie said. 'Isn't that how the Son of Sam got caught?'

'Yes,' said Winsome. 'It's possible, isn't it, Guv?'

'It would certainly be a lucky break for us,' Annie said.

'It'll probably take a day or two,' Banks said, 'but it's worth checking. Can you get the numbers of all cars ticketed in the area on the dates in question and feed them into HOLMES, see if anything comes up?'

'Can do,' said Winsome. 'We don't exactly have a lot of number plates to cross-reference on this one, but I'll see what I can do. There might be something on the CCTV cameras, too. They're all over the place these days.'

'Good,' said Banks. 'Definitely worth checking.' He finished his chicken and left the chips, then drank some beer and leaned back in his chair. 'This still doesn't let Whitaker off the hook,' he said, 'even though it seems now that it wasn't his Jeep Cherokee at the scene of the boat fires.'

'We'll check the petrol in his car against the accelerant used at the Gardiner scene. That might tell us something. And if we can dig out any connection, however remote, between Whitaker and Masefield . . .'

'Maybe,' said Banks. 'Anything new on those Turners?' he asked Annie as casually as he could manage.

Her tone hardened. Pure professional. 'Phil couldn't say at first glance for certain whether they were forged or genuine,' she said. 'Not without a more comprehensive examination. But he did say they *looked* genuine, the style and the paper, that sort of thing.'

'Which means they could be very good forgeries?'

'Yes,' Annie agreed.

'I've heard that McMahon was a good copyist,' Banks said. 'Apparently he didn't have much original talent, but he did have a gift for reproducing the work of others.'

'Where did you find this out?' Annie asked.

'From someone who knew him.' Banks said.

'What next?'

'I'm going to Leeds.'

'What for?'

'I want to visit Tina's grandparents. I rang them earlier and they agreed to talk to me. They might be able to tell me something about Tina's relationship with Patrick Aspern.'

'Surely you don't think they *knew* what was going on and that, even if they did, they'll tell you?'

'Give me some credit. I'm not that stupid, Annie. I just want to sound out their feelings, that's all.'

Annie shrugged.

'What?' said Banks.

'Nothing.'

'Come on. Out with it.'

'It's just that I'm not sure the girl has anything to do with all this.'

'What do you mean by that?'

'Aspern's clothes came out clean, didn't they?'

'Yes,' said Banks. 'That's the problem. So did everybody else's.'

'To be honest, Guv,' Winsome said, 'he could have given me any old clothes. I don't know what he was wearing that night.'

Annie gave Banks a hard look. 'We don't have any evidence against Patrick Aspern at all,' she said. 'I think you're going off on some sort of personal crusade against the man.'

'So all of a sudden you're SIO on this case, are you?' Banks shot back.

Annie's mouth closed to a tight white line. Winsome looked away, embarrassed. Banks wondered if Annie had told her all about the row they'd had over Phil Keane's involvement in the case. Maybe after a couple of drinks in the hotel bar last night.

He immediately regretted his sarcastic remark, but it was too late to take it back. Instead he bade Annie and Winsome a curt goodbye and left the pub.

•

One thing Banks hadn't told Annie was that he was intending to stop off at Phil Keane's cottage on his way to

Leeds. Well, it wasn't exactly on his way, but he thought it was worth the diversion.

Puddles from yesterday's rain spread out from the gutters and sent up sheets of spray as Banks drove just a little too fast into Fortford. Still annoyed with himself for his outburst over lunch, he parked on the cobbles in front of the shops by the village green and headed towards the cottage. Maybe Annie was right and he *was* on some sort of personal crusade against Patrick Aspern. But so what? Someone had to bring the arrogant bastard down.

Across the street, on top of a grassy mound, stood the excavated ruins of a Roman fort. What a bitter, lonely and dangerous outpost it must have been back in Emperor Domitian's time, Banks thought. Wild country all around and enemies everywhere.

It was another mild day, vague haze in the air, and perhaps a hint of more rain to come. Banks had no idea whether Keane would be at home or not, but it was worth a try. The silver BMW parked in the narrow drive beside the cottage was a good sign. It was 51 registration, Banks noticed, which meant that it had been registered with the Driver and Vehicle Licensing Agency – the DVLA – between September 2001 and February 2002. A pretty recent model, then, and not inexpensive. How much exactly did an art researcher make?

Banks's knock on the front door was answered seconds later by Phil Keane himself, looking every inch the twenty-first-century country squire in faded Levis and a rust-coloured Swaledale sweater.

'Alan,' he said, opening the door wide. 'Good to see you. Come on in.'

Banks entered. The ceilings were low and the walls rough-painted limestone with nooks and crannies here and there, each filled with delicate little statuettes and ivory carvings: elephants, human figures, cats.

'Nice,' said Banks.

'Thank you. The place has been in my family for generations,' Keane said. 'Even though I only remember occasional visits to my grandparents here when I was a child – I grew up down south, for my sins – I couldn't bear the thought of losing it when they died. Most of the knick-knacks were theirs. Do sit down. Can I get you a drink or anything?'

'Nothing, thank you,' said Banks. 'It's only a flying visit.'

Keane sat on the arm of the sofa. 'Yes? Is it about the Turners? If indeed they are by Turner.'

'Indirectly,' said Banks. 'By the way, our fingerprints expert has finished with them, so you'll be able to carry out further testing.'

'Excellent. Did he find anything?'

'Not much. Do you want to pick them up or should I have them sent to your London office?'

'I'll pick them up at the police station tomorrow morning and take them down, myself, if that's OK?'

'As long as you're not worried about being hijacked.'

'Nobody but you and me would know what I was carrying, would they?'

'I suppose not,' said Banks. 'Look, in your opinion, would it be very difficult to forge such a work?'

'As I told Annie,' Keane said, 'the actual forging would be easy enough for an artist who had the talent for such things. Turner isn't easy to imitate – his brush strokes are difficult, for example – but he's not impossible, as long as the artist got hold of the correct paper and painting materials, which isn't too hard, if you know how. Tom

Keating claimed to have dashed off twenty or so Turner watercolours. The problem is the provenance.'

'And you can't fake that?'

'It can be done. A man called John Drewe did so a few years ago, caused quite a furore in the art world. You might have heard of him. He even got into the Tate archives and doctored catalogues. But they've tightened up a lot since then. The last owner is your real problem. I mean, it's easy enough to fake who owned paintings years ago – there's no one to question it, as they're dead. But the last owner is usually alive.'

'I see,' said Banks. 'So you'd need an accomplice?'

'At least one.'

'Anyway,' Banks went on, 'as I said, my visit is only indirectly related to the Turners. It's actually the artist himself, Thomas McMahon, I wanted to talk to you about.'

'Oh?'

'You told me you didn't know him.'

'No, I don't. Neither him nor his work.'

'Yet someone told me you were seen in conversation with him at the Turner reception last July.'

Keane frowned. 'I talked to a number of people there. That's where I first met Annie, too, as a matter of fact.'

'Yes, I know that,' said Banks. 'But what about McMahon?'

'I'm sorry. I still can't place him.'

'Short, burly sort of fellow, didn't shave often, longish greasy brown hair. Bit of a scruff. He'd been drinking.'

'Ah,' said Keane. 'You mean the chap with rather disagreeable BO?'

McMahon had smelled of burnt flesh the only time Banks had been close to him. 'Do I?' he said. 'I can't say I ever smelled him. Not when he was alive.'

'Artist. A bit pissed, if I remember right.'

'So you did know him?'

'No. I hadn't a clue who he was.' Keane spread his hands. 'But if you say he was Thomas McMahon, then I'm sure you're right.'

'But you talked to him?'

'Just the once, yes.'

'What did you talk about?'

'He was a bit intense. I do recall that. I think we just chatted about some of the paintings on the walls. He thought they were pretty dreadful. I actually quite liked one or two of them. And – yes, now I remember – he made some disparaging remarks about Turner, said he could easily dash off the other missing Yorkshire watercolour.'

'The one we've just been talking about?'

'The very same.'

'And you've only just remembered this?'

'Yes. Well, since you jogged my memory. Why? Is it important?'

'It could be. So you had an argument with McMahon?'

Keane smiled and a bit of an edge came into his tone. 'I wouldn't exactly call it an argument, just an artistic disagreement. Look, what are you getting at? What is all this about?'

'Probably nothing, really,' said Banks, standing and heading over to the door. 'I'm sorry to waste your time.'

Keane's tone softened again when he noticed Banks was leaving. 'Oh, that's all right. I'm just sorry I can't help you. Look, are you sure you won't have one for the road? Or is that against police regulations?'

Banks laughed. 'I can't say that's ever stopped me before, but not this time, thanks very much,' he said. 'I'll be on my way. If you do remember anything else about that conversation, you'll be sure to let me know, won't you?'

'Of course.'

Banks paused at the open door. 'Just one more thing.'

'Yes?'

'We're putting together an identity parade, and you're the same general build and colouring as the suspect. Seeing as you're practically one of the team, would you consider helping us out and being an extra?'

'How exciting,' said Keane. 'I've never been in an identity parade before. Of course. I'd be only too happy to help.'

'Good,' said Banks. 'Thank you. I'll be in touch. Bye for now, then.'

14

Banks pondered over Phil Keane's response to his visit and his questions as he drove down to Leeds that afternoon. Quite often, he knew, it wasn't so much what a person *said* that was revealing, it was what he didn't say, the way he said something, or the body language he was unconsciously displaying at the time he said it. No matter how often he ran over it in his mind, though, Banks couldn't fault Keane's performance. Even the hint of irritation at being questioned was reasonable, realistic. He'd have felt the same way himself.

But there was something that niggled away at him. It wasn't until the roundabout at the Leeds ring road that Banks realized what it was. Keane's performance had been just that: a *performance*. He was anxious to know if Burgess had been able to dig anything up, but decided he'd leave it until the morning. If he hadn't heard by then, he'd phone Scotland Yard.

For the moment, though, he had a rather difficult interview with Tina's grandparents, the Redferns, to concentrate on. He found their house easily enough, a large bay-windowed semi on a quiet, tree-lined Roundhay street, and parked outside.

'Mr Banks,' said the matronly woman who answered the door. 'We've been expecting you. Please come in. I'm Julia Redfern. Let me take your coat.'

Banks gave her his car coat, which she put on a hanger

in the hall cupboard. The house smelled of baking. Mrs Redfern led him into the kitchen, where the smell was even stronger. 'I hope you don't mind if we talk in here,' she said. 'The study and the sitting room are just too formal. I always think the kitchen is the real heart of a house, don't you?'

Banks agreed. Though he spent most of his time in his living room reading, watching television or listening to music, he loved his own kitchen. In fact, the kitchen was the main reason he had bought the cottage in the first place, having dreamed about it before he saw it. The Redferns' kitchen was much larger than his, though, done out in rustic style, with a heavy wooden dining table and four hard-backed chairs. French doors, closed at the moment, led out to a small conservatory. Banks sat down.

'Besides,' Mrs Redfern went on, 'the cake should be ready. I'll just take it out and let it cool a minute.'

'I thought I could smell something good,' said Banks.

'I always like to do something a bit special when we have company,' Mrs Redfern said, taking a fruit cake out of the oven and setting it on a rack. There was something surreal about the whole scene, Banks was beginning to feel: rustic kitchens, cooking smells, fruit cake fresh from the oven. It was a far cry from Mark's and Tina's world. He wondered if Mrs Redfern felt that she needed some sort of activity to take her mind off his impending visit, or to calm her nerves.

Dr Redfern strode in. He looked fit and energetic despite being in his seventies, and he still had a full head of silver hair. His handshake was firm. Banks wondered if he had been a good doctor. 'Maurice Redfern,' he said. 'Pleased to meet you.' Then he sat opposite Banks.

'First of all,' Banks said, 'I just want you to know that

I'm very sorry about what happened to your grand-daughter and that we're doing our best to find out who did it.'

'I don't see how we can help you,' said Dr Redfern, 'but we'll do as much as we can, of course.'

His wife fussed over tea, then set the pot and three cups and saucers down on the table and cut them each a slice of cake.

'Milk and sugar?' she asked, tapping the teapot.

'Just as it comes, please,' said Banks. She poured and sat down. She seemed on edge, Banks thought, unable to keep still. Perhaps it was just her nature. Banks sipped some tea. It was strong, the way he liked it. Sandra always used to say he could stand a spoon up in his tea. She preferred hers weak, with milk and two sugars. In his mind's eye, he saw her walking away from him in the rain, pushing the pram. 'I'm just after some background, really,' he said. 'You'd be surprised how helpful little things can be and you don't know what they are until you find them. Rather like a doctor's diagnosis, I suppose?'

'Indeed,' said Maurice Redfern. 'Very well. Go ahead, then.'

'Were you close to your granddaughter?' Banks asked.

The Redferns exchanged glances. Finally, Maurice answered. 'Christine lived here with us until she was five years old,' he said slowly. 'After that, she was a frequent visitor, and sometimes she even stayed with us for longer periods. We'd look after her if her parents took a short holiday, that sort of thing.'

It was a very evasive answer, Banks thought. But maybe his question was too difficult, or too painful, for the Redferns to answer. 'Did she confide in you about things?'

'She was a quiet child. A dreamer. I don't know that she ever confided in anyone.'

'What about when she got older? Did you remain close?'

'Do you have any children of your own, Mr Banks?' Julia Redfern asked.

'Two,' Banks said. 'A boy and a girl.'

'Grandchildren?'

'Not yet.'

'Of course not,' she said. 'You're far too young. But you'll know what I mean when I tell you how relationships change when children become teenagers.'

'You didn't see as much of her?'

'Exactly. The last thing a teenage girl wants to do is come and visit old Grandma and Grandad.'

'Boys, too,' said Banks. 'I was the same, myself.' Banks's grandparents had all lived in London, so he hadn't seen them that often, but he remembered endless rainy train rides with his parents and his brother Roy, remembered the old Hornby clockwork train set his grandad Banks kept for him to play with in the spare room, the old war souvenirs in the attic – a tin hat, a shell casing and a gas mask – and the rabbit hutches in the big back garden of his grandad Peyton's house, facing the railway tracks, the long trains rumbling by in the night, through his sleep. All four grandparents were dead by the time he was seventeen, and he was sorry he hadn't had a chance to know them better. Both his grandfathers had fought in the First World War, and he wished he'd asked them about their experiences. But back when he was a kid, he hadn't cared so much. Now the subject interested him. He hoped that if Brian or Tracy had kids it wouldn't be so far in the future that he was a useless old man. 'But you did see her on occasion, didn't you?' he asked.

'Oh, yes,' Maurice Redfern answered, 'but she was uncommunicative.'

'Did you ever suspect there was anything wrong?'

The muscles on Maurice's face seemed to tighten. 'Wrong? In what way?'

'Did you suspect drug use, for example? It's not uncommon among teenagers.'

'I never saw any evidence of it.'

'Was she happy?'

'What an odd question,' Maurice said. 'I suppose so. I mean she never said, either way. She was very much in her own world. I assumed it was a benign place. Now it appears that perhaps I was wrong.'

'Oh? Why is that?'

'You'd hardly be here asking all these questions otherwise, would you?'

'Dr Redfern, I'm sorry if I appear to be prying into private family history, but this is a murder investigation. If you know anything at all about your granddaughter's state of mind prior to her death, then you should realize it might be important information.'

'We don't know anything,' said Julia. 'We were just a normal family.'

'Let's go back a bit,' said Banks. 'How old was Christine's mother when she got pregnant?'

'Sixteen,' said Maurice.

'Was she a wild child?'

He thought for a moment, fingertip touching his lips, then said, 'No, I wouldn't say that, would you, dear?'

'Not at all,' Julia agreed. 'Just foolish. And ignorant. It only takes once, you know.'

'And the father was an American student?'

'Apparently so,' said Dr Redfern. 'He soon disappeared from the scene, whoever he was.'

'What kind of a mother was Frances?'

'She did her best,' said Julia. 'It was difficult, her being so young and all, but she tried. She did love little Christine.'

'Was Dr Aspern on the scene then?'

'I've known Patrick Aspern for nearly thirty years,' said Dr Redfern. 'He was my junior at the infirmary, and we even practised together in Alwoodley for a period.'

'So you were his mentor?'

'In a way. His friend too, I hope.'

'How did you feel about Dr Aspern's interest in your daughter?'

'We were pleased for both of them.'

'How early did you notice it?'

'What do you mean?'

'I assume Patrick Aspern was around the house a lot. Did he seem interested in Frances *before* she had Christine?'

'Don't be absurd,' said Maurice. 'She would have been under sixteen then. He knew her, of course, had done almost since the day she was born. But Frances was twenty-one when they got married, well above the age of consent. There was nothing untowards or unhealthy about it at all. Besides, an older man can bring a bit more stability and experience to raising a family. Frances needed that.'

'So your daughter was grateful for Patrick Aspern's interest in her?'

'I wouldn't say "grateful" is the right word to use,' Maurice argued.

'But his interest was reciprocated?'

'Of course. What do you think it was, an arranged marriage? Do you think we forced Frances into it?'

'What are you getting at, Mr Banks?' asked Julia. 'What's this got to do with Christine's death?'

'How long were they courting?' Banks asked her. 'These things don't happen overnight.'

'You have to remember,' Julia explained, 'that there was Christine to think about. Always. It was hard for Frances to lead a normal life, make friends and go out with boys like other girls her age. She didn't get out very often, so she had no chance to meet boys. Patrick took her out a few times while we looked after Christine. Just to the pictures, that sort of thing. More as a favour, really, to get her out of the house for a while. Sometimes he'd take the two of them to the country for a day out. Whitby, or Malham. Somewhere like that.'

'Weren't you worried?'

'About what?'

'That they might be up to something.'

'Why should we be?' said Maurice. 'Patrick was my closest and dearest friend. I trusted him implicitly.'

'But didn't it bother you, him being so much older than Frances? Weren't you concerned that he might take advantage of her?'

An edge of irritation entered Maurice Redfern's tone. 'Not at all,' he said. 'Why would we be concerned? Frances was twenty and Patrick was in his thirties when they first started "stepping out" together. She was a very attractive young woman and he was a dashing, handsome, talented doctor with a great future. What could be wrong with that? Why should we object or feel concern? We'd almost despaired of Frances finding anyone, and then . . . this happened. It was perfect. A miracle. An occasion for joy. Two of the people I loved most in the world finding one another. I couldn't have wished for a better match.'

So that was it, Banks realized. The reason for all the edginess and embarrassment he had sensed. The Redferns had wanted to get Frances married off and baby Christine had been an impediment to that. They were the ones who were grateful for Patrick's interest in their daughter. After all, not many young men are willing to take on a young woman *and* a baby, especially if that baby isn't his own. When the good Dr Aspern took both Frances and the child as well, it would have been easy for the Redferns to turn a blind eye to any number of things. Perhaps they had even encouraged him, left the two alone together, offered to babysit? But to what, exactly, had they turned a blind eye?

'What was their relationship like?' Banks asked.

'Perfectly above board,' said Julia Redfern. 'There was no hanky-panky. Not in this house. And, take my word for it, we'd have known.'

'Were they affectionate? Demonstrative?'

'They weren't always touching and feeling each other like some of the kids today,' said Julia. 'It's disgusting, if you ask me. You should keep that sort of thing private.'

'And they didn't get much privacy?'

'I suppose not,' she said. 'It was difficult.'

'We were just happy that Patrick took an interest in her,' Maurice added. 'He brought her out of her shell. It had been a difficult few years. Christine wasn't always the easiest child to deal with and Frances was becoming withdrawn, old before her time.'

'Christine was five when Patrick and Frances married?'

'Yes.'

'How did he take to fatherhood?'

'He was very good with her, wasn't he, darling?' Julia said.

'Yes, very,' Maurice agreed.

Well, what had Banks expected? That they'd suddenly come out and tell him that the pure and holy Patrick Aspern was a daughter-diddling paedophile? But the portrait of utter mind-numbing ordinariness that they were painting just didn't ring true. Had they suspected something and tried to ignore it? People did that often enough, Banks knew. Or were they really blissfully, wilfully ignorant of Aspern's sexual interest in Tina? And when did that start? When she was six, seven, eight, nine, ten? Or before? Had he been interested in Frances when she was a child, too? He wished he could find out, but he couldn't think of a direct way of getting an answer to these questions. He would have to see if he could get there indirectly.

'Did the marriage have any effect on Christine?' he asked.

'Well, it gave her a father,' said Maurice. 'I'd say that's pretty important for a child, wouldn't you? No matter what some of these special-interest groups say.'

'Did she behave any differently after the marriage?'

'We weren't with her so much, so we wouldn't know. They had their own house by then, out Lawnswood way, not far from where they are now. I'm sure she had her problems adjusting to a new routine, though, as we all do.'

'When they brought Christine to visit, did she seem the same as usual?'

'Yes,' said Maurice. 'Until . . .'

'Until when?'

'What I told you earlier. Until she became a teenager.'

'Then she became uncommunicative?'

'Somewhat, yes. Rather quiet and brooding. Sullen. She could be quite snappy, too, if you pushed her on any-thing. Hormones.'

Or Patrick Aspern, Banks thought. So he had his answer. It had started, in all likelihood, when she hit puberty. What's a cut-off point for some paedophiles is the starting point for others.

'Did you see her after she left home?'

The Redferns looked at one another, and Julia nodded. 'She came here once,' she said, close to tears. 'Maurice was out. Oh, she looked terrible, Mr Banks. My heart just . . .' She shook her head and grabbed a tissue from the box on the window ledge. 'It just went out to her. I'm sorry,' she said. 'It was just so upsetting.'

'In what way did she look terrible?'

'She was so thin and pale. Her nose was running con-stantly. Her face was spotty, her skin terrible. Dry and blotched. She used to be such a pretty young thing. And I hate to say it, but her clothes were filthy and . . . she *smelled.*'

'When was this?'

'Shortly after she'd left. About a year ago.'

When they were living in the Leeds squat, before the boat, perhaps even before Mark. 'What did she come for?'

'She wanted money.'

'Did you give her any?'

She looked at her husband. 'Fifty pounds. It was all I had in my purse.'

'Did she say anything?'

'Not much. I tried to persuade her to go back to Patrick

and Frances. They were beside themselves with worry, of course.'

'What did she say to that?'

'She said she wasn't going back. Not ever. She was quite emotional about it.'

'Did she say why?'

'Why what?'

'Why she wasn't going back. Why she left.'

'No, she just got very upset when I mentioned the subject and refused to talk about it.'

'Why did you *think* she left?'

'I thought it must be something to do with a boy.'

'A boy? Why? Did Patrick Aspern say that?'

'No . . . I . . . I just assumed. She was the same age as her mother was when she . . . I don't know. It's a difficult age for young girls. They want to be all grown up, but they don't have the experience. They lose their hearts to some no-good layabout, and the next thing you know, they're pregnant.'

'Like Frances?'

'Yes.'

'So you saw history repeating itself?'

'I suppose so.'

'Did you ask your daughter or her husband why Christine left home at sixteen?' Banks persisted.

Julia put her hands to her ears. 'Please stop! Make him stop, Maurice.'

'It's all right, Mrs Redfern,' said Banks. 'I'm not here to badger you. I'll slow down. Let's all just take a minute and relax. Take a deep breath.' He finished his tea. It was lukewarm.

'As you can see, Mr Banks,' Maurice said, 'this is all very upsetting and I can't see what any of it has to do with Christine's unfortunate death. Perhaps you'd better leave.'

'Murder's an upsetting business, Dr Redfern, and I haven't finished yet.'

'But my wife . . .'

'Your wife is emotional, I can see that. What I'd really like to know is why.'

'I'd have thought that was quite obvious.'

'Not to me it isn't.'

'You coming here and—'

'I don't believe that's the reason and I don't think you do either.'

'What are you getting at, man?'

Banks took a deep breath. Here goes, he thought. 'There have been serious allegations that Patrick Aspern had been sexually abusing his stepdaughter, probably since puberty.'

Maurice Redfern shot to his feet. 'Are you insane? Patrick? What allegations? Who made them?'

'Christine told her boyfriend, Mark Siddons, that that was partly why she started using drugs, drugs she got from her stepfather's surgery, to escape the shame and the pain. He also suggested that Patrick Aspern later let her have the drugs in return for her silence and perhaps for her sexual favours.'

'I don't believe it,' said Maurice, sinking back into his chair, pale. 'Not Patrick. I *won't* believe it.'

'So that's what she meant,' Julia Redfern said, in a voice hardly louder than a whisper.

'What?' said Banks. 'What did she say?'

'Just that I was better off not knowing, that's all. And that I wouldn't believe her, never in a million years, she said, even if she told me. And that *look* on her face.' She turned to her husband, tears welling up in her eyes again. 'Oh, my God, Maurice, what have we done?'

'Get a grip on yourself, Julia,' said Maurice. 'It's all lies. Lies made up by some drug-addled boy. We've done nothing to be ashamed of. Our daughter married a good man and now someone's trying to blacken his character. That's all. We'll deal with this through our solicitor.' He stood up. 'I'd prefer it if you left now, Mr Banks. Unless you're going to arrest us or something, we don't want to talk to you any more.'

Banks had nothing more to ask, anyway. He already had his answers. He nodded, got up and left, the slice of cake still untouched on his plate.

•

It was well after dark when Mark got off the No. 1 bus outside the Lawnswood Arms, just past the Leeds Crematorium. His journey had taken so long because there weren't that many buses from Eastvale to Leeds, and he had to change in Harrogate. Then he had to buy a street map at W. H. Smith's to find out how to get to Adel. He had never visited Tina's parents before – never had any reason to – but the address was on the inside cover of some of the books she had kept with her in the squat and on the boat, and he remembered it. He also knew the security code you had to punch in to stop the burglar alarm from going off. Tina had made him memorize it. A month or so ago Danny Boy had suffered a brief disruption in distribution, and to keep Tina sane Mark had pretended to go along with a half-baked scheme to break into her stepfather's surgery and steal some morphine. Luckily, Danny Boy had come through before things really got out of hand.

There was nothing but fields across the main road, and beyond them, down the hill, Mark could see the clustered lights of Adel village. Still unsure of exactly what he was going to say or do, Mark was drawn by the lights of the Lawnswood Arms and went inside. He hadn't eaten any lunch, so he was hungry for one thing, and maybe a few drinks would give him Dutch courage.

The Lawnswood Arms seemed more of a family pub than a local watering hole, though at eight o'clock that evening there were hardly any families in evidence. Mark went to the bar and ordered a pint of Tetley's cask and looked at the menu. Steak and chips would do just fine, he decided. The first pint went down so fast the barman gave him a dirty look when he ordered a second. He'd seen that look before: 'I've got my eye on you, mate. I know trouble when I see it.' Well, maybe he *was* going to be trouble, but not for the bartender.

He got two pints down before his food was ready and ordered a third to wash down the steak. He wasn't showing any signs of drunkenness, so they had no reason to refuse to serve him, and they didn't. He just sat quietly in his corner, smoking and thinking. If they knew his thoughts, then maybe they'd call the police, but they didn't. The more he drank, the darker his thoughts became. Surges of emotion, sometimes anger, shot with red, black and grey.

He'd been wandering aimlessly, he realized now, with nowhere to go and nobody to talk to, nobody to share his grief with, nobody to hold him when he cried. But he never had had anyone. He had always been alone. Just him and his imagination and his wits. The only difference was that he was even more adrift than ever now that Tina, his anchor, his burden, his reason for being, was gone.

He thought about Crazy Nick lying bleeding on the floor; he thought about his mother, how she'd never wanted him because he got in the way of her good times, though when he heard she was dead he had felt oddly alone in the world. But most of all he thought about Tina. He had never seen her body, he realized, so her parents must have identified her. The thought of Aspern gloating over her, touching her, made his flesh crawl. His last memory of her, the one he would carry for ever, was the frail figure huddled in the sleeping bag, needle barely out of her arm, giving a little sigh of pleasure, and Beth Orton playing quietly on the CD. Not 'Stolen Car' but a more recent one, a song about being on a train in Paris, as he snuffed out the candle and left her, to sneak off to the welcoming arms of Mandy. If only he'd stayed with her, the way he'd promised, the way he had always done before . . .

'You all right?'

The voice sounded far away, and when he looked up, Mark noticed it was one of the bar staff collecting glasses, a young girl, perhaps not much older than Tina, though he knew she had to be over eighteen to work in a pub. She had a short spiky haircut and a gold stud through her lower lip, just like Tina, and in a way she reminded him of her, the way she could be when she held the darkness at bay.

'Yeah,' he said. 'Fine. Just thinking.'

She stared at him, an assessing look in her eye. 'Not good thoughts, by the looks of you.'

'You could say that.'

She lowered her voice. 'Only, old misery guts over there has been giving you the evil eye all night. One wrong move and you're cut off. You weren't thinking of making any wrong moves, were you?'

'No,' said Mark. 'Not here, at any rate.'

'Well, that's all right, then.' She smiled. 'I've not seen you here before.'

'That's because I've never been here before.'

'Not from around these parts?'

'No.'

'Cathy!'

The new voice came from the bar. 'Oops,' she said, grimacing. 'Got to go. Old misery's calling. Remember, tread carefully.'

'I will,' said Mark.

The brief conversation had brought him back to a world of normality, at least for a few moments, and he wondered if his life could ever be good again. The girl might not have been trying to pick him up, but she was definitely flirting with him and he could tell she fancied him. If his world were normal he'd have pursued the matter and maybe gone home with her, if she had her own flat. She probably did, he thought. Looked like a student and the university wasn't far down the road. The bus had passed it on the way out of town. But after what happened to Tina, and him being with Mandy at the time, somehow it made it so he just couldn't contemplate anything like that, even though this girl Cathy reminded him of Tina.

The barman gave him the evil eye again when he ordered his next pint, his fifth, he thought, though he was still steady on his feet and his speech wasn't slurred. The look told him, 'This is your last one, mate. After that you're on your bike.' Fine, he didn't want any more. It was nearly closing time anyway.

Mark lit another cigarette, the last in his packet, and tried to work out exactly what he wanted to do or say when he got to Aspern's house. The way he felt whenever he thought about Patrick Aspern, he thought he'd probably do what he did to Crazy Nick, or worse. He didn't know about Tina's mother. He'd nothing against her and didn't want to hurt her, but she hadn't been there for her daughter any more than his mother had been there for him. True, he'd never been sexually molested by any of her men friends, but more than one of them had beaten him up and more often than not they just used him to fetch and carry for them and clean up their messes. Mothers ought to be there for their kids, they were supposed to love them and nurture them, and Tina's had failed in that as much as his own mother had, no matter how far apart they were in social status. When it came right down to it, a doctor's wife could be just as useless a mother as a whore, because that was what his mother had been, he had no illusions about that.

A bell rang and someone called out time. Mark had about half a pint left in his glass. He'd had five and he still didn't feel in the least bit pissed. He fiddled for change in his pocket and bought another packet of cigarettes from the machine. When he'd finished his drink, he stuck a cigarette in his mouth, lit it and headed for the door.

'Goodnight,' a voice called out behind him.

It was the girl, Cathy. She was closer than he thought, a cloth in her hand, wiping down the tables.

'Goodnight,' he said.

'Maybe I'll see you again?'

Was that a note of hope in her voice? He wondered. He

managed a smile for her. 'Maybe,' he said. 'You never know.'

Then he walked out into the chilly night air.

•

'Have you thought any more about New York?' Phil asked Annie as they lingered over café noir and crème brûlée in Le Select, Eastvale's prestigious French bistro. Already well sated with several glasses of fine claret, Annie was feeling warm and relaxed, and the idea of a weekend away with Phil held immense appeal. Especially New York.

'I can't go, Phil, really I can't,' she said. 'I'd love to, honestly. Maybe some other time?'

'If it's a matter of money . . .'

'It's only *partly* a matter of money,' Annie chipped in. 'I mean, you might be able to go swanning off to America on a whim, but I *do* have to think about the expense.'

'I told you I'd get your ticket. Security consultant.'

'That's very sweet of you, but it doesn't seem right,' Annie said. 'Besides, if I went with you to New York, I certainly wouldn't want to go as your employee.'

Phil laughed. 'But that would only be on paper.'

'I don't care.'

The waiter came over with the bill and Phil picked it up.

'See what I mean?' Annie said. 'You're always paying.'

'I'll split it with you, then?'

'Fine,' said Annie, reaching for her handbag. The Visa wasn't maxed out, she was certain. How embarrassing it would be, after all her bravado about paying her own way, if that obsequious waiter with the phoney French accent trotted back and told her her card had been rejected.

'You don't know what you're missing,' Phil went on.

'We could stay at the Plaza. A carriage ride in Central Park, top of the Empire State Building, the Tavern on the Green, Saks Fifth Avenue, Bloomingdale's, Tiffany's . . .'

'Oh, stop it!' Annie said, slapping his arm and putting her hands over her ears. 'I don't want to know, OK?'

Phil held his hands up in mock surrender. 'OK, OK, I'll stop.'

'Besides,' Annie said, 'we've still got a major crime investigation on the go.'

'Still stumped?'

'We don't have a lot to go on. Even the rented car turned out to be a dead end. Literally. The man who rented it died six months ago.'

'Oh,' said Phil. 'Then how . . . ?'

'Don't ask. All I know is it's a real bloody headache, and it's nice to take my mind off it even for a few hours. Christ, I even had to spend last night in a motel outside Redditch fighting off the attentions of two travelling salesmen from Solihull.'

Phil laughed. 'Successfully, I hope.'

'Yes. I had Winsome with me. She can be quite fearsome when she wants.' Annie smiled. 'Fearsome Winsome.'

The waiter returned with their credit-card receipts to sign. Annie breathed a sigh of relief. When they had finished, they picked up their coats from the rack by the table and walked out into the cobbled alley off King Street at the back of the police station.

'Ooh,' said Annie, when the cold night air hit her, 'I feel dizzy. I think I've had a bit too much wine.' She linked arms with Phil.

'Come on,' Phil said. 'My car's just around the corner. Where did you park?'

Annie was wearing high heels and it was difficult walking on the cobbles, especially with the effects of the wine and the patches of ice that were forming as the temperature dropped. 'Police station car park,' she said.

'Leave it there, then. I'm perfectly OK to drive.'

And he was, Annie knew. She had never seen Phil drunk, never known him to drink more than one glass of wine with dinner. 'But what . . . ?'

'Look,' he said, 'I'll take you home, if you like. Or if you want . . .'

Annie looked up at him. 'What?'

'Well, you could come back to my place, if you like.'

'But how will I get to work in the morning?'

'Maybe you won't. Maybe I'll keep you there. My love slave.'

Annie laughed and pushed him.

'Seriously,' he said, 'I'll drop you off there in the morning. I have to pick up the Turners to take them to London, anyway.'

'You're going back down?'

'Have to.'

'Pity.'

'Work goes on. Anyway, how about it?'

'You'll bring me back in the morning? You'll do that?'

'Of course. Unless I decide to keep you prisoner.'

'Go on, then.'

'But I'm warning you. I know you've had a bit too much to drink and I might take advantage of you.'

Annie felt better than she had in a long while about that prospect, but she was damned if she was going to let Phil know it. 'I'm not *that* drunk,' she said. 'And I'm definitely not that easy.'

'Well, I'm sure we'll find some way of keeping your mind off your work for a few hours more, at least.'

Annie tightened her arm around his and they turned the corner onto King Street.

•

'Dad? I'm sorry to ring so late, but I just got back in.'

Banks glanced at his watch. Almost midnight. 'Where've you been?'

'The pictures. With Jane and Ravi.'

'What did you see?'

'The new *Lord of the Rings*.'

'Was it good?'

'Brilliant. But very long. Look, Dad . . .'

Banks turned down the old Jesse Winchester CD he was playing and settled back in the armchair with his glass of Laphroaig, his used paperback copy of Ambler's *The Mask of Dimitrius* open face-down beside him. The peat fire crackled and filled the small living room with its warmth, the acrid smell harmonizing with the taste of whisky. He didn't like the ominous tone of his daughter's 'Look, Dad.' 'What?' he asked.

'I was talking to Mum earlier today,' Tracy went on.

'And?'

'She'd said she saw you. In London.'

'That's right. I was down there on business.'

'She said she thought you were watching her. Stalking her.'

'I was doing no such thing.'

'Well, she says you were hanging around her house. In the rain.'

'It wasn't raining. That started later.'

'Dad, she's worried about you.'

'I don't see why.'

'She thinks you're becoming weird.'

'Weird?'

'Yes. Hanging around her house and all. It *is* pretty weird. You must admit.'

'I had a few questions I wanted to ask her.'

'About a case?'

'As it happens, yes. About an artist she once knew when she worked at the community centre. It's part of a case I'm working on.'

'The burning boats. Yes, I've read about it in the paper.' Tracy paused. 'She didn't tell me that.'

'Well, it's true. What? Don't you believe me? Do *you* think I'm getting weird in my old age?'

'Nobody said anything about old age.'

'Still . . . my own daughter grilling me.'

'I'm not grilling you. Can't you see she still cares about you?'

'She's got a funny way of showing it.'

'You scare her, Dad. She just can't cope with you. You always seem so angry with her. She thinks you hate her. All she can manage is to go cold when the two of you talk to one another.'

Banks remembered that from their marriage. Whenever Sandra couldn't deal with a situation emotionally, she would just sort of turn off. Sometimes she would even fall asleep in the middle of an argument. It used to infuriate him. 'I don't hate her,' he said.

'Well, that's how she feels.'

'It's a funny turn of events, isn't it, my own daughter giving me advice on marital relationships?'

'I don't have any advice to give. And you're not married any more. That's the problem. How's your girlfriend?'

'Michelle? She's fine.'

'Seen her lately?'

'No. We've both been too busy.'

'There you go, then.'

'And what's that supposed to mean?'

'Dad, you've got to make time to have a life. Stop and smell the roses. You can't just . . . Oh, I don't know. What's the point?'

'I stopped to smell the roses last summer,' Banks said. 'But it didn't last.' He remembered the two weeks of bliss he had spent on a Greek island, the sun, the light on white and blue planes of the houses straggling down the hill, scents of lavender, thyme, oregano, a whiff of dead fish and salt spray. He also remembered how restless he had felt and how, though it seemed a great wrench at the time, he was secretly pleased to feel himself being called back home to a case. And to the lovely Michelle Hart. How he wished she were with him tonight, but he wasn't going to let his daughter in on his longings.

'That was because you came running back to get involved in another case,' Tracy said.

'Tracy, Graham Marshall was an old friend of mine. How could I—'

'Oh, I know. I'm not saying you shouldn't have come back. Of course I'm not. But remember the time before, when we were supposed to be going to Paris for the weekend, and you went off searching for Jimmy Riddle's runaway daughter instead? There's always something. Always will be. You just have to . . . I mean, you can't solve the world's problems single-handedly. You're not the only detective in the country, you know. Sometimes I think you just use your job to hide yourself from yourself. And from everybody else.'

'What's that supposed to mean?'

'Oh, it's too complicated to go into right now.'

'Quite the philosopher you've become. And here's me thinking you were a history student.'

'You know what Socrates said: "The unexamined life is not worth living."'

'Well, I wouldn't examine it *too* closely, if I were you. You never know what you might find.'

'Oh, Dad. You're just playing word games now.'

Banks felt the urge for a cigarette peak and wane. He took another sip of whisky. 'Look,' he said. 'I'm sorry for being facetious. It's just been a long day. A long week, as a matter of fact. I haven't had much sleep and I've got a lot on my mind.'

'When was it ever any different?'

'Tell your mother I don't hate her.'

'Tell her yourself. Goodnight, Dad.'

And Tracy hung up.

Banks held the phone in his hand for a few moments and listened to the buzzing sound. He'd been about to tell Tracy that seeing the baby for the first time had been a shock, that he hadn't been prepared for the way it made him feel. But she'd hung up on him.

He put the phone down and went into the kitchen to top up his glass. As he stood there pouring the Laphroaig, he felt an overwhelming sense of melancholy envelop him. But it came from the *outside*, not the inside. Though he didn't generally believe in the supernatural, he had long believed that the kitchen contained some sort of spirit. It usually gave him a strong sense of well-being, and he had never felt its sadness before.

Banks shuddered and went back to the living room, turned up Jesse Winchester singing 'The Brand New Tennessee Waltz' and settled down gloomily to get drunk. He knew he shouldn't, knew that tomorrow would be just as busy as today, and that the hangovers only got worse as he got older. But his daughter had hung up on him. He thought of phoning her back, but decided against it. He didn't feel he had the emotional energy to deal with the sort of discussion Tracy seemed to have in mind tonight. Best wait till they'd both slept on it. He was sure she would ring him again tomorrow and patch things up. Still, it was a sour note to go to bed on, which was why he had refilled his glass.

He wanted to talk to Michelle. The way things had turned out he hadn't called her from London, hadn't spent the evening in Peterborough. It was after one o'clock, but he would ring her anyway, he decided, reaching for the phone. But before he could pick it up, it rang. He thought it might be Tracy ringing back to apologize, so he answered it.

'Alan?'

'Yes?'

'Ken Blackstone here. Sorry to bother you at this hour, but I thought you might be interested. I just got a call from Weetwood.'

Banks sat up. 'What is it?'

'Another fire. Adel. Patrick Aspern's house.'

Banks put his glass down. 'I'll be there as soon as I can,' he said.

'I'll be waiting.'

Banks took stock of the shape he was in. Luckily, he had only taken a sip or two of his second drink, and he knew he wasn't over the limit. He put the kettle on and poured plenty of fine-ground coffee into a filter. While the water was coming to a boil, he stuck his head under the tap and ran cold water over it for a couple of minutes. Then he poured the boiling water into the filter and watched it drip through, filled it once again and brushed his teeth and sucked on a breath mint. Just before he left, he filled a travel mug with hot black coffee and carried it out to the car. The night was cold and hoar frost had formed on the trees and drystone walls, giving them a ghostly white outline in the night. The sky was studded with stars.

There was no time for Jesse Winchester's bittersweet musings now. Banks flipped through the CDs he carried in the car and went for the Clash's *London Calling*. If that and the hot, strong coffee didn't keep him awake all the way to Adel, nothing would.

15

The fire engines were gone when Banks arrived at Patrick
Aspern's house shortly after two in the morning, and two
police patrol cars were parked diagonally across the street,
blocking it to all traffic. He hadn't known what to expect
in terms of damage, but from the outside, at least, the
house seemed intact. The local police had sealed off the
path and a line of blue and white tape barred the gate-
way, where a young constable, who looked to be freezing
his bollocks off even in his overcoat, was logging everyone who came and went. Banks went up to him and asked
for DI Ken Blackstone.

The PC wrote something on his clipboard and gestured
with his thumb. 'Inside, sir,' he said with a wistful tone.

Banks walked down the path. The front door was
closed, but not locked, and there were signs of forced
entry. The firefighters, or someone else?

Banks found Ken Blackstone and the local DI from
Weetwood, Gary Bridges, in the living room. DI Bridges
presented quite a contrast to Banks and the elegant,
dapper Blackstone. In some ways he resembled DS Hatchley, though he was in far better shape. He was a big man
in a baggy, creased suit, an ex-rugby forward with arms
and legs like steel cables, a thick head of sandy hair and
piercing green eyes. Traces of his Belfast accent were still
in his voice, even though he'd spent most of his life in
England.

Banks looked around the room. There was no trace, or even smell, of fire or smoke damage anywhere. Sitting on the sofa, where he cut a slight and lonely figure indeed, was Mark Siddons. The room was warm, but Mark had a blanket wrapped around his shoulders and was trembling slightly. He looked over when Banks walked in, then quickly averted his eyes. What looked like streaks of dirt, or blood, stained his face and the hands gripping the blanket. There was also blood on the side of his head.

'What's going on?' Banks asked, after greeting Blackstone and Bridges. 'Where's the fire?'

'Gary here rang me at home as soon as he heard the location,' said Blackstone. 'His lads had been helping us check up on Aspern, so he knew I had an interest.'

'It started in Dr Aspern's surgery,' Bridges said. 'At the back. An addition, really. The damage isn't serious, and it's pretty well contained.' He gestured towards Mark. 'Seems this lad here snapped into action with the extinguisher real sharpish.'

Banks looked at Mark. 'That right?' he asked.

Mark nodded.

'Was it you who broke in?'

Mark said nothing.

'Sure you didn't start the fire yourself?' Banks went on.

'I didn't start it.'

'I warned you to stay away.'

'I didn't do it.'

'What makes you think he did?' Bridges asked. 'What's going on here? DI Blackstone said Dr Aspern was involved in a case you're working on, but that's about all I know. Do you think this might be related?'

'The personnel's the same,' said Banks, then he explained about the other fires and Mark's problems with

Patrick Aspern. Mark said nothing. He seemed to be lost in his own world, still trembling.

'So what happened?' Banks asked.

'We're still not clear yet,' Blackstone said. 'But the fire's not the main problem.' He looked at Mark. 'And the leading firefighter told me the front door was already open when they got here. Do you want a look at the scene?'

Banks nodded. Blackstone glanced at Bridges. It was a courtesy to seek his permission because they were on his patch. 'It's OK,' Bridges said. 'Looks like we'll be working together on this one, anyway. I'll take the lad here down to the station.'

'Why are you arresting me?' Mark asked. 'I haven't done anything.'

'Where else would you go at this hour?' Banks asked. Mark just shrugged.

Bridges looked over at Banks. 'Breaking and entering?'

'That'll do for starters. And see if you can get a doctor to have a look at him, would you? We'll talk to him tomorrow.'

'OK,' said Bridges. 'Be careful in there. The doc's been and gone, but the photographer's not finished yet, I think, and the SOCOs haven't done their stuff. Can't seem to get the idle buggers out of bed.'

'It's pretty grim,' Blackstone said as he and Banks walked down the plush-carpeted hall to the back of the house.

Banks remembered the scene on the boats and in Gardiner's caravan. He didn't imagine it could be much worse than either of those. And it certainly couldn't be worse than what he had witnessed in that tall, narrow terraced house all those years ago.

'There's just one connecting door through from the

main house,' Blackstone said, turning the handle. 'And there's a separate entrance from the outside into a small waiting room for the patients. They're mostly private and I expect they pay a little bit extra for the olde worlde charm. I'll bet the doctor paid house calls, too.'

There wasn't much olde worlde charm in evidence when Blackstone opened the door to Aspern's surgery, but whatever damage had been done there hadn't been done by fire. Even with the slight charring and spray of foam from the extinguisher, it was plain to see that the walls and floor were covered in blood, and that the blood came from the body of Patrick Aspern, well beyond the help of any doctor now, spread-eagled on the floor, the entire front of his body ripped open in a glistening tapestry of tissue, organ, sinew and bone.

Banks glanced at Blackstone, who was looking distinctly peaky. 'Shotgun?' he said. 'Close range? Both barrels?'

'Exactly. Gary's bagged it and tagged it.'

'Jesus Christ,' Banks said under his breath. In such a small room the impact must have been tremendous. Even now he could still smell the powder mingled with burned rubber, surgical spirit and blood. Banks could only imagine the deafening noise and the spray of arterial blood, the gobbets of flesh blown clean off the bone, leaving dark slimy trails on the walls. Even the eye chart was splattered with blood and the hypodermic syringe on the floor by the chair.

'Who did it?' Banks asked.

'Looks like the wife,' said Blackstone, 'but she's not talking yet.'

'Frances?' Banks said. 'Where is she?'

'Station.'

'And the boy was in the room too? Mark?'

'Yes.'

'What does he have to say for himself?'

'Nothing. You saw for yourself. I think he's still in shock. We'll have to wait a while before we get anything out of him.'

Banks kept silent for a few moments, looking around the room. A shambles, in the original meaning of the word. He noticed several strands of cord on the floor by the doctor's chair. 'What's that?' he asked.

'We think the boy must have been tied to the chair.'

'Why?'

'Don't know yet. But Mrs Aspern must have cut him free.'

'And the fire?'

'Hardly got started before the kid turned the extinguisher on it. As you can see.'

He pointed to a burnt patch on the carpet, which had spread as far as the cubbyhole used to store patients' files and singed the crisp white sheets on the examination table.

'Who set it?'

'Again, it looks like the wife.'

Frances Aspern. Well, maybe she had reached snapping point, Banks thought. If what he suspected had been going on, and if she had known, then he could only guess at the power of the emotions she had suppressed, or how warped and dangerous they had become under the pressure of the years. But something must have happened to make her snap. A trigger of some sort. Maybe they would get something out of her or Mark later.

The outside door opened, letting in a draught of icy night air. 'Sorry, lads,' said the photographer, tapping his

Pentax. 'I finished the video, then I had to go back to the car for this.'

The young photographer didn't seem at all fazed by the scene of carnage in front of him. Banks had seen the same lack of reaction before. He knew that photographers often managed to distance themselves through their lenses. To them the scene was only another photo, an image, a composition, not real human blood and guts spilled there. It was their way of coping.

Banks wondered what his way of coping was and realized he didn't really have one. He looked upon these scenes as exactly what they were – outbursts of anger, hate, greed, lust or passion, which left one human being mangled and split open, the fragile bag of blood burst – and he didn't have any way of distancing himself. But still he slept at night, still he didn't faint or puke his guts up over someone's shoes. What did that say about him? Oh, he remembered them all, of course, all the victims, young and old, and sometimes his sleep was disturbed by dreams, or he couldn't get to sleep for the images that assaulted his mind, but still he lived with it. What did that make him?

'Alan?'

Banks turned to see Ken Blackstone frowning at him.

'All right?'

'Fine, thanks.'

'My sofa?'

'Why not,' said Banks, with a sigh. 'It's a bloody long way home, and I'm knackered. Got any decent whisky?'

'I think I could rustle up a dram or two of Bell's.'

'That'll do nicely,' said Banks. 'Let's leave it to DI Bridges and go. We'll sort this mess out tomorrow.'

•

Annie was in the office early, despite a mild hangover and a mostly sleepless night. Phil had picked up the Turners and set off for London after dropping her at the front doors of Western Area Headquarters. She made a pot of strong coffee in the squad room and settled down to some much neglected paperwork. She was just starting to enjoy the relative early-morning peace and quiet when the place started springing to life. DC Rickerd was first in, followed by Winsome. Then Kevin Templeton and the others came and went, attending to the varied tasks and minutiae of a major investigation. Annie felt embarrassed to be wearing the same clothes she'd gone to dinner in the previous evening, but nobody noticed, or at least nobody said anything. Banks wasn't there, anyway. She could only imagine the kind of look she'd get from him. Sometimes she felt as if he could smell the sex on her, no matter how long she had showered.

It wasn't long after nine when an excited DC Templeton came up to her waving a sheet of paper. 'I've got it!' he said. 'I've got it.'

'Alleluia,' said Annie. 'What have you got?'

'McMahon and Gardiner. The connection.'

Annie felt the excitement of a big break spread around the squad room like the first breath of spring. Everyone put in hard and long hours on a case, and something like this was pay day for them all, whether they'd worked that particular angle or not.

'Come on, then, Kev,' she said. 'Give.'

'They were at university together,' said Templeton. 'Well, it wasn't actually a university back then, but it is now.'

'Kev, slow down,' said Annie. 'Give me the details so they make sense.'

Templeton ran his hand over his wavy brown hair. He had some sort of gel on it, Annie noticed, which made it look wet, as if he'd just walked out of the shower. He always did fancy himself a bit, did Kevin Templeton, she thought, and he was a good-looking, trim, fit lad who probably did really well with the girls. He had a touch of the Hugh Grant boyish charm about him, too, the sort of quality that called out for a bit of mothering, but just enough to make it an attractive proposition for the right type of woman. Not Annie. She wasn't the mothering kind.

'OK,' he went on, reading from the sheet. 'Between 1978 and 1981 both Thomas McMahon and Roland Gardiner attended the former Leeds Polytechnic, since 1992 known as Leeds Metropolitan University. Back then it was made up of the Art College, the College of Commerce, the College of Technology and the Cookery School. Thomas McMahon attended the Art College, obviously, and Roland Gardiner went to the College of Commerce.'

'Did they know one another?'

Templeton scratched his forehead. 'Can't tell you that, Ma'am. Only that they were both there at the same time.'

Winsome shot Annie a glance. Annie smiled at her. One day she'd get Kevin Templeton out of the habit of calling her 'Ma'am', too. Coming from a handsome young lad like him, it really did make her feel like an old maid.

'In my experience,' Annie said, 'it's pretty unlikely that art and commerce students shared the same interests. I doubt they'd ever mix.'

'Not the same subjects, maybe,' said Templeton, 'but that's only a part of what college is all about, isn't it? There's the pub, student politics, the music scene. Leeds

Poly always had great bands. They could have met through something like that.'

'"Could have" isn't good enough, Kev. If we're to make any sort of link, we need to know for certain. And we need to know who else they hung out with. There's a fair chance that whoever killed them met them back then, someone who was maybe part of the same scene. I certainly don't believe it's a coincidence that two men who were murdered so close together and in much the same way just *happened* to go to the same poly at the same time. But we need a definite connection, if one exists. And there's the late William Masefield to consider, too. How was he linked with the others, if he was?'

'Well,' said Templeton, 'I could always get onto the authorities in Leeds. I'm sure their records go back that far.'

'And what do we do then? Check up on every student who attended Leeds Poly from 1978 to 1981? It'd be like looking for the proverbial needle in a haystack.'

'Can you think of any other way?'

'I've got an idea,' said Winsome.

Annie and Templeton looked at her. 'Go on,' Annie said.

'Friends Reunited dot com. I'm a member. I've used it before to locate people. I admit it's a short cut, but it might help narrow things down a bit. Of course, you've only got the people who have taken the trouble to register on the site, but there's a chance one of them might remember McMahon or Gardiner. We can send out an email to everyone on the list who left Leeds Poly in 1981, asking if they knew a Thomas McMahon and a Roland Gardiner, and see what kind of response we get back. Plenty of people are constantly online these days, so if we're lucky we might even get a speedy reply.'

'It's worth a try,' said Annie, getting to her feet. 'Come on, let's do it.'

•

The interview room was the same as just about every interview room Banks had ever been in: small, high window covered by a grille, bare bulb similarly covered, metal table bolted to the floor. The institutional green paint looked fresh, though, and Banks fancied he could still smell traces of it in the stale air. Either that or the Scotch he had drunk with Ken Blackstone the previous night was giving him a headache. He massaged his temples.

Frances Aspern sat opposite Banks and DI Gary Bridges, who was not only wearing the same suit as he had last night, but looked as if he'd slept in it too. Dressed in disposable navy overalls, Frances Aspern seemed listless and distant, and much older than she had when Banks first saw her. The dark circles under her eyes testified that she hadn't slept and she was fidgeting with a ring. Not her wedding ring, Banks noticed. That was gone.

'Are you ready to talk to us?' Bridges asked, when he had issued the caution and set the tape machine rolling.

Frances nodded, a faraway look in her eyes.

'Can you speak your answers out loud, please?' Bridges asked.

'Yes,' she said in a small voice. 'Sorry.'

'What happened last night?'

Frances paused so long before answering that Banks was beginning to think she hadn't heard DI Bridges's question. But eventually she began to speak. 'We were asleep. Patrick heard a noise downstairs. He took his gun out of the cabinet and went down.' Her voice was a monotone, disconnected from her feelings, as if the things she was saying were of no interest to her.

'What happened then?'

'I waited. A long time. I don't know how long. Then I went downstairs. He was going to hurt the boy. I picked up his gun and shot him, then I cut the boy free and told him to go.'

'What about the fire?' DI Bridges asked.

'Fire cleanses,' she said. 'I wanted to purify the house.'

'What did you use to start it?'

'Rubbing alcohol. It was on the table.'

'What happened?'

'The boy came back and put it out. I told him not to, but he didn't listen. Then he made me sit down and he rang the police. I just felt so tired I didn't care what happened, but I couldn't sleep.'

'I'm trying to understand all this, Frances,' Bridges said. 'Why did you kill your husband?'

Frances looked at Banks, not at Bridges, her eyes burning with tears now. 'Because he was going to hurt the boy.'

'He was going to hurt Mark?' It was DI Bridges who spoke, but Frances continued to look at Banks.

'Yes,' she said. 'Patrick is a cruel man. You must know that. He was going to hurt the boy. He was tied to the chair.'

'But why did he want to hurt Mark?' Bridges asked.

Slowly Frances turned to face him, still fiddling with her ring. 'Because of Christine,' she said. 'The boy took Christine from him. Patrick couldn't bear to lose.'

Banks felt a chill ripple up his spine. Bridges turned to

him, looking confused. 'DCI Banks,' he said, 'you're familiar with the background to this case. Is there anything you'd like to ask?'

Banks turned to Frances Aspern. 'You're saying that your husband was going to harm Mark because Mark lived with Christine on the boat, is that right?'

'Yes.'

'Did Patrick go to the boat last Thursday evening? Did he start the fire?'

Frances looked up sharply, surprised. 'No,' she said. 'No, we were at home. That much is true.'

'But was your husband sexually abusing Christine?'

The tears spilled over from Frances's eyes and rolled down her cheeks, but she didn't sob or wail. 'Yes,' she said.

'For how long?'

'Since she was twelve. When she . . . you know, when she started to develop. He couldn't stop touching her.'

'Why didn't you stop him? She must have known what was happening, that it was wrong? She could have gone to the authorities.'

Frances wiped the tears from her eyes and cheeks with the sleeve of her overalls and gave Banks a what-do-you-know look. 'He was the only father she had ever known,' she said. 'He was strict with her when she was growing up. Always. She was terrified of him. She never dared disobey his demands.'

'And you knew about the sexual abuse from the start?'

'Yes. From very early on, at any rate.'

'How did you find out?'

'It's not hard to recognize the signs, when you're around all the time. Besides . . .'

'It happened with you, too?'

'How do you know?'

'I'm just guessing.'

She looked away. 'I tried to tell Daddy, but I couldn't. He wouldn't have believed me, anyway, and if he had, it would have broken his heart.'

'So you did nothing about Christine, either?'

She leaned over towards Banks, her eyes imploring. 'How could I? I was terrified of him.'

'Even so, after your experiences, your own daughter . . .'

She slapped the table with her palm. 'You've no idea how cruel Patrick could be. No idea.'

'Why? Did he hit you? Did he hit Christine?'

She shook her head. 'No. What he did . . . it was worse than that, much worse. Cold, calculated.'

'What did he do?'

Frances looked away again, at a spot on the wall above Banks's head, her eyes unfocused. 'He . . . he knew chemicals.' She gave a harsh laugh. 'Of course he did, he was a doctor, after all, wasn't he?'

'What do you mean, Frances?'

She looked directly at Banks, her expression unfathomable. 'Patrick knew drugs. Not illegal drugs. Prescriptions. What made you sleep. What made you stay awake. What made your heart beat like a frightened bird inside your chest. What made you sick. What made you have to go to the toilet all the time. What made your skin burn and your mouth dry.'

Banks understood. And wished he didn't. He looked at Bridges, who seemed to have turned a shade paler. Just when he thought he'd seen and heard it all, dug about as deep as anyone can into the darkness of the human soul and remained sane, something else came along and knocked all your assumptions out of the window.

'Now you understand,' Frances Aspern said, a note of shrill triumph in her voice. 'But even that wasn't it. I could have stood the pain, the cruelty.'

'What was it, Frances?' Banks asked.

'My father. He worshipped Patrick. You know he did. You've talked to him. He rang us after you left. How could I tell him? It was like before, like I told you. Even if I could have made him believe, it would have broken his heart.'

'So for the sake of your father's trust in Patrick Aspern, you let your husband abuse both you and your daughter? Is that what you're saying?'

She leaned forward, her eyes imploring. 'What else could I do? Surely you understand? If it came out what kind of man Patrick was, what he *did*, it would have destroyed my father. He's not a strong man.'

He had looked healthy enough the other day, Banks thought, though appearances could be deceptive. But there was no point in pursuing this line of questioning. Whatever her reasons, Frances Aspern knew the enormity of what she had done and she knew she had to live with the consequences.

'What about Paul Ryder?' Banks asked.

'Who?'

'Paul Ryder. Christine's birth father, remember? We haven't been able to find him.'

Frances looked down at the scarred table top and ran her fingertips over its rough surface.

'There was no Paul Ryder, was there?' Banks said.

She responded with a barely perceptible shake of the head.

'Patrick was Christine's real father, wasn't he?'

'Yes,' she said, still looking down at the table.

'Remember when we first met, when Patrick wanted to drive you to Eastvale to identify the body?'

Frances just looked at him.

'You said, "She's *my* daughter." I took it to imply that you were putting him in his place, reminding him that he was only Christine's stepfather, but that wasn't it, was it?'

'When you live a lie for long enough,' Frances said in little more than a whisper, 'you come to believe it.'

Banks let the silence stretch, with only the hiss of the tape and muffled sounds from the station in the background, then he looked at Bridges, who shook his head slowly. 'Let's suspend this interview for now,' Banks said. Bridges nodded and turned off the tape machine.

●

'Alan out again, is he?' asked DS Stefan Nowak, popping his head around the squad-room door close to lunchtime that day.

'Another fire,' Annie said. 'In Leeds, this time. I've just been on the phone with him, and it seems that Mrs Aspern, the doctor's wife, has killed her husband and tried to set fire to the body.'

Stefan whistled between his teeth.

'Indeed,' said Annie. 'Have you got anything new for us?'

'I might have.' Stefan walked into the room and sat down opposite Annie. He looked as handsome and regal as ever, and just as remote and unreadable. Not for the first time, Annie wondered what sort of private life he had. Did he have friends outside the force? Family? Was he gay? She didn't sense that in him, but she had been wrong before.

Stefan opened the folder he had brought with him.

'What do you want first,' he asked, 'the good news or the bad?'

'I don't care,' Annie said.

'Well,' Stefan went on, 'apart from the soil and gravel samples, which do match samples from the lay-by, we drew a blank with the Jeep Cherokee. The car-rental company had done a bloody good job of cleaning it, inside and out. We did find some hair, fibres and a partial print under the front seat, but it's not much more than a smudge. We might be able to do some computer enhancement, but don't expect too much.'

'That's what I figured,' said Annie. 'I wouldn't be surprised if our killer gave it a good going over, too. He seems to be the meticulous type.'

'And we checked a sample of petrol from the fuel tank of Leslie Whitaker's Jeep Cherokee with the accelerant from the Gardiner fire.'

'And?'

'It doesn't match.'

'Shit,' said Annie.

'We do have the Nike trainer impression, though. That's pretty distinctive. If he hasn't ditched them, we can match them when we find a suspect.'

'Was that the good news or the bad news?'

Stefan smiled. 'It might be nothing, but one of our lads found traces of candle wax puddled near the point of origin in Roland Gardiner's caravan.'

'You mean he'd been having a romantic evening?'

'No,' said Stefan, 'that's not what comes to mind. Not my mind, anyway. Call me a cynic, but I see it in a different light altogether.'

'Joke,' said Annie. 'Never mind. Wasn't there also a candle beside the girl who died on the boat?'

'Yes,' said Stefan, 'but that's different. The fire didn't originate on the boat and it was pretty clear she'd used the candle to prepare the heroin she'd injected. Also, the boyfriend said in his statement that he made sure the candle was out before he left.'

'Mark Siddons? I can't understand why everybody is so quick to believe anything he says. He could easily have been lying.'

'No, this is something else.'

'I think I know what you're getting at,' said Annie.

'Yes. It looks as if it was used as some sort of primitive time-delay ignition device. It's not unusual in arson cases.'

'So the killer makes sure Gardiner's fast asleep, pours out the petrol, then lights the candle and leaves?'

'And an hour, or two hours later, the candle burns down, meets the petrol, and *pouff*! Up it goes.'

'Can you estimate how long?'

'If we can discover exactly what make and length of candle it was, and if we assume it hadn't been used previously – was still whole – then, yes. But don't hold your breath. We don't have a lot to go on.'

'An estimate?'

'Well, an ordinary household candle is seven-eighths of an inch in diameter, and it burns one inch every fifty-seven minutes in a draught-free environment.'

'The caravan could hardly have been a draught-free environment, could it?'

'Agreed,' said Stefan. 'But there was hardly any wind that night. Anyway, let's say you've got a six-inch candle, that gives you nearly six hours of burn time before ignition, all factors being equal.'

'How could the killer rely on Gardiner's remaining unconscious for that long?'

'He couldn't. Look, Annie, it could just have been a candle stub. Half an inch, an inch. Half an hour, or an hour at the most.'

'Or it could have been two hours, or three?'

'Afraid so. It could even have been one of those fancy, thick candles, which would burn much more slowly. We're doing what tests we can on the wax, but as I said don't get your hopes up.'

'What about Thomas McMahon's barge? Anything there?'

'No signs of candle wax. It looks as if that fire was set directly.'

'But not the Gardiner fire?'

'No.'

'Isn't using a candle like that unreliable?'

'Extremely. Very crude and unpredictable. Not to mention dangerous. Any number of things can, and do, go wrong. You could accidentally ignite the accelerant when you're lighting the candle, for example. Or you light it and leave and a draught blows it out. Or it topples over and sets the accelerant off sooner than you'd hoped. It's amateur, but it can also be very effective, if it works. I'm sorry it's not very much to go on,' Stefan apologized, 'but it does tell us one thing, doesn't it?'

'Yes,' said Annie, already turning over the implications in her mind. 'It tells us that whoever set the second fire needed time, most likely time to arrange for an alibi. And which of our suspects seems to have a watertight alibi?'

Stefan thought for a moment, then answered. 'Leslie Whitaker?'

'Exactly.'

'But what about the petrol?'

'He must have been bright enough to siphon some

from someone else's car. Maybe he knew there was a chance we'd be able to trace it. Don't you see, Stefan? It makes sense. Whitaker said he went out for an eight o'clock dinner in Harrogate with nine other booksellers. They all vouched for him. We already know that he supplied Thomas McMahon with the special paper he needed to produce his forgeries. They were in it together. He practically admitted as much. One reason we almost ruled Whitaker out was that he's got an alibi for the Jennings Field fire, but not the one on the barges.'

'But this timing device puts paid to his alibi?'

'Yes,' said Annie. 'If he was in Harrogate for that dinner at eight o'clock, then he must have left Eastvale or Lyndgarth, where he lives, at about seven. But surely it would have been possible for him to use a two- or three-inch candle and gain a couple of hours or more burn time before the accelerant ignited?'

'Easily, assuming it all went according to plan.'

'This time it did,' said Annie. 'We'll have him in, Stefan. And then we'll have him.'

●

After the interview with Frances Aspern, Banks picked up a coffee in the canteen and remembered that he had intended to ring Dirty Dick Burgess. He found an empty office and took out his mobile.

'At last,' said Dirty Dick. 'I've been leaving messages for you in Eastvale all bloody morning.'

'Bit of a crisis up here,' said Banks, giving a brief explanation of his night and morning. 'Anyway, what have you got?'

'Not much, I'm afraid. Business above board. Solo operation. No partner. No employees. Philip Keane is a well-respected and popular member of the art community. Judgement valued, pals with all the movers and shakers: dealers, collectors, gallery owners, that sort of thing. Not exactly Anthony Blunt, but you get the picture.'

'Blunt?' said Banks. 'Why mention him? Wasn't he a spy, along with Philby, Burgess and Maclean? The fourth man?'

'Yes,' said Burgess, 'but he was also surveyor of the queen's pictures and director of the Courtauld Institute.'

'Of course,' said Banks. 'Yes, I remember. Interesting. A master of the art of deception. Anything else?'

'Nothing. Philip Keane has lived a completely blameless life. At least for the past four years.'

'Four years? And before that?'

'There's the glitch. Before that, there's nothing. Nada. Zilch. Bupkis.'

'What do you mean?'

'I mean that he appeared fully formed on the scene four years ago, like Athena from the head of Zeus. And if you're thinking of teasing me about classical analogies, Banksy, don't. I got a first in classics at Oxford.'

'Bollocks,' said Banks. 'Go on, though. You've got me interested.'

'Like I said, there's nothing else to tell. The trail stops there. It's as if Keane didn't exist until four years ago.'

'He must have been born, for a start.'

'Oh, well, if you'd like me to send a team to the General Register Office . . . Or perhaps I should go myself? Shouldn't take long. Let me see, unusual name that, Philip Keane. I suppose you've got the details of his date and place of birth?'

'All right,' said Banks. 'I get the point. Give it a rest.

Look, maybe Keane studied and worked in museums and galleries abroad. Maybe that's where he was before?'

'Maybe he did, and we can certainly check that, too, given time and resources. How official do you want this to be?'

Banks thought for a moment. He didn't want it to be official at all just yet. Not unless he got something more concrete to go on. On a whim, he asked, 'Can you check if anyone called Philip Keane was connected in any way with a fire four years ago, and if he was ever associated with someone called William Masefield?'

'Fire? Where?'

'I don't know,' said Banks, explaining about William Masefield's stolen identity. 'It's a long shot. But if it *is* him, it could be an MO. He might have done it before.'

'So you want me to keep digging?'

'If you can. But still discreetly. This case is confusing enough already. It just keeps shifting in the wind. It'd be nice to get some good solid information for a change.'

'I do have one practical suggestion to make,' offered Burgess.

'Oh, and what's that?'

'You could talk to his wife.'

16

'Mark,' said Banks, 'we must stop meeting like this.'

Mark Siddons grunted and sat down.

'How are you feeling?' Banks asked.

'I'm all right. A bit tired. And my head feels like it's stuffed full of wet cotton wool.'

'Must be the tranquillizer the doctor gave you last night. Are you ready to talk?' Banks and Bridges had already agreed that Banks would do most of the questioning, as he had interviewed Mark before and knew the terrain.

'If you like. Can I have some water first?'

Banks asked the constable waiting outside the door, who brought in a jug and three glasses. Mark filled his, but Bridges took nothing and Banks stuck with coffee.

'Are you going to charge me?' Mark asked.

'What with?'

'Breaking and entering.'

Banks looked at DI Bridges. 'That depends,' Bridges said.

'What on?'

'On how co-operative you are.'

'Look, Mark,' Banks said, 'we know it was you who put out the fire and you who rang the police and the fire brigade and waited with Mrs Aspern until they arrived. All that will work in your favour. You're not being charged with anything just at the moment, but you'd better tell us exactly what went on. OK?'

'Can I have a smoke?'

Smoking wasn't allowed in the police station any more, but Bridges took out a packet of Silk Cut and offered Mark one. He also lit one himself. Banks felt no craving at all, just a slight wave of nausea when he smelled the smoke. Mostly he was trying to put what he had just heard from Dirty Dick Burgess out of his mind. And its implications for Annie. For the time being, at any rate. He had got the London address of Keane and his wife, Helen, and checked train times from Leeds. After he'd finished with Mark, he'd head straight down to London on an early afternoon train and talk to her, get things sorted. But until then he had Mark Siddons and Frances Aspern to occupy his mind.

'There is one question I'd like answered before we start,' Bridges asked.

'What?' said Mark.

'The burglar alarm. How did you disable it?'

Mark told them about the scheme Tina had come up with and how he had memorized the code.

'All right,' said Bridges, looking over at Banks. 'Your turn.'

'What time did you get to the Asperns' house?' Banks asked.

'I don't know. It was late, though. After closing time. I came out of the pub and put it off for a while, just walking around, then I went there.'

'Put what off?'

'I don't know. All I know is that I was going the wrong way and it didn't make sense any more.'

'What do you mean?'

'Scarborough and all that. That was why all those things happened. The bloke in the car. Those plainclothes cops on the seafront. Because I was going the wrong way. It was Adel I had to go to, not Scarborough. I couldn't get on with my life until I'd faced them.'

'What happened with the bloke in the car?' Banks asked.

'Nothing,' said Mark. 'He . . . you know, he tried to proposition me. I said, like, no way, and he just stopped the car and made me get out.'

Banks didn't believe him. There was the matter of the mysterious two hundred pounds, for a start, but he let it go. Either Mark had capitulated and earned the money with his body, or he had stolen it. Either way, no accusations had been made against anyone as far as he knew, so best let it lie. 'What were you going to do in Adel?' he asked.

'I don't know. I didn't have a plan.'

'So what *did* you do?'

'I had a bit too much to drink in that big pub on the main road, to get my bottle up, I suppose. Anyway, like I said, I just got into the house. They were in bed. I walked around a bit, wondering what the hell I was going to do now I was there. I mean, was I supposed to go upstairs and strangle the bastard, or what? I found a bottle of something, brandy I think, and I took a few swigs of that, just sitting in the kitchen in the dark, thinking. Or trying to. I didn't even hear him coming.'

'What happened next?'

'I don't know. I felt this sharp pain on the side of my head and everything went black.'

'And when you came round?'

Mark paused and stubbed out his cigarette. He looked over at DI Bridges, who sighed and pushed the packet towards him. Mark fidgeted with the packet, but didn't open it immediately. 'I was in the surgery, wasn't I? All the lights were on and *he* was there, standing over me with that evil fucking smile on his face.'

'Patrick Aspern?'

'Who else?'

'What was he doing?'

'Filling a syringe with morphine. He had me tied to the chair so I couldn't move my arms, and he'd shoved some sort of cotton-wool gag in my mouth so I couldn't scream out.'

'How do you know it was morphine?'

'He told me. That was all part of the fun for him. He wanted me to know what was going to happen to me, to be scared thinking about it for as long as he could draw it out.'

'What else did he say?'

'He said he was soon going to inject me with a fatal dose of morphine, that it was more than a piece of scum like me deserved because it was quick and merciful, and if he had his way he'd make me suffer for much longer.' Mark glanced at Banks. 'He was enjoying himself, you know. The power. Enjoying every minute of it.'

'I believe you, Mark.'

'He said the thought of me in bed with his daughter disgusted him, that she was a no-good ungrateful slut who deserved to die for betraying him like that, and now I was going to die, too.'

'He referred to Tina as his daughter?'

'Yes.'

'Did he say anything about being responsible for her death?'

'He didn't say he killed her, if that's what you mean.'

'Did he mention his wife?'

'No.'

'All right. Go on.'

'He said nobody would shed any tears about a piece of junkie filth like me being found dead of an overdose in a back alley somewhere, which is exactly where he was going to dump me.'

'What happened next?'

Mark lit his second cigarette and looked away. His voice became quieter. 'I could see her standing behind him, in the doorway. Just standing there. Watching. Listening. He didn't know she was there, but I could see her.'

'Mrs Aspern?'

'Yes. At least, I guessed that's who it was.'

'You'd never seen her before?'

'No, never.'

'Not around the boat or anything? She'd never come to visit Tina?'

'No. I'm not even sure she knew where the boat was.'

'Carry on.'

Mark swallowed, took a sip of water and went on. 'He said . . . he started talking about the things he did to her, to Tina, you know, and how much she loved it when he touched her and put himself inside her and all the things she did to him. He was making me crazy, but I couldn't break free. I couldn't yell out and make him stop. And I could see her behind him all the time, her face just going paler and paler. It was sickening what he said. I mean, I know Tina told me he'd abused her, but she . . . I mean, the details. He had to go into every little detail. She never told me all that . . . all that stuff he said, what he did. I wanted to shut my ears, but you can't, can you? And all the time he was doing it, he had this strange sort of distant smile on his face and he was fiddling with the syringe, giving a little squirt, like they do on television.'

'What did Mrs Aspern do?'

'The next thing I knew, she was holding the shotgun – he'd left it in the doorway – and she told him to leave me alone, that I hadn't done anything.'

'What did he say to that?'

'He turned to her and he laughed. He just laughed.'

'Is that when she fired?'

'No. He started telling her to put the gun down, the way you'd talk to a child, said that she hadn't the courage to pull the trigger, just like she hadn't had the courage to stand up for her daughter, that she was weak and cowardly. Then he started moving towards her with his hands out, like he expected her to hand him the gun. Then it just exploded.'

'She fired?'

'It was deafening. My ears are still ringing, but I was tied up, so there was no way I could have covered them up.' He shook his head and rubbed his face with his hands. 'It was . . . I was covered in stuff, blood and stuff . . . I don't know . . . It was just like he'd burst open, you know, a bag full of blood, like those water balloons you burst, and it went all over the place, all over me. The smell was awful. I closed my eyes, but I couldn't close my nose any more than I could my ears. Gunpowder. And his insides. Shit and stuff. I had bits of him all over me. Slimy bits.' Mark shuddered and finished his water. He refilled his glass with a shaking hand.

'What happened next, Mark?'

Mark took a deep drag on his cigarette. 'She cut me free with some scissors or something and just told me to leave.'

'She didn't say anything else?'

'No. Just to leave. Then she took that stuff they put on you before they stick the needle in. You know what I mean. He had it on his desk, though I don't think he was going to use it on me.' Mark gave a harsh laugh. 'I mean, what would it matter if I got an infection when he was going to kill me anyway? I was backing out of the room and she was pouring the stuff on the floor. You could smell that, too, some sort of surgical spirit, along with every-thing else. I was feeling pretty sick by then. Anyway, I saw a small fire extinguisher in the hall and I took it. She'd already started the fire by the time I got back, but it wasn't a very big one. Just a small patch where she'd poured the spirits. It was easy to put out.'

'What was Mrs Aspern doing while you put the fire out?'

'Nothing. She didn't even try to stop me, if that's what you mean. To be honest, she looked as if she'd had it, like she'd given up and didn't care any more. When I was sure it was out, I took her into the other room and she went with me, quiet as a lamb, like she was in a trance or some-thing. I rang nine-nine-nine.'

Banks and Bridges said nothing for a while as Mark smoked and the tape recorder ran on. Finally, Banks asked, 'Is there anything else?'

'No,' said Mark.

Bridges turned off the tapes.

'What are you going to do now?' Banks asked Mark. 'Are you charging me?'

Banks looked at Bridges, who shook his head. 'I don't think the CPS would find much of a case there,' he said. 'You're free to go. But you're an important witness and the CPS will want to talk to you, as well as Mrs Aspern's lawyers. Whatever you do, you need to stay close, stay available, make sure we know where you are.'

Mark nodded. 'I know. I've still got some money left. I suppose I can buy myself some new clothes and find a place to stay for a while.'

'Why don't you come back to Eastvale? Give my contact on the restoration project a call? He's always looking for keen apprentices.'

'Dunno. I might do. To be honest, right now, I just want a bit of space, some peace and quiet. I want to try and get all these horrible pictures out of my head.'

Good luck, thought Banks, who hadn't succeeded in getting the nightmare images out of his own head after years of trying.

•

Leslie Whitaker seemed to have done a runner. His shop was closed and he wasn't at his Lyndgarth home. Cursing herself for not keeping a closer eye on him, Annie set the wheels in motion to track him down.

They had at least been lucky with Friends Reunited, Annie thought, pulling up outside the small detached house with Winsome late that afternoon. Elaine Hough lived on the outskirts of Harrogate, where she worked as an executive chef in one of the spa's best restaurants. Elaine wasn't the only one to reply to Winsome's request saying she remembered both Thomas McMahon and Roland Gardiner – two others out of the 115 alumni registered at the Friends Reunited website had also responded quickly and said they remembered them – but she was by far the most easily accessible of the three – one being in Eastbourne and the other in Aberdeen – and she also said that Gardiner and McMahon had been good friends of hers.

Elaine Hough seemed a no-nonsense sort of woman with a brisk manner and short black hair streaked with grey. If she ate what she cooked, she didn't show it on her tall, lean frame.

'Come in,' she said. Annie and Winsome followed her through to the sparsely decorated living room, all exposed beams and stone and heavy oak furniture.

'Nice,' Annie said, but if truth be told, it wasn't her favourite style of interior decoration.

'I'm glad you like it. It's more a reflection of my husband's taste, really. I spend most of the time in my little den when I'm at home.'

'Not in the kitchen?'

Elaine laughed. 'Well, it's true, I still *do* love cooking, and I don't get much of a chance to do any at the restaurant any more. It's the old, old story, isn't it? You work your way up in an area you love, and then you find you're so successful you spend all your time running the business side and you don't have time to do what you love best any more.' She laughed. 'But I can't complain. And I don't. I know how lucky I am. Would you like tea or coffee or something?'

'Coffee would be nice,' said Annie. Winsome nodded in agreement.

'Come through to the kitchen, then. We can talk there.'

They followed her into a modern kitchen with a stainless-steel oven and fridge, copper pots and pans hanging from a rail over the central granite-topped island, and a wood-block of expensive-looking chef's knives. Annie had sometimes thought that she would like such a well-stocked and attractive kitchen herself, but her cooking skills extended about as far as vegetarian pasta and ordering an Indian takeaway, so most of the fancy equipment would be wasted on her.

Elaine put the kettle on, and while it boiled, she ground coffee beans and dropped them in a cafetière. The aroma was delicious. All her movements were economical and deft, Annie noticed, betraying her occupation and her training. Even something as simple as making coffee got her full attention. She probably even knew how to chop up a string of onions quickly, and without crying too.

They sat on stools around the island while the coffee brewed and Annie went through her mental list of questions.

'You said you knew both Thomas McMahon *and* Roland Gardiner at Leeds Poly?' she started.

'Yes.'

'Did you know them together, or separately?'

'Both, actually. Look, I was at the school of cookery – surprise, surprise – but four evenings a week I worked behind the bar in the student pub. My parents weren't well off and my grant wasn't exactly huge. At least we still got grants back then, not loans like today. Anyway, that's where I first met Tommy and Rolo. That's what we called them back then. I was so sorry to read about what happened, but I couldn't see how it could be at all relevant to me until your email. Otherwise, I'd have come forward sooner.'

'That's all right,' said Annie. 'How were you to know what we were looking for? Anyway, we're here now.'

'Yes.' Elaine poured the coffee. Winsome asked for milk and sugar while Annie and Elaine took theirs black. 'Actually,' she said, 'I went out with Rolo a few times. Just casual, like. Nothing too heavy.'

'What was he like?'

'Rolo? Well, I heard he was living alone in a caravan when he died – very sad – but back then he seemed ambitious, bright, ready to take on the world. I remember we all used to get into a lot of arguments because Rolo was a Thatcherite and the rest of us were wishy-washy liberals.' She laughed. 'But he was fun, and intelligent. What can I say? We got along fine.'

'Even after you split up?'

'We remained friends. It wasn't a serious relationship. You know what it's like when you're a student. You experiment, go out with different people.'

'Did you go out with Thomas McMahon, too?'

'Tommy? No. Not that he wasn't attractive, or that he had any shortage of admirers. We just . . . I don't know, we just didn't hit it off on that level. Besides,' she added, 'you may have noticed I'm a bit taller than the average woman, and Tommy was short. Not that I've got anything against short men, you understand, but it's always been, well . . . just that little bit awkward. Even Rolo was only just about the same height as me.'

'I understand what you mean,' said Winsome, looking up from her notebook and smiling.

'Yes, I bet you do,' Elaine said.

Annie sipped her coffee. It was still hot enough to burn her tongue, but it tasted as wonderful as the ground beans had smelled. 'So Tommy and Rolo were good friends?' she went on.

'Yes. They met in the pub, liked the same music, and even though he was studying business, Rolo was no slouch when it came to the arts. I think he liked hanging around with the arty crowd. He said more than once that most of his fellow business students were boring. I remember, he used to write. Stories, poetry . . . His poems were quite good. What he showed me, anyway. Not your usual adolescent rubbish. Thoughtful. Some of them even rhymed. And he was well read.'

'So they weren't such odd bedfellows?'

'No, not at all.'

'Did you ever know anyone back then by the name of Masefield? William Masefield?'

'No. I can't say I did. Why?'

'Doesn't matter. What about a Leslie Whitaker?'

'Can't say that rings a bell, either.'

'Was there anyone else?'

'What do you mean?'

'Was it just the two of them hung out together, or were they part of a larger group?'

'Oh, I see what you mean. Well, there used to be quite a few of them sat in the back corner. Mostly art students, and a few guests from outside. But it was the three of them stuck together most of all.'

'Three of them?'

'Yes. Rolo, Tommy and Giles.'

'Who was Giles?'

Elaine smiled and, to Annie's eyes, even seemed to blush a little at the memory. 'Giles was my boyfriend. My real boyfriend. For the second year, at any rate.'

'And he was a friend of Tommy's and Rolo's?'

'Yes. Thick as thieves, they were.'

'This Giles, what college was he attached to?'

'He wasn't. Giles went to the uni, Leeds University.'

'To study what?'

'Art history.'

That was interesting, Annie thought. 'He wasn't a painter or a sculptor?'

'No.' Elaine laughed. 'He said he had no talent for it, but he loved it. The same with music. He liked to listen – classical mostly, but he did often come to see bands with us – although he couldn't play an instrument.'

'How did he know Rolo and Tommy?'

'I don't know. They probably got talking in one of those pubs on Woodhouse Lane near the campus. The three of them just came as a package.'

'And you say you went out with Giles?'

'For a year, yes. My second year.'

'Serious?'

Elaine looked down into her coffee cup. 'Yes, I suppose so. For me. At least, that was what I thought at the time. Young love. It's all so long ago. It feels strange to be thinking back after all this time, all that's happened since.'

'What happened to Giles?'

'He vanished.'

'Vanished?'

'Just like that. I don't mean he was abducted or anything. At least I don't think he was. He just disappeared as quickly as he'd arrived on the scene.'

'Had he finished his degree?'

'No, that was the funny thing. It was only the end of his second year. He never came back.'

'What did you do?'

'I tried to find out about him from the department, but they wouldn't tell me anything, of course.'

'Did you have a row or something?'

'No. Honestly. He just . . . One day he was there, and everything was fine, but the next day he was gone. Maybe not quite like that. I mean, we were all away for the holidays, but he just didn't come back. Not a trace. It was sad . . . I mean, I don't know if you've ever experienced this, but he was one of those people who leaves a big hole in your life when he goes.' She laughed. 'Listen to me. Aren't I being silly? Anyway, I suppose what I'm saying is that I was a little bit in love with him.'

'Can you tell me anything more about him?'

'Not really. He was a bit of a dark horse. That's probably one of the other things that was so exciting about him. The mysterious quality. But he was great fun to be around. And generous. He always seemed to have plenty of money.'

'Do you know where he got it from?'

'His parents were wealthy. His father had something to do with defence work, government contracts. Knew Maggie Thatcher personally, apparently. If you ask me, I think he was an arms dealer. Come to think of it, Giles was a lot closer to Rolo in his political ideas than any of the rest of us. And his mother was related to the Duke of Devonshire. Only distantly, mind. Anyway, they had a big old family mansion house outside King's Lynn.'

'Did you ever go there?'

'No. Not inside, at any rate. Giles drove me past it once, perhaps because I nagged him about it so much. But we didn't go in. He said his parents were away in Italy and the place was locked up. Very *Brideshead Revisited*.'

'He didn't have a key?'

'Apparently not. They had to give him money, he said – it was some sort of inheritance or trust fund, and it belonged to him – but they didn't actually get on. They weren't on speaking terms.'

'Did you ever try to get in touch with them after he'd disappeared?'

'No. After a while I just gave up and got on with life. You know what it's like when you're young. A broken heart feels like it'll never mend for at least a couple of weeks. You pull out all your sad, romantic records and indulge in a bit of tearful melancholy for a while, maybe go out, get rat-arsed and fuck a stranger, then you move on. Pardon my language.'

'I remember. Neil Trethowan.'

'Sorry?'

'The one who first broke my heart. Neil Trethowan was his name.'

'Yes. Well, Giles . . . It was so long ago, but now you've got me talking about it, it seems just like yesterday. Some of it, anyway.'

'Did you ever see him or hear from him again?'

'No.'

'Do you know if Tommy and Rolo kept in touch with him?'

'If they did, they didn't tell me. We all lost touch when we graduated, of course, as you do, though we had every good intention.'

'What was his last name?'

'Moore. Giles Moore.'

With the name and some of the details Elaine had given them, they would be able to dig a little deeper into the background of this enigmatic Giles Moore, Annie thought, perhaps even locate him. Of course, he might have had nothing to do with recent events, but at least he sounded a promising start. They were looking for someone who was linked with both Thomas McMahon and Roland Gardiner when they were at Leeds Polytechnic, and it looked as if they'd found that someone.

'Do you have any photographs?' Annie asked.

'No. They disappeared after one of my many moves.'

'Pity,' said Annie. 'This might sound like a strange

question, but was there ever any connection between Giles or the rest of you and a fire?'

Elaine frowned. 'A fire? No, not that I remember. I mean, I'm sure there were fires in the city, but none of them concerned us. Surely you can't think Giles had anything to do with what happened to Tommy and Rolo? Not after all this time.'

'I'm not saying he did,' said Annie. 'But don't you think it's a big coincidence that two men living about ten miles from one another, both killed in suspicious fires only days apart, happened to be at Leeds Polytechnic at the same time? I do. Not only that, but since we've talked to you, we now also know that they were close friends over twenty years ago. And then there's this mysterious third: Giles Moore.'

'But Giles wouldn't hurt anyone. Why would he do that?'

'Is there anything else you can tell us about him that might help us find him?'

'No,' said Elaine. Annie could sense her closing down. She didn't like the idea of her old lover being in the frame for a double murder. Annie didn't blame her; she wouldn't feel too good about it, either.

'What did he look like?'

'He was very good-looking. A bit taller than me, slim. Wavy hair, a bit long. Chestnut. But that was years ago.'

'How old was he at the time?'

'Twenty-one, a couple of years older than the rest of us.'

'Any distinguishing marks?'

'What do you mean?'

'Like birthmarks, scars, that sort of thing.'

'No,' said Elaine. 'His skin was smooth, without a

blemish.' She blushed at a memory. 'Apart from an appendectomy scar.'

'Any regional accent?'

'No. A bit posh, maybe, but not too much. Educated, upper class. Just like you'd expect, coming from the background he did.'

'Smoker? Drinker?'

'He smoked. We all did back then. I mean, it's not as if we didn't know what it did to you – it was nineteen-eighty, after all – but we were young, we felt invulnerable. I stopped ten years ago. As for the drinking, we all did.'

'To excess?'

'Giles? Not really, no.'

'Was there anyone else on the scene you think we might be able to locate and talk to?'

'It was so long ago. I've lost touch with all of them. Can't even remember most of their names. You do lose touch, don't you? Move away, get married, have kids or concentrate on your career.'

Annie realized that even though she was younger than Elaine, and not so distant from her past, she didn't know a soul she went to school or university with, hadn't kept in touch at all. Still, given the police life, the frequent relocations, the unreasonable hours, it was hardly surprising. Apart from Phil, the only friends she had were colleagues from work, the only social life an occasional drink with Banks or someone else in the Queen's Arms. 'Do you have any ideas who might have done this to Tommy and Rolo?'

'Me? Good Lord, no. I just don't believe Giles had anything to do with it.'

Annie gestured to Winsome, who put away her notebook. She hoped Elaine was right, though perhaps a part of her also hoped that they could track down this Giles Moore and prove that he *was* the one who did it. At least then the case would be solved and a murderer would be off the streets. In the meantime, it was time to see if any progress had been made on tracking down Leslie Whitaker.

•

As Banks walked out of the underground station onto Holland Park Avenue, he was grateful for yet another mild evening after the previous night's cold snap, and thankful that he was in Leeds when he got Burgess's message. He was also lucky that both the trains and the tube were running on time that day. As a result, it was a little over two and a half hours since his train had pulled out of Leeds City Station, and now he was heading for Helen Keane's flat – the one she shared with her art-researcher husband, Phil (now short for philanderer in Banks's mind) Keane – in one of the residential streets across the main road, overlooking the park itself. Maybe it wasn't Mayfair or Belgravia, but you didn't live around here if you couldn't afford the high rents.

Banks didn't know what to expect when he pressed the buzzer. For obvious reasons he hadn't rung ahead, so he didn't even know if Keane himself would be there. He hoped not, but it didn't really matter. He needed to know what the hell was going on. It wasn't just a question of Annie's feelings being hurt, but of someone being not exactly the sort of person he presented himself as. It probably meant nothing, but coming hot on the heels of the lie about not knowing McMahon, Banks wanted some answers.

A cautious voice came over the intercom. 'Yes?'

Banks introduced himself and said he wanted to speak to Helen Keane. Naturally, she was suspicious and nervous – people always are when the police come to call – but he managed to convince her that it was information he wanted, nothing more. She agreed to let him in, but said she would keep her chain on until she had seen his identification. Fair enough, Banks thought, climbing the plushly carpeted stairs. Foyers, halls and stairs said a lot about the quality, and cost, of the place you were visiting, Banks always thought, the way bath towels and toilet paper said a lot about the hotel you were staying in.

As promised, she kept the chain on while she examined his warrant card, then she let him in.

The flat was an interior designer's paradise, all sharp angles and reflective surfaces, colours named after rare plants and south-west American states. There was no clutter. The stereo was state of the art, brushed steel, hanging on the wall next to the large plasma wide-screen TV, and if the Keanes owned any books or CDs they were stored elsewhere or hidden well out of sight. A couple of artfully placed art and design magazines were the only reading materials in plain view. At the far end of the high-ceilinged room stood a narrow black chair with a fan-shaped back. When he looked more closely, Banks couldn't be sure whether it was a chair or a work of art. At any rate, he wouldn't want to try sitting on it.

The woman who came with the flat was every bit as much of an expensive package and a designer's wet dream – beautiful, chic, petite, dark-haired, thirty at most, with intense blue eyes and a pale, flawless complexion, she was wearing ivory silk combats, high-heeled sandals and a delicate lace top that didn't quite obscure her skimpy black bra.

She bade Banks sit on the modular sofa, and sat opposite on a matching armchair, the colour of which Banks couldn't name. Pink, or coral, came closest, but even they were a long way off.

'It's all right, Mrs Keane,' said Banks. 'There's no need to be nervous. As far as I know, nobody's done anything criminal. I'd just like a bit of background information, if you don't mind.'

'About what?'

'Your husband.'

She seemed to relax a bit at that. 'Philip? What about him? I'm afraid I don't know where he is right now.'

Banks noticed a trace of an accent. It sounded vaguely Eastern European to his untrained ear. 'How long have you been married?' he asked.

'Three years now.'

'How did you meet?'

'At a club.'

'Where?'

'In the West End. I was working there. It was a gambling club. A casino. Philip used to come there to play cards. We talked once . . . he asked me to dinner . . . you know . . .'

'Where are you from?' Banks asked.

'Where from?'

'Yes. Your accent.'

'Ah. Kosovo,' she said. 'But everything is legal.'

'Because of the marriage?'

'Yes. I have a British passport now. Everything is legal. Philip did that for me.'

'But when you met?'

She smiled. 'You know . . . I was Jelena Pavelich then, just another poor refugee from a war-torn country trying to make a simple living.' She gestured around the room. 'Now I am Helen Keane.'

'It's a nice flat,' Banks said.

'Thank you. I designed it myself.'

'Is that what you did? In Kosovo?'

'No. I studied at university there. Languages. To be a translator. Then the fighting came. My parents were killed. I had to leave.'

'How did you escape?'

'People helped me. It was a long journey. One I want to forget. I saw many terrible things. I had to do many bad things. But you said you wanted to know about Philip?'

'Yes,' said Banks. 'Do you know what he was doing before you met?'

'He said he was working abroad. In galleries and museums, in Italy, Spain, Russia, America. Philip is very clever. He has travelled all over the world.'

'Yes, I know that,' said Banks.

Helen's eyes narrowed as she studied him. 'Has he taken your girlfriend? Is that why you want to ask me about him?'

Banks felt himself blush. 'Why do you say that?'

She smiled the way women do when they think they've gained the upper edge, put their finger on your weakness. 'Because Philip is a very attractive man, no?'

'I suppose so,' said Banks. 'But what makes you think he would have another woman? Has he been unfaithful before?'

She laughed. It was a deep, hoarse, almost crude, kind of laugh, not at all the sort of sound he would have expected from such an exquisitely petite woman, but more like the way you'd laugh at a dirty joke in a smoky pub. Banks liked it. It made her seem more human to him, less of an ethereal beauty. 'Philip always has other women,' she said.

'And it doesn't bother you?'

She made a little moue, then answered, 'Ours is not that kind of marriage. We do what we want.'

'Why stay together, then?'

'Because we like one another. We are friends. And because, well . . .'

'Go on.'

She looked around the flat and ran her hand over her lace top, all the way down over the rise and fall of her small breasts. 'I like nice things. Do you not think I'm pretty?'

'Very.'

'I think for Philip I am a business asset also, no? He likes to be seen with his pretty young wife on his arm. All his friends and colleagues envy him. They all want to go to bed with me. I can tell by the way they look at me.'

'And Philip enjoys that?'

'Yes. We go to openings and dinners and galas together. All sorts of official functions with many important people. And all of them look at me the same way. Young men. Old men. Some wives. It is good to be married when you have a business, yes?'

Banks agreed that it was. For some reason, marriage gave the semblance of both conservatism and stability that people require from a business. Potential clients were much more inclined to be suspicious of a bachelor of Phil's or Banks's age than they were of a married man. And the fact that his wife was a mysterious Eastern European beauty would certainly do no harm in the circles he moved in. If anything, it might make him seem a little more daring than most. Not too much, but just enough of a risk-taker to be worth running with.

Yes, if Phil Keane wanted everyone to think he was a traditional, solid and dependable sort of fellow, he could do a lot worse than step out with Helen on his arm. And for her part, she had already indicated that she loved the trappings of wealth, the opulent lifestyle. Perhaps she had lovers too. It seemed to be an open sort of marriage, according to what she had said, so no doubt she had plenty of freedom. Banks felt a little uncomfortable now as his eyes strayed to the outline of her skimpy bra under the lace top, and the exposed black strap against her pale shoulder. He found himself wondering just how much Phil Keane's lifestyle cost him, and whether ArtSearch made enough to support it.

'Did your husband ever mention a man called Thomas McMahon, an artist he knew?'

'No.'

'You never met anyone called Thomas McMahon?'

'No.'

'What about William Masefield?'

'No.'

'Leslie Whitaker?'

'I haven't heard the name. But Philip never talks about his friends. If he's not here, then I have no idea where he is or what he's doing.'

'Does he have many close friends?'

'Close friends? I don't think so. Mostly it is work.'

'You mean colleagues he's met through work, in the art field?'

'Yes.'

'Does he have any partners, anyone he works closely with?'

'No. He says he doesn't trust other people. They only mess things up. If he wants to do something, he does it himself.'

'Does Philip ever take you to the family cottage in Fortford?'

'What family cottage?'

'Apparently it belonged to his grandparents. In Yorkshire. He inherited it.'

'I know nothing about any grandparents. All Philip told me about his family is that his father was a diplomat and they were always moving from one country to another when he was young. Where did you hear about these grandparents? Who told you?'

'It doesn't matter,' said Banks. 'Did you ever meet his parents?'

'They're dead. They were killed in a plane crash ten years ago, before we met.'

'And he never said anything about owning property in Yorkshire?'

'Never. Whenever we go away we go to California or the Bahamas. But never to Yorkshire.' She hugged herself and gave a little shiver. 'It is cold there, no?'

'Sometimes,' Banks said.

'I love the sun.'

'Helen,' said Banks, mostly out of exasperation, 'do you know *anything* about your husband?'

She laughed again, that deep, throaty sound, then spread her hands as if to display her body. 'I know he likes the good things in life,' she said, without a hint of false modesty.

Banks realized there was nothing more to be learned from her, so he said his goodbyes and made a speedy exit, more confused than when he had first arrived.

17

After a good night's sleep and a morning spent catching up with the previous day's developments – especially the candle wax found in Roland Gardiner's caravan and Elaine Hough's statement – Banks asked Annie if she fancied a cup of tea and a toasted teacake at the Golden Grill, just across from the station. He needed to build a few bridges if they were to continue working together.

He'd been struggling with the dilemma that Helen Keane posed all the way home on the train from London the previous evening, and all that morning, and he still hadn't come to any firm decision. Maybe he'd probe Annie a bit, find out how she really felt about Phil. It wasn't fair to charge right in, he realized, and tell her outright. Especially as Keane's marriage was definitely the unusual kind. On the other hand, he was concerned about her feelings, and he didn't want her getting in too deep with Keane before she found out he was married. Still, he could only imagine how his news would be received, especially as their relationship was hardly on firm ground at the moment.

The bell over the door pinged as they entered. The place was half empty and they had their pick of tables. Banks immediately headed for the most isolated. As soon as they were settled with a pot of tea and teacakes, Banks stirred his tea, though there was nothing added to it, and said, 'Look, Annie, I'd just like to say that I'm sorry. I was out of line the other day. About bringing Phil in. Of course it made sense. I was just . . .'

'Jealous?'

'Not in the real sense of the word, no. It just feels awkward, that's all.'

'He thinks you don't like him.'

'Can't say I have an opinion one way or another. I've only met him a couple of times.'

'Oh, come on, Alan.'

'Really. He seems fine. But when it comes down to it, how much do you know about him?'

'What do you mean?'

'I mean about his background, his past, his family. Has he ever been married, for example?'

'Not that he's mentioned to me. And I don't think he has. That's one of the refreshing things about him.'

The remark stung Banks, as he thought it was intended to. His failed marriage and the baggage thereof had been a constant bone of contention in his relationship with Annie. The wise thing to do would be to move on, not to retaliate with what he had learned from Dirty Dick Burgess. He teetered on the brink for a moment, then asked, 'Anything new this morning?'

'Not a lot,' said Annie. 'Winsome's been looking into William Masefield's background and come up with one piece of interesting information: he was at Leeds University at the same time as McMahon and Gardiner were enrolled at the Poly. 1978 to 1981. There's no evidence that they knew one another, however, and Elaine Hough says she's never heard of him.'

'Pity,' said Banks. 'Still, it does give us a tenuous link. Wasn't Giles Moore at the university?'

'That's another thing. I checked with the university this

morning and they say there's no record of him ever being there.'

'Interesting,' said Banks. 'Maybe he didn't get accepted, felt he needed to impress people.'

'Even so,' said Annie. 'It's a pretty odd thing to do, isn't it?'

'He sounds like an odd person altogether,' Banks agreed. 'Which gives us all the more reason to be interested in him. He's got to be somewhere. He can't just have vanished into thin air.'

'We're looking,' said Annie. 'The only problem is that we're running out of places to look. As far as we can tell so far, there aren't any Moores living in mansions near King's Lynn. We haven't actually asked Maggie Thatcher or the Duke of Devonshire whether they knew a Giles Moore yet, but it may come to that.'

Banks laughed. 'So he's a liar, then?'

'So it would seem.'

'What we need to do,' Banks said, 'is have the Hough woman look at a photograph of Whitaker. I know it was a long time ago, but she may still recognize something about him.' And a photo of Phil Keane, too, if he could get his hands on one, Banks added to himself. 'I seem to remember there was a framed photo on the desk in the bookshop. As he's missing, and people have been dying, I suppose it's reasonable for us to enter the premises, wouldn't you say? I mean, he could be lying dead in the back room soaked in petrol, with a six-hour candle slowly burning down beside him, for all we know.'

'Good idea,' said Annie. 'I'll get onto it. What's going to happen with the Aspern woman?'

'Frances?' Banks shook his head. 'I don't know. From

what Mark Siddons told us, she might have a damn good case for pleading provocation.'

'What about diminished responsibility?'

'I'd leave that one to the experts. She needs psychiatric help, no doubt about it. She's not clinically insane – at least not in my layman's opinion – but she's confused and disturbed. I think she just couldn't accept that her husband was sexually abusing his own daughter the same way he'd sexually abused her. It was easier in her mind to embrace the lie they'd lived right from the start – from when he first got her pregnant – that this fictitious American, Paul Ryder, was the father, and that Patrick was Tina's stepfather. Maybe sometimes she actually believed it. It's a thin line.'

'It certainly is,' Annie agreed. 'I suppose this knocks both her and her husband off the list of suspects?'

'Yes,' said Banks.

'And how seriously are we taking Andrew Hurst and Mark Siddons?'

'Not very. Hurst's weird. I mean, if it turns out that the art-forgery angle's a blind alley and the fires were set by some nutter who just likes to set fires, then I'd look closely at him again. But he's got no connection with McMahon, Gardiner and the rest. Neither does Mark Siddons, except that he happened to be a neighbour of McMahon's. Mark has his problems, but I don't think arson is one of them. Besides he has a good alibi. You said so yourself.'

'I could talk to Mandy Patterson again. Go in a bit harder.'

'No,' said Banks. 'What could she possibly gain by giving Mark Siddons an alibi for murder? If Mark had wanted rid of Tina, there were far easier and more reliable ways of doing it than fixing himself up with a dodgy alibi and setting fire to Thomas McMahon's boat.'

'Which brings us back to Leslie Whitaker,' said Annie. 'What's his educational background?'

'He attended Strathclyde University from 1980 to 1983. Unfortunately, there's no evidence that links him to either Gardiner or Masefield, but we're still looking. And the way he's taken off certainly makes him seem more suspicious. That and some of his recent financial idiosyncrasies. According to the auditor, his business' books are a bit of a mess, to say the least.'

'I suppose if he was involved in some sort of scam with McMahon, he had to hide the profits somehow. Tell me your thoughts, Annie.'

'McMahon was known to be a good imitator and he gained access to period materials through Whitaker's bookshop, and no doubt from other sources. Maybe Whitaker, Moore, or whoever set it up, enlisted his old buddies to help him in a forgery scam and they fell out?'

'OK,' said Banks. 'That makes sense up to a point. But what parts did Gardiner and Masefield play?'

'Masefield provided the identity for the killer to remain anonymous in his dealings with McMahon,' said Annie. 'Whenever they met, he hired a Jeep Cherokee in Masefield's name, no doubt so we wouldn't be able to trace him. Remember, when Masefield died, or was killed, our man had his post redirected to a post-office box, used his bank accounts, paid his bills. Assumed his identity.'

'What about Gardiner?'

'I don't know yet. But he must have played some part in it all. Don't forget the Turners and the money we found in his safe. They can't be just coincidence.'

'No, I haven't forgotten them. But none of this gets us

any closer to who that person actually *is*,' said Banks. 'Even if it *is* Giles bloody Moore, he's not going by that name now and that name probably won't lead us to him. He's slippery. We're dealing with a chameleon, Annie. A damn clever one, too. Did you find out anything else about Moore? Anything at all that might help us?'

'No,' said Annie. 'Not yet. It's a lot of legwork. And legwork takes time, and more legs than we've got right now.'

'I can talk to Red Ron about manpower.'

'Thanks,' said Annie. 'I could do with a couple more good researchers, at least. But for the moment, my money's still on Leslie Whitaker. Just because we haven't been able to find a past connection between him and Gardiner doesn't mean one doesn't exist, or even that we need one. I mean, maybe McMahon himself is the link. Maybe Whitaker put the idea to McMahon and McMahon recruited Gardiner.'

'Maybe,' said Banks. 'We'll have to ask him when we find him.' He finished his tea and let the silence stretch a moment before asking, 'How are you and Phil getting along, by the way?'

'Fine,' Annie said. 'Why do you ask?'

'No reason. Where is he, anyway? I haven't seen him for a couple of days.'

'He's down in London dealing with the Turners. You know that. Why the sudden interest?'

'Nothing. Just wondering, that's all.'

Annie looked him in the eye. 'Phil's right, isn't he? What I said earlier. You denied it at the time, but you didn't like him right from the start, did you? I mean, you never really gave him a chance, did you?'

'I told you, I've got nothing against him,' Banks said. But if truth be told, he had a very uneasy feeling about

Phil Keane, like an itch he couldn't quite scratch, and though he wouldn't tell Annie this, he was going to keep on digging into the man's background until he was satisfied one way or another. 'I don't want to start another argument, Annie,' Banks said. 'I just asked you how you two were getting along.'

'Yes, but it's not as simple as that, is it? It never is with you. I can tell from your tone of voice. There's always another agenda. What is it? What do you know? What are you getting at?'

Banks spread his hands. 'I don't know what you mean.'

'Is it jealousy? Is that what it is, Alan? Because, honestly, if it's that, if that's what it is, I'll just get a fucking transfer out of here.'

Banks didn't remember ever hearing Annie swear before, and it shocked him. 'Look,' he said, 'it's not jealousy. OK? I just don't want to see you get hurt, that's all.'

'Why should I get hurt? And who do you think you are? My big brother? I can take care of myself, thank you very much.'

And with that Annie tossed her serviette on the remains of her toasted teacake and strode out of the cafe. Was it Banks's imagination, or did the bell ping just that little more loudly when she left?

•

Annie spent the rest of the day avoiding Banks. It wasn't difficult; she had plenty more paperwork to hide behind, and she took Winsome along to Whitaker's shop, which they entered through the back door, leaving no sign that they had been there, and borrowed the photograph. A quick trip to Harrogate didn't provide the conclusive answers she had hoped for. It was over twenty years ago, after all, said Elaine Hough, and Whitaker's chin and eyes were wrong. Even so, that didn't let Whitaker off the hook for the fires as far as Annie was concerned.

Had she overreacted to Bank in the Golden Grill? She didn't know. There had just been something about the way he kept on bringing up the subject of Phil that irritated her. Perhaps she should have let it go; after all, that would have been easy enough. But if she were going to carry on seeing Phil and working with Banks, then something would have to change, and it wasn't going to be her.

Banks clearly had something on his mind and she wished she knew what it was. Had he been investigating Phil behind her back? Had he found out something? If so, what? Annie dismissed her fears as absurd. If Banks had found any dirt on Phil, he would have made sure she was the first to know. Otherwise, what was the point? Except to hurt her. Lash out because of his jealousy.

But the suspicion and anxiety persisted throughout the day and made it hard for her to concentrate. Late in the afternoon, by which time Annie already knew she was going to be working late into the evening, the phone rang.

'Annie, it's Phil here.'

'Well, hello. It's nice to hear from you, stranger.'

'I just thought I'd let you know that the consensus of opinion is that the Turner sketches and watercolours are forgeries.'

If Annie was a bit disappointed that Phil was calling her on business, she tried not to let it show in her voice.

'Oh. Why's that?' she asked.

'It's nothing specific. Just a number of things adding up, or not adding up. Some of the scientific tests indicated the paper used was slightly later than the dates of the sketches. Then there's the style. Little details. I told you Turner was hard to fake. When you add to that the lack of provenance, the loose sketches and the coincidence of these pieces turning up so quickly after the major find, then . . .'

'What about fingerprints? In the paint, I mean.'

'There were none. So no help there.'

'Would there have been if the painting were genuine?'

'Not necessarily.'

'OK, Phil. Thanks,' said Annie. 'Does this cast doubt on the other watercolour?'

'Not at all. We've got some provenance there and the same tests didn't turn out negative. I think that one was a genuine find. It must have given someone the idea of forging the other missing piece.'

'McMahon?'

'I've no idea who did it, but if you found it at the site of the caravan fire and you've managed to link the two victims, yes, I'd say you're probably on the right track. They must have hatched some hare-brained get-rich-quick scheme. It's quite possible to be a fine artist and pretty useless at almost everything else.'

'Tell me about it,' said Annie, thinking of her father. She had grown up surrounded by beards and endless arguments on Impressionism versus Cubism, Van Gogh versus Gauguin and the like. While Ray seemed reasonably well equipped to handle the real world, he could lose himself in his work for days on end and forget about petty irritations like bills and house-cleaning.

'Anyway, that's all I've got to say, for better or worse. I'll get them packed and have them couriered back up to you. They're worthless, but I suppose you might still need them as evidence.'

'Thanks,' said Annie.

'How are things up there?'

'Fine, I suppose.'

'Closing in for the kill?'

'Maybe,' Annie said. 'Whitaker – you know, the bloke who supplied McMahon with the paper – he's disappeared.'

'As in been killed?'

'No. As in legged it.'

'Oh, I see. Best of luck then.'

'Thanks.'

'What's wrong? You sound a bit glum.'

'Oh, it's nothing. I had a bit of a barney with Alan, DCI Banks, this morning. It's left rather a bad taste in my mouth.'

'What about?'

'Nothing. That's it. Just me being over-sensitive. I wish the two of you could get on better.'

'Why, what's he said about me?'

'Nothing. It's just . . . I don't know, Phil. It's me. Don't pay any attention.'

'Did he say anything about me?'

'No. He just asked about you, that's all. See what I mean about being over-sensitive?'

'I shouldn't worry about it, then,' said Phil. 'I've got nothing against him. I've only met the man the once and you were there.'

'Like I said, Phil, it's just me. Where are you? Will you be up tonight?'

'Afraid not. I'm still down in London. I'll try to make it tomorrow or the next day, all right?'

'OK. See you later, then.'

'See you.'

Annie put the phone down and looked at the piles of

actions and statements on her desk. Well, at least it would keep her from thinking about Banks. And about Phil.

But before she could even pick up her pen, DC Templeton dashed into the squad room. 'We've got him,' he said. 'We've got Whitaker. He's downstairs.'

•

'Well, Leslie,' said Banks. 'It's quite a merry dance you've led us, isn't it?'

'I had no idea you'd been looking for me,' said Whitaker. 'How could I?'

They were in the same interview room as last time, only today Whitaker was already wearing the disposable red overalls. He hadn't been charged, but he had been arrested and read his rights, and the tape recorders were running. The duty solicitor, Gareth Bowen, sat beside him. Banks could still sense some tension between Annie and himself, but he knew they were both professional enough to do their jobs, especially now they seemed close to the end. If they could break Whitaker, it would be drinks all around in the Queen's Arms, and there was a good chance Banks would get to see Michelle this weekend.

'Where were you?' Banks asked.

'I needed to get away. I went to visit a friend in Newcastle.'

'Rather an opportune time to go away, wasn't it?'

'As I said, I had no idea you would want to talk to me again.'

'Oh, I think you did, Leslie,' said Banks. 'In fact, I'm sure you did.'

'Why don't you tell us about it?' Annie said. 'You'll feel better if you do.'

Whitaker curled his lip. 'Tell you about what?'

'About Thomas McMahon. Tommy. And about Roland Gardiner. Rolo. How long have you known them?'

'I don't know what you're talking about. I've already told you I saw Thomas McMahon in the shop from time to time, but I don't know the other person you're talking about.'

Banks sighed. 'All right, we'll do it the hard way.'

'Lay a finger on me and I'll sue you.' Whitaker looked over to Bowen, who just rolled his eyes.

'What I meant,' said Banks, 'is that I'm tired, DI Cabbot's tired, and I'm sure you and Mr Bowen are tired, too. But we'll stay here as long as it takes to get the truth.' He glanced at Bowen, 'with all requisite meal breaks and rest periods, as required by the Police and Criminal Evidence Act, of course.'

'I don't have to tell you anything,' said Whitaker.

'No, you don't,' Banks agreed. 'In fact, if you remember that bit in the caution about later relying in court on something you *didn't* say when we first asked you, you'll understand exactly what it means not to have to tell us anything. But let me lay my cards on the table, Leslie. At the moment, you're our main suspect in the murders of Thomas McMahon and Roland Gardiner.'

'But I told you, I was in Harrogate at a dinner party. Surely you must have checked?'

'We checked.'

'And?'

'Everyone we talked to corroborates your statement. You were there.'

Whitaker folded his arms. 'I told you so.'

'I wouldn't look so smug if I were you, Leslie,' Banks went on. 'We now have evidence to suggest that a timing device was used in Roland Gardiner's caravan.'

'A timing device?'

'Yes. A candle. Crude but effective. It allowed the arsonist to prepare the fire scene but leave before the blaze started. A good couple of hours before. Easily. Wouldn't you agree DI Cabbot?'

'Yes,' said Annie, turning the pages of Stefan Nowak's report. 'Easily.'

'But do you have any evidence specifically to connect Mr Whitaker to the scene?' Bowen asked. 'All you're saying is that *anyone* could have set that fire.'

'Have you ever heard of a man called William Masefield?' Banks asked Whitaker.

'No. Never.'

'All right. We'll leave that for the moment. Did you or did you not supply period paper to Thomas McMahon?'

'He bought books and prints from me. It's my business. It's what I sell.'

'But did you sell them to him for the purpose of forging works of art?'

'Chief Inspector Banks,' Bowen cut in. 'Mr Whitaker can hardly be held responsible for what a client did *after* a purchase, or even know what he intended to do.'

'Perhaps in this case he can,' said Banks, 'if money was involved.'

Whitaker looked sheepish.

'Leslie?' Banks went on. 'What's it to be?'

'I told you,' Whitaker repeated. 'I sold him what he wanted. It's what you do when you're in business.'

'You own a Jeep Cherokee, am I right?' said Banks.

'You know I do. Your men have been taking it apart since we last spoke.'

'And,' Bowen added, 'might I say that they have come

up with nothing to connect my client's car with either crime scene.'

'Not yet,' said Banks.

'In fact,' Bowen went on, 'I understand that a Jeep Cherokee *has* been connected with the Thomas McMahon fire, and that it was rented to this mysterious, and late, Mr William Masefield by a garage outside York. Are you now saying that my client is this Mr Masefield?'

'I'm saying that it might be the case that your client has taken Mr Masefield's identity,' Banks went on.

'Have you any proof of this?' Bowen asked.

'The investigation is ongoing.'

'In other words, you haven't?'

'This is ridiculous,' said Whitaker. 'I've already got a Jeep Cherokee. Why would I rent one?'

'To avoid exactly the kind of situation you're in,' said Banks.

'But I'm in it, anyway, aren't I?'

'There are several counts against you. First, you're a minor art dealer and one of the victims was a forger you supplied with paper. Secondly, you drive a Jeep Cherokee and such a car, or one very much like it, was spotted at the scene of the Thomas McMahon fire.'

'But you've already found—' Bowen started.

Banks cut him off. 'That doesn't mean Mr Whitaker's Jeep was *never* there.' He went on, 'Add to this that you have no alibi for either murder, and that you lied to us in your previous interview, I'd say it adds up to a pretty strong case against you.'

'Circumstantial,' said Bowen. 'You've no proof my client had ever heard of, let alone knew, Roland Gardiner; the car in the lay-by spotted near the scene has been identified; the accelerant used did not come from Mr

Whitaker's fuel tank; and there's no connection between Mr Whitaker and the man whose credit card was used to rent the car. I'd say that adds up to nothing.'

'Except,' said Annie Cabbot, 'that Mr Whitaker's business has been reporting a loss for two years in a row now, yet he has recently made several rather expensive purchases. For cash.' Annie opened a file folder. 'To whit, a thirty-two-inch television and a home theatre system, a state-of-the-art Dell desktop computer system, and he's had his house repainted and added a new conservatory. Do you deny these purchases?'

Whitaker looked at Annie. 'I . . . er . . . no.'

'Where did you get the money?'

'I won it. The horses.'

'You don't bet on the horses.'

'How do you know?'

'Do you think we overlook the bookies when we're investigating someone's financial status, Leslie?' Annie said. 'Do you really think we're *that* stupid?'

'It was a gift. A friend gave it to me.'

'Which friend?'

'He wants to remain anonymous. A tax thing. You understand.'

Banks was shaking his head and even Gareth Bowen looked anxious.

'Where did you get the money, Leslie?' Annie repeated.

'You don't have to answer,' said Bowen.

'Right,' said Banks, standing up. 'I've had enough of this. Interview terminated at six thirty-five p.m. I'm going home and the suspect is going back to his cell.'

'You can't—'

Bowen touched Whitaker's sleeve. 'Yes, they can,

Leslie,' he said. 'For twenty-four hours. But don't worry. I'll be working for you.'

Whitaker glared at the solicitor. 'Well,' he said, 'you've no idea how bloody confident that makes me feel.'

•

Annie munched on a salad sandwich Winsome had brought her from the bakery across Market Street and started reading through the statements again. Andrew Hurst. Mark Siddons. Jack Mellor. Leslie Whitaker. Elaine Hough. There had to be something there to link Whitaker more closely to the killings, but if there was she was damned if she could find it. It didn't help that she was having trouble concentrating, partly because she still couldn't stop herself wondering what Banks was up to, and partly because of something else, something she couldn't quite put her finger on. It would come, she knew, if she let her mind drift.

Phil had suggested that McMahon and Gardiner were involved in some art forgery scam, an ill-advised and ill-timed attempt to come up with a Turner watercolour that had been lost for over a century. Annie agreed. But if that were the case, her questions remained: who killed them and why? Leslie Whitaker still seemed the most logical culprit, despite the Jeep Cherokee rented under William Masefield's name. Perhaps that was a red herring, another issue entirely?

Annie ruled out the Siddons–Aspern angle, as she had done almost from the start, despite her mistrust of the boy. Tina's death was an unfortunate but irrelevant distraction; she had died because she was at the wrong place at the wrong time and in the wrong state of mind. In other words she wasn't the intended victim. Thomas McMahon was.

And in Gardiner's case there was no question. He lived alone and in isolation. The two knew each other from their time at Leeds Polytechnic, and they had also once been close to a mysterious character named Giles Moore, who had misled all his friends about being a university student.

Why? What possible reason could he have had, unless lying was an essential part of his character? If it was, it could easily be put to criminal purposes. This Giles Moore had claimed to be studying art history, and according to Elaine Hough had seemed to know plenty about the subject, whether he learned it at university or not. Was this, then, the person who had assumed William Masefield's identity when hiring cars for meetings with McMahon? Meetings about their scam. Because she was certain it was him, not McMahon or Gardiner, who was the brains behind it. And was this person Whitaker?

But again the question remained: why had Moore-Masefield-Whitaker, or whoever he was, killed the goose that laid the golden eggs – McMahon? Unless . . . unless, she thought, the Turners weren't part of his master plan, and he believed they would ruin everything and expose him. Phil had said that any forger worth his salt goes for lower-level stuff, artists who fetch a decent price but don't draw too much attention to themselves, like Turner or Van Gogh. And Phil should know. He was in the business. An expert. Dead artists were a better bet, too, especially if they'd been dead so long that nobody living had known them because the provenance was easier to forge. So who was it?

Winsome walked by with a handful of papers she had been keying into HOLMES.

'Anything?' Annie asked.

'My fingertips are bleeding,' said Winsome. 'I don't know if that counts as anything.' She dropped the papers on Annie's desk. 'The list of parking tickets from the Askham Bar area. You'd think with all those vehicle numbers something would jump out, wouldn't you?'

'Son of Sam?'

'Like that, yes.'

'Fancy a drink?'

Winsome grinned. 'You're talking my language.'

Annie glanced over the list of car numbers that had been given parking tickets in the area around Kirk's Garage, where 'William Masefield' had rented his Jeep Cherokee and she saw one that immediately jumped out at her. It couldn't be right, she thought. It wasn't possible. She looked again. Maybe she'd remembered the numbers wrong. But she knew she hadn't. She never did.

•

Banks felt irritable when he got back to his cottage that evening. It was because of his argument with Annie, he knew. He didn't think he'd been too heavy-handed, so maybe she had simply over-reacted. Love can make you feel that way sometimes. Was Annie in love with Keane? The thought didn't make Banks feel any better, so he poured himself a generous Laphroaig cask strength and put some Schubert string quartets on the CD player. Should he have told her about Helen? Probably not. What he should do, he realized, was talk to Keane again and suggest he tell Annie himself. After all, if it was such an open marriage, what had he got to hide? Annie wouldn't like it, would no doubt promptly end the relationship, but that was Keane's problem, not his.

He was trying to decide whether to get back to his Eric

Ambler or watch a European cup match on TV when someone knocked on his door. Too late for travelling salesmen, not that there were many around these days, and a friend would most likely have rung first. Puzzled, he put his glass aside and answered it.

Banks was surprised, and more than a little put out, to see Phil Keane standing there, a smile on his face, a bottle clutched in his hand. He'd wanted to talk to Keane again, but not in his own home, and not now, when he was in need of solitude and relaxation, and the healing balm of Schubert. Still, sometimes you just had to take what you were offered when you were offered it.

'May I come in?' Keane asked.

Banks stood aside. Keane thrust the bottle towards him. 'A little present,' he said. 'I heard you like a good single malt.'

Banks looked at the label. Glenlivet. Not one of his favourites. 'Thanks,' he said, gesturing towards his glass. 'I'll stick with this for now, if you don't mind.' No matter how paranoid it seemed, he felt oddly disinclined to drink anything this man offered him until he knew once and for all that he was who and what he claimed to be. 'Would you like some?' he asked. 'It's an Islay, cask strength.'

Keane took off his coat and laid it over the back of a chair, then he sat down in the armchair opposite Banks's sofa. 'No thanks,' he said. 'I don't like the peaty stuff, and cask strength is way too strong for me. I'm driving, after all.' He tapped the bottle he'd brought. 'I'll have a nip of this, though, if that's all right?'

'Fine with me.' Banks brought a glass, topping up his own with Laphroaig while he was in the kitchen and bringing the bottle with him. If he was going to have a heart-to-heart with Keane, he might need it.

'You know,' said Keane, sipping the Glenlivet and relaxing into the armchair, 'when it comes right down to it, we're a lot alike, you and me.'

'How do you get that?' Banks asked.

Keane looked around the room, blue walls and a ceiling the colour of ripe Brie, dimly lit by a shaded table lamp. 'We both have a taste for the good things in life,' he said. 'Fine whisky, Schubert, the English countryside. I wonder how you manage it all on a policeman's salary.'

'I do without the bad things in life.'

Keane smiled. 'I see. Very good. Anyway, however you work it, we have a lot in common. Beautiful women, too.'

'I assume you mean Annie? Or Helen?'

'Annie told me about you and her. I didn't know I was poaching.'

'You weren't.'

'But you're not happy about it. I can see that. Are you going to tell her?'

'About Helen?'

'Yes. She told me about your little visit yesterday.'

'Charming woman,' Banks said.

'Are you?'

'Don't you think it would be better coming from you?'

'So you haven't told Annie yet?'

'No. I haven't told her anything. I've been trying to decide. Maybe you can help me.'

'How?'

'Convince me you're not a lying, cheating bastard.'

Keane laughed. 'Well, I *am* a bastard, quite literally. I admit to that.'

'You know what I mean.'

'Look,' Keane went on, 'the relationship Helen and I have is more like that of friends. We're of use to one another. She doesn't mind if I have other women. Surely she told you that?'

'But you *are* married.'

'Yes. We had to get married. I mean, she was an illegal immigrant. They'd have sent her back to Kosovo. I did it for her sake.'

'That's big of you. You don't love her?'

'Love? What's that?'

'If you don't know, I can't explain it to you.'

'It's not something I've ever experienced,' Keane said, studying the whisky in his glass. 'All my life I've had to live by my wits, sink or swim. I haven't had time for love. Sure you won't have a drop of this?' He proffered the bottle.

Banks shook his head. He realized his glass was empty and poured a little more Laphroaig. He was already feeling its effects, he noticed, when he moved and decided to make this one his last, and to drink it slowly. 'Anyway,' he went on, 'it's not a matter of whether Helen minds if you have other women or not, it's how *Annie* feels.'

'Still her champion, are you? Her knight in shining armour?'

'Her friend.' Banks felt as if he was slurring his words a bit now, but he hadn't drunk much more since he'd poured the third glass. There was also an irritating buzzing in his ears and he was starting to feel really tired. He shook it off. Fatigue.

Keane's mobile played a tune.

'Aren't you going to answer it?' Banks asked.

'Probably work. Whoever it is, they can leave a message. Look, Alan, if it makes you feel any better, I'll explain the situation to Annie,' said Keane. 'She's broadminded. I'm sure she'll understand.'

'I wouldn't be too certain of that.'

'Oh, why? Know something I don't?'

'I know Annie and deep down she's a lot more traditional than you think. If she's got strong feelings for you, she's not going to play second fiddle to your wife, no matter how convenient the marriage or how Platonic the relationship.'

'Well, we'll just have to see, won't we?'

'When?'

'The next time I see her. I promise. How's the case going?'

Banks wasn't willing to talk about the case to Keane, even though he had assisted as a consultant on the art forgery side. He just shrugged. It felt as if he were hoisting the weight of the world on his shoulders. He took another sip of whisky – the glass was heavy, too – and when he put it down on the arm of the sofa he felt himself sliding sideways, so he was lying on his side, and he couldn't raise himself to a sitting position again. He heard his own telephone ringing in the distance, but couldn't for the life of him drag himself off the sofa to answer it.

'What about this identity parade you mentioned?' Keane said, his voice now sounding far away. 'I've been looking forward to it.'

Banks couldn't speak.

'It was very clever of you,' Keane said. 'You thought your witness would identify *me* not Whitaker, didn't you?'

Banks still couldn't make his tongue move.

'What's the problem?' Keane asked. 'A bit too much to drink?'

'Go now,' Banks managed to say, though it probably sounded more like a grunt.

'I don't think so,' said Keane. 'You're just starting to feel the effects. See if you can stand up now. Just try it.'

Banks tried. He couldn't move more than an inch or two. Too heavy.

'Eventually, you'll go to sleep,' Keane said, his voice an echoing monotone now, like a hypnotist's. 'And when you wake in the morning, you won't remember a thing. At least you wouldn't remember a thing if you *were* to wake up in the morning. But you won't be doing that. I'm really surprised you don't have more security in this place, you being a policeman and all. It was child's play to get in through the kitchen window just after dark and add a little flunitrazepam to your cask-strength malt. Plenty of strong taste to cover up any residual bitterness in the drug, too. Perfect. They call it the "date rape" drug, you know, but don't worry, I'm not going to rape you.'

•

'What's wrong, Guv?' Winsome asked, leaning over her.

'This number.' Annie pointed. 'I know it. It's Phil's BMW.'

'Are you certain?'

'Yes. I don't know why. I just remember these things. There's no mistake. He got a parking ticket two streets away from Kirk's Garage on September the seventeenth.'

Winsome checked with her file. 'That's one of the times Masefield rented the Jeep Cherokee,' she said. 'Look, it doesn't make sense. Maybe the bloke who wrote the ticket made a mistake?'

'Maybe,' said Annie, as the thing that had been bothering her rose to the surface of her mind. Banks had said during their argument that morning that he had met Phil a *couple* of times, but later Phil had said he only met

Banks *once*. The three of them had met the previous weekend, several days ago, but Banks had also said he hadn't seen Phil for a *couple* of days. Why was that? Had he been to see him since? And if so, what was it about? What were they keeping from her?

It might be nothing. An easy mistake to make. But now this. The BMW number. And it was true that Phil had only come onto the scene last summer, when both Roland Gardiner and Thomas McMahon had told people their fortunes were on the rise. Annie had only met him herself at the Turner reception, and he had phoned her a month or so later, determined not to take no for an answer.

Annie didn't like the direction in which her thoughts were turning, but even as she fought against the growing realization, she found herself remembering the night she was called away from her dinner at the Angel with Phil to the Jennings Field fire. Of course the accelerant didn't match the petrol from the Jeep Cherokee's fuel tank. Phil had been in his own car that evening, the BMW. He could hardly turn up for dinner in the rented Cherokee the police were all looking for, and he wouldn't have had time both to return it and to get cleaned up. Worth the risk for the alibi. Annie herself. A perfect alibi. And a source of information on the shape the investigation was taking. The horse's mouth. Horse's arse, more likely.

'There could be a simple explanation,' Winsome suggested. 'It was well before the murders, too. Maybe it's just coincidence?'

'I know that,' said Annie, remembering that it was also around the time he had phoned and asked her out for the first time. 'But we have to find out.'

Her hand was shaking, but she dialled Phil's mobile number.

No answer. Just the voicemail.

She phoned Banks at home.

No answer. After a few rings she was patched through to the answering service. She didn't leave a message. She tried his mobile, too, but it was turned off.

That was odd. Banks had *said* he was going straight home. Of course, he could have gone somewhere else, or maybe he just wasn't answering the telephone. There were any number of explanations. But when Banks was on a case, especially one that seemed so near to its conclusion, he was always on call one way or another. She had never, in all the time they had worked together, been unable to get hold of him at any hour of the day or night.

Annie felt confused and uneasy. She couldn't just sit there. This had to be settled one way or the other, and it had to be settled *now*.

'Winsome,' she said, 'fancy a drive out in the country?'

18

It was a struggle just to cling to consciousness, Banks found. But the longer he stayed awake, the better his chances of staying alive. He could hardly move; his body felt like lead. He knew that he had to conserve whatever strength he had, if he had any, because when Keane set the fire, as he was certain to do, he was going to leave, and Banks might have just one slight opportunity to get out alive. *If* he was still conscious. If he could move. Neither McMahon nor Gardiner had got out alive and the thought sapped his confidence, but he had to cling to what little hope he could dredge up.

'I'm doing this,' Keane said, 'because you're really the *only* one who suspects me. Annie doesn't. And she won't. I know you haven't shared your suspicions with her or anybody else. I'd have been able to tell from the tone of her voice. I'm not an official suspect. And I'm pretty certain I've covered my tracks well enough that, with you out of the way, I'm in the clear.'

Burgess, Banks found himself thinking, in his muddled, muddied way. *Dirty Dick Burgess*. Keane had no way of knowing that Banks had enlisted Burgess's help. He also knew that if anything happened to him Dirty Dick would have a good idea who was behind it, and that he wouldn't rest until he'd tracked Keane down. But a fat lot of consolation that was to him if he was dead.

Banks felt himself slipping in and out of consciousness

as Keane's words washed over him, some of them resonating, some not connecting at all. All he could think, if you could call it thinking, was that he was going to die soon. By fire. He remembered again the image of the little girl etched for ever into his mind, sculpted by the fire into an attitude of prayer, kneeling by her bed, a charred angel. 'Now I lay me down to sleep, I pray the Lord my soul to keep.'

Banks heard the door open and felt a brief chill as the draught blew in. It revitalized him enough to make that one last attempt to move, but all he could manage was to roll off the sofa and bang his head on the sharp edge of the low coffee table. As he lay on the floor, the blood dripping in his eye, fast losing consciousness, he heard the door shut again and then the sloshing of petrol from the can. He could smell it now, the fumes overwhelming him, and all he wanted to do was hug the floor and fall asleep. The *andante* from 'Death and the Maiden' was playing, and Banks's final thought was that this was the last piece of music he was ever going to hear.

•

Annie felt no real sense of urgency as they drove along the dale to Banks's cottage. Only that she had to see Banks, to talk to him about what she had discovered and what she was beginning to suspect. But Winsome was behind the wheel, and whatever inner alarms were ringing in Annie seemed to have communicated themselves to her, and she was doing her best Damon Hill imitation.

She slowed down as they passed through Fortford. A few lights showed behind drawn curtains, and here and there Annie could make out the flickering of a television set. One bent old man was walking his collie towards the

Rose and Crown. There was a long stretch of uninhabited road between there and Helmthorpe, nothing but dark hills silhouetted against the night sky, distant farm lights and the sleek shimmer of moonlight on the slow-flowing river.

There were a few people out on Helmthorpe High Street, mostly heading for folk night at the Dog and Gun, Annie guessed. The general store was still open and the fish-and-chip shop queue was almost out into the street. Annie was still hungry, despite the salad sandwich. She thought of asking Winsome to stop. She didn't eat fish, but if the chips had been cooked in vegetable oil, then they might go down nicely with a pinch of salt and a dash of malt vinegar. But she held her hunger pangs at bay. Later.

Winsome turned sharp left past the school, with only a slight screeching of rubber on tarmac, and slipped smoothly down into second for the hill up to Gratly. Just before the village was a narrow laneway to the right, leading to Banks's cottage, and as they approached, a car came out and turned right, heading away from them. It wasn't Banks's Renault.

'That looks like Phil's car,' she said.

'Are you sure?' Winsome asked.

'It can't be. He told me he was still in London.'

Winsome stopped before turning into Banks's drive. 'Shall I follow it?'

Annie thought for moment. It would be good to know for certain. But if it was Phil, what on earth had he been doing visiting Banks? 'No,' she said. 'No point in a car chase over the moors. Let's do what we came here for and see if Alan's in.'

Winsome turned into Banks's drive, and ahead she and

Annie could see the flames climbing up the curtains in the living room. *Christ, no!* Annie thought. No. Not after all this. She couldn't be too late. But they were flames, all right, and they were all over the front room.

'Call the fire brigade,' Annie said, unbuckling her safety belt and jumping out before the car had even come to a full halt. 'And tell them there's danger to life. A police officer's life.' That might speed them up a bit, Annie thought. The local station was staffed by retained men, and it would take an extra five minutes for them to respond to their personal alerters and get to the station. Rural response time was eighteen minutes and there'd be nothing left of the cottage by then.

Annie couldn't just stand there and watch the place burn. She knew that the worst thing you could do with a fire was open the door and supply more oxygen, but opening the door was the only chance she possibly had of getting Banks out alive. If he was still alive.

Annie pulled the wool blanket from the boot of the car. Luckily, the rain had left a few puddles in Banks's pot-holed drive, so she rolled it around quickly to soak it, then she wrapped it around herself, paying special attention to covering her hair and face.

Winsome had her car door open by now, mobile still in her hand. 'What are you doing, Guv?' she yelled. 'You can't go in there. You know you can't.'

'Did you ring?'

'Yes. They're coming. But you—'

Annie went up to the door.

Locked.

'Guv!'

Rearing back, she kicked at the area around the lock. It took her three tries, and it hurt her foot like hell, but she succeeded in the end. The door flew open and the fire surged, as she had expected. She heard Winsome shouting behind her against the roar of the flames, but she couldn't stop now. She took a deep breath and rushed inside. She had only seconds, if that.

The smoke was thick and the petrol fumes seeped through the blanket she had wrapped around her mouth and nose. As soon as she was inside, Annie could feel the intense heat licking at her, the tongues of flame on her legs and ankles. She hadn't believed fire could make so much noise. She called out Banks's name, but she knew he wouldn't be able to answer. He would be drugged, just like the others. It was a small living room and Annie was fortunate to know her way around. She had been there often enough to know about the low coffee table between the sofa and armchairs, for example, so she wasn't going to trip over that.

The flames roared and smoke billowed. A painting fell off the wall and the glass smashed. Annie's eyes were stinging. She needed to breathe again. Her lungs felt as if they were exploding.

Then she saw him, just a leg, through the smoke down on the floor near the table. She rushed over to him. No time for subtleties now, Annie, she told herself, as she threw the table over, grabbed Banks's legs with both hands and tugged. The limp body slid across the carpet. Annie's arms strained at her shoulder sockets.

Banks banged his head on the leg of the table as Annie pulled him around its edge. She couldn't see clearly, but she sensed that the open door was right behind her. All she had to do was keep on pulling him, moving backwards. She thought she was going to keel over from the heat and smoke, but she kept dragging him, and soon she felt the chill of the outside piercing the blanket over her back. Almost there. A part of the ceiling fell down close to her, and flames singed her eyebrows. Annie couldn't go on. She felt her strength waning, her legs beginning to buckle under her. So close. Her vision shimmered. Her knees bent and she started toppling forward.

Then she felt herself bodily lifted and practically thrown across the lane. As she landed unceremoniously in the mud, she was able to rub her eyes and see Winsome finish the job, drag Banks's body out of the doorway to safety. Annie breathed the fresh air deeply and let herself fall back, hair and arms spread out in the mud, still wrapped in her damp blanket.

Winsome was outside the cottage now, and a few more feet would free Banks from the flames. His head bounced down the steps. Annie didn't know if he was dead or alive. She didn't even want to look at him, for fear he would be grotesquely disfigured by the fire, or just lying with his eyes wide open.

Finally, Winsome set Banks down a few feet from the cottage and hurried over to Annie.

'You all right, Guv?'

'I'm fine,' said Annie.

'That was a bloody stupid thing to do, if you don't mind my saying so.'

'Alan . . . ?'

'I don't know, Guv. It took all I had to get the two of you out of there.'

Annie flung off her blanket and took a deep breath. And another. The cold, fresh air made her feel dizzy. The two of them went over and squatted beside Banks. His clothes were smouldering, so Annie put the damp blanket on him. His face was blackened by the smoke, and she really couldn't tell if he was badly burned or not. She didn't think so, hoped to God not.

Holding her own breath, Annie leaned forward and listened for his. She thought he was still breathing. She wished she had some oxygen, wished that the firefighters and the ambulances would hurry up. She didn't even know whether it would help to give him the kiss of life, or if it would only make things worse. *Live, you bastard, live*, she whispered, Winsome beside her, hand on her shoulder, and in the distance she heard the welcome sound of a fire engine.

•

It was the middle of the night when Annie finally got home from the hospital, exhausted beyond belief, leaving Detective Superintendent Gristhorpe to keep a bedside vigil. There was more paperwork to do, of course, always more paperwork, but that could wait until morning.

Banks wasn't out of danger yet. He still wasn't conscious, for a start. Annie told the doctor that he had most likely been drugged with Rohypnol, or something similar, probably mixed with alcohol. The flames had done *some* damage, mostly to his right leg and side, which had been closest in proximity to one of the seats of the fire, and to one side of his face. They were second-degree burns, with blistering, which would be extremely painful and cause some scarring. Banks's shallow breathing had prevented the high level of smoke inhalation that might have done more serious damage more quickly, and the bumps on his head from the table and steps were superficial.

Annie moved around like a zombie. She knew she should go to bed, but she was certain she wouldn't be able to sleep. She needed a drink; she knew that much at least. She didn't often drink spirits, but tonight called for something stronger than wine, so she poured herself a stiff cognac and coughed when she first tasted the fiery liquor.

When she caught a glance of herself in the mirror, she was surprised at the muddy hair, sooty face and the frightened eyes that looked back at her. The doctor who had examined Annie and Winsome had been reluctant to let her go, but there was no real damage and no real reason to keep her. She had insisted she was fine. And she was, physically. Her muscles ached, and her foot was bruised and swollen from kicking the door in, but other than that she had been spared the ravages of fire and smoke. She had probably been in the burning cottage for no more than thirty seconds, she reckoned. Of course, the station officer had given her a bollocking for going in at all, but she sensed that he did so because it was expected of him, because it was his job, and that he secretly approved. He must have known, as Annie did, that there was nothing else she could have done to save Banks's life.

Phil. Phil Keane had done all this. He had enlisted his old polytechnic pals McMahon and Gardiner to help him with the art scam, and they had got together and turned on him. For that, he had killed them. It had to have happened that way. It was the only thing that made sense now. Philip Keane, not Leslie Whitaker, was Giles Moore. Philip Keane, not Leslie Whitaker, had assumed William Masefield's identity and perhaps even killed him, too.

Annie would never understand in a million years how she could have felt so close to someone capable of doing what he did, of thinking she was in love with him, of sharing his bed. The thought made her skin crawl.

She realized that Phil, or whatever his name really was, was one of those rare creatures indeed: part charming con-man, part cold-blooded killer. Con-men didn't usually kill, not unless they were cornered and could see no other way out. And that was what must have happened. The threat of exposure. Of ruin. Of prison.

Phil Keane made people feel special so that he could manipulate them. Chameleon-like, he metamorphosed from one identity to another, leaving chaos in his wake. And he did it for profit and self-protection. Annie shook her head in disbelief at her own blindness. How little we know even those closest to us, she thought. Phil Keane kept his true self locked in a dark, secret place nobody could ever penetrate. You saw what he wanted you to see, believed what he wanted you to believe.

And he made you feel special.

Annie tossed back the cognac and poured herself another large one. What the hell. She felt as if she had been raped all over again, and right now she didn't know if she hated Phil more for killing McMahon and Gardiner, and for almost killing Banks, or for deceiving her so completely. He had used her all along, of that she was certain. While he hadn't known he was going to kill McMahon and Gardiner, he had been in a criminal partnership with them by August, when he had pursued Annie, and he had no doubt thought it would be useful to get close to someone with inside knowledge of what the local police were thinking and doing.

And, to cap it all, the bastard had got away.

There was a huge manhunt going on, even now, but Annie doubted they'd find him. After all, he *was* a chameleon. If it had been a television drama, of course, they would have hushed up Banks's survival, let the world believe he was dead, and Annie would have waited for Phil to get in touch, to come and offer his sympathy and condolences on the loss of her friend.

But the reporters were on the scene almost as quickly as the fire brigade. This was big news. Banks was a well-known local detective with a number of successful cases under his belt. In no time flat, the local news on TV and radio was informing the good citizens of Eastvale and, no doubt, the rest of England, that DCI Alan Banks had been pulled from his blazing cottage by his heroic DI Annie Cabbot and DC Winsome Jackman, and that he was now in Eastvale General Infirmary. There was no way Phil wouldn't hear that, and when he did he would know the game was up. He would disappear and reemerge as yet someone else.

Annie smelled of smoke, and she wanted to go up and have a shower and get clean. She took her cognac to the bathroom with her. They would go over Keane's cottage with a fine-tooth comb, she thought. Meticulous and fastidious as Phil was – and she had no doubt that he would have cleaned up behind him – the odds were that they would find *something*. A hair. A fingerprint. *Something*.

She stripped her clothes off and dropped them in the laundry basket. Already, she noticed, her foot was turning yellow, black and blue. At least it wasn't broken. The doctor had told her that much.

Annie paused at the sink, gripping its edge, again looking at her black face. Like a soldier going into battle. She couldn't understand the expression in her eyes now, didn't know what she was feeling. Just before she turned to get into the hot shower, she noticed the toothbrush lying on the sink. It wasn't hers. She remembered when Phil had stayed a few nights ago she had given him it to use, and it looked as if he had. She knew she hadn't cleaned up the bathroom since.

Taking a plastic bag from the cupboard under the sink, she dropped the toothbrush in it. You never knew. It could contain Phil Keane's DNA. Because one day they'd catch the bastard and then they would need all the evidence they could get.

●

It was two days before Banks was allowed visitors at Eastvale General Infirmary, and Annie was the first to go in. Beyond the window occasional shafts of sunlight shot through the cloud cover. Cut flowers brightened up the drab olive room.

Banks lay propped up on his pillows, one side of his face bandaged and smeared with antibiotic salve, looking at the rain through his window. He looked spent, Annie thought, but there was still life in his eyes, life and something that had not been there before. She didn't know what it was.

He had lost everything. Banks's cottage didn't exist any more. She had seen it with her own eyes reduced by fire to nothing more than a roofless shell. Everything he owned had gone up in flames: his CDs, clothes, furniture, stereo, all his memorabilia, family photographs, papers, letters, the lot. He had nothing left except his car and whatever personal effects he kept in his office. Did he know this? Surely someone must have told him.

'How are you doing?' she asked, laying her hand on his bare forearm, near the spot where the needle rested.

'Can't complain,' Banks said. 'If I did, no one would listen.'

'Are they treating you well?'

'Fair to middling. Mostly I'm bored. Did you—'

Annie passed him the hip flask. 'It's not Laphroaig,' she said.

'Good,' said Banks, slipping it in the drawer. 'I'm not sure I could stomach that stuff again.'

'What has the doctor said?'

'I should heal up, OK,' Banks said, 'but there might be some scarring. We'll have to wait and see. At least the headache's gone. Worst I ever had.'

'Pain?'

'Pretty bad, but they keep me dosed up. Ever burned your finger?'

Annie nodded.

'Well, multiply the pain by a few thousand and you'll have some idea. Thing is, with second-degree burns the nerve endings stay intact. That's why it hurts. I didn't know that. The hair follicles and sweat glands too. It's only the upper layers of skin that are burned. You know what the worst thing is, though?'

'What?'

'The memory loss. I can't remember a bloody thing, from the moment I answered the door to the moment I woke up here. Except for the taste of the whisky. The doctor says it might come back or it might not. Which is a pretty bloody useless thing to say, if you ask me.'

'Tracy's been by a couple of times,' Annie said, 'and she'll be back. Brian rang. He's in Amsterdam with the band. Wants to know if you need him.'

'I shouldn't think so,' said Banks. 'I'll be home in a day or so.'

Christ, thought Annie, the poor sod. He *didn't* know. 'Alan,' she said, 'look, I wouldn't . . . you know . . . the cottage, I mean. The fire caused quite a lot of damage.'

Banks looked at her as if she were confirming what he already suspected and nodded. 'Well, I'll be out of *here*, at any rate,' he said.

Annie handed him a gift-wrapped package. 'Everyone in the squad room put together for this.'

Banks opened it and inside found a new personal CD player and a copy of Mozart's *Don Giovanni*.

'We didn't know what you'd want,' Annie said. 'It was Kev's idea. I think it's the only opera he's ever heard of. There's batteries already in it.'

'It's fine,' said Banks. 'Thank everyone for me.'

'You can do it yourself soon.'

Banks turned the CD player over in his hands for a few moments and looked away, as if the emotion were too much. 'Have you caught him yet?' he asked.

'No,' said Annie. 'Not yet. But we will. It's just a matter of time.'

'Tell me what you've found out.'

Annie sat back in her chair. 'Quite a bit, actually,' she said. 'Greater Manchester Police found his BMW parked at the airport, which means he could have gone anywhere. We're pursuing enquiries with the major airlines and at the railway station, but nothing yet. And the cottage hadn't been in his family for generations. It was leased from a couple who lived in south London. We've got fingerprints and DNA, but there are no matches with anything on record yet.'

'So he's clean?'

'No quite,' said Annie. 'Spectral analysis matched the petrol in the BMW's fuel tank with that used at the Gardiner scene and . . .'

'And?'

'And at your cottage.'

'So he used his own car to visit Gardiner, too?'

'Had to,' Annie said, looking away. 'He was having dinner with me at the Angel when the fire started.'

Banks said nothing for a moment. 'Anything else?' he asked finally.

'His prints match a partial the SOCOs found on the rented Jeep Cherokee, which confirms what we already suspected.'

'That the killer was using Masefield's identity?'

'Yes. The accountants digging into Masefield's investments have discovered that he was dealing with someone called Ian Lang of Olympus Holdings, registered in the British Virgin Islands, but they're not having a lot of luck tracing Mr Lang or his company.'

'They wouldn't have, would they?' said Banks. 'Any more on Masefield?'

'All we know is that he was at university in Leeds at the right time, so I assume "Giles Moore", if that's who we're looking for, must have known him somehow and kept in touch. There's every chance that Keane had something to do with whatever lost Masefield all his money and that he killed him. But we can't know for sure. Maybe it was just opportune. Maybe Masefield did commit suicide – everyone said he was depressed and drinking too much – and Keane found him dead, stole his identity and started the fire. But, one way or another, he was involved in the death.'

'Yes,' said Banks. 'And it would have been easy for him to pass himself off as Masefield if the two of them had a passing resemblance. It's amazing what you can do with a pair of glasses, a different hairstyle or colouring, maybe a slight stoop and a little paunch.'

'Anyway,' Annie went on, 'I talked to Elaine Hough

again, and she reluctantly dug out a couple of old letters Giles Moore had written to her. She said she hadn't wanted anyone else to read them. No detectable prints, unfortunately, but we do have samples of Keane's handwriting, and our expert cautiously admits they might match. But they're years apart, so it's hard to be certain. Nothing that would stand up in court, at any rate.'

'It's a start,' said Banks. 'Can you show her Keane's picture?'

'We don't have a picture,' Annie said. 'Another problem is that we can't seem to dig up any background on Giles Moore. He definitely existed for Elaine Hough, and for McMahon, Gardiner and Masefield, and whoever else he hung around with in Leeds, but outside that, we have no record of him. You do realize we might never find out?'

'Someone like him,' Banks said, 'is bound to be clever. Keane and Moore are probably only two of his identities. Maybe he's Ian Lang, too. God knows who he is now, or where, but if I read him right, he'd have an escape route – and a new identity – all set up for an eventuality like this. I'll bet he's overseas already. He's been at this all his life, Annie. Conning people, stealing identities. Maybe this is the first time he's killed, maybe not. But he's been at the game for a long time. Look how he conned *us*.'

Annie produced a cheap pocket-sized notebook bound in stiff cardboard covers and tapped it with her forefinger. 'We found this at Keane's cottage,' she said. 'One of the SOCOs discovered a false ceiling in the wardrobe. The measurements didn't agree. In it we found the notebook, a passport in the name of Ewan Collins, and about twenty thousand quid in fives and tens.'

'So he didn't have time to get back there and pick them

up,' said Banks. 'Which means maybe he doesn't have a passport – not one he can use, at any rate.'

'Which means he may well be still in the country.'

Banks looked at the notebook. 'What's that?' he asked.

'Roland Gardiner's journal. It looks as if he started keeping it when Keane first came to visit, and it stops on the evening of his death. It's quite touching, really. Elaine Hough told us Gardiner fancied himself as a bit of a writer when he was at the poly.'

'Does it tell us anything?'

'Not really,' Annie said. 'It's more of a personal, poetic record than anything else. Gardiner was taken in by the excitement and romance Keane offered. It does help explain why they had to die, though. It was mostly McMahon's fault. Not only did he get greedy, he also intended to try to pass off the Turner as genuine. According to Gardiner, he was embittered. He wanted revenge on the art world for failing to recognize his great talent, and he thought the best way to get it was to put one over on them. A big one.'

'And Keane?'

'Ever the pragmatist,' said Annie. 'McMahon tried to blackmail him into helping authenticate the Turner. Said if he didn't he'd pass on the names of all the fakes he'd channelled through Keane to the press, the police, the galleries, the dealers. It would have ruined Keane, and he'd probably have ended up in jail. McMahon could have claimed that all he did was paint them, not try to pass them off as genuine. Keane obviously realized what trouble McMahon could cause him, so the artist became more of a liability than an asset. And Gardiner was a loose end.'

'Why did Keane hang onto the notebook? Why not burn it?'

'Vanity,' said Annie. 'It never names him, but it's all about him.'

'What was Gardiner's role?'

'Forger of provenance, letters, old catalogues, bills of sale. That sort of thing. Go-between for non-existent owners, dealers and auction houses. McMahon could dash off the paintings, but that's as far as his contribution went.'

'As we thought,' said Banks.

'Yes.' Annie paused. 'We've also talked to Keane's wife, who was less than useful, and we've been having a close look at his business. It was clever,' Annie went on. 'Very clever. He chose lesser-known artists. Eighteenth-century English landscape painters. Dutch minimalists. Minor Impressionists. And McMahon churned them out in quantity. Sketches. Small watercolours. Nothing big enough to draw too much attention to itself. Ten thousand quid here, fifty thousand there, twenty, five. It all adds up to a tidy sum.'

'Christ,' said Banks. 'Keane *told* us all this, you know. He told us everything we needed to know. He was toying with us. We just weren't listening.'

Annie said nothing.

'Anything more from Whitaker?'

'I've talked to him again. He admitted supplying the paper and canvas for a small cut, most likely from McMahon's take. He knows nothing about the real magnitude of what was going on, knew nothing about Keane, but he *did* know why McMahon wanted the materials and what he did with them. He also confirmed what Gardiner wrote, that McMahon was bitter and bragged about "showing them all".'

'Are we charging Whitaker?'

'What with? Being an arsehole?'

Banks managed a weak smile, but Annie could tell it hurt. 'Have you seen or heard anything of Mark Siddons?' he asked.

'No,' said Annie. 'We've no unfinished business with him, have we?'

'No,' said Banks. 'I was just wondering, that's all.' He glanced towards the window again, and Annie could see he was looking at the scaffolding around the church tower.

Annie tapped the notebook again. 'It really is odd,' she said, 'the way Gardiner seemed to look up to Keane, hero-worship him, as if their scam was all that made life bearable, and when it was over . . .' She dropped the notebook on the bed sheet. 'Well, you can read it for yourself.'

'Keane made him feel special?' Banks suggested.

'Yes. He made him feel special.' Annie leaned forward. 'Look, Alan—'

Banks touched her hand. 'Later,' he said.

Then the door opened and Michelle Hart popped her head in. 'Not interrupting anything, am I?'

Banks looked over at her. 'Well,' he said. 'You're a sight for sore eyes.'

Annie left the room.

18 January

He'll be coming for me soon. Today, tomorrow, or the next day. I can feel his dark mind reaching out to me. It doesn't matter. I'm tired now. I'm the cancer patient who lives longer than the doctors have given him, the sad father who outlives all his children, the condemned man who receives a stay of execution. But now it's time. Soon he will come.

In my weak and foolish moments, I dream we go away together, start anew, embark on another escapade, but in the cold, dark reality of my caravan, I know he likes to travel light, and I know he doesn't like loose ends. I don't think he enjoys killing. Yes, there is a coldness at the core of his being, and I doubt that he's overly troubled by conscience. But I don't think he actually enjoys it. My murder will be dispassionate, calculated, a necessary end.

The irony is, of course, that I would never betray him. I'm not like Tommy, the fool, who let his greed and his pride ruin everything. Why did he have to spoil it all? These past few months have been a great adventure, full of camaraderie, romance and the thrill of the game, but Tommy had to let his ego ruin it for everyone. So we weren't getting enough money. I could have lived with that easily, so long as he still came to visit me in the caravan and we had our long talks into the night with the rain tapping against my flimsy roof.

I can hear him coming up the rickety steps. Now he's knocking at my door. When I open it, he will be standing there with a smile on his face and a bottle in his hand. Quick. I must stop now. Another drink, another pill, Beethoven's 'Pastorale'. We have come full circle.

Acknowledgements

First of all, I would like to give special thanks to Fire Investigation Officer Terry Calpin and to the firefighters of Pontefract Station, White Watch: Sub Officer Peter Lavine, Leading Firefighter Barry Collinson and Firefighters Gary Dixon, Andy Rees, Richard Beaumont, Dave Newsome and Arran Huskins. Thanks for your time, and an extra thank you to Gary for setting it all up. Also, for their professional help, I would like to thank Detective Inspector Claire Stevens of the Thames Valley Police and Commander Philip Gormley of the Metropolitan Police. As usual, any technical mistakes are entirely my own and are usually made for the benefit of the story.

Thanks also to those who read and commented on the manuscript: Dominick Abel, Dinah Forbes, Trish Grader, Sheila Halladay, Maria Rejt and Sarah Turner. Your help is invaluable when I can't see the wood for the trees.